BRINGER OF DUST

Also by J. M. Miro

Ordinary Monsters

BRINGER OF DUST

J. M. MIRO

FLATIRON
BOOKS
NEW YORK

BRINGER OF DUST. Copyright © 2024 by Ides of March Creative Inc. All rights reserved. Printed in the United States of America. For information, address Flatiron Books, 120 Broadway, New York, NY 10271.

www.flatironbooks.com

Designed by Donna Sinisgalli Noetzel

The Library of Congress Cataloging-in-Publication Data is available upon request.

ISBN 978-1-250-83383-9 (hardcover)
ISBN 978-1-250-83386-0 (ebook)

Our books may be purchased in bulk for promotional, educational, or business use. Please contact your local bookseller or the Macmillan Corporate and Premium Sales Department at 1-800-221-7945, extension 5442, or by email at MacmillanSpecialMarkets@macmillan.com.

First Edition: 2024

10 9 8 7 6 5 4 3 2 1

For my brothers,
Kevin and Brian

It happened as he expected. He turned his head
And behind him on the path was no one.

—*Czeslaw Milosz*

LIGHTS WERE GOING OUT all OVER the WORLD

·

1883

1

KINDRED

Alice Quicke stood under a ragged plane tree in the gloom of Montparnasse, her hat brim dripping, the collar of her oilskin coat turned high against the rain.

She was quiet, dark-eyed. She carried a finger-blade hidden in her sleeve, another at her ankle. In one hand she gripped a four-foot-long iron bar, like a cudgel. A fiacre rounded the corner, clattering and splashing past, its driver hidden, side lanterns swaying. Otherwise Paris was dark. The rain was dark.

She looked ordinary, to the ordinary eye. That was the thing about monsters: the real ones always did. She'd been in the city nearly a month, spreading a ripple of unease through any crowd. It wasn't the clothes she wore, the trousers, the stained oilskin coat; in Paris, at least, a woman in a man's clothes drew little interest. Though her knuckles were bigger than most men's, and the backs of her wrists were scarred like a blacksmith's, and there was clay clumped in her tangled yellow hair, none of that mattered. What mattered was the thin crescent of light in her eye, like a blade turned sideways, that warned off most inquiries. Four months ago she'd killed her partner and friend, shot him in the heart while looking into his eyes, and before that she'd seen horrors that belonged only in fairy tales, children afflicted with strange talents, and monsters too, real monsters, the kind she couldn't stop seeing even after she'd shut her eyes. She'd been hurt badly by one of those monsters, impaled by a tendril of smoke on the roof of a speeding train. Whatever it was that had infected her then was in her still. In the mornings she'd awake in pain and press a hand to her ribs, to the old wound of it, imagining some monstrous thing uncoiling there, just under the skin, a part of her.

Now a figure in a mud-spattered cloak turned onto the boulevard, walking fast in the rain. It was Ribs. She carried a bull's-eye lantern clipped to a belt at her waist. Alice stepped out of the shadows and together they hurried to a manhole cover in the street. Alice pried it up with the iron bar, the rain foaming over the edge, over the rusted iron rungs, pouring down into the sudden blackness. Ribs clambered in. Alice followed.

And then, clinging to the iron rungs, Alice reached up and dragged the heavy covering back into place, cutting off the rain. And in the darkness she followed her friend down, deep into the catacombs of Paris.

"Jesus," she muttered, when she felt her boots collide with the bottom. Her voice echoed back. "Some light here, maybe?"

After a moment the shutter on the lantern opened. It was an old-fashioned candle lantern with a fish-eye lens, a beam of weak yellow light illuminating the gallery. Ribs had taken it off her belt and leaned it against the wall. Alice could see the girl drawing back her wet hood, smoothing her red hair. The air was cold, sour.

Ribs was grinning, gap-toothed, at her. "Not Jesus. Just me."

Alice gave her a flat look.

"What?"

"I waited nearly an hour."

The girl winked. "It weren't my fault you was there early. Anyway I got us lunch. I don't reckon you remembered to?"

"No one saw you?"

"*Saw* me?" Ribs's tone was wounded. She sniffed, opened her cloak to reveal a package in brown paper, tied off under one arm. "Look at this. A baguette an half a cheese. No reason we got to be all bones, just because everyone else down here is, right?"

Alice suppressed a smile. Ribs was maybe fifteen or sixteen years old but there was something about her that made Alice think she'd never been a kid, not really. And something else that made her think she'd never quite be a grown-up.

The catacombs were thick with silence. Three tunnels branched off in different directions, tall and arched. Alice closed her eyes, and the dark ache bloomed in her side.

They were seeking the second orsine, a door between worlds, a way to cross into the land of the dead and find a living boy trapped within. It was somewhere under Paris. Dr. Berghast had told Alice as much, in his sunlit greenhouse at Cairndale long months ago, a bonebird clicking weirdly at his wrist, his eyes cold and dead. And almost as soon as she'd arrived in Paris she'd *felt* it, an ache radiating up out of the old wound in her side, a coldness that seeped down her left arm into her fingertips. It was as if the infected dust that Jacob Marber—corrupted talent, servant of an evil more terrible than anything Alice had imagined—had left in her was stirring, waking up. As if it knew an orsine was near. And like a hook in her side, tugging at her, it had led her forward, first through the crowded lanes and boulevards, across the bridges, then down into the maze of the ossuaries. Ribs, who'd come with her, could only trail along, watchful. Alice, for her part, just went where it hurt worst.

But they weren't in the ossuaries now. There were miles of ancient quarries under Paris, tunnels and stairs carved out of the limestone, submerged chambers, wells hidden in the absolute darkness. Only a small part of it was known. There were stories of things living deep in the underground, pale creatures, vengeful spirits. Cutthroats and pick-pockets. Stories of servants lost in the black when their lanterns extinguished, their bodies only found years later. Stories of sudden drops, of dead ends, of ceiling collapses.

Maybe some of it was even true. But Alice, for her part, figured probably the worst thing in that darkness was her own self and the thing that was inside her.

Ribs was looking at her funny. "So? Which way, then?"

Alice grimaced. She started down the left-hand tunnel, retracing their steps from the night before, following the line of red chalk they'd slowly been adding to. Ribs came along behind.

The tunnels were wide at first, dry. The lantern's beam was weak and wobbled as Ribs walked. They could see a few feet ahead, nothing more. The tunnel turned and turned again, then they descended an iron staircase put in sometime in the last century, and crept past a well and through a fissure in the limestone. All the while they watched for the line of red chalk that marked their way. They came out in a long gallery, the ceiling supported by pillars, their shadows crooked and silent in the black. The air was colder. They hurried on.

They'd stop now and then for a sip of water or a twist of bread but they did not linger long. Ribs would climb up onto a block of limestone and sprawl out with her arms dangling, or flop down onto the ground if it was dry, and she'd breathe wearily in the bad air.

It was during one such rest that Ribs mentioned their friend, the dustworker Komako. She'd gone to Spain in search of an ancient glyphic, and its secrets about the second orsine. She'd insisted on going alone. "So bloody stubborn. Je-*sus*. I guess she's probably all right, though?"

"That girl can handle herself," Alice murmured. "It's the glyphic I'd be worried for."

She heard Ribs snort.

The darkness seemed to lean in, muffling their voices. Alice didn't like the new tiredness she heard in her friend. She said, "We're going to find this second orsine. You know that, right?"

The girl was quiet.

"Ribs?"

"Sure," Ribs said at last. "But it's *after* we find it what worries me."

"After, we'll get Marlowe out. That's what'll happen."

Ribs rolled onto her side, raised her face. In the glow of the lantern it looked unearthly and pale. "It's what else gets out I don't like to imagine. Charlie was awful scared when he come out, back at Cairndale. I remember it." The damp turned suddenly colder in the gallery. "I keep thinking bout him, like. At night. When I try an sleep."

"Charlie?"

"Not *Charlie*."

But Alice knew who Ribs meant. They didn't talk about Marlowe, not often. She thought of the little boy she'd known, the calm certainty in his face, the way he'd chosen to believe in her goodness despite everything, the strange power that had been in him. It felt like a lifetime ago. That night she'd first seen his talent, the blue shine in that sideshow tent outside Remington. The rough men watching him with tears in their eyes. She wasn't sure what to say. Ribs had sat up now and was pushing the tallow higher into the lantern, then taking out the spare candle she'd brought.

"You go into the dark because it's where the bad things are," Ribs murmured. "Because it's the only way to fight them. I get it. But in the dark, it's easy to start thinking evil is stronger than it is."

Alice was quiet. Ribs surprised her sometimes. She could feel the little blade strapped to her wrist, the consolation of it. Sometimes, she thought, the bad things weren't in the dark at all. They were right in front of you, in the light, the whole time.

She got to her feet. The rock overhead felt heavy, crushing. Beyond the candlelight, the dark seemed to go on forever.

"We should keep going," she said softly.

Nine hundred and seventy miles to the south, in an overgrown garden on the south coast of Sicily, Abigail Davenshaw walked barefoot below a villa, her long skirts swishing at her ankles.

The night air was warm with the scent of the potted basil plants near the old gardener's shed. She could hear voices and children's laughter spilling out of the shuttered windows. All her life she had been blind but her lord and benefactor, the man who had raised her and educated her, had refused to allow her blindness to stand in the way of who she might become. Blindness and seeing were not opposites, he'd told her. That was just the prejudice of the sighted. She had learned in the years since that there were many kinds of seeing. It was not darkness that she walked through, but a faint snowy haze at the edges of her vision, always there, night or day, and in the presence of a stark light—a bright lamp, the sun on a fierce day—she would sense the glow and turn her face toward it. She was thin and straight-backed still, like the schoolmistress she had been at Cairndale, but she was something else now, too, some-thing new, and the weight of her responsibilities for the children she had brought out of England, and for this new refuge they were building, had changed her.

She'd come to like this hour of the day, when the rescued children were being settled by Susan, and she could slip out into the gardens and be alone with her thoughts. They were scattered now, those teenagers she'd come to know and love: young Oskar here with her, protecting and guiding the little ones; Ribs, under Alice's shadow in the grand boule-vards of Paris; her eldest ward, Komako, somewhere in Spain, hunting the glyphic rumored to live in that country. Charlie would be somewhere in northern waters, she hoped, perhaps already arrived back in Edinburgh. She worried about him most of all, his haelan talent lost—*stolen* from him, really, ripped out of him at the edge of the orsine by Berghast—his young mind overbrimming with anger, blaming himself for what happened at Cairndale. Well, nearly most of all. Always at the back of her mind was Marlowe, little Marlowe, adrift somewhere in a world of the dead, maybe not even alive.

She smoothed her already tight hair, grim. No, she must not think that.

What she wanted, above all, was to bring them all back together, to offer them a safe harbor, a place where they could just be young and protected and learn the limits of their talents and how to conceal them in a world that feared their difference.

But that, she thought sadly, pausing to trace her fingers through the leaves of a bougainvillea, might not ever be possible.

They were lucky to be here at all. The villa had been held in trust by the Cairndale Institute since the last century, an ancient refuge for talentkind. By chance, they'd found the documents attesting to this among Margaret Harrogate's papers in London, and she'd made the reckless decision to move all of them south. Perched high on a rocky promontory near the sea, the main house had been shuttered by an Englishwoman eighty years earlier, while Napoleon marched burning through Europe, and not inhabited since. The roof had given way in places. A tree was growing out of the carriage house. There was an air of deep sadness around the property. Perhaps it was just the feeling of time passing. It was in the second week that Charlie and Oskar had found the room hidden below the wash-house, a long room carved from the rock, with inscriptions chiseled over every surface. She'd run her fingers over the writing, amazed, listening to the echo of the boys' footsteps, beginning to hope. She studied the crude images of orsines, of talents, of a horned figure she knew must be the drughr, that ancient evil that had fed on young talents, and seduced Jacob Marber into its service. Secrets were contained here, old truths, if only they could be deciphered.

But mostly the days were spent in the difficult labor of restoring the villa. Abigail Davenshaw would rub the backs of her hands against her cheeks, reading the hard raised veins there, wondering at how the years seemed to grow up out of her skin. She still wore her hair drawn sharply back from her face and up off her neck, as she had done at Cairndale, and a long cloth was still tied over her eyes. That was for the children's benefit, as it had always been. But her old blindfold—a gift from her benefactor a lifetime ago—had been lost in the institute fire, when Jacob Marber had attacked them, and now she wore simply an ordinary black cloth, purchased at a market in Palermo as they were arranging supplies for the long ride out past Agrigento.

When she reached the stone fountain at the center of the garden, she stopped. All the paths converged here, like the spokes of a wheel. Under the fragrant hibiscus and magnolia, a rotten stink was in the air, like the heavy murk of a slaughterhouse.

She turned her face. "Mr. Czekowisz, please tell Lymenion to step *out* of the fountain."

There was a scrambling sound from the bench to her left, and the boy hissed, "Lymenion! I told you *not* to go *in* there. It's not appropriate." The boy made a noise of regret. "I'm sorry, Miss Davenshaw, I am. He just likes the feel of the water on his feet. He gets so hot here."

"Rruh," said the flesh golem. She could hear the wet pulpy shift of its weight as it climbed out.

"There is a water barrel beside the gardener's shed, Lymenion," she said sternly. "You know that."

But she wasn't annoyed, not really. She was thinking about how brave the creature had been in that terrible conflagration in the autumn, the way it had sacrificed itself fighting Jacob Marber, been torn to pieces. In their final days in Palermo, Oskar had disappeared, and when he returned two days later Lymenion had been refashioned. She did not ask where the boy had found the flesh to do it.

Oskar was changed now, too. He had taken it upon himself and Lymenion to keep the other children safe and she'd been surprised at how seriously he had grown into the role. He was still shy, still hesitant, and yet there was an undercurrent of steel in his voice now. He was only thirteen and yet he had faced terrible things, and survived. Whatever else, he was no longer an innocent, and would not ever be so again.

But that was true of all of them, she thought with a pang. Their childhoods had never been theirs, not really, not ever.

"Jubal and Meredith have almost finished rebuilding the wall, like you asked," the boy said now. "Lymenion's been helping. I know they're both clinks but they're still little, they can't get strong for long. The wall should be strong enough soon. Whatever's been digging around it will have a harder time of it. Lymenion thinks it must be a dog. Oh, and Miss Crowley wanted me to tell you the larder is low again on flour and salt. She said the delivery wagon is late. She wanted to know if maybe you wanted her to find a new dry goods seller?"

The town was a good hour away. Abigail Davenshaw shook her head dryly. "Miss Crowley is used to English schedules. I believe we will all need to adjust to the ways of the Sicilians."

"Rrrr," said Lymenion in agreement.

"And what of Mr. Ovid? Have we had any word?"

"This morning. A shop boy from town ran up the post. Charlie's arrived in Edinburgh, he's safe. He doesn't say anything much."

"Nothing about the inscription? No word yet of the alchemist woman, if she will help us?"

"I think he'd just arrived when he wrote." Oskar hesitated. "You know what his letters are usually like? Well, this one was even shorter. But, Miss Davenshaw—"

"Yes?"

"Lymenion found something outside the walls, this morning. Something . . . unnatural."

She turned her face, interested.

"I . . . I think it was a dog, maybe. Or it used to be. One of the wild dogs from the hills. It was hard to be certain. Its head was missing. And something had got into it, pulled it apart. Made a mess of it. Where I come from, they'd say it was the work of wolves. Except the insides weren't eaten, Miss Davenshaw. They were all just sort of . . . pulled out, and laid in a circle around the kill. Like a kind of . . . warning."

Abigail Davenshaw was suddenly alert, disturbed. She felt for the ledge of the stone fountain and sat and then she ran one hand through the cool water.

"There are no wolves in Sicily, Mr. Czekowisz. Where is the carcass now?"

"It's still there. I didn't want to touch it. Something about it just felt . . . wrong. What do you think it could be?"

"Maybe nothing," she said softly.

She could feel the boy's eyes on her. Lymenion was breathing heavily to her left, like a horse after a hard ride. Someone had started playing the old pianola in the villa's ruined ballroom and the eerie tinkling, out of tune, carried across the garden. She thought of the secret room below the wash-house, with the ancient runes and carved images of talentkind. She thought of the wild dogs prowling outside the walls. She thought of the children brought out of England, their talents still weak and uncertain, and she thought of Susan Crowley, the way she fussed over them all like a protective mother. This was supposed to be a good place, she thought, a safe place. She got to her feet, suddenly tired.

"What do you want me to do about it?" the boy asked.

"Bury it," she replied. "Bury it where no one will find it."

·   ·   ·

Komako Onoe lowered herself down from the iron railing, hanging suspended for a long moment, the morning rain of Barcelona in her face. Then she dropped.

A knife was held between her teeth.

She landed without sound on the cobblestones. The man with the black dog, the sinister talent known as el Vicari Angles, had already vanished around the corner. The sky was bright despite the rain and the old city with its textured stone blocks and uneven streets felt confusing to her eye. She knew it best by darkness. She kept lifting a hand to her face, blinking in the shine. The rain came down in blooms of mist.

She wore a dark cloak soaked with rain and magenta skirts darkened by the water and her hands were gloved because of the rashes on them. Under her cloak her braided hair dragged heavy and whiplike at her spine. The streets of Barcelona's Gothic Quarter were narrow and twisting and she crouched in the early light, listening. At this hour the streets were still deserted and she was, thank God, alone. She'd learned the hard way that this was an hour in which a girl alone in the street would be taken as an invitation to mischief, and she had little time just then to teach a man respect.

Not that it would be hard for her to do.

She'd been stalking el Vicari Angles for two weeks, night after night. It was said he prowled the streets alone, a black dog at his heels, a malevolent figure who'd appeared after the burning of Cairndale. He ran with a small group of talents, petty thieves, hidden somewhere in the city. The dye-worker in Valladolid had sworn they'd know the way to the Spanish glyphic, had sworn it with terror in her eyes, a rope of Komako's dust tightening at her throat, leaving black stains like burns. Komako had chosen to believe her.

The figure's footsteps receded. She set out at a low run, blinking the rain from her eyes, violence like a flare of steel in her eyes.

She was different now. A new coldness was in her, a harshness. She'd asked to come to Spain alone, asked to be the one to track down the Spanish glyphic, in part because she couldn't bear to be around the others. The littlest ones who'd survived Cairndale, who she'd been unable to protect. Ribs, her best friend, nearly murdered by Jacob's litch. Charlie, with his sad eyes, who observed her now as if from a great distance, as if he didn't quite know her anymore. It was like the loss of Marlowe had driven them all apart somehow, though the grief of it was the very thing they all shared. And the dark truth—the really awful, dark truth of it, though she'd confess it to no one, not ever—was that, buried deep in some secret chamber of her heart, she didn't believe Marlowe had survived. He was just dead, dead and gone, like her sister Teshi, like anyone. Because that was what the world was like.

Truth was, something *had* changed in Ko, after that terrible night. It was like the hopeful part of her was diminished. It had to do with seeing Jacob again, she thought, Jacob who'd once offered her kindness and solace, like an older brother, who'd sat with her on the roof of the old Kabuki theater under the stars and whispered to her of family and love and how he'd never abandon her. But then he'd been seduced by the drughr—no, she told herself, say it like it was: he'd *allowed* it to happen, had *chosen* it—and was made into a kind of monster himself. And she was too much like him, she knew. She'd always been.

And that was what scared her.

But now she was the only dustworker left, the only one who could fight. The old talents were gone, Frank Coulton was gone. She'd come to Spain alone because of the danger and because she didn't want anyone else to get hurt, yes, but if she was truthful, it was also because she didn't want her friends to see what she was willing to do.

And what was that, exactly?

Whatever it was she had to.

She followed the figure and his black dog up las Ramblas, weaving between the plane trees, and when he reached the Boqueria she hurried left into the maze of streets behind it. Beyond the ancient walls lay the new construction of the Eixample, hazing the air, the fashionable squares and new apartments rising by the week, rain be damned. But in the oldest parts, in the labyrinthine alleys where she'd let rooms above a rope maker's shop, all was shadow and the scrape of cartwheels and puddles of filth. That suited her fine. The man crossed a small plaza with a fountain of a satyr and at the corner of a crumbling alley he slowed. She saw a scarf and stained top hat with the brim pulled low against the weather, the collar of a greatcoat turned up. He was very tall. She couldn't see his face. He swung his silver-tipped cane like a weapon, the black mastiff trotting at his heels.

He reached a black door with an iron knocker nailed into its center, and withdrew a ring of keys. The mastiff turned its face in the rain, peering back at Ko. She caught her breath. She wouldn't be able to manipulate her dust in the rain and so was only as useful as the knife in her fist. But the man didn't see; he ducked his head and went inside and the dog like a living shadow slid in after.

Komako followed. The door was still unlocked. Inside was a small whitewashed antechamber, with a corridor leading off into gloom. A candle in a dish stood in an alcove. She took off her gloves, crushed her fist tight around the wick, and after a moment the candle bloomed into flame.

She only wanted to talk. She needed these talents to help her, to tell her how to find the Spanish glyphic. That was what she wanted. She didn't want to fight; she didn't want to hurt them.

But you brought the knife anyway, didn't you? she thought. *Not that you'll need it indoors.*

For a moment she wished Ribs or Charlie was with her and then she scowled at her own weakness. She could see wet boot prints where el Vicari Angles had gone and she followed to a cellar door. A strange metallic smell was in the air, and something else, something foul.

She went down.

In the cellar were brick pillars, stone-block arches. The floor was packed dirt. Komako put away her knife and instead felt the old pain in her skin as she drew the dust toward her. The smell was close, stale. And there, in the far corner of the cellar, was a second light.

A man was stooped over a rough table, his back to her. It was the talent she'd been stalking. She didn't see the dog. The man had taken off his top hat and she saw that his hair had been burned away on one side of his head. The ear there looked melted and malformed. He turned his face just slightly as she approached; the huge black mastiff growled from the darkness. In the gloom she could see splashes of water where the rain had leaked in, and what looked like bundles of clothes in the shadows.

"Por qué me molestas aquí?" he said in a hoarse voice.

And straightened, and turned.

At once she drew a tight ring of dust to her free hand, the pain sparking all along her arm. Because the candle on the table was behind him, she could not at first make out his features, only that he was taller and wider than she'd thought. His hands were huge, and badly scarred, and one held the silver-tipped cane like a weapon. When she raised her own candle the light played over his features and for a moment she had trouble making out what she was seeing: a sunken cheek grizzled with stubble, shriveled lips split as he breathed. He looked like he'd been crying. One eyelid, paper-thin, trembled like a leaf in a wind. Wisps of hair were adrift from his savaged scalp. Then the pieces came together and she understood: his face had been horribly burned.

That was when she caught her breath in amazement. She *knew* him.

"Mr. Bailey?" she whispered.

He was watching her, a hulking presence. And suddenly the recognition bloomed in his eyes—recognition, and disgust. "Miss Onoe," he said. "By God, what do you want? Why are you here?"

She was surprised at how fast her heart was beating. They'd all been so frightened of this man back at Cairndale. He'd been Dr. Berghast's manservant, sent to summon the children to the director's study at all hours. He'd never smiled, rarely spoken, cared nothing for the fear he instilled.

She'd hated him.

Now she was shaking her head, trying to understand how he could be here. Miss Davenshaw had found him dead, hadn't she said so? On that last night at Cairndale. His throat ripped open. How was it he lived yet? And then she realized she didn't care—she looked at him, at his hateful scarred neck, at the glistening on his face that might have been rain, might have been tears—for he was the closest thing living to the man who'd caused it all. For a moment the Spanish glyphic was forgotten; her search was forgotten. There was only anger.

The dust thickened at her closed fist. "Did you know?" she demanded. "Did you know what Dr. Berghast was planning? That he just wanted the drughr's power for himself? That he used us, used *Marlowe*—"

But Mr. Bailey just continued to stare at her, his cheeks wet. "Does it matter?" he said quietly. "Look around you. He failed. Now we must live with the consequences."

She saw then to her horror they were not bundles of clothes in the shadows, but bodies. She counted four of them. Three women and a man. They'd been badly mutilated, ripped apart. They lay glistening in the weak light, wet, fresh. Their faces, mercifully, had been covered by coats, shirts. A thick smear of blood led off toward one wall, then ceased abruptly.

"There was another, a little boy," said Mr. Bailey. "Juan Carlos. He was a caster."

"He got away?"

"No one gets away," he replied. "It took him."

Komako made herself look at the bodies, one by one. Then she said, "What did this, Mr. Bailey?"

But she knew the answer, even as she asked it. When he said the word—*drughr*—she felt something cold and terrible pass through her. She glared at him, black dust thickening at her fist. His eyelid wouldn't open fully and the eye beneath it, she saw, was opalescent. He wasn't lying. But he didn't know what she knew either, that the drughr was dead, that it had been destroyed by Dr. Berghast at the orsine.

"It's not possible," she whispered. "Did you see it? Did you *see* the drughr do this?"

"Nowhere is safe, Miss Onoe," said the man. "Not now, not for any talent. Not even for a dustworker such as yourself."

Komako let herself look at the man then. Really look. She'd heard enough. "I'm seeking the English Vicar," she said coldly, controlling her fury. "A talent with a black dog and a silver cane. I've been told he knows the way to the Spanish glyphic. Is it you?"

"Ah. No." He sat heavily. "Not anymore."

"What do you mean?"

He ignored her question. "It'll be back. This won't be finished until it's found me. It's me it's after, I think. Yes. Yes, me."

Komako couldn't keep her voice from shaking. The rainwater was dripping from her cloak onto the floor. The man was half-mad. "We need your help, Mr. Bailey," she said. "You owe us that much."

The ancient walls creaked around them.

"Us?" Slowly Mr. Bailey raised his ravaged face. "What us?"

"I'm with Miss Davenshaw. And some of the other children. We got out."

He studied her. She could feel the calculations in his gaze. "And why does Miss Davenshaw seek the Spanish glyphic? It is the oldest and most dangerous of all glyphics. It is hidden for a reason."

"For Marlowe," Komako replied sharply. She felt a flare of anger. "He disappeared the night Cairndale burned. He sealed the orsine first, but after, he was . . . lost inside it. Trapped. We think the Spanish glyphic can help us get him back. We think it might know a way."

Mr. Bailey's eyes widened. "The shining boy? He is lost?"

"For now. Not for long."

The man's voice was hoarse with relief. "He is lost. It's a mercy, then."

Komako wasn't sure she'd heard him right. She thought of Marlowe, what he must have gone through; and she thought of this man, still alive, when so many children had perished. Suddenly she was drawing the dust to her and encircling the man's arms and dragging him upright. A cold fiery pain rippled through her wrists, the heels of her palms. The mastiff whimpered and crawled deeper into its straw. Mr. Bailey staggered unnaturally before her, like a figure carved out of wax, propelled by the force of her anger. She was strong now, stronger than she had been at Cairndale. Let him see it. She allowed a tendril of dust to slide, brutally, deep into his nostril, and then thicken, choking him. He started to cough, and retch, and gasp for air.

"You *will* help me, Mr. Bailey," she said. Her voice was dark. "And you *will* help Marlowe."

There was something in his good eye, a kind of frightened understanding. But the fear wasn't what she thought.

"You don't know what that boy is," he whispered, "or you'd leave him in there. The Dark Talent is rising, girl. It will destroy everything."

A GUEST
in the HOUSE
of the DEAD,
PART I

·

1883

2

THE SUMMONS

The old woman shuffled under an arch, into a dripping lane, making for the dark mortuary. Sixty-seven years old and crooked as a bad candle, Caroline Ficke, who'd once walked out of Cairndale a bride.

That was a lifetime ago. Now the years were in her, bent like a soft nail, and there was just no getting them out. She was too old, she thought some mornings. Too old for what living demanded.

And yet she went on, long-widowed, always weary. She lived in a chandler's shop off the Grassmarket with her brother, Edward, but her real labor was the dark study of talentkind. In the rooms above the shop, she and her brother cared for seven children, children half-twisted into glyphics by a madman now dead, children who had lost their talents but not their courage to try to keep this world safe. It broke her heart to see it. The fingers on her good hand were red and blistered from the lye and vinegar of her trade and she put them in her mouth as she walked, and sucked at them to warm them. She'd lost half her other arm years ago. Buckled to the stump, amid leather straps and lashings, was a thin blade of her own devising. She wore a green shawl two sizes too big to hide the injury but there was no concealing the crooked slant of her shoulder, the way she leaned into her broken side. That shawl was patched in places and the blue dress under it faded to gray, its hem stained and clumping with muck like a witch's wardrobe out of a fairy story. She'd made a study of alchemy all her life and she knew enough to know one thing didn't change into another without something being lost. She was evidence enough her own self. But there were secrets to be gained in the turning, too. The glyph-twisted children she loved and lived among had taught her that. She'd always liked hidden things, and darkness, and here in this grimy coal-blacked alley there were only candle-lanterns, suspended by chains over doorways, guttering in their smoky glass, and plenty of darkness between.

Slowly the dusk deepened to soot. The air felt like snow. She cast a fierce glance in both directions; then, satisfied, she hurried across, her ankles creaking in their boots.

The mortuary bell clattered as she entered.

It was colder maybe inside than out. It filled her with sadness, this place. A low light, cast by a single gas sconce behind the counter, spread a hush over the narrow receiving room. Her eyes took in the same two upholstered chairs, the same frayed red scarf on the hat rack, the same waterfoxed copy of *Punch* from last autumn. The heavy smell of flowers made her nostrils itch.

After a moment a man came through from the back, wiping his hands on a leather apron. She knew him: Macrae, the proprietor. A crown of oily hair encircled his pate, gleaming in the lantern light; his groomed muttonchops were uneven and stopped short of his mouth.

"Mrs. Ficke," he said.

She nodded in greeting. "I come about the body. Out of Loch Fae."

"We near give up on you," he said. "'Tis a recent find, you understand. A drowning. Nothing to do with that fire."

She allowed herself a flicker of annoyance. "But you sent for me, all the same?"

"Aye, we did. On account of its . . . queerness. I remembered what you said about the others, about if we'd seen any sort of strangeness in them. Well, here it is all over." He scratched at his wrist, clearly unhappy. "I ought to warn you, it's not a natural thing. There's a devil in this one."

"I'd reckon the devil a better swimmer."

"You'd be wrong. Water's the death of him. I said it to you before, Loch Fae's no natural place. You know it yourself. There's not many as like to go near it, nor Cairndale neither. Get a bad feeling at the gates, a person does. Mr. Macpherson grew up out that way and he says it wasn't ever a place for God-fearing folk. He's the one says this body's got the evil of the loch in it. We ought to have sent it over to the lime-pits days ago, if you want to know the truth. Makes us uncomfortable, knowing it's down there in the dark."

"It's only frightening until you know what it is," said Caroline. "Then it's just—"

"Aye?"

"—science."

The mortician gave a bitter laugh. He lifted the hinged part of the counter for her to come through.

"I'd best just show you," he said.

Caroline had wept when she heard about Cairndale. That was the truth.

Knowing her own part in it, reading about the bodies as they came down to Edinburgh in the police wagons, one by one. Seeing in her mind's eye curtains of unnatural fire, blown across the great stone edifice, the old talents spread out in a flickering line while Jacob Marber strode toward them in the darkness, feeling the silent roar of the orsine crumpling in upon itself and the ancient wych elm in the loch ablaze upon it. Four months now had passed, and still she'd not gathered the strength to go to the ruins.

Yet she'd gone to this mortuary and stood over the dead and paid the coin that saw them buried, day after day, sparing herself nothing. The little bodies of the children were the hardest to bear. But the servants and groundsmen and the old talents, many mutilated in terrible ways, had left her shaken too. An aged woman in rough-spun clothes with skin reddened by labor. Whatever Mr. Macrae and his assistant thought, they were always respectful of her grief. Some of the dead she'd known by name. Others were laid in unnamed graves under skies the color of steel, she and her brother the only mourners, riding to the cemetery in the black Albany Chandlers carriage so often their mare learned to pick her slow way unguided.

Not a night passed now without her seeing the Cairndale wards as they'd been, as they'd first come to her, seeking answers about the glyph-twisted all those months before. Komako, Ribs, Oskar. Filled with a fury and sureness that was wrong all the way through. She'd explained how they could destroy the orsine, how they must carve out the glyphic's heart and pitch it into the portal. Never quite believing they would do it. There had been such anger in her then, such fury at what Berghast was doing. But who could say that she was right, with all the suffering that followed? Some nights now with her eyes closed she'd remember the aftermath, hear the panicked battering on the shop door the night it all happened, see the American detective, Miss Quicke, tattered and bloodied on her stoop, a horde of frightened children huddled in the wet dawn around her, Komako and her friends among them.

They'd stayed two weeks, haunted by the horror of it. Crowded into her cellar, into the corridor upstairs, lurking in the shop aisles when no customers were present. Long enough for the broken to mend a little, for the oldest students—Komako, Oskar, Ribs—to accept that no one else had survived. Two weeks of thin gruel and crusts of bread to feed so many.

Two weeks of her brother, Edward, shy, keeping to his rooms, afraid to go among them. Two weeks of Caroline drifting through the mortuaries, then returning to the shop to tell Alice Quicke about it. She'd liked Alice for her toughness and uncomplaining silence but saw such sorrow in the woman that it staggered her. Sorrow, and some darker thing under it. It was Alice who decided one night to take them all south, to Harrogate's old address in London, checking the chambers of her revolver by candlelight as she said it. They were too many for Caroline and her brother to feed, and the Grassmarket was just too close to the ruins. Alice's voice was quiet, measured as she worked it through. And it was Alice who later wrote in a careful hand to say she feared the drughr was not destroyed; that Caroline ought to be cautious, for her wards might yet be in danger; worse, that they all feared the boy Marlowe was alive and alone in that other world.

Caroline had studied that letter by the light of a taper, brooding. Alice's handwriting was surprisingly poor. The envelope had been posted from Palermo, Sicily, at the close of the year.

It had been four months now since the burning of Cairndale. There'd been no word since.

The mortician led her along a brick corridor, up a ramp, into a room at the back. Waterstained wallpaper that maybe once had been yellow was peeling badly all over. Caroline took in the narrow tables, the rubber hoses suspended in coils from the low ceiling, the large cabinet with two drawers missing. There was a dead woman strapped upright to a chair, with tubes sticking out of her arms and her neck. She was covered crookedly in a stained wool blanket. An assistant with a long red beard tucked inside his apron was at work on the body.

"No papers on the devil, of course," said Mr. Macrae. "But he can't have been in the water more than a day or two, I'd think. Either he fell in or he walked himself in, if you take my meaning. But there's not a one as reported him missing. Local lad found him, washed up under the cliffs."

"On the Cairndale side?"

"Aye. Could be he went up that way to see the ruins. There's been a few of that ilk wandering about, souvenir-hunters an such. Became a bit of an attraction, it did, after the broadsheets got wind of it. But if I know anything it's that he wasn't there seeing the sights. Not a devil like that." There were stairs at the back leading down into the cellar and Mr. Macrae hesitated at the top of them. "An inspector come up from London, even. Scotland Yard, he was. On account of all what happened at Cairndale. I'd not have expected a man from London. Maybe a priest."

"An I'd not have taken you for the superstitious type."

"You can close your eyes to a thing, or stare it full in the face, Mrs. Ficke." Mr. Macrae just gave her a dark look. "I tell you, it's not a natural thing, this one."

The mortician took out two plugs of cork and inserted them in his nostrils. Then he held out two more in his seamed palm, for her.

At the bottom of the stairs the mortician unlocked a door and lifted a smoke-blacked lantern from its hook. They passed through a large windowless room with white walls and bodies stacked on wooden shelves. The air was very cold.

The next chamber was smaller. The body lay under a sheet on a table. Mr. Macrae hooked the lantern on a ring over the table and the light swayed and then steadied. Then the mortician drew back the sheet and stepped away.

The dead man was naked, of course. He didn't look like he'd been in the water for long. He'd had a thick black beard in life and heavy black eyebrows. His eyelashes were curiously long and pretty. One cheek had been ravaged, sliced four inches from the corner of the mouth up toward his ear. Caroline could think of no fall that would cause that kind of injury; only a blade would do that. There was bruising on his throat and buttocks and thighs, and claw marks on his ribs, as if he'd been attacked by an animal. But that was not the strangest part of it. His hands and arms and his entire chest were covered in tattoos.

"Look closer, Mrs. Ficke," the mortician said from the doorway.

She did; and that was when she saw.

The tattoos were *moving*. She'd thought it was the lanternlight at first but it wasn't the lanternlight. The tattoos twisted lazily under the dead man's skin, like curls of pipe smoke. When Caroline stepped back she noticed something in the air, level with her face. A smudge of darkness. She squinted. A cloud of what looked like dust or soot hung suspended above the dead man's chest, collapsing slowly inward upon itself, over and over. It was about the size of a human heart.

"Follows him from room to room, it does," the mortician said from the doorway. "Don't matter where you put him. The inspector thought it were some sort of magnetism. The devil's work, more like."

But she was only half listening. She walked the length of the body and crossed to the other side and came back. The blood was loud in her ears. She felt suddenly afraid. For she knew: this was the corpse of the corrupted dustworker, the monster Jacob Marber.

The shadows in the mortuary shifted.

Cautiously, Caroline reached out her hand, waved it at the twisting ball of dust. All at once the dust bloomed with a blue shine, as if lightning were flickering deep within it. As she drew her hand closer, a strong wind seemed to rise within, swirling the soot and dust violently. She felt the faintest cold lick of it against her fingertips, and something stirred inside her, a feeling she'd not known since she was a girl. She recoiled sharply, as if burned. Wiped her fingers in her skirts. The blue shine went out.

"By God," the mortician whispered. His face looked craggy and strange in the light of the lantern. "It never did that before, not in all our examinations. And we run our own hands through it aplenty . . . What is it, Mrs. Ficke? What did they bring into my mortuary?"

Corrupted dust. That was what it was. But she said nothing, just tried to think it through. Henry Berghast, when he was alive, would have paid her handsomely for it. But she knew there were many who would want it, even still. Dangerous characters, ones it would be better never learned of its existence. The London exiles in their fury, for one. That terrible woman in France, the Abbess, and her acolytes, for another. Those who had heard the old stories about the other world, about what the dust of it could do. How it could make whole again what had been rent asunder, how it could rewrite the language of this world.

She realized she had already decided something. She didn't trust herself with the corrupted dust; she could already feel it, the way it wanted to bind itself to her, corrupt her as it had corrupted Jacob Marber. But she couldn't leave it here either, unprotected.

She turned to the mortician. "Do you have a jar I can take? A vial? Anything clean will do."

He went out and came back with a small corked bottle that might once have held ink and Caroline carefully scooped the dust from the air. It seemed to cling to itself, and once some was trapped the rest almost flowed in after, as if of its own accord. She stoppered the bottle with the cork and held it up to the light. She could see it adrift within, a constellation of miniature galaxies, all of it swirling, the motes glinting when they caught the light like tiny metal shavings. Staring into it, she felt as if she were descending a steep hill, and she had to shut her eyes to break the spell. Quickly she slid the vial into the lining of her shawl.

"Hard to take your eyes off, isn't it?" the mortician murmured. He drew the sheet back over the corpse, its tattoos still coalescing in the dead skin, and then he unhooked the lantern to go. "Ach. If you gather anything out of this line of work, it's that death's a door that opens two ways. So who was he, then?"

Caroline hesitated. "If the stories are to be believed, he was a dangerous man. Perhaps the very cause of the fire itself."

"He done it on purpose?"

"Aye," she said quietly.

She felt the light slide from her face. For a long moment, neither spoke.

"It was awful sad, seeing all those little ones," the mortician said finally. "I won't forget it all my days. Worst thing I ever saw, Mrs. Ficke. The very worst." He folded his hand over his whiskers, as if to squeeze out water. "What should we do with the body, then?"

Caroline gave it a withering glance. "Burn it, Mr. Macrae. Burn it until nothing is left."

She made her tired way back through the night streets of Edinburgh, to the Grassmarket, her shawl pulled up over her head. Still thinking about the shining vial in her pocket, how the dust had felt as her fingers brushed it. That sudden bloom of strength inside her, as if all the candles were lit at once in a house that had stood dark for years, room after room after room. She needed to understand what it meant. A solitary streetlamp burned in the square as she neared the chandler shop. Edward had locked the door; she glanced at the upper windows, all painted over with lime, as if afraid she might see one of the glyph-twisted there. But there was no one, of course, and no light visible. She walked around the building to be sure and came back and bent low to unlock the door when she heard a voice.

"Mrs. Ficke?" it said.

She turned. In the shadows, a figure. Tall, broad-shouldered, with a bowler hat drawn low. His shabby coat was unbuttoned and torn badly at the shoulder. He came forward out of the liquid darkness and she saw a boy halfway to a man, seventeen maybe, face still soft, with dark skin and eyes lost in shadow. He'd spoken like an American. She took a grim step back, squaring herself to face him, sliding the vial of corrupted dust into a pocket in her skirts. She had her blade already naked under her shawl.

But the boy just fumbled for a cord around his neck, held it out. Threaded upon it was a ring, with the Cairndale crest. Even in the weak streetlight of the Grassmarket, she could see how strange the object looked, its bands of dark wood and metal, the metal very black and glinting as if edged with frost. The thing seemed to suck up the light. She looked again at his features. And then she knew.

"You're Charlie," she said softly.

A shy smile. "I didn't mean to alarm you," he murmured.

Charlie Ovid. The haelan. The boy Alice Quicke had told her about, in those days after the institute burned. He had lived through terrible things, had withstood the drughr and Henry Berghast and the world of the dead, and lost to the orsine his only friend, the shining boy, the one they called Marlowe. At the time Alice had feared his death too, and it was only later, in that letter from Sicily, that Caroline had learned otherwise.

But something was wrong.

Caroline looked closer at the boy before her. A gash on his forehead, a glister of blood at his nostrils; the knuckles of his hands, swollen and sore. It shouldn't have been possible. Then she saw his face more clearly, the pimples darkening his cheeks, the scar under one ear.

His own eyes watched hers. His eyes were old for his years, and careful, as she would have expected, and he seemed to know what she was thinking.

"I . . . I lost my talent at the orsine, trying to stop Dr. Berghast," he said. "I'm not a haelan anymore. I'm just ordinary. I'm just . . . me." There was a tightness in his voice as he said it. "I came a long way to be here, Mrs. Ficke. I wanted to write ahead, let you know I was coming. But Miss Davenshaw didn't think I should. She didn't think it was safe."

"Abigail Davenshaw? From Cairndale?"

The boy nodded. "It was her idea I come find you. Hers and Alice's."

Caroline became aware of the cobblestones, the square, the stillness all around. The solitary streetlamp shining aslant over the rough setts, like coins of light on water. The blood was loud in her ears. An uneasy feeling came over her, as if she'd been waiting for this, as if she'd known something like this was coming, ever since Cairndale burned, since Alice and Komako and Ribs and the rest had gone. She had the glyph-twisted children to think of; she had her brother. But she looked hard at the boy in the shadows and knew that was not all that she was responsible for.

He'd taken off his bowler hat, was running a long thin hand over his scalp. The darkness crawled across him like a living thing. "We need your help, Mrs. Ficke," he said softly. "Please."

It's strange to consider, she'd often thought, how one decision in a life can change all others. *You and your foolish soft heart, Caroline Albany Ficke*, she scolded now. *It'll be the death of you yet.*

But she didn't listen to her own better self. Instead she stumped into the shop, standing aside to let the boy pass, and then she pulled the knee-level bolt back into place and led on through the gloom to the cellar stairs. She lit a taper as she descended, gesturing for the boy to shut the door fast behind him. A pool of light fell in staggered steps ahead of her. This cellar had been her laboratory for thirty years. A long plank table stood in front of a hearth, hammered together by Edward decades ago; glass alembics and clay beakers and dusty distillery equipment were scattered among stacks of leatherbound books and her collated parchments, records of her experiments. She hung her shawl on a hook, snagging it with the blade of her artificial arm, and then she took out the shining vial of blue dust and set it carefully on the table.

The boy had taken a scroll tied with twine from his cloak. He looked at the vial. "What's that?"

Caroline hesitated. She held the taper sideways, the flame standing tall. "I've been to see a body," she said quietly. "The body of Jacob Marber. I took that from it."

Charlie's nostrils flared. "Jacob Marber?"

"Aye."

"You're sure? You're sure it was him?"

"Black beard, disfigured? Tattoos moving all over his arms an chest? A knot of corrupted dust suspended in the air above him?" She allowed herself a faint smile. "I'd say I'm fair-to-right certain."

"So he's dead," the boy breathed. "Jacob Marber is dead."

"Did you doubt it?"

But the boy could only nod.

"Then you are wiser than most, Charlie Ovid," she replied, in the dim light. "Now, what is it you have in your hand. A message?"

But when she took the scroll and slowly unrolled it, pinning each corner flat with a heavy tome, she saw it was not a message but a charcoal rubbing. She lit a candle in its dish for the extra light and then leaned over the long table with the flaring taper held low, to see the ancient writing.

"Why bring this to me?"

"Miss Davenshaw said you were the only one left who could read it."

"It's very old, Charlie. I don't know as I can."

"But you know what it is? You recognize it?"

She nodded. "Where did it come from?"

"At the villa, outside Agrigento," the boy told her. "There's a . . . a secret room. It's filled with these symbols all over the walls. The villa used to belong to talents, centuries ago. It's how Miss Davenshaw knew to take us there. Cairndale held it in trust. It was really just a ruin when we got there, but everyone's been working on it. Miss Davenshaw says this writing might hold a clue to opening an orsine. She says it might help us get Marlowe back."

"The Agnoscenti," she murmured. "That is who lived there. They weren't talents but they lived alongside talents, protected them, preserved their knowledge."

"Agnoscenti," murmured the boy, tasting the strange word. "How do I find them?"

"*Find* them? Ach, they're long gone, Charlie. They haven't been heard from in centuries." Caroline watched the disappointment drag at his shoulders. She turned back to the rubbing and brought the taper very close, reading from right to left. "It isn't Latin, but a derivative of Latin. See here, where tis mixed with the Greek. And this marking, this is an ancient Gallic rune. Here. This is describing a door that can open in any wall. It says the door is one but the key is many. I don't know what these symbols here mean. This one might be . . . sun? Or, morning?"

"Maybe it would make sense if you saw it all together."

Caroline looked at the anxious lines at the boy's eyes. He'd been sent here for this; he was afraid she might say no. But Sicily was a very great distance away. "I can't just leave, Charlie," she said gently. "I have the children upstairs to care for. And Edward. My whole life is here."

"So bring them with you. What's in Edinburgh, anyway? Cairndale's gone. Bring them."

She grimaced. "I'm old for such a journey. It's been a long age since I traveled."

The boy picked up the vial of corrupted dust, unconvinced. She could see he was trying to think of something persuasive. The vial began to shine brightly, at once. She glanced back at the rubbing, intrigued despite herself; because of this, she didn't see until too late that he'd unstoppered the bottle. The glowing dust swirled up around his knuckles, like chimney soot caught in a flue, a strange cycloning of particles.

"Set that down—!" she said sharply.

But then she stopped, and just stared.

For the gash on the boy's forehead was closing itself up, just as if the skin were stitching itself together. He raised a slow hand to his face. The blood remained, smearing under his touch.

"It's healed," he said in wonder. "My hurt. It's gone."

"Extraordinary," she breathed.

She swept the bottle from his hand, set it on the table. She saw the shining particles dance, now, around her own knuckles. That same difference was in her, she could feel it, like at the mortuary earlier, but filling her now, like water overflowing a cup. She gripped the edge of the laboratory table as hard as she could. Her fingers left deep divots in the hardwood. Just as she'd used to do, when she was a girl, and still a clink.

"Mrs. Ficke?" He looked up at her, his eyes shining. "What's happening?"

She was blinking furiously, trying to understand.

Charlie stepped nearer. He sounded shaken. "Am I . . . better?" he whispered. "Is my talent back?"

"No," she said at once. "Once a talent dies out, it can't ever be rekindled. Your talent's gone, Charlie, as is mine. 'Tis the corrupted dust what's done this."

She stoppered the vial so that the dust was sealed away and felt, instantly, the sleek river of power leave her body. She tried to crush the table again. This time her immense strength was gone.

In the stillness that followed she could hear her brother, Edward, in the aisles above, restocking the shelves, his heavy tread creaking.

The boy rubbed at his healed forehead. She could see the disappointment in him. But he didn't look at the shining vial with the kind of hunger she'd have expected. He was still, she thought, very young. Still innocent. She remembered how Alice had described him, the goodness in him. Then she thought of the power in that vial, the danger of it. Of those who would want it for themselves.

"Did you know it could do that?" Charlie asked, interrupting her thoughts. He was shivering slightly, half-visible in the gloom. "Did you know it could make our talents work again?"

"I didn't," she said.

"It didn't feel right, though," the boy went on. "It wasn't like it used to be. I could *feel* it there, the dust. Do you think it was like that for Jacob Marber, anytime he used his talent? Like . . . like there was someone else with their hand on his hand, moving it for him—?"

"I don't know, Charlie," she said softly. She picked up the vial with great care. The shine was all around her, casting everything into strange relief, as if it were hungry, eager for their touch again. The scroll with its charcoal rubbing was blue in the blue light. "We'll want to keep it secret. I need time to think. I need to learn more about it."

"Okay," said the boy. Then he looked at her. "Secret from who?"

Caroline regarded him in the shadows, his wet bowler hat beginning now to smell, his anxious eyes. "A thing like this has a way of making itself known. There'll be others looking for it, soon enough."

"But the drughr's dead, Mrs. Ficke. Cairndale's gone. Who would come here?"

Caroline lifted the candle in its dish and the corona of light sharpened.

"The world of the talents is vaster and stranger than Cairndale ever was, Charlie," she said grimly. "And you haven't met the half of what's in it, yet."

3

THE BONE WITCH

As a little girl, in the night, Jeta Wajs would lie in her uncle's wagon and *feel* the wet, living bones of the tabor's women all around her, thrumping with blood, sucking and shifting and stiffening in their bodies' flesh. And in that darkness she would *know*: a witchery was inside her.

She told no one, not even her aunt. Her parents had died of sickness when she was two and she did not remember them. They were a small family, but they would meet up with other families of eastern Roma and follow the lungo drom between Graz and Zagreb, a tribe of clattering wagons, swaying fabrics, silver bells. Both her father and uncle had been auctioned together as boys at the Monastery of St. Elias in Wallachia in 1852, and when slavery was abolished four years later they traveled west out of Romania and away from their kin with nothing in their pockets but a heel of bread and their tinsmithing tools. Her uncle's left hand had been cut off when he was nine by his boyar, and he displayed the stump with a fierce pride to any gadji that were near. He wore silver coins sewn into the front of his coat, that would catch the light like a cold fire, and black mustaches that hung down past his chin. He rode at the front of the caravan with the other men, Jeta and the women in the wagons behind, and it was he who got down at the crossroads to read the patrin signs left by other Roma, twigs tied with a bit of rag, bones cut just so. And then he would decide which road to take.

There were wolves in the southern forests still but the great cities like Dubrovnik or Trieste had long since been given over to humans. They'd circle the towns, trading and mending, and though Jeta hated the church-yards and slaughter pens at the edge of the town commons, she hated worse the evening chore of plucking and carving chicken carcasses. The bones were just so *alive*. But it was the human dead that filled her with the greatest dread. Human bones were brittle and dry and she, a small girl still in her colorful skirts, had to be careful; they would dance for her at just the curl of a finger. She remembered sitting alone at her daki dej's death-side, making the old woman's arm rise and lift to her cheek in the lanternlight, just like her daki dej used to do in life, and she remembered how it had felt, the illicit power in her at that moment, while the tabor sang and wept around the fire outside. But there was an answering ache in her own bones, all throughout her little body, a sharp throb that she felt as her power manifested and that made her gasp and cry out. She was five years old the night the old woman died. Five years old, and newly afraid, for that night she understood what it was she could do.

The knitting and unknitting of bones.

That was her curse. There were 206 bones in every human body, give or take, and Jeta could feel each one, had always been able to, had counted them over and over. The soft clavicle, like a coat hanger for the body to hang from. The tiny horseshoe-shaped hyoid in the throat, connected to no other bones and instead afloat in the soft tissue, like a stone in a jar of jelly. The femurs, as long and strong as her uncle's pry-bars. She could feel the chalky grind of the old men's knees when they trudged alongside the horses. On summer nights she would sit among the new babies at the fire, feeling the plates of their skulls fusing together, while the hairs on her arms stood up. It was like standing in a river while the current tugged at her; that's how it felt. The pull was weak from living bones, at least at first. But right from the beginning, among the dead, she had to set her feet wide and brace herself or risk being swept away.

Gradually, she could not shut out the rustle of blood in the bones around her, she could not hide what she was. She grew light-headed in the company of too many bodies. She buried her face in her aunt's skirts. Her family did not understand it but they saw how she longed for solitude and fresh air and how she would turn pale and begin to shiver as they neared villages and towns and soon her uncle, afraid, steered the tabor into the high forests north of Mostar. And then one spring afternoon when she was chopping kindling there the hatchet slipped and cut off the middle and index fingers of her left hand, and a new horror emerged. Jeta's uncle came running through the pines at her screams and wrapped her bloodied hand in his shirt and carried her down the slope to the wagons. She was dizzy, nauseous with the pain. But when her aunt untied the bandages to clean the wound, they all saw the stumps of her two fingers, the glistening red meat, the phalanges already growing back out of them. Nubs of white bone, pushing out, like shoots in spring. There was no hiding what she was, not after that.

She was disfigured; she was a monster. The first could be borne, the second not ever.

The tabor declared her mahrime, unclean. It was in those same terrible days that a stranger came to them. In Jeta's memory, it was all mixed up, as if everything happened at once, the axe and the blood and the new bones and the gadjo crunching up through the cool pine needles, red-faced, thumbs hooked at his waistcoat, though she didn't think it could be true. The sun in her recollection was orange and cast long treelike shadows across the mountain dirt. He wore a yellow waistcoat spattered with dried mud, a black hat with a narrow brim. He looked a little like the mentalist out of Vienna they had met on the roads the previous autumn. He'd journeyed by ship and by train and by cart and by foot out of the west, from a vast city called London. His name was Coulton.

He had come, he said, for Jeta.

She was afraid. All her life she'd been taught to fear the gadjikane world. They had enslaved her people, mutilated her uncle, they spat and jeered and taunted from their doorsteps when the caravans passed through. But this gadjo sat by their fire late into the night, seemingly tolerated by her uncle, speaking in a broken Romani, and from where she lay alone under the stars, unwanted, cut from the circle of the wagons, she could hear her uncle's low, rumbling replies. She could hear the heavy click of the coins on his coat, the slow unhappy sighs. The next day her uncle cut off her hair, her aunt took her shoes and washed her feet in a basin. They stood her barefoot and crying as the tabor packed up its wagons and made the signs of the dead over her, just as she'd seen done for her daki dej all those years ago, except she wasn't dead, she wasn't. She stood with her weird skeletal fingers folded up into her armpit, the pain of it like a rope keeping her upright, and she cried over and over, while the wagons turned and rolled creaking out of her life forever, and the frightening Englishman just sat brooding at the ashes of the fire. She was eight years old.

She never saw her aunt and uncle again. The bones of her two severed fingers regrew but the flesh around them did not, the skin around them did not, for what was put asunder by that axe would not ever be whole again.

That was six years ago, half a continent away.

She was a different person now. Fourteen years old, with quiet eyes. Jeta stared unseeing out the rattling window of a hired carriage, watching the Scottish landscape pass by, remembering. How it had been, what she had lost. Snow had fallen in the night and the white lanes were already slashed black with muck from passing wagons.

She had not lived a good childhood since. What she had become would have frightened her when she was small. She had killed grown men and women in the murky alleys of Wapping, and not because she had to; she had killed in Aldgate and Southwark, for profit and for purpose; and now she killed in any borough, at the bidding of the man who'd saved her. She was dark-skinned like her uncle, and her hair was the same liquid black as her aunt's had been. She wore it in twin braids that fell over either breast in the manner of her daki dej. She had thick eyebrows that joined in a long severe line, full lips. Her eyes were as black as her hair and hard-looking except when they took the sunlight. Then the little girl she had been shone through. But the anger she felt at what her tabor had done had never left her, and was visible in the set of her jaw, in the ferocity of her glare. That fury had been in her so long it was now just a part of her, like her talent, like the polished yellow fingerbones of the first two fingers on her left hand. And what she hated most of all—what she blamed for all the rejection and pity and suffering, for all the grimy loneliness she'd known in her brief time on this earth—was the very thing that made her different: the talents, her own and others'. Damn them all.

She raised her face. Miss Ruth, seated across from her in the carriage, watched her.

"It will not be long now," she told Jeta, smoothing the blanket at her lap. Miss Ruth was much older than Jeta and resentful by nature and disliked leaving the underworld of the Falls. She'd been a turner once, long ago, before her talent left her and she was sent down from Cairndale, frightened and alone, still a girl herself. For five years she'd acted as Jeta's procurer, running messages between her and Claker Jack. It was Ruth who'd set her up in that seedy rooming house in Billingsgate, who paid her way, a bone witch for hire.

With her steel-gray hair and her pale blue eyes and dark blue cloak, Ruth looked as cold and still as winter itself. "You must take your medicine," the older woman said now.

The carriage shifted sharply in the slush of the road. Ruth withdrew a little cut-glass vial from the satchel at her feet, droppered three clear drops into a flask of cold tea. The other bottles in the satchel clinked softly, poisons, acids, darker potions.

"I'm not your pet," whispered Jeta, almost to herself. "I will not be kept."

Ruth smiled thinly. "As you say. Now, drink."

For just a moment Jeta resisted, as if to prove it was her own decision. But she reached for the flask, as she always had and always would, and drank the cold tea in a few swift gulps. The numbing she felt, a rippling in her bones, was almost instantaneous; she winced and passed a trembling hand over her eyes, as her sensitivity receded; and though she didn't know what was in Claker Jack's medicine, once again she understood the power of it. It did not reduce her talent entirely, only diminished it. It was like closing a blind: some light still trickled through, but very little. If it made her less of a danger, it also muffled the agony she felt, being around so many living bones. She'd heard once from Claker Jack that most bone witches lived in solitude, hermits in mountain caves, madwomen in forest cottages, for they could not shut out the pull of other bodies.

She raised her eyes to the window. They were just passing under a copse of snowy trees and she caught her ghostly self, reflected there. The plain cloak, and under it the old dress of multicolored patchwork. Mismatched buttons of brown whalebone. A single sleek red kidskin glove on her left hand, concealing the two skeletal fingers. At her throat glinted a silver coin on a tight necklace. Her eyes were lost in the reflection.

"You have not seen Cairndale before, I think?" said Ruth, stone-faced, wiry, dressed in a coarse gray cloak. "It is a wretched place. You will see."

Jeta was careful to show nothing. She knew the woman despised her, despised her and dreaded her in equal measure. Like all exiles—like their leader and lord, Claker Jack himself—Ruth hated talents; she hated them with the passionate fury of the scorned; her loathing ate away at her, a raw anger that some other could live in the full shining of a gift that had once been hers.

It was true, she'd never been to the institute before. It sometimes seemed to Jeta that she was always left out, not allowed entrance to places others got to go by natural right. For she'd never been down to the Falls either, where Claker Jack and Ruth lived, had never dared walk among the exiles in their underground misery. It was no place for a talent, Claker Jack had warned her; if ever they caught her, the exiles there would tear her limb from limb. He'd kept her very existence a secret, to keep her safe. He was the only one, the only one in all her awful childhood who had not abandoned her. *You're like a daughter to me,* he'd told her once. Reaching out to smooth her hair. She held those words hidden in her heart and had never said them out loud, certainly not to Ruth, knowing how the older woman would sneer, would spoil them.

Gradually, the hired carriage slowed to a stop.

The driver got down and pulled the door wide and folded down a little wooden step, much worn. "This is the place, ma'am," he said to Ruth, touching his cap. "Not much here now, I'm afraid. An the horses don't go further than this."

Jeta followed Ruth out. The thin snow crunched under her boots. They were stopped at the gates to Cairndale. She'd imagined this place so many nights, over the years, at first with longing, then later with a terrible anger, praying for the most awful things to befall it. The black gates were closed and chained together though it was clear they hung badly on their hinges. Narrow cliffs of snow overhung the cross-posts and the snow had been trampled in front. A faded sign hand-painted in red warned trespassers to stay away.

"That's on account of all the tourists, see," explained the driver. He caught himself, as if afraid of giving offense. "Now, it's only natural to want to see the sight of a tragedy, of course. To pay respects, mind. But these aren't safe ruins, not for the walking about at least. A lady visitor twisted her ankle in the autumn, she did. An would you know they pulled a body out of the loch only a few weeks back? A sailor it was, on shore leave. He must have read about it in the papers I reckon, and come to get an eyeful. Say he slipped and fell in and drowned himself, they do."

Ruth was wrestling on her gloves. She drew her satchel crosswise over her cloak, the bottles there clinking. "A sailor drowned himself? In the middle of Scotland?"

The driver rubbed at his whiskers. He peered curiously at the satchel, as if wondering what sort of drink might be concealed there. "Aye. Rotten luck, that."

"How did they know it was a sailor?" asked Jeta.

The driver blinked in surprise. "Why, on account of the tattoos, miss. Peculiar, they was. My cousin knows the lad what found him. Said he were awful shaken by it, such a tragedy. If you insist on going in, I'd advise the two of you to be careful. Stay well back from the loch, now. I could come with you, if you like. Carry your . . . bags, an such." He nodded at the satchel.

"We do not require a porter," said Ruth sharply, "nor a chaperone. Be sure to wait until we're back. It wouldn't do to be stranded here."

Jeta crossed to the gates, peered through. Her breath stood out in the cold. The snowy fields beyond were smooth and unmarked, as if no one had ever set foot there, as if nothing had ever happened. She walked some few feet along the stone wall and cleared off the snow with her elbow and hoisted herself up. After a moment Ruth followed.

"How long do you and your daughter expect to be, ma'am?" the driver called. "If you don't mind my asking?"

But the older woman didn't bother to reply, and Jeta, who had dropped over the wall into the strange still air of the Cairndale estate, had already forgotten the question.

It was not a long walk. Jeta stopped at the edge of the courtyard, glanced back. Their crooked tracks led back across the white field, to the distant wall, to the carriage waiting beyond. Ruth came up alongside her. An eerie quiet rang out in the cold air.

"It's a peculiar feeling, arriving at a ruins one once knew," Ruth said softly.

Jeta drew her cloak in close.

In front of them, the ruined manor house loomed up out of the snow, a blackened shell standing against the white sky. The size of it, its deep age, impressed Jeta. A massive edifice of stone and dark promise. She imagined all the children who had come to this place, who had found refuge here, and felt an old bite of fury. The second level stood open to the weather in places, its walls blasted wide, the interiors lost in gloom. The whole of it, she saw, must have burned hot in its destruction, for the stones were scorched and the glass had melted from the frames. A wrongness hung in the air, even now, like smoke.

The hairs at the back of Jeta's neck were prickling. She felt a sudden dark pull in her bones, painful, arthritic, such as she had not felt before. The pull was summoning her, drawing her toward the manor.

She looked sharply at Ruth. "You said the estate was abandoned."

"It should be. Why? Do you feel someone?"

"Not someone." Jeta frowned. "Some*thing*."

"The dustworker's bones?"

"No. Something . . . alive, I think."

"An animal, perhaps." Ruth reached into her petticoats, withdrew the knife she carried there, tested the blade against her gloved finger. "But let us not linger. We'll begin at the orsine, if it is still there. Come."

Reluctantly, still feeling the pull from the ruined house, Jeta turned and let herself be led down across the snow to the loch. The water was glassy and reflected the silver of the sky. The dock leaned crookedly, half-submerged now on one side, black water seeping through the boards when Jeta stepped out onto it. No boat was in sight. Jeta peered across at the island, the shell of the ancient monastery there. For a moment, in the distant shadows, it looked like a small figure was staring out at them.

Ruth came up beside her, the dock creaking. "Fires don't cross lakes," she said, nodding over at the burned island. "What happened here was no fire. There used to be a tree there. A wych elm. It grew right over the orsine. With gold leaves, even in winter."

Jeta frowned. "Even in winter?"

"Some said it was the glyphic who fed it. Others said the glyphic fed *on* it." Ruth adjusted the neck of her cloak in the chill, regarded Jeta with her pale eyes. A web of fine lines appeared as she squinted. "I was very young. But I used to stand here and look out at it and it seemed to me the glyphic and the tree were one and the same. I used to think it was singing to me." She made a face. "I was a foolish girl. I should have hated this place. I should have hated its director."

Vaguely, Jeta remembered a tall figure, severe, terrible. A silhouette who'd sent her to the workhouses. "To hell with him," she muttered.

"Mm. I expect that is precisely where Henry Berghast is."

She spat. "I'd have sent him there myself."

"You'd have tried, perhaps," said Ruth quietly, as if she'd feared him in life. "He didn't live as long as he did by being weak. You are not the only one he refused. But Claker Jack raised a glass when he learned of his death; did you know that? He raised a glass, as he does for all those whose lives are cut short by *talentkind*."

The last word came out with disgust.

Jeta tried to imagine it. Claker Jack had always taken care of her, watched out for her, *loved* her, even, maybe, despite her talent. But there was a hardened core inside him, a core of hatred for Cairndale. She looked out at the island. She saw now how half the surface had been pried back, like the lid of a tin can. A ruined nest of pale roots from the great wych elm stuck sideways out, like the thin arms of the dead.

But she felt nothing in her bones, no ache, no dark pull at all from the monastery. There could be no mistaking it: if the glyphic had truly existed, it was long since obliterated. The island was dead.

They had come for the corrupted dust.

They'd departed King's Cross Station in a roar of steam in the early darkness and were already nearing Peterborough when the red sun cracked the winter darkness. From Edinburgh they'd made the long wearying journey out to Cairndale. Jeta was to be Ruth's bloodhound. She was to sniff out the bones of a dead talent, a dustworker who'd perished in the blaze: a killer of children, servant of the drughr, a man named Jacob Marber. If his body was not at Cairndale, they would scour the cemeteries and streets of Edinburgh next. For the body must be *somewhere*; and its dust was still powerful.

And Claker Jack wanted it.

All this Jeta knew because Claker had chosen to tell it. She wasn't so foolish as to imagine there weren't things he chose not to tell. Why both of them were needed for such a task, for instance. Or how the drughr could be a real thing, and not just the stuff of nightmares. Rumors had reached London quickly about the burning of Cairndale, the dying of its glyphic, the collapse of its orsine. Even Jeta, who kept to the shadows, a shred of darkness against a greater darkness, had heard within days about the institute's fate and the death of its feared director, Henry Berghast. She'd felt a sharp twinge of pleasure, hearing it. Had walked into the first chocolatier she saw and ordered a box of caramels, ignoring the looks of the other patrons. She was surprised, then, when Claker Jack arranged to see her in person months later, on account of Cairndale.

They met at a slaughter yard and walked between the hanging carcasses, still bleeding out. Ruth waited in a doorway. He'd aged, since last she saw him. Or maybe she had. Regardless, he looked different, frailer—that was the thing she sensed—and there was a nervous flicker in his eyes, as if he didn't quite trust her. She didn't like seeing that. She wanted to tell him how grateful she was, how much she owed to him. How he was a kind of father to her. Wasn't he the one who'd saved her, who'd plucked her out of that terrible Ladies' Aid Society, who'd known about her talent and taken her in, anyway? Didn't he tell her she could be more than just her talent? Why would he look at her like that now?

His gray face was grave, his eyes fierce. She was to find Jacob Marber's body. From the corpse Ruth would remove the corrupted dust, and isolate it, and preserve it; Jeta would erase all evidence of his passing. In Edinburgh they were to learn what they could of the fate of Cairndale. What had happened to Henry Berghast's experiments? What had happened to the old talents? Had they truly all perished? Oh, it was most curious, Claker Jack told her softly, threading his hands between the hanging chains, and parting them like a curtain. Most curious indeed.

"I knew Henry Berghast, of course," he whispered, moving closer. "Oh, not as a boy. But long after I was sent down from Cairndale. We corresponded for many years. I watched him change. I did not much agree with him. But when we cease to listen to the world, we cease to understand it. Berghast was a brilliant mind, I grant you. But one with a terrible vision of what might come."

The lowing of cattle in the pens outside drifted through. Their boots left bloodied prints across the concrete floor.

Jeta and Ruth turned now from the lake, their skirts sweeping the snow. The white sky was darkening with weather. Far up the slope the black manor house crouched, patient as a spider.

Jeta wouldn't grieve for Cairndale, what it had been. Not for the glyphic who had located her in his dreams, far off in the eastern forests north of Mostar, not for the orsine that had given him the strength to do so. Not for the man Coulton who'd brought her to London, riding at first on a train out of Vienna, the hordes of human bones making her faint, and then later, more slowly, through the empty countrysides when Coulton saw how her talent pained her. Because in the end he'd left her, too. Nor would she grieve for the terrible Harrogate woman in her black veil, who'd held her in that basement room, testing her, probing her with questions. Nor for all those children who'd lived here, happy, a kind of family, all of them cared for and beloved, in exactly the ways she'd never been. No. And she'd never—*never*—grieve for that monster Berghast, who'd traveled to London to see her, who'd stood over her in the crooked lantern light one night, terrifying, disapproving, and shaken his head in refusal.

She is not for us, he'd said.

He hadn't wanted her; Cairndale hadn't wanted her.

And the next morning Coulton had left her on the doorstep of the Orphan Working Home in Stepney with a donation of two guineas for her keep and a folding box with a single change of new clothes. She used to crush her eyes shut at night while the other children slept around her, the pull of their bones making her dizzy and sick. This was her tabor now, these gadji. The whole world was unclean. She'd imagine the grand hall of Cairndale as Coulton had described it to her, the laughter of children like her, bone witches, talents, all running through its corridors, gathering together for hot meals. And, just eight years old, understanding English badly still, she'd cry herself to sleep. She hadn't lasted long in Stepney; they'd been only too glad to give her bed over to a new orphan; and she'd lived rough after that, drifting among the guttersnipes in the rookeries around St Giles High Street, stealing and fighting for scraps, clutching her skull for the pain of all those bodies and their thousands of little bones, wrapping her bone fingers in rags like a leper to hide what she was really. Until one day, when a tall, dirty man in mismatched clothes appeared. He'd kneeled next to her, taken off his silk hat, whispered that he knew what she was. And reached down and touched her wrapped fingers gently.

That was her first meeting with Claker Jack.

He took her from that place, from that life, whispering all the while of the wickedness and evil that Berghast and Cairndale had done to her, whispering that he too had been abandoned by them once, many had, that he and Jeta were not so different, her talent notwithstanding. They could almost be a kind of family. In a shabby carriage waiting at the curb she met Miss Ruth, who looked her up and down as if assessing a cut of meat, and then turned her face away.

"We will feed you and care for you, child," Claker Jack told her, rapping the partition for the driver to start. "And in time, you will find a way to repay us."

London had been a brown sooty horror, unimaginable to a little Roma girl growing up in the eastern forests of the Balkans. It was Cairndale's doing—Berghast's doing—that had plunged her into it, then left her to die. They'd all seen what she was, and reviled her for it.

All except this strange, dirty man.

"But you must trust no one," he added, "no one but me. What is the matter? Is it the bones all around us? Ah, but I have a medicine that can help with your sickness. You would like that, yes? Come now, steady yourself. You will be my secret, and I will be yours."

She felt the sway of his bones, plucking at her, the metacarpals of the woman Ruth picking at her skirt, the scaphoids and lunates in the wrists of the driver up front.

"You won't . . . hurt me?" Jeta had said, in a small voice.

"Oh, child," said Claker Jack. "I will keep you safe, forever and for always."

And he'd reached across slowly, as if toward a skittish animal, and drawn her close. The feel of another human touch, even through his overcoat and gloves, his arm heavy at her shoulders, had made her begin, quite suddenly and helplessly, to cry.

Jeta was thinking of that first meeting, the sway of the carriage, the pipe smoke in Claker Jack's wool coat, and how long ago it seemed. Ruth had led her across to the snowy courtyard, the shattered front entrance of Cairndale Manor, and now she stopped.

"Well?" said the older woman. "Is the dustworker buried here, or not?"

But Jeta wasn't sure. She went in. The roof had collapsed. She raised her eyes to a white sky, dazzlingly bright. Charred beams stood out in silhouette. A great staircase was white with untouched snow and where the snow had not reached it was black from the firestorm. The railings were gone, half the steps had fallen through. And yet despite all this Jeta felt herself dreaming, saw in flashes moments she had long imagined. Running through the foyer hand in hand with another girl, laughing, late for breakfast. Counting the steps of the stairs as she went up, in a girlhood game. Staring in wonder at the great stained glass window as the sun rose beyond it. She turned. An entire wall had been blown out and the famous stained glass was gone and there was now no trace of the beauty that had been.

Then she felt it. A pull, almost like a current of cold water, tugging at her hair, at her clothes. "Ruth," she whispered sharply.

And pointed at the ceiling.

She picked up her skirts, her gloved fingers brushing the loose balustrade, and started upstairs. Halfway up, she had to turn sideways and jump to get past. Ruth, unsteady, her bottles of potions and tinctures clinking in her satchel, followed.

The upper floor lay in darkness, broken by shafts of sharp light falling aslant the scorched walls. They made their way slowly along the wide corridor, passing burned-out rooms, broken bedframes, shreds of curtains. The dark pull that drew her onward was unlike anything she'd felt before. Impossibly strong. The pain bloomed in her marrow, an ache that made her rub her wrists and wince and step gingerly.

It led her to a room at the end of the hall. She stepped through the clinking rubble on the floor and found herself blinking in the sudden daylight. The back half of the room had fallen away, and she could see where the snowy fields descended to the slate-gray loch. There on a pile of rubble sat something she didn't immediately understand, or recognize.

Until it turned its head, and she saw.

It was a bird, made entirely of bones. Bones, and ragged feathers. Its furcula and sternum fused together and held compressed under a breastplate. The eyeless sockets stared at nothing. The bird, the creature, whatever it was, clicked its reedlike carpals and digits in a shivering movement and then fell still.

As if in a kind of trance, Jeta stepped forward, very gently, so as not to startle the thing, and removed the glove on her left hand, and reached out her own two bone fingers. The creature hesitated only a moment, and then hopped stiffly down and onto her fingers, and was still.

"My God," whispered Ruth, from the doorway. "It's a bonebird."

Jeta raised her other hand and traced her fingers over its delicate architecture. How beautiful it was. "A bonebird," she murmured in wonder. She'd never imagined such a thing. She could sense the exquisite artistry that had built it, the webbing of knots and invisible strings, bones fused to bones. Its caudal vertebrae shivered. Somehow she understood it was the work of a powerful bone witch, far more powerful than she.

"It feels . . . old," she said.

Ruth grimaced. "They were all thought destroyed. There were nineteen of them, once," she said. "Or so I have read. Created by a bone witch nearly a hundred years ago. She's long dead, and yet this remains." Ruth shook her aged head, her eyes pale and creepy. "Extraordinary that Dr. Berghast kept it, all this time. It is said they were messengers, from our world to the other. What messages they could take to the world of the dead, to what end, for *whom* . . . no one ever wrote that down. That is the problem with histories. We have only what the once-living chose to preserve. And who is to say how much has been lost?"

A scroll of paper was tied with twine to one leg. Jeta removed it, studied it. It was a warning for Henry Berghast from before the fire. It mentioned Jacob Marber and a litch and something about the glyphic's dying. She passed it across to Ruth, who read it and looked up.

"It's from London. From months ago. It didn't arrive in time, it seems." Ruth regarded the creature on Jeta's fingers. "This . . . thing has been here since the fire. Just waiting."

"London," Jeta said slowly. "It must have come from Nickel Street West. From Harrogate."

"Most likely. God only knows what Margaret was up to. A despicable, interfering woman, she was." Ruth folded the paper and slipped it inside her glove. "Was it this you sensed earlier, downstairs?"

"I don't know. Maybe. It's hard with . . . the medicine."

"I expect it was. Evil calls to evil, yes? Well, a bonebird won't lead us any nearer the dustworker's body. Give it to me." Ruth held out her two hands.

The bonebird clicked and shivered on Jeta's fingers. For a moment she didn't understand the woman's meaning. Then she drew the bonebird out of Ruth's reach. "No," she said sharply. "You wouldn't."

"What, destroy it?" Ruth raised her eyebrows. "Why ever not?"

Jeta swallowed. She wanted to say something convincing, something Ruth would understand. Instead, she murmured, unable to help herself: "Because it's beautiful."

Ruth laughed scornfully.

"Don't," said Jeta, with a deadly softness. "I could snap your neck, like this."

"And disappoint your precious Claker Jack?" replied Ruth, unafraid. "I think not, *pet*. What would you do with that? Keep it in Billingsgate?

Do you imagine your landlady will never see it? That no lodger will catch sight of it? You cannot conceal what you are and still keep a creature like that."

Jeta moved back, nearer the wall. "You'll not touch it," she said again.

The older woman interlaced her fingers, her pale lizard-like eyes unreadable. She raised her eyebrows slowly. "Perhaps," she said at last, "we had best divide our efforts. It gets dark early, this far north. I want to be on the road before nightfall."

"Go on, then," said Jeta.

Ruth smiled thinly, holding her gaze a long moment. Then she swept from the room.

When she was alone, Jeta exhaled loudly. She walked to the ruined wall and stared out over the snowy fields. She was shaking. She was a child and yet she was no child. The world had done that to her. She ran her two skeletal fingers over the skull of the bonebird, feeling a faint bright tingling in her arm.

"And if you could talk," she murmured, "what would you say, hm? I don't suppose you know anything about a dustworker named Jacob Marber?"

The bonebird was still.

But, very slowly, Jeta became aware of something else. She stared out at the snowy world, her breath visible in the air, and she tried to make sense of it. The hairs at her nape stood up. It was like a whisper in a crowded room, very near. But the grounds were deserted, only her and Ruth's footprints visible, tracing a path sidelong up from the loch. She turned to leave, and stopped.

"Oh—" she breathed.

For in the doorway stood a small boy, very pale, much younger than Jeta. She could see the wall through his body. He was dressed in grubby clothes, the cuffs rolled back. A faint blue light was coming off his skin and there was about him something blurred, as if the edges of his face and body had been drawn in charcoal and a thumb had smudged them out. His hair was very black and it drifted up off his head as if underwater. He was obviously a talent but she'd never seen one like him.

"Who are you?" she said, more sharply than she'd intended. "What do you want?"

He didn't move. Time seemed to slow then. Shadows lengthened. Something about the child filled Jeta with pity and she wet her lips, the cold world receding all around. She remembered her own aloneness in London as a little girl, her own fear, the seep of yellow fog under a doorframe as she huddled for warmth next to the other guttersnipes. The dap of slow water in a dark alley. How cold Mr. Coulton's naked hand had felt, leading her up the steps of the Orphan Working Home, how she'd shivered as the doctor took Coulton's guineas, then adjusted his waistcoat, and told her sternly never to let anyone see her bone fingers—

Jeta blinked in confusion. At her wrist the bonebird clicked, went still. All around her the great manor creaked, as if something moved through the rooms. Something was wrong.

And all at once she knew what it was: there was no pull from the boy's bones. Nothing. He could have been just dust, and light, and sadness, as insubstantial as a memory.

A ghost. The boy, flickering, watching her with dead eyes, was a ghost.

You're not Charlie, he whispered.

4

DARK ASSISTANT

On his first nights in Edinburgh, despite the windblown sleet, Charlie would go out alone with a lantern in one fist and Alice Quicke's Colt Peacemaker in the other, walking north up West Bow into the streets of Old Town. In his mind was the feeling of the corrupted dust in Mrs. Ficke's cellar, the way his talent had bloomed in his flesh again, how it had felt, the sweetness of the little hurting fires.

It had been there, in him, *real*; and then it was taken again. He didn't know what to feel. So he would leave Mrs. Ficke and her brother, Edward, asleep in their shabby chandler's shop, and go out into the night streets, thinking about his friends—how strange that word still felt to him, *friends*—scattered now, some in that villa outside Agrigento, others on a steamer in firelit waters somewhere east of Alexandria, Komako stalking the streets of Barcelona. They were safe at least, he would think, safe and dry. Always then his thoughts would turn to Marlowe. The way he'd looked at him some nights as they sat up at Cairndale, whispering; the feel of his small hand folded in Charlie's bigger one; the little hiccuping sound he'd make when he laughed and couldn't stop. At such moments Charlie would dip the peak of his hood, grateful for the dark, the water streaming down his face not all from the sleet. The stone churches in the squares would loom squat and black out of the mist; his cloak would drag heavy with damp; and he'd walk with Marlowe's pale face in his mind's eye, as if seeking it out. But in truth what Charlie sought on such nights was just trouble and violence and the still-new sensation of lingering pain, for everything, since the burning of Cairndale, was changed, changed utterly.

Including himself.

There were scars on him now, for one thing. Mrs. Ficke wasn't the only one to see it. All the others looked at him now like he was a breakable thing. He hated it. Ko couldn't bear to be near him. Alice had given him her revolver and a fistful of bullets for safety. And he saw what they saw: a long scar under one ear, another on his throat, scratches on his hands. His nails, bitten to the quick. He had pimples where his skin had always been smooth before. He wasn't any taller than at Cairndale but he'd filled out through the shoulders and chest and so seemed taller because of it. When he caught his reflection in a window his eyes were still the same wide-set and dark eyes he'd always known but there was a new sadness in them. It wasn't only what had happened to Marlowe. It was also the forgetting of it, that other world, all the terrors it held, and knowing Mar was trapped in it like a leaf in amber and not able to remember what that meant.

But most of all it was his new weakness. The way he hurt now and didn't stop hurting and how the healing came slowly, ordinarily, if at all. The strangeness of this left him uncertain of who he was, what he was. All his life he'd been the untouchable one. The one whose wounds stayed hidden. All that was gone; his talent was gone. Berghast had ripped it from him at the edge of the orsine. In his second-class stateroom, night after night, all the long voyage back to Edinburgh, he'd sat at the edge of his cot in the darkness carving up his forearms with long horizontal cuts, feeling the pain of it in disbelief and smearing away the blood and wondering if maybe it would come back, if his talent would ever come back. It never did. The fact of it was, he was ordinary now, just like anyone. And ordinary would be no use at all in saving Marlowe.

You have to find a way, Mar had said to him that last night. *A way to bring me back. You have to. You have to.*

Mar's small voice was in Charlie's head all the time, steady, calm as it had been on that last night. So certain that it was possible. Filled with trust. None of the others, much as he loved them, not Ko or Ribs or Oskar or Alice, *none of them* had been there, none had failed Mar the way he had. They didn't live with it like he did, they weren't the ones who walked the deck of that hired freighter all through the Mediterranean, sleepless, haunted, thinking not of the life to come but of a life cut short. Miss Davenshaw had led them south to an ancient villa outside Agrigento, in Sicily, a villa that had been held in trust by Cairndale for over a century. It had been a refuge for talentkind once; it would be so again. A new Cairndale. Such was her dream. And then, in a secret room below the wash-house, they'd found stone inscriptions, in a language even Miss Davenshaw, running her fingertips across the walls, hadn't known. But the ancient tapestry behind its altar made its subject clear: an orsine being opened, figures emerging from it, figures all in darkness. It must be, Miss Davenshaw hoped, instructions on how to manipulate an orsine, perhaps even how to locate a talent, lead him back up into this world. If only they could read it.

You have to find a way. A way to bring me back.

And so Charlie had sailed alone all the way back to Edinburgh, almost to the source of his grief, to ask for help from the only one still living who had knowledge of such things, Alice's revolver rolled in a nightshirt in his small trunk, the ring his father had given his mother on a cord around his neck. In truth they should've sent Ko, or Ribs, or Oskar; any of them knew this old alchemist better than he, any of them would've been more persuasive.

But he was the one who could be spared, he was the one without a talent. He was good for errands such as this, he thought bitterly. Errands without danger.

So be it.

Except Mrs. Ficke didn't give him an answer, not on that first night. And he'd scarcely seen her since.

He'd glimpse her coming back to the chandler's shop at all hours, never mind the weather, her old shawl drawn up over her face, obscuring it. Or he'd hear the scrape and knock of heavy objects through the locked cellar door, the old woman lost in her researches, brooding over the eerie corrupted dust. He'd lie awake in a small room in the back with a moth-eaten blanket pulled to his chin, Alice's revolver under his pillow, and he'd wonder if Mrs. Ficke had felt the same shock and agony as he, when she brushed the corrupted dust, an ancient strength blazing in her corded muscles.

Few customers entered the shop. He'd hear them from the back room. On such occasions he'd listen to the heavy tread of Mr. Albany, the old woman's brother, coming down to assist. But he never saw the man, not at first. When he'd emerge, after the street door had clattered shut, the shop would once again lie still and deserted, the air thick with dust, Mr. Albany gone again somewhere upstairs. Charlie'd go up and down the aisles, scanning the dim shelves, their stacks of candles, ropes, wicks, sparkers, his boot prints tracking over the floorboards. Light would flood in through the dirty windows.

He went upstairs. At the top he stopped with a hand on the balustrade, one boot suspended on the step. A dark hallway extended the length of the building, windowless, with several doors along one side. He didn't see the shopkeeper.

"Hello?" he called out.

In the stillness he moved to the first door, pressed an ear to its wood. There was no sound within. As he reached for the pull he heard a low keening from the next room, and tried that door instead.

He wasn't sure, at first, what he was looking at. A strange room, oddly furnished, with its windows painted over. In one corner was a bed with a kind of railing attached, like a crib. Pasted to the walls at waist level were odd reproductions from daily broadsheets, black-and-white engravings of foggy nights and men in courtrooms and the like. Dried flowers hung in knots from the wall beside the bed table.

And there, in the middle of the floor, rolling a ball with great deliberation against the wall, was a girl unlike any Charlie'd ever seen. She wore a white dress, but it had been cut and altered to fit her form. He saw the way her skin thickened into bark along one side of her face, the fingers of one hand crooked and twiglike, he saw the knots and knurls of wood where her legs were twisted up under her, and he remembered Mr. Thorpe, the Spider, the glyphic at Cairndale who'd terrified him so, who had been slaughtered by the litch, whose heart he'd carved out in a moment filled with terror. This girl was like Thorpe had been; she was one of the glyph-twisted whom Ribs and Komako had described, one of the exiles Dr. Berghast had experimented on. There would be others, in each of the rooms, mute, locked in their terrible deformities. He felt sick.

"The nuns would not take her," said a deep voice.

Charlie turned in alarm. A hulking figure, bearded, grim, loomed in the dim hall. There was red wax or paint on his knuckles where he held a jar with something floating in it and Charlie watched him root around in the liquid with two meaty fingers and pull out a pickled onion. His eyes were bright, oddly shiny in the gloom, and he seemed to stare at Charlie without blinking.

"Jesus," Charlie said angrily. "You scared me."

The huge figure stopped his chewing, the pickled onion belling out one cheek. He seemed to think about it. "Sometimes it's good to be quiet," he said.

He swallowed the onion.

Gradually Charlie's heart slowed. He took an uneasy step to one side, trying to make out the man's features. Heavy beard. A big nose, squashed sideways. Long delicate eyelashes. A chest so wide he had to turn sideways in the door. Of course he'd heard the stories from Ko and Ribs; he knew the man. "You must be Mr. Albany?" he said.

The man cleared his throat, as if wanting to get the answer right. "My name is Edward."

"Edward. I'm Charlie."

"I know."

"I came to talk to your sister. I . . . I didn't mean to intrude."

"Okay."

There was something in the way the man absorbed what Charlie said, and thought about it, and then replied as if each word were a stone he was laying down in front of him. He was like a child, in some ways. An innocent.

The man fished out another pickled onion. He said slowly, "Caroline is going to go away."

Charlie looked up. "Did she say that?"

"It will be too far for me to visit. It will be lonely."

Charlie felt a sudden sharp guilt. There was no recrimination in the man's voice. Old as he was, Edward Albany had lived with his sister all his life and now Charlie was here, trying to take her from him. *But not forever*, he told himself. *Just until she can read the inscription, translate it, help us find a way to get to Mar.* "You could come too," he said, furrowing his brow. "There's plenty of things to be done there. You'd be needed, Edward. We're building a new home, a home for talents. Where they'll be safe. Your . . . wards, they'd be safe there."

"They are safe here."

Charlie looked at the glyph-twisted in front of him, a girl, very deliberately rolling the red ball against a wall. "Maybe," he said quietly. "But
they look sad, if you ask me. My friends knew some of them, before. I
bet they'd like to see their old friends again."

The giant moved closer and looked down at Charlie. He raised one
enormous hand and set it, heavy as a sack of feed, on Charlie's skull, a
kind of benediction.

"You are sad too," he said softly.

Mrs. Ficke sent for him, at last, on the third day.

Her laboratory in the cellar was cluttered with barrels and crates and
sealskin bags stacked in piles. A strange smell of singed iron and something bitter, like almonds, was in the air. A fire was roaring in the hearth,
liquids were bubbling in their alembics. He came down uncertainly to find
the old woman unbuckling and removing her artificial arm, its gears and
levers glinting dully in the lanternlight. She massaged the tender flesh of
her stump, scarcely giving him a glance, then untied a leather apron nim-
bly with her one hand and hung it back up on a hook. He watched her,
wary. He thought of Edward and the glyph-twisteds and he wasn't sure
how much he trusted the old alchemist.

"Come," she said to him. "Knowledge is not the property of any one
person. I will tell you what I've learned."

She reached for a second arm, with a malleable hook on its end, and attached the buckles and straps using her teeth to help her. Charlie watched,
fascinated despite himself. Then she led him to a bookcase and pressed a
catch and, to Charlie's amazement, the shelf swung outward, revealing a
small chamber beyond. The walls were lined with ancient books. It was
lit by several candles, burning low now, and held a cramped writing desk
covered in books. He saw the scroll he had brought, curled open. He saw
the vial of corrupted dust.

"You will be wondering why it worked on us like it did," she said. "How it brought our talents back."

Charlie nodded.

The old woman gave him a dark look. "Well, it never did; that was all illusion. There is much I still don't know. But the dust, it is like a . . . a parasite. It feeds on its host. It grows stronger inside them. And in return, it makes possible certain . . . impossibilities."

Charlie thought of Jacob Marber's whips of dust, and shivered.

"'Tis a thing of wrongness," she continued. She squeezed in behind the desk, moving the candles around for a better light, casting strange shadows across her face. "It eats away at a person, the corruption does. Consumes them whole. Until they're like Jacob Marber: no longer what they was."

"Is it safe to hold?"

"Aye."

Charlie picked up the shining vial. He had a sharp memory of Jacob Marber leaning over Marlowe in the land of the dead, ropes of silver dust pinioning the boy's wrists to a chair. Then it was gone. "He was so terrifying," he said quietly. "Jacob Marber was . . . brutal. And cruel. But I think, on some deep level, he really did love Mar. He wanted to protect him. He just . . . I don't know. He was willing to destroy anyone in order to do it." He set the vial back down on the writing table; the shine dimmed as his hand pulled away. "It's strange to hold it, knowing all that."

"Such is the nature of corrupted dust, Charlie. It belongs on the far side of the orsine. Not here. Not with us. Tis a part of the world beyond."

"You mean the world of the dead."

"The world of the dead, aye. An of the drughr. When Jacob Marber fell under her spell, the drughr infected him with this part of herself. The very substance of which the drughr was made."

Charlie stopped. "Wait. The drughr was . . . made?"

Slowly the old woman nodded. Her crooked shadow loomed large on the wall behind her. "Tis an old story. A made-up story, some say. But there is truth in the old stories, Charlie, if we are willing to see it.

"According to the Agnoscenti chroniclers, long ago, in a place called the Grathyyl, 'under the dish of the world,' there was a gathering of the strongest talents. It was a place of power, a place where the worlds of the living an the dead met. Not an orsine, not a door between the worlds. No, the Grathyyl was something else. An in-between, a place neither wholly of one world nor of the other.

"It was a time of great upheaval. There were a struggle among talent-kind, a struggle over how they ought to exist, whether to reveal their abilities and influence the world, for good or for ill, or to remain concealed. At the Grathyyl, five talents volunteered to go into the other world forever, as guards, to protect the gateways between the worlds. The orsines. There was one for each kind of talent: a caster, a clink, a turner, a dustworker, a glyphic. It would be their task to stop any evil from crossing back over to our world. An to prevent any talents from trying to break through from this side."

Charlie looked sharply at her. "Like Dr. Berghast was doing. At Cairndale."

The old woman rested her tired hand on the books.

"Is that how the drughr got loose?"

"No. Listen." The old woman's face was unreadable. "The five talents what volunteered needed to be altered, so as they could survive in that other world. You've seen it, Charlie, you've walked in it. You understand tis no place for the living. At the Grathyyl, their talents were . . . bent. Changed." Mrs. Ficke gestured at the shining blue vial. "It were this substance what was used to do it. It comes from that place. The Grathyyl. And when they was all changed fully, they entered the world of the dead, and weren't ever seen again. What happened to them, how they perished, no one knows. But there was one what did not perish. You've seen her."

The darkness seemed to bend nearer.

"The drughr," whispered Charlie.

Mrs. Ficke nodded. "Aye. What corrupted Jacob Marber, what fed on the littlest talents. But she weren't nothing like the talent she'd once been, when first she entered the orsine to protect the gateways. Twisted, she was, by all her long years in that terrible world. It was said she could appear in the dreams of the living, taking on the resemblances of those she'd known. She could walk through walls, come an go at will. An she could cross between the worlds to pick apart the living, like a bit of cod on a plate. She'd become something else entirely, an was no longer human.

"This dust, Charlie, tis all that remains of her in this world. That were the drughr's touch you felt, when your forehead healed. That were her."

Charlie stared at the shining blue vial, feeling a sickening in his gut.

"Are you afraid?" she asked.

"It's not that. I've . . . seen this, before. This kind of glowing. In Mar. He used to shine like this, too."

Mrs. Ficke pursed her lips in a thin line. "The shining boy," she murmured. "I had not thought of him. Alice spoke of him too, of course. Not like the rest of you, was he?"

Charlie didn't tell her about what Jacob Marber had said, about the drughr being Marlowe's mother. About the hunger that was in her, her terrible desire for Mar. The memory of it was murky and there were holes in it but he was sure of it all the same. He rubbed his face with his hands. He needed to think. "Miss Davenshaw never said what kind of a talent Mar was. But Ko and Ribs said he was . . . different."

"We all of us heard stories about him, when he was a baby. How Jacob Marber tried to steal him away."

"I heard those stories, too," said Charlie. "He wasn't like those stories. He was just . . . Mar."

The old woman was looking at him strangely, her lined face grooved and etched in the lanternlight. "You miss him," she said quietly.

Charlie swallowed back the lump in his throat. He passed his hand over the blue vial and the shine intensified, pulsed, faded. "It's strange how it felt, having my talent back. Even if just for a moment. But it wasn't real, was it?"

"Would you want it again, even so?"

Charlie shuddered. "It's an evil thing. No. No, I wouldn't."

Mrs. Ficke seemed to relax. "Alice Quicke was right about you. She said you were stronger even than your own talent. She said the strength was inside you."

Charlie felt the heat rise to his face. He wasn't used to hearing such things. He turned to go and was already at the hidden door when Mrs. Ficke spoke again, stopping him.

"There is one thing else," she said. "One thing important. The corrupted dust is still connected to the drughr, wherever she might be. And tis still powerful. The drughr might have lost her strength to Henry Berghast, but this dust would be a way for her to . . . reacquire it."

Charlie shook his head, confused. "But Dr. Berghast destroyed the drughr. At the orsine. I was there, Mrs. Ficke. The drughr was dying, she had no power left. She took hold of Dr. Berghast, she dragged him under, but . . . she was dying. I could see it."

"Think, now. Did you *see* the drughr die?"

Charlie hesitated.

The old woman raised her troubled eyes, the candlelight glinting in them like twin flames. But whatever she was thinking, she seemed to decide against it. "The drughr belongs to the world of the dead," she said instead. "She's existed at the edge of that world for centuries. Became what she was because of it. I don't know what it would mean to say now: *She is dead.* She always was, Charlie. And she never can be."

Charlie felt a coldness go through him. He was thinking of Marlowe, trapped in that other world. The shining blue vial pulsed brighter as he reached for it. "You're saying this can bring the drughr . . . back?"

"I'm saying it is a possibility."

"We should hide it, then," he said, his voice hardening. "Or destroy it."

The old woman smiled angrily. "Hide it? The drughr's no police inspector, Charlie, fumbling about in the dark, taking breaks for her tea. She will smell out the dust, like a wolf. The two are *connected.* Where would you hide it? Nowhere is safe."

"So we destroy it."

"An how would you do that? 'Tis the very stuff of which the drughr is made. You cannot burn it, or break it, or drown it, or crush it. You cannot scatter it any more than you could scatter the drughr herself."

Charlie felt his impatience boiling up. He thought of the drughr, still alive maybe. He knew Marlowe would not be safe, afraid and alone in that other world, not once the drughr returned to strength. Even if they could get him out, he'd not be safe.

"I don't know how," he said sharply, "but we have to try. There's got to be a way."

The old woman leaned back on her stool. When she spoke, her voice was deadly soft. "Even though it could make you a haelan, again? Even though it could bring back your talent?"

Charlie glared. "I don't care about that."

"No?"

"No."

The old woman watched him, her expression lost in shadow.

Just then the cellar door beyond banged open, and Edward called down. He came stomping down the steps, heavy as a workhorse, and he was swinging his gloves and smiling, a great shaggy bear of a man.

It was like a spell broke then. Half a head again higher than any other man Charlie'd known, even than the flesh giant Lymenion, with a belly that overhung his waistline and a powerful neck that gave his shoulders a narrow look, Edward Ficke crowded the cellar until the very walls seemed to buckle. His beard smelled of the pickled onions he liked to eat. His nose was red and running from the cold and he was still dressed in his greatcoat and hat. He'd bartered away the dark Albany Chandlers carriage to a wainwright, he said, for a wagon and two horses.

"Come see, come see," he said excitedly.

Charlie didn't understand; and then, suddenly, he did. The wagon would be suitable for transporting the strange brood of children. As they followed him up, Charlie watched Mrs. Ficke's face with apprehension but saw nothing in it. What Edward showed them, proudly, in the narrow mews behind the shop, was an ancient Burton wagon, with small wheels and a wooden roof, all of it painted in yellow and red stripes. It had been used by a menagerie showman's family in days gone by. In fraying harness stood two bony and skittish horses, better suited for the tannery than the road. Charlie watched Mrs. Ficke walk the length of it, banging her hand in distraction against the rails, clearly unhappy with it. There was a patched and weather-faded awning over the driver's bench, tied with different colors of rope, and when Charlie opened the little door in the back he saw loose slats and nails bent every which way and no seating to speak of. Mrs. Ficke was looking at her brother with a strange expression.

He just smiled happily. "It even come with extra nails," he said, pulling out a long box from behind the driver's seat. "And an oil slicker for when it rains. Do you like it?"

Mrs. Ficke sighed. Charlie suspected the value of the old carriage must have far exceeded this.

"Your nose is all adrip," she said.

He ran his sleeve over his whiskers, his mouth half-open in antici-pation.

She gave a tired smile. "You did good, Edward. It's perfect."

"Yeah," he breathed. He moved behind Charlie to get a better look at the rickety wagon. Charlie could feel his hot breath on the top of his head, like a great horse.

"Yeah," Edward said again.

Charlie was beginning to see that that was the thing about Edward. There was a clarity to him, a singleness of purpose to whatever he did. He did one thing, and then he did the next thing. He didn't let himself get tangled up in fifty tasks and obligations, he didn't let his mind run off in every direction at once. His thinking was like water running downhill, seeking its channel, following it down. Charlie bet most of Edward's life people had treated him like he was stupid, but that wasn't it, that wasn't it at all.

"Now." Mrs. Ficke turned to Charlie. "I've decided I'll go with you to Agrigento," she said. "But the children will come too. They ought to be with their own kind. But I must pass through London first; we can hire a vessel off Miller's Wharf. There might be more information on the drughr's dust at the institute's old offices. I want to be sure of it. You are familiar with Margaret Harrogate's residence? Her old offices?"

Charlie nodded, his relief giving way to unease. He'd hated Mrs. Harrogate's row house; he'd been afraid there, and alone, attacked by a litch while sleeping, and barely surviving. Some nights he still had nightmares. But it was there he'd first met Mar, too, first felt that fierce protective love for him, first sensed what it was to maybe have a brother. He looked at Mrs. Ficke, and nodded.

She turned back to her brother. "Edward. Did you chance to see Deirdre this morning?"

Charlie remembered the glyph-twisted girl upstairs. He watched the concentration in Edward's face as he thought about it. "Yes," said Edward.

"What's to be done?"

"She don't want to go." He shook his massive head. "She's afeared of going. She wants to stay. They all do."

Mrs. Ficke was frowning. Her arm was sore and she'd reached two fingers in to massage the cloth folded at the stump. She and her brother looked nothing alike, Charlie thought, and yet all their lives they must have had only each other. Now watching Edward's aged face he saw suddenly that the gentle giant wasn't just thinking about the girl, little Deirdre, he was thinking about himself, too, about how he would live and all his days to come with his sister far away, and Charlie felt again a sudden upwelling of sadness. It was his doing. He would have to live with it.

Caroline left Edward at the wagon, with the Ovid boy.

Back inside, along the ancient low stone corridor, into the shop with its tumble of packed trunks, cases, cloth-bundled goods for the journey. Up the rickety stairs, to see the girl.

A feeling was in her, a feeling of significance. Something was changing in all of their lives, never to be undone. The corrupted dust worried her; she knew it would be safest, perhaps, at the villa outside Agrigento; but she knew too that to carry it would bring other dangers, dangers she didn't like to think too deeply on.

The children were in their rooms. Silent and curled into their stuffed toys or seated on the edge of their cots, peering down at their hands. She greeted each and refilled their glasses and brushed their leaves with her fingers, Wislawa and Brendan, Maddie, Chester. These were the glyph-twisted, grown treelike and stilled and no longer what they'd once been. In the eyes of any, they must seem horrors, mutated beyond all recognition. Berghast had done this, had tempted them into this change, desperate to make a new glyphic before the old one died, desperate to keep the orsine whole. He had failed; he was dead now; these poor children remained.

And this is what they did, how they lived. Locked inside their own silences, or humming through the hours, alive and separate and no longer like the children they had been. It broke Caroline's old heart to see.

Deirdre, the second eldest, was not in her room. She frowned in the soft afternoon light. She found her in little Seamus's room, running her fingers along his scalp, down his neck, soothing him. Deirdre was like that. Caroline stood at the door watching until she turned her small face. Caroline knew the abomination of the girl, the skin encrusted like bark, gleaming as if burnished by the light, the leafy twigs like spines sprouting from the backs of her arms, the one leg twisted already into solid wood, the roots pushing always against the floor as if seeking purchase. She knew this and yet saw none of it. What she saw was the shine in the girl's eye, the eager sweet smile she turned upon her, slow as it was, the glow of recognition in her face. Caroline's heart was a dark assistant to the task at hand: she knew she was not to have favorites, that all of them were darling in her eyes, and yet she could not help the smile that came to her face unbidden, whenever she saw young Deirdre.

But something was wrong with the girl, something was different.

The girl's feet had always been twisted but now new knuckled tendrils of wood had spread across the floorboards, under the carpet, as if seeking purchase.

Caroline had never seen anything like it. It was this Edward had been trying to explain. She went in carefully and kneeled before the girl and little Seamus, feeling her old knees ache, and she ran her liver-spotted hand lightly over the spreading tendrils. It was, she thought in horror, as if the girl were sending out roots. She wondered what effect the corrupted dust might have on these little ones and then she stopped herself. She loved them as they were; they didn't need any kind of changing.

"Was Seamus frightened, my little bird?" she murmured to Deirdre. "Did you come here to let him know he weren't alone? It was good of you."

The girl blinked her yellow eyes. Her head, creaking, nodded.

"Ah, Seamus, little one," she said. "What is it, what's all this? We're to be goin in the morning, child. It won't do to be so afraid, hm? There, now. You're not alone; you'll never be alone."

The light came whitely in through the limed-over window. Caroline could feel the great stillness of the shop below, and was troubled. The corrupted dust would be a beacon of danger, to any who were near it. Yet somehow she must smuggle these strange, wonderful children south with her. They could not stay. There would be no safety here, not with her gone.

Safety. What a word it was.

Well, she thought. *We build the door, but have no say in who will knock at it. All we can do is answer.*

5

THE PRESENCE

What are you?" Jeta asked the apparition, afraid. "Are you a . . . spirit?"

The institute was cold; an evil wind came in through the broken wall. Somewhere in the ruins Ruth would be picking through the debris, looking for traces of the corrupted dustworker.

The boy, flickering, watched her. A gauzy blue shine seemed to blow across his features, like cobwebs pulling apart. She saw no sign on his rags of the Cairndale crest and yet some part of her, somehow, understood that he was one of those who'd died in the fire. The spirit dead, they were called. She knew there had been an orsine on the island and she knew of its breaking and perhaps, she thought, the world of the living and the world of the dead had got tangled up in the process. Perhaps this poor boy had slipped through, or failed to. He was very young, even for a Cairndale ward. He kept parting his bloodless lips, as if to speak.

Where . . . am I? he said.

Jeta filled with a sudden pity. "You're at Cairndale. What's left of it."

A shadow rippled across the shining boy's face. He was so small. It seemed to be a terrible effort for him just to remain visible, to remain in front of her, the darkness eating away at his edges.

Cairndale . . . , he whispered. *But it's gone. It's all gone.* He raised his face and the darkness upon it seemed to recede, like a hood being drawn back. *I have to find someone,* he said. *Jacob Marber. He will know what to do.*

Jeta went still. "Marber. The dustworker?"

The apparition watched her.

Slowly, she shook her head. "Jacob Marber's dead. He died here, in the fire."

The apparition was quiet. Then he looked up. *You're a talent. I can feel it.*

The flat midday light shifted, as if a great wing had passed overhead, and the wall was visible through the boy's form. The wallpaper was scorched in a strange pattern, as if tendrils of fire had lashed across it. She should be angrier, or more afraid, she knew. But something in the boy's words made her heart hurt in ways she hadn't known for years. It made her remember the girl she had been in the orphanage, after Cairndale had refused her. The world of the dead and the world of the living were close here, where the orsine had been. There might be many dead within these walls.

You've come for it, too, the apparition said softly. He raised a flickering blue hand, very small. *Don't be afraid. You need the dust too, Jeta, don't you? We can help each other—*

She startled at that. She took a step back, reaching involuntarily for the coin at her throat. "How do you know my name?"

The ghost gave her a quick look of deep cunning, unexpected and frightening; then it was gone, and he was just a child again, a boy.

Because we are the same, he whispered unhappily.

·   ·   ·

The little ghost had something to show her.

Somehow she knew this, without him having to say it. He turned and vanished into the house and she followed, the bonebird at her wrist, her long patchwork skirts swishing. The corridors twisted and split into narrower passages and the faint ghost seemed always to be just ahead, turning a corner, slipping through a doorway. Past rooms dark where ceilings had collapsed, blocking out windows. Past rooms open to the white sky. She reached a narrow staircase, saw the ghost disappear through a little door at the top.

It was a long flat portion of the roof, with a low wall on three sides. The daylight was dazzling. A cold air stirred Jeta's skirts, ran its fingers through her braids. She paused with the bonebird on her wrist, studying where flames had eaten away the center of the roof. She could see down through the gloom, nearly to the basement, could hear meltwater dapping from below. The ghost was nowhere to be seen.

Jeta cursed. On the far side of the roof stood an iron dovecote, orange with rust, its doors ajar, and while she stood, squinting, the bonebird lifted lightly from her wrist and flew across. A strange halting flight, buffeted by the air, as if it were made from paper.

"For God's sake," she muttered.

It had alighted on a perch inside the cage. Carefully, she followed. On the cage floor Jeta saw the crushed remains of two other bonebirds, half-covered in a dusting of snow. There was no mistaking what they were, what they had been. She frowned, wondering at it. The fires had not done that. In the courtyard below, Ruth trudged past, her satchel hanging heavily. She did not look up.

All at once the bonebird launched itself in a clatter from cage wall to cage wall, banging down hard into the bones of its brethren, and then shooting off out past Jeta, into the sky. She watched it go, feeling something in her chest compress.

That was when she glimpsed him, the little boy, the ghost. Through the hole in the roof. He was standing all the way down in the basement, like at the bottom of a well of darkness, peering up. His face was impassive, his blue hair flickering.

Then he turned, stepped out of sight.

"Wait!" she called in annoyance.

If he wanted her in the cellar, why lead her to the roof? But she leaped unsteadily along the ruined wall and hurried back down the steps, along the burned-out corridor, working her way into the ravaged belly of the manor. The air was thick with the smell of snow and charred things, and in the gloom the floor was littered with debris. She stumbled, caught herself, hurried onward until she found the servants' stairs leading down and scrambled over a pile of charred wood and stopped, breathing hard, in the ruined cellar.

The only light filtered down from the hole in the roof three floors above. It cast crescents of shadow over the melted jars, the knocked-over shelves. She could hear the slow sound of dripping water.

And then there he was.

He stood at the edge of a deep blackness. It was a tunnel, she realized, leading away into the earth. Darkness seeped from it like a cold air, like a faint whispering.

This is how he got in, said the ghost. *Through here. It was a long time ago. It's so . . . strange. I can almost remember him here . . .*

It wasn't the voice of a child. Jeta felt a sudden sharp fear, wondering what could have happened to him, and shuddered despite herself. Everything he said sounded jumbled, like it almost made sense, like in a dream. "Who?" she asked. "Who got in?"

Jacob.

Jacob Marber. The dustworker who'd served the drughr. She still didn't understand what he could have to do with this child, how they had known each other. Had Jacob killed this little one? Ruth would be most interested in this child.

An expression of pain distorted the little ghost's features. *It's all connected*, he said, with a sudden anguish. *That's what they didn't know. It's all connected, Jeta. Jacob didn't come here for the reasons he said.*

She hesitated. "What reasons?"

He didn't come here for me.

"Who were you?" she asked.

I was the one he loved most, the ghost whispered. *That's what he always said.*

Jeta walked around the well of daylight, her thoughts racing. She was afraid he would vanish again. But the apparition turned with her, his child's gaze steady. He was a part of this, a piece of the puzzle. What was she not understanding? The boy had known Jacob Marber in life; he knew of the corrupted dust. She wet her lips.

"How did you die?" she asked.

But something shifted in the boy then, as if a change had come over him. His face seemed somehow older, more knowing. Whatever world he walked in, it was not quite the world Jeta herself knew.

He did not answer her question. Instead, he said: *We can find it together, Jeta. The dust. Jacob's body. If you'll . . . let me.*

"How?"

I'm . . . connected to him. To Jacob. I don't know how to explain it.

"Is his body here, at Cairndale?"

The apparition's face flickered, an eerie blue in the darkness. *I don't feel him. Not here.*

"But you could feel him? If he were close?"

The ghost drew nearer. It did not glide but seemed somehow to be suddenly next to her, extending its small, flickering hand. And then it passed through her own wrist.

It felt as if she were immersing her arm in icy water. And then the cold was climbing up to her shoulder, enveloping her, and she was seeing in her mind's eye that terrible last day at the tabor, her uncle cutting a coin from his coat and pressing it into her unclean hand, the wagons creaking slowly away over the rutted roadbed, and Coulton in his bright waistcoat watching all of it. And she saw Berghast at Nickel Street West, lifting her chin with his two fingers, studying her dark eyes, and refusing her. *She is not for us.* Damning her—a child, a dark-skinned Roma girl with too little English, alone in all the world—damning her to the workhouses and desperation. And she saw, too, Claker Jack's long grimy body, folding itself over her in that alley, she felt the fear and hopelessness and burning gratitude again as he led her through the fog to the waiting carriage. And somehow she knew the apparition could see all this too, could feel it, *know* it as only she knew it.

And she saw, then, how they were the same. How the child too had been refused in his time. She saw darkness and felt herself awakening alone, her loved one stolen from her. She saw train tracks, vanishing into mist. Darkness that was like a light, shining with its own horror. She saw a powerful man, bearded, with tattoos all over his arms and throat, tattoos that were moving—

She stumbled backward, gasping.

You blame your talent? said the ghost, a confusion filling his face, a sadness. *Oh. Oh. You think you can't be loved, because of it. You can be. I used to think that way, too. So much bad happens. But it isn't our fault, what happened to us. It's theirs. One day they'll see it. They'll see what you are, and they'll be sorry. They'll be afraid.*

Her head felt gluey, thick. "It doesn't matter. It's done. There's no changing what's done."

But tomorrow doesn't have to be like today. It could be different. You could be different.

"How?" she asked. The voice seemed not to belong to her but to another, far away.

First, we have to find the dust, said the boy. *Then I can show you.*

She rubbed at her arms. The cellar darkened. Almost against her will, as if she couldn't stop herself, she whispered: "All right. Yes. We'll find it together."

But we have to hurry. They'll be coming.

Jeta looked up. "Who? Who will come?"

Them.

It sounded almost like a threat. She felt a deep dread, watching the faint outlines of the tunnel through his flickering form. They were so alike, she and this child. Unwanted. Unloved. Condemned for a talent they'd never sought and didn't desire. And yet, rising up out of the back of her mind, as if out of a still pool, came the knowledge that he wasn't telling her everything, that he was more than he seemed, that there was a dark and complicated story behind him. It would be madness to trust him. Then she thought of Claker Jack—distant, cold, autocratic, yes; but also the one person in all her life who'd sheltered her, accepted her for what she was. He'd set her a difficult task because he believed in her; she would not disappoint him.

The little ghost was fading, thin as muslin.

"Wait. Can you even leave this place?" she asked in alarm. "Can you come with me, back to Edinburgh? How will I *find* you?"

She turned and turned in place, staring around at the shadows.

But the ghost of the child was gone.

The winter sun was low and the shadows long over the snow when she found Ruth in the Cairndale courtyard. The woman stood waiting for her, the snow crisscrossed by her tracks as if she'd been pacing there, her cloak weighed down by a satchel stuffed with charred books, old manuscripts.

"You found books," said Jeta.

"And you, I see, found nothing," replied Ruth.

Jeta drew her red glove back over her bone fingers. She started to answer sharply about the ghost child but then did not. She didn't know what stopped her. She watched Ruth's eyes, pale and creepy, and bit back her words, and told herself there would be time enough.

But then the moment was gone, and something lurched inside her, like a warning, and she looked up and saw the bonebird descend out of the white sky with a suddenness that made her catch her breath. It alighted on her wrist, clicked its strange wings. The answering pull in Jeta's own bones was painful.

"Not nothing," she said with a grimace.

Ruth drew the hood of her cloak over her gray hair. She began walking across the snowy field, toward the gates, the waiting carriage beyond. "Bonebirds are evil things, child. Harbingers of the dead. You are unwise to draw this one to you."

"It wasn't my doing," Jeta protested. "It just . . . came."

"You should destroy it, while you have the chance. Who knows what will follow it to you? There is no telling who its master is."

Jeta followed along, quiet. It did not *feel* like an agent of evil.

There was a new soberness in them both as they rode from the gates of Cairndale, the carriage springs creaking and jouncing, Jeta lifting the lace from the window to watch the old iron gates recede. On her lap, hidden in her cloak like a parcel, was the bonebird.

Ruth, for her part, took out a small notebook and a pencil and wrote for a long while. She'd withdrawn from her glove the message that had been tied to the bonebird's foot, and consulted it from time to time, as Jeta watched. The carriage rattled and sped on, the satchel clinking at their feet.

"Ruth?" Jeta said after a moment, tentative.

"What?"

"How many do you think died there, at Cairndale?"

"I don't know. Many."

"What happens to them? To the spirit dead, I mean. How do they cross over to the other side, without an orsine? Are they trapped in this world forever?"

Ruth looked up in impatience. "The dead don't use an orsine, child. When you die, you cross over. It has nothing to do with an orsine. An orsine is a doorway for . . . other things."

"Like the drughr?"

Ruth set down her pencil and closed her notebook over it to mark her page. "The drughr, yes. But also Henry Berghast's experiments. He used to send talents through, into the world of the dead. I don't know why. It was something the other children at Cairndale used to whisper about. As to the orsine's exact purpose, where it came from?" She studied Jeta with a grim, pale stare. Adjusted her hat. "The world of the dead and the world of the living abide uneasily. What exists on the one side cannot exist on the other, *must not* exist. That is what makes the creature you carry with you so . . . unnatural." She nodded at the bonebird, buried in Jeta's lap. "It bears the taint of that world like a pestilence. And no, not all who die become like the spirit dead. Some just seem to be lost. But of those who do, it's said they drift through the other world shapeless, lost, slowly forgetting who they were in life. It is the forgetting that is usually described, in the old books. Why? Why are you interested in the spirit dead all of a sudden?"

"I was just . . . thinking. About what will happen now."

"The world will not suddenly be filled with the newly dead, child," Ruth said dryly. "You may be sure of that. The sun will rise and set. The dead will go into the ground."

Jeta flushed. She hated the older woman's condescension, but she either suffered it or learned nothing. "What about the corrupted dust we've been sent to find?" she pressed. "What does it do, exactly?"

A cold smile creased Ruth's eyes. For a moment Jeta expected her not to reply. But then she seemed to decide something inside herself, and said, "Do you remember what our driver said about the sailor's tattoos? The man they pulled from the loch? He said they were . . . peculiar. Jacob Marber was said to have marks in his skin that *moved*. The marks—Marber's 'tattoos'—were made of a very unusual substance. You see, the dust that Marber manipulated came from that other world, from the far side of the orsine. It was put inside him by the drughr. It increased his strength, but also tethered him to the monster. And that dust, which helped to destroy Cairndale, is more terrible than anything you or I have ever seen. It is powerful, and dangerous, and very old."

Jeta felt her blood go cold. She saw again that strange image from the ghost child's mind, the image of a bearded man with twisting tattoos. That would be Marber, surely. She felt like she was trapped in someone else's story, like she didn't understand all of what was going on around her.

The day was going and the driver stopped the carriage and walked all around it lighting the lanterns and then he climbed heavily back up and they rode on.

When they were moving again, and the driver could not overhear, Ruth continued.

"How the drughr's dust can exist here, no one, not even Claker Jack, can explain," she said. "All that is known is that somehow Jacob Marber became its vessel. He was a corrupted thing not because he *did* evil. The evil was literally *inside* him. And is, evidently, inside him still. The Abbess wrote to Claker Jack with news of the body, and instructions on how to recover it. We shall search the mortuaries next."

Jeta tugged at the fingers of her glove. "Who is the Abbess?"

"Someone even Claker Jack fears."

Jeta couldn't imagine Claker Jack afraid of anyone. Gradually the road under the coach gave way to the clatter of cobblestones. Soon there were figures moving through the darkness, dim lanterns along the streets; they'd entered the outskirts of Edinburgh. Ruth turned her lined face to the window, gloved fingers interlaced over her notebook.

"I still don't understand," said Jeta. "How could the Abbess know about the body? Does she live near here?"

"How do any of them know anything?" muttered Ruth. "But if she lived near Cairndale, I should think our presence here unnecessary. I do not ask Claker Jack his business; I only follow mine. You should learn the same, child. When we find the dustworker's corpse, we will see if the dust is still there."

"Still there?"

"Surrounding his body. Floating above it. Yes."

Jeta hesitated. Ruth had never been so forthcoming and she didn't know what to believe. The bonebird clicked in her lap like a strange clock. "What does it *do*, this dust?"

"Ah," said Ruth softly. The lanterns on the outside of the carriage cast a swinging light across her features; they were turning now up the cobbled side street where they'd taken lodgings. "That, child, is a very good question."

The very next morning she and Ruth began their grim search through the city's deadhouses, asking after the drowned man from the loch at Cairndale. It did not snow again but the air was bladed with cold and the stone city was hard and dark and still.

Days passed. The apparition of the child did not appear; the bonebird remained. In the early hours, Ruth would come to Jeta's room with the tincture in hand, and Jeta would catch her peering at the covered birdcage, at the bonebird hidden there, with a barely concealed wrath.

They'd tried the cemeteries first in the hope that a clerk or a groundskeeper might have word of the recent dead but what the locals knew was nothing useful. After that they tried the mortuaries. Even with the tincture to mute her talent, the pull of the dead's bones on Jeta was sometimes so powerful she would have to close her eyes, clench her jaw, suffer the condescensions of whatever gentlemen were nearest. If they only knew; it was not faintheartedness that plagued her.

At last they came to the mortuary of one William Robert Macrae.

His was a shabby, dark establishment of stone and brick. At the threshold Jeta sensed at once that something was different. She hesitated until Ruth pushed her in and even then she went unwilling. It was dim inside, lit by a single candle in a dish on a low wooden counter. A bell rang as the door swung shut. The candle stood sideways in its wax, then steadied.

"Is it him? Is he here?" Ruth whispered, studying her face.

Jeta shook her head. "I don't know. Something's . . . different."

They were in a narrow antechamber, with a half window greasy from smoke and long disuse. A sharp metallic stink filled the gloom and Jeta knew it was the chemical smell of the mortician's art. She could just make out a hatstand, with two silk hats askew upon it, both cheap-looking. A small table with an out-of-date copy of *Punch*. Beside the candle stood an inkwell, an ancient bronze paperweight of Wellington on a horse. A pale green door with a pewter handle led into the back.

After a moment there came a creaking of floorboards, and then a stout man in shirtsleeves entered—the mortician, Jeta guessed, by the leather apron he wore. He left the door standing wide behind him.

And there, in the shadows beyond, stood the apparition of the boy.

Jeta froze, alarmed. The dark corridor where he'd materialized was cut by a lantern burning someplace just out of sight. Her blood was loud in her ears. His hair was still adrift in its invisible waters, the faint blue shine was still there at his edges, smudging them. He watched her with his serious, childlike face.

She looked quickly to Ruth, but the older woman did not see him, though he stood in plain sight. Nor had the proprietor taken any notice.

Jeta felt once more that sudden, overwhelming pity for the ghost she had felt back in the cellar at Cairndale, that same powerful longing.

With great difficulty, she forced herself to look away.

The proprietor was short, nearly bald; his muttonchops stood out in a frazzle along his cheeks. The tin clasps on his apron glinted in the candlelight. He scratched at a sore on his chin, eyed Ruth's satchel with a wary eye, as if afraid she might be selling something. "Mr. Macrae, at your service. What is it I can do for you?"

While Ruth explained about the dead man they were seeking, Jeta risked a look at the ghost boy. He turned slowly, casting a flickering glance over his shoulder, filled with an inexpressible sadness. Then he receded into the mortuary dark.

When he was gone, it was like a great heaviness was removed from Jeta's heart; she shook her head slowly, and came back to herself.

Ruth had finished talking. The mortician nodded. "Drowned man from up Cairndale way? Aye, I know him. Queer business, that. There's some as said he had something to do with it all, though I don't see how it can be so. I've been working the dead for forty years and there's no possibility this one died last fall."

Ruth's eyes flickered. "I beg your pardon. He is *here*?"

"Aye. Forgive me," he said, suddenly anxious. "Are you and the lass here relations? There wasn't any papers on him, and the clothes was as good as rags when he come in here. We just didn't know who he was."

Ruth's teeth glinted in the candlelight. "That is so," she said. "We are relations."

"I allowed that maybe you were. I'm sorry for your loss."

Ruth nodded. She took off her gloves, finger by finger, and caught Jeta's eye, Jeta who still hadn't reacted, who'd said nothing. "The dust-worker is *here*, Jeta," she said grimly. "In this building."

The mortician, disconcerted, cleared his throat. "Did you say *dust*, missus?"

For just a moment the lights seemed to dim, as if a wind had passed through. The mortician told them about the body and the tattoos that moved of their own accord over its hands and arms and chest. He supposed as family they maybe knew something about that their own selves, he couldn't say. He hooked his blackened thumbs in the cords of his apron and explained then about the dust, suspended in the air. If they didn't believe him, well, he wasn't the only one who'd seen it. There was his assistant, for one, and that detective inspector sent up from London to investigate the body. They could verify it, also. The body ought to have been disposed of by now but it was just luck that they hadn't sent it away. He'd have some papers for them to fill out, of course. He paused. "Did you want to see him, then?"

"Yes."

He hesitated. He glanced at Jeta. "'Tis not a sight for young eyes, miss. A man in a place like this isn't the same as what you'd see in a drawing room at a wake."

"Oh, my granddaughter's seen death before, Mr. Macrae," Ruth replied. "In all sorts of places, I assure you."

He gave her a funny look at that, but said nothing more. He led them down a short sloping corridor to the embalming room, where a man in spectacles stood abruptly, as if hoisted on cables. This was the assistant. He was working on a body on a long table. There were tubes and jars of green liquid and gears and leather bellows. Jeta felt the dark pull of the bones of the dead all around. She cast a sharp glance around but saw no sign of the ghostly child. The mortician did not stop but passed down a shadowy set of stairs to a cold cellar and there he lighted a lantern and led them deeper, past stacks of bodies on the walls. At the end of the room, a heavy door opened onto a small chamber. The mortician hooked the lantern and adjusted the burn and then they saw it, the thing itself, what they had come in search of: the dustworker's corpse, the fearsome Jacob Marber.

Jeta caught her breath, suddenly afraid.

For some shadowed thing crouched atop the slab. Then she saw: it was the apparition, the little boy, straddling the body. But his mouth was too big for his face, and he was ... *licking* the white skin of the dead man's chest. He had no eyes and his teeth were black and there were far too many for his mouth. He raised his dripping face toward her; Jeta stumbled backward in horror.

Then, in a blink, he was gone.

Once again, the others had seen nothing. Ruth entered the room, oblivious, and circled the body, her satchel clinking. A stained cloth had been laid across its privates for modesty but the markings on its arms and chest were clearly visible. The tattoos moved in the firelight. Jeta, her heart still pounding, approached.

The dustworker had been handsome, in life. His thick beard was black and long, his eyebrows expressive. But his face had been slashed, from mouth to ear, and one eye was marbled shut. There were bruises along his ribs and one of his legs. How anyone could think he'd drowned puzzled Jeta; here was one who'd died violently.

"Miss, if it's a bit disturbing for you—" said the mortician, uneasy.

But she ignored him. She ran her gloved hand lightly over the dead man's arm, tracing the strange shifting tattoos. What the ghost had been doing, she couldn't imagine. She could see no sign of rot in the flesh, no decomposition at all. The body, uncorrupted, glowed whitely in the cold light.

"It's him," said Ruth softly, raising her lined eyes. "It's Jacob Marber."

"Is that his name, then?" called the mortician, from the doorway. "We never did know what to call him. It's good for a man to be buried under his own name."

"I do not see the dust you spoke of," said Ruth.

It was true, Jeta saw with a sudden disappointment: there was no dust.

"Ach," replied Mr. Macrae. "That'd be the doing of old Mrs. Ficke. She was managing the affairs of all them poor wee ones that was taken in the fire. Didn't know who else to summon. She took a bit of it off the body, she did. Not without permission, mind." He wiped at his forehead with his naked palm, then rubbed it on his apron. "We didn't imagine there'd be relatives, you see. An it all disappeared after that. But it was there, missus, I promise you." He scratched at his whiskers in the dimness. "You don't seem much surprised by it, now. Was it always like that with him? What was the matter with him? The inspector up from London reckoned it was magnetism. Mr. Macpherson is of a mind he had a bit of the devil in him. Respectfully, of course."

"I beg your pardon. She *took* the *dust?*" said Ruth sharply, ignoring all the rest.

The mortician blinked. "Aye. In a wee bottle. Should I not have allowed it?" He looked from the woman to Jeta and back. "It's a queer thing to do, I grant you."

"It is gone, then. She will be from Cairndale, you can be certain." Ruth's face was tired, angry. To the mortician she said, "How do we find this Ficke woman? You will have her details, I trust?"

"Aye, missus. We keep a careful record. There was that sad time last November when poor Mrs. Ficke was in here every other day, nearly. Mr. Macpherson upstairs can find you the address." He cleared his throat, uncertain. "Shall I leave the two of you with Mr. Marber, then?"

But Ruth didn't answer. She took off her satchel and perched it on the edge of a little table and removed the bottles with great care.

It was time. Jeta knew—had known, from the moment the mortician showed them the body—just what it was Ruth expected her to do. And she felt herself making a space in a corner of her heart, a space where all the parts of her that were afraid or filled with pity could go to and hide.

Ruth brushed her hands together as if clearing them of dust and uncorked the first bottle and poured out a fine black powder the length of Marber's body. The mortician made a small sound of surprise from the edge of the room.

But he didn't speak. For Jeta had already removed her red glove in the lanternlight and raised her hands and she felt the familiar pain bloom in her bones. She shivered, could not stop shivering. She was reaching out, feeling for the little knucklebones of vertebrae in his neck. There were seven and she worked her way carefully, as if with invisible fingers, until she felt the first of them, at the base of the skull. She knew from experience that snapping the lower vertebrae would lead to something going wrong with the victim's breathing and then to massive heart failure and a messier death. She was more efficient now.

With a sharp twist of her wrist, she snapped the uppermost vertebra in Mr. Macrae's neck and severed his spinal cord. His legs went out from under him. He was dead before he struck the floor. *Be merciful*, Claker Jack had told her. *Know mercy*.

She didn't even know what the word meant anymore.

The answering pain in her bones was a deep ringing sort of pain, and she balled her hands into fists to contain it.

The dustworker's body was letting off a strange gray smell. Jeta could hear a faint hiss as the powder ate away at the flesh. Ruth was uncorking a second bottle, a bottle of clear liquid, and dabbed it into a cloth and began to run the cloth over the corpse's arms and chest.

"Will you be able to get any dust from the tattoos?"

The older woman examined the cloth. "Nothing. They are just residue. They are . . . inert." She gave Jeta a pointed look. She prompted, "There is the other one upstairs, yes? The assistant? Be certain to get the Ficke woman's address first, hm?"

Jeta nodded. She lifted her skirts and stepped over the mortician in the doorway and went back up through the darkness to the embalming room.

Mr. Macpherson again stood as she entered and he waited for the others but Jeta just gave a little shrug. Her arms were crossed at her breast, the bone fingers hidden.

"They are still below," she said. "I did not like it. I do not like the dead, sir."

"Ah. It's natural, miss. My own daughters don't like the smell of it in my clothes when I come home. 'Tis not for the young, I always say." He gave a nod of understanding. He shifted his chair so that he was blocking the body he was working on, out of politeness, and Jeta felt a twinge of guilt.

"There was a woman who came here, a Mrs. Ficke," she said. "Mr. Macrae was telling us about her. My grandmother was wondering if you took any record of her whereabouts. Her address, perhaps?"

"Aye, it'd be Caroline Ficke you want. Come here regular for a time, after the fire. Awful sad, that was." The man went to a small cabinet in the corner and withdrew a registry and brought it to her. He flipped to the back and on the second-to-last page his finger found something of interest. He stood near and she could smell the rank chemicals of his trade and a faint unwashed reek of his skin and she saw that he was much younger than she'd supposed.

"This'd be the one," he said to her, balancing the registry. "Mrs. Caroline Ficke, lives out at Albany Chandlers in the Grassmarket. 'Tis her brother's establishment, I believe. Paid for all the burials, she did. Worked for the institute in some fashion. Here it is, miss."

She followed his finger down the columns and saw the woman's name and address.

"Where is this? Is it far?" she asked.

He told her it was not; she could walk the distance in a half hour easy.

He gave her a shy smile and closed the leather registry and it was when he turned away that Jeta snapped his neck. She left him where he fell. She tore out the page with the Ficke woman's address.

In the meanwhile Ruth, displeased, had finished with the dustwork-er's body. When Jeta returned below there was a soft waxy-looking mess where the corpse had been. The old exile had already packed up her bottles. She unhooked the lantern.

"Is it done, child?" Ruth asked curtly. "The other one is dead?"

Jeta nodded.

Upstairs again, the older woman moved about the embalming room, looking for flammables. She overturned a jar of chemical preservative and poured out paraffin oil over everything. She went back down to the bodies below and Jeta could hear the scrape and crash of objects. Soon, she knew, it would all burn.

And there, standing over the body of the mortuary assistant, was the ghost.

She froze, afraid. He no longer looked twisted or dark, as he had in the cold-room below, but there was something about the way he lurked, flickering in the shadow, that made her shudder. Particles of light glit-tered, shifting his features, making his expression difficult to discern. She felt again a kind of fog come over her, as if the back of her skull were lifting lightly up, away.

You killed him, whispered the child.

But Jeta shook her head fiercely, glancing at where Ruth had gone. "What are you?" she hissed. Suddenly her anger was taking over. "What were you doing to that body? You're not a boy, don't tell me you were—"

The little ghost looked so sad. There was nothing monstrous about him now. *Please*, he whispered. *It's not like that. I'm not a monster, I'm not . . . what I was. I just shouldn't be here, on this side. Not like this. It's changing me. I need to cross back over . . .*

But Jeta was shaking her head, furious.

I'm sorry, he whispered. *I'm sorry. I'm sorry.*

"Where have you even been?" she continued. "You didn't *help* me find the body. You *followed* me to it. You used me."

The apparition's eyes seemed to darken then, as if a cavity behind them were opening. She saw again the image of his eyeless face, his blackened mouth, the insect-like way he'd crouched over the corpse. She had the eerie sensation of losing her balance.

The dust isn't here, he whispered. His lips parted, were sad. He turned his face as if hearing something. There was an urgency in him. *But it's close. I can . . . taste it. Whoever has it is nearby, in the streets. They're taking it somewhere. Come, I'll take you—*

Jeta put out a hand on the table to steady herself. She knew Ruth might come upstairs at any moment. "I don't trust you," she hissed.

I just need a bit of it, the child begged. He looked so small, so helpless. The pity she'd felt at Cairndale was rising in her again, a longing to protect him. *Just enough to cross over. You can keep the rest. Please.*

"Ruth will never—"

But the apparition cut her off. *They're taking it! Please!*

How small he was, how alone. His blue shine faded down the corridor to the front of the mortuary. Jeta went out to the little room at the front and unlocked the door, blew out the candles. It was like she was in a dream, and the air was slow around her, still. Her head hurt; the bones in her arms hurt. A small part of her was warning her not to trust him, the ghostly child, spirit dead, whatever he was.

And yet she put on her cloak, regardless; she opened the door. The shining child was already moving away, down the street. Just then, there came a whoosh; a sudden warm glow illuminated the mortuary behind her. It would burn hot and fast. Ruth would be through the door in a moment.

She felt for the coin at her neck, rubbed at it numbly, feeling as if everything was happening very far away. The child could lead her to the dust, she thought faintly; the child needed her.

And Jeta, fourteen years old, black-haired, black-eyed, a creature of bone and darkness, strode out of the light into the cold city.

6

FROM DUST

Caroline Ficke hurried uphill through the winding streets, uneasy.

In the deepening twilight the Ovid boy was a taller darkness at her side, his breath standing out in the cold. She carried a brown paper parcel under her arm, filled with provisions for the journey south; the boy carried several more, all tied with twine. A carriage rattled over the cobbles, lanterns already lit and swaying.

She'd been having dreams, disturbing dreams, dreams she knew better than to ignore. When last that happened, the world had been ripping itself asunder, the dustworker Marber had been stalking Cairndale, the glyphic had been dying. Those dear, irascible children had come to her door determined to learn a truth she'd had no business telling. Though she'd lost her own talent a lifetime ago, that talent had been a clink's strength, muscle and sinew, nothing to do with dreams. Oh, but there were mysteries beyond talentkind, too. As her dear Mr. Ficke, long dead, who had been tall and thin as a willow in winter, used to remind her, in those early years of their marriage, when they both would lie late into the morning simply because they could not bear to rise from each other. *There are many kinds of gifts, Caroline,* he would say, *not all of them talents, for the human mind is multifold and mysterious.*

She looked at Charlie askance. He was so young to bear the loss of a talent. They all were. It was good he had friends around him to help; maybe if the other exiles hadn't been sent away, if they'd been offered some kindness, maybe they wouldn't all have collapsed into that terrible underworld of malice and crime down in London. She knew enough about it to know she was among the lucky ones, the spared.

And what were they up to now, those exiles? Too quiet. She'd heard little of London's affairs, and that worried her. Ever since the orsine at Cairndale had been sealed, the world had taken a darker turn, though few yet could see it. She'd heard of strange discoveries abroad, of talents born without eyes, without ears. A local man she knew on the far side of Loch Fae told her of monsters eating out the wombs of sheep that strayed too near the ruins of Cairndale. In Istanbul there'd been a sun as black as ink, and yet still too bright to look at; in Iceland, two moons were sighted in the sky, drifting away from each other. A seer in Tokyo wrote with news that no new talents had been discovered in her country in two years. A community of talents outside Accra had fallen silent, returning none of her letters, as if they'd all vanished. Worst of all, from an exile she trusted in the grimy streets of Vienna, she heard rumors that the lost drughr, the four who'd vanished centuries ago, were once more stirring. She didn't see how it could be so; and yet, bearing the small vial of shining dust in a secret pocket of her cloak, turning now in the direction of the Royal Mile, she understood: these were days dark with dread.

They had spent the afternoon on errands. Now was just one last thing to be done: a meeting with a notorious pickpocket and forger, to acquire transit papers for her little ones.

She hitched up her skirts, and hurried on.

.   .   .

Charlie, stumbling along in Mrs. Ficke's wake, said nothing of the girl behind them.

She'd been following them through the darkening streets for some time. He wasn't sure why he didn't draw it to the old alchemist's attention. Maybe it was just that she kept her own counsel, had her own secrets. Maybe he was just stubborn that way. Komako certainly thought so. But he turned his chilled face and fumbled the parcels in his arms and tried to keep a silent sidelong eye on the girl. A kitchen maid perhaps, nothing more, younger than he was. But she moved like smoke in the twilight, her long hair in dark braids spilling from the hood of her cloak, and the scarlet gloves on her hands were too fine for her station. She was being careful, or trying to be, and it was this that unsettled him. She kept some thirty yards back with her cowl low.

What he didn't know was why.

They would depart south as soon as the glyph-twisted children had their papers. There was some urgency to it now, of course, after the discovery of Jacob Marber's dust, what it could do. That ethereal, electric blue of its shining. He'd felt a revulsion, learning what it was, what he'd brushed up against, even if only briefly. A living poison that fed on a talent, that ate them away from the inside. A part of the very evil that had hunted Marlowe all his life. Worse: the seed of its power, which could bring the drughr back to strength, even now.

He caught the sharp profile of Mrs. Ficke as they passed a lighted public house, the downturned nose, the prominent brow, the way her chin jutted forward and her gizzard-like throat trailed after. They splashed through a sunken puddle and turned up a nameless court. They came out in the thick of Old Town on the Royal Mile and shouldered their way through the crowds of clerks until they'd reached the square at St Giles'. Mrs. Ficke's fist held one half of her skirts, her other hem dragging with water. Under her artificial arm she carried a parcel; in her petticoats was a bundle of banknotes she'd tried to keep Charlie from seeing. Payment, he supposed, for whatever came next. She wasn't much forthcoming, for a woman who wanted his trust.

What would Alice say? He had a good idea of it. *If your head tells you one thing, Charlie, and your heart tells you another—listen to your heart.*

Yes.

The old woman stopped at the statue of Charles II, shifting the parcel to her other elbow, grimacing. Charlie took off his bowler and wiped his forehead and scanned the square. The servant girl who'd been following them wasn't there. He looked back down at Mrs. Ficke.

"Well?" he said.

"I need you to wait for me here," she said. She reached into her cloak and took out the vial of corrupted dust, folded in a handkerchief. "Hold this for me. Keep it safe. The man I'm going to meet has . . . clever fingers."

Charlie took it, feeling a sudden apprehension. As if he were holding something impossibly precious. He screwed up his face. "The man's a thief?"

"Among other things, yes. A rather gifted one." Her little eyes were made smaller by the cold. She gestured past the cathedral to a pillared edifice. "Those are the Goodline shipping offices. I'll meet with a Mr. Pillins there, when the first business is done. If we can arrange passage from here, all the better. You watch the parcels. Buy yourself a pie if you get cold."

Charlie peered around the darkening square, uncertain in the chill. "You want me to just stand here, until you're done? How long will you be?" He took the old woman's elbow, concerned. "Will you be safe with this thief of yours? Can he be trusted?"

"Oh, I'll be safe enough," Mrs. Ficke replied softly. She reached up and patted Charlie's cheek with a cold hand. "Don't you worry. I've known him long; he's no different than the rest of us. Trustworthy from a certain point of view. And no more violent than the world what made him."

Jeta Wajs watched the old woman stride away into the dusk.

The last light shone slickly over the setts, all dazzle and umber. She started to follow but the apparition didn't. An old distrust of the gadjikane world was in her, a fear from her uncle's tabor, a fear of so many strangers all around. Narrow-minded and vicious and filled with hate for what she was, if ever they knew. Even with Ruth's tincture still in her, she could feel their bones tugging gently at her, a wind plucking at her skirts.

It's for Claker, she told herself, to steady her nerves. *He needs this.*

The ghost of the child was staring not at the Ficke woman's retreating figure, but at the companion she'd left behind. It was a young man, almost a boy still, tall, dark-skinned. Half-black, he seemed. The old woman's servant, maybe. But then he took off his hat and ran a hand over his hair and put his hat back on and she thought he didn't seem like a servant, somehow. The ghost child wavered, translucent as the skin of a bubble, his black eyes peering with an undisguised hunger.

"What is it?" Jeta murmured. "Shouldn't we follow the Ficke woman?"

The dust isn't with her now, whispered the boy. *It's with . . . him.*

He pointed. Jeta bit at her lip, trying to think. Something didn't feel right. She'd do nothing untoward, she told herself. Not until she'd seen the corrupted dust, held it herself, made sure of it. And then? She thought about the dead assistant at the mortuary, the quiet stillness in his body. The apparition squatting monstrously over the corpse on its slab, its twisted features. Ruth's vitriol.

"If you're mistaken," she whispered to the ghost, "if there's no dust—"

He has it. A hint of impatience in his child's features. *Go. Take it from him.*

Jeta crossed the square. The young man was taller than she'd thought, and looked thickset in his heavy wool coat, though his neck was slender. He turned as she neared, betraying no surprise. Even in the gloom she could see his open, trusting face, the handsome eyes, the long dark lashes. He would be a foreigner in the eyes of all in this city, just like her. An outsider. The sadness around his mouth gave her pause.

"You've been following us," he said. It wasn't a question.

"I'm a ... friend," she replied, from within the hood of her cloak. She took a gamble. "I come with a warning, about what you're carrying. What Caroline Ficke gave you. The dust."

He looked startled. "What—I don't have ..." His eyes hardened. "How do you know Mrs. Ficke?"

"Please," she said. "We can't talk out here. Come."

She took her patchwork skirts in her fist and led him across to the great doors of St Giles'. An elaborate carved arch, fallen into shadow. A greasy lantern on a metal rung, unlit. The cathedral was closed for renovations but she'd seen the stonemasons filing out ten minutes earlier and when she tried the door it opened easily.

"In here, if you please," she said, and stepped aside. "It'll be safer inside."

It had started to rain, a faint cold webbing blowing in over them in the settling dark. He wiped his big hand over his face where the mist was catching in his eyelashes, as if deciding something.

"Safer than what?" he said.

But he went in anyway, to her satisfaction. She caught the smell of wet wool and old pipe smoke as he passed, like a scent from some distant part of her life, and then she was closing the heavy doors behind them both. The apparition of the little boy, already somehow within, shimmered faintly in the gloom.

Jeta? it whispered suddenly. *I think ... I think I know him.*

"Forgive me," she said, drawing her wet hood back. Her voice echoed in the stony darkness. "What is your name?"

The young man was quiet only a moment. "Ovid," he said firmly. "Charles Ovid. But where I come from, it's impolite to ask. Not without offering your own name first."

There was something about him that made her want to answer. But she knew it would be madness. *Charlie,* she thought suddenly. The ghost child had mentioned a Charlie, back at Cairndale. She saw he'd drifted close to the stranger, a faint blue crackling in the gloom, and he was leaning his little face near as if to breathe in the smell of his damp. His eyes were utterly black.

Charlie? he whispered, but there was no recognition in it. *He's . . . changed, I think. Different. What's happened to him? He scares me, Jeta.*

Jeta scanned the darkness; they were quite alone.

The apparition, she thought, didn't sound scared.

Caroline chewed at her lips as she climbed a stair and stumped into the black garden at Dunedin Close, just beyond a kirk. The roar of the Royal Mile faded, the clatter and bustle of Old Town. An ancient stillness closed around her, like a fist. At a blackened oak she stopped, and sat savagely, and glared all around. The small gardens were empty.

At last a figure came between the hedgerows, worn silk hat on his head. He sat gingerly on the bench, turned a bespectacled eye upon her. "Mrs. Ficke," he said.

"I come about the papers. For the little ones."

He nodded. "I can't say for certain they'll be good at an English port. But it was the best your money could buy. You'll see they've been completed according to your instructions."

She waited.

"You have the payment?"

She took out the banknotes. He gave a quick dark glance around, then unbuttoned his greatcoat and withdrew a thick packet of letters, tied with yellow string.

"If they are refused," Caroline Ficke said calmly, taking them from him, "you will answer for it."

"I would expect no less," he replied, unruffled. "Safe passage to you, Mrs. Ficke."

And he touched his hat, and rose smoothly, and walked off into the coming darkness. After a moment she too rose, and walked back the way she had come. She gave little thought to Charlie, waiting with their parcels outside St Giles'. She was thinking, instead, about this city she'd known for so long, its invisible web of connections. She would lose that, soon. It filled her with an unexpected melancholy.

The door to the Goodline shipping offices was located off a stub of a lane, so narrow as to seem an alley. A mist was blowing in against her face sidelong and Caroline turned her bad shoulder into it. The man she sought within was no friend of hers but he was happy to ask few questions in exchange for a higher fee and that, she understood, was the best she could hope for.

He was working late, bent over a small desk, a candle in a dish burning low. He wore a checkered waistcoat and a cheap-looking watch on a chain and his hair had been brushed greasily flat on his head. As she came in he looked her way, waved a hand, then continued with whatever it was he'd been writing.

She sat and withdrew the packet of papers and set them on the desk.

"That's for all of them," she said. "I expect you will complete the paperwork now?"

The clerk grimaced. "You'll be sailing on the *Bad Chance*. Never mind the name; she's a fine vessel. She'll get you straight to the port of Palermo, no questions asked. Unless there's any trouble with the port authorities in London."

"When does she sail?"

The clerk gave her a wink. "Within the fortnight. I'll send word of your coming, of course."

"Will she wait for us?"

"She'll wait on the tides. I can't promise more than that." His hair had been pomaded and there was a faint reek of perfume coming from his clothes. "You'd best be in London and at Miller's Wharf within the fortnight."

When she left the shipping offices she did not go back in search of Charlie outside St Giles', as she had promised. She went, instead, to the Police Chambers in the adjoining street. She stood at the counter and asked the receiving officer if Mr. Tooley was on duty, and then sat on a hard bench across from a rather forlorn-looking man clutching a hatbox.

Mr. Tooley was an old acquaintance, small, sober, gray. His hair once had been as orange as an oak in autumn. He'd been a friend of Cairndale's, in his way. He came out with his polished buttons winking in the light and his fine blue uniform soaking up the dark and he beckoned her through.

At his desk he said, "Can I get you a cup of tea? I never thought to see you in here, Mrs. Ficke. What is it I can do for you? Mr. Albany is all right?"

She furrowed her brow. "Well, Mr. Tooley sir, it's Mr. Albany I wanted to see you about. I'll be leaving shortly on a trip. I won't be back for a long while."

"Leaving Mr. Albany on his own?" said Mr. Tooley in surprise. "Is that wise?"

"Oh, he's clever enough in his way. He knows his business and how his days ought to look. But all the same, it'd be a relief to me if you could look in on him, now and again. Just to see how he's getting on."

Mr. Tooley paused. "Is there some sort of trouble?"

"Ach. It's nothing like that."

There was an open newspaper on the desk and now Mr. Tooley ran one hand over it, as if smoothing out the words. He looked up. "You know I'd be glad to look in on him. He's a good one, your brother. Heart as big as a four-poster."

Caroline smiled at that. "Yes he is, Mr. Tooley. And I will take that tea now, thank you. Just a quick drop against the weather."

Charlie's boots scraped. A weak glow was coming in through a stained glass window, casting the scaffolding and the stacks of lumber and worked stone in a red and blue light. The air was cold; the cathedral smelled of dust and waterlogged wool and lantern smoke. He could make out thick stone pillars in the half-light, row upon row, and white sheets laid over objects in the darkness. A clutter of workmen's buckets and trowels and a mess of tarps to his left.

The girl, whoever she was, was already halfway up an aisle but Charlie stopped. He took off his gloves and folded them together and stuffed them in the same pocket as Alice's revolver.

"Who sent you?" he said.

He saw now, as she walked slowly back, that she could not possibly be anyone's servant. She wore a strange patchwork dress that might have been sewn by a madwoman; her two braids were entwined in a pattern he'd never seen before; she wore a coin at her throat like payment for the ferryman. Her eyes, her expression were too old for her face, as if she had suffered horrors and survived them. Her face was dark in the darkness and her thick eyebrows were drawn low. On her hands she wore scarlet gloves of a very fine material. He understood she was a talent or had been once but there was a wariness about her that he did not know what to do with and he was surprised at the feeling that was in him.

"You're like me," he said quietly. "You're a talent, aren't you?"

Her eyes narrowed. "Don't tell me what I am. You don't know me."

"That's not . . . I didn't mean that. I just meant, you're alone too. Like me."

He saw it then, in her dark eyes: the person she was maybe when she was alone, unguarded, pensive, saddened. Then it was gone. She glanced to one side, as if a third stood there. But there was no one.

"I've been out to the ruins," she said briskly. "You've not been back, not since the fire, I take it?"

This surprised him. "Cairndale? There's nothing there now. Just . . . memories."

"But there is. Or, was. Something important, I think?" She let her eyes go up and down his person. "It was taken from Loch Fae to William Macrae's mortuary, where Caroline Ficke acquired it. But it does not belong to her. I've been sent to retrieve the dust, Mr. Ovid. I'd rather take it gently. I don't wish to hurt you."

Charlie said nothing. He'd fought the drughr, worse; this girl did not frighten him.

"I work for a man named Claker Jack," she continued, slowly peeling off her scarlet gloves. In the dimness he saw the two yellowing bone fingers, curling there. It wasn't something he'd seen before. "You may have heard of him. He is master of a community in London, a community of exiles, sent down from Cairndale. If I return without Jacob Marber's dust, he will send others to retrieve it. They will not be so . . . polite. Please."

He didn't know why he did it; later he would think back and wonder if something had compelled him. But nothing had; it wasn't anyone's doing but his own. He *wanted* to show her the vial of dust; he *wanted* to see where all this would lead.

He withdrew the handkerchief and unwrapped the glass vial. He held it delicately in his fingers. The dust within began to whorl and shine with that same blue luminescence he'd seen at Mrs. Ficke's. The blue shine was reflected in the girl's face, casting it into eerie relief, so that she looked suddenly distorted, frightening. She seemed unable to speak, unable to look away.

Charlie said, "This? Is this what you want?"

She nodded slowly.

"Do you know what it is?" he asked.

"The dust of the drughr," she whispered.

He watched her carefully. "And did your Claker Jack tell you what it does? No? It's dangerous, more dangerous than you imagine. It'll bring the drughr *to* you. Whoever carries it is like a beacon for the drughr. And you're a talent; you're exactly who the drughr would be drawn to. You should leave this, leave me. Go."

"The drughr," said the girl. "I used to think it was just a story."

Charlie closed his fist around the vial. The blue light died away.

"I've seen it," he replied. "It's real."

The girl shook her head then, as if rising from a dream. On her face he saw hunger and fear and some other thing entirely, something like joy, all of it there and then gone. She didn't speak. She just raised her hands into fists and squeezed them until her skin whitened and she shut her dark eyes in concentration and all at once Charlie felt the bones in his littlest finger snap.

He screamed.

His finger was bent weirdly out of his fist, the fist that held the vial. He stumbled backward, gasping, and spun behind a pillar. The pain was terrible. He ran deeper into the darkness. But he felt a second crack, as his ring finger too was broken and splayed back, and he screamed again. It was as if, somehow, the girl was prying open his fist, finger by finger, ripping the vial from him.

"I don't want to do this," she said calmly. "Please, Charlie. Give me the dust. I have to bring it to Claker Jack. He needs it."

"Stop!" he shouted, crouching behind a scaffolding. "Did you not hear what I said? Wait!"

He could see the girl walking calmly down the nave.

"Oh, Charlie," she said. "This is nothing."

That was when he felt truly afraid. She was too composed, too steady. Alice's revolver was in his greatcoat pocket but he didn't take it out. Even now, even like this, he knew he could never pull the trigger. Alice had taught him to shoot but it wasn't in him, not really. Not even against a talent like this. *You'll die because of it*, he thought bitterly. *What would Alice say?*

Her footsteps ceased; then they began again, stepping slowly nearer.

"Wait—!" he called again. His voice echoed off the walls. "Just, wait. For God's sake—"

"Let me face your drughr, Charlie," she called from somewhere close by. "Or whatever you saw. Let me lead it away from you. Give me the vial. I won't harm you further."

He leaned flat against the pillar, wincing. The door was some thirty feet to his left. Too far to run. But the cathedral felt vast; he might lose her in the maze of its renovations. If he could only get far enough ahead of her. He shifted the vial to his free hand and then, with a groan, he snapped his broken fingers back into position. There were tears on his face. He thought about the dust, what it could do for his talent, if only he used it now. He grimaced. No. He wouldn't do it.

"I can . . . feel you, Charlie Ovid," the girl whispered. "I know where you are."

And then, as if to prove her point, Charlie felt the small bones in his third finger snap. He let out a strangled gasp, muffling his pain, and stumbled deeper into the cathedral's darkness. *Pull Alice's gun, just pull out her gun*, one part of his brain was telling him. And the other part was screaming at him: *Run!*

He ran.

But he didn't get far; he was cradling his broken hand against his chest, the vial of dust held tight in his other fist, moving as softly and

swiftly as he could, when he came around a pillar and saw the girl standing very still, staring right at him. He froze. She looked so small, so
young. Charlie spun back behind the pillar, gasping.

Of course she'd seen him. The bones in his last finger and his thumb
cracked sharply then, yanked backward, and he could not help himself,
he shrieked. He doubled over, fell to his knees on the cold floor, afraid
even to shift his hand a little because of the waves of pain. His face was
twisted in agony and his cheeks were wet and he was breathing in quick
short sharp breaths. Faintly, through the hurt, he could hear the girl's
shoes as she walked closer.

It all happened so fast, after that.

The bones in his wrist snapped, like dry sticks underfoot, and his
crushed hand flopped painfully loose. He wasn't thinking clearly by
then. In his agony he'd squeezed his other fist tight, the fist that held
the vial of corrupted dust, and he had a vague awareness of something
crunching there—the glass, crushed—at the same moment that he rose
in a furious anger and stepped out from behind the pillar and opened
his fist and swung his big broad palm clumsily toward the girl's head, the
shattered pieces of glass falling away from his hand in an arc of glinting
confetti.

But something was burning where he'd broken the vial, burning into
his flesh, boiling it, even as he struck the girl on the side of her head. And
there was dust in the air, brightly illumined, dust in the broken shards of
glass. The skin of his hand and wrist was whorling with shadow, as if a
darkness were inside him, and in that very same instant his blow landed
on the girl's head, a clumsy slap, not nearly as forceful as he needed.

She screamed. Her eyes rolled back up into her skull, and she collapsed.

Everything went suddenly still.

Charlie's ears were ringing. He staggered sideways. The bones in his
left hand were horribly broken. His right hand felt like it was on fire.

The girl was on the ground, unmoving, but he didn't care. His skin was crawling with an inky darkness, as if alive. He thought of the dust, parasitic, feeding. A wave of sickness came over him. There were many small cuts in his palm where the glass had gone in but they weren't bleeding, they were just shining feebly with a blue light. Slowly even that faded.

And then he was running raggedly for the door of the cathedral, stumbling out into the cold night, confused, in pain, looking wildly about for Mrs. Ficke, for anyone at all.

Jeta didn't lose consciousness, not all at once.

Instead it happened slowly, as if the young man's hand were striking her underwater. A slow heavy movement in the gloom that she saw as it descended and yet which she couldn't step out of the way of. The ghost boy shimmered in the darkness, full of a sadness and a hunger, but he said nothing, did nothing, as if he was giving up, accepting that all was lost.

Damn him too, she thought briefly.

And then she saw the rising glow of blue between Charlie Ovid's fingers as if his fist held the shine itself and some part of her brain understood: the dust was *inside* him now; he had broken the vial and the living dust had *infected* him; and then she felt the blow, like a kind of slow caress, and the dust, whatever it was, suddenly stripped away all of the muffling powers of Ruth's tincture and her own talent exploded within her, impossibly strong, so that all the wet living bones in all the bodies in all the vast city around her, and all the bones of all the dead deep in their pockets of decay, all of them, came roaring in upon her, overwhelming her, and the agony of it filled her own bones like a vessel filling with water, filling and filling, until it was too much and she was overbrimming with pain and with light and gasping for breath, and she felt the person that she was grow smaller next to it, diminishing, over-flowing and undone.

Claker—! she thought, *I tried, I tried*—!

And closed her eyes to it, and was lost.

Charlie had only a faint awareness of stumbling out into the square at St Giles', of leaning up against the base of the statue there, a cold rain on his face, of Mrs. Ficke crouching over him, cradling his broken hand. There was a hansom, jouncing painfully in the darkness. And then Mrs. Ficke's brother, Edward, his enormous arms lifting Charlie, carrying him like a child into the chandler's shop.

The thing was, when he came to, all of what happened in the cathedral felt dreamlike and strange. A fear was in him, a fear he didn't understand, and he worked his lips dryly and blinked and squinted at the fire burning in the grate, at Mrs. Ficke where she sat in a rocking chair.

"You're awake," she said. "I allowed you might sleep a bit longer. Easy, now. You've been holding the wrong end of the pan a bit, haven't you?"

But he swung his legs down, and rose painfully to the edge of the bed. He lifted his two hands carefully in front of him. They were each a mess.

The fingers of his left hand had been set and wrapped with gauze and the wrist too had been set. He would be lucky to ever get the use of it like he'd had before. But under the wrappings it felt . . . peculiar. Pained and prickling and peculiar. Not like when he was a haelan; different. As if tiny biting insects were in the bones themselves. The rest of the arm hurt to move and he lowered it gingerly back to his chest, Mrs. Ficke watching him the while.

If his left hand felt strange, the right felt like there was a furnace stoked in its skin. Mrs. Ficke had cut away the sleeve and he stared now at his forearm. It was smooth, untouched. But from the wrist down, it was marked with strange dark burns. Burns, that were not burns. For he knew what he was looking at. It was what he'd seen on Jacob Marber on the roof of a speeding train, in what seemed a different life, a sight he'd never forget: the bizarre, witchlike patterns in the skin. He felt afraid.

Mrs. Ficke held her good hand over the marks on his palm, so close she was almost touching him, and all at once the patterns began to shift and crawl under the dermis, as if alive.

Charlie swayed, suddenly dizzy. "It's . . . in me?" he whispered. "Mrs. Ficke? The drughr's dust, it's . . . it's *in* me? What will it do?"

He stared up at her, afraid. His heart was going very fast.

But there was both wonder and pity in her voice, when at last she replied. "See what it's already done," she said.

She unwrapped the bandages on his shattered left hand. The bones were whole again; the skin was unmarked; the swelling already had gone down. It was this he'd been able to feel.

"It's bonded to you," she said, gentle.

He was crying. He curled the healed fingers, turned his wrist. It felt like someone else's wrist, someone else's hand.

"Charlie? I need to know what happened."

"Will I become like him?" he whispered suddenly, his cheeks wet. "Will I become like Jacob Marber now?"

"No," said Mrs. Ficke firmly. "It wasn't the dust that made him what he was. What was wrong in Jacob was wrong in him from the start."

"But I don't *want* this, Mrs. Ficke. I *don't.*"

"Aye. But you're a vessel now, want it or not. Try to remember: what happened?"

Charlie swallowed. He told her what he could about the cathedral, and the girl who'd approached him in the square. How she'd been following them, how she tried to take the vial of corrupted dust. "She was just young, maybe Oskar's age. She said she had a warning for me. About . . .

the dust. She knew your name. Dark hair, an odd-looking coin on a necklace. A dress all patched up like a quilt." He looked up. "She had two fingers on her left hand that were just bones. I wasn't afraid, not at first. Then she broke my fingers. Without even looking."

"A bone witch," Mrs. Ficke replied quickly. "You were attacked by a bone witch. They're a rare talent, Charlie. And terrifying. You're lucky to be alive."

He gave an involuntary shudder. But he remembered the look on her face, how alone she'd seemed, and he wasn't so certain. She could have killed him at any point. She hadn't. "I had the vial in my fist and must have crushed it, and I cut my hand up. Then I . . . I hit her. The dust was shining. The cathedral was dark so it was really easy to see. I watched it sort of suck itself up through the little cuts in my palm, here. Mrs. Ficke, when I hit her, the girl just . . . crumpled. It wasn't the blow that did it, I didn't hit her that hard. It was like the dust did it, like the dust made her fall down." He worked the fingers of his tattooed hand, feeling an overwhelming revulsion. "There was another name. Claker Jack. She's working for him. Does it mean anything to you?"

The older woman grimaced, turned to the fire. "Claker Jack runs the empire of the exiles. In London, where we must go."

"I thought the exiles hated talents? Why would they hire a bone witch?"

"Aye, it's a bitter hatred the exiles hold for talents. It's the one thing they all agree on. And Claker Jack's the worst of them." There was a darkness in Mrs. Ficke's voice when she added, "But if he's hired a bone witch to take the dust—the dust that's in you now, Charlie—then he must be desperate. You may be sure we've not seen the last of her."

He shivered. He steeled himself and looked hard at the old woman. "Can you . . . can you get it out of me? The dust, I mean?"

"Does it cause you pain?"

He shook his head. "It's not the hurting. It's more like something's crawling there, under the skin." He watched her. "Please, Mrs. Ficke. I just . . . I don't want it in me."

The old woman chewed at her bottom lip, considering. "There may be a way," she said at last. "But it is not without its risks. In London, at the old institute offices, Henry Berghast kept a chest of unusual texts. Old books he didn't want in the reach of other talents, and the like. There may be something in there." She frowned. "This is a dark business. I don't know that I can help you, but I can try."

He looked at her gratefully. "And the bone witch? What will we do about her?"

"What our kind have always done," she said. Her old eyes glistened in the firelight. "We will wake the children, and run. While there is still time."

The GLYPHIC of MOJÁCAR

·

1883

7

THE GIRL
FROM TOKYO

The Barcelona rain stopped sometime in the night and there was only the dap of water from the railings and the knifelike gleam of wet stones in the alley. Komako looked up from her chair at the window.

A bonebird hopped crookedly in out of the darkness, a slender twig-like thing, its eyeless skull turning, its bone wings clicking. Komako's skirts were still damp but she wore a blanket over her shoulders and her hair was mostly dry. Though she was tired from the night's work and hadn't been expecting the creature, she rubbed her face and reached out and smoothed its wings, careful not to cut herself on the blade of its scapula.

"Oh look at you, come all this way, hm?" she murmured.

In a tiny copper cylinder on its leg was a letter.

Komako wasn't surprised. She knew it would be from Miss Davenshaw, knew it had to be, knew the woman would be seeking word of her progress in Spain. The poor woman had enough to do, trying to build a new Cairndale in that ruined villa in Sicily, caring for the littlest talents, protecting them, without also managing the search for Marlowe. It made Ko sad, and then angry. The world was shit. So what.

How the bonebird had found her, she couldn't guess. Its workings were a mystery to her. She glanced back to where Mr. Bailey slept, fully dressed, on the four-poster, his long legs twisted, the wet laces of one shoe untied. She could hear the rattle of his breathing, as if he was afraid even in his dreams. Which he probably was.

The *drughr*.

That's what he feared. That the drughr was living yet and had torn his companions apart and taken the boy talent Juan Carlos, whoever that was. A caster, he'd said. That boy would be dead now too, she knew. Or maybe the kid was the one who'd turned on the others. There was no way to know. Bailey was half-mad of course, with his gruesome burns from Cairndale and the scars at his throat where he'd been clawed open and, worse, the deeper injuries that were hidden from the eye and that would never heal. He'd said little after she forced him from that cellar, forced him to leave the bodies in their rags, walked him back across the Quarter like a prisoner, to these rooms she'd let above a rope maker's shop, his black dog following for a time and then fading into the rain. She'd carried his walking stick in one hand like a threat, her knife in the other. He didn't explain what he'd meant about the Dark Talent, how it was rising. But the terror in him was real. He'd told her only that the Spanish glyphic dwelled in the south, in the dry foothills facing the Alboran Sea, and that it was nothing like poor Mr. Thorpe, whom the children had called the Spider back at Cairndale. "You'll see," he'd whispered, afraid. "You'll be fortunate to leave with your life."

She didn't trust Mr. Bailey; she certainly didn't like him. He'd been a part of whatever Dr. Berghast had intended for Cairndale, and that was enough for her. It seemed to fill him with sadness now, whatever the true extent of his crimes, but what about all the dead kids and sacrificed talents and those poor glyph-twisted children at old Mrs. Ficke's chandler shop? No, Mr. Bailey could pay for his part in it, could pay through all his remaining days, and meet no mercy in her. But she needed help finding the second orsine, *his* help. For Charlie was broken inside from everything, and wouldn't heal until he knew for sure about Marlowe; and so she'd tolerate this man, this monster's assistant, if it brought her closer to that.

All this was in her as she reached for the bonebird. "Easy, Bertie, it's all right," she whispered, untying the letter.

Bertie was the name Ribs had given it, on the long sea voyage south from London, when the creature had been kept hidden in their stateroom. "Well that's what it is, right? A bone-bertie?" Ribs had said with a grin. They'd taken only the one bonebird from the institute's old terrace house at Nickel Street West, at Miss Davenshaw's insistence. But if the creature knew Ko, or recognized the nickname, it gave no sign. Its sockets were filled with darkness.

Ribs. Jesus. How Ko missed her, terribly. All of them. It felt like she'd been alone and angry forever.

She unfolded the letter. Then reached for a candle and crushed her fingers together around the wick and felt a prickle of pain as the dust rubbed itself hotter. A flame bloomed; she took her hand away quickly; the tiny script came clear. Oskar's handwriting.

It was mostly a query about her search, as she'd thought. No word about Ribs or Alice. She was surprised to learn Charlie had sailed to Edinburgh, to try to locate old Mrs. Ficke. What Miss Davenshaw could want with the old alchemist, Ko couldn't guess. She worried about Charlie though, his talent gone, grief filling the space where it had been.

She crossed the room and retrieved a stub of pencil and then sat in the candlelight and turned over the little paper and wrote out a reply on its back:

I have found the way. Will depart in the morning. If the Spanish g. is real, I will find it. One caution: something has been killing talents here in Barcelona. There are rumors that the d. is back. What do you know of the Dark Talent?

—K.

She screwed the letter into its canister and fitted it to the bonebird's leg and watched as the creature exploded out into the night and was gone.

Mr. Bailey slept on.

Komako blew out the candle. The smoke hung pale in the darkness. In the morning they would leave this city behind. But there was a sadness in her that would go with her always now, she knew, no matter how far she went. She leaned back in the chair, peered out at the night. Slowly the wreath of smoke dissolved.

She didn't like to sleep, because she didn't like to dream.

She was so tired, so filled with anger. But when she closed her eyes she saw again the children at Cairndale, the littlest talents, on that terrible last night, that night when Jacob and his litch attacked them, Jacob whom she'd trusted once, had even—say it—loved. Loved as a brother, as a friend. She saw etched into her eyelids the flames at Cairndale, the old talents slaughtered, the children, the others. She saw their bodies, littering the dark courtyard. She heard their cries. And she knew, deep inside herself, that it was she—Komako, the dustworker—who should have found a way to save them. That was the truth of it. Her talent, above all others, was suited to fighting. Now she'd left Miss Davenshaw, and Oskar, and Charlie, at the villa outside Agrigento, had left the few youngest talents who'd survived, because being around them all was too painful. Too much a reminder of what she'd failed to do, during the razing of Cairndale.

And even the dreams and memories that were not filled with horror left her feeling hollowed out and devastated. Since arriving in Barcelona she'd found herself dreaming of her little sister, Teshi, who had died back in Tokyo all those years ago, her sister whom she'd raised as a litch without meaning to, in those early years, when she didn't understand what her talent could do. It was Jacob who'd located her, who'd helped her see the unkindness—the *selfishness*—in keeping Teshi from death. Jacob, who'd betrayed her, betrayed them all.

She was so sick of all the death. All the suffering. And if she was honest with herself, she knew, then the truth was she wondered sometimes, in the darkest hours of the night, if Jacob Marber had been wrong, if it would have been better to have kept Teshi alive, even as a litch, instead of losing her only family to oblivion. If she'd failed her little sister a second time, by letting her die.

She'd sworn to herself it would not happen again; those she loved would not die.

She would not let them.

And then there was Marlowe, poor little Marlowe.

He was dead. She knew it, every part of her reasonable self knew it. She hated to see the hopefulness in Charlie, the way he held on to his own faith. Marlowe was like Teshi, like her mother, like Mr. Coulton or Jacob himself. You loved a person and they died anyway. It hurt her heart, knowing it, of course it did. But you couldn't just walk into an orsine and disappear beyond it and stay alive for all these months. No one could. Whether he was now one of the spirit dead, or some other thing entirely, she couldn't say. She just hoped Marlowe hadn't, please

God, suffered. When the gray light sifted in through the shutters she rose and folded the blanket and went to the covered washbowl in the corner. Her eyes were dark with the awfulness of it. Marlowe.

She splashed her face, stared at her reflection in the pier glass. Pulled the skin at her face into a grimace. "It's your own doing," she whispered at the mirror. "You should have been stronger. You couldn't even stop Jacob. So how could you have kept him safe?"

A cough from the gloom within; Komako turned her head.

"What is the hour?" Mr. Bailey emerged, tall and rumpled, the stubble on his ravaged face catching the morning light like steel shavings. His one hooded eyelid. The milky eye beneath it.

Seeing him, she felt all her old anger flare up. Berghast's manservant. The only one who'd known enough of his master's intentions to have stopped him. And he'd been relieved—*relieved!*—to hear Marlowe was lost inside the orsine. Had just muttered his ominous warning about a Dark Talent rising, and then gone sullen, silent with fear. If Komako was honest, she'd admit it had felt good, gathering the dust to her and roughing him up and seeing the weakness in him. She chewed at her lip. Something was wrong with her. It shouldn't feel *good.*

She stepped back from the washbowl, drying her face and hands, gathering her hair at her shoulder. "You should wash up, Mr. Bailey," she said coldly. "You look like death."

His good eye peered disconsolately around the apartment, then back at her. "You did not sleep," he replied.

"Someone had to watch for your drughr."

He flinched.

"Last night," she went on, "you said the Spanish glyphic resides in the south. You've been there before, then?"

A wary glance as he crossed to the window, peered out. "Once. In the early time of my employment at Cairndale. Dr. Berghast sent me."

"Why?"

"Mr. Thorpe was ill. Dr. Berghast understood that Cairndale, its orsine, would become . . . untenable without a glyphic." Mr. Bailey stood very still with half his face in shadow and the slats from the shutters carving the rest of him into pieces. His voice was deep. "We understand so little about glyphics. We know they can access a plane of existence that is hidden from us, that they are . . . *connected* to each other, and to all talentkind. That is how Mr. Thorpe would dream of the young talents, how Cairndale would find them. They live to a great age, Miss Onoe. But glyphics . . . merge with their environments, as they age. Like Mr. Thorpe and his tree."

"So the Spanish glyphic is a tree?"

"No." Mr. Bailey's huge hands were gnarled as he raised them to his face. "No, the Spanish glyphic is not a tree. It is old, even for glyphics. So old as to no longer be . . . human. It exists inside its own dreaming. I do not think it concerns itself much with what we want. It resides in a cavern beyond the village of Mojácar, in Almería. In the Sierra Cabrera. It is said to have come from the east, following the rivers underground, out of the deep caves of Bulgaria, more than a thousand years ago. It was here before the Moors, before Spain itself. You will find, I believe, that it shares my feelings about the shining boy. That he is best lost, and not recovered."

Komako glared. "Yeah, we'll see. Are you hungry?"

"Yes."

"Too bad. You can eat on the train. You'll want your coat and hat."

The man shuddered; he didn't move. He looked stricken. She might almost have pitied him. "I've met it once," he said slowly. "Once was enough. You don't know what you are asking. Please."

"I'm not *asking* anything." Komako glared at the clock. It was not yet six and if they hurried they might be in time for the train to Madrid. Her small steamer trunk stood open near the bed but there was nothing in it she needed, not really. Just her billfold and coin purse and her kidskin gloves for her sore hands.

She summoned a fist of dust to her, then crossed to the apartment door and stood with one hand outstretched menacingly toward Mr. Bailey. The dust writhed darkly at her wrist.

"Take your time," she said. "I'd like that."

Mr. Bailey watched the dust, shrinking back against the wall. "Even if you find it, it won't do you any good," he muttered. "The glyphic doesn't speak English. It speaks Latin."

"Latin?"

"As I said," continued Mr. Bailey. "It is a very old creature."

But if he'd spoken with the Spanish glyphic once, she decided, then he could bloody well find a way to speak with it again. She unhooked the big man's coat and hat, opened the door onto the stairs.

"Anyway, it's not a *creature*," she said coldly. "The glyphic is a *person*, Mr. Bailey. You would do well to remember that."

They walked to the train station through the early streets, past carts and wagons on their way to market, past stalls opening up along Las Ramblas. They carried no luggage. In the daylight Mr. Bailey looked worn, his trousers and hat spotted with grime. They must have made a strange pair, the slender foreign girl with her imperious glare and her kidskin gloves, the scarred manservant with his blinded eye, hulking at her side. The station was a yellow two-story building huddled against the low gray sky, with men in frock coats hurrying out through its doors. Mr. Bailey swung his silver-tipped walking stick, his tall black hat stained and scuffed. A smell was coming off his coat.

A most strange pair indeed, thought Komako, pushing her way in past the crowds of arriving clerks.

And yet it turned out to be useful, she found to her displeasure, having Mr. Bailey as her companion. He peered down gravely at the smaller Spanish men. The ticket sellers spoke to him, not to her, even though it was her purse that opened to pay; his Spanish was excellent, though hers was perfectly passable; he glided unnoticed through the crowds, while she suffered strange looks. She'd learned that Barcelona, urbane as it was, saw few Asian faces, excepting those that sailed in on the trading ships; a young half-Japanese woman, well-dressed, fascinated.

They did not have long to wait. Mr. Bailey had stopped at a handcart to purchase several pastries when a whistle sounded. Komako hurried outside to the platform, the tracks reeking of smoke and coal.

It was an old green-and-gold Tardienta locomotive waiting there, with a low-slung boiler for the steam and a ridiculous tall chimney, like a stovepipe hat, built by the English decades ago. It pulled four wooden carriages, each painted green and golden-brown, ladies in skirts and men in silk hats climbing up into their compartments. All morning it creaked and swayed its slow way through the hills to Zaragoza, the fierce Spanish landscape sliding past, eventually the flat expanse of the Ebro shining like hammered steel. It was seven hours and twenty-two minutes to Delicias station in Madrid and Komako watched Mr. Bailey in their compartment the whole way, fuming. They were not alone in the compartment and the old Spanish woman who sat beside Komako was dressed all in black, and carried a cloth-covered basket on her knees. There were things Komako wanted to ask Mr. Bailey and might have tried asking in English but instead she rode in silence. At Lleida Mr. Bailey had unfolded his little square handkerchief and eaten the pastries that were to have lasted the day and an hour later the basket on the old lady's lap stirred, and a kitten poked its face up out of the cloth, then vanished again. It was early afternoon when they arrived at the soaring new iron-and-glass station in Madrid, amid the roar and steam of the platforms, and Komako purchased one-way tickets for the two of them on the Córdoba line and then had to run to make the connecting train.

They were alone this time in the polished wood-and-brass compartment. The narrow door swung closed from the outside and was locked fast by the conductor before departure and as Madrid slid away outside, Komako leaned forward and tried the release. It didn't open.

"It's because they keep falling out," said Mr. Bailey, cracking one eye. "The passengers, I mean. They're not used to trains in this country, not yet. And so the carriages must be locked."

Komako regarded him flatly. "The Spaniards keep falling out."

"Yes."

She shook her head. "Not everyone is stupid, Mr. Bailey, simply because they are not English."

The train rattled and shunted tracks. Mr. Bailey swayed in his seat. He took off his hat, brushed at the brim with his wrist. "Indeed, Miss Onoe," he said. "Not everyone. You have been watching me all day. Do you fear I might try to run? That you will have to use your talent to restrain me?"

Komako shrugged. They were passing now through a brown landscape of stunted trees, hills of blasted grass. "No," she said quietly.

"No?"

She met his eye. "You believe the drughr is hunting you, Mr. Bailey. And that I'm the only one who stands any chance at all of fighting it. You'd be a fool to run."

His good eye stared at her. "You imagine you can fight the drughr, girl? Your talent is nothing. An amusement."

"Then why are you still with me? Why didn't you contrive to vanish in the crowds in Madrid?"

"There are reasons," he said softly.

She didn't understand. And then she did: he believed he could feed her to the drughr, if ever it came back. That she could be the distraction that let him escape. She scowled in disgust.

"Tell me about the Dark Talent," she said abruptly.

He stopped turning his hat in his scarred fingers and studied her.

"Your Miss Davenshaw didn't teach you about the Dark Talent, in all your classes at Cairndale?"

"My time there was interrupted."

He smiled raggedly. There was no kindness in it. "It is an old foretelling. Dreamed up by an ancient glyphic, a powerful one. A glyphic who saw the fall of kingdoms, who saw the rise of Cairndale and its orsine. A glyphic so old that its flesh has given way to the dream of its flesh." He waited, a strange expression in his opalescent eye. "Would you like to know which glyphic I mean?"

"Let me guess. The Spanish glyphic."

"The very creature we seek. Yes."

Komako rubbed at her sore hands, the rash rising there. Unimpressed. "What was seen?"

Mr. Bailey moistened his lips. "That a talent would be born, different from all others. A living child, emergent of the dead. A child to cut the worlds like cloth, and remake them anew, and so bring about the destruction of all talentkind."

"Oh, is that all?"

"You jest. The foretelling is widely known."

"So is the story of the three little pigs. Doesn't make it true."

"I am ashamed, Miss Onoe, of my part in what happened at Cairndale. More than you can know. But I am certain of one thing. The Dark Talent is a danger to all of us."

"Marlowe wasn't fulfilling anything," Komako said angrily. "He was just a kid. A good kid."

Mr. Bailey paused. "Was?"

"*Is*. He *is* a good kid. Don't make him the scapegoat for whatever evil you and Dr. Berghast were up to. Maybe Dr. Berghast is the Dark Talent. Maybe I am."

"Dr. Berghast believed—"

"Don't tell me what he believed," she snapped. "You have no idea. He didn't tell you his intentions, or you'd be a damn sight less ugly right now." She gestured at his burns, his ruined eye.

Mr. Bailey's face twisted. "You've grown cruel," he said quietly.

"I've learned to save my kindness for those who deserve it," she replied.

At Córdoba they purchased tickets to Málaga and caught the last train of the day and in Málaga they stepped down into inky darkness. Mr. Bailey had turned up the collar of his coat and drawn his hat low to obscure his scars but there was almost no one about to see. Komako felt a vague guilt at how she'd spoken to him but then she grew angry at herself. He deserved no one's pity, hers least of all. She sent him to find accommodations. In the quiet waiting room at Málaga station there was a little Japanese girl with a folded parasol, seated on a wooden bench, her governess at her side. A Spanish woman approached and began to speak to the child in Spanish. Komako stared. It had been a long time since she'd seen anyone that looked like her sister, Teshi. She remembered the creak of the old wooden theater in Tokyo, the smell of dust and wash-water, the glint of her sister's eyes in the firelight. The sound of her little feet running down the hall. That.

They slept that night in a public house in the dark town and in the late morning they found a cart and driver to take them north along the coast road. The rain held off. Komako, exhausted, folded herself up against the side-rail and tried to sleep. Mr. Bailey watched the road.

Instead she found herself remembering, remembering something that had happened long ago, something she'd lost. An afternoon when Teshi, very small, had found little kimonos almost their size in the ward-robe at the theater where they lived, kimonos of delicate blue and white stitching, folding soft against their cheeks. They'd snuck them, giggling as they dressed each other, and then gone out into the bustling city clutching the few coins they'd saved, walking all the way to the Sazaido in the golden light, to see Mount Fuji, just like other children, just as if they'd had a mother and a father who loved them, clothed them, wanted them. It must have been spring, for white blossoms were in the air. Teshi had gripped her hand tightly as they entered the gate, crossed the temple gardens, climbed the spiral staircase all the way up to the third story, and stared out across the marshes at the great mountain, monumental and shining. The beauty of it. How her little sister had smiled up at her, flecks of red seaweed sticking to the corners of her mouth from the nori they'd bought. The sweetness of that moment, its inescapable goodness. In the cart, Komako folded her arms tighter, trying to hold on to the memory.

It was twilight when they came upon the village and even then it was beautiful. A cluster of whitewashed houses and narrow twisting lanes, Mojácar perched in the foothills of the Sierra Cabrera, placid, ancient, unchanging. Komako saw green shoots and plants on the balconies despite the season. The roads were cobbled badly from centuries of use and the stones rutted with cart tracks. They stopped at a small square, got down.

The rooms the driver had led them to were in a small house overlooking a garden, behind thick stone walls. He stabled his horse on-site and went out to a small cottage as if he lived there. The landlady was a widow all in black, short and squat and fierce, who shook her head to see Komako with Mr. Bailey. She spoke no English and only a rapid-fire Spanish that Komako could not follow. Mr. Bailey she waved furiously away into a room at the back of the house but Komako she led to her own bedchamber, muttering the while, lighting lamps and turning down the bed.

Komako was so tired. She knew the next day would be longer yet. At dinner she sat with Mr. Bailey and the driver at the long table, and ate the old woman's dishes, the onions and red peppers roasted on the out-side, then peeled and soaked in oil, and the chicken cooked with prawns in a ceramic dish, and she nodded dully when it was done. Mr. Bailey too ate in grim silence, a huge figure looming over them all. Komako didn't care. And then she was taking off her boots, her gloves, climbing into the bed, blowing out the lamp. Later still, the old widow came into the room carrying a candle, and undressed behind the dresser, buttoning a nightshirt to her chin, genuflecting to the crucifix nailed to the wall. And then, without a word, she blew out the candle and climbed into bed beside Komako.

Her hairy feet, when they brushed Komako's legs, were cold as ice.

In the middle of the night Komako opened her eyes to find Mr. Bailey standing over her bed, watching her sleep. He was barefoot in a night-shirt. She lay very still with her eyes open to be sure she was seeing what she saw. Then she whispered, "You are in the wrong room, Mr. Bailey."

He said nothing. His eyes were caverns of shadow. He drew in a long ragged breath. "You looked like you were . . . like you weren't sleeping," he whispered.

"Because I'm not. Not anymore."

"I mean you looked dead," he whispered. "Like the drughr had come for you. I thought—"

The old widow snorted loudly beside Komako, and rolled over. The bed sank low toward her weight. Komako waited to be sure she was still asleep and then she hissed, "For God's sake, you're safe here, Mr. Bailey. For tonight, at least. Go to sleep."

"Tonight." He nodded. "But tomorrow? What then?"

In irritation Komako raised up onto one elbow, the mattress shiver-ing slightly. The widow snored on. The little whitewashed room looked spare and strange in the moonlight. "Tomorrow we go up into the hills.

Tomorrow we find the Spanish glyphic. After that you're free to go wherever you choose."

In the silver light the man's long face looked corpse-like. "None of us are free, who were at Cairndale," he said quietly. "The drughr has marked us all."

Komako felt her impatience flare up. "The drughr's dead, Mr. Bailey," she whispered angrily. "It's *dead*. Dr. Berghast destroyed it at the orsine. Charlie was there, he saw."

Mr. Bailey began to laugh then, a quiet laugh, more like an exhalation of breath. It was an ugly, not entirely sane sound. He folded his long arms over his head in a weird gesture, his borrowed nightshirt baring his hairy knees. "You can't kill the drughr, girl. It's already dead. You can't kill a thing that's already dead."

The old widow was making a chewing sound with her mouth, near Komako's ear. Komako, fuming, folded her pillow over her face. Her heart was black. Who was he to say she couldn't?

He had no idea what she was capable of.

8

Adversus Solem
ne Loquitor

In the pale wash of morning they set out, unlikely pilgrims, trudging up into the dark foothills as if fleeing the day.

There were paths invisible in the sharp rocks and steep scree of the hills, paths only Mr. Bailey could find. Small black scorpions and stinging ants and snakes would come out with the day but it wasn't quite the hour. Still Komako watched the landscape warily.

Mr. Bailey, scraping at the rocks with his walking stick, was different now. He seemed changed. Komako wasn't sure of the difference at first and then she knew what it was. He was no longer afraid. As if in the night he'd come to some decision about his own fate, and his fear of the drughr had receded. She glimpsed in his milky eye an increased sadness, a regret that had risen in the night, but this only made her the more angry. She didn't want to forgive anything.

The skin on her knuckles was red and chafing. A rash always broke out when she used her talent, as if her own body resisted it, as if she was allergic to herself. Her boots crunched through the loose rocks. They came over a rise and the yellow foothills were bathed in the morning light and she stopped, amazed. Far below and behind them lay the long sandy beach of Mojácar. White combers rolled endlessly in. Ahead lay the scooped and ragged mountains of the Sierra Cabrera, green and murky brown. There were low bushes and wind-twisted trees in the valleys where water lay. The slopes were long with grasses. And over everything lay a sky as vast and limitless as the world.

Mr. Bailey watched her. He said nothing, only took out a waterskin and offered it to her. Then he drank for himself and set off walking again.

It had been a long time since Cairndale burned. She knew this. The sun rising over the smoky rubble while she and the little ones and Alice rode away. The dead in their stone boats behind. She'd been struggling against her own darker impulses ever since, not liking who she was becoming, not knowing how to stop it. What she feared was Jacob, still, becoming like him, because there was a part of her too that would have bonded with the drughr to get those she loved back. She used to sit up in the night watching Teshi sleep, while their mother lay sick with fever on the tatami near the door, and she would hold her breath until it hurt telling herself no bad would come to the baby, she'd keep her sister safe, just like her mama would want. While the waterwheel creaked slowly outside and the stars turned and all the other poor huddled with them on the floor, snoring or groaning or rustling in their rags. And later how she'd cried and held Teshi in the heat of the theater, begging her, too, not to die, and how her sister had woken up pale and wrong in the morning, with three thin red lines at her throat and a part of her hungry for oblivion. Oh, she understood Jacob too well. It scared her.

In the early afternoon Mr. Bailey led her to a low rocky hill, with a stone escarpment facing east, and he crouched down in the lee of a boulder and stared hard across a valley. She didn't know what he was seeking. His good eye scanned a slope of loose rock, watchful. She did so too. There was a boulder with starflowers on it, a bush the shape of Ribs's head. Nothing else of interest.

Suddenly Mr. Bailey stood. He gestured bleakly.

Next to the boulder, where there'd been nothing before, Komako now saw the jagged dark entrance of a cave. It might have been there all along, she thought. Maybe the light had shifted.

"Is that it?" she muttered. "Is that what we're looking for?"

"It has found us," he said softly.

The cave was a narrow, twisting passage of dirt and loose stones, leading down into darkness. Komako took off her gloves for a light to see by but Mr. Bailey set his big hand on her shoulder, shook his head no.

So she descended with him into the dark, trailing a careful hand along the rough wall. The air turned damp. They did not go far before a light could be seen up ahead. Mr. Bailey's breathing was loud and ragged.

The tunnel ended abruptly at an underground pool of water, about the size and shape of the old theater in Tokyo where she had lived as a child. There were shafts of sunlight filtering down from the rock ceiling above. Komako shivered. The water lay silver and flat and absolutely still and it filled the entire chamber, from wall to wall. To the left the water lay in darkness, where the ceiling sloped low. There were stalactites and pale mineral deposits in weblike formations overhead.

"You are disappointed," Mr. Bailey whispered. His voice bounced off the cave, distorting. "You thought maybe the second orsine would be here?"

As soon as he said it, Komako realized it was true. It made no sense, but it was true. She'd hoped she'd reached the end of something.

She watched as Mr. Bailey removed his hat, his coat, his shoes. He rolled up his trouser legs to his knees and then he waded noiselessly out into the water.

After a moment, Komako did the same.

The splash of their steps echoed around the walls. The light fell in cathedral shafts. The water she walked through was cold, metallic, strangely viscous. But it stood only as deep as her ankles, and she was surprised to feel the bottom of the pool to be as smooth as glass.

Mr. Bailey kneeled in the waters, and trailed his fingers around him, and breathed.

Then suddenly she knew it: they were not alone. Komako felt a presence. Something was uncoiling from the rocky ceiling, dripping slowly, a gelatinous thing sagging out of the narrow darkness, dipping toward the still waters. Komako's eyes couldn't make sense of it. It was the size and shape of a human brain, with a single blue eye affixed in its slime, and it oozed slowly down out of the shadows toward the water.

Komako stared, fascinated. But even as it neared the surface the water itself lifted upward, and cradled the thing, and surrounded it, and there were tiny spectral worms, glass eels, thousands of them, all wriggling in the water as it rose. The water was gurgling, sputtering. And gradually it took on the form of a child, a child made entirely of writhing eel larvae, and its one eye was very blue and stared unblinking at Komako.

Mr. Bailey had not stirred.

A cavity of darkness formed in its face, as the eels parted, and out of it came the low, sweet voice of a woman.

Textor pulvis, the glyphic murmured. The words gave off no echo in the cavern, hanging heavily in the stillness and then simply ceasing. *Iam nostis. Venisti ad me. Me roga et videberis.*

Komako swallowed uneasily. "Mr. Bailey?" she whispered.

He was kneeling with his hands on his thighs and his ravaged face upraised. "It knows what you are," he said softly. "It knows why you are here."

"Right. Okay. That should make this easier."

Lutetia Parisiorum, the glyphic murmured. *Debes ire ad Lutetiam.*

Komako's glance flickered again over to Mr. Bailey. "What did she say?"

"It said you must go to Paris. That the orsine you seek is in Paris."

"Paris," Komako whispered, the echo of her words fading. "I already knew that. I have friends there even now, looking for it. Where in Paris?" She looked at the glyphic, rippling and glassy and slick in the shaft of sunlight, as if soaked by the light itself, as if the light itself were dripping. "Does she say *where* to look?"

The shafts of daylight shifted in the cavern. The pool dimmed. Slowly the glyphic glided nearer; the eels on its face, surrounding its one eye, wriggled sickeningly. *Clausa est. Glyphic fuit illic semel. Eius cor clausit omnia. Petas Abbatissam.*

"It says . . . the second orsine is closed," Mr. Bailey translated. "The orsine lies dormant. A glyphic's heart has . . . has already closed it. Sealed it. You will not be able to pass through. You must seek out the Abbess."

"Wait. The second orsine is *closed*? Like at Cairndale?"

The glyphic's blue eye did not blink.

Komako whirled on Mr. Bailey. "What good is it, then, if it's sealed? Is there a way to reopen it?" She spun back to face the glyphic. "Who is this Abbess? Will she help us?"

"If it is who I think," interjected Mr. Bailey softly, "then she will be little help. In Paris is a commune of powerful talents, women all. They live chastely. That is, they have sworn off use of their talents. Their leader and Dr. Berghast . . . corresponded for many years. They did not agree on many things. I did not know she controlled an orsine," he added.

Komako gave a bitter smile. "Well, if she disagreed with Berghast, how bad can she be?"

"She murdered her orsine's glyphic," whispered Mr. Bailey. "She cut out its heart and sealed her orsine with it. Slaughtered any of her followers who objected, one must presume. She is ruthless, Miss Onoe. Can you not feel the pain in the waters here? The grief? It is an evil place, that commune."

Komako remembered with a pang their own intentions back at Cairndale, on that terrible last night. How the alchemist woman Ficke had told them to do the same. That the only way to seal an orsine was with a glyphic's heart. And how, as Jacob Marber and his litches strode through the dark fields, and the old talents gathered to meet them, Charlie had slipped away to find the Spider. She thought of the blood that would have been on their hands. Who was she to judge?

But the glyphic now was gliding toward her, out of the half-light. She felt the waters at her ankles tighten, as if to grip her fast. A heat was rising from the mass of wriggling eels. It was like standing before a fire. She saw the glyphic's blue eye fix upon her.

The glyphic reached out a writhing limb. Touched Komako's wrist. She braced for the slither of eels but instead a bubble of shimmering water encapsulated her hand and arm and grew, spreading slowly up, past her elbow, toward her shoulder. It felt exactly as if she'd plunged her arm into a moving river. The sleeve of her dress floated within it. She flexed her fingers slowly in wonder, and the water, pulling as if in a current, flexed with them.

The glove of water surrounded her chest and ribs and hips and down to her ankles, where it met itself, and then it rose up over her throat and mouth and nose and last of all her eyes. And yet Komako found she could breathe, somehow, even under the water, while her hair drifted like webbing slowly around her. The waters refracted the light, bent it, so that now the cave around her looked distorted and strange. The glyphic rippled in the light. Its blue eye was piercing.

You have a part to play in all that is to come, Komako Onoe, it said in its calm, melodic voice. *You must resist what you are, to become what you will be.*

Komako stared. All around her the waterlight danced. "You . . . you speak English? I can understand you—?"

The glyphic paid her no mind. *The Bringer of Dust brings more than he knows,* it continued. *Only those touched by his dust can pass through the orsine. Jacob Marber was not the only conduit. There is a second. Fear the dust.*

"Jacob?" Komako whispered. "What does he have to do with anything? What's the Bringer of Dust?"

I dreamed this age long ago, Dust Weaver. That a child would be taken from the talent world and raised unknowing. A child unlike any other. A child who would wield the talents of the five as if they were one. Who would face down the First and bring about his ruin and the ruin of his kind. The Dark Talent is rising, Komako Onoe. Our time is nearing its end.

Komako lifted her arm. It felt so heavy. The water moved thickly around her.

"Please," she begged. "I don't understand. You mean the foretelling? What is . . . the First? And the dust? Is it Marlowe you dreamed of, is he the Dark Talent?"

The glyphic wavered in front of her, a writhing mass of eels. Its face when it turned its head looked to be melting. Komako felt a sudden fierce heat bloom in her skin, as the glyphic's blue eye came very close to her own.

Not a foretelling, it murmured, and there was a hint of scorn in the word. *I dreamed a possible future, long ago. It does not mean it will come to pass. I have dreamed others. The dream changes, for the future is not yet written.*

"But Mr. Bailey believes—"

Oh, they are all so eager to believe. But not you.

And all at once Komako crushed her eyes shut, and asked the question she'd been afraid to ask.

"Is he even alive?" she whispered. "Is Marlowe alive?"

A long stillness followed. She could hear the ripple of waters. Mr. Bailey's breathing. She opened her eyes, afraid.

And then, at last, the glyphic's voice rang out, like a bell. *He is not gone yet.*

Komako gave out a low moan. He *wasn't* dead. Marlowe *wasn't dead.* She hadn't realized how much hope she'd still had inside her, how desperately she'd wanted to believe. In the water her eyes were stinging with water.

"Thank you," she whispered.

The glyphic writhed and folded over itself and turned its eye away. *You have brought me your offering. I accept. No other gratitude is necessary. You will depart now.*

Suddenly the cocoon of water was collapsing all around Komako, crashing flatly into the pool. She heaved and gasped and sucked at the air. Put her hands on her knees, coughed and coughed.

Nunc dimittis, the glyphic whispered, releasing her from its spell.

She was still spluttering when the glyphic poured itself toward Mr. Bailey. He kneeled yet in the shallow waters, his burned face upraised, his gaze fixed on the glyphic. Komako felt a scaly coil flick past her ankle. There were things in the water, small biting things, very quick. She stumbled backward, uncertain, to the dry tunnel they'd climbed down through. Her mind felt slow, clouded. A fin broke the surface, like a little blade, and then a second, a third. In an instant they'd flickered away.

"Mr. Bailey!" she called, shivering. Her wet hair was in her face. "Get out of the water! There's something in it—"

But he only looked at her, a calmness in his eye.

And all at once she understood. Understood what the glyphic had meant by "offering," its "acceptance." Why Mr. Bailey had spoken of the glyphic in horror. It had answered Komako's questions, in exchange for a life. His.

"Wait! No!" she cried. "Mr. Bailey—!"

But there wasn't time; the glyphic was leaning slowly in toward him. Already the tiny glass eels were dropping in clumps from the glyphic, dropping into the waters, then boiling up all around Mr. Bailey's kneeling form. He didn't move. She saw then a dark red cloud of blood fill the waters around him. He started to shudder, then convulse. His head was banging loosely around on his neck. His back was twisting, cracking. She stared in horror as a patch on his shirt bloomed red, then a second, and then all the blood was seeping together and there was blood running down his face and his throat. And that was when she saw the eels, the little glass eels, dozens of them, furrowing up out of Mr. Bailey's skin, frothing and pink with his blood, then wriggling back under, eating their way through Dr. Berghast's manservant, carving their way into his imperfect heart.

But the glyphic wasn't done with her yet, either. All at once she felt something pierce her thoughts, an image, an image in motion. It was, she saw in horror, the dream itself, the vision the Spanish glyphic had discerned all those centuries ago. She saw a man with no eyes, blood pouring from his sockets, a man of great strength, imprisoned in a world of darkness and swirling dust; she saw a child, alone and suffering in darkness. His face was hidden. Yet somehow she sensed a resemblance between them, even across the centuries, a shared bloodline. And she saw what that child would become, how he shone with an eerie blue light, shone so brightly she could not see his face but only the skull and veins and muscles under the skin. And there were little ones, talent children, all fallen like rag dolls and lying dead in a ruined house. The mutilated man was on his knees, clawing at his own face. A drughr loomed near, with a clawlike hand outstretched, against a sky the color of blood. But the child ignored the drughr, and stood over the fallen man, merciless.

And at last everything blurred, as in a fog, and Komako saw a face—the face of the Dark Talent, a face twisted by its own power—and, in the seconds before everything went dark, she threw her hands over her eyes in horror.

For she *knew* him.

9

FINGERTIPS OF FIRE

S he came dazed down out of the narrow cave and fell in the sunlight, her shadow pooling beneath her, and she dialed her slow face to the sky. She wanted to scream. The insides of her eyelids were red with light. Behind her loomed a crevice between white rocks, a crevice exploding in starflowers, and she saw a stony slope and prickly scrub and a wall of sunlight beyond but the cave of the glyphic had vanished, the cave with Mr. Bailey and the glass eels, it had vanished just as if it had never been.

Something in her was not right. She sat in the rocks, and started to cry. She saw the tiny eels pricking through Mr. Bailey's flesh, saw the quiet smile on his face as they ate out his throat. The blood flowering in his clothes. She rose, took a slow unsteady step downhill. Then a second. Somehow she knew the scorpions and ants would not sting her. The world was bright with meaning. She walked in it.

Gradually horror gave way. A hollowness took over. And then there below were the orchard trees, bare and ragged. The sun was shifting in the cold sky. She walked out past the village with her hands loose at her sides and in the dirt road down out of the foothills she did not stop. It was dark, the stars were wheeling all around. She walked on. It was daybreak. The sky was red. It was noon.

When she came to, she was alone on the winding road back to Málaga. A chill wind was up. Her dark skirt was white with dust. In the distance a cart was approaching.

Komako worked her dry lips. She thought suddenly of the glyphic and all it had shown her. The terrifying vision, the eyeless man. The drughr and the child under blood-drenched skies. She thought of what it had told her: Marlowe, alive yet; the second orsine in Paris, controlled by the Abbess. That dream was just a possible future; nothing was fixed until time made it so. She sat down in the dirt and waited for the cart to get nearer and she knew she had to get back to Sicily as fast as she could. She thought of Mr. Bailey and how he had known and then she felt something harden inside her, a cold dark hard spot in her chest, where her heart should have been, and she got back to her feet. The cart was pulled by a thin-shanked mule and driven by two boys and they slowed as they neared her. Staring, as if at an apparition.

"Málaga, por favor," she said creakily. "He estado caminado mucho tiempo."

Her hands were raw in their ragged sleeves. Her face felt tender. It hurt to speak.

The two boys, eyes wide with alarm, gestured her into the back among the barrels and crates.

It was only much later, when they stopped to water their mule, that Komako leaned over the still surface of the pool and pulled back her hair and saw her reflection.

Her face stared back at her, like something diseased. The skin all over had turned a painful red, and was starting to peel, as if she'd stood too close to a sun.

A GUEST in the HOUSE of the DEAD, PART II

·

1883

10

THE SHAPE OF THINGS WE LEAVE BEHIND

As they rode south, Caroline Ficke could see how the boy's hand hurt him.

Not the shattered hand, with its fingerbones already fusing back together, its wristbones tender but strong, though the pain there must have been excruciating. No, not that one, but the other, the infected one, the one with dark tattoos of dust in its skin.

Not that he complained; he just clenched his jaw as they rode, a tightness at his eyes, working his fingers open and shut as if the tattooed skin were a glove he could peel away.

It had been three days since their ancient showman's wagon had left Edinburgh, picking its slow way south on the Great North Road, three days since he'd faced down a bone witch and lived. Behind them lay snow and the north that Caroline had come to love and her brother, Edward, Edward who would be all right, she told herself, Edward who would manage, who would have to. There'd been no reasoning with him, bless his heart; he wouldn't leave the home he knew, not for any reason, not for her, not even to keep himself safe. *Well*, she thought. *If the bone witch comes hunting, at least it isn't Edward she's wanting.*

But she'd left their forwarding address in plain sight, just in case.

It was after they'd passed the coaching inns at Durham, riding with a slate-colored sky low at their backs, when Caroline heard the keening from inside the wagon. Soft, high-pitched, almost like a song. The old horses in their traces slowed and raised their heads, their ears flicking nervously.

She got stiffly down and pulled her shawl close. She hadn't traveled in such a fashion since she was a young woman and her body was not what it was. She limped around the small wheels and unlatched the rear door.

Her children were inside, all seven of them, Brendan turning his face to see her, Seamus blinking against the daylight. They sat or hunched or lay in a rough circle in the warmth of the wagon, Wislawa and Maddie and Tobey holding hands, twisted figures malignant and knurled and made more strange by the strange twilight within. It was how they had traveled since leaving Edinburgh, silent and unmoving, still and uncomplaining, patient as the trees they were slowly resembling. All around them leaned the lashed crates filled with Caroline's alchemical objects, crates of glass beakers packed in straw, boxes of ancient books, jars of powders and iron filings and rare ingredients. She let go of her shawl, gripped the door-bar for balance.

"All right, now," she said, more for herself than the children. "It's all right. There, now."

The keening came from little Deirdre. It was like back at the chandler's shop, she saw: pale shoots had spread from under the girl's blanket, crisscrossing the wall of the wagon behind her, disappearing among the crates. A small colored pane of glass under the gable at the front of the wagon drenched everything in a yellow light. Deirdre's sweet face was obscured by her hair.

It was Charlie, coming up behind her, who broke the spell. "Hang on, Mrs. Ficke," he said. And then, to the children within: "What's all this? What is it, Deirdre? Everything okay?"

And he squeezed in past Caroline, his head bumping the roof, the wagon groaning and shifting under his weight. Close to the glyph-twisted, the skin of his tattooed hand began to fill with shadows, the marks writhing sluggishly. The children followed that hand with their eyes. She'd been surprised at how quickly Charlie had grown used to her strange wards, surprised and pleased, and was even more pleased to find the children liked him too.

Now the other children began keening also, in their strange not-quite-human voices. A low thrumming song, as in a church, subtle and quick and intelligent. There was a melodic beauty threaded through it.

Gently, Charlie traced the pale shoots back to Deirdre's body, finding their sources. He had to lean up against a box of glass alembics to do so. His hand was mottled with darkness as he ran his fingertips over her collarbone and the back of her neck, tracing the new rough bark growing there. The bark had grown up over her ear and enclosed one side of her face. It looked, thought Caroline grimly, as if the girl were being slowly entombed alive. Charlie unhooked the water flask from its nail and leaned over and gave the children a drink, one by one, with an infinite patience. Then he corked the bottle and met Caroline's eye. Sometimes, she thought, he was so much older than his years.

Outside again, she watched him busily brush at his bowler hat, one-handed. A fine pair they were, him with his infected hand, her with her missing arm. He was a person, she was coming to see, who accepted that there were things that could not be explained. He was comfortable with the not-knowing. She had met few people in her life she could say that of, talents or no. More even than that, he could stand before her infected with the dust of the drughr and still be worried for a little girl he scarcely knew.

"Is there no help for her?" he repeated, for the third time. "None of the others are changing. Could it be because we moved her? Could it be the travel?"

She shook her head. "Ach. It started before."

"Maybe she knew she'd have to go." He was quiet for a moment. "Or maybe it's something to do with me. With this . . . dust. Maybe it's my doing."

"It's not your doing," she said firmly. "There's no knowing what's natural or normal or right for these children, now. They're glyph-twisted. We just have to do our best, like."

"She's hot to the touch, Mrs. Ficke. We should be summoning a doctor."

"There's not a doctor alive who can help," she replied.

That night they camped behind a wet hedgerow feeling the damp creep into their clothes. Charlie had managed a small fire with the dry wood brought down from Edinburgh. But there wasn't much and what little he'd scavenged from nearby was too green or too wet to burn well and turned the smoke greasy and thick.

Caroline sat huddled in her shawl. Her bones ached, her teeth hurt. She listened to the quiet road in the early dark, the wood popping in the fire. They had seen few other travelers this far north. The horses, hobbled near an oak, dipped their heads and raised them and their eyes shone weirdly in the firelight.

She had brought out the charcoal rubbing of the Sicilian inscription, the old runes from the Agnoscenti. But the light was failing even as she did and she couldn't see much and so she rolled it back up, set it aside. Charlie sat near the fire with his hands cradled in his lap and his bowler drawn low so that she could not see his eyes but he would turn his face now and again to glance over at the wagon where the children slept. She could feel his concern. They were not monsters in his eye but kids, just kids, with just a steeper path to climb than most. The boy took off his hat, wiped his face carefully with his handkerchief. His young eyes were large and naked.

"We'll be more at risk in London," said Caroline suddenly. "It would be best if we arrived after dark. We'll want to make as few ripples as possible. The cobblestones have ears. If we're lucky, we'll leave Nickel Street West before Claker Jack and his exiles even realize we've arrived."

"Will the bone witch be there before us?"

"Tis unlikely." She shook her head. "But she'll regret it, if she is. I'm old, but not without resources. And you will be something of a surprise to her now."

The boy raked at the fire with a leafy stick, making sparks. "What kind of a danger is he, this Claker Jack? I heard rumors of the exiles, back at Cairndale. But never that name. I read about an RF in London—"

"That would be Fang. Ratcliffe Fang."

"Ratcliffe Fang," said the boy softly, as if testing it on his tongue.

"Mr. Fang has been dead since autumn," said Caroline. "Murdered in his doorway. His task was to watch over the exiles in London but he only had dealings with the . . . better sort. The destitute, the addicted, the petty thieves what he could keep out of prison. But there are all manner of exiles, many far worse. It's like when they lose their talent, they lose some will to live. You might have felt it. I did, for years. A kind of listlessness, and anger. At what I'd used to be, you understand." She gave Charlie a long look. "Aye. Well, that sort lives belowground, in a place called the Falls. Full of spite and venom, it is. And pity any talent what they get their hooks into. It's pain first and death like a kindness later. And all of it's under the eye of Claker Jack. He was the first exile to be sent down from Cairndale, some say. I don't see how he can be quite that old. But he's the first what set out to build his own version of Cairndale, his own . . . community. And a wicked one it is."

"My father was an exile," said Charlie.

Caroline paused. She wasn't sure she'd heard him right. "Talents don't run in families," she said gently.

"Mine did," the boy replied.

She'd never heard of such a thing. The emergence of the gifts was random, children born anywhere, to anyone. She fumbled for the kettle on the flat rock at her foot and carefully set it into the fire.

"I found a file on him," the boy went on, fiddling with his bowler. "In Dr. Berghast's office, at Cairndale. His name was Hywel Owydd. He came to Cairndale when he was twelve."

"He was Welsh," she said.

He nodded, mistaking her meaning. "It was my mama who was black. The file said he was sent to London when his talent started to go. So he would've been one of them, wouldn't he? One of the exiles. Maybe he even knew this Claker Jack."

She saw the question in his eyes. "Knew *of* him, I'd expect. But you said he died taking you and your mother west, in America. That doesn't sound like one of Claker Jack's exiles. Your father must have been very brave, Charlie, to lose his talent and not lose himself in the process."

"I wish—" he began, in a whisper. "I wish I'd known him."

"Aye. But there's none of us as know our parents. Not really."

The boy looked at her.

"I don't even know how he died, Mrs. Ficke. My mama never talked about it. She said he got sick. That's all."

With her hooked arm, Caroline lifted the kettle out of the fire. She watched as Charlie reached into his shirt and took out the ring he wore on its cord, the delicately shaped ring he'd shown her on that first night, the ring with the Cairndale crest. Its eerie black metal and wood sucked up the light, shone as if with a darkness all its own.

"He gave my mama this," said the boy. "When she passed, I kept it safe. It's the only thing I have from her. From him. I saw this symbol on Mr. Coulton's papers when he and Alice came for me or I wouldn't have gone with them. So it kind of saved me, I guess, this ring. Like my father wanted me to know about it, Cairndale. Like he wanted me to know where I could be safe."

"I'm sure that's true, Charlie," she said, watching him carefully. She didn't say: *Cairndale sent him away, into the horrors of London.* She didn't say: *He was running as far from that place as he could get.*

"Did Dr. Berghast ever say anything to you about . . . artifacts?" he asked her.

"Artifacts?"

Charlie nodded. "He seemed to think this ring is what kept me safe when I was in the orsine. He said the metal had been reworked, but that he knew it anyway. What it was. He said there were three artifacts, once. Two were lost. This was one of the lost ones. They made it so you could go into the land of the dead."

"Why would your father have such a thing?"

Charlie wet his lips. "I don't know. I don't know anything about him. You didn't . . . you didn't know him, did you?"

"No, Charlie," she said, as gently as she could. "I'm sorry. There've been a fair lot of talents at Cairndale over the years. And my time there would have been long before his."

Caroline arranged the two chipped teacups, poured out the cooling kettle. The fire was warm on her face. She passed across a teacup to Charlie and paused, glimpsing his hand, the intricate patterns whorling eerily there.

The boy saw her looking. He leaned across and set the little teacup down on a rock and gingerly took off his greatcoat and, using his healed fingers, he unbuttoned and folded high the sleeve of his infected hand, all the way to the elbow. The tracks of corrupted dust like arteries under the skin. "I don't know if I'm part drughr now, or what," he said. "I wonder what my father would think, to see me like this. Or Mama."

"They would love you just as you are," she replied firmly. "Who you are on the inside hasn't changed."

Charlie held his tea to his lips but he did not drink. His eyes were twinned in the firelight.

"Our skins are stories about how we've lived," she went on. She unbuckled and removed her artificial arm. She held the ruined limb up like an exhibit, brushing it gently with her fingertips. The soft pink scarred skin there, the folds of old tissue. "I thought I was ugly, after this. My Mr. Ficke taught me I wasn't. He said a scar is just our body remembering the world. There's a story there, he'd say, about how you got to be you. He was kind like that, and wise. You can't be ashamed of what's happened to you, Charlie. It's the world's doing. And you're still here."

He smiled a little, at that. "Do you miss him?"

"Every day." She blew on her cup of tea, drank. "But he passed away a long time ago. And he'd lived a good life, a long life. At Cairndale I was a clink, one of the strongest. Sometimes a talent goes slowly, when it goes. But not for me. I was eighteen. I was lifting a barrel—I don't even remember why, I think we were cleaning out a storeroom—when it just washed out of me, my strength. The barrel came down hard on my arm. Crushed it. I was lucky to be alive. Henry Berghast allowed me to stay in the infirmary until I was strong enough to travel."

Charlie watched her in the firelight.

"It was Mr. Ficke who was there in the infirmary with me, as I was recovering," she said, feeling the smile creep across her features. "I was disconsolate. But he was kind, and patient with me. He was an unusual guest at Cairndale. Not a part of the talent world but allowed in anyway. Henry Berghast had work for him to do. He was an anatomist and a scientist and an illustrator who'd studied in Naples. He was made a member of the Royal Academy, later. On account of his watercolors.

It's true. I think I fell in love with him first, before he did with me. The difference in our ages was much harder for him to accept. He was forty-three years old when we met and sixty-eight years old when he died. I had twenty-five years with him. And I've never loved another man in all my life since." She threw the last of her tea on the fire. "It's extraordinary to me now, to think of it. In those days there was a chaplain at Cairndale, a caster named Mr. Wooley. He's long passed too, now. But he married us, the day before we departed. I rode away from the institute a bride. I'm sure I'm the only exile ever to do so."

His eyes were dark with the imagining of it. She saw then how young he was still, despite the life he'd had. They sat for a while in silence.

To her surprise Charlie began, haltingly, to talk about Marlowe. He'd not said much about the shining boy. Maybe it was because she'd talked about her husband; maybe it was just in him and needed getting out. Whatever it was, in the low firelight at the edge of that quiet wood, he started to describe their parting. That had been at the edge of the orsine, as its darkness flooded the monastery on the island in Loch Fae. He described his friend's courage, while the spirit dead stood screaming all around, and his sadness, and how small his hand was in Charlie's own. Charlie's eyes were wet in the firelight but he made no move to wipe them. She hadn't understood just how young Marlowe was and she was surprised to hear it. Charlie poked at the fire, raked the coals. His face was half in darkness, and he would pause sometimes to reach for a word, unhurried, wanting to get it right. "I never asked to be a part of all this," he said, across the faint hiss of the fire. "I didn't want to be a talent. I hated it. And then when I lost it, I didn't want it gone. Sometimes it's like life is just all about taking what you can't say no to, and going on anyway, you know?"

"I do," she whispered.

"I was alone after Mama died. That was nearly most of my childhood, Mrs. Ficke. When Alice and Mr. Coulton took me out of Natchez, I had no idea what a family could be. I'd lost the idea of it. I've done some awful things. You just had to, to stay alive. But Marlowe, right from the first days we were in Mrs. Harrogate's row house, it was like he saw something in me, something good, and because he saw it I could see it too. I don't know. I didn't used to know how important that is. Being seen, I mean." Charlie ran a slow hand over his eyes. "I hate thinking where he is, what he must be going through. I don't remember much, but it was a frightening place. I know that. And I let him go through the orsine alone. I lost him. Now there's this hurt inside me worse than when I had my healing. Right here." He tapped his heart. "And there won't be any fixing it unless I make things right."

"You will," she said. "You'll make it right."

The night deepened. He was sleepy at the fire and his eyelids were heavy when he said, "Mrs. Ficke? You're not like other grown-ups, none I ever knew. Not even Alice."

"How do you mean?"

He yawned, folded himself deeper in his blanket. "I don't know," he mumbled. "I saw how you were when your brother bought the wagon. You didn't like it. But you pretended like you did."

She was quiet.

"I'll tell you a secret," she said gently. "There aren't any grown-ups, Charlie. Not in the way you mean it. There's only just children what's gone and got too far away from their own childhoods. Sure, their bodies is all grown. But on the inside, everyone's all just about the same size."

But the boy was already asleep, snoring softly, and she didn't know if he'd heard any of it. Caroline took herself up to the steering bench, where she'd laid out a blanket. She could hear the little ones inside the wagon, keening. She emptied her mind of all that was in it, her fears, her memories, her fascinated horror hearing about the bone witch, the inscription from the Agnoscenti, she let all of it recede, in order to take away some of the humanness in her, and let the pure dark of the night fill the spaces where it had been.

For she'd seen something else, something that frightened her. When the boy had folded back his sleeve, she'd seen the dust under his skin, creeping slowly up his arm, like a black stain.

It was spreading.

11

THE FALLS
OF LONDON

They were three: a boy and two girls, each sinister, and they lurked in an alley in Wapping.

Micah was the boy. His two sisters wore the same ragged brown coats as he, chewed the same frayed cigars at their mouths. Micah was the eldest yet no more than twelve himself and all three had eyes like molasses. Both sisters swung short wood clubs loosely in their begrimed hands. Micah wore a satchel low on one hip and rested a long-fingered hand upon it, as if it held some precious thing. Hawk-nosed, slope-shouldered, with hair as white and fine as cobwebs, they none of them stood taller than a grown man's rib cage yet each was feared in any street that knew them. They were born of three different fathers but the one mother, a vicious woman, dead by her own hand, and they might have been her progeny only with just the one blood in their veins for how much they resembled her and how little their fathers. Yet the truest blood they shared was the blood they'd wash from their hands each morning in a tin bucket in the echoing tunnels running under London.

Rain dripped from their hats.

Across the street, a carriage came to a slow stop; a driver in a black cape got down, unfolded the steps, opened the carriage door.

A gentleman in a silk hat and white gloves emerged, taking the umbrella from the driver. He might have just come from the theater district, except that he clutched a doctor's bag under one arm. He crossed the muck of the way. Only when he'd stepped out of the lanternlight of his carriage did the littlest sister, Timna, glide forward.

"It is done, then?" The gentleman tilted his umbrella and beads of silver water rolled off. "I had nearly given up on you lot. Where is your master?"

Timna spat the chewed cigar away, into the dark. "He isn't our master," she said. "An you never said there'd be three. Your mark weren't alone, like."

"And yet here you are, child, perfectly fine." The gentleman held up the doctor's bag. "I brought your master's fee. I trust this concludes our business."

"Three costs *extra*, mister," she whispered. "An I told you, he isn't our master."

The gentleman set down the bag, turned to go. Back in the street, the driver of the carriage had got back up onto his seat, and huddled there in the wet, his whip leaning elegantly out like a fishing line.

Just then, out of the darkness, a grimy hand reached up and tugged at the gentleman's sleeve. He turned sharply, knocking the second sister aside with the back of his hand.

"By God," he muttered in disgust. "How many of you are there?"

As he did so, out of the darkness he had just turned away from, a new hand materialized, reaching up, unhurried, and it drew a blade across the gentleman's exposed throat. A look of astonishment crossed his face.

Then, as if opening a faucet, a bib of blood poured suddenly out over his coat. His umbrella fell away. He sank to his knees.

Across the street, the driver turned at the noise, peering across at the darkness. "Mr. Brackthwaite?" he called. "Sir? Is everything all right?"

The littlest sister, Timna, wiped the rain from her face. Picked up the doctor's bag, opened it.

"Well?" said Micah softly.

Behind them the driver of the carriage had got down now, and was unhooking one of the side lanterns, lifting it high to see into the alley.

Timna looked up, unhurried. She nodded. "It'll do."

The boy turned at that, and crouched beside the dead man. He tilted the man's chin to one side and then swiftly sawed off one ear with his blade, not caring about the mess.

And then the three of them vanished into the alley, leaving the mutilated gentleman in the rain.

He was an agent of the Abbess, Micah was. Up to his pits in blood. Left in London to do her bidding, to protect her interests in the foul underground Falls of Claker Jack.

And his sisters were even bloodier than he. If any had a last name, they'd never used it, and it was lost now in their mother's grave. They were blood but not family. What kept them together wasn't love but hate, hatred for the whole smoldering fog-thick hell of the world. Never mind their ages: the only satisfying work they'd ever done was the killing kind.

Prudence, the middle sister, had her own meanness. It was quieter and therefore more frightening. She never spoke. She was thin like a shovel turned sideways and in silhouette her forehead looked dented. She had small grimy hands with fingernails as black as if they'd been painted and she moved with a deliberate slowness. Sometimes Micah thought her simple. Sometimes he thought her the cleverest of all. He'd catch her watching him from under her greasy hair with a look of mingled fear and hatred but he didn't care.

There was no such fear in Timna, the littlest, not of him nor of any other. She had two teeth out in front and a scar across her back like she'd been cut open as a baby and her insides moved around. She was birthed under an archway, a slippery bloodied screaming thing, and Micah had been there to see the horror of it. She used to cut the legs off living rats and then throw them into the Thames. She'd once paid an urchin every coin in her pocket in exchange for the urchin kicking his own father's mouth in, while he drunkenly slept. She felt neither hunger nor cold nor pity nor despair and this made her useful to the Abbess. But the world had got into her at some point, and never got out, and it was this more than anything that had turned her cruel.

Micah knew if ever his sisters had to choose they'd take each other and leave him to the quicklime. But they were all he had in the world except for maybe the Abbess herself, and they weren't much.

He was himself broken inside in a million little ways, and there was no putting him back together. He knew it but the knowing meant nothing to him. Of the many articulate tools in his leather satchel, his favorite was a pearl-handled corkscrew he'd picked out of the gutters in Marylebone one night when he was eight. It could do things to a person's eyeball you wouldn't think possible, and yet still allow the bastard to see, and that was what he liked. The seeing. He'd been a clink long ago at Cairndale, a strong who could condense his flesh into something hard and impregnable and powerful, taken from his little sisters by that witch Harrogate and sent like cattle north to the institute. When he'd lost his talent, he wasn't even eight years old. The Abbess had greeted him at King's Cross, a woman six and a half feet at the shoulder, monstrously tall in heels and in an outsized feathered hat, daring any man's stare. With her were two women in red, silent as spilled blood. She'd taken Micah to a sumptuous hotel room, and there he'd found his tiny sisters, plucked from the workhouse, stuffing their faces with pastries. He'd feared no one, even then, and yet he knew to fear the Abbess. Her eyes were silver like the edge of a knife and her enormous hands were hot to the touch. He'd later hear such terrible stories, that she held sway in a hidden corner of Paris, that talents did not affect her, that she was immune to their powers. Some said she'd lived hundreds of years and in all that time she'd stalked and killed talents without remorse, like a drughr. Some said she was part drughr herself.

He was not so foolish as to believe all that was said. But he knew, even at seven years old, newly weak, no longer a clink, learning all over again to be wary of the swiping canes of gentlemen as they strode past in the streets—even then, he'd known there was no refusing the Abbess. What she wanted were eyes and ears in the London underworld known, among the exiles, as the Falls. She offered him employment. He took it.

And soon discovered, among the filth and misery of that place, that he had other gifts, terrible ones.

He'd been pleased to hear about the burning of Cairndale, all those months back. In the weeks that followed, there had been some survivors who'd made their way south to London, a few desperate talents, some of them injured, in pain. With the Abbess's blessing, Micah and Prudence and Timna had combed the streets, hunting them.

Yes, that had been a good season.

They slipped now across a dripping court and down a cobblestone stair and ducked under an arch into a doorway. Micah went first. Behind him, Timna carried the doctor's bag with its banknotes and coins, and silent Prudence followed last. A stone tunnel, echoing with the sound of running water. A dark passage, a second turning, a wash of torchlight on a wall far ahead.

At last he could hear the faint low roar of water, tidal and distant still. A bearded giant in a shabby top hat loomed up out of an alcove, cudgel in one fist. "He's expectin you," he growled.

The siblings ignored him.

And then they turned a corner, and descended a narrow slippery set of wood stairs, and came out into the smoky crowded roar of the Falls.

Fact was, there were two Londons. Not many knew about the second one. The first was cramped, gaslit, its foggy streets filled with crowds even at night, when the roar of carriages and voices and industry carried out over the flickering Thames, past the moored barges and the passenger ferries lit by lanterns, all of it vibrant and alive with the bustle of human filth. That was the London all the world knew. Britain's capital, jewel of the modern world, seat of Empire and power.

But hidden inside that city was a second London, a London every shade of gray.

An under-London, is how its denizens thought of it. City of the exiles, of all those who'd been sent away from Cairndale, or who'd lived outside its walls and lost their talents all the same, a seedy under-city located at the end of crooked alleys, down shabby courts, off wooden steps two leaps above the Thames where only dead men went, behind damp cellar walls and beneath crumbling tunnels. A city of cutthroats and pickpockets and addicts. Since the murder of Ratcliffe Fang all those months ago—Fang, who had watched over the exiles in the streets above, those too *pitiful* or *weak* or *moral* to descend into the Falls—their numbers here had swelled. Now it was an underworld crowded with hawkers, pie sellers, indigents. And all of it was run by a reclusive exile, lord of the poor, a man who'd hardly set foot aboveground in sixteen years. Claker Jack, he was called. And the seat of his empire was the vast underground chamber of tumbling water and rope bridges and lantern-lit alcoves known, in whispers, as the Falls.

Micah came out now at the edge, and lifted his eyes. It had been constructed at the end of the 1860s, before he was born, to hold some great machinery for the sewer lines being built at that time. But plans had changed, the pumping station at Abbey Mills had been erected, and the conduits been rerouted through. This hollow chamber remained. It was vast and domed like St Paul's Cathedral, constructed of brick and stone, its ceiling lost in darkness. Three main lines met high up along the walls, their heavy flows controlled by knife gates, and the foul waters poured down to a staggered floor. And there, at its center, was a great drop: the reeking effluent was sucked whorling down into the shaft below. It was said if you dropped a ha'penny in, it'd wash up out in the Thames.

There were levels, platforms built crazily upon platforms, linked by ladders and wood stairs. Suspended in the very middle of that pit, above the falls, like the heart of their world, was a caged platform with rows of stands for the crowds. A caged-in passage led away from it, into the cells. Micah could see figures gathering already for the night's fights.

Timna had already begun to cross the gap on the rickety bridge, and he hurried to catch up. High along the walls swung wooden catwalks, and rope ladders, all leading to tunnels, iron doors. Torches were hung in brackets as high as the eye could see, like small fiery stars. Ropes criss-crossed the high gloom, tying off the platforms, securing beams, hauling up loads of goods. Patched and mismatched tarps had been strung up on platforms, making weird tents where the exiles conducted their sour business: selling ale, or opium, or stolen goods.

Not all who lurked in the Falls had once been talents, of course. There weren't nearly so many as that. Micah had come to suspect that most, in fact, were the ordinary poor, some drawn to the danger and strangeness of the place, others trapped in it like flies in molasses.

He didn't much care.

At the far side of the gap he climbed an iron ladder and paused in an alcove, frowning. A figure in a brown robe had caught his eye, a figure drifting casually among the crowds at the cage fight. The figure was methodically picking the pockets of the watchers. Timna and Prudence saw it, too.

"Stupid buggers," muttered Timna.

Now the first fight of the night was beginning. A bearded fighter had climbed up into the cage, through the little iron door. He was shirtless and tattooed and even at that distance the boy could see how big his fists looked. On the far side stood the caged-in passage, what everyone had really come to see. A complicated system of ropes and pulleys was hauling open a metal door, at the far end of it.

For a long moment nothing seemed to happen. The fighter stayed where he was, wiser than some. And then, with a sudden explosion, something thin and white and blurred hurtled outward the length of the passage along the roof of the cage and clung upside down, its weird face elongated and blinking, its long teeth like needles. The crowd roared in approval.

It was a litch, Micah knew: Claker Jack's pet litch, collected years ago, its master long since dead. And it would tear the fighter to pieces in a few minutes' time.

He turned, bored. Prudence watched him, wary. Timna was still standing transfixed with the doctor's bag in her arms.

"Jesus hell, come on," he muttered.

They left the fight behind and continued upward, to a wide stone ledge, and a windowed office behind it. Two burly men in red waistcoats stood guard. And inside, seated at a long walnut desk, was Claker Jack himself.

"You're late," he said.

He looked nothing like a man who ruled an empire. His skin was yellowed and there were small red sores around his mouth and low at his throat. His gray hair was long and greasy and hung in tangled ropes over his eyes; he wore a waistcoat with mismatched buttons. He sat sideways with his legs crossed, in trousers stained with old foodstuffs.

He raised his ancient eyes as the three of them entered. His lined face bore an expression of a very old, very deep regret. Outside, the crowd at the cage roared.

"Your pet's in fine form this evening," said Micah.

"Ah," replied Claker Jack. "Well. She keeps the rabble satisfied."

"We got your fee, Mr. Jack," said Timna. She set the doctor's bag on the desk. "We already took the Abbess's cut."

Claker Jack made no move to open it. He seemed not to care in the slightest. "And its owner?" he said instead. "Has he been suitably . . . chastened?"

Micah nodded. He held up the bloodied ear, then winked it away in his little fist. He did not take his eyes from the crime lord as he said, "Chastened his throat with my bloody knife, didn't I?"

"Mm. Good."

"You was lookin for us?" said Timna.

Prudence, of course, all the while said nothing.

Claker Jack shifted his gaze, slowly, between the three of them. A pale tongue moistened his lips. "Your Abbess will want to know," he said. "I have had a letter from Ruth. She is still in Edinburgh. She has not yet located the dustworker's body. Or, rather, its particular dust."

"Bloody useless, she is," Micah muttered. He hated the woman, hated her condescension, hated her dry husk of a face. He didn't trust her. He'd followed her once up into Billingsgate, seen her in the company of a dark-haired girl wearing scarlet gloves, a foreign coin on a ribbon at her throat, the two of them going about at night in the shadows like footpads. That girl had the stink of talentkind about her.

Claker Jack steepled his fingers. "But the dust she seeks is no longer in Edinburgh. I have reason to believe it is being smuggled south, to London. Ruth has . . . *disappointed* me." Claker Jack weighed them in his sallow gaze. "I trust you will let the Abbess know how strenuous my efforts have been."

"I'll let her know all of it," sneered Micah.

"All?" Claker Jack rose to his feet, his ancient joints creaking, and he took up a bull's-eye lantern from his desk. He said softly, "But you do not know all, Micah. It is time I showed you something. Something the Abbess will find . . . interesting. Come."

Micah turned his hat in his hands. He watched the crime lord a moment and Timna watched him. At last he nodded and put on his hat and followed.

Claker Jack led them through a wooden door in the back corner and down a dark stone corridor, over an iron grate, into a long low-ceilinged chamber. The lantern he carried cast a steady orange beam of light. A sound of rushing water could be heard all around.

Few passed into that chamber and lived. The boy knew this. He and his sisters had been back only a handful of times before and each time the walls had been bloodier than the last. For it was here that Claker Jack— among the very oldest of the exiles, rumored by some to be the first— liked to take the talents that were caught walking the streets of London. He would tie them up and unseam them, and sift through their innards looking for . . . what? Some said the source of their talents.

But there was no talent's corpse cut up in the chamber now. The crime lord led them past the creepy tables where he worked and around a cistern's overflow, the lantern flickering behind the pouring water. And here Micah and his sisters found themselves in a second, smaller chamber, hidden from sight, that they hadn't known existed.

It was very dark, except for the light of the lantern. The crime lord opened the shutter of his lantern wide, and the room bloomed with orange light.

In the middle stood a murky pool, inside a low stone wall. The boy hesitated. It was not a pool of water at all, but a large tank of reeking mud, foul and thick, its surface shivering slightly as if from some vibration.

Timna put a sleeve to her mouth. "It's a tub of shite," she whispered.

"Shut your gob," hissed Micah.

For a moment it seemed Claker Jack did not hear. He was peering down into the muck with a strange expression on his face, an expression almost of joy. But then he said, "I do not often ask for politeness or decorum from those who speak for the Abbess." And he looked up at Timna and his eyes were shining and Micah, despite himself, gave an inward shudder. "It would be best, however, if you held your tongue, child, and showed respect."

Prudence took a step forward, as if to protect her sister.

Claker Jack paid her no mind. "Do you know what a glyphic is?" he asked softly.

"There was one at Cairndale," said Micah. "I remember. He was a sort of a . . . tree."

"There are several kinds. And they can be most . . . useful. Did you never wonder how I knew when a talent was near, or when a talent was among us?"

Micah said nothing.

Claker Jack reached his hand into the muck and stirred it and a faint blue glow trailed behind his fingers. As he lifted his hand, it came out clean, without anything sticking to it. And then the muck began to move, to stir of its own accord, thickening and deepening more quickly.

Claker Jack scratched at the sores on his neck. He said, "I would like you to meet my other . . . pet."

Slowly the whirling muck began to rise up, like a great molten shaft of darkness, reeking, clumps of itself falling heavily down into the pool. It swayed, a thick column of mud, sentient, strange, as if listening to their breathing in the lantern light.

"Three weeks ago," said Claker Jack softly, "your Abbess wrote to you from Paris. A letter with the most extraordinary details. She wrote an account of what happened at Cairndale, what happened to Henry Berghast, an account that is scarcely to be believed. She wrote that the body of Jacob Marber had surfaced in the ruins, and that the corrupted dust was still . . . active. Oh, I have read the letter. Do not be surprised." He gave a thin wry smile. "Your Abbess sent a similar one to me. But she included one further detail in mine. She said I was to send *you*."

"Us?" Micah looked sharply up. "But you never did."

"I thought you might be of more use here." Claker Jack waved his hand at the mud glyphic. "Show them," he said. "Show them what you showed me."

And suddenly, to the boy's astonishment, the muck fell apart and re-formed, fell and reformed, over and over, until he saw himself staring at a building, a terrace house, set into the corner of a busy crossing. There were tiny melting carriages passing and figures hurrying along and the boy saw the crooked gate and the dripping windows and he recognized 23 Nickel Street West for what it was.

"I know that place," he said. "It's the institute offices, here in London. Where that witch Harrogate used to—"

But even as he spoke the mud shifted and took on the form of crossed hammers against a rising sun. That was the Cairndale crest, of course. Gradually the muck smoothed itself into a ring, a ring with the crest on it, held up between the melting thumb and finger of a man. The man had no features.

Micah looked at Claker Jack in the gloom. The old man had taken off his own Cairndale ring, the one he always wore, and he held it out in his seamed palm.

"This is a copy," the old man said softly. "The original was stolen from me, years ago. It was a . . . keepsake, from my time at Cairndale. It was stolen by an exile, a young man I trusted. A far bloodier and more capable man than any I'd yet known. You would have found much to admire in him, I believe."

"What is that, then?" said Timna, unable to tear her eyes away from the melting figure of mud. "Is it your own bloody ring we're seein?"

"Indeed. The thief was a man named Hywel Owydd. He took my ring, and vanished. I'd heard reports he had drowned. Others said he'd sailed for America." Claker Jack shrugged, as if to lend such reports no credence. "It would appear he is back."

"How can you tell? He don't got any face."

"The glyphic's word is true. That is my artifact. I am not mistaken."

"It's his what?" whispered Timna.

Micah watched a buried anger twist in the old man's features. He'd never heard Claker Jack admit to such a weakness, a betrayal and theft from someone close to him. He felt a mixture of pleasure and dread. Claker wasn't one you wanted to know the secrets of, not really. He ran the back of his wrist under his nose, wiping it. "Right," he said. "So you want us to get your bit of glitter back, then. An that's why you never sent us north. You want us to stick him, this Owydd? Is he at Nickel Street, then?"

Claker Jack gestured at the glyphic. "Patience, Micah. Keep watching."

The figure studying the ring was already dissolving, clumpily, the muck falling away. What rose in its place was the figure of an old woman, her features, too, melting away so that he could not see her face. She seemed to be missing one arm and in its place she wore some peculiar apparatus. She was walking through what seemed to be a forest, touching the leaves. Beside her walked a second figure, a figure with a ring on a cord at its throat. The thief. Then both dissolved into a lumpen wagon, dragging through the muck of the glyphic's surface, slowly, slowly. Until this too melted away into nothing.

"Bleedin creepy," whispered Timna, unable to stop herself.

"The old woman has the dust," Claker Jack said softly. "I am certain of it. And it appears my good Mr. Owydd is keeping her company."

"That one-armed woman? She's what got the dust before Ruth? We can handle her, an whatever she's brung with her."

"I trust that is so," said Claker Jack. "They will be coming to Nickel

Street West. Do not underestimate Mr. Owydd's nature. He is most dangerous. As for the woman . . . is she a talent? Was she once? I do not know. She is familiar, and yet . . ." He tapped the side of his nose in a curious gesture. "Find them. Go to Nickel Street and wait for them there. Kill the thief. Collect my ring from his corpse. As for the old woman—"

"Bring her in whole?" asked Timna.

Micah scowled. "He don't want her in pieces, you ass. He's got questions to ask of her."

Claker Jack's eyes glowed in the darkness.

"Whole is preferable," he said.

12

A CANDLE
MADE OF BONE

Edward Albany knew he wasn't supposed to stop in the street on his way home from the stalls. His sister wouldn't like it. What was it Caroline said to him last night, before riding away? *Follow the path. Always follow the path, Edward, and you'll be all right.*

He knew by the way she said it that she meant more than just always take the same route to market and back, to church and back, wherever, he knew it by the serious voice she used, like she was worried for him, but he wasn't quite sure of her *exact* meaning. It was always like that with Caroline. She was the smart one, she knew things. He was okay with her telling him what to do, never mind that he was the eldest, or the biggest. He liked knowing she was watching out for him. They'd both got old, they'd got wrinkles. His bones hurt him in the mornings now. And still she watched out for him.

Except now she couldn't. Now she was gone, gone south to London with all the little ones, with young Charlie and his unhappy eyes, she was gone and maybe never coming back, rolling creakily away in that big painted wagon last night, and he, Edward, was left to manage all alone.

The morning was cold and he had come out without lacing his boots because the knots were difficult, sometimes, and because Caroline used to do that for him. So he stopped in the street where a crowd was gathering, and stamped his feet to warm them, and watched laughing with the others while a drunk man tried to put on a coat backward, liking the funniness of it. He'd made that same mistake himself before, too. Though not from drinking, he knew better than to do that. Some of the street boys were there, making fun of the drunk, and Edward thought their jokes were very funny, and he laughed, laughed with all his belly. He was happy that they weren't laughing at him for once. *Old Man Donkey*, they called him most days, when he went out to buy vegetables, on account of his being so slow-witted and so strong. But he wasn't slow-witted, really. Caroline had told him so. He just liked to think his way through a thing at his own speed. There was nothing wrong with that. *You're all right just the way you are*, she'd told him. *Don't you let anyone make you think different.*

He had a big box of foodstuffs under either arm and he left the crowd and hurried on his way. The food list Caroline had left him was in his pocket, folded carefully. He knew his letters some but it was hard for him all the same, so Mrs. Tilley at the market had helped him, made sure he got the right coins back and such, and he was grateful. She was nice, Mrs. Tilley was.

His sister had left him instructions on what to do. It took him a long time to read them all but he did it anyway, even though she'd just gone, because he missed her and he could hear her voice in his head when he read them. *Remember to turn the sign in the door to Open*, she'd written. *Remember to eat. Mrs. Tilley at the market will help you. The paraffin oil is in the cellar cabinet under the stairs. Coal deliveries are every second Tuesday.*

Mind you remember the saved money is under the third floorboard in my bedroom. Use it only for emergencies. I love you Edward. I will write you.

Back at the Grassmarket there were delivery wagons clattering over the cobblestones, sellers hollering their wares at shoppers and workers and clerks in the morning crush. Albany Chandlers occupied a small shabby corner building, grim and uninviting, but to Edward it looked impressive. Its walls were streaked with grime, maybe, the paint on its trim peeling and worn, but he didn't care. It was where he'd lived half his life, with Caroline and later with the little ones, and it was home. And because Caroline had kept it going, even if it was his name on the sign, and because she was the one who used the cellar for her work, it always seemed to him to be her shop, mostly, and he liked that too. He didn't want it to be his.

Thing was, it had always only just been the two of them, all their lives. Their mother died when Caroline was born and Edward didn't hardly remember her at all. Their father worked as a blacksmith until he got sick and Edward took any work he could find from the age of nine to help. Even when they were little, it was Caroline who seemed to take care of Edward, not the other way around, even when she got married to Mr. Ficke, a kind man but very old, who drew pictures of birds for a rich man down in England, even before that, when she was taken to live on that fancy estate at Cairndale on account of what she could do, and even after she met Mr. Ficke and lost her arm in the accident and was sent away from the institute, always still she made sure Edward was cared for. And maybe he missed her more than anything he'd ever missed in his life, maybe so. But he knew she wanted him to make good here, without her, that she was depending on him to be okay, so he was going to do just that.

He had to put down one of the boxes on the rough step and fish around in his pocket for the key to the shop. The air was cold on the back of his neck. When he let himself inside, he stood a moment in the gloom, breathing in the old smell of candles and dust, listening. He pretended for a minute that he could hear Caroline upstairs, with the little ones, maybe singing to them. That used to be a good thing.

He set the boxes down on the counter in the back and unpacked one of them and then he took the second downstairs to the cellar. He stopped on the stairs, two steps from the bottom.

"Oh," he said in surprise.

A slender figure stood in the gloom, at the far end of the long table. How she had got in, he couldn't explain. She was cloaked and a book of Caroline's was open in her hands and she closed it softly, drew back the hood from her face. A corona of candlelight caught her features. She looked like she hadn't slept. Her skin was dark and her black hair hung in twin braids, one over either breast. The cloak was dirty and splotched with streaks of pale stone dust but under it she wore a high-necked dress sewn of various colored patches and Edward liked it, liked the colors in it, and because he knew no one who wore such dresses he understood she had come from far away. Her right hand was concealed in a red glove but her left was bare. At her throat a coin on a leather cord shone brightly in the candlelight, like a silver moon. One side of her jaw was marbled purple from an enormous bruise. Her mouth looked angry.

"I am looking for Caroline Ficke," she said fiercely.

Edward swallowed. He was pretty sure he was supposed to say something, but he wasn't sure what. "Okay," he said.

The bruised girl waited. A flicker of impatience crossed her features. "Well? Is she here or not?"

His sister was always telling him he had to mind his manners. It wasn't mindful to blow his nose in his hand, or pass gas in company, or say bad words. He was sure about those things. But this wasn't any of those things. He said, as politely as he could, "Miss, I'm very regretful to say Caroline's not here."

He thought that sounded pretty good. Caroline would like it. He was still holding the big box in his arms and he didn't put it down because it seemed to him maybe more polite to just stand where he was and pay full attention to the girl when she was speaking to him but the box was starting to get heavy. He shifted his grip.

"Will she be back soon?" demanded the girl.

"No," he said.

"And who are you? What is your name?"

He felt the heat rising to his cheeks. He should have introduced himself. "Edward Michael Albany, miss. I'm . . . I'm her brother."

Again, that long pause, as if she expected him to say something more. He tried to think what it might be, what Caroline might do.

"Would you . . . like a cup of tea?" he asked.

Now the girl stepped fluidly forward, full into the light, setting the book aside and smoothing out her dress. Her eyes were strange, dark. "I would *like*, Mr. Albany," she said in a soft, dangerous voice, "for you to tell me where she has gone."

Jeta lifted the candle high for the light, wincing as the hot wax ran over her knuckles.

So. This was the Ficke woman's brother.

He was huge. A big, burly beast of a man, with a thick gray beard obscuring half his face, and tiny eyes blinking out at her, and an enormous belly crushed up against the crate he carried. Much taller even than the young man, Charlie Ovid, who'd struck her down the night before with the corrupted dust. A rank smell of rust and brackish water came off him, as if he hadn't changed his clothes in days. She felt the pull of his bones in her own, aching.

But if he meant her harm, he gave no sign; instead he seemed without anger, eager to please. And his voice, she realized uneasily, was like the small voice of a boy, pitched high, unsure of itself, afraid.

Well. He would have to do.

"Mr. Albany," she said now, as if she were the grown-up, at her own establishment, and he were the guest. "*Edward.* Don't just stand there. Set that crate down. Come closer."

And he did, with evident relief, setting it on a stack of other crates and turning to face her in the gloom. His shoes crunched heavily on broken glass, splinters of wood. She lifted the candle in a semicircle, illuminating the cellar. It was a laboratory of some kind. A long worktable of rough wood ran the length of one wall and she moved behind it, keeping it between her and the hulking chandler. A massive old hearth stood beyond, black and cold, leaking a drafty air. Cauldrons, a shelf of books. As she set the candle down amid the clutter of scales and jars of powders, shapes shifted and materialized in the gloom, crates and barrels with their lids knocked off, trays of bottles overturned in a rush. Whatever Caroline Ficke had been involved in, whatever her connection to Cairndale and the corrupted dust, it was not innocent.

"Where is your sister now?" she asked.

The man blinked rapidly. For a second she thought he was going to cry but he didn't cry. "She went away," he said.

"That was sudden. She was just here last night. Where did she go to?"

He shrugged his huge shoulders. "I'm not supposed to tell."

Jeta fingered the coin at her throat, thinking. "I would not want you to get in trouble, Edward."

He looked at her gratefully.

"But it's important I find your sister. For her own safety. The young man she's with is dangerous."

"No, no, no. Charlie's a good boy."

"He wanted you to think so. But he's not."

"Caroline's the smart one, she's always been smart. She told me not to worry."

"But she's far from home now, isn't she?"

He nodded.

"And you're worried now, aren't you? It's all right for you to tell me. I'm from Cairndale. She would want you to talk to me."

"Okay."

"Where did she go to?"

He swallowed. "I'm not supposed to tell," he said again.

His hands were hanging loose at his sides, his big belly overhanging his trousers. He looked like an overgrown, errant child. Jeta didn't like the feeling that was in her: the pity. She thought of Claker Jack, how his lidded eyes would darken with sadness when she told him she'd failed. She took off her red glove slowly, baring her bone fingers, and walked the length of the wooden table drawing her fingers rasping along it. She knew the effect this had, usually. The chandler saw, but seemed unconcerned.

"Tell me about Charlie Ovid," she said, trying a different approach. "He was carrying something with him, something of importance. A little blue glass vial. I must find him, Edward. I must speak with him."

"Okay."

She breathed quietly. Waited. "He went away with your sister, yes?"

"Yes."

"Are you allowed to tell me where *he* is?"

The man thought about it. He rolled his lips tightly shut, shook his head.

Ruth, she knew, believed there were several ways to get answers out of a person, pain being the first and most effective. Jeta was glad suddenly that the older woman was not with her. She had awakened that morning in the cathedral, a stonemason leaning over her, a weak red sunlight filtering in through the stained glass. She'd risen bleary and confused, trying to remember what had happened the night before. There had been the young man, Charlie, and the dust shining in his flesh . . . She'd shrugged off the stonemason's hands and stumbled out into the early cold, the city dark and lovely. She saw no sign of the apparition. On the church steps she'd rested her head against the cold stone, felt her head swim. She thought she might throw up but she didn't. Slowly her thoughts took shape. The Grassmarket. The woman . . . That was where she would go.

But she didn't return first to the hotel, didn't go in search of Ruth, though the records keeper would surely make her suffer for it later, she knew. Instead she'd found the chandler's shop and let herself in using a set of burglar's tools she carried deep in the pocket of her cloak, and stood in the quiet shop, listening for the bones of the living all around her, waiting.

Now Edward shuffled forward, a look of anxiety in his face. Jeta took a smooth step back. But he was only going to the book that Jeta had been reading, in order to put it back in its place on the shelf.

"Caroline always says, 'A place for everything, and everything in its place,'" he said shyly.

"She is wise, your sister."

"She's the smart one," he said again. "I have to go to work now. I have to follow the path."

Jeta didn't understand what he meant. But he stomped back upstairs, the wooden steps shivering under his weight, and after a moment she followed. It was becoming clear to her, with a sense of increasing urgency, that she wasn't going to get the answers she needed.

She didn't *want* to have to hurt him. She didn't even think it would work.

The shop was dim, quiet. Edward was behind the counter, leaning his face close to the wall, reading something. His lips formed the words soundlessly. "I have to sweep the floor," he said. "Then I can open."

Behind the counter, Jeta saw what he'd been reading. It was a letter from his sister in spidery script, two pages, each page nailed to the wall. A list of instructions for Edward to follow, each day. The list made Jeta's heart heavy. And there it was, at the bottom of the second page, her forwarding address.

23 Nickel Street West, London.

Jeta ran her hands over her face, amazed. It couldn't be so easy. It couldn't.

In the near aisle, Edward was leaning against his broom, solemn, blinking his little eyes. Dark shapes moved in the grimy windows at the far end of the shop, figures hurrying past in the street. Edward was watching her, and it was like he was trying to remember something important. She braced herself. Then his face lit up as it came to him.

"Would . . . would you like a cup of tea, miss?" he asked.

Jeta left Albany Chandlers quietly, dark rings under her eyes, her bruised jaw stiffening so that it hurt to talk.

The sun had tracked across the white sky. She thought of the big, childlike man behind her, whom she had left sweeping the floor of the shop. The matter-of-factness of his answers. She knew what Ruth would have had her do to him.

Well. Ruth would be angry at her disappearance but interested to hear all she'd learned. An omnibus clattered past, light tracking across its windows. Something about it made her think of the mortician's assistant from the night before. He was an innocent too, in his way; a deep revulsion arose in her, remembering the thud as his body fell, making her catch her breath; and she understood suddenly that, no matter how much she loved Claker Jack, thought of him as a kind of father, she was done with this sort of work.

She was done with the killing.

Just then, a violent pain seized her ribs, her breastbone, her hips. It radiated outward and all through her body. She crumpled, gasping, into the crowded pedestrian way.

She'd never felt anything like it. Onlookers began to stop, to watch her. No one moved to help. She forced herself to her feet and hailed a passing hansom and when she got to the lodging house she gave the driver whatever coin she had and hoped it was enough and stumbled upstairs.

The pain worsened as she neared her room. It seemed to come over her in waves, increasing in frequency as she stumbled along the carpeted hall.

And then she was leaning into the door pull, folding over herself onto the floor. Still dressed in the stained and rumpled clothes from the night before. The door swung shut behind her. Something sharp and fine was on the carpet, crunching under her weight, and she raised her bruised face; she raised her bruised face and she saw.

The bonebird.

That was her pain, *that* was what she'd felt. The creature had been smashed into little pieces, ground into the carpet. The curtains hung ragged at the window, the brass birdcage was tipped over, its door torn from the hinges. And Ruth, with scratches still bleeding all up and down her forearms and on her face, stood in the middle of the destruction, breathing hard. It must have only just happened, moments ago.

"Ruth—?" Jeta gasped. "This, this isn't—"

"Summon the devil and look what appears," she said grimly. "And look at the state of you. What's happened to your face? Were you in a fight?" Her own steel-gray hair was a mess. "You left me to finish at the mortuary alone. You *left* me, child."

"What . . . what have you done?"

"What you would not." The older woman made a face. "Please. The creature *attacked* me. You should thank me. I have spared you the task."

The pain Jeta felt was dizzying. It had to be her connection to the bonebird, the bond there. She hadn't imagined it was so strong.

"Perhaps if you had not *left* me, girl, you might have been here to control it. I have already written to Claker Jack, reporting on your truancy. He will be displeased. Where have you been? What have you got into?"

Something in Ruth's expression, a kind of satisfied pleasure, cut through Jeta's confusion. It wasn't just that she was tired, and frustrated, deeply drained by her encounter in the cathedral, it wasn't just that. It was something else, too. She thought of the bonebird, the delicate beauty of it, the surprise she'd felt that such a thing was even possible. It had been a kind of future, a future in which her talent did more than simply kill.

She was shaking. She watched Ruth take out a handkerchief, dab at her scratches. She had just enough clarity in her to close her fists slowly, focusing on the slender ribs near Ruth's heart, crushing it gradually.

The older woman gasped, her eyes goggled. She turned and stared at Jeta in astonishment. She *knew*; she knew *exactly* what was happening.

"You *dare*—?" she exclaimed.

It all happened very fast then. Jeta squeezed and squeezed, cutting the blood to the heart, until Ruth's face had turned a dark red. The older woman's body crashed sideways onto the fragments of bone and feather near the hearth. Still Jeta squeezed, crushing the older woman's heart, until she was sure, absolutely sure that her procurer was dead; only then did she release her grip, and lean her shoulder into the wall, exhausted.

It was strange. She could feel her talent flowing out, away from her, rippling like a long ribbon in a wind. But her anger remained; her fury and hurt and pity for the bonebird remained. The horror of what she'd done came to her slowly, mingled with her exhaustion.

Ruth was dead.

Dead by her, Jeta's, hand, by the hand of a talent, and if ever he found out, her Claker Jack would not forgive. She'd lost the corrupted dust; she'd killed her keeper. Jeta closed her eyes. Claker must never know.

The day lengthened. She kneeled on the carpet, trembling, and began to collect the tiny fragments of bone. Dizzied by their touch. *Her* bone-bird: her poor creature.

Nothing beautiful, she understood, nothing fragile or rare or precious, in this world or the next, would ever be permitted to survive.

That night the ghost child came to her in a dream.

The dream was very real. The fire in the grate had died out. She sat up and drew the heavy wool blanket close for the cold and watched his blue silhouette waver and take form. The bedchamber was silver with the moonfall and the boy stood at the far window, the blue drift of his hair clearly visible. It was as if some part of her had been waiting for him. She knew it was a dream and yet it didn't feel like a dream and she looked at the boy and he looked back at her with a darkness where his eyes should have been. The faint blue light caught in the glass of the chandelier and cast shadows over the ceiling. He seemed less solid, somehow, than before. She could see the wallpaper and the bureau through his figure.

"I killed her," she said slowly, dreamily. "Ruth. She broke the bone-bird and I killed her for it. I'm afraid. I'm so afraid of what Claker Jack will do, when he finds out."

The apparition shivered. He said nothing, a small boy lost in a different grief.

"He'll hate me. I just . . . I wanted to make him proud. He trusted me here, he trusted me to—"

To get the dust. That's what he wanted.

She stared at her hands. Nodded, dreamlike, slow.

But you didn't, Jeta. You didn't take the dust, at the cathedral. You could've, but you didn't.

"No," she whispered, ashamed.

Now the little boy turned his face. There was anger in his eyes. *I don't have much time. They'll find me. I know they will. It hurts, being here. On this side.*

Her cheeks were wet. "That was Charlie, wasn't it," she whispered. "At the cathedral. Charlie, who you wanted back at Cairndale. Who is he? Is it his fault, what happened to you?"

It's Henry Berghast's fault, said the ghost child. *His and no other. I blame him.*

Berghast. The hairs on Jeta's arms prickled. She folded her bone fingers into her fist. The dream was already changing, the apparition fading.

"What happens now?" she asked thickly.

Follow the dust. Go to London. Take it from them.

"London?" she said, even as the moonlight filled the space he had been standing, even as the dream was dissolving. "Is that where he's gone? Wait! How do you know? What *are* you?"

Are we not . . . all we can . . . imagine . . . , the dream replied, distorted and strange.

If there was more, she did not hear it. She awoke in the hotel bed, the strangeness receding, until the dream was only a half-remembered thing, and what remained was a single overwhelming clarity: Go to London.

Find the dust.

Go.

13

BLOOD IN THE WATER

Two days passed, two nights. It was early on the third night and a brown fog was descending over Spitalfields when Micah's sisters returned from Nickel Street West. He had been collecting from an illegal rat-baiting and had just stepped out into the murk, sliding the envelope into his pocket, when he saw them. Timna wore a hat that overhung her eyes. The elbows of Prudence's coat were frayed.

"Well?" he said.

"No one's come there yet," Timna replied. Sullen eyes glittered in shadow. "Every window's about as dark as old Claker's arse. You think the Jack's maybe gone unstitched on us? Should we write to the Abbess?"

Calmly the boy buttoned his ill-fitting coat, calmly he folded up the collar. "You saw what I saw. In the mud."

"In the *shite*, more like. Maybe Claker dossed our drinks. Maybe we didn't see nothing."

Micah paused and looked at his sister. Two streaks of soot were on her cheek. Her eyes were lined and hollow and dead-looking, like the eyes of an old woman. Nearby, workmen passed in the fog, drunk, their buckets clattering. None of the three spoke.

"You saw what I saw," Micah repeated.

Prudence yawned loudly, as if bored of all this.

Micah didn't like the way his sisters looked at him, sometimes. And he didn't like how Timna could creep up out of an alley in silence and suddenly materialize in front of him, hands empty or no.

But he said none of that. Instead, he said, "Go back, watch the row house. The wagon will come, you'll see. Don't you come find me again, not unless that woman's arrived. Remember, the thief is dangerous. Ruth buggered it up. We won't."

Timna tipped her chin at his bulging pocket. "Fine skim tonight?"

"Fine enough. Claker won't be unhappy."

"You ever reckon how far it'd get you? Like, all the way to America?"

Prudence gave her sister a sharp, dark look.

Micah caught it, and went menacingly still. "What're you two up to?" he said quietly. His long pale fingers adjusted his hat. "Don't go on gettin ideas. You steal from Claker, it's like to get you just about as far as Blackfriars Bridge. Even the Abbess won't protect you. Some mudlark'll be going through your pockets an pulling out your teeth."

A smoldering red sun was rising blurred above the Thames when Micah turned his back on London and the wet reek of its alleys, and went down into the tunnels.

The nights were long. He was tired but the tiredness didn't bother him as much as the quiet in the streets. Something didn't feel right. He walked splashing through the tunnel, the grates overhead casting shafts of reddish daylight down through the dark, listening to faint sounds of the city far above. He was thinking about his sisters and about the terrace house on Nickel Street West and about the strangeness of Claker Jack's glyphic.

Gradually the concrete tunnel widened and then it came out at a wooden platform. He stood for a moment suspended over the Falls, wrapping his knuckles around the railing, staring down. Slowly he took off his hat, clawed his fingers through his white hair. The sleeves on his coat were double-folded back because he was so small. He put back on the hat, drawing the brim low. Then he made his way down the crooked stair, swaying on the ropes, high over the murky waters. The air was thick with the reek of rot and dead things. He glanced up at Claker Jack's rooms, at the two burly men standing watch there. He'd been seen. Everyone here was always seen.

Then he was down, in the crush of bodies, making his way down steps and across the platforms and ducking under guylines and passing through tarps strung up as makeshift stalls. There were figures dazed and half-asleep on straw ticking, the poppy in their blood sold by shabby men with pockets in their hats. There were penny hangs heavy with the bodies draped across them, men and women both. Painted ladies, whispering their wares. The destitute, adrift with clawlike fingers. But all of them fell silent and drew aside as the boy passed. Many had been clinks or turners or casters or dustworkers, once. In their dreams they were such still. He saw hunger in their looks, grief-crazed grins, and he knew what they would do if they learned Claker Jack kept a living talent in his office, a glyphic no less.

Sweet hell. Even Claker Jack wouldn't be able to calm them.

Which made Micah all the more troubled. He didn't understand why Claker Jack would risk betrayal, showing the boy and his sisters the mud glyphic now. He knew it would serve some purpose, though; the old bastard was nothing if not resourceful. Micah spat. He'd write it all out in his letter to the Abbess, and let her sort it.

He walked out over a swaying rope bridge to the concrete platform at the center of the vast chamber. Here were rough plinths nailed together to form rows of seats—all empty now, stained—and in the middle of it all stood the big iron cage where the fights took place. He could see the sawdust on its floor, the trace of splatter patterns where blood had been shed.

He crossed a second swaying bridge to a brick tunnel on the far side. Two more heavyset men, peering down at him, wary. They didn't try to stop him. The tunnel was lit by a solitary oil lantern and it ended in a stone chamber. It was there he found what he was seeking.

The litch was naked and curled in the straw of its cell, like a hairless white dog, knees tucked up into its belly. It had been a woman once. Its face was folded into its arms, so that Micah could not make out its features. But he knew them well. He could see the three red lines at its neck, even in the bad light. Filth streaked its thighs. Muck had flecked its slack breasts, dried blood had stained its arms to the elbows. It had always been here, so it was said, some saying it had been here before Claker Jack himself, others that he'd brought it with him when he founded the Falls. Micah remembered that first night he saw it fight, how he'd felt the wild thrill of it. He loved it like other boys his age loved racing stallions, or greyhounds. He still didn't know, after all these years, if it slept, if sleeping was the word to describe what it did. Its chest seemed scarcely to rise or fall. It ate nothing. Its tongue had been cut out at some point and so it never spoke. Alone in its cell it seemed diminished, almost to be pitied.

"They say a litch without its maker is a lost thing," said a voice from the darkness.

Micah turned.

Claker Jack stepped slowly forward, his shoes crunching softly. He leaned on a walking stick. "I've seen her tear a man apart in under a minute flat. But somehow, when I see her here, I've always thought she seems to be just waiting. What would she be waiting for, I wonder?"

"Her freedom," said Micah.

"Is that what anyone desires, really? You, for instance? Do you wish to be free, child?"

Micah met Claker Jack's eye. "I am free," he said.

"Oh, but you're not, my pet. None of us are. That is what it means to go on living, after losing something so much a part of ourselves. We are all captives to that which has made us."

"Nothing made me. I made me."

Claker Jack's eyes glittered in the lantern light. "Your talent made you, Micah. And then it unmade you."

"I don't miss it. Not like them out there."

He saw the crime lord's hand moving, and for just a moment he thought the old man carried a weapon. He tensed. But it was just the light catching his ring. The false ring, the ring with the Cairndale crest, hammers crossed against a rising sun.

"I am told you come down here often," said Claker Jack. "You watch her for a time and then you go on. But you never stay for the fights. You never bet on the outcomes."

Micah kept his expression empty, but his mouth went dry. He hadn't realized his movements were being tracked so closely. No good ever came of Claker Jack's notice. Micah ran a long-fingered hand over the back of his neck, and then, casually, he made himself shrug. "I've seen them some."

"There are times," said Claker Jack quietly, "I get the feeling like she's trying to tell me something. I don't understand it. It's more like a song than anything. A song being whispered to me, in the back of my skull. But I can't make out the words."

Micah watched the crime lord with a careful eye.

"You've felt it too, haven't you?"

Micah nodded.

"A word of advice. Do not listen to that song, or you will find your throat opened in short order." The crime lord ran his tongue over his teeth, slowly. It was like his thoughts were elsewhere. "For some of us, we go on living almost connected to the talent we lost. There's just a thin barrier between us and our gift. But a barrier that's never been breached. Hm?"

Micah let his gaze drift back over to the litch. It was watching them with silent red eyes.

"There is no knowing a litch's heart," said Claker Jack softly. His voice had changed. "But hers I've felt. You are nothing to her, Micah. A means to an end. You wonder what she desires? Not her *freedom*. Not that. She hungers for *me*."

The crime lord turned to go, stopped. He tapped his walking stick twice on the stone floor. "What of Mr. Owydd and the old woman? No word yet?"

Micah buttoned the middle two buttons of his coat. "You'll know when she arrives. My sisters an me, we're not Ruth. We can locate a simple bloody crow."

"Ah," Claker Jack replied softly.

But if he was pleased or displeased, Micah couldn't tell.

Later that afternoon Micah awoke from a bad sleep in the alcove that was his and his sisters'. It was carved out of the warren of tunnels branching off from the Falls, and had been outfitted with a heavy wooden door. The room might have been meant to house pumping machinery of some kind, but now it held their three small cots, a wardrobe, a trunk with their few possessions. A basin of cold water fetched for him daily by one of the more pitiful exiles.

He rose in the absolute darkness and reached for his flint and lit the candle by touch. His feet kept growing and the bad shoes he wore pinched worse by the day. There was a dark shadow at his upper lip that wouldn't wash away. All his brief life, he'd known he would not live to see twenty.

The candle in its dish bloomed with light. It was such a small room, barely large enough for what it held. But it felt luxurious, compared to the squalor of the Falls.

He relieved himself in the chamber pot and then he dressed and opened the trunk and carefully took out a cloth-wrapped bundle. It was a mirror, smooth and fine, and it caught the light and brightened the room. He leaned it up against the top of the wardrobe. Poured out some water from the basin into a bowl. Then he stood and stared at his face and saw his dead mum in his own reflection. Last of all he took out a little wooden box he'd had for as long as he could remember. Inside, each one twisted and black like a dried fig, was his collection of human ears.

The door opened. The candle flame stood sideways. The water bowl rippled once and went still.

It was Timna, alone. Her coat unbuttoned, white hair wet and dripping.

"Where's Prudence?" said Micah, narrowing his eyes.

"Outside." Timna spat. She looked very small. "She don't like comin in. Reckon she don't trust you."

"I'm her brother."

"So?"

"So I wouldn't never hurt either of you. You tell her that."

"Tell her yourself."

Micah closed the lid on his box of ears. It was maybe good, he thought, to have them a little afraid. "You never come here to tell me that," he said. "What is it?"

"They've come," replied Timna, sullen. "That one-armed crow, an old Claker's thief. They're here."

14

23 Nickel Street West

Then Caroline and Charlie and all her little ones were in London.

They hadn't been followed. Not by the bone witch, not by Claker Jack's exiles. Caroline could scarcely believe their luck.

She hadn't been back to the city in thirty years. Seeing it again, by God, she understood why. Everything was darker, grimier, more crowded and noisy than she remembered. The air was brown with coal smoke and fog and there were lanterns lit already over the pubs on the streets, though it was early yet in the afternoon. They made their way to 23 Nickel Street West, Charlie navigating the crush of wagons and hansoms and old-fashioned flies and the tall swaying omnibuses with the outside riders dangling their legs and hollering down at the pedestrians. They passed the Thames in its slow brown sluggish current, passenger ferries steaming between the moored barges, glowing like small red embers. The air was cold. They passed lampposts and benches draped in the bodies of the poor. There were menders and hawkers screaming their wares and ladies with fashionable dresses from Paris and sailors just in off the ships with ragged coats and pockets heavy with coin. Ragmen wheeled their barrows piled high. Crossing sweeps—children mostly—leaned into their brooms, faces covered in grime, or hollered out jeers at the passing carriages. Caroline had thought Edinburgh a fine modern city, but seeing London's sheer multitude on street after street, block after block, she came to understand there was no truer city in the world than this. It *was* the world.

And then Charlie was guiding the old Burton wagon away from the Thames and the bridge at Blackfriars and nosing their way through the traffic and drawing the horses up short at a bollarded pedestrian walk. A closed iron gate stood before them.

Caroline raised her eyes.

The house at 23 Nickel Street West loomed above her, black against the darkening afternoon. There was rust on the iron railings. The shingles looked loose, dangerous; paint was peeling from the posts; the dark bricks were greasy with soot.

"They brought you here, too?" asked Charlie, mistaking her expression.

"Ach, not as a girl," she replied. "Twas not in use, in those days. I came down here later, with my good Mr. Ficke. Twas much different then."

Yet she knew enough, knew 23 Nickel Street West had belonged to the institute for more than a century, and that for years the orphans were examined here by Margaret Harrogate, sometimes painfully, their talents' strengths and natures determined. Some of her own little ones still had bad dreams about it: old Mrs. Harrogate draped in black, her face obscured, like a witch out of a fairy story.

Charlie got down and worked the rusted gate until it shuddered and swung inward. Then he climbed back up. "I really hate this place," he muttered.

The Burton wagon rolled, creaking, in.

It didn't *feel* familiar. The cobblestones were chipped and uneven.

There was a covered alcove for carriages built in an old-fashioned continental style and they drew the wagon up short, obscured from the street. Caroline stayed with the horse, watching Charlie break a window and clamber through, leaving blood in the glass. When he opened the door, his knuckles were already healed. She turned his hand in the bad light, wiping away the blood, looking for the cut.

"Is it fully back, then?" she asked quietly. "Your talent, I mean?"

He nodded gravely.

"As it was before?" she said.

"No," he replied. "It's . . . different. Stronger, maybe. But it's not mine. I can feel the dust in me, doing the work. It's like . . . it's like if you had a tongue in your mouth, but it wasn't your own." He gave a little shudder.

Caroline could hear the rising panic in his voice and turned away, in part to give him a moment to contain himself. She didn't know what to think, not yet.

"Ach. Best to get the wee ones in," she muttered.

They brought the glyph-twisted children inside, all of them, even Deirdre, who had grown heavy as wet wood. In the sitting room Caroline found an old barrow that had been converted into a kind of rolling chair, of all things, with only one piece taken off for firewood, and with some difficulty she and Charlie managed to wheel Deirdre up into the house.

Under her shift, the poor girl's torso had thickened and twisted. Pale branches, budding with silvery leaves, shivered at her shoulders when they moved her. The bark was soft to the touch, and white, like wood that had been left in water too long. But her lower half was forked still like a person, like the person she had been and maybe still was; and though her mouth remained closed, her lips stitched together by weird rootlike threads, she kept making that low soft humming noise, like a song.

The house was vast, gloomy, smelling of dust and rats and the foul reek of the streets outside. In the parlor Charlie started a fire in the grate.

The glyph-twisted children, without seeming to, followed him with shining eyes in the shadows, uncurious, lost in the maze of their own minds. Caroline drew back a curtain and a weak twilight entered the chamber. Back in the foyer she saw stairs leading up into darkness. A door standing open. She tried a different door and saw an office, Margaret Harrogate's presumably, stuffed armchairs and a vast polished desk. She shivered.

When she turned, she saw the Cairndale crest carved into the lintel, heavy, dark with age.

Charlie met her in the hall, his infected hand folded under his armpit. "You'll look for those books now, Mrs. Ficke?" he said, peering down at her. "The ones you said were here?"

She knew the books he meant. She sighed. "I don't know as it'll work, Charlie," she warned. "Might be best to leave it be. If the dust doesn't hurt you none."

"But you *promised*," he said, studying his shoes. He suddenly seemed very young to her, despite his height. "You promised you'd cut it out of me."

"I promised I'd *try*," she said.

And wrinkled her old face up, unhappy.

The truth was, she'd been thinking about that promise. Thinking maybe she'd spoken too soon. She'd never heard of a drughr's dust bonding to an exiled talent, nor—*of course*—ever heard of such a bonding being severed. She didn't see *how* the dust could be drawn out.

But she didn't say this to Charlie. She could see the desperation in his eyes. He didn't complain their whole journey south, but there was a pain there, a steady pain that hadn't gone away, and she could only nod and draw her shawl close and start to go through the rooms, her artificial arm clicking as she adjusted its gears, looking for Henry Berghast's old crate of books. Books on the subject of talent physiology, surgical procedures, the unusual physical nature of talentkind, sent to Margaret Harrogate to aid her, she realized now, in her examinations. Books which she knew had once been here, for she had helped Henry pack them herself, long years ago.

Maybe, just maybe, Margaret Harrogate had kept them safe. And maybe, just maybe, there would be something in one of them, a clue as to how to proceed. She pitied the poor boy, if there wasn't.

But she pitied him the more, if there was.

Caroline sent Charlie down to Miller's Wharf, below the docks at St Katharine. She gave him their papers and the address of the London shipping line and the name of the vessel they were to take. Last of all she told him to bring back pies and mash from a street seller, any street seller. She needed time, and he was underfoot. He left through the old delivery door at the rear of the house, letting onto the mews, and she stood at the window watching his tall figure vanish into the fog. He'd be safe enough, she told herself.

And then she kissed the tips of her two fingers for luck.

Eventually she found Henry Berghast's ancient books in a storage cupboard under the stairs, in a chest that might not have been opened in twenty-five years. With her good arm she dragged the chest across to the office, too old and tired by half for the effort needed. The volumes were bound in a creamy leather and their pages were soft as vellum. She took out the first three books, and lit an oil lantern, and settled down in the armchair to read. It occurred to her, now that Henry Berghast was dead, and all of Cairndale burned, that she herself would be one of those few who remembered how it had been, what had come before. Who knew the old books, and what they contained. The thought made her sad.

She found what she was looking for in a slim green book, untitled. It was very old, written in an antique hand.

It told of an account in the early seventeenth century, in an enclave in Bohemia, of a girl tainted by the dust of the drughr. She had been assaulted in the middle of a span of a covered bridge, in the deep hours of the night. There was some supposition she had summoned the creature to her. Midway between two landfalls was a location of strength for the drughr, the old source claimed; midway between sunset and sunrise was a time of its power. Caroline, intrigued, turned the page.

The girl had been found unconscious. Why she had been allowed to live, no one knew. The corrupted dust, the account went on, was located in the basal cell layer of the skin, the innermost layer of the epidermis. The only way to remove the corruption involved the flensing of the girl's infected shoulder. A gruesome woodcut illustrated the event. In the margins someone had written, in a faded brown ink: *Stilleduste?*

Caroline crossed to the curtains and peered out at the murky fog, brooding. The girl's wound had contained, according to the account, only a small portion of dust. But Charlie's infection was already widespread and, worse, he was a *haelan*; Caroline doubted she could cut the skin away before it began to heal. Perhaps, she thought, if she worked very quickly, or if she cut away very small portions, over and over—

It would be a gory business, regardless. And painful.

Just then there came a knocking at the front, rather soft, as if someone in gloves were brushing their knuckles against the door. It would be Charlie, of course. The office window gave no view of the stoop, and Caroline went at once to let him in. But the front steps were empty.

The cobblestoned street seemed darker, more sinister. For the first time, Caroline felt an uneasy sensation of being watched. The cold air struck her face and bare hand; the roar of the city overwhelmed her. Two men passing in dark coats glanced up, their eyes hidden by their hats. A crossing sweep beyond the traffic leaned into his broom, pale face dialed toward her. Even the horses in the street looked somehow evil.

She shut the door fast; she drew the sidelight curtains, for good measure.

The sooner they got out of London, the better.

·   ·   ·

When Charlie returned, she was ready.

She'd retrieved from the Burton wagon a small box of sharp instruments and they were already boiled and wiped dry and folded into a cloth. She'd prepared several glass vials filled with a solution designed to suspend the corrupted dust for transport. She ate quickly, watching through the bay window as shadowy figures crossed in the fog. Charlie'd already eaten. He'd located the vessel, and its second mate, and confirmed their cabin bookings and the hour of embarkation in the morning. The ship would follow the tide.

Caroline did not mention the knock at the door. No sense in worrying the boy, she thought.

She needed a room to work, a room that would be quiet, away from the little ones, muffled from the street should Charlie start to scream. She was remembering something from her visit long ago, a room under the house, a room without windows. It might do. She found the staircase to the cellar but it ended in a thick door, locked, and Charlie took one look at the locking apparatus and shook his head.

"You know what's through there, Mrs. Ficke?" he said.

There was something in his voice, a kind of fear she'd not heard there before. She searched his face. "Did Mrs. Harrogate take you in there, Charlie? Did she . . . examine you?"

The boy wet his lips. His eyes were hard. "Yeah."

Of course. She'd been so stupid. "Ach, we don't need to go in there," she said. "I wasn't thinking. I just reckoned—"

"—that we wouldn't be interrupted. Is that it?"

Slowly, she nodded.

He looked at his infected hand. Frowned. "Come on," he said, "there's another way in."

He led her back up to Margaret Harrogate's office. Behind the desk, he traced his fingers over the wallpaper. There was a thin, nearly indistinguishable line. She watched as he followed it to a small button on the underside of the wainscotting. With a click, a panel swung noiselessly inward on invisible hinges. A gust of bad air came out. Beyond lay an ancient stairwell, crooked, extending down into darkness.

Caroline set down the folded cloth with the instruments, the glass vials clinking, and she rummaged in Harrogate's desk until she found a stub of candle.

The stairs led deep below the building, into a narrow corridor. When she held the candle high, she could see at one end the thick locked door blocking the cellar. On either side the walls were slick with wet, coming in maybe from the drains, or perhaps from a buried river running under the street. In London, you never knew. Charlie led her in the other direction, to a thick iron door. It was unlocked. The candle flickered over the room's walls. They were painted white with lime and the wide brushes had left streaks. There was a drain in the middle of the floor and a chair set over it and in the guttering light she shuddered, imagining its purpose. This had been a room of cruelty, of fear.

Well, she thought to herself. *It will be something different now.*

Though still a room of pain. Still that.

She glanced sidelong at Charlie but couldn't see if he was nervous or not, nervous the way she was nervous, not at the task ahead of her but of the possibilities after. She dragged over a small table and began to lay out her cleaned instruments and the little glass bottles. Charlie had sat himself down in the chair over the drain. She saw there were manacles at the wrists and ankles. He clicked the leftmost tight at his wrist.

"Ach, that won't be necessary," she said sharply.

"It might be," he replied. "Close the other, Mrs. Ficke. When you start cutting, we don't know how the dust will react."

She pursed her lips and then nodded and tightened the other manacle.

Then she took out the scalpel and cut into the skin on the back of

198 ◆ J. M. Miro

his hand, a quick light incision, the blood welling up like dark ink. The corrupted dust was shining faintly, a brilliant blue, and she could see it swirling and twisting in patterns away from the blade. Charlie's jaw was tight with the pain.

Quickly Caroline carved out a wide flap of skin and began to peel it back away from the underlying flesh. The dust spiraled out and away and the loose skin was suddenly blank, the dust scattering like a school of fish. Charlie grunted.

And then, just as quickly, the incisions closed up again into white scars and the scars darkened and Caroline wiped away the blood and saw his skin was whole again.

"You have to cut faster than that," Charlie said softly.

She looked at him. "I don't know as this will work—" she began.

"You promised," he said again.

She took out a long flat scraping tool, wickedly sharp, and held it in her artificial claw. Then she cut again, and again the corrupted dust split away and scattered as if it could sense what she was doing. And she cut again, high up his forearm, quickly scraping away a long ribbon of skin, catching just the smallest pinch of the shining dust in the underlayer, the blood pouring from the boy's arm, and when she looked worriedly at his face she saw his eyes had rolled back in his head and he'd fainted.

With great care, she set the curl of infected skin in a small vial, corking it quickly, watching the dust glow and drift away from the dead flesh and begin to spiral on its own, giving off a blue shine.

It was such a small amount. And there was so much in Charlie.

She blinked the water from her eyes, and leaned back over the unconscious boy, and tried again.

Charlie's body went rigid. He could feel the corrupted dust as it was torn from him—small as it was—and it was like his very flesh was singing in agony. A great wave of darkness washed over him, the room was spinning, and then he was out.

At some point, he started to dream.

He was back at Cairndale. Only it wasn't Cairndale as he'd known it, but older, strung with rot, a dank soft floor beneath him. He was standing in the foyer of the great manor, the walls waterstained and dripping all around. The air was gray, thick with gloom. The great staircase led up into darkness.

And there he was, Marlowe, walking softly toward him out of the shadow. His face was very pale. His black hair was wet and plastered to his forehead and Charlie could not see his eyes.

I thought it would be you, said Marlowe. *I thought you would be the one to find me.*

And Charlie felt a sudden shock of fear go through him. His friend stopped some feet from where Charlie stood in the entrance, just at the edge of the darkest shadow. He looked like Marlowe. And yet somehow Charlie understood it wasn't Marlowe, or not the Marlowe he had known, the Marlowe he had loved. This apparition had changed so much; he had lost so much. It was like if you turn a glove inside out, so all the bad stitching and uneven seams show, he thought. That was what this Marlowe was like.

"Who are you?" Charlie whispered. "Why do you look like Mar? What have you done to him?"

The boy's face was old with sorrow. *Will you help me? Will you find me?*

In the dream Charlie felt his dread rise. "What are you?" he said again.

The child stared at him, his cold lips parted. The rags he wore were grimy and hung from his skeletal shoulders. *They are coming for us. We do not have much time. We cannot stay.*

"Am I dreaming? Are you real?"

Bring me the dust, Charlie Ovid. Before it is too late.

200 • J. M. Miro

"No," said Charlie, shaking his head. "Don't pretend to be him. What have you done? Where is he?"

He had the creeping feeling that Marlowe was near, in the darkness, listening.

"Mar! I'm coming for you!" he cried. "I'll find a way—!"

You left me to die, Charlie, said the not-Marlowe. He held up his hands; they were shining. *You left me. Why?*

He opened his eyes.

His skin felt like it was on fire. He was seated still in the chair in the white room. The manacles had been undone. The blood-soaked cloth was balled up on the little table beside him. The floor was sticky with blood and so were his shirt and trousers. But he could feel at once that it hadn't worked: the corrupted was still inside him. Despair overwhelmed him.

He raised his infected hand and saw the tattoos moving there, under the skin. Mrs. Ficke cleared her throat. She was standing near the door, watching him. Her face was filled with pity.

"It didn't work," whispered Charlie. He swallowed, feeling desperate, feeling like he might cry. "I thought it would work, I thought ... Mrs. Ficke? It didn't—" His voice choked.

"Ach, I'm so sorry, Charlie," she murmured.

"What do I do now? What do I *do*?" He heard the pleading in his voice as if it were someone else's.

Mrs. Ficke's face was heavy. "Sometimes ... sometimes it's a question of choice, Charlie."

"I didn't choose this!" he cried.

"No, lad," she replied gently. "But you do get to choose what you do next. You get to choose how you live with what you've been given."

She reached around her artificial arm and pressed a hidden catch and withdrew something from inside it. A small glass vial, glowing bright blue. There was a bit of dust in it. Seeing it, Charlie felt something inside him lurch. He thought he might throw up.

"Tis all I could get out of you," she said. "Carved away at you like a roast, I did. The dust just wouldn't come. I had no way of drawing it out. I'm sorry, Charlie."

The lantern light was soft. The room steadied. He could see how much it had hurt Mrs. Ficke to have to cut into him. He suddenly remembered his dream, the Marlowe-that-was-not-Marlowe standing in the rotting front hall of Cairndale Manor. The suffering in his little face. He wiped at his own eyes.

"Is it all right?" the old woman asked, anxious, gesturing at his arm, the tracks of dried blood all over it. "I couldn't see it healing. Will you be able to travel in the morning?"

He cradled his arm, the pain in it real. But he could feel the dust crawling there, doing its work, a bit slower maybe, but still healing. "I'll be ready," he said.

"We could wait. I could send to the shipping company, inform them of a delay—"

He got shakily to his feet. "I'll be ready, Mrs. Ficke," he said again, but quieter. He stumbled toward the door, and the old woman caught his arm. He could smell the sweat and lantern smoke in her clothes. But some part of him was still far away, still hearing Mar's voice in the dream, over and over, a fading echo.

You left me to die, Charlie.

You left me.

You left me.

15

A FOLLOWING LIKE SMOKE

The old showman's wagon rode up out of the carriageway, and turned east, toward Shadwell.

Micah straightened, tipping his hat back. Timna and Prudence, grimy and sullen, each opened one red eyelid. None spoke.

They simply detached themselves, thin as knives, and stepped out into the flow of people. Three small street urchins, in oversized coats, white hair sticking out from under their shabby hats. The yellow and red paint on the sidewalls of the wagon was garish and flaking and highly visible, easily followed, and the wagon itself rode high among the carts.

The old woman was in it, and Claker Jack's thief. But he was much too young, Micah thought: a black kid in a bowler hat and a seamy overcoat with the elbows worn. Broad shoulders. One heavy gloved hand rested on his knee. The kid's other arm was not in its sleeve; and that hand he could see was wrapped in a scarf, as if against the cold. He looked, Micah thought, a bit like a damned police constable, except for the fact of his age and the color of his skin, of course; like the kind of constable that didn't want to be noticed in the streets in the early hours of morning, but was the only one walking about in a coat and hat and whistling away and so you couldn't help staring. Well, no matter. Dangerous or no. Micah ran the back of his hand across his mouth, considering it. Then he started forward, following the slow progress of the wagon, his murderous sisters at his side.

The precious dust would be in the old woman's clothing somewhere, of course. Bring her in whole, Claker Jack had said. Right. Snatching was a job they didn't do often anymore but had used to do, when they were very small. Difficult in the day, but not impossible, not in a city like London. Except now they'd need a different approach. Maybe something more sly.

Or maybe something less so.

They loped along in the muck of the street, dodging the horses and wheels of the carriages, careful not to lose sight of the ridiculous painted wagon. It followed the river east along Upper Thames Street and when it reached King William Street it joined the flow of traffic heading north. Prudence was breathing unhealthily as she ran. The one-armed woman was guiding her horses toward Aldgate when she turned south again, away from Houndsditch, and the crush of traffic brought them all to a walk. It was then Micah realized where she must be going. The river. The docks.

He swore and gripped Timna and Prudence by the sleeves and dragged them under an awning. A fruit seller looked at them suspiciously.

"She aims to sail out of the city," he muttered.

Prudence shook her head, doubt in her eyes.

"An so what if she do?" replied little Timna. "She could aim to *fly* out of London in a goddamn *balloon* an with all what's in that wagon, it's no matter. I don't give a fig about Claker's thief. But the Abbess still wants what she wants, Micah." She tightened her jaw, watching the wagon creep slowly in the crush. "What you reckon she's got packed up in there, anyhow? A circus?"

Micah glowered. He'd been wondering the same and whether Claker Jack would want the entire cargo or just the woman herself. No doubt it was all her life's belongings. How Ruth had let this ridiculous contraption get away from her amazed him.

The mud glyphic had shown both the old crow and her wagon, but Claker Jack hadn't asked for both; that was what decided him. "You take the woman," he said. "An bring her in delicate-like, unless *you* want to explain it to Claker. Or worse, to the bloody Abbess herself. I'll get Claker's glitter."

The wagon had drawn level to Swan Street by then but the road was filling with workmen in shirtsleeves and ragged coats, trudging north as if on a holiday, up away from the docks. Those would be the day laborers, unhired, leaving the gates without wages or work. Some few looked angry but most were just tired, resigned. The horses had stopped in place and the wagon could not move forward nor back and the boy understood their opportunity. They could drag the one-armed woman clear, and vanish into the crowds.

He looked over. Timna had taken out two long, thin knives. She held them backward in her little fists, and folded her arms up, and grinned.

"What're you doing?" Micah scowled. "I said delicate-like. Put those away."

"I got me methods, an you got yours," she said, showing her small brown teeth, the gap in the front. "These are to play with Claker's thief."

"Put those away," he said again.

For a long moment she hesitated. Prudence had gone very still, watching them. The grin slid off Timna's face. Then, sullenly, she pocketed them inside her coat.

"Take them out when we need them. Not before. Prue, you get the crow away from the wagon."

Prudence nodded.

"An that other bastard? You got a plan for him?" asked Timna.

"What do you bloody well think?" Micah reached into his satchel. He slid on a set of iron knuckles that were too big for his hands but the best fit he'd found and then he drew his cuff low to conceal them. Elsewhere in that satchel he carried a double-bladed knife as long as a grown man's forearm.

The crowds were flowing past. The wagon stood stopped in the traffic, its horses with their heads dipped, unmoving. He could see the black kid and the woman on the bench, slouched, tired-looking, unaware.

"You just get the crow clear," he growled again at Prudence. "We'll find you when we're done. It won't take long. Come on, Timna."

And then they all three pushed their way into the crowd.

Across the city, amid the blur and steam of Piccadilly Station, Jeta Wajs strode away from the platforms with neither traveling case nor trunk. Her hair was badly messed and her patchwork dress was rumpled from sleeping on the Express. Ladies paused to stare disapprovingly as she passed. Porters in caps and brass buttons stroked their beards, watchful. The tips of her scarlet gloves were dirty with soot. She rubbed the coin at her throat between forefinger and thumb, trying to steady the ache that was washing over her, the ache of all their thousands of breakable little bones. The sweet, sweet pull of them, without Ruth's tinctures to dull her talent.

As she exited the station she caught a glimpse of herself in the glass. Eyes dark as the grave. A face sunken and grooved from exhaustion. Then she pushed out into the roar of the morning haze and left that self behind.

She wanted to go to Claker Jack at once, to beg his forgiveness, to explain all that had happened in Scotland. But she couldn't. For one, she'd never been to the Falls, not once in all her years, kept from Claker Jack's realm out of concern for her own safety: her kind, talents, were slaughtered in that place, cut into pieces and dumped in the Thames. And though she knew ways of finding it, she was afraid too of Claker's disappointment, of showing up empty-handed, no corrupted dust, no Ruth. She knew Claker cared for her, cared for her in ways he'd never have expected to, when first he'd plucked her from the streets. She'd been just a tool, a ready weapon at first, a child who might yet prove useful. He'd told her this himself, just last year, seated on the roof of a warehouse in Deptford in the dark hours of the night. But he'd grown fond of her, just as she had of him; and now they were a kind of family, in their way. Isn't that what he'd said to her? Something like it, at least. Claker had his own gruff kind of tenderness, at least with her. And it was true, she knew it was true, knew it deep down in her heart, even if Ruth would have laughed at her for thinking it.

Ruth, damn her. Jeta was glad to be rid of her. She regretted nothing, even as she felt exposed, walking unaccompanied in daylight, no Ruth at her side. It felt . . . good to be alone. She'd slept on the train in the third-class carriage and when she awoke even the shining blue figure of the ghost boy was gone.

Now, alone in the city in almost as long as she could remember, she knew exactly where she had to go.

She hired a hansom and sat back and pinched her eyes shut. She could feel the millions of bodies adrift in the streets as she passed. The smells of the city, its smoky air, the reek of effluent and hot-pies in the street-ovens and horses.

At 23 Nickel Street West, she got down, paid with coin from Ruth's purse. The terraced house loomed above her, dark and forbidding. The curtains were drawn in every window but one.

She knocked.

After a moment she took off her scarlet glove and rested her palm flat against the door, and closed her eyes. She could feel something within, something powerful and strange, not unlike the pull she'd felt back at the ruins of Cairndale. Of the Ficke woman, or Charlie, she sensed nothing.

She picked up her skirts and swept back down the steps and made her way along the little iron railing at the front, to the rusting gates that led below. They stood locked. There were respectable people in the street, passing her, trying not to look too closely. She furrowed her brow and went back up to the door and withdrew the little locksmithing tools from a hidden pocket at her waist.

She was inside in a moment.

Twenty-three Nickel Street West was dark, and silent, and cold. She stood in the entrance hall, listening. Something pulled at her, drew her in, but she resisted. She had been here once, nearly six years ago. Mrs. Harrogate, with a veil at her face. Dr. Berghast in the night, dressed in a suit as if he'd only just arrived, holding a candle over her bed. Shaking his head in disapproval. And then in the morning, waiting in the hall upon a small trunk, the sound of the clock on the landing. And that man Coulton, escorting her gruffly to the orphans' home.

Damn them all.

She glared at the furnishings, the ferns dead in their pots, the heavy coat pegs standing empty. When she turned she saw the Cairndale crest above the door, its crossed hammers. She turned angrily away.

It was clear to her that someone had been here, only just recently. They had not stayed long. There were footprints in the dust of the parlor rug, and marks as if something had been dragged or wheeled there. Blankets and sheets were piled messily on the sofas.

She went to the large window overlooking the street and drew back the curtains just slightly and tried to decide if she ought to wait. The Ficke woman and Charlie Ovid might yet return.

She began to make her slow way through the rooms, feeling always that dark pull in her wristbones, in her hipbones, a tugging that led her up the stairs. It was coming from somewhere near the top of the house, she understood. But she was cautious and stopped at each floor and went from room to room. A stained glass window illuminated the first floor landing. A huge, ancient clock stood at the second floor landing, its hands stopped. The bedchambers were all empty, tidy for the most part, but the air was cold and musty as if it hadn't been disturbed in months, and there was an old razor and strop in one of the rooms, a bed with ropes at its posts in another.

At last she reached the top of the house, and went up a rickety staircase, and stood in the attic, letting her eyes adjust. After the dimness of the house, the brightness of the attic was startling. French doors, paned with glass, filled the back wall. Dusty chests, shelves of jars and tin cans. And then she heard the eerie clicking sounds, in cages silhouetted against the brightness, and saw them.

Bonebirds.

Two of them, in a cote near an ancient writing console. She crossed the space quickly, and kneeled down, and stared in at them. They were so beautiful. Delicate, filigreed things, their bones like lace. That strange iron brace at their chests and wrapping over their skulls, as if to hold them together. The little hook on one leg, for the messages. She thought of the poor creature crushed underfoot, in that hotel room in Edinburgh, Ruth's cruel joy at the destruction. She thought of Ruth.

You're too late, said a small voice. *It's gone. They're gone.*

She turned smoothly. The ghost boy stood in the attic shadow, watching her. His blue hair wavered and drifted, shining. His eyes were darker than usual, just black holes in the gloom.

"You mean . . . Charlie," she said. "Charlie's gone." That dreamlike fog was descending over her again. Something about the apparition didn't seem right.

Charlie. Yes.

She gave her head a slow shake. The bonebirds clicked softly. "Then I won't be able to find them," she said, feeling a fierce disappointment rise in her. "London's too big. It's not possible. How did they get away? I'm here, I came as fast as I could—!"

The little apparition guttered, as if in a wind.

She looked up, suddenly hopeful. "Couldn't you *sense* the dust? Like at the cathedral?"

In Edinburgh I'd just . . . tasted it. It's gone now.

Jeta remembered the mortuary, the ghost child crouched like a spider over the dustworker's corpse, mouth gaping, teeth blackened as if he'd been drinking ink. She shivered.

The little apparition seemed to sense her despair. *You can still find it, Jeta, I know you can. You're powerful, more powerful than you think. I see it. Your talent can find the dust, it can, and together we can—*

But she crushed her eyes shut, scarcely listening, and turned away. There was nothing to be done; she'd lost the corrupted dust; she'd failed. Her heart hurt. There was no way forward, she saw.

"I have to go to the Falls," she said quietly. "I have to talk to Claker. He . . . he told me never to go there. But I have to."

She felt the ghost child drift nearer. His voice, soft, came from very close. *He'll be mad. You should find the dust first. There are still ways—*

"No." She swallowed a knot in her throat, looked down at the apparition. Looked *through* him. "Claker's always looked out for me, even when Ruth was against me. He'll understand. I'll just explain what happened. He'll tell me what to do next."

But she was afraid all the same, afraid that he wouldn't, afraid that he'd look at her differently. Tell her he didn't need her.

And Ruth? What will you tell him about her? whispered the boy. *Going there won't help us find the dust. It's a bad idea.*

Jeta felt sick. She glared at the apparition, feeling a faint doubt seep in, staining the pity. What did he really want? Through the grimy French doors, the city roofs disappeared in the fog. She unlatched them, stood them wide. The air was cold and tasted of soot. She could just make out the sluggish expanse of the Thames beyond; then all was haze. Somewhere out there was the alley where the urchins lived, the ones Claker Jack used for errands. At her elbow she could feel the little clockwork skeletons of the bonebirds, their eyeless skulls swiveling, tracking her. She remembered the tiny bones on the carpet in Edinburgh, crunching. The horror of it. She unlatched the peg of the cote, stood the door wide.

The first creature exploded outward. It took to the sky, its strange wings snapping and creaking. She watched it vanish crookedly into the smoke above the rooftops.

But the second bonebird did not go.

Her thoughts were still murky. She poked at the bars. "Go on," she muttered.

Carefully she lifted it out and held it high in the open wall of the attic and when it did not fly she threw it bodily from her. It snapped into flight and circled twice and flew away.

They would've been safer here, whispered the ghost.

Jeta frowned. "Nothing belongs in a cage."

Some things do, he replied.

She left the terrace house alone, and turned east, seeking the poorer parts of the city. The air was cold. If the apparition was near, he did not show himself. She walked swiftly, her braids swaying against her back, her cloak billowing out around her. The streets were filled with all manner of people, hawkers, shoppers, clerks, ladies in their finery, wainwrights, cabmen. All of them jostling and calling out and muscling their way past. At each dank lane she would pause and turn in and seek the sort of indigent she needed. At last she found an urchin squatting in a doorway, watching a vegetable seller with hungry eyes.

She took him by the scruff of his neck, spun him around. He couldn't have been older than five. His shirt was ragged, his trousers ripped at the knees. He was barefoot. He swung on the end of her arm, glaring.

She held out a penny in the flat of her scarlet glove. "I've got a second one for you, if you can get me where I need to go."

He eyed her suspiciously. "Where's that, then?"

"The Falls." She released him. "Do you know it?"

When he glanced up and down the alley, there was fear etched in his face. "You isn't working for the beaks or nothing?"

Nuffink, it sounded like. She gave him a hard shake but didn't bother to reply.

His eyes suddenly looked older, cagier. "Double it an I'll go far as Cooper's Runs," he said. "It's easy to find from there."

She leaned down so that her eyes were level with his. She said nothing for several heartbeats. She could feel the pull of his little bones. "See that you lead me directly," she said softly, "and I'll pay you in full. But lie to me, and I'll break your legs and dump you in the Thames."

The urchin gave her a grin. "Just try to keep up, miss."

She hitched up her multicolored skirts and followed the urchin down a crooked lane, into a crumbling court, along a passageway, into a second alley. They passed the huddled poor on the doorsteps, wizened indigents picking through bundles of rags.

As they went, Jeta felt a painful tugging at her bones. She raised her face and saw, high up between the mews, what looked like the silhouette of a bonebird, following her; but then the urchin ducked under an arch and down a passageway of dripping stairs, and whatever was up there in the sky was gone.

16

THE PRIZEFIGHTER'S PRAYER

The hands were small and grubby with bitten nails, grime in the seams of their palms. They curled beseechingly up toward Charlie from out of the street's crowds, little claws of hunger, tugging at his clothes, pawing at him.

But he had nothing to give. Their wagon was nearly at Miller's Wharf. He could see through curtains of mist the tall iron gates of the west entrance to St Katharine Docks, looming over the crush of the crowd. Unhired laborers and sailors on leave and night stevedores were flowing past, a sudden crowd, spooking the horses in their traces. In the back of the showman's wagon were the glyph-twisted children, silent, still. Charlie kept a tired ear trained for any sound from them, but there was none; they seemed calm. Even Deirdre. Soon they'd be on board a ship, and setting out for safer shores.

Gradually he became aware that the little hands were still there.

That was when, to his astonishment, he felt one take hold of his loose sleeve, another reach around his knee, a third his elbow. One wore, incongruously, heavy iron knuckles. All at once they started *pulling*— pulling with an unexpected strength—and he buckled sideways off his perch, like a wet sack of grain, his weight somehow working against him. Men in the crowd swore as he fell, shoving at him. His head cracked the cobblestones.

"Charlie?" cried Mrs. Ficke from above. "*Charlie!*"

He was too surprised to speak. He shook his head, dazed, not sure what had just happened. His infected hand exploded in a constellation of pain. There were so many people. He saw his bowler crushed under a boot and he started to reach for it when it was kicked to one side, then kicked away again.

But already the crowds were making a space around him, as if an eddy were opening in the current of a river. In all that movement there was one point of stillness; and he lifted his eyes, and looked, and he saw the beggar kid.

The kid was thin and dirty with hair as white as dead grass. He wore a battered satchel over one shoulder. He couldn't have been much more than twelve years of age but he stared at Charlie with terrible eyes, trembling with intent. Charlie knew that look, had seen it in kids and men alike in the American South, white folk, black folk who'd hit the breaking point and then been pushed past. It was a look of raw fury. Then he saw, low at the boy's side, the glint of iron knuckles. The other hand held a long knife. He knew who the boy must be: an associate of the bone witch, an underling for the infamous Claker Jack.

Charlie got to his feet, unafraid. "What're you doing?" he called across, feeling his own anger rise. "I don't want trouble. Put that down, you don't want to be doing this."

The boy took a lazy step forward, catlike, saying nothing.

Charlie didn't hesitate. He wasn't a damned fool; he'd learned his lesson at the cathedral in Edinburgh. He reached into his greatcoat and withdrew Alice's Colt Peacemaker and he cocked the hammer.

Now the crowds took notice. Men stopped and others took unsteady steps backward and one shouted something at him.

He was aware of Mrs. Ficke, leaning over the driver's bench, the reins looped in her hand. She started to get down but stopped when she saw the boy with the knife. "Charlie?" she said uncertainly.

"Keep going!" he called back. "Try to get the wagon through. I'll catch up." Because of his infected hand, his greatcoat hung at a strange angle. He turned square to the beggar kid, the revolver steady. He thought of the bone witch in Edinburgh and looked at the kid and knew he, too, would be dangerous. Never mind how small and grubby he seemed. "We're leaving the city," he called across. "You can tell your Claker Jack that. His bone witch failed. You'll fail too. Don't do this."

The boy began circling over the uneven cobblestones, unconcerned.

"You don't look so dangerous, like," the urchin called. "But I reckon you got to be, comin back into Claker's city an all. You got the ring, Mr. Owydd? It's only just the ring old Claker wants. Give it over."

Charlie paused, confused. Had the boy called him *Owydd*?

"The *ring*, lad," the urchin called again. "At your *throat*."

But Charlie was shaking his head, the gun already lowering. It couldn't be. "Wait. What you called me, Owydd. Is it Hywel Owydd you mean?"

The urchin's narrow eyes were bloodshot and unreadable. He took a soft step forward.

But before Charlie could ask more, could ask what he knew about Hywel Owydd, Charlie's father, who had fled Cairndale as an exile in his youth, and washed up here in this awful city, a father Charlie had never known—he caught a movement from the corner of his eye, a flickering in and out of the thin brown fog.

A second urchin, a little girl.

Charlie scarcely dared risk breaking his eyeline with the kid. But he glimpsed her pale head, narrow shoulders. He lost sight of her and when he saw her again she was on the back of the wagon, clambering lightly up, impossibly fast, then running across the roof and dropping down onto the driver's bench beside Mrs. Ficke.

"Mrs. Ficke—!" he shouted, too late.

The urchin landed lightly beside her and in the same instant reached around, as if to embrace her, skinny arms snaking around the older woman's waist. And then—all of it was so fast!—the ragged child just leaned backward, still grasping Mrs. Ficke tightly, and both pitched sideways, over the far side, into the crowds and lost to view.

Caroline Ficke rolled painfully off the child, her surprise absolute. She'd bitten her tongue and blood was in her mouth. Out of the crowd, an old man in a heavy wool coat stooped to help her up. His white beard was yellowed around the mouth where years of tobacco had stained it.

When he saw the urchin sprawled under her he paused, adjusted his cap in disapproval.

"Taint all rait nowt, is it, missus?" he said. His eyes went to her artificial arm.

She was shaking. A sharp pain radiated through her hips, but nothing was broken, thank the lord. She knew Charlie with the corrupted dust at work inside him would be all right. But she feared what would happen if the children in the back of the showman's wagon were exposed, and so she didn't have time to deal with the old man, chivalrous or no.

"'Tis nothing," she said coldly. "Off with you."

The little girl who'd attacked her scrambled up. She was a pitiful creature. Ten years old, perhaps. Unkempt and stinking with a face streaked with soot, grime all down the front of her ill-fitting clothes. But she wasn't a talent; that much Caroline felt sure of. Could she be a servant of Claker Jack's? An exile?

"There are other ways, child, we might do this," she said calmly. "Speak your business with me. I'd not wish to hurt you."

Slowly the urchin wiped her hands on her legs. For just a moment Caroline could see the child within—blinking, confused, small and vulnerable and alone in all the world.

But then she heard Charlie hollering from the far side of the wagon, and the horses shied skittishly, and the girl's eyes hardened.

Caroline untangled her cloak. She pressed a catch on her artificial arm and twisted it counterclockwise and then she turned a small wheel at the elbow. Silently the blade at the end extended, until it was nearly two feet in length. Its serrated edge glinted in the murky day.

"Ach, you poor creature," she murmured. "The world never gave you a choice, did it?"

The girl crouched.

Caroline raised her blade.

At that same moment, Charlie was wiping the sweat from his eyes.

"Mrs. Ficke!" he shouted. "Mrs. Ficke! Are you all right?"

He couldn't see her; the showman's wagon was in the way. All thought of his father, and the white-haired boy's bizarre demands about his Cairndale ring, had vanished. He felt confused, and fearful, and angry; anger, like a small hard seed, was lodged in his throat. He crept sidelong around the front wheel toward the horses, trying to get around to the old woman, where she'd fallen. The ragged boy moved to block his way.

Charlie aimed Alice's revolver steady at the kid's heart. He didn't know if he could pull the trigger. He didn't want to know. "Stay back," he shouted. "I mean it!"

It was then that he sensed movement. Something—some*one*—was crawling spiderlike out from beneath the axle, low to his left. A child.

A third urchin.

She was smaller than the other two but with the same white hair and frayed clothes and before he could react she had run straight at his back. She kicked hard at the bend of his knee and it folded forward; he staggered down, off-balance. Suddenly she was clambering up his back, onto his shoulders. In her tiny fists were two daggers, which she plunged—swiftly, furiously, over and over—into his back, into his shoulders, into the fold at the base of his neck, and with each strike long lines of gore whipped out around him.

They were killing strokes. Charlie cried out. The cry was his, and not his; it came from some deep source inside him; and he spun and thrashed, all instinct, and hurled her off. Alice's revolver had fired wildly down at the cobblestones, the bullet ricocheting off with a spark, God only knew where. The horses screamed. The tiny girl skidded across the cobblestones. He tried to get up but suddenly the boy was in front of him, scything his long blade at Charlie's stomach. It was all he could do to scramble backward, once, twice, clawing at the ground with his infected hand, wincing in the agony of it. He dropped the Colt Peacemaker. The kid cut at him again. Clumsily, Charlie lurched onto one knee and swung back, a big loose fist aimed at the boy's head. But he caught only air.

Everything seemed to slow down then. Vaguely he sensed the crowds fleeing, men hollering in the fog. He heard over the roar his good Mrs. Ficke shouting somewhere. When he'd tried to strike the kid, his shirtsleeve had lifted away from his wrist, and he'd glimpsed the marks of dust all along his forearm, the tattoos. Writhing, as if alive. Mrs. Ficke's incisions already, of course, healed over, leaving thin white scars.

Come on, then, he thought in sudden fury.

He stumbled toward the bollards lining the pedestrian way. A watery fog was adrift in the street. There were stalls at the edge of the road, proprietors in aprons and shirtsleeves stepping forward open-mouthed. But now the urchin and the tiny girl were both on their feet, each circling slowly from separate directions, their knives in their fists, and they cut off Charlie's retreat. They said nothing, explained nothing. Charlie's eyes were wet with the pain and he ran his hand across his face and ripped off his greatcoat and wrapped it bulkily around his infected hand and forearm and he held this out in front of him to block the knives.

He was shouting at them, a fierce sound without words, only half knowing that he was doing so. It was like all the rage he'd felt since Marlowe had vanished, all the sorrow at his lost talent, all the fear he'd felt for Alice and his friends and now for himself with this evil coalescing under his skin—all of it came roaring out of him. He'd seen pugilists in barns throughout his boyhood and pain for them was like a prayer they'd learned to release, to find strength in. But a tiredness was coming in its place, and the dust's healing was different in him from how he'd used to be, and he could lift his arms only heavily.

And then the blades came at him, as he'd known they would, fast, impossibly fast, ribboning his clothes, carving into his ribs, the bite of metal turning coldly inside him. He screamed. The knives cut deeper.

Then he was collapsing, and the dockside street and its cold fog and all the roar and clash faded, faded with his fear and his anger, and in its place was only darkness.

Caroline stumbled around the horses where they shied in fear just in time to see Charlie fall, to hear him scream, to see his legs kick out and go still.

Charlie. The dust. His talent, corrupted.

Her mind was reeling. They were *children*. Two children, white-haired, crouching over poor Charlie's body, holding knives gone black in the flat daylight, their rags spattered in blood. Caroline looked fearfully at the wagon. She was thinking in alarm of the glyph-twisted children in the back, afraid suddenly what would happen if these urchins threw open the door. She didn't know what it was they wanted but some part of her understood it had to do with the corrupted dust. But they didn't know where it was; they didn't know, or they'd not have cut down Charlie.

She turned on the third urchin, the girl with the raggedly cut hair, and swung the blade she'd attached to her stump in a quick, expert slash. It caught the girl in the meat of her upper arm and her face twisted in pain but she made no sound.

She fell back, clutching her bloodied shoulder, watching Caroline warily. Her small eyes were half-hidden by her greasy hair.

Caroline backed away from the wagon, toward an alley. She wanted to draw her attacker away. Maybe she could lose her in the labyrinth of narrow streets near St Katharine Docks and double back for the children, for poor Charlie? She remembered the little bit of dust she'd hidden inside her artificial arm. If only it hadn't bonded to Charlie, she could have run her fingers through it, she could have overpowered this child—

That was when she saw the two other urchins, bloodied, murderous, stalk around the back of the wagon. Her heart sank. If they had left Charlie, it could mean only one thing. She and the children were truly unprotected.

But the urchins didn't stop at the wagon, didn't try to open the back door, didn't attack her glyph-twisted wards. Instead, they strode past. Toward *her*.

She ran.

She ran in her long skirts, in her stiff leather boots. She ran for all she was worth, cursing her lady's clothes, her old legs, her tired lungs, everything the years had done to her body. She ducked down a narrow alley and tried the first door she came to but it was locked. She ran on. The morning fog was already thickening, creeping in tendrils along the cobblestones. She knew she'd not be able to outrun her pursuers. She turned up a grimy lane, half fell down a slick stair, crossed a street, ran for a second alley. She was stumbling by then. There were old women like her sitting on the steps, blocking doorways, watching her panicked run with dull eyes. No one rose to help. When she glanced back she saw the boy and the littlest urchin jogging along, unhurried, letting her run.

She swore at that. It made her angry to think these miserable little ones could toy with her. Gasping, her gray hair all undone, she turned sharply into a court and came to a stop, her sleeve unpinned and flapping. She looked ahead and froze. In the small arched exitway stood the third urchin, the one that had dragged her out of the wagon, swinging a cosh languidly. She could see the blood congealed on the child's shoulder, the arm hanging at her side.

Caroline whirled about, blade held dangerously in front of her. The other two urchins had come now to the edge of the court behind her.

"Aw, now," grinned the littlest. "I think she wants to play, Micah."

"She's old as a bloody Bible, Timna," said the boy. "She isn't going to *play*. She don't know what she wants." On a cord at his throat was Charlie's ring, the ring that had belonged to his mother.

The littlest—Timna—was holding small knives in both her tiny hands. Those hands were red with blood, right up to the wrists. Charlie's blood.

"What did you do to him?" she shouted. "What did you do to Charlie?"

The boy reached into his satchel and took out a yellow kidskin glove. Charlie's glove. It was dark with blood and crushed up into a strange shape. Slowly the boy unfolded it and held it out. There was something bloodied and soft curled in it, like a rubbery shell. An ear. A human ear. Caroline started to shake, seeing it. Her disgust and fury made her stagger. *Charlie—?* she was thinking. *Charlie, my God, no—!*

"Now, we don't *have* to hurt you neither, missus," the boy was saying. "We just need you to come with us, like."

Caroline's vision narrowed suddenly. She felt a dangerous calm come over her. She saw mud and dried blood spattered across the boy's nose and forehead, like freckles. She heard his voice, reasonable, as if he were playacting at being a grown-up.

"Come *with* you?" she whispered. "Ach, no. You walk away now, and I won't follow you. How's that for an offer?"

"I think it's sweet," said the young Timna. "I think it's a awful sweet offer, lady."

There were faces, pale, lifeless, adrift in the open windows all around the court. Men in shirtsleeves and dented hats stepped into the doorways, watching. No one made any attempt to interfere.

"What is it you want?" Caroline demanded. "Why would you come after us?"

"Aw, just *you*, missus. Our employer would like a word with *you*, is all. On account of Cairndale. An what you took."

She was still trembling from the run and she fumbled with her good hand for the edge of a cart that stood nearby. She could smell the reek of the Thames in the fog. She must be only a few streets away from the docks. If she could make it there, perhaps she could lose them in the crowds. Or attract someone—anyone—to help her.

"You mean Claker Jack," she said, trying to buy herself time. "We already met his bone witch. You think you're worse?"

"Micah," interrupted the littlest, suddenly bored. "We got to go. There's like to be beaks here soon enough."

Caroline lifted her blade again, trying to look fierce. "God help me, I will carve at least one of you into pieces. You hurt a good young man. A friend. And I'll be damned if—"

But all at once she felt the air shift behind her, and spun around in time to see the third urchin, who had climbed soundlessly up onto the cart at her back, swing a stubby cosh high in one fist.

There was a burst of pain. Caroline Ficke felt her boots slip; she raised her arms. The muck of the yard came spinning up toward her.

While all around that dark court white faces withdrew, one by one, back into the gloom.

17

Witching Hours

The street urchin led Jeta swiftly down through the dripping alleys, his naked feet splashing ahead, his scrawny body twisting first left, then right, then vanishing down a stair, then twisting left again. He was so small.

She ran to keep up. When they came out above the embankment and hurried down a rickety wooden stair, all the way down to the Thames, she was at first blinded by the white sky and the pale fog hugging the shore. She glimpsed the dark hulls of passenger ferries in the mist, feeble orange lanterns swaying from their housings.

But then the boy slipped under a railing into ankle-deep muck, the muck a queer sulfurous color, and it was all she could do to follow. The river was low. Twenty paces on, he stopped, his feet slucking in the mud. The knifelike silhouettes of birds were circling in the fog above and Jeta could feel, among them, the tight painful pull of a bonebird. It had followed her.

"Right. That's Cooper's Runs," the boy said sullenly, gesturing at a dark tunnel. "Now where's me tuppence, then?"

A rusted iron gate blocked the tunnel. Jeta frowned. "*That's* Cooper's Runs? It's a sewer."

He spat. "One end of it. Aye."

"How far up will I need to go?"

"You was hopin maybe they's all just standin round inside, like? Just waitin for you?" He gave her a sly grin. "It's a ways in yet, it is. But keep to the right an you'll find it. Or it'll find you."

"How many ways in are there?"

"Aw, there's any number of ways *in*."

"And you bring me to this one? A sewer?"

"Aye. There's just only the one way *out*, though." The child drew a grimy finger across his throat, still grinning. "Don't much take to visitors, them lot."

She thought about snapping his little vertebra. It would be so easy; the pull of his young bones was strong, and it was the safest way to avoid his betrayal. But instead she opened her glove and dropped his coins one by one in the yellow muck and when he swore and set to clawing them out with his fingers she took off the glove from her left hand. "Do you believe in monsters?" she asked softly.

He stood with a quick reply on his lips but then he saw her fingers and froze.

"You should," she said in a sweet voice.

And ran her bony fingers slowly down his cheek, staring into his face as she did so. Then she put her glove back on and hitched up her skirts and waded toward the tunnel. When she looked back, he'd fled.

The iron gate had been pried from its hinges, then propped upright. As she squeezed through, she caught sight of something alighted on the mud some feet away. It was the bonebird—the very one from Nickel Street West. She stood looking at it through the iron gate. "Go," she whispered. "You're free. Go on, *go!*"

It cocked its skull, its eyeless sockets seeming to take in her gaze.

Then it hopped lightly over the muck and took flapping to the sky. She turned away.

It was a relief to go into the tunnel, like taking off a heavy coat, the thickening pull of the city's bones receding, growing muffled. She thought of Claker Jack, what he might say to see her. What she might say to him. But she hadn't crept twenty feet into the darkness when she saw, shimmering and blue, as if rippling with water, the ghost child. She hissed in surprise. "I should put a bell on you. Jesus."

He said nothing, watchful.

"Don't try to talk me out of this. I won't be."

Still the boy watched her.

She shook her head. She hadn't brought a lantern or candle of any kind. "Well, make yourself useful," she said. "Go on, be a light. Scare off the rats. I'll not be much use to you if I get eaten now, will I?"

The tunnels were wet, cold. She made her way cautiously by the blue shine of the boy ahead of her, keeping to the right at each turning. There were marks scraped into the walls, only just discernible in the gloom, and the waters—green, brackish, reeking with effluent and soft lumps of matter—pushed steadily past.

At last she reached a dark, dry passageway. She hesitated, looked at the ghost boy. He was shining at its entrance.

"This way?" she whispered.

Don't you feel it? he replied softly. *The bodies within?*

And she could; she closed her eyes and it was like a wind was tugging her gently forward. She opened her eyes. "Ruth used to give me medicine, for my talent. To keep it . . . smaller. And it hasn't been right since the cathedral, either. Whatever Charlie did to me, it . . . affected me. It comes and goes now, like it's too close to me, or too far away. I don't trust it."

That's the dust. It opened your talent too completely, and overwhelmed you. You weren't ready.

She frowned. There was in the boy something new, something she didn't like. A hunger.

Fifty yards in, a hulking figure stepped out of the darkness, barring her way. She could hear a distant roar of water, of voices. The figure held out a meaty hand. He held a club low in his other. She couldn't see his face.

"An where is it you're going, little flea?" he said.

Jeta could see the ghost child, flickering and indistinct. He had stopped some ways beyond the guard and simply stood, waiting. She ran her tongue along her teeth in annoyance.

"The Falls," she said.

The man scratched at his beard. "The Falls, is it? An what exactly is that, then?"

She frowned. She hadn't thought through how she'd talk her way in. "I came down from Cairndale," she began. "I'm one of the . . . exiles? I need to see Claker Jack. I have something important to tell him."

The man nodded slowly. When he stepped closer she could smell his unwashed skin. "Is that right?" he whispered. "There's a toll to get past, of course. How you aim to pay it, then?"

She reached into her skirts for her coin purse but the man cleared his throat.

"It ain't coin you got to pay it with," he said.

She paused. She looked past at the ghost child where he wavered, she looked up at the massive guard. And with a quick twist of her wrist, she felt for the bones in his neck and crushed them, one by one. His legs went out from under him and he fell, dead, into the dried muck of the tunnel.

"Bastard," she muttered.

They'll know you're here, the apparition whispered. *We can still go back.*

She glared at the ghost and then looked down at the dead man and then she dragged him by the armpits awkwardly back down the tunnel. He was heavy and the going was difficult. When she reached deep water at the first junction she rolled the body, with a splash, into the sluggish current. It would have to do. Then she retraced her steps and continued on.

When at last she came out onto a platform above the Falls she caught her breath in amazement. She'd imagined a dark warren of tunnels, arches, dank rooms lit by meager candles. Not the vast and thundering cistern that she stood at the edge of, the staggered wooden platforms built up out of the water.

It might have been erected to house some kind of machinery, once. At three different places around the upper walls, a torrent of brackish water thundered down, swirling in increasing speed toward a vast central drain. There it was sucked away into the earth, toward a labyrinth of drainage tunnels.

But suspended over that pit was an enormous platform, with a tall roofed-in cage, as in a menagerie, though no creature lurked within. And radiating outward, like the spokes of a wheel, or the strands of a web, were bridges and flats filled with rickety wooden structures and figures milling about in the mist. There were more platforms attached to the walls, linked by ladders or wooden stairs, and archways built in, vanishing into gloom. From high above came a weak daylight; it was filtering in through deep shafts in the ceiling. And not only light; she saw pigeons roosting high along the walls, crackling here and there in sudden flurries.

It was, she saw in amazement, an entire world.

She descended the stairs and went into the crush of people, her skull buzzing with all their bones. Cutthroats, pickpockets, cardsharps, buzzers, all those who trafficked in the cruel and the dangerous. Some few caught her eye with suspicious looks but she was careful to glance away, to keep moving, though the pull of their bones was sickening.

An hour passed. She went up and down ladders, making her way.

When she asked an old woman where she could find Claker Jack she got no reply and when she asked a sullen kid carrying a bucket of slops the kid looked at her with such suspicion she didn't dare ask anyone else. When she'd circled through the crowds twice, she found a hollow high on the far side of the cistern where she could huddle down to think, arms crossed over her knees. It gave a good view of the platforms. If Claker Jack appeared, she'd see him.

The weak daylight was already fading, high up where the birds were still crackling, when movement caught Jeta's eye. Three small urchins with white hair had come in, and were descending one of the rickety stairs. Something about the way the denizens of the Falls withdrew, watchful, as they passed, made her sit up and take notice. The boy at the front wore a bloodstained yellow glove on one hand. They were escorting, she saw, an old woman in a ruined blue dress. She had only one arm.

Jeta scrambled to her feet, suddenly awake.

Micah nudged the old woman forward, almost gently. He was feeling pleased with himself. How Ruth had let this old crow slip through her fingers, he couldn't imagine.

It had been easy; it had been *fun*.

Claker Jack's ring was on a cord at his throat; the dead boy's ear was in his pocket. The yellow kidskin glove taken from the body was ruined by the blood. When he'd peeled it away, he'd been surprised to see the hand beneath covered in tattoos, in ink that seemed almost to move in the weak fog-thick daylight. It wasn't like any kind of talent he'd ever seen. The glove was too big for his own hands, outsized as they were; but Micah could cut out the fingers and wear it easy enough.

He and his sisters led the old woman down through the warren of tarps and crates and barrels, to the stair that led up to Claker Jack's.

There was a man at the base of it with a bad eye and he stepped aside
to let them pass.

If the old woman was afraid, she gave no sign. She stared ahead with
dignity. This seemed to infuriate Timna, and she would poke the woman
in the small of her back, now and then, to try for a reaction. Micah had
taken the artificial arm off her after Prudence had struck her down; it
had been difficult, what with all the buckles and straps, and none of them
could figure out how to retract its long, wicked-looking blade. It stuck
out now from Micah's satchel like a fishing pole.

He raised his head as they climbed the stairs, and peered out over
the Falls. He had the strange feeling of being watched. Pigeons roosting
in the high ceiling. Figures milling about on the platforms. Across the
gloom, in the mist sprayed up from the roaring waters, he saw a figure get
to her feet. She was maybe his own age, black-haired, wearing a strange
patchwork dress. A mudlark, maybe. It seemed to him, even at that distance, that she'd locked eyes on him. A coldness went through him. He'd
seen her somewhere.

What's this, now? he wondered.

But then they'd reached the narrow platform outside Claker Jack's
office, and he thought no more of it. The two guards in their red waistcoats stood aside and Micah saw Timna give them a smug grin as she
passed. They stepped into the little brick chamber, lit by a lantern on
Claker Jack's desk, and there was the crime lord seated behind it, his
fingers steepled, just as if he'd been expecting them. He wore a black suit
with stains on the front, black trousers. The blacks didn't match. On his
greasy head he wore an old-fashioned stovepipe hat.

"Mr. Jack," said Micah calmly. "Caught a bit of rabbit for the Abbess,
we did."

He took out from the satchel the old woman's arm, and set it on the
big desk with a clatter. Then he pulled the ring free of his shirtfront,

pulled the cord over his head. For just a moment he hesitated, rolling the peculiar ring between his fingers. Then he dropped it heavily down onto the table.

Claker Jack scooped it up at once. "Ah," he said. "And the man?"

"Dead. But he weren't old enough to be your thief. Just a lad, he was."

"Is that so? Curious." The crime lord rose to his full height, slow, thin as a spider. His yellowing skin, his red-rimmed eyes. He turned his attention to the old woman, who stood startled, defiant. Claker Jack touched the brim of his hat with two fingers.

"Well, well, well," he murmured. "And what have we here?"

"Ought to be ashamed of yourself, treating God-fearing folk like this," snapped the woman.

Claker Jack raised his eyebrows. "Come now, Caroline," he said softly. "Do you not remember me?"

And smiled an awful smile.

Jeta Wajs moved across the gap, the roar of the waters swirling up below her. She watched the old woman be taken up a set of roughly nailed stairs to a kind of room cut into the wall of the chamber. She could see men standing guard at the railing. She saw the white-haired kid turn, peer in her direction.

There. It had to be Claker Jack's office.

She herself had to be careful. Claker couldn't protect her here. Among the cutthroats and thieves in the Falls were many who hated talents, who slaughtered talents. At the high cage in the center of the Falls, she stopped. The floor within was sawdust but even still she could make out dark stains, blood. The bars were made of heavy iron. The door was toothed along one edge.

The platform was wide and rose in tiers on two sides to allow, she supposed, for spectators. She tried to see a way up into Claker's offices, where the Ficke woman had been taken. The best way maybe was just to walk up and request to see Claker Jack, she decided, like she was any exile, like she was a part of all this.

She didn't get far.

She'd ducked under a line of washing, her hood drawn low, when she felt a dark pull in her ribs, and gasped. A man in a red checked suit appeared. He wore a bank clerk's spectacles but there was no glass in them and his long whiskers were clotted with some gray matter. He looked angry.

"Oi!" he snapped, waving a rag. "What's that, then? T'ain't yours, now?"

Jeta followed his gesture. The bonebird from Nickel Street West, that had followed her to the Thames, had perched on a railing not two feet from her. She grimaced, scarcely believing it. She looked wildly up at the pigeons in the high roof, then back at the man. "No," she muttered, "it's not my—"

She tried to kick at the bonebird but it flapped and crackled out of reach. When she turned back the man was glaring at her in suspicion.

"Queer-looking bird, that," he said softly.

That was when it alighted suddenly on her shoulder, its sharp talons digging into her skin, and she twisted and reached for it but it took off again, circling.

"Why, it's a bloomin bonebird," the man whispered.

An old woman emerged around a line of washing. "Archibald! Will you bloody well look at this!"

A second man, her husband maybe, ducked his greasy face around, knife in one hand.

Jeta was shaking her head by then, starting to back away. A crowd was forming. She glanced up and saw the urchin with the white hair standing way off at the railing, peering down. The pull of everyone's bones was sickening, too strong for her. All the while the bonebird continued to try to alight upon her, as if it could not help itself. She could hear whispers all around. A chill went through her.

"A *caster*," someone whispered. "That's what she is—"

"A *bone witch*, Martha—!"

"She's one of them what come out of Cairndale—"

"—bleedin *talents*, just like Claker Jack says—"

A hand grabbed at her arm and without thinking she made a fist and felt with her mind for the ulna and cracked it cleanly. Someone cried out in agony. She saw a man step in to block her way and she held out her hands and felt a surge of pain in her own wrists. But the man's knees both split sideways and he fell heavily to the floor and she tried to get past him. But now there were too many, the pull of their bones washing over her in skull-splitting waves, and someone grabbed her from the back, pinning her arms to her sides, and someone else hit her hard on the side of the head, twice, and her vision blurred, and the last thing she saw was the bonebird in a panic above the outstretched arms of the gathering crowd, its small explosions of feather and bone as it flew back and forth.

The glyph-twisted children sat huddled inside the showman's wagon, silhouettes of stillness, each draped in a dark cloak given them by Mrs. Ficke.

Listening.

Waiting.

Their thoughts rose slowly, like bubbles in tar. *Where?* they thought. *When?* Their eyes glinted a metallic yellow, their vision weak now and catching only vague forms in the gloom. But it was with their skin they saw most clearly. Every inch of what they were was alive and prickling with sensation. Time for them was a river they could taste, time had a scent that lingered. They spoke each to each in a language that had no words and no sound but it was in the wisp of their breathing that they understood, gradually, in the way the sun slides across a sky, that they were not alone. For the human children they had been once, the talents they had been, were gone, fading like a dream badly remembered.

How long did they wait, unmoving? The air within the wagon grew warm. The wheels shifted slightly on the cobblestones as the horses shied. There had been shouts earlier, scufflings, a gunshot, but now there was only the weak red drift of daylight coming in through the stained glass, and silence. One raised her face. Another made a high noise in the back of his throat.

When?

A dark one was speaking through them, reaching for them. A true glyphic. But she was all wrong on the inside, wrapped in her own sorrows, and she was telling them a story, a story that had not yet happened. They saw a city under the city, a city ringed by falling water. Darkness, and smoke, and torches on the walls. They saw the tunnels leading in, like roots through the earth. They felt the thrump of blood in Mrs. Ficke's veins, they felt the heat of her body as she moved, alive. All this was in the web of light and web of darkness they read the world by. All this they knew and did not know. There were those with the faintest of outlines, talents once, picking their desolate way through the earth. There was blood. And they saw as one what they must do, where they must go, and only the one known as Deirdre was strong enough to resist.

She, with great effort, opened the rear door of the wagon.

Light.

Noise.

A fog had descended and thickened in the street and yet the brightness made her stagger. She came down in a slow rolling gait, down the wooden steps, into the muck of the cobblestoned street, followed by the others, seven shrunken figures in all squelching across the puddles, cloaked and cowled and quiet. There was a body lying facedown in the street nearby and as they emerged a woman with a barrow stood up from over his body, and hurried away. The body was Charlie Ovid's. Some passerby had taken his greatcoat and pocket watch and another had turned out his pockets for the coins and a third had unlaced and taken his boots. The bandages on his infected hand had unraveled and were stained. They saw the curlicues of dust whorling under his skin. There was blood all seeped up through his shirt on his back and when the children rolled him gently onto his side they could see the blood all over his front as well. One ear had been cut away and there was blood all down his neck but already they saw the bud of a new ear growing back. The cuts on his face were closing, but leaving tiny white cobwebbed scars. They could feel the wrongness in the healing; it was the corrupted dust at work.

Yet they gathered there around him in their dark brown cloaks, looking for all the world like mendicants at prayer, and laid their twisted hands upon his flesh. They began to cry softly, a sound filled with grief.

The fog parted, closed in again. Figures in the doorways of the shops watched. A man was shouting: "Hey, hey! You can't leave your horses stopped here. Get a move on!"

But all of that seemed somehow to be taking place far away, at a great remove, the human voices muffled, their movements eerie and slow. The glyph-twisted children leaned closer, their strange song rising over the body. They could feel a web of sound casting between them, fragile as moonlight. Then, all as one, ringingly, their singing ceased. The street sped up; the roar of the city came rushing in upon them; shopkeepers stepped forward, wringing their hands in their aprons, calling for police.

And Charlie Ovid, battered, bruised, opened his bloodshot eyes.

18

THE HOSPITALITY
OF LESSER MEN

Often, across the years, it had seemed to Caroline Ficke that those who had faith in a higher power, in their God, whatever form it took, were the lucky ones. Easier by far to withstand suffering, if you believed there was a shape to things.

She herself had no such illusions. Misfortune descended, then lifted, all of its own accord; she saw no purpose in it. The death of her and Edward's father, collapsed in the street. The loss of her talent, her slow ride out of Cairndale with Mr. Ficke at eighteen, Henry Berghast in silhouette at his study window watching her go. The death of her good husband, in the guest quarters of an estate in middle England, a sketch of some rare bird half-finished on the table by the window. There was no shape to any of it; it was chance and fortune, and you just faced it as best you could, and kept going.

Her brother, bless his soul, had taught her that.

And now, bloodied, sore, afraid, she stared at this infamous phantom in his lair, leaning against his desk, shabby and cold-eyed and cruel, and she accepted the roll of the dice. Charlie was probably dead, the dust not enough to heal what had been done to him. She'd seen the knives go in. And she'd felt what was in the dust, its power, and its limitations. Her poor glyph-twisted children would welter alone in the showman's wagon, turned out of it after it was seized by some salvager. Their ship at anchor in the Thames would sail without them. And she was here, with the infamous Claker Jack, helpless to do anything about it.

"You do not remember me?" he said quietly. "But I remember you. Caroline Albany, the famous beauty. What a loss, when you were sent down."

She blinked. "You were with me at—?"

"At Cairndale. Of course." He waved a dismissive hand at the three white-haired urchins. They slipped sullenly out. His red-rimmed eyes were still fixed upon her, assessing. His face was clean-shaven, the skin sallow and slack, a cluster of red sores around his mouth. "Jack. Jack Renby. I was nine years old. You, the older ones like you . . . I was in awe of you all." He permitted himself a brief smile. "I was in the courtyard that day you tried lifting the barrel, when it crushed your arm. Is that not what happened? Your strength just . . . gave out?"

"That was the beginning of its going," she said slowly, trying to think. This was unexpected. "I thought I was invincible," she added.

"Mm. I understood it later, but at the time it just seemed frightening. You were so powerful. And then, suddenly, you were . . . not." He studied her. "Caroline Albany," he murmured. "My goodness."

She didn't like the way he said it. "It is Ficke, now. It's been Ficke for fifty years."

"Ah. You married him, then. The artist."

She said nothing.

"He is passed, I presume?"

"It was long ago," she said.

"Everything was, I rather fear." His yellowing face was full of regret. "Do you know, I was glad when you were taken away. We all were. It was just too uncomfortable, catching sight of how fleeting our abilities might be." He sighed. "I thought of that day often, after my own talent started to go. Of course, my loss was less dramatic. I was a dustworker. And one day when I drew the dust to me, less came. And then less again. Eventually, none at all. Even the pain was gone. Oh, I could see everyone watching my face, I saw their expressions. I saw Berghast's expression. He was there, yes. That was when I knew."

He did not seem ferocious or terrifying. Just an old, ill man, destitute and heavy with regret. And yet Caroline knew this man—Jack Renby, the notorious Claker Jack—was both terrifying, and worse.

"Your little ones did a terrible thing to my friend," she said.

"Ah, not mine," he said. "They are agents of the Abbess. Here to see that her bidding is done. The boy was a clink at Cairndale, five years ago." He pronounced the words with a sarcastic precision, watching her face for a reaction. "Your *friend* was in possession of a stolen ring. My ring. I merely desired its safe return."

"Charlie never stole anything in his life."

"No? I wonder." Claker Jack opened his fist. She could see Charlie's ring, its leather cord pooled around it. The bands of black wood and iron sucking up the light. Then Claker Jack held up his other hand, limply. She could see an identical ring on his finger, glinting. "Which is the copy, which is the real? If you understood what I'd gone through to find this ring, to *obtain* it, then you would understand why your friend is lying in an alley even now. How did he come to have it?"

Caroline swallowed. She was suddenly afraid. "I don't know," she said.

"Ah. But I don't believe you," he replied.

Claker Jack picked up her artificial arm and turned it in his fingers and then put it back down on his desk, gently. He crossed the little stone chamber and looked out at the Falls, the roar of the waters there, his bony wrists sticking out of his cuffs. "It is an awful feeling, isn't it? Gnawing away at you. That emptiness. It is like a part of you has been cut away. Half of the exiles down there are broken by it. On the inside, I mean. The other half are simply ... empty. They fill their pain with opium and rum. But not us. We have managed our losses rather well, haven't we, Caroline?"

She glared. This man had sent the bone witch to Edinburgh. He'd ordered Charlie's death, her own kidnapping. Untold terrors onto other talents who stumbled across his exiles.

Claker Jack turned in the lantern light, hands clasped in the small of his back. "I have heard that Henry Berghast became one of us too, in the end. That even he lost his talent. I hope it caused him much pain, before he died. I expect he never ceased searching for a cure? For a way to regain his talent?"

A shadow crossed his face; his voice darkened. "Come, I am not so ill-informed. You were in Berghast's employ for decades, concocting your recipes, supplying him with ... what shall we call them? Medicines?"

"What is it you want, Mr. Renby?" said Caroline.

"The same as Berghast. To become whole again."

"That's not what I did for him," she said.

"Ah. But you sell yourself short." He held up a long crooked finger, the ring on it glinting. "I have made a study of what we are, what we were. Of talentkind. Would you like to know what I have discovered?" When she said nothing, he continued, "Consider: there is the brain, and there is the mind. There is the muscle, and there is the strength. They are one and the same. So it is with the talents. I have sought the organ in our bodies where the talents reside."

Caroline shook her head. "There is no organ for the talent."

"The spleen, I thought for a time. Perhaps the gallbladder. I conducted several studies, but the results were inconclusive. I am now of the opinion that the talent resides in a singular part of the *brain*, in the frontal lobe, a part that is not developed in non-talents. In exiles, it seems to lie dormant. Like a seed in the earth. And yet, like a seed, it can be cultivated, Caroline. With the proper . . . stimulation."

Caroline bit back her retort. "You didn't send a bone witch after us in Edinburgh, and kill Charlie, and drag me here to tell me about your *research*, Mr. Renby."

"I didn't send Miss Wajs after *you*, at all," he said quietly. "I didn't know you were involved. Yet you *are* involved. You have brought the corrupted dust into my city. My glyphic has seen truly."

His *glyphic*.

She held her breath, unsure she had heard him right. His shadow rippled across the wall. His eyes were black and chipped as basalt. He picked up her artificial arm. Then he opened a wooden door she hadn't noticed before, and stood at the edge of a darkness.

"Come," he said. "I will show you something."

She could not make out his face. She glanced back at the burly guards at the door, heard the distant roar of the Falls drifting up. She looked at her mud-stained boots.

Then she rose, grimacing at the pain in her legs, and followed.

Something was going on down below, some kind of disturbance. Micah left the one-armed woman with Claker Jack and waded down into the thick of it, the yelling and the shouting, exiles swarming over someone in the tarps.

It was a girl, not much older than he. Dark-skinned. The same he'd seen across the Falls earlier, whose glare he'd felt like a slap. And now he knew her; he'd seen her with Ruth, in the streets of Billingsgate. She'd been struck unconscious and lay in her rags and there was blood smeared over her forehead, her nose. Her patchwork dress was ripped at the shoulder.

"Tis a bleedin bone witch, Micah," said a man, still breathing hard. He doffed his hat. "Brung some cussed bird in with her, she did. It were all bones, like."

Micah poked her with one boot. A *talent*. His nostrils flared. "You're certain?"

A second man stepped forward, cradling a broken arm. "I never done this to meself, now, did I? Look at her damn fingers."

Micah regarded the angry exiles through hooded eyes, then he turned and peered down at the girl's hand. Two fingers were smooth and polished bone. He let his gaze drift off, to the roofed-in cage over the roaring waters. He'd seen Claker Jack's litch tear a man to pieces in seven seconds, once. Pull a man's tongue clean out of his mouth like unwinding a thread from a jumper. He looked back down at the girl, and spat.

They took her to a small secondary cell, in the under-tunnel. Micah was careful to pour the muting powder around the bars. Its effects wouldn't last forever; he'd seen a turner outlast it once; but it would work for as long as this one was inside. Micah had never really understood what was in that powder. He knew it was uncommon and that Claker Jack had reworked the recipe himself and that it seemed to dampen a talent's abilities for a time. There were many kinds of prison, the worst being one's own body.

Micah watched her through the bars for a while. Then he went to the far wall and crouched on his haunches to wait. She was pretty, he decided, in a sullen sort of way. He rummaged through his satchel and took out the bloodstained glove and a pair of long gardener's shears.

The girl woke. She got stiffly to her feet, limped up to the bars. She was trying to do something with her fingers, he saw. Panic came into her face.

"Go on," said Micah, grinning a slow grin, "keep at it. It won't matter.

It's sort of why you was brought here and not left out there, if you take my meaning. There's no talents in here."

The bone witch glanced sharply past him at the doorway, at the ramp leading out. She rubbed the coin at her throat. "What will they do with me?"

"They?" Micah shrugged, enjoying himself. He started slowly snipping the fingers from the glove. "*They* won't do nothing."

"Who then?"

"Ah, well. It'd be Claker Jack you'd want to worry over. But it's my mistress you'd best be frightened of. She's what tells old Claker what to do."

"No one tells Claker Jack what to do," she said quickly.

"An she's like to be wondering, for starters," he went on, ignoring this, "what's a full-grown bone witch such as yourself doing in the Falls? Was you looking for someone? Not our dearly beloved Ruth, now?"

Her face betrayed nothing.

"Oh, I seen her with you, all right. Up in Billingsgate, last year. Her dark little secret, you are. Was you up in Edinburgh with her, then? An you come all the way back to London without her?" Micah arched an eyebrow, as if waiting for her reply. "Hm? Nothing? It's no matter. We're in no hurry. Claker Jack'll be down when he's ready."

She gripped the bars, leaning her face into the firelight. "Tell him I'm here. I . . . I need to talk to him."

"Ah." Micah brightened. "About the dust, is it? You never come down into the Falls on account of *that*, I hope? You needn't have worried so. It's all taken care of. We brung it in our own selves, my sisters an me. Not even a bloody hour ago, we did."

The girl looked all around at the dark. "You had the woman with you. The Ficke woman."

He snapped his fingers at her, grinning. He liked her company. She was so . . . desperate. They were nearly the same age, by his reckoning.

He said, "You ever wagered at a rat-baiting? No? Not even just for a lark? See, at a rat-baiting, you don't wager whether the rats survive. Because they don't. No, you wager on *how long it takes* for them to be ripped to pieces. Thing is, we got our own rat-baiting tonight. I'll be taking wagers."

"You're Micah," said the girl, her eyes narrowing. "Ruth talked about you."

"Course she did. I'm right famous."

But he saw she was staring now at the bloodstained glove. He moved it casually from hand to hand and her eyes followed it. He finished cutting it to size, then put it on, wiggling his fingers. "What do you think?" he said, and winked. "I reckon it might be a better fit. A shame it come in just the one size."

"The young man you took that from," she said slowly. "Where is he?"

He grinned, wiggled his eyebrows.

"What did you do to him?"

"Oh, me an him had a *chat*, we did. Just a nice, polite chat."

The bone witch gripped the bars, lowering her voice in her anger. "You bloody idiot," she swore. "He's the one Claker Jack wants, not the old woman. You need to find him."

But Micah wasn't fool enough to listen. He knew how a person would carry on, say anything, anything at all, anything to keep their own skin, when they were about to die.

Caroline Ficke stopped at an iron grate, the glow of light ahead of her. She bit back her dread, and went in.

A long low-ceilinged chamber. There was a water outflow pouring down one wall and a channel of the filthy water was cut into the floor. Three ornate lanterns, very bright, were burning on tables along the wall.

There were two other tables, with leather straps hanging from them like tongues. Stains all over the floor and walls. It made her think of the secret room beneath Nickel Street West. A room of horrors.

Claker Jack had taken off his stovepipe hat and his forehead glistened in the orange light. Ropy strands of gray hair fell across his eyes. He'd set his hat and Caroline's artificial arm on a cluttered table beside a glass cabinet and he was watching her, a long thin sickly figure. In the cabinet were rows of specimen jars.

"Do come closer, Caroline. I do not bite."

"Where is the glyphic?"

"Ah, not here in my workshop," he said. "Watch your step. I do not often have guests."

He opened the cabinet and showed her the jars. They held human brains, spleens, gallbladders, all of them labeled and dated. Caroline had never been squeamish but she thought of the living talents who had been cut up by this man and felt a sickness in her stomach. On a second shelf were boxes of ingredients, metals, herbs. Items she knew from her own alchemical labors. She was careful to keep the table between herself and Claker Jack. And he in turn, she saw, was careful to keep her artificial arm and its long blade out of her reach.

"We have heard such . . . stories about Cairndale. Accounts that are scarcely to be believed." Claker Jack spoke with a quiet calm but there was a hunger in his yellow eyes. "I do not labor on my own behalf. Or not only. The Abbess writes me."

"She is your keeper, then?"

Claker Jack smiled. "Keeper? Ah, no. She will set me a task now and then, that is all. In return for her . . . favor. Whether I fulfill it in just the way she wishes, well . . ." He raised his mild eyebrows. "It is she who learned of Marber's corpse. That it had been recovered. She understood the nature of its dust."

"I know the Abbess."

"But do you? Do you really?" He ran a finger under each eye, as if they wept. "I have corresponded with her for thirty years, and been in her presence four times, and I would not claim to know her. She is older than Cairndale itself, Caroline. And yet she carries no years upon her person. She has lost herself to legends and books and ancient mysteries. She is not like any talent I have ever seen and yet she is not human, either. I fear her, yes. Anyone would. But I do not serve her."

Caroline said nothing.

He lifted his eyebrows. "I confess, I am more curious to know why you would bring the corrupted dust south with you. Where were you hoping to take it?"

"Why should you care, Mr. Renby? It can be of no use to you."

"What if I told you, Caroline, that I had discovered certain forgotten . . . truths? That we, as a society of talents, have done a rather poor job of preserving our heritage?" Claker Jack crossed to a small bookcase and withdrew an old, handwritten volume. He found the page he needed, and began to read: "*For the drughr is dust and not-dust both. For the drughr infects the human talent with what is and is-not. For the talent may die but the drughr may not. For the dust may die and the not-dust may not.*" He looked up at her, expectant. "Fascinating, yes? The original is in Latin, of course." He clapped the book closed, ran his yellowed fingertips lovingly over the leather. "I took it from an old talent who had just arrived in London. He'd come from a village in Bavaria, of all places. Rather an innocent, alas. He'd heard about Cairndale and wished to see its library. He came to me seeking directions."

Caroline blinked furiously. "You killed him?"

"Ah. Not because I wanted to." He opened the book again where one knuckle had marked the page. "*For the not-dust and dust are one. And the talent is the spring, and the talent is the autumn. And the drughr will bring forth the shoot.*"

"Either that is a poor translation, Mr. Renby, or you've been deceived. That sounds like bad poetry. What exactly are you trying to tell me?"

"That we are each of us the *shoot*, Caroline. And the corrupted dust is the soil and the sun. *That* is what I'm trying to explain. Jacob Marber's dust is the very thing. It will *bring back our talents*."

She stared. Somehow, he *knew*.

"Everyone doubts the new thing," he replied, mistaking her silence. "Until it is accomplished, that is."

"It would kill you, Mr. Renby," she said, suddenly sober. "It isn't a *cure*. It would draw the drughr to you, like a pikefish to blood."

"Oh, but have you not heard?" He waved a long skeletal hand, a faint smile playing at his lips. "The drughr is slain. Killed by good Henry Berghast, while Cairndale burned around him."

"It doesn't matter," Caroline said desperately. "Jacob Marber's dust was destroyed in Edinburgh, when your bone witch tried to take it. It's gone."

"Oh?"

"It's the truth."

Claker Jack's glittering eyes held her own. She could smell the rank scent in his clothes, the unwashed fug of his skin. "But not *entirely* the truth, I think. Do you know all that a glyphic can dream?"

He walked back to the table and emptied his pockets. Dumped the cord with Charlie's ring on it in a little silver dish. Then he picked up her artificial arm in his long fingers, avoiding the blade, and after a moment she heard the unmistakable click of its mechanism. The small catch slid back and opened and from the hollow behind the elbow he withdrew the little glass vial. He held it to the light.

Caroline caught her breath, afraid.

It was just the tiny pinch of corrupted dust she had managed to extract from Charlie's flesh—only the faintest, smallest amount—and yet even still, in Claker Jack's hands, the vial glowed with a quick flickering blue light.

"Don't try to use it," she said quickly. "Mr. Renby—"

"All my life," he replied, "I have been misjudged, according to my appearance and circumstance." The blue shine flickered over his features. "But I am more than that, Caroline. As are you. We are more than we are imagined to be."

Charlie Ovid was bloody hard to kill. That was the truth of it.

Most of his life he'd hated it. It just hurt like hell, and left him worse off than before. But there were times—he thought grimly, wiping the blood from his face, leaning into the reins of the old showman's wagon—times when it was *damned useful*.

Like right now.

He rode with little Deirdre, burrowed in her brown cloak, beside him. The others were in the house of the wagon, working their strange magic. His infected skin was still sore to the touch from whatever it was Mrs. Ficke had tried to do. He could feel the dust crawling there, inside his flesh, slowly repairing his injuries. One of his eyes had been kicked half-shut and wasn't focusing quite right. His left ear had been carved from his bloody head, for God's sake, but a new nub of an ear was already forming. His balance was somehow confused. He'd been stabbed in the back and stabbed all up and down his ribs and one of the blades had gone in dangerously close to his stomach lining so that he had to press his bad elbow up against the flesh to keep it from separating. The worst of it was already healed but the healing was wrong, and left slender white scars where the skin stitched itself together. But he was alive. Alive, and angry. Those little bastards. They'd taken Mrs. Ficke—he was sure of it—and the only thing they'd made a mess of was not making sure he was dead.

Because he'd found Alice's revolver. It had been kicked behind the wheel of the wagon and when he turned the horses with difficulty he saw it lying there in a puddle the color of molten steel and he got back down to retrieve it. Then they rode north away from St Katharine's Dock, rolling bumpily over the cobblestones, his wounds on fire with each bump, just as quick as the traffic would allow.

Because that was the other thing, the strangest part of it all. The glyph-twisted children, helpless in Mrs. Ficke's telling, unable to speak, seemingly lost inside themselves, had somehow *revived* him—and not only that, but now they were guiding him where he needed to go. He didn't understand it. Mrs. Ficke had told him, during their long ride south, that they were malformed glyphics. It had made no sense to him at the time. Now it did. Little Deirdre, beside him on the driver's bench, would turn her gnarled hand where it lay in her lap, just slightly, to indicate which direction Charlie ought to go. While the others in the back made their strange soft keening, like a dirge.

"This way?" Charlie would mutter, at each new alley or lane. "Did Mrs. Ficke come this way?"

And Deirdre would brush his arm, face hidden in her brown cowl, and Charlie'd fill with a sudden warm feeling of certainty: *Yes. Go. That way. Go.*

They stopped at a ruined court, under a crumbling tenement, the slow creep of fog pressing in around them. When Charlie got down and leaned up against the side of the wagon, his fingertips came away black with soot. The air was bad. He looked at Deirdre.

"Here?" he said, looking across at a darkened doorway. "You're sure it's here?"

The girl made no response. Grimacing with the pain, he lifted the girl carefully down and took her around to the back of the wagon and opened the door.

"I need all of you to wait here," he said. "Be safe. I'll get Mrs. Ficke out. And then we'll find that ship."

He swallowed. Their shining yellow eyes were fixed on him, unblinking.

"Don't look at me like that," he said. "I'll figure something out."

He took a moment to fumble with his revolver, reloading the chambers. It was difficult with only the one hand. His shirt was torn and loose and he had no shoes. He entered the doorway and followed a passage down and came to a turning and stood listening. He could hear faint sounds to his left. He went on. At each turning, he caught sounds and noises and continued deeper into the earth. Finally he came around a corner and a massive shaggy figure detached itself from the shadows and looked him over, a guard.

Charlie tensed. But whatever the man saw—a broken black boy, destitute, shoeless, badly beaten—must have satisfied him, for the guard just grunted and stepped back into the darkness.

And Charlie continued around a corner, and came out at the edge of the Falls.

19

IN THE CELLS

Someone came to Jeta's cell with a bowl of brown sludge, a spoon sticking out of it. She didn't eat. The bruises from her encounter at St Giles' were receding but still it hurt to move her face.

Later someone brought a bottle of ale. That she drank greedily, wiped at her mouth. The bottle, she thought, might be useful.

Later yet two men came and took the bowl and spoon and bottle away.

She sat on a bed of straw, her head between her knees. She could hear something, a kind of low moaning, from elsewhere. Her cell was one of three, the others empty, all on the leftmost side of a brick tunnel that curved away into darkness. The moaning came from that darkness. She didn't know what it could be.

At last he came down and stood at the bars staring in at her, sickly, frail-looking, the man she had come to find, the man she'd learned to trust, the man who had kept her safe all these years. Claker Jack wore a mismatched black suit, with stains on his collar. She clenched her fists, feeling for some pull—*any* pull—from his bones. But it felt as if a wet towel were wrapped around her skull, muffling her talent. In the poor light Claker Jack looked different from how she'd seen him before, he looked like an ashman or slop collector. But then he took off his hat, laying his long yellow fingers across his scalp, and she saw the man she'd known and come to love, and she shivered.

"Oh, child," he said at last, enunciating slowly. "What were you thinking? You were never to come here. Now Micah has seen you. They have all seen you. A *talent*. In *the Falls*."

"Ruth is dead," she said.

"Ah," he said softly, unmoved. "You came to tell me this? I sent you to recover the dust and you failed me, Jeta."

"Ruth failed you. Not me."

"Oh? So you have the dust, then?"

She shook her head. "But I know how to find it." She told him then about the mortuary in Edinburgh, and the cathedral in the rain, and how she'd confronted the young man Charlie and tried to take the drughr's dust from him. She told about being struck in the head, and the sudden obliterating roar as the dust hit her. "I *tried*," she said, hating the look of disappointment in his face. "I *tried*, I *did*. But it was like suddenly I could feel every bone all around me, inside of me . . ." She shuddered. "When I woke up, he was gone. I went to the Ficke woman's residence, but she'd fled. I followed them here, to London."

"You followed them . . . *here*."

She nodded. "The Ficke woman's in your offices, even now. I know it; I saw her come in. But she won't have the drughr's dust. She never did."

Claker Jack's shoes scraped on the stone. "She says it was destroyed, all but a tiny amount. Is she lying?"

Jeta rattled the bars of the cell. "Will you unlock this? I'd rather not talk through a cell door."

"Ah. But then, who would?"

Jeta went suddenly still. He made no move to free her. She remembered Micah's snarling little face, his sinister grin. Rat-baitings, he'd been talking about.

"Tell me about this young man from the cathedral," whispered Claker Jack, leaning in closer. "You are saying the dust is not destroyed?"

Her blood slowed. She told him then, haltingly, about the apparition of the little dark-haired boy. How she'd encountered him in the ruins at Cairndale, one of the spirit dead, and how he'd stalked her at the mortuary. She explained how he needed the dust himself to find peace, to cross back over into the land of the dead. She told how he was able to sense the dust, how he'd led her to St Giles', and to Charlie Ovid, who'd struck her. "Charlie's the one who has the dust. He's the one we need to find. Micah left him for dead in the streets when he took Ficke, but he won't be there now, he'll have vanished."

"Ovid? That is his name? You're certain?" She could see the anger in Claker Jack's jaw, as he sawed his teeth back and forth. But his voice was still soft, calm. "And this apparition can find him? It can sense the dust?"

She nodded. "It's more like he *smells* it. The dust has a . . . taste."

Claker Jack turned aside and ran his fingers along his chin. She'd been afraid he'd doubt the truth of her account but he didn't seem fazed by it. "And is he here, now?"

She bit her lip. "No."

"A strange ability, for one of the spirit dead. Curious that Ruth's telegrams did not mention any Charlie, nor any apparition."

"She didn't know. I didn't tell her."

"You have given me much to think about. I thank you." Claker Jack, all regretfulness, turned to leave.

"Wait, Claker—" she said. "You can't just *leave* me. Unlock the door. Please."

He peered in at her. She saw the lines at his eyes, the red sores at his mouth. Something shifted in his expression. "Ah. But you have been seen. I can do nothing."

"What . . . what do you mean?" she asked slowly. "What will happen to me?"

"You will be sent to the cages, child," he said, his voice softening. "You will stand against a litch, and be ripped to pieces. They will demand it."

Jeta looked at the old man in slow understanding. A *litch*. A horrified attentiveness took hold in her. She rubbed at the coin at her throat. She'd heard stories of litches, terrible stories.

"Why?" she said in soft disbelief. "Why? I . . . I've done everything for you. You said I was like a daughter to you. I . . . I *loved* you."

The old man's pupils were black. "Love?" he whispered.

He curled his fists around the bars, sweetly, gently, so that he was only a few inches from Jeta herself, and she saw the heavy ring he wore, with the crest of crossed hammers. "What is love, to a litch? To a litch that has lost its master? A litch cannot live after its master has died; but if its master becomes an exile, one of those you saw out there? Then it lives on, alone, separated from its maker, in pain." His pale tongue moistened his lips; his greasy face was very close to the bars. "I believe it is love that keeps the litch alive, but also love that makes it go mad."

"Let me out!" she said suddenly. She gripped the bars. "Please! Don't do this."

Claker Jack ran his tongue over his teeth. He looked down at her a long moment before he answered. "My mother always said, *Look into the face of the man what kills you. Know him, Jack.*" There was an unexpected sadness in his face. But his voice was clear and cold. "Look into my face, Jeta Wajs. You are nothing to me. You were always nothing."

Then he turned, and left Jeta in the shadowed cell.

She crushed her forehead against the bars. When she looked up at last, she saw, in the darkness, the blue flickering visage of the ghost child. He had come, after all. He watched Jeta with his face quiet, his eyes dark.

I'm so sorry, he whispered, small.

. . .

All that while, Caroline Ficke was left in the keeping of the little white-haired girls, the sisters.

They were sullen and small and vicious. She was afraid of their intentions. She thought of her own little ones, alone in that wagon near the docks, abandoned, most likely discovered by now. And Charlie, maybe dead. She thought of her brother, in the quiet chandler's shop back in Edinburgh, how deeply he loved the children. She thought of his face, trying to explain to him what happened. She could not bear it.

The girls took her out into the smoky roar of the Falls and crossed a swaying rope bridge and led her up an iron ladder to a brick tunnel. The climbing was hard. The smallest—Timna—lit a bull's-eye lantern and led her to a metal door. Inside, Caroline was given a bowl of scummy water and a rag and told to wash. The second urchin tried to clean some of her cuts but Caroline smacked her hand away. The child smacked Caroline back, hard, on the side of her head, but otherwise left her alone. They brought her a bowl of porridge, a mug of watered-down ale. She was surprised at how hungry she was.

Time passed. They led her back.

"Ah, you look refreshed," said Claker Jack, rising from his desk in his stained suit. "Thank you, Timna, Prudence. That will do."

Whatever had called him away had troubled him; Caroline could see it in the deep groove between his brows. She was trying to think of how to get away, to retrace her steps and find her glyph-twisted children. She'd seen no opportunity yet.

"Come, Mrs. Ficke," Claker Jack called, passing again through the wooden door into darkness. "I promised you a glyphic. Watch your step, now."

The water was pouring down the long wall, runnelling through the drainage-cut in the flagstones. He led her past one table with its straps and buckles dangling ominously, stopping at a second to take off his jacket, roll back his shirtsleeves. The surface was cluttered with jars and glass beakers and ancient books.

She studied the table before her with interest. He was preparing a kind of serum. She saw iron powder, a dish of liquid mercury. Shavings of basalt. Turquoise powder. There was a small bottle of amber liquid which she didn't recognize.

"Patience, Mrs. Ficke," he said with a little smile. "It is nearly prepared. One of the benefits of a well-stocked alchemical cabinet."

"You are determined to try it, then. You will use it on yourself?"

"Well. You did not bring me much. It would hardly do to restore another's talent, would it? Yours, for instance. But it is a risk . . ."

He led her to a second door at the rear of the chamber. Claker Jack brought in a lantern. Caroline's eyes, adjusting gradually, took in a wall of slimy pipes, old machinery long out of use. Filling almost the entire floor was a low stone cistern, some reeking muck visible within.

At once Claker Jack stirred his fingers through the muck, and where they trailed a faint blue shining followed in their wake. The muck began to move of its own accord.

"This—?" Caroline whispered, despite herself. "Your glyphic is—"

"Yes," he nodded. "Mrs. Ficke, I'd like you to meet Miss Laqueur."

The muck was shifting, clumping, falling away. Caroline stepped forward, fascinated despite herself. "What's the matter with her? Is she all right?"

"What is the matter with any of us? Time. Grief. Choices made and not made. She was delivered to me in a barrel from a vessel whose crew had been struck down by illness. A *barrel*. Imagine it."

But Caroline was scarcely listening. Slowly, thickly, the glyphic rose up, a lumpen foul-smelling column of soft muck, melting and shimmering in the lantern light. A column of brown matter, very still, without shape or resemblance to anything. It rose up until it loomed over both

Caroline and Claker Jack, just shy of the ceiling, and there it hung, suspended. She stared up at it, unable to speak.

"Show her," Claker Jack commanded.

Caroline tensed. But the glyphic did nothing; in the weird shadows cast by that lantern it remained silent, still, like a feature of the earth, like a thing that had always been there. And yet something was happening, like a light appearing at the back of Caroline's mind, a faint glow that grew brighter. She saw a girl in a field of flowers, a long parade of torches in a village square. She saw an ancient body pulled out of a bog, under skies the color of beaten metal. She felt an immense sadness, a weariness the likes of which she'd never in all her own long life known. Grief. The gravestones of those she'd loved. A long lonely silent time, without ceasing. A night sky wherein the stars were crushed out, one by one, until only blackness remained—

And then all of it was subsumed by a vision of gray dampness, water dripping softly, a world submerged under its own rank decay. And she saw in the gloom something moving, antlered figures, silhouetted, though she could not make out their number.

"She wishes for release," Claker Jack interrupted. There was an edge to his voice. "As do we all."

Caroline sagged backward, ripped from the dream. Her heart was loud in her chest. The glyphic sank back down into its tank, a few small bubbles rising sluggishly to the surface.

"Did she show you her grief? Ah. But Miss Laqueur is not here because it pleases *her*. She has her purpose. And what did you see, Miss Laqueur? What does Mrs. Ficke know of the remaining dust?"

Then, to Caroline's horror, the mud began to reshape itself in the low glow of the lantern. She saw herself, leaning over Charlie in the basement of Nickel Street West, trying to extract the corruption. Except Charlie's face was smooth, featureless, like a mask. The mud fell apart, reformed. Now she saw the wagon in the street near the docks. Charlie was sprawled on the setts where he'd fallen, where the boy Micah had stabbed him, but again his face was missing, his features smoothed out as if with a trowel.

"What is this rubbish?" Claker Jack demanded. "Show me his *face*."

But the surface of the glyphic just rippled, fell still. It either could not, or would not.

Claker Jack swore. He swept up the lantern. "That is the boy whom Micah cut up and left? The boy, what is his name—*Charlie*? Of course it is. I am tolerant, and tolerance breeds incompetence." He swung around to face her, the lantern held high. "Damn the Abbess. He was carrying the rest of the dust, I presume. Was it *in* his person?"

Caroline's head was still buzzing from the glyphic. She said nothing.

He did not press the matter, not then. He just led her back, past the tables, the lanterns, the channel of water in the floor, through the passage to his office. He brought her to the railing of his balcony, the smoke and roar of the Falls all around her. Micah and his hateful sisters were lounging idly by. Something was happening at the cage far below.

"You!" he barked at them. "You left the boy in the street. *He* had the dust, you imbeciles."

They stared at him, silent, furious, but wary enough not to protest.

"Tell me, Mrs. Ficke," he said, rounding on her, his voice softening with difficulty. "What was in the wagon? Did you and this boy come to London with any other? Don't tell me it was just the two of you, in such a contraption, on your way to the docks?"

Caroline felt a new kind of fear go through her. She tried to focus her thoughts.

"It was just us," she whispered.

20

THE LITCH'S HEART

They came for Jeta, six men, powerfully built, and they dragged her struggling out of the cells and up toward the cage. After the quiet gloom below, the Falls roared with sound and movement. The crowds parted as she came up, faces jeering, and then she was being thrust into the large iron enclosure, and the door swung shut on its rusting hinges, and the bolt was shot through. She stood peering through it, her heart horrified, her ears ringing yet with Claker Jack's words. *You are nothing to me. You were always nothing.*

Lock after lock was secured in place.

She turned slowly. Crowds on all sides, shouting, jostling. Faces filled with a vicious hunger.

On the far side of the cage was a tunnel, long and straight, leading out across the rushing waters to a heavy iron door. It stood closed. Jeta balled her hands up into fists; her despair gave way to anger.

The litch would come from there. Claker Jack's *pet* would come from there.

She couldn't feel the pull of bones. It was a kind of blessing, maybe, with so many around. The muting powder in the cells below had helped with that, at least. But there was something else, a faint pressure at the back of her skull. She knew what it was: her talent, rising sluggishly in her. If she could live long enough here in the cage, her bone talent would come rushing back.

That was when she saw, in a rack beside the door, the weapons.

So. They wanted to make sport of it after all.

She walked slowly over, studying the blades. They were old forged objects, chipped, scoured. A sword, a serrated pike, a spear on an eight-foot-long shaft. An axe, with a long light handle and a wide blade.

She picked up the axe, her heart loud in her chest.

All at once the crowds went suddenly, terribly silent. She raised her face. The iron door at the far end was opening; ropes on pulleys were straining, working the door wider.

Jeta swallowed, adjusted her grip on the axe. There was darkness beyond, and in the darkness some long, thin, pale thing was moving. Stillness.

"Come on, then," she whispered.

Then, like a spell breaking, the crowds erupted, surging forward for a clearer view.

Charlie was crushed up against a barrel, half-hidden on a damp platform high over the Falls, wincing in pain, when the girl was brought out.

He knew her at once.

He was bloodied and light-headed, his clothes were in rags, and yet he knew her. The girl from St Giles', the girl who'd broken the little bones in his hand, in his wrist, taking a malevolent pleasure in it. The girl with the bone fingers. He stood barefoot in a filthy puddle, with the blood from his savaged ear all down his collar and into his clothes, the corrupted dust already healing him, stitching him painfully together, and he tried to make sense of what he was seeing.

It was a fighting pit, of course. He'd known such stages when he was a boy in the barn fights in Mississippi. The girl had been locked into a cage on a central platform, suspended over the thundering waters. But she was alone. Crowds were shouting and jeering all around. He watched her pick a weapon from a rack on the wall—an axe, it was—and then she turned in place, as if studying the faces.

He couldn't make sense of it. What she could be doing there, why she would be fighting for sport. There were few things in this life he'd come to fear, but this girl was one of them. He ran his hand over his eyes, wiping away the sweat. The strange tattoos were writhing and crawling under his skin. And then he looked across the gap again.

He'd been watching Mrs. Ficke and the man ever since they'd appeared at the railing. It looked to him like she didn't have her artificial arm. Why they would take her, yet leave him for dead, he couldn't imagine. She had lived a long life of secrets and he knew so little of it that he understood—grimly, without self-pity—that this, too, was likely one part of a long feud which he'd walked unwittingly into. He let his gaze slide to the urchins with the white hair, on the stair below the balcony. As for them? He'd drown the lot of them.

Well. Maybe just scare them a little.

Thing was, he was trying to think how he could get Mrs. Ficke out. He was in no shape to fight. He'd be lucky if he could just run. He had Alice's revolver but it would be no use against so many. There were big men on the balcony, and that tall man in the stovepipe hat, gesturing. He would be the one, Charlie knew. He would be the key to all of it.

The crowds below fell silent. A metal door had opened at the end of the caged-in passage. Charlie saw the girl crouch suddenly, her axe held at the ready. Something stirred at the end of the passage; and then all at once the crowds erupted into a frenzy of shouting, and cheering. Charlie glimpsed teeth, long pale limbs, something red and shining at a throat as the thing scrabbled forward, impossibly fast, banging its way up along the sides and ceiling of the caged passage, rocketing toward the girl.

He started to shake. He couldn't help himself, he was just shaking, shaking out of pure fear. Because he knew what it was.

A litch.

A damned *litch*.

The metal door behind it slammed shut. From the height where he watched he could see the ropes on their pulleys controlling it, he could see where they vanished into the rooms below. A moment later two men in shirtsleeves and leather aprons came hurrying up one of the ramps, afraid to miss the fight.

Faintly, from someplace deep inside his fear, an idea began to take shape.

Everything was just a blur. The cage was rattling and shaking and Jeta saw the pale thing hurtling up toward her, leaping from wall to wall and along the ceiling of the passage, the bars shivering under its power.

A *litch*, for God's sake. Claker's own *litch*.

Move! she told herself. *Run!* But her legs were slow to react. One part of her brain had turned animal, was all instinct and fear. But a second part—a deeper, slower part—seemed to be narrating all that was happening. *What would Ruth say to see you now?* it asked her. *She'd say I told you so. She'd say Claker never thought of you as anything but a weapon because how could he, look at you, what are you? This is why you don't just trust anyone, not the man who'd rescue you from a hateful world, not his procurer, not a bloody ghost child come to you in the ruins of—*

Thinking all this in a flash, as all the while the litch rocketed up toward her. It exploded through the opening, launching itself across the cage, clawed hands outstretched as if to tear open Jeta's throat. She swung the axe, her body dropping sideways. But the litch twisted, somehow, in midair—

And her axe passed through the space where the litch had been.

But as it hurtled past, it reached out one long claw, and hooked the haft of Jeta's weapon, and plucked it—so gently, as if taking it from a child—out of her hands. Then it spun off sideways, the axe in its grip.

Jeta was knocked to the floor. It had all taken maybe three seconds, and already she'd lost her first weapon. The crowds were roaring. The weapons rack was behind her and she backed up and pulled down the long spear and swung it whistling through the air.

Now she could see the creature clearly. It was crouched on the far side of the cage, hairless. It seemed very old. Its slack breasts overhung its ribs, its collarbone stood out stark under its gray skin. Three red lines at its throat, like a twisted necklace. It held the axe high near the blade, balanced on one thigh, and it studied Jeta.

There was more animal than human in what crouched across from her. Its black eyes were dull with pain and hunger. Its nostrils flared as it took in all the scents around. When it opened its mouth, slowly, Jeta saw the long needlelike teeth. There were too many teeth, she thought.

There was something else, too. A pressure in the back of her head, as if an enormous hand were crushed against the base of her skull.

Her *talent*.

Her talent was coming back.

But not quickly enough. The litch rose fluidly to its feet and sidestepped a thrust of Jeta's spear and skittered spiderlike up the wall of the cage and across the ceiling, too fast to follow. It dropped behind Jeta, almost before she could turn. The spear was too long. As the litch came down, it drew one long sharp claw down Jeta's back, as if undoing a zipper, and Jeta felt her skin unseam itself.

She screamed. She whirled around, dragging the long spear sparking over the floor of the cage. But the litch already had slipped back, to the edge of the cage, out of reach.

Jeta was gasping, feeling around clumsily at her back for the wound. It was not deep. Her clothes hung strangely and her blood was hot and seeping there. She clenched her fists, willing her talent to rise up. The litch had turned its back on her, as if she was nothing, and she saw how it stared up at the balcony where Claker Jack and the old Ficke woman stood, watching. She saw how it looped both its clawed hands into the cage. She felt the quiet stillness in it. She knew its longing.

And then just as suddenly it had turned and bared its teeth at her and again was clambering along the outer wall of the cage, racing toward her. Jeta was learning its speed, was ready this time, and yet even still it came so fast it was all she could do to raise the spear in front of her, like a bar, and push at the litch as it threw itself toward her.

When it collided, she was surprised at how light it was, how bone-less. The shaft of the spear smacked its ribs, sending the litch through the air. And yet it wasn't fazed; it just reached its two long claws, almost lazily, up to Jeta's shoulders as it swung past, and raked its fingers down the flesh of both her arms. She grunted in agony. Blood poured out; her sleeves were in ribbons.

She knew then the creature was toying with her. Some in the crowd were throwing things against the cage, the bars rattling. She'd dropped the spear. She started to back up again, seeking the rack of weapons, but her legs were slow now, tired.

Across the cage the litch rose up again, watching her. She sensed nothing in it, neither pleasure nor triumph. It stood unmarked, uninjured.

It came at her before she could reach the rack, before she could do anything more than throw her arms in front of her, catching the litch's wrists in her grip. She tumbled backward, fell hard, and the litch was on her in a moment, its knees pinning her down, its teeth biting the air.

And suddenly, like a sluice bursting wide, her talent came flooding over her in great thick waves of pain, and she felt the hiss and pull of the bones all around her, living and dead, and yet somehow still she held on, still she kept the litch from tearing her into pieces. There were tears leaking down the sides of her face; her sliced back where it was grinding into the floor was on fire.

And she summoned her talent, poured it through her bloodied arms, and with everything she had she willed the litch's skull to crumple in on itself, she willed every little bone in its chest to splinter and drive inward toward its heart, she willed that damned monster to *die*.

The litch just leaned in closer, scrabbling with its claws, hissing.

Jeta was sobbing with the effort. She couldn't do it, it was as if the creature's bones were slippery, somehow, and she just couldn't get a firm grasp of them. It dipped very close, so that its hot breath was in her face, a long line of spittle shivering there, its needlelike teeth getting closer, closer to her throat. Its skin was dry, papery. Jeta fought with all her strength, kicking out, thrashing there, but the litch kept her pinned fast and it was all she could do to hold its wrists back, to keep its claws from her throat.

And somewhere deep inside her belly a guttural sound rose up, animallike, a fury of terror and rage and helplessness. She didn't *want* to die, not like *this*—

The litch's jaws snapped nearer, nearer.

Jeta crushed her eyes shut, and screamed.

In that same moment, in the dripping tunnels that wound under the streets of London, six figures shuffled forward in the shadows. They moved with a slow, hunched, rolling gait. They went cloaked and silent, two by two, like monks in a procession of dark piety.

The seventh, the strongest among them, the glyph-twist known as

Deirdre, had stayed behind. Only she had been able to resist what called to them.

For the dark glyphic was singing to them, summoning them onward. They'd left the ancient showman's wagon, left it as they had been warned not to do, left it in a ruined court with the rear door standing wide and the horses in their traces likely to be stolen. They were seeking the drainage tunnels that led toward the Falls, vast swift currents of sludge and runoff. In their minds unspooled an image, a memory of a thing not yet happened, a memory shared between them, carried with great gentleness. *The waters*, it said to them. *The sluices. Go.*

A city below the city. It was in their minds, a ripple in the talent world. Filthy water thundering down into a vast drain, far below. Men and women in ragged clothes, fleeing in fear. Three vast stone and steel barriers, high in the thick walls, crumbling.

All this.

And also poor Charlie Ovid, in pain, perched above the rising flood. And dear Mrs. Ficke, who loved them, her dress torn and spattered, her careworn eyes full of fear.

And so they moved forward, with a steady deliberate strength, and when they reached a branching in the tunnel they did not hesitate but together pried the iron grating from the stone with the strength of roots, and two of them went that way. And when the remaining four reached a second branching, two others took that route, also. There was muck and grime smeared all over their cloaks, by then. Their yellow eyes glowed in the darkness. The tunnels widened, the foul waters running more swiftly.

The roar of the Falls grew louder.

They shuffled on.

Charlie was limping painfully along the outer edges of the crowd when he heard the girl in the cage scream. It carried even over the roaring and cheering. He didn't stop. He thought of her in the cathedral, the flicker of loneliness in her. Then he remembered the look in her eyes as she snapped his fingerbones.

Don't fool yourself, Charlie Ovid, he thought sharply. *There's two monsters in that cage.*

He hurried along the railing and onto a rope bridge that spanned the whirlpool below. He could see where the waters whorled faster into the vast central darkness, where they were sucked down into the earth and the labyrinth of sewage tunnels beyond. Waterfalls of foul matter were thundering down the walls around him from vast sluices overhead—a redirected river, the overflow from the tannery yards, the filth of tens of thousands of citizens. By God it stank.

Charlie held his breath, hurried on.

He was still shaking with fear. No one stopped him, no one questioned him. Alice's revolver tugged heavily in one pocket but he didn't need it. Nearly everyone had gathered at the cage. He hunched his shoulders to hide his face and forced himself to go slow as he neared the place he'd seen, the arched doorway the two men had come out of. Beyond lay a dimly lit tunnel. There were cells here, all empty—three of them—and Charlie hurried around a corner. There he found a man, a guard in a tanner's apron, seated on a low stool against one wall. He had his arms crossed over a bottle of stout and he looked up in surprise.

Charlie didn't hesitate; he hit the man hard, hit him like he'd been born a fighter in the barns in Mississippi, and the man's mouth exploded in blood and spit and he fairly flew off his stool into the muck and lay unmoving.

There was a lever of some kind on the wall, attached to a wheel, and he could see the mechanism of pulleys and ropes leading overhead to what must be the metal door. He made himself take the time to understand it, how it worked. The cell itself was low-ceilinged and filthy and Charlie could see the dead bodies of rats smeared along the floor.

The cell door itself was locked. That wouldn't do. He needed to draw the litch back this way, let it find its freedom and cross the rope bridge and set the whole bloody under-city into panic.

That was his plan, at least. He fumbled a ring of keys from the man he'd punched and he unlocked the litch's cell. His knuckles were bloodied, but already beginning to heal. He stood the door wide. Then he walked to the far end and peered up at the metal door. He could hear the crowds. That would be it; that would be the passage out. He went back, stepped over the guard, reached for the lever on its wheel.

And paused. What would he do if it worked? He hadn't thought of that. The litch would come ripping through here and would carve Charlie himself into pieces, first thing. Would the dust that was in him now be enough to heal him from it?

Maybe.

He allowed himself a bitter smile. Komako wouldn't approve. Of course, she'd never accused him of thinking a thing through too deeply. Ribs, on the other hand, would already have the door open.

Just let it work, he thought. *Just let the litch see the door's open. Just let it get loose.*

And then he threw his poor, aching body against the lever, leaving bloodied handprints where he gripped it, and with everything he had left, he cranked the wheel.

21

Rising Waters

Caroline squeezed the wooden railing hard, feeling its splinters prick her hand.

That was *a litch* down there.

And squared off against it in that cage was Claker Jack's bone witch, the girl who'd assaulted Charlie at St Giles'. Claker Jack said nothing. He leaned beside Caroline, his thin body thrumming with intensity, and yet she knew it, knew it with certainty; she saw the strange mosaic of the girl's dress and the thick black braids and the coin flashing at her throat, and she knew. Why his bone witch would be here, caged, Caroline couldn't guess. What kind of a man would do such a thing, to one of his own?

The girl stumbled, faltered, lashed out; an axe was ripped from her hands.

Caroline held her breath, rapt. It wasn't fear or pity she felt, not exactly. And she was too far away to see the fight clearly. Not through all the smoke, not through all the bodies moving in excitement around the cage. And yet at one point she saw the gray creature rise up at the bars, and grip them tightly, and stare up at Claker Jack himself, almost with a kind of longing.

"You keep a litch, Mr. Renby" was all she said. "For your own amusement, then?"

He smoothed back his greasy hair. His hands, she saw, were ropy with veins and his fingernails were black with dirt. He spoke softly so that only she could hear. "Not for my *amusement*, Mrs. Ficke. For my . . . penance. She is not what she was. But this," and he touched with two fingers the pocket where the corrupted dust was kept, "will do more than bring my talent back. It will bring her back, too."

Caroline took a breath, suddenly understanding. "*You* made her?"

He inclined his head. "I was six years old when she died of fever. Or nearly died. I . . . *made* her, as you say. As she once made me. And when I was taken up to Cairndale, she followed. I kept her a secret, in the tunnels below the manor. For years in the night I would sneak down under the kitchens to be with her. And when I was sent away . . . she followed again. Here, into London. But when a litch's master loses his talent, he loses control of his litch as well. She does not die—the bond between them is too strong—but she does not simply obey her maker's commands, either. I have kept her here because I cannot bear to do otherwise." His eyes were dark in their sockets. It was almost like he was speaking to himself. "What is left of her, in there? Is there anything that knows her son now?"

Caroline was stunned. "She's your *mother*?"

He looked at her. "My mother. Yes."

"Oh, Mr. Renby."

But he was watching the creature below with a mixture of disgust and sorrow. Something had changed in him. He'd grown more focused, more calm. "There are those who matter to us, though they shouldn't. We cannot help who we love."

Caroline nodded at the white-haired children on the stairs, lurking, sullen. "Do they know?"

"The Abbess knows. Has she told them?" He shrugged. "Who can say?"

"The corrupted dust will kill you, Mr. Renby," she said, trying one last time. "It is not what you think it is. It will not bring your mother back to you. It will only draw the drughr to you, and be your death."

"Well. We shall find out soon enough. Micah," he called, in a liquid voice. "See that I am not disturbed."

The urchin raised his face, nodded sullenly.

Claker Jack turned toward her, taking her elbow almost like a gentleman. But then Caroline ground her teeth hard. His bony fingers dug painfully into the soft meat of her arm.

"My lady," he said softly.

Jeta was screaming.

She thrashed and swung her weight from side to side but she couldn't dislodge the litch. Its needlelike teeth snapped at her throat. Her own teeth were bared in a rictus of fury.

But then, suddenly—the litch lifted its face. It peered back, down the caged-in passage, its nostrils flaring. Jeta was still gasping, struggling. The crowds were a faint buzz of noise; the air was dense with smoke.

And then it was gone, leaping lightly away, leaving Jeta scrambling backward on all fours to the cage edge and sobbing and shaking. Her hands were bloodied and left smears on the floor. Her foot had kicked aside the axe and she grabbed it now and held it in front of her. She was looking wildly for the monster but she couldn't see it; it had vanished.

Slowly, she got to her feet. She was aware that the mood of the crowd had shifted; and she stumbled forward, and peered down the long caged-in passage, and saw the thick metal door standing open. Beyond it lay darkness. She held the axe low at her side, exhausted, and turned in place, and then she stared again at the metal door, not understanding. Was the fight over? Had someone called off the litch? Had Claker—?

No, she thought bitterly. *Not that.*

Her talent was surging through her, her veins on fire, and she could feel the millions of bones in the bodies all around her, slick, thrumping with blood, pushing on her skull and making it hard to think. She drew a bloody hand across her eyes. Her bone fingers gleamed.

Stillness descended.

Gradually, out of her exhaustion, she became aware that something was happening. She took an unsteady step forward, peering through the bars. Some sort of commotion. She saw two burly men in leather aprons, each gripping clubs, disappear toward the cells. She could sense the crowd's uncertainty. Some at the edges, nearest where the guards had disappeared, began to peel away.

All at once, explosively, there came a terrible rending sound, unlike anything Jeta had heard; one of the men in aprons stumbled to the edge of the ramp, and then the man just seemed to burst apart, like a wet sack of blood, as something large carved through his torso and passed clean out the other side, hurtling up the swaying rope bridge, into the gathered onlookers outside the cage.

It was the litch.

Loosed. Drenched now in blood and gore, carving a ferocious path through the crowd.

The exiles were screaming. Jeta staggered backward, back toward the long, caged-in passage. At the far end, the scarred metal door was still open.

Something dark and fine sprayed the bars of the cage.

Jeta hesitated only a second. She dropped the axe, and ran.

·   ·   ·

Micah saw the litch explode outward, into the gathered crowds, scattering them like pigeons. For a moment he didn't understand what he was seeing.

The jeering below turned to screams. Micah was standing halfway down the sagging stair, watching the blood-covered figure of the litch leap and carve and spin its way deeper, away from the cells, over the roaring waters, into the fleeing exiles. Claker Jack had just taken the one-armed woman back inside; he wouldn't know what was happening. Micah started to go inside, then hesitated.

The two guards in their red waistcoats had stepped forward, eyes narrowed at the disturbance.

Micah's eye too tracked the litch's path. Suddenly he understood. The creature was making its way toward the stair, toward Claker Jack's offices. Toward *them*.

She hungers for me, the old man had said earlier.

Micah had no intention of getting in the way of a bloody litch. Claker Jack had ordered him to stay put but that was before the litch got free. But then his eye caught a second movement, slow, shuffling *against* the crowd, a figure limping and dragging itself along in the litch's wake. Dressed in rags and shoeless, hands bloodied. A tall black kid. He was making his solitary way across the rope bridges, stumbling over the torn bodies, finding a back route, making for the stair also.

Micah felt a heat rise to his face. He'd killed the son of a bitch dead. He was sure of it. It had to be the dust that bone witch of Ruth's had been on about, keeping him somehow upright. *Well an how upright can he stay if his head gets cut clean off?* Micah wondered. Then he thought about it. It was like a bloody gift, wasn't it? A second chance? Here was the one thing the Abbess wanted, delivering its own self at Micah's feet.

He stood very still with his mouth half-open and his eyes hardening. He looked at the litch, slaughtering her slow way through the exiles. He looked at the black kid's approach. And he saw who would reach him first.

He wasn't the only one. The two men standing guard at the office door muscled past, bulky in their waistcoats, sleeves rolled up, the steps thundering under them as they ran down and away.

Micah scowled. "Prue," he called quietly. "You get old Claker's peepers out here. I reckon he's about to have a visit from his . . . pet. Timna—you stay out here."

Timna spat. "What's it to us?"

"That pet'll go through us like butter, she don't get Claker out in front of it. Right?"

"An what about you? You goin to just run, then?"

Micah nodded at the black kid still approaching. "You an me, we got a card won't stay dealt."

Prudence, saying nothing, went to the railing to see. Her eyes were black with worry. Then the little girl disappeared off inside, her ragged coat gray with dirt, and Timna pulled her knives out of her pockets. Micah tried to decide what to do. He didn't often wish his talent was still in him, but for a moment he let himself wish it. A clink would have no fear of litches. Truth was, if he was smart he'd run, just like Timna had accused him of. But with a grim little frown, he sat instead, and fumbled in his satchel. He took out the bloodied handkerchief and unfolded from it the kid's severed ear, and held it up, considering. Then he flipped it, like a coin, the rubbery thing spinning end over end, and caught it in one fist.

Heads, Micah thought.

And grinned at his own cleverness.

The black kid—Charlie—had reached the base of the stair, far below. Micah started down.

·   ·   ·

The dark glyphic was singing to them all, singing them onward, a song without words, and the six glyph-twisted children crawled into the sluices, in her thrall. In the world above stood the painted wagon, with their seventh, Deirdre, alone inside it. There were three knife-gate sluices and the children, separated two by two, had found their way to all. The waters in all three were moving very fast. All was darkness. Currents of effluent filled and swirled back upon themselves in the cisterns, pouring out through a sequence of grilles and traps. A metal gate in a groove, controlled by a hand-lowered chain, restricted the outflow. The waters sucked under, poured through the far side and out, down into the Falls.

And the glyph-twisted children, silent, worked free of their brown cloaks and dragged their strange, treelike bodies down into the murky waters. It seemed to each of them that a silver thread connected them, humming with a vibrant sorrow, and they pulled against it and felt its pull against them.

And yet, beneath that, faint but vibrating with regret, was a second thread, a thread cast out from Deirdre herself to each of them, whispering: *Come back! Come back!*

But her whisper was lost against the glyphic's dark song. The greasy sewage was cold even against their roughened skins and they gripped the concrete with rootlike strength and their limbs were twisted and strong and terrible. And they made their slow steady way down, down beneath the waters, closing their lungs against it, down to the very edges of the gates where the sucking waters were strongest. The currents tried to rip them free. But they gripped with their powerful limbs, feeling the web of cracks and imperfections in the cement all around them, and steadied, and for a long while it seemed they had taken root. And then, with great slowness, they leaned into it.

That was when they began to *push*—to push with the slow tendril-like power of what they were, of what they *truly* were—until the concrete shivered, weakening.

The waters were black. Their eyes glowed like yellow fires deep in the murk. For a long silent crushing time—it might have been minutes, hours—the vast constructed sluices stood fast. And then a crack widened; the rushing waters forced their way in, widening, doing the children's work for them; all at once the cement buckled, splintered, crumbled apart.

The dark glyphic ceased her singing.

And with a mighty crack, the great muscular waters burst through.

When the sluices gave way, Charlie fell to his knees. He stared up in horror. A burst of foul water thundered down into the Falls. He saw a great dark crack open, spidering up one wall, and then suddenly the concrete toppled outward, plummeted. The rope bridges below rocked wildly. An array of platforms crumpled under the weight, washed away.

He didn't know what was happening. No one did. The screams were terrible.

He glanced quickly back up, where he had to go. Mrs. Ficke was gone. The urchin—the white-haired boy who'd attacked him in the street—had descended the rickety stairs and stopped. He was maybe six feet away. Two steps back lurked the littlest sister, the one with the terrible blades.

This time Charlie saw the knives. He took out Alice's revolver and thumbed back the hammer. But he knew he couldn't do it, couldn't pull the trigger, couldn't kill someone, for God's sake, no matter how wicked.

You're a damned fool, Charlie Ovid, he swore at himself. *You deserve what you get.*

The boy was out in front, grinning at him, grinning like he knew it, like he knew Charlie was too softhearted to do what needed to be done. He raised one grubby hand to the side of his face, as if to scratch his ear, but he was holding something small and discolored, and suddenly

Charlie saw what it was. The kid was holding Charlie's own severed ear up, as if trying on an earring.

"What I need," the boy called down, "is a bleedin *pair*. What do you reckon?"

The little sister laughed.

Charlie bared his teeth. It wasn't a smile. He turned his head so that the ruined ear—grown back now, because of the dust, but tender still and weirdly soft, like toffee—could be seen clearly by the urchin. "You can keep the ear," he called up. "Where's my father's ring?"

"Your what, now?" The urchin's clever little smirk flickered. "Your *father*? Hear that, Timna? Won't ol Claker get a sackful out of that, like?"

The little sister laughed again.

"It weren't never his ring to begin with," the boy added with spite. "Your *fa-ther* were a bricky, like. A meater. Stole that ring from Claker when he got scared an run away. Me an the girls were just collectin it back, like." Charlie's expression must have betrayed him, for the boy grinned and went on: "Aw, what? He never told you? Your papa were ol Claker's right hand. Right trusted he were, til he buggered off with that ring."

The stair was shuddering dangerously. The waters were roaring below, overturning the platforms and wooden structures. The urchin reached for the railing to steady himself. And Charlie raised the Colt Peacemaker and fired.

He wasn't aiming for the urchin. He just wanted to scare him. But the bullet hit the post that held the railing and the wood exploded into kindling. The railing buckled and fairly leaped away, pulling the urchin off-balance, and in that same moment Charlie threw himself forward at the boy.

But Charlie was slow; his body was slow, badly beaten and healing wearily; and the two urchins moved with a snakelike grace. The boy danced back out of Charlie's reach, the drop to their left now sheer and unprotected, and then, before Charlie could regain his balance, the little girl coiled low and launched herself, boots first, at Charlie's face. He raised his arms in a block and her filthy boots hit Charlie's sore wrists, slid off. He cried out, fell back.

His head landed at the edge of the gap, the furious waters rising below, and he rolled away and struggled upright. The little girl had fallen funny on the stair below him, and was getting to her knees, one knife lost, the other still in her fist. Something was wrong with her ankle. Her little face was twisted in pain and for just the briefest of moments Charlie saw, again, the little girl she was, the girl she might have been, had her life only been different.

But then it was gone. He swung his foot with all the strength he had in him and struck her fist, feeling the small bones in her wrist snap, the knife skittering away over the edge into the waters far below. She screamed in pain.

That was when he felt the rip of a blade down his back, and twisting, he saw her brother, the urchin boy, bring his long knife down on Charlie's throat. That knife was wet with Charlie's own blood and left long arcs of gore in the air as he swung. There was blood in Charlie's filthy shirt and pouring now from a deep cut at his collarbone. He still had Alice's revolver somehow but he couldn't lift it.

And then he felt the little girl at his back. She'd climbed up onto him with her arms around his throat and she was biting him, biting and spitting out the bits of his neck and back, and he writhed in agony.

Enough! he was thinking. *End this now! End it, Charlie!*

And then, somehow, he knew what he had to do. The brother came at him from the front with the long knife and Charlie reached out, he seized the boy's fists, and he helped him, he helped him with all the strength he had left, he forced the blade to its very handle deep into his stomach, so that it punched clear through his back, and impaled the little girl behind him.

And then they both collapsed, both young ones, Charlie and the girl, and he rolled off in agony to see her gripping her own side where she lay. It had gone in under her ribs, not a killing stroke. But the boy had lost the knife and he stood now with his red hands loose at his sides, staring in horror at his sister. Then he raised his eyes, and looked past her.

That was when the thing came loping along up the stairs, gore-stained and monstrous, its limbs leaving red smears where it climbed. Charlie saw it moving very fast and he scrambled back away from the girl, three steps, four steps, five steps and higher, just as the litch reached her. There was a scrabble of claws, and a scream, and something fell to the stair—the girl's small *hand*, for God's sake, it was her *hand*—and then the murderous little child was spinning away sidelong off the stair with her arms splayed wide, and Charlie where he lay watched as the girl pitched, already dead, surely, down into the thundering waters far below. She struck the surface, went under. Charlie saw her white head reappear for a moment and then vanish in the foaming roar and not surface again.

There was a strangled cry from above. He saw the boy, Micah, stumble back, fleeing in terror up the stairs and into the offices of Claker Jack.

Charlie himself didn't run. Ten stairs below him, the litch was crouched, breathing hard. It glared up at Charlie with terrible eyes.

Everything—the roar of the waters, the roar of the blood in his own skull, the roar that was coming out of his own mouth, that was both his own terror and not his own, somehow—all of it seemed to quieten, as if it were happening to some other, not himself.

And then the litch leaped.

Jeta heard the sudden crack, as the sluices gave way, then the screams of the crowds trapped below. A great thundering sheet of filthy water smashed into the far side of the cistern, upending tents and platforms and crushing exiles into the foam of it.

The apparition's voice was in her ear. *Go! Hurry! The dust is here . . .*

She hesitated only a moment. Then she spun and broke free of the panicked exiles all around her and hurtled over a barrel, across a mess of sacking, down a ladder. She landed painfully on the lowest platform. The waters were already rising, creeping over the boards, swirling muckily around her ankles. She splashed her way across to the stair she needed, the stair to Claker Jack's offices.

Nearly everyone else was running for an exit; there was no one on this level. A few foolish exiles, trying to grab what they could. But Jeta wasn't trying to get out. Not yet.

She started up. She didn't know what she would say to Claker, or do to him. There was vengeance and fury in her heart but also something else, something to do with the apparition of the little boy, the corrupted dust he sought. *He'd* not betrayed her; *he* was with her yet. She gripped the shivering railing, climbed fast. The apparition stood, small and blue and flickering, on the steps just ahead of her. Its face was filled with a terrible excitement. Through the slats Jeta glimpsed a flicker of movement above: a gray, blood-spattered thing.

The litch.

Blocking her way. Ripping someone to pieces, by the sound of it. Her cuts where it had slashed her were on fire, as if infected with some kind of poison. She felt a fear enter her. It was too powerful, impossible to fight. Her talent had no effect on it. Its claws had nearly torn her throat out. She looked wildly around for some other way up but there was only this one stair, this one route to the dust. The reeking waters were engulfing the lower levels of the Falls, now. She could see bodies in the tumult, bits of wood and cloth, all of it sucked down into the foaming central whorl. Nothing would get through that alive.

Jeta, the apparition called to her. *It's this way. Come!*

The stair ran alongside the curved wall of the cistern and Jeta followed the apparition's gaze. There were struts and supports under the slats, like a weird kind of webbing.

She understood. "I can't," she said in horror. "No—"

The apparition said nothing, only watched her with its feverish dark eyes.

And somehow, slowly, she swung herself over the railing and lowered herself into the narrow gap between stair and wall. With her knees folded high, and her hands gripping the edge of the slats, she began to crawl along the underside of the stair.

Below her the Falls spun crazily. All the blood rushed to her head. Her braids were dangling heavily, her skirts were dragging her low. As she went her hands ached, her forearms grew thick with blood. She was so tired. When she neared the litch she felt herself want to freeze up in fear, eyes wide. She was staring through the slats upside down at the creature. But it didn't turn, it didn't sense her presence; there was a figure above it on the stair.

She scrambled hand over hand past the bare feet of the young man who faced it, not catching sight of his face, of who he might be. When she reached the underside of the balcony she was careful to hook her ankle up over one post, and then, with great care, drag her exhausted body onto the level.

She lay, gasping.

Then she got to her feet.

The apparition stood before her, hair flickering in the blue shine. It was watching the litch on the stairs below. But Jeta's attention was seized by the white-haired child emerging out of the doorway in front of her, barefoot, her long coat rolled at the sleeves, and for a moment she thought it must be the boy, the boy who'd talked to her in her cell, Micah. But it was a girl. She held a little knife in her small hand and stared at Jeta, silent as smoke, her child's eyes running with tears. Then she dropped the knife and pressed herself back against the wall, terrified. Jeta didn't hurt her, but swept past, her long wet skirts leaving a trail of muck behind her.

Claker! she wanted to scream. *Claker! Where are you?*

That was when she heard a gun fire, again and again, on the stairs below. She paused. The white-haired child had crushed her eyes shut. Outside, bullets crunched into wood, rang singing off the walls.

Charlie's hand was shaking. The dust under his skin crawled itchingly over his knuckles, his wrist, up his forearm. He blinked the sweat from his eyes. The litch had bared a mouthful of long, glistening teeth and even after everything, after all the pain of the last weeks, Charlie still was taken right back to that awful night at Mrs. Harrogate's, when the litch scrabbled over the ceiling with its teeth clashing, and he felt himself starting to weep out of fear. He fell backward and pulled the trigger wildly, and Alice's revolver bucked in his hand. He fired it again and again, watching the bullets divot up out of the wood around the litch. One hit its shoulder and the creature spun bodily and a second hit its leg knocking both out from under and it smashed chest-first onto the stair. Charlie was still firing, the Colt Peacemaker clicking through its emptied chambers, his mind in a panic.

But the litch just picked itself up, just as if the bullets were nothing, as if the pain it felt was nothing, and sidled crablike to the far railing again. Charlie, tears on his cheeks, swore. He hurled the weapon at the monster, uselessly, and scrambled to his feet.

And ran.

He didn't know what else to do. He was hardly thinking now. He ran up the stair, falling and stumbling and clawing his way upright and running harder.

Please, he was thinking. *Please please please please—*

The balcony was just ahead of him, the landing where he'd seen Mrs. Ficke standing at the rail. If he could just make it there, he might get inside, bar a door or something. But he was gasping, the pain everywhere in him was just too much. The dust in him felt like it was on fire. He turned. The litch was clambering spiderlike across the wall, impossibly fast—

Charlie's head spun. Just then his foot missed a step and he fell hard and the pain made him retch. For a long moment he just lay there, his heart hammering.

And then the creature was upon him. He could smell the reek of death in its gray skin. At its throat were three thin red creases, like folds of skin. Its teeth were long and sharp. It crawled over him and crouched above him and he saw it was wilder, fiercer, more animallike even than the litch Walter, who had attacked him at Mrs. Harrogate's. There was only reflection and shine in its eyes. Nothing human. Blood—too much blood—stained its arms and thighs and slack breasts and rib cage. It reached for Charlie's throat.

And froze.

Something stayed its hand. The litch shifted. It drew a long claw-like fingernail up Charlie's sleeve, slicing it away, and then it grasped his wrist and lifted his infected arm. The ink-like marks in his skin were shining with a bright blue light, coalescing through their peculiar patterns, a storm of glowing dust. Charlie, dizzy with fear, stared at the thing in horror.

It raised its eyes, studied him back. Its eyes were eerie, its pupils hourglass-shaped and catching the light in a queer way. An intelligence flickered across its features—a kind of recognition, as if it were remembering something important, or struggling to—and for just an instant Charlie glimpsed the woman the litch had been, her eyes sad, her face narrow and pinched. She was breathing strangely, as if in her breathing there was a sound, a word almost.

Then she was gone, faded again into some deep place in her skull, and in her eyes was only the flat expressionless stare of the litch. Its claw released him; it bolted upright; it gave a fierce screech, a terrible sound—and fled.

Jeta was so close; Claker was near, somewhere down the dark passage beyond the desk. She had no real idea what she would do when she saw him again. Her heart was too full, full with anger and betrayal and her own stupid faith in a man who could never have loved her, not as a father, not as a friend. She saw that now.

And yet, close as she was, she paused. She didn't know why. She felt a strangeness rising in her, a kind of prickling in her skin, like a thousand little hooks were in her and lifting her painfully. The apparition had not followed her in, and maybe it was just that, just his own hesitation that drew her back. She turned. Below, the murky waters were rising, frothing. The balcony shuddered under her weight.

And there he was, the apparition, flickering, transparent and blue as ink, his boyish hair adrift, staring downward. She followed his gaze, and saw.

It was *him*. Charlie Ovid, whom Micah had sworn he'd left for dead in the streets of London.

And over him hunched the litch, folded like a spider. Claker's *pet*. She saw in her mind's eye that creature as it crushed the breath from her in that cage. Terror overwhelmed her. As she watched, the litch lifted the young man's arm and sniffed at the skin and then she saw it, too, the very thing the apparition must have sensed: under Charlie Ovid's skin a blue smoke was swirling.

The corrupted dust.

It was *in* him, *infecting* him. All at once the litch let out a heartrending scream, a scream that filled Jeta with dread. The creature leaped backward, its skull-like face twisting in fury; and then it hurtled up the stair toward her.

Jeta froze.

And yet it simply scrabbled on past, taking no notice of her, its long claws clicking furiously on the stone wall, colliding sidelong with the doorframe and splintering the wood there, before vanishing into the offices of Claker Jack.

The balcony shivered at its passing, the raw struts groaning. Jeta put out a hand to steady herself. Her heart was going too fast. For one impossible moment she wanted to leap after it, scream out, warn Claker that it was coming. But then her heart turned cold. *Let it find him,* she thought fiercely.

And passed her hand across her eyes.

Across the way, chunks of concrete were toppling from high up the walls, crashing into the waters.

Jeta, the small ghost whispered, suddenly near, startling her. There was a dark urgency in his voice, a hunger. *It's bonded to him, to Charlie Ovid. The dust, Jeta . . . We're almost too late, there's only one way to get it now—*

Kill him.

That's what the child meant.

She couldn't think clearly. She tried to shake the fog from her thoughts, knowing somewhere deep inside her that it wasn't right, not entirely, that what the apparition was telling her wasn't quite what she herself wanted. And yet she stumbled to the edge of the balcony, as if half-asleep, as if pulled by a will not her own. She raised her bone fingers in a kind of benediction. She saw Charlie, his wet eyes, the tears on his cheeks. He'd got shakily to his feet.

He was looking up at her, his hands empty. His eyes were clear: he knew what she would do.

"Don't do this," he called up. "Please. You don't have to do this."

Do it, whispered the apparition. *You have to.*

And she did; or began to. But just then there came a shrieking, and the wood balcony turned sideways under her feet, and all at once she was sliding, sliding sharply, sliding through the spin and roar of the air. It was the balcony itself. The struts had broken loose, torn sheer away from the wall from the force of the rising waters, and Jeta swung out wildly now over the Falls. Her legs were tangled up in the railing; she gripped the edge of a board, staring back at the stairs she'd stood above only moments before. They hadn't pulled loose yet. Charlie Ovid was on his feet, calling across to her. The gap between them widened. She couldn't make out his words. For what seemed an impossibly long moment the broken balcony swayed, suspended over the whirlpool, attached still to the wall by a single last stubborn strut.

Jeta's mind was clear. It was without fear or surprise or regret. So. She would drown. The apparition of the boy—hungry, no longer quite human, if ever he'd been—had vanished.

She started to shout something to Charlie but before she could even finish her thought the wood all around her groaned, groaned exactly like a living thing in pain, and then crumpled, and it was like all of the joinings and nails gave out at the same moment and Jeta Wajs felt her heart leap into her throat as she plunged, in a scattering of shattered wood and a whipping of braids, down into the cold rushing dark of the waters below.

In the laboratory chamber, Caroline Ficke was quiet. Her arm was pinioned to her side. She lay on a dissection table, lashed fast with the leather straps.

Claker Jack removed his hat, his coat, folded back his sleeves with slow care. He took down an alembic and several beakers and began weighing and pouring and mixing various powders. Some of them she knew by sight. She could see much of the work had been done already and yet he moved with deliberate care, not hurrying, checking often to make sure his levels were right. Gradually she became aware of a new sound, faint, coming from the passageway back out to the Falls. The sounds of shouting, screaming. There came the faint report of gunshots. Claker Jack went to the doorway and stood listening. Then he returned to his labors, more tense. He took the vial of shining blue dust from his waistcoat, and set it carefully on the worktable. At last, with great care, he picked up the vial in his long fingers and began to work the stopper free. The tiny pinch of dust within was shining very bright.

She wet her lips. "It won't bond to you, Mr. Renby. No matter what you do. The dust, it . . . it already has a host."

"Indeed. A dead host."

"Not Jacob Marber. Someone else."

He paused. His cold gaze shifted to her. "Why would it respond to my presence, if it's already bonded?" He held his hand over the vial and the dust whorled in a vortex of sudden brightness.

"That's just what it *does*! I have the same effect upon it. That is not *bonding*. But if you ingest it, or absorb it, it will *reject* you, Mr. Renby. It will take whatever you have to offer and eat its way through that, and then it will eat its way through to the other world, to where it—"

He made a cutting gesture with his hand. His face twisted in disgust. "Oh? And have you tried?"

"Of course not—"

"Then you cannot know."

"You're like Henry was," she whispered. "You're no different."

"And you, Caroline? What are you? After all you did to aid in his *experiments*?" He nodded. "Ah, yes. I know about the *children*."

There came a flurry of movement from the doorway, and the white-haired urchin—Micah—stumbled in, his face and hands bloodied. His eyes were wild. His boots left bloody little prints where he hurried.

"Prudence!" he cried. "Prue! Where is she, Claker? The litch is loose. An it's coming here. It . . . it tore Timna into pieces . . ."

"Enough." Claker Jack made a cutting gesture with his hand. He looked angry. The boy went quiet, standing near the back shelves so that Caroline could only just see him by twisting her neck.

But now Claker was tapping the shining dust into the drink he'd prepared. He raised the glass to his lips. The liquid was glowing. His eyes, reflective, found Caroline's own and fixed on her. She held her breath.

And then he drank it down.

Immediately she could see something was different in him. He set the glass with a click back on the table and rested his hand there for a moment and turned in profile and stood like that, as if posing in the faint light. Micah gave out a low moan. She felt a fourth presence and glanced back and saw something standing in the doorway, a creature, its arms and torso dark with some wetness. The litch, she realized in shock. It was the litch from the cage fight below. The litch was staring at Claker Jack, its long teeth glinting.

"Mother," he murmured. "I was . . . coming for you . . ."

The litch made a strange choked noise in its throat.

But Claker Jack's eyes were already filling with pain. A blue shining was seeping out from under his eyelids and out of his nostrils and dissipating away, like smoke. He looked afraid. He started to shake his head. All of a sudden he scrabbled at his shirtfront, ripping away the buttons and cloth, and Caroline saw between the cracks of his fingernails that same blue shining light, seeping away.

"Get it off, get it off—!" he cried in a strangled voice.

A gash was opening in his chest, a slash of raw-looking flesh. And deep behind it something else, a darkness, a darkness that filled with an unnatural light at its edges. Caroline didn't understand what she was seeing. Forgotten now was the litch, forgotten the urchin, the straps that held her fast.

Claker Jack screamed: a scream that seemed to go on forever. The blue shine was fierce. As she watched, his features smoothed themselves out, his nose and eyebrows and cheekbones and eyes, all softening like hot wax and blurring together, as if a great thumb were rolling across him, until there was only the gaping hole that had been his mouth, and the scream issuing from it.

Caroline could not look away.

The hole in his chest gaped, shining with that eerie blue light. It seemed to be drawing the man's flesh into itself, drinking it deeply. He shuddered, smashing into the table in front of him, shattering the jars and alembics. His shoulders crunched gruesomely inward. His spine buckled, as if under a terrible weight.

Now the man's body was folding over itself. All at once the shrieking ceased. It was as if he was being sucked inside his own chest, drawn smaller and tighter and smaller again, sucked into a tiny point in space. Caroline watched as the tiny opening widened, until it was the size of a fist, of a human heart, and she saw through the strange window that it was a second world, a different world, a world not her own. There were dark figures in silhouette, monstrous figures stirring and rising, four of them. And then one turned, as if hearing a sound, and fixed its terrible eyes directly upon her. The eyes were ablaze with a fire that gave no light, and its terrible skull was antlered, and it seemed made of a darkness that was somehow solid. Caroline could not look away, so absolute was her terror. The horror came striding toward her, unfathomably fast. But then—all at once—the rip in Claker Jack's body began to tremble. His skull was bending into the space where his lungs should have been, his legs were folding forward into his chest, and the opening crushed itself smaller and smaller.

Until the compressed shining thing that had been Claker Jack could not withstand the pressure, and suddenly gave way, and burst.

Blood and gore and bits of bone splattered the ceiling and floor and walls. Caroline screamed. Where the lord of the exiles had writhed moments before, now there was only a crushed speck of swirling blue dust. Then that, too, blinked out, and was gone.

The stillness was absolute. It seemed to go on for a long time. Caroline's ears were ringing. She turned her face away and saw the litch had collapsed, lifeless, to the floor. Its pitiful ribs were showing, like a starved dog. It would not rise again; its creator was dead. The vicious urchin, Micah, was crawling on his hands and knees in the mess, his clothes and hair dripping, and then he got to his feet and ran banging out over the litch's body, away.

Caroline was alone. Her eyes were wet. She didn't understand why. She kept seeing the antlered horrors that had been in the beyond, their eyes that were like lights, but burning with darkness.

All around her the walls shuddered, as if the earth itself were afraid.

The roar was deafening. Charlie watched the balcony shear off from the wall, lean weirdly out over the swirling flood, the bone witch scrabbling for a hold. He tried to holler to her but she couldn't hear. She looked young in that moment, so much younger than Charlie, so afraid. Then, all at once, the entire structure collapsed and she plunged into the murky water below.

She was gone.

But just as it all collapsed, as the bone witch sheared sideways off the platform, he felt a sudden pain in his skin, as if the dust there were prickling with a fiery current. And he glimpsed something, a figure, blurred and indistinct and yet somehow real, somehow there, on the collapsing structure with the bone witch. A figure of darkness and smoke. It looked almost like a woman, a woman in black.

He was on his hands and knees by then, gasping, feeling the stairs under him tremble, too. Below him the dark waters were rising. The lower half of the stairs already had been sucked out into the current. He felt the structure sway. Two steps above him, the broken stairs ended in emptiness. He could see the splintered stub of balcony some eight feet above him, where the door to Claker Jack's offices stood. It was there that Mrs. Ficke had been taken, there that the litch had vanished.

Charlie rubbed at his eyes. He couldn't leap that far. He couldn't.

And even if he could, what then? The litch lay in wait, somewhere above. That murderous little monster, Micah, was up there too. And the waters were rising; they would all drown, regardless.

The dust in his skin was crackling, like a fire in his flesh, and he cradled his infected arm and tried to think. His wounds were healing, the corrupted dust doing its work. Suddenly he remembered the night Dr. Berghast had tried to kill Marlowe, how he, Charlie, had reached for the knives. The mortaling. He'd done the mortaling.

He crawled nervously to the edge of the balcony and shut his eyes and tried to find the stillness in him, that same quiet calm he'd found before, when his body had torn and reshaped itself. If he could reach out to the doorway, if he could just pull himself up . . .

He crushed his eyes shut. Willing it to be so. But when he opened his eyes, he saw it was no use; if the corrupted dust had restored his talent, it hadn't restored the mortaling. He couldn't.

The rickety stair shivered. Charlie grabbed for purchase.

And just then he saw a movement in the doorway far above. It was a child, one of the white-haired sisters—the quiet one who'd not spoken—and she was peering down at him with a grave, still face. She vanished from sight and a moment later returned with a coil of rope. This she tied off against some brace within, and then she threw the rope down to Charlie.

He caught it, uncomprehending. She was gesturing at him, at the thundering waters below. He didn't know if she meant to cut him loose, to let him drown, if she'd seen what happened to her sister when the litch got to her. He didn't care. He couldn't see any other options.

He gripped the rope, and staggered his bare feet against the wall, and climbed.

She was so small. She stood pale as a ghost in her ragged coat, eyes dark and big, and when he was halfway up the drop she turned and peered behind her, as if some other were approaching.

Micah, filled with terror, drew his wet hands across his eyes as he ran, wiping the gore away. His hair was already going stiff with Claker Jack's blood.

He'd seen terrible things in his life but nothing like what he'd just witnessed. His stare was hollow and haunted though he could not know the horror he bore on his face and when he stumbled up out of the dark corridor into Claker Jack's ruined office, he stopped, puzzled, trying to catch his breath.

Claker had ripped apart, from the inside. There'd been a . . . a window inside him. And terrible creatures moving there.

He couldn't unsee it. Some part of his brain was telling him the Abbess would want to know. Would surely explain what it was. But mostly he was just thinking he had to get out, had to find Prudence and get out. There was an old maintenance shaft in the ceiling of Claker Jack's office. He started to shove the big desk toward the corner when he saw the balcony had collapsed. At the gaping doorway, his sister was fumbling with a rope, tying it into place. She turned and looked back at him and the look on her face was filled with fear.

He didn't understand.

"Prudence, for quim's sake," he shouted at her. "We're not going back *down*. We got to *climb*."

And he scrambled up onto the desk and found the pull-latch to the hidden door and swung it down. The ladder inside was bolted to the walls with rusting bolts and it vanished up into the darkness. He thought he could make out a light, very faint, high up, where they could get free.

But his sister didn't move. She was watching him with such horror.

"Aw, it's not mine," he said, wiping more of the blood away. "It's old Claker's. He's in bits back there. An his pet litch is dead too. Now *move* your bleedin *legs*, Prue!"

But she was inching away, not toward him. That was when he saw the way the rope sang in its traces, shifted tightly as if a weight were moving on it. And then he saw a hand, two hands, grappling with the ledge, and the face of that bastard Charlie appeared, gasping, up the rope.

Micah jumped down, wrath rising sharply in him. He fumbled around, looking for a weapon. A blade, anything. His fucking sister, what was she *doing*? "Bloody hell—Prudence! What'd you do?"

He saw something come over her then, something fill her eyes with a deep, profound terror. A terror of *him*. And then she stumbled backward, took a single decisive step away, over Charlie's struggling body, toward the gap, toward the maelstrom below. Her eyes never left Micah's face.

And then she was gone. Just like that. Plummeted into the roar, and gone, like Timna, like the whole damned Falls itself.

Micah, stunned, didn't understand it. He started forward, stopped. He was shaking his little head, as if he could refuse what had just happened, as if he could make sense of it. But he couldn't. He couldn't.

He watched Charlie drag himself up into the office. And then Micah, Micah who had never turned from a killing when it was so easy, Micah who was born in blood and would die in it, Micah of the two sisters who now was only just himself, and alone in all the world—Micah turned and leaped up the desk and into the maintenance shaft, and started to climb.

His eyes were stinging with tears.

Charlie felt, rather than saw, the child lean out past him, into the gulf of air, and drop.

It all happened so fast. She made no sound. Grunting, he heaved himself up over the bits of broken wood and into the doorway, and lay gasping. The office was a mess. He rolled to his side and peered down at the whorling waters but saw no sign of the white-haired girl.

That was when he heard a racket and twisted in alarm in time to see the white-haired boy, drenched in blood, staring at him with absolute hatred. The office was dark in the back corners and the boy hovered there, as if suspended in air, pale and bloodied and awful.

And then he twisted lithely upward, and vanished into a hole in the ceiling.

For a long moment Charlie stared, shocked. Then he got to his feet in fear, thinking of Mrs. Ficke. That was when he saw the little wooden hatch hanging open in the ceiling. It was an access ladder, built for use by workers, no doubt, back when all this had been constructed for the sewers. The shaft vanished into blackness. He could hear, he thought, the faint exaggerated echo of boots scraping on rungs, of a steady slow breathing. So. He'd got out, the vicious little urchin.

He hurried through the wooden door and down a passage and came to the dimly lit laboratory of Claker Jack. And there he saw, crumpled in the doorway, the slack corpse of the litch, dead by no human hand. The room itself was splattered with bits of flesh. Tables, cluttered with jars and alembics, dripped with human matter. Blood was everywhere. A channel of filthy water was overflowing into the room. Lying buckled to a dissection table, half-drenched in blood not her own, was Mrs. Ficke.

Alive. Stunned, maybe, but alive.

Charlie could see how the leather straps bit into her skin and he hurried to her, his feet splashing in the muck. The ceiling shuddered. He didn't know how long they had.

"Mrs. Ficke?" he said in a rush. "We've got to go, the whole place is going to come down. Mrs. Ficke? Can you walk?"

She turned her slow face. She looked so old. "I saw them, Charlie," she whispered. "I *saw* them."

He didn't know what she was talking about. The litch, maybe, or Claker Jack himself. "Right. Okay. But can you stand? We got to go."

But she waved him away, leaning up against the table. "It was the drughr, Charlie," she went on. "I saw the drughr. On the other side. They're awake, they're . . . *listening*."

She gave a peculiar shiver, and closed her eyes in horror. Charlie nodded quickly. The candles were guttering and he feared they'd be plunged into darkness soon. He hurried across to a table and picked up Mrs. Ficke's artificial arm, the long blade of it still extended. In a silver dish he saw his father's ring, still on its cord, clumpy with bloody matter. He snatched it up, strung it back onto his neck.

The old alchemist had turned away and splashed across to a door at the far end of the chamber. Charlie called to her but she didn't stop.

Charlie hurried after her. She'd entered a small chamber, lightless but for the blue shine emanating from a stone tank. Mrs. Ficke sank to her knees before it. It contained a dazzling muck. And as he watched, the muck rose up, a congealed and dripping thing, lumpen and oozing over the lip of the tank and falling into the water on the floor. It sloshed its slow way into a corner.

"What—? What is—?" he whispered.

But Mrs. Ficke, fierce, intense, just held out her one hand, fingers splayed. "You tried to show me," she said to the living mud. "You *knew* about them. How did you know?"

But the living muck twisted and folded over upon itself and gave no indication that it even knew she was there.

"Are they awake?" the old woman pressed. "Are they coming for the children? For all of us?"

The muck writhed and fell away.

"We need to go," said Charlie again, more forcefully. The ring was swinging at his neck. "Please, Mrs. Ficke. Please!"

The old woman stood, wiping her hand on her sleeve. When she looked at Charlie her face was clear, her eyes were clear. "He used the dust, Charlie, Mr. Renby did. The little that I'd taken out of you. And something happened, a kind of . . . window opened. A window onto another world. And they were there, watching."

He felt his blood run cold, even as he said it: "Who were?"

"The drughr. All of them. She tried to warn me, Miss Laqueur did. I didn't understand."

Neither did he. Not a word of it. But there wasn't time; he half lifted her in her weakness and then he was running, falling sidelong against the walls, catching himself and her and running onward. He stumbled over the dead litch, the waters lapping at its body, and then on up the dark passageway, into Claker Jack's office. The roaring waters of the Falls had ceased rising, and begun to recede a little, though the ruin was total, and Charlie could see no way out below.

Mrs. Ficke stopped, haggard and thin, at the sight of the destruction. "How—?"

"Can you climb?" he asked instead. "There's an access panel up here. We can get out this way. I don't know how far it goes, though." His voice was strange in his throat and he cleared it and then he realized he was crying. His heart ached. His infected arm was on fire.

Mrs. Ficke turned then, and walked to him, and laid her hand on his cheek. "I was afraid you were dead," she said.

And then she held him. He leaned in, exhausted. "Not me, Mrs. Ficke. It's never me. I just . . . don't ever."

At last the old woman wiped her eyes, composing herself. "Yes. Well. Are the children safe? Deirdre and the others?"

Charlie nodded. "I left them in the wagon in an empty court. The horses might be gone. The little ones should be fine."

Some premonition of fear flickered in the old woman's face, but she didn't speak. She took her artificial arm from him, buckled it into place. Charlie peered up the maintenance shaft. He could see the bottom rungs of an iron ladder. He craned his neck and tried to see how far it went but the shaft was lost in darkness. He knew the vicious urchin had escaped that way and yet somehow he knew, too, the kid was gone, that he would not be there still. Mrs. Ficke gathered her skirts in her fist. When she was ready he lifted her lightly up and she started to climb, slowly, wearily, into the blackness, folding her elbow over the rungs for purchase, breathing raggedly, and when she was far enough along, Charlie swung himself up, the marks on his hand and wrist writhing, and he left that place for good.

They were six and they were each themselves and the dark waters all around them thundered and ripped at their purchase. They held on with all their strength, as the dark glyphic sang, singing such a thin threnody. *Release, release, release.*

And as they held on they leaned into the music, even while the rushing waters stripped away their twigs, their delicate leaves, while their clothes whipped sideways in the current. They held on. The concrete was giving way, giving way all around them, the waters were a black cold pressure. They held.

They could feel her song changing, the overwhelming sadness in it softening, easing, as something close to relief entered the music. She sang of Mrs. Ficke, free, crouching before her in the gloom, and she sang of Charlie standing over the body of a litch. She sang of the drowned and of the lost. She sang of a great and sweet destruction. For the dark glyphic herself was dying; she was grateful; her time was nearing its end.

The force of the water was impossible. One of the six felt his fingers peel back, slowly, and then give. He was flickering in the rush, battering side to side, still holding on, and then the waters overwhelmed him and he gave in to the current and spun suddenly away, over the drop, plummeting into the floodwaters below. And then a second of the children lost her grip, and was carried away; and then a third. One by one the children could not withstand the fury of the waters and were washed, battered and crumpling, into the destruction.

The last child—little Seamus, kindest heart—felt the others peel away and vanish, and closed his eyes, and let go. The waters carried him lightly away. He felt nothing.

In the ancient showman's wagon, Deirdre gave out an awful cry.

And the dark glyphic's song went out, like a phosphorous match to smoke.

22

THE QUICKENING

Jeta burst up out of the roiling water, gasping, sobbing, in the dark sewers under London.

Alive.

She'd hit the surface like concrete as she fell and felt her bones shatter and then she'd been washed hurtling down through the sewers, dragged along the walls, plunged under and raked against the bottom. Her bones fusing themselves back together even as she blacked out and came to in the darkness and the roar.

The tunnel was wide, curved. All around her now floated detritus from the Falls, broken bits of wood, bodies facedown like soft logs. A weak gray daylight was falling aslant the walls from some hidden shaft above, illuminating the green waters. She had no idea where she was, how far the flood had carried her. For a long time she stooped in the shallows, hunched and shivering. There was blood on her hands and arms and blood running down her face and her body was bruised all over. Her skirts were thick with the foul water and they dragged heavily at her hips as she climbed out. Her long hair had come loose and fell in ragged knots all about her face. With her two hands she parted the curtain of it, the bone fingers smooth and gleaming.

She couldn't stop shaking. It all came rushing back to her, the litch, Claker, his cruelty, his betrayal. He had never loved her. She was no daughter to him. She doubled over and coughed and retched and coughed again. The slow waters tugged at her skirts, foamy and discolored. In the gloom the walls were streaked with foul matter. He would be dead now. Claker would be dead.

It was then she heard the voice.

The dust is gone, Jeta Wajs, it whispered, sorrowful. *The boy is gone.*

A blue glow bloomed behind her.

She turned slowly. The apparition wavered on the walkway of the drainage tunnel, his ink-black eyes unreadable and still. Something about the ghost was changed. She felt her own grief and swallowed and didn't know what to say. None of it mattered; what would she do now?

The child apparition tilted its head. The gesture seemed, somehow, not quite human. Then, as if she'd spoken her thoughts aloud, as if it had understood, it replied: *What you will do, what you will become . . . is it not already decided?*

The air turned colder. Jeta was aware that something had altered between her and the apparition.

I am not what you think, it whispered, and its voice was strange, too old for a child. *You have not seen me as I am. This is not my face.*

She wiped at her cheeks. The tunnel seemed to darken. "What . . . what do you mean? Who are you?"

This is my boy. My son.

Jeta stared at the ghost, his small face. The eyes were not right, not the eyes of a child. It was like something else, some other not quite human thing, was peering out from behind a mask.

I did not wish to deceive you. But there are those who will tell you I mean you harm . . . I've been afraid, Jeta. Afraid to be who I am with you.

The skin on her arms was prickling. She wanted to scream, lash out, cry that she didn't care, she was sick of the dust, and Claker's lies, and this ghost and whatever lies it had been telling, all of it. But she simply stood transfixed, black hair lank and dripping, her patchwork dress soaked and heavy.

A great power is in you, Jeta Wajs. If only you will let yourself become what you are meant to be.

"What . . . what are you?" she whispered.

Oh, child. Are we not all we can imagine?

All at once the apparition was changing, its edges blurring, its face shifting in the brilliance. Jeta glimpsed an old man with long whiskers, his eyes white with blindness; a girl on crutches; a tall man in old-fashioned robes. Each visage gave way to another, until at last the apparition took on the form of a woman with dark hair, a woman wearing an old-fashioned high-collared dress, her eyes dark with knowing. She wore a cloak and she raised her hands and her hands were corrupted and gray and wizened like the hands of the dead. Jeta stumbled backward. But the apparition was changing again, growing taller, filling out, until it seemed to loom over her, crushing up against the tunnel ceiling. Its hands in their silhouette grew long and in the blur it folded a second pair of arms before its chest, rippling, monstrous. All around it the darkness intensified, turned liquid and black, as if any last vestige of light was being sucked up into it and absorbed; and the shine that blazed out from within grew impossibly bright.

Jeta stared in horror.

The thing's face was elongating now in the brilliance. Its jaw seemed to distend. Something was twisting from its forehead, like antlers, though Jeta could not make them out in the dazzle. She held a hand to her eyes, afraid in the way she'd been afraid as a girl, abandoned by her family, taken by that gruff Englishman Coulton into a world of noise and filth and machines, afraid like that for the first time since she could even remember.

Do not be frightened, murmured the drughr, casting its arms wide in benevolence. *I have gone by many names, and most are fearful. But to you, Jeta Wajs, I am what I always was. A friend. But there is a world beyond this one, a world where terrible things are awakening. And my boy walks there, even now. My son. He is in such danger.*

Jeta shielded her eyes, trying to catch her breath. The brightness was too much. She could feel the drughr, near. Now its breath was soft on her wet cheek, inviting.

Will you help me, Jeta? The dust can yet be found. Will you come: come, and make a difference in the world?

The CROSSING

·

23

SHINING BOY

Against a white sky they wheeled, the bonebirds, frail and trembling.

The child in his rags watched them. Having made himself small, his clothes gray against the darker gray roof tiles, his little hands and cheeks streaked with dirt. Small as a rabbit. Small as a pebble in a shoe.

You had to, if you wanted not to be seen.

All around him the city of the dead stretched away, the rooftops dim with fog, the dark spindles of their chimney stacks still and cold. Below in the dripping lanes a white mist coalesced, whispering. Spirits. Always they whispered, hungry. It was how you knew they weren't fog.

He wasn't afraid anymore, not like he'd been at first, in the beginning. As long as you stayed hidden, as long as you stayed small. He let his eyes, near feral, flick down to watch the spirits seep past the rotting timber-frame doorways, the sagging abandoned carts. He made no sound. The spirits were drawn to his talent, to the blue shine that burned in him. He'd learned in this place to fear what he could do, the way he'd feared it as a little boy in Eliza's care, mudlarking in the reaches of the Thames, hiding what he was.

The bonebirds, silent as death, circled away.

When he was sure they were gone, he crawled out of his hiding place. Eight years old, with blue eyes, hair as black as a crow. The damp in his clothes now, always. His skin was still pale, but made the more pale by the strange half-light of that world. He'd nearly forgotten the feel of sunlight on his face. His childhood was like that too now, like a thing remembered only in pieces, like it was long ago. But even so he was still just a kid, the same kid he'd always been, a foundling from a railway carriage in England, lifted from the straw by a woman fleeing for her life. He had no name but the one she'd given him that night, the name of the first village they'd come to, and so Marlowe it was and Marlowe it would be, all the rest of his days.

Marlowe, little one. Hopeful by nature, even in the shadow of the gray rooms. Sometimes he'd put his left hand into his right, and grip it tightly, and pretend Charlie was with him.

But he wasn't alone. Not on that rooftop, and not in that world.

A spirit was near him, protective. She'd not left his side since first she appeared. She wavered now at the edge of the roof, a long silver braid down her back, just like in life. But she wasn't like in life, not really. When he squinched up his eyes and looked sidelong at her he could see the city through her massive form, as if she were made of gauze, and sometimes she would ripple and her face would look younger, or older. Why Brynt—for it was *his* Brynt, or the echo of her, what she'd become in this place—should be different from the other spirits, the ones who wanted to hurt him, he didn't know. But she was. She never smiled, only watched him with grave eyes, silent. Filled with a terrible longing he didn't know what to do with. It was Brynt who'd warned him of the dangers in this world, who knew the bonebirds here were to be feared, who knew he was in peril from more than just the dead.

Brynt, who explained that he could not stay.

Across the river. That was where he had to go, she'd told him, and he knew it now too, he did. To the far shore, where spirits drifted in their countless ranks. Then along the old tracks, past the gray rooms—but do not go inside them!—to the Passage of the Drughr. Fear the wall of carykk; fear the house itself. For there, she'd explained, stood the only door that could be opened from this side of the divide, a door guarded fiercely by the drughr themselves. There was a time, once, when it had been their way of coming and going. But they had other ways now, she whispered.

They.

More than one. More drughr than just the one that had hunted him, that had claimed him for its own, that Jacob Marber had told him was his mother. The drughr Dr. Berghast had summoned to the orsine, and killed. The terror of it all was in him for a time and then it dulled as everything seemed to dull in this world until now it was just another bad thing he had to hide from, another evil fact in this place of wrongness. And he was running out of time; the bonebirds would find him soon, and then their masters, the drughr, would come.

And so the black river drew him, like a song; it was like a shadow version of the Thames he'd known in his boyhood, like if the Thames had been turned inside out and all the light and movement were sucked from it, so that all that was left was its cold. But even if he got across, even if the terrible ferrymen—the carykk, Brynt called them—were to let him pass, somehow, how would he ever get through the crowds of spirits? He'd resisted at first, not wanting to try, for she could not go with him.

What I am . . . cannot cross back over, she'd whispered. *Not like that. The carykk bring my kind only the one way.*

He hadn't understood. "But not me?"

You are not what I am. The river will not stop you.

"Then why are you afraid?"

You are known, Marlowe, though you do not see it yet. She'd turned her quiet face toward the river. *There is something over there. Something . . . wrong. I don't know what it is.* She wavered in the weird light and said nothing and then added, *There are things in this world that fear the drughr, and things the drughr fear. Who can say which is which?*

A yellow fog was parting slowly, allowing a glimpse of the river. The carykk were carving their skiffs across its surface, like blades in glass. Too many to count, vanishing in both directions. Their vessels were filled with spirits on the way into the city; they were empty, always, on the way out. For the dead came only the one way; and the carykk fed on their memories, leaving their passengers hollowed and lost.

"Is that what happened to you, Brynt?" he'd asked. "Did they do that to you, too?"

I . . . couldn't remember you. Not at first . . . Not when I found you.

"But then you did," the child said sturdily. "You remembered."

He'd been so afraid, at first.

The orsine shuddering all around him, his arms aching, a fire burning through his hands. Knowing Charlie was just up there, on the other side, hurting and afraid too. He'd dragged the torn surface of the orsine closed, darkness all around him, wanting to cry and not crying and feeling the watery whatever-it-was like a great pressure, crushing his lungs. Everything that mattered to him was on the far side, in that collapsing cavern, at the stone edge of a flooding pool; and he'd left Alice and the others too, he'd had to, because the orsine was rupturing, and he was the only one who could seal it. He knew Dr. Berghast and the drughr were somewhere already below, he'd watched them sink away, dying, and yet he held on, he held and he held, feeling the light of the orsine dim and go out, like a coal, into darkness.

That darkness had lasted a long time.

He'd awoken shivering and damp at the bottom of a rotting staircase, in a moldering building that was both Nickel Street West and not. His little hands were sore, blistered from dragging the bark-like skin of the orsine shut. In his flesh a pain was only gradually shuddering away, like a cymbal struck in an empty hall. He'd sat up. And he'd known—for the first time in all his short life, a life of abandonments, of betrayals—what it felt like to be absolutely, utterly alone.

There was only the slow dap of water, the stillness. A faint charred scent in his nostrils. He'd looked at once for the bodies of Dr. Berghast and the drughr, but there was no one, no one at all. The door was open on its hinges; outside in the street drifted a mist, flickering with faces, like water poured from a bowl of light.

The spirit dead.

He'd leaned back into the shadows, afraid, and made no sound.

What was he supposed to do? He didn't know. Behind him the stairs led up into darkness. That was the way back to the ruined orsine. He peered up, hoping maybe Charlie would appear somehow up there, maybe he'd find a way. He waited. After a long while, he screwed up his courage and climbed the stairs himself, gripping the banister in his sore hands, but the stairs went on and on, and the darkness was total, blacker than anything he'd ever known, and it seemed to thicken as he ascended until it filled him with such fear that he had to turn back.

After that he didn't know what to do. Charlie didn't come for him, Alice didn't come, no one did. He folded his little knees up to his chest and rested his chin on his arms and stared out at the gray world in its soft decay, and he started to cry.

Maybe it was the quiet crying, or the tiredness. Whatever it was, he didn't notice that he had begun to shine, softly at first, a smoldering blue glow that brightened and brightened. The veins within his hands grew visible, then the blurred dark shapes of his bones. From the street outside, a tendril of mist curled around the bottom of the rotting door. Spirits. Soon a twisting ribbon of them were drifting closer, surrounding him. When he raised his wet face, it was like he was peering through a shifting prism of mist, and then something was in his mouth, a dry taste, like ashes, and then it was in his nose, too, the spirits surrounding him, and then he was trying to breathe but it was like he was underwater—

He kicked out, and scrambled backward, choking. All at once, in a panic, the blue shine burst outward from him, in a great slicing heat—arcing through the spirits, shivering them away into wisps, into nothing.

He was on his hands and knees, gasping. His skin was returning to normal. The spirits were gone but he knew there would be others, countless others, in the streets outside. He looked up. And that was when he saw, in the doorway, a familiar outline.

"Brynt?" he whispered. His cheeks were wet. "Is it . . . is it you? You're back?"

She flickered in the doorway, translucent.

"Brynt! It's me! It's *Marlowe!*"

Marlowe . . . ? Slow recognition filled her face. She'd appeared to him at the orsine, and earlier when he and Charlie had been lost in this world. And yet it was like she'd forgotten, like she'd not seen him in a lifetime. He watched the confusion on her face. *You do not . . . belong here, Marlowe. The spirit dead will be coming. Hurry—*

She beckoned.

He fled with her out into the decaying streets, hurrying through the puddles and leaping across the dripping lanes and crouching in doorways, under crumbled arches, until it was safe to go on, the spirits being drawn somehow to the talent, the power he'd used, and him just following the ghostly figure of a woman he'd loved when she was alive, not thinking anything at all, just breathing, trying to keep quiet.

And so began the days of hiding, if days they were, days that passed unchanging. At first he worried simply about how to keep hidden, to keep safe. Gradually he learned how to stay above the dead in the streets, to move along the rooftops and balconies with quiet feet. He kept hoping Charlie would come for him but after a time it seemed less and less real, less and less likely. That was when he began to try his own luck. He and Brynt followed the city east, followed the city west. It made no difference; always he arrived at the edge of the black Thames, peering across, as if the city of the dead were encircled. And yet it had no center; when they walked north, he and Brynt never reached the middle. He found again the strange room where he'd located the artifact for Dr. Berghast in that other lifetime, the room with the dead talent slumped within, the white tree in the street outside. It brought back a sudden violent memory of Charlie, so real it was like he could feel him.

For a while he stayed close, running back in when the spirits caught scent of him. But gradually he learned to conceal himself; and because Brynt could not enter the room, and there was nothing of use to him there anyway, in time he left that behind as well.

All the while, day after day, he watched the spirit of Brynt in wonder, not sure what she was. She *looked* like his beloved Brynt, seemed to guard him as she had in life. And yet something was different, something was off. She wasn't the same tough, grim, careful giantess who'd allowed Miss Quicke and Mr. Coulton to take him, and then pursued him when she understood his peril, who'd fought off a litch and saved them all on that train north to Scotland. There was in her too much . . . emptiness.

He tried not to think about that.

But she was right about one thing. He couldn't stay; he would have to cross the river.

The day came. He padded silently along the edge of the rooftop, swung himself down onto the crumbling balcony. The spirits drifted away over the poisoned water in the puddles, like a slow-seeping gas, leaving just the ordinary fog. Brynt was already descending. He hurried down through the ruined building, into the street, and ran at a low crouch across to the embankment. The fog was cold and clinging to his ragged shirt as he reached an ancient wooden stair.

He made his slow way down, Brynt following. The stair turned and turned, the wood soft and rotten underfoot, and it ended in a slimy dock half-submerged in the glittering black water of the river. He knew this place, had been watching it for weeks. A roofless shack stood at one end—a ticketing shack, Marlowe knew—though it had decayed and stood long empty. He crouched, waited. The fog was thicker here. He could just see dock after dock, stretching away both upriver and down. There would be slow ferries beyond, poled in by their cloaked and hooded guides, crowded with the dead, bumping softly against the landings. Then the translucent threads of spirits would slide up, and off, and away.

There was something, a kind of hissing coming from under the dock. Marlowe risked a look. He saw his own face, pale, watery, reflected in the black surface; but then it was fading, as if sinking from view, and the hissing was the sound of soft voices, of Charlie, of Alice, calling to him. There was someone moving in the river, someone down there—

Mar-lowe—

Brynt's voice, as if from afar. He fell back, breathing hard. Brynt was at his side, her eyes dark with fear. He wasn't sure what he'd seen but it filled him with dread.

You must not look into the river, she whispered. *That is not water. And do not let it touch you.*

Marlowe shuddered. The puddles on the dock looked slick and molten, like quicksilver. They seemed to eat away at the wood.

"I won't," he said.

Soon a gray prow was emerging out of the mist, paint peeling from it like dried skin. He'd not come this close before. It wasn't a skiff, as he'd thought, but a small steam ferry, its rails slick with a gray slime, its deck riding low in the black river. It was crowded with the spirit dead, flickering, mournful. A burning stack with its hatch standing open rose up from the middle of the deck, a dark red fire burning within, like a terrible eye. Marlowe shuddered. The carykk in dark robes leaned out over the river, a hooked pole held high. It caught a snare of rotting rope on the pier; the vessel glided in.

The carykk was a female. Her black cowl was folded back, revealing a skull-like visage, the skin gray and pulled so tight that it seemed to tear in places. Long teeth, where the gums had pulled back. A wreath of black smoke obscured her eyes, like a halo of darkness. She turned her grinning face from side to side, as if sniffing the air. The hood and long robes she wore were a part of her, like loose skin, gathering at her neck and elbows. A grimy iron chain was wrapped around one arm and crosswise at her chest; and Marlowe saw in horror that the chain was moving, making a soft liquid clatter as it slithered, and that it pierced her flesh in places and crawled along under the skin and then burst out again, wrapping her in its coils, moving slowly from arm to arm. Her hood and long robes gathered at her neck and elbows, like loose skin.

Marlowe put his head down, terrified. "Brynt?" he whispered. "Brynt, what if she sees me? What do I do?"

She is blind. You must be quiet.

Marlowe tried to make himself brave. "This isn't goodbye," he said.

I will find you. I will find a way across.

He looked up at Brynt's translucent face, her flat eyes. He wanted to believe her but he'd been left so many times. "I know you will," he whispered. "Don't forget, okay?"

The spirit dead were already dissipating, sliding uncertainly past and along the steps and away, up into the city of the dead. Without pause, the dark carykk began to unmoor the ferry. Her chains slithered. Marlowe stood. His feet were naked and cold and he stepped with caution over the pier and—without thinking any more about it—he climbed into the ferry.

Its deck was slick with mold. He stood with one hand on the slippery railing and made himself very small and he stared at the robed figure in the prow. The creature was tall—far taller than she'd seemed—and moved slowly, her limbs popping as she unhooked the ferry and swung the pole slicing through the air. Marlowe felt it pass dripping near his face. The ferry cast off and groaned as it started across.

Brynt vanished from view, almost at once. Marlowe felt suddenly the weight of his aloneness. Soon there were only the mists all around, the lapping of the river against the boat.

He held his breath, willing his heart to silence. He was afraid the carykk would hear it, reach out one terrible long arm and snatch him up, hurl him overboard.

But she stood unmoving in the prow with her face down and her wide shoulders slumped, as if lost in thought. The chains crawled over her throat, down her back. She was working something in her hands, he saw. It was a child's yellow ribbon. The carykk was tying and untying it around one skeletal finger, like a memory knot, running the fabric through her hands as if savoring the feel. Marlowe, fascinated, felt a sudden upwelling of pity. It might have been her daughter's; it might have been her own. Who had she been, in life? He craned his neck to get a closer look.

The creature stopped. She raised the grinning horror of her face.

Marlowe froze; he didn't dare breathe. The wreath of smoke obscuring the carykk's eyes whorled and smoldered with intensity. She tilted her chin, and *sniffed*.

It was like she could smell him, Marlowe, as if she could smell the wrongness of the boy, the lifeblood still inside him. She turned her awful head from side to side. And then suddenly she rose to her full height—up, up, ten feet, twelve feet, robes billowing in the sudden movement—and she advanced slowly across the deck toward him.

They'd passed the midpoint of the river by then. Marlowe saw with a sinking feeling that the far shore was thick with spirits, as if a great cloud of the dead had descended.

Still the carykk came nearer, towering. She swung her hands back and forth before her, the long knuckled fingers opening and closing on the air, popping quietly, but she was so tall, and he so little, that they clawed emptily over his head. He made himself smaller, gripping the railing.

The dark chain rose up from the back of her arm, serpentlike, and slowly extended blindly toward him. Marlowe watched it in fear. It swayed and came nearer. Swept past him, came back. Stopped not two inches from his face.

The carykk dipped her head, and *looked* at him. Her yellowed bone fingers extended.

It was then Marlowe realized, in horror, that the blue light was leaking up out of his skin. He could see the veins in his hands, dark against the shine, like tiny maps. He couldn't stop it. And he did the only thing he could think of doing: he reached up and snatched the faded yellow ribbon tied to the carykk's finger, and *pulled*.

And the ribbon came away in his grip, loose, rippling.

The creature whipped back, as if burned. The chain burrowed into its flesh. A wave of malice poured from the carykk, fierce, awful, as Marlowe ran past, stumbling behind the smokestack. "Don't!" he cried out. "Don't come closer, or I'll throw it in the river! I'll do it! I mean it!"

His voice sounded small and petrified, even to his own ears.

The carykk turned with a clicking sound and faced him. She loomed at the railing, massive, powerful, and swung her grinning face from side to side.

Marlowe's heart was pounding. His entire little body was shivering with fear. He held the ribbon crushed up in his fist, ready to throw, as if she could see. "Take me to where there aren't so many spirits," he demanded. His voice cracked with fear but he got it out. "You can have the ribbon back when I'm safe."

But the ferry didn't turn. It just continued sluggishly onward, without any visible means of steering, and Marlowe saw the shore slide nearer. Now through the mist and fog he could make out long weeds, the crumbled edges of a cobbled road long collapsed into ruin. A stone pier, a lantern glowing weakly in the fog.

And everywhere: the spirit dead, in their assembled mass. They seethed and folded over themselves.

"Not here," Marlowe cried. "Don't stop here! Turn the ferry!" And then he added, foolishly: "Please?"

The carykk watched him, grinning.

Marlowe didn't know what to do. He wished Alice was with him, he wished Charlie was with him. He held the ribbon high in his fist, like a lantern. The blue shining cut through the gloom, making him more afraid.

But then the prow was scraping against the rising shore; the weeds folded themselves around the sides; onshore the spirit dead in their ranks hung back, confused, as if sensing the living boy.

The carykk's eyeless face was fixed on Marlowe. And then she *spoke*.

He cannot sleep, she whispered. *He cannot sleep with you in his dream. He awaits you.*

Her voice was like iron dragged over rock. Marlowe shook. He hadn't known she could speak and something about it made her even more awful. Maybe it was the dark hatred in her voice. Maybe it was the eagerness.

She clawed her hands in front of her eyes, where the wreath of darkness hovered, as if drawing away a veil; and Marlowe saw what lay beneath. In the grooved and pitted sockets of her face, he saw two light-brown eyes, human-looking, a child's eyes, filled with sorrow, and the eyes stared at him as he stared back, confused, and they were wet with pity.

Then she opened her grinning mouth, and screamed.

A ripple went through the spirits onshore. They began to shudder, as if a dark wind were rising from within them, and their flickering visages twisted in pain. Then they were whirling faster and faster. Marlowe watched in horror as a cyclone of the dead thickened and roiled on the bank of that black river.

"Stop it," he cried. "Stop it!"

But the carykk with her too-human eyes kept screaming. That was when he saw, in the hazy skies over the river, the distant shadows of wings. Bonebirds.

He whirled around, cold with fear. Throwing the yellow ribbon at his feet, he clambered over the slippery railing and plunged, heart pounding, into the maelstrom.

At once his face and hands were lashed and stinging. The spirit dead were screaming in his ears, screaming as they crackled past. The gray light darkened. Soon he could see nothing but his own terrible blue shine, reflecting off the gauzy layers of the dead, dissipating in the storm. There was stone underfoot, uneven and damp, and he fell to his knees, gasping. He rose and tried to go on but could not. The veins in his arms were whitening. The blue shine was weakening. He couldn't breathe—he kept gasping and trying to inhale but just hacked and coughed. Something was wrong, there was something wrong inside him, he could feel it, it was like there were a thousand other lungs breathing *his* air, a thousand other hearts pumping *his* blood.

Then he was on his side. The wet ground was seeping through his rags.

He covered his face.

How long did he lie there? The screams of the dead were deafening. Through his fingers he saw a figure in a gray cloak, arms and legs padded with rags tied every which way, leaning into that wind, trudging through it, something cupped in the hands at its chest. One hand was bulky, not human. Its head and face were wrapped in a long scarf.

The stranger came on. He kneeled at Marlowe's side.

"Fool boy!" he hissed, eyes glittering. "You will bring them all to you!"

And he unwrapped his one good hand, and pressed his palm to Marlowe's little cheek so that an unsettling heat rose up in him. And he, Marlowe, felt a thing he'd almost forgotten, the living touch of another, and he closed his eyes, while a deep and unnatural sleep rolled over him and consumed him.

24

OTHER MONSTERS

Much later, Marlowe, shivering, opened his eyes.

The light was cold. He was alone, in a cavern, the walls slick. Water trickled over pebbles near his feet. He'd been laid down against one wall, on a sulfurous bed of old rags, and he rubbed his arms for the chill. A makeshift table stood in the gloom, on it a broken dish, two bent spoons. Pale equations had been carved into the walls, equations he could make no sense of, a madman's scrawl.

He slept again. When he awoke, someone stood in the entrance, a masked figure. The man from the maelstrom.

"You're awake," he grunted, through his scarf. "Good. We haven't much time."

His voice sounded as if it hadn't been used in a long time. Marlowe turned to see him stoop into the cave, half-blocking the eerie light from outside. A living man. He wasn't prepared for how that unsettled him. The stranger wore rags on his arms and legs, lashed together by belts and straps, like some miserable medieval armor. An ancient knife was tucked at the front of his belt. As Marlowe watched, he unbuckled something from his hand, a kind of apparatus, and at the same moment that Marlowe knew what it was, the man unwound the scarf, and Marlowe saw his face.

It was Dr. Berghast.

He was much changed. One cheek and ear was red and blistered. His dark eyes flickered over Marlowe. His scalp was hairless, his beard gone, so that his eye sockets looked deep and hollow. Old blood had bloomed and dried in the rags of his shirt. "It was madness to challenge a carykk, child," he said sternly. "You're lucky to still be whole. It will have called down the bonebirds by now. Are you well enough, can you walk?"

Marlowe shook his small head, confused. Slowly, as if through a haze, it all began to come back to him, everything, everything that had happened on that last terrible night at the edge of the orsine. The relief he'd felt at seeing another living soul suddenly vanished and in its place was a fury that surprised him.

He scrambled to his feet, balling up his little fists. "What'd you do? *What'd you do?*" he shouted. "You killed her! You killed Mrs. Harrogate! And you hurt *Charlie* and, and—"

"Enough," snapped Berghast. "I did not pull you from the dead for this. They will be hunting us both now. And their ears are keen. Hold your tongue."

Berghast crouched over the remains of a small fire and raked the ashes and gradually a grim little flame caught. It gave off very little heat but the strange dark red coloring of the fire made Marlowe shudder. He felt a lump in his throat but he was too angry and he wouldn't cry, not in front of this man, this terrible man.

"All this time," Berghast went on, "I thought I was searching for the Tracks. The hidden way. But I wasn't searching; I was *waiting*. For *you*." His voice was cold, brisk, filled with authority. "I was allowed to find the Tracks the same day you appeared. I do not believe in coincidence, child. This world *wants* us to proceed together. It has its own will."

He didn't know what the older man was talking about, but he didn't want to let go of his anger. There was a crazed smolder in Dr. Berghast's eye, a look that made Marlowe think of Jacob.

Dr. Berghast straightened. He turned his back and Marlowe saw a seeping stain from a wound in his back, the rags discolored and foul. The old man caught him looking. "It doesn't heal," he said softly. "That is where Charlie put his knife. It doesn't get worse, but it doesn't heal." He touched his blistered face with two fingers. "This, too."

Marlowe glared. *He'd* done that to Berghast, at the orsine, he'd burned the man with his shining on that terrible last night. It hadn't been enough. "What about everyone at Cairndale, all of *us*?" he demanded. "The orsine was *open*. You just left *everyone*. The dead were coming through. *You* did that!"

The older man's face was craggy in the firelight. He passed a hand across his eyes. "Ah, but your precious Charlie did that, Marlowe. By interrupting my work. By delaying the transference." For only a moment he looked tired, sad; then his face hardened. "Charlie tried to *seal* the orsine. Before I could take in the drughr. Because of him, I did not absorb all her power. I am not . . . strong enough for what must be done. What I took from her, what I took from *him* . . . it is not enough."

From him. Marlowe blinked slowly, afraid. "What did you do to Charlie?"

"Nothing . . . deliberate. His talent was caught in the transference. I believe it is keeping me alive, in here—along with this artifact, and what I could drain from the drughr."

"You took Charlie's talent?" Marlowe balled up his little fists. "You just wanted your own talent back! You never cared who it would hurt!"

"Why should the cost prevent it?" said Berghast harshly. "Why should I cease to do the right thing, because it is hard?"

"But it's *not* right. Alice wouldn't ever do what you did. Mr. Coulton wouldn't. I *hate* you. Why did you bring me here? I just want to get home."

"The world does not care what we *want*," answered Berghast. "Soon there will be no home to return to, there will be no safe place left. Not for your Charlie, or your friends, or your Alice. A darkness is waking, child. It may be too late already."

Marlowe swallowed, suddenly unsure. "What . . . what do you mean?"

"My work here is important, and it is not yet finished. You have not asked about that. About what it is I mean to do, now that I am here."

Marlowe glared. "I don't care. You don't tell the truth. You hurt my friends."

Berghast looked at him. He began to gather his things. He winced as he double-wrapped his hands, as he tightened the rags on his shins. He kept touching the hilt of the ancient knife, as if to reassure himself it was still there. "Come, hurry, child. You have no other option but to wait here for the carykk."

"Maybe I *will*. I'm not afraid."

The older man's eyes glittered.

"But you are afraid," he said calmly, and the calmness seemed worse somehow than any anger he might have. He tightened the straps on his arms, reached again for the plated glove. "And you are right to be."

A half hour later, when Berghast left the cavern, Marlowe went too.

It wasn't just the fear, or the veiled threats, or because he was supposed to. All of that was in him, it was true. But mostly he wanted not to be alone, not here, not again. He followed the older man out, into the eerie gray light of that world, down a long slope of scree, into a stand of trees blackened with rot. Far off, the dark Thames cut like a wound; the city of the dead rose up out of the mist beyond, its spires and chimneys and crooked rooftops. Somewhere there, he knew, Brynt's spirit would be adrift, maybe already forgetting him.

His legs were short, and it was hard to keep up. Berghast had wrapped Marlowe, too, in rags, covering every part of his skin. It made the running awkward, stiff. His breath was sour and hot against his own scarf. He could see a road below, winding toward a sunken roadhouse, the spires of a village in the fog beyond. The skeletal ravages of stone walls, stretching away over the land. Mist moved unnaturally across the fields, that same mist, uncurling and gathering itself and drifting on. The dead. In the far-off, Marlowe could see what looked like storm clouds, blue flashes of lightning illuminating the pan.

They passed into the trees and across the road and through a marshy undergrowth. Their footprints left deep squelching cuts in the muck. Berghast's strides were long, but he'd pause every twenty steps or so to listen to the stillness all around.

Solitary wisps of the dead drifted between the trees, drifted away. The air was cold. After a minute Berghast would rise and continue on, Marlowe following.

Soon they came to a gray path in the undergrowth. The ground sloped slightly upward and they reached a stone wall, collapsing. Beyond it stood a ruined farmhouse, its walls soft with decay. Its interior stood open to the sky. In the shadow of its walls Berghast crouched and raised a finger to his lips and gestured back the way they had come.

Marlowe looked. He saw the high crag where Berghast's cavern stood, hidden now. Above it, circling slowly in the sky, were three bonebirds. As he watched, their circles widened and they lifted higher and they began to drift away, in the direction of the river.

"They have the trace of us, now," Berghast whispered with a grimace, pulling the scarf down to regard Marlowe squarely. "They will bring the drughr down on us. We must go quietly, and in haste."

They'd rested only a brief time at the ruined farmhouse when Berghast led him away, across a rotting orchard, through a collapsed gate. He walked along the crest of a ditch and then, at a particular spot, leaped it, and Marlowe followed him up a slope. That was when he saw the Tracks.

"They are not easily found," Berghast whispered, turning in place, "though they do not look hidden. I've been searching for them a long time. A talent found them for me once, long ago. According to his map, he followed them to the gray rooms. That is the beginning of where we must go."

It was like spirit-Brynt's instructions: *Along the old tracks, past the gray rooms, to the Passage of the Drughr.* But Marlowe didn't tell Dr. Berghast. He felt an ache bloom in his chest, when he thought of her.

Out of breath, they staggered up the slope. A long straight line of iron rails, red with rust, led away into the undergrowth. The crushed stone ballast underfoot was leached of color. Black weeds sprouted between the ties. Here and there the gray wood of the sleepers was rotten and coming apart. Marlowe kneeled, laid a wrapped hand on the track. Even through the rags he could feel the cold metal. A dread rose up in him, and suddenly it was like all of his insides were being yanked forward, ripped out of his chest. He withdrew his hand, shaking.

"Who made these?" he whispered. "How come there are tracks here at all?"

"Who made any of this?" Berghast replied.

Marlowe thought about that. "The drughr?"

"The drughr never made anything but sorrow. This world makes itself." Berghast glanced at his face, watching his reaction, then back at the sky. "You don't understand yet, because you're not supposed to. Come. We should go while we can."

Marlowe stared off down the Tracks in both directions, uneasy. "But where do they lead?"

"To the drughr, child. And to what they are protecting."

Marlowe swallowed. He'd almost forgotten the feeling he got with Dr. Berghast, that feeling like he was doing something he didn't want to do, and like he wasn't being told everything he ought to be told. He knew he was supposed to ask more but he just didn't want to.

"Dr. Berghast?" he said quietly, and made himself look at the old man directly. "I just want to go home."

Berghast's eyes were pitiless. "And this is the way to that, too. Come."

They trudged on, then, under the ruined trees, along the rusted rails. After a time the trees thinned and Berghast stopped and Marlowe, raising his tired face, saw what lay before them.

The Tracks came out at a sudden steep trestle. A vast plain opened out beneath them. Pillars of clouds hung suspended from the sky. The plain was gray and pocked with crevices and in some of them Marlowe could see the dark red glow of fires. He could see thick hordes of the spirit dead, drifting slowly across the plain, spirits by the thousands. Along their edges he saw the lean dark figures of carykk, dozens, carrying staffs like shepherds and herding the dead onward. Some were moving in the direction of the river, the city of the dead beyond. But others were being led away. He could see other trestles, vast networks interconnected, vanishing in the fog of the plain. Marlowe, exhausted, sat on the railway sleeper, feeling the wood crumble softly under his weight.

There was something else, a structure being erected out on the plain. A kind of platform, or dais, surrounded by standing stones. There were carykk laboring there, dragging up buckets of muck, their chains glinting, and others were leading the spirit dead to a deep pit in the center. There, as Marlowe watched, the spirits slipped and fell, vanishing into the darkness. A flash of blue lightning would crackle now and then from the pit.

"What is it?" he whispered. "Dr. Berghast? What are they digging for? What are they making?"

Berghast's eyes were troubled. "An orsine," he said, and the dread in his voice was evident. "They are building an orsine. Here. *Inside* this world. The spirit dead, their longing . . . it will be the engine to drive it."

The old man's fear made Marlowe, too, afraid. "Is it so they can . . . get out? For good?"

"The drughr can already pass from world to world, child. They do not require orsines." He turned the armored glove at his side. "No, these works will be for something else. Or some*one* else."

He fell silent then, considering. Then he turned sharply. "Come," he said. "We should not linger. It is not safe."

Ahead, the wooden trestle extended impossibly long and high, leading far away across the plain. It seemed to have no ending but the fog.

Marlowe thought of the strange works on the plain below, of the terrible drop. He shook his head. "I don't want to go out there, Dr. Berghast. Please."

But the older man had walked to the edge of the drop and stood now watching the skies. There was something terrible and powerful in him. "So *this* is what was on the map," he said softly. "I could never tell . . ." He seemed to come to a decision. "We will be exposed, child. Walking the trestle. It is dangerous. We must trust to speed and the unexpected. But I see no other way. And if the bonebirds come . . ."

Marlowe watched him with worried eyes. But Berghast didn't finish his thought. He just set a tentative foot out onto the trestle. The wood sagged but did not give.

"It will hold," he called back. "You must keep to the rails. The supports are soft."

He took a second step, a third. Then he glanced back and nodded.

"Wait," called Marlowe. "Can't we go down? What if we get trapped?"

Berghast was wrapped and counter-wrapped like a man in a sandstorm and the armored glove on his hand was black in the pale light. The blade at his belt was like a warning. He held his arms out for balance.

"We are already trapped, child. Come!"

And Marlowe, not knowing what else to do, followed unhappily. He was small, much smaller than Dr. Berghast, and the structure did not creak and sway so sickeningly under his weight; but he could see through the gray webbing of slats and struts to the distant plain below. His head swam. He got down onto his hands and knees and crawled forward. There was black moss hanging like slime from the undersides of the boards. The trestle was dizzyingly high. He closed his eyes. He didn't think he could do it.

Then he felt a firm grip on his arm. It was Berghast, come silently back to him. "Come," he said gently. "You will be all right. We did not come all this distance, only to fail here."

Marlowe allowed himself to be lifted to his feet. He opened his eyes.

"There is an end to this, too," said Berghast. "As there is to all things. Be brave. We must go on, just a little further. Until we cannot."

They'd been walking slowly for some hours in the dizzying cold when Marlowe noticed they were being followed. A shape, far back along the trestle. Bent low to the sleepers like an animal, creeping. It might have been nothing at all, except it paused when they paused, continued when they continued.

Berghast had seen it also. "It's been following us since before we reached the plain," he said.

Marlowe stopped with a hand on his head, staring back. "What is it, Dr. Berghast? Is it a carykk?"

"I don't think so."

"Is it a . . . drughr?"

The older man shook his head slightly. He looked down at the drop below, the plains with their eerie fires flickering, the other trestles skeletal and distant, and his eyes hardened. "No," he said.

There was nowhere for them to go, Marlowe saw. It might have been only a spirit, or a trick of the weird light. But if it was something terrible, there'd be no escaping it. The span vanished into fog ahead, fog behind. Far below, the plain with its slow-moving herds of spirit dead, and their carykk guards, stretched off into the strangeness. Had they thought to look up, they might have seen through the fog their two silhouettes, the one very tall, both peering back the way they'd come. A third thing, like a glimmer of darkness, far behind them. But nothing looked up.

"Well, let it follow," said Berghast after a time. He sounded, now, slightly out of breath. The skin around his eyes looked pinched. "We cannot do anything about it. Come."

There was something else, something moving high off in the sky. Like a faint shadow in the fog. Marlowe cupped a hand to his eyes to make it out and then suddenly he felt Berghast's hand pulling him down onto the rails. The trestle groaned and shuddered.

"Stay down!" Berghast hissed.

It was a bonebird, half a league away. Hurrying past on its way someplace. For a long moment Marlowe held his breath, afraid even to take his eyes off the little speck. Then it seemed to him the creature continued on, vanishing into the mist.

But Berghast must have seen more clearly for he swore and drew Marlowe sharply to the far edge. The bonebird was coming back. Berghast swung his legs out over the drop and fumbled until he was standing on the skeletal understructure and his armored glove was leaving divots in the soft wood. His face was level with Marlowe's.

"There is plenty to hold on to down here," he said in a rush. "Hurry! It is coming!"

He held out his good hand and Marlowe reached for it and the older man—still strong, still powerful—drew him close. It was the nearest Marlowe had been to another living body. Berghast pulled him to his chest and hissed, "Don't let go. Hold tight." And he began, with a slow careful loping movement, to clamber over the under-struts, like a spider.

He crawled to the middle of the trestle and found his footing in a join and pinioned his shoulders into place, to free up his hands.

Then, with great care, he shifted Marlowe, until the boy was cradled between his knees. He raised a finger to his lips, and turned his head upward.

Marlowe let his eyes drift down to the distant earth below. It was maybe a hundred yards down. His heart was beating very fast. In the silence he heard, faintly at first, the scissorlike snicking of wings. He peered up through the slats and ties. Something big and dark passed quickly over them, turned, circled back again.

He could see Berghast's eyes, strained, fierce. One hand had gone to the knife at his belt.

The presence scissored past again. Searching.

But then suddenly, like that, it was gone. Berghast turned his head slowly to try to follow its flight. Something behind them had drawn it off. A silence stretched out around them.

"Did it see us?" Marlowe whispered at last.

"It's you they want," Berghast hissed.

For just a moment the watery otherworldly light filled the older man's eyes, turning them a dazzling blue. Then he looked away.

Gradually the fog deepened. They walked on, hour after hour, along the endless creaking trestle, the plain below dissolving from view. They saw neither bonebirds nor the dead. And whatever it was that had followed them had disappeared in the gray.

Marlowe was so tired. He stumbled along on the rusting and twisted rails, seeing the moisture gather and drip from the slats into the nothingness below. Berghast was just a dark silhouette in the fog, bundled and shapeless. For a time they traversed a section of the trestle that was fallen into ruin, and Marlowe had to be carried across the gaps, and Berghast would run powerfully and make the jump without fear. Later still they came to a crossing where a second trestle joined and went away up and down the plain, but Berghast kept them walking in the one direction. Marlowe was thinking, as he went, about that older man, the way he'd carried Marlowe without hesitating under the span to keep him safe. There'd been gentleness there, as well as fear. Something like what he'd remembered from Brynt, from Eliza, from Alice Quicke. It was like Marlowe mattered as much as the peril.

At last out of the fog a darkness loomed, and the trestle ended at a second cliff. A cluster of decaying buildings emerged from the gloom. It was a railroad depot, he saw, with a turntable bridge spanning a vast pit, and tracks leading away into crumbling sheds. Immediately beyond the buildings lay a river, sluggish and dark, and a stone bridge curving across it. A vast rockface rose up on the far side, with three dark entrances. Caves.

Berghast followed his gaze, shook his head. "Those are the gray rooms," he said. "We'll not go in there. We can follow the river on the far side."

"What's in them?" asked Marlowe.

Berghast grunted through his scarf. "I'd not care to find out."

They stopped for sleep in one of the abandoned outbuildings, a slung-roofed wooden shack with a porch out front and half the floorboards rotted away inside. The ground underneath was wet and littered with debris.

Marlowe was so tired he sank to the floor and let his hands rest beside him. But he found he couldn't sleep. As soon as he tried to, all of the thousands of questions he had came flooding back to him. He opened his eyes. Dr. Berghast was sitting with his back to the far wall, holding the armored glove gingerly on his knees.

Marlowe pulled his scarf away from his face. "Dr. Berghast?"

Berghast raised his eyes. It was as if he'd been waiting for the boy to speak. "What is it?"

"The bonebird today . . . You were afraid of it. But at Cairndale—"

"The bonebirds at Cairndale are different, child."

"But if—"

Berghast made an impatient noise in his throat. "They are *different*. They were created by a bone witch only a hundred years ago. They are smaller, more . . . docile. But these creatures that hunt us here? These are as old as the orsine itself. Or nearly so. They serve the drughr." He was quiet for a moment and then he shifted onto one elbow. "The first bonebirds were created to be messengers. Travelers between the worlds. They were a way for talents and drughr to communicate, across the divide."

"To communicate with the drughr?" Marlowe, despite his exhaustion, was astonished. "What for?"

"It is a long story, child."

"Okay."

But Berghast seemed reluctant to say more. He took off the armored glove and unwrapped the rags at his hand and began to massage the discolored skin there. Marlowe watched, fascinated.

At last he said, "You hate them, don't you? The drughr?"

Berghast grimaced. "Hate is not a strong enough word."

"Is that why you hate me, too?"

Berghast paused. "Does it matter to you so much, what I think?"

Marlowe shrugged, suddenly uncomfortable.

"After all, I am the villain, am I not?" Berghast went on. "The betrayer of you and your dear Charlie? I am the one who does not care what happens to all the talents at Cairndale, yes?"

"That's right," Marlowe said bravely.

Berghast's dark eyes glinted. "I do not hate you," he murmured. "And you are no drughr. You are something else, a . . . new thing." Berghast rose and crossed to the ruined door and stood listening a moment. "Talents manipulate dead tissue. That is where our power comes from. But your gift manipulates *living* tissue. That is not something a talent or a drughr has ever done."

Marlowe chewed at his lip. "But I'm still a monster, aren't I? You said—"

"I said, I said," said Berghast sharply. "Don't quote me to myself, child. You're no monster; you're just different."

There was a sudden lump in Marlowe's throat. It was like he'd been waiting to hear it said, like he'd been afraid of it and wanting to hear it both. He swallowed. "Miss Davenshaw said that, too," he mumbled. "She said being different isn't the same thing as, as—"

A deep groove appeared in Berghast's brow. Something hardened even further in his voice. "My life has been long, Marlowe. Longer than you can imagine. I have done terrible things, things that fill me with shame. And I have failed to do things, too, difficult things that were wrong, maybe, but would have prevented much harm later. I am ashamed of these, too." He breathed quietly. "Who we are acquires its shape through the choices we make, and go on making. Do you see? There is no right course. We just do what we can. And after a while the choices we make are all in conversation with the ones we've made before. It took me a long time to see this. I'm making a choice now, here. To make up for choices I made before, in my life. That's why I've come." He gestured at his ruined face, at the artifact he wore on his hand. "Why I've done this to myself."

Marlowe didn't understand half of the older man's confession. But he thought about that last part, and about Brynt, and about Eliza who'd looked after him before Brynt, and how they'd always told him that he wasn't as bad as he feared. It was like Dr. Berghast had never had that, never had anyone to tell him that.

He raised his little face. "I know what it's like to feel bad about yourself," he said firmly. "But it isn't right, if that's all you see. You have to see the good parts, too."

The older man looked faintly amused. "Wisdom from a boy in breeches," he said. "If you live long enough, truly you meet with everything."

But there was no real bite to his words and Marlowe didn't mind it anymore, for some reason. He was thinking about the last part of what Dr. Berghast had said. "Dr. Berghast? Did you come here on purpose?"

Berghast nodded.

"Why?"

Berghast's eyes darkened. "What do you know of Alastair Cairndale?"

Marlowe hesitated. "Only what you told me. What Miss Davenshaw taught us."

Berghast came back over and sat. "You should know the truth of him," he said. "He was the greatest of our kind, the First Talent. Not first to exist, but first in order of power. I saw him once, though I was still very young. This would be three hundred years ago, Marlowe. And he was old even then. I do not know where he was born, or when. He was a tall man, severe, red-haired, bearded. Physically powerful. There were other talents before him, but none like him. For of the five talents—the clinks, the casters, the glyphics, the dustworkers, and the turners—Alastair Cairndale wielded all five. Imagine it. There's never been another like him, to rival his power. I pray there never will be.

"What is a god, if not a being with power over death? I've tried to make sense of that question. Time corrupts all things, drughr, haelan, all. Life has meaning because it ends. Talents are not more worthy or deserving than the weakest among us, merely because of our talents. We draw our gifts from the dying cells in our own flesh, but we are neither wiser nor more righteous nor more deserving than ordinary people. Alastair . . . did not agree. He did not think this way. He'd seen our kind hunted, branded as witches, quartered and burned. He'd survived in a Europe that was terrible and stained with superstition. Nevertheless, it does not excuse his beliefs. His . . . choices."

Berghast breathed quietly, as if deciding how to go on. "Alastair Cairndale purchased the land at Loch Fae and began construction on his manor in those years. He never imagined a . . . school. A safe haven. What he wanted was a fortress, something impregnable and secluded. He gathered his own kind to him.

"There were those who opposed him. An ancient brotherhood known as the Agnoscenti, who lived alongside talents, who hid them, nurtured them. A collective of talents in medieval Paris. Powerful talents from the kingdom of Ghana. Others. Alastair believed it was time the talents revealed themselves to the world, and took their rightful place. A great struggle broke out. A war, lasting thirty years. Terrible things were done on both sides. Talentkind was diminished and has never recovered, even to this day." Berghast lowered his face so that Marlowe could not see his eyes. "It was Alastair Cairndale's pride and ambition that led to his destruction."

Marlowe picked at the rags tied to his hands. "You told me Alastair Cairndale went into the orsine and disappeared. That he died fighting the drughr."

"Did I?"

"You did."

"Ah. But he is very much alive. Only sleeping."

"Sleeping?"

Berghast nodded. "Alastair Cairndale found a way to connect himself to all of talentkind, to tie himself into the threads that the glyphics use. He called it the Dreaming. And because of this, it was believed he could not be killed, not without severing the rest of talentkind from its source, not without risking the destruction of all we are. And so what was to be done with him? He was banished—banished here, by the

Agnoscenti, into this world, imprisoned in an unnatural sleep that was to contain him forever. I cannot imagine how it was done; such skills are long since lost, vanished with the Agnoscenti themselves. But the greater part of Alastair Cairndale's power—the part of him that was tied to the Dreaming, his 'sixth talent,' as it was sometimes called—was cut out of him, and hidden where no one would ever find it. As if it were an object, to be locked away in a box somewhere. So the old stories claimed. In this way the First Talent was subdued, and weakened, and warded.

"But the Agnoscenti could not leave him unguarded, all the same. Five talents—one from each class of power—volunteered to come through the orsine, to watch over him and be sure that he never awoke. Each was powerful on their own, but together they were . . . immense. But this place is different from how it was imagined. It corrupts our kind, twists us into things we do not want to become. Those five talents began to change. A darkness spread through them. And in time we heard less and less from them. The bonebirds were sent in to act as messengers. Gradually they too ceased to return. The talents continued to change."

Marlowe was nodding despite himself. "They're the drughr, aren't they?"

"Those five became the drughr. Yes."

"So my mother—?"

"Was one of them. They are all lost now, lost to us and to what we hold dear. We did not imagine how powerful the First Talent could be, even in his sleep. His dreams called to them, ensnared them; now they serve him. They gather their strength. They wait. For it is said the First Talent will wake again; and I believe that time is near."

Marlowe shuddered. "Is that why you're here? To stop it from happening?"

Berghast took the ancient knife from his belt and turned it in his hands. "Indeed, child," he said softly. In his eyes flickered an otherworldly fire. "I must find him, and kill him."

Marlowe stared. "But . . . that's *awful*, Dr. Berghast. Isn't there another way?"

"No," said the older man.

"Maybe he's not really waking up. Or maybe he's . . . changed."

"Oh, child," said Dr. Berghast. His ravaged face was grim. "He is more terrible than you can imagine. No, I must find him and kill him, before he awakens. No matter what it might mean for talentkind. This world wants it; can't you feel it? And I believe it has sent you here to help me."

Marlowe looked at him in bewilderment. "I don't want to hurt anybody!"

"The drughr fear you. The bonebirds are hunting you. You have a part to play in all of this."

Marlowe shook his head, recoiling. "I . . . I just want to go home. I just want to see Charlie again, and Alice, and everyone."

Berghast crouched in front of Marlowe, his long legs folding up, and with his ungloved hand he lifted the boy's chin. "But the orsine is sealed behind us, child. You did that. There is only one way home from here. I will take you there myself, after we have destroyed the First Talent. I will send you through it."

There was something in the way he said it that made Marlowe pause. "Won't you be coming too? Don't you want to get home too?"

Berghast ran a hand across his jaw. "Home," he said softly, as if tasting the word. "When you have lived long enough, the word means nothing. I will not be leaving this world."

"You can't think like that, Dr. Berghast. There's always a way."

"You are still very young, child. Home isn't a place you go to. It's something you carry with you. And I lost mine a lifetime ago."

"Can't you make a new one?" said Marlowe. But he felt a lump form in his throat. He thought of being alone in this world and having nowhere worth going back to.

The light in Berghast's eyes darkened. He withdrew across the room. Whatever openness had passed between them faded, like a lantern going out. "The pity of a child," he muttered. He folded his arms across his chest, and shifted onto his side, and closed his eyes.

For a long time after that, Marlowe watched the old man sleep. The rise of his chest, the dry rattle of his breathing. He was surprised to realize he didn't hate him anymore, not the way he probably should, and he didn't understand it. Goodness and evil didn't make sense, not the way they used to. Sometimes it seemed everyone was a little bit good on the inside. He curled his knees to his chest for warmth.

Thing was, you just had to keep your eyes open, if you wanted to see the good in a person. Just look close. Maybe you had to look a little closer with some people, like Dr. Berghast. And maybe the good wasn't always equal to the bad. But it was in there somewhere all the same, he decided. Even if it made your heart hurt to think about it, even if it made the world a little harder to be in, still it was there. The goodness was there.

25

Into the Cold to Come

Marlowe awoke after a fitful sleep. The light had not changed. Dr. Berghast was standing in the doorway, peering out, the armored glove on his hand. The wound on his back was seeping afresh. His head was not covered and the shorn scalp looked mottled and scarred where he stood and something in the man's manner made Marlowe afraid.

"Dr. Berghast?" he whispered, getting to his feet. "What is it? What's out there?"

"Our pursuer," the man replied softly. "What followed us on the trestle."

It was a spirit, hovering in the middle of the decaying yard. Columnar and twisting in the eerie light like a rope of water. Its faces flickered rapidly in passing but all seemed fixed on the doorway, on the two living figures within. Its size, its sadness, these were what betrayed it. Marlowe swallowed, suddenly overcome.

It was Brynt.

"You know her," murmured Berghast. Marlowe glanced up, startled. It was not a question; the older man had been watching his face.

Marlowe nodded, unable to say anything. She'd promised she'd find him, that she'd find a way. And she'd done so. He felt awful about leaving her behind and he felt awful about her being here and he looked at her and he could see something wasn't right. She wasn't right.

"She's my—"

But he felt Berghast's powerful hand on his shoulder and went quiet.

"She's not what you think," he hissed. "And she's not alone."

That was when he saw Brynt's spirit, too, had turned. It drifted now toward the corner of the building, out of sight. The air was cold, silent.

"What is it? Is it a bonebird?" Marlowe whispered. He scanned the pale sky.

Berghast put his hand over Marlowe's mouth, drew back from the doorway. The floorboards groaned under their weight. His eyes were fierce. "Stay close," he hissed. "If I run, you run. Understood?"

"But . . . what is it?" Marlowe whispered.

Berghast blinked sharply. "They've found us."

Berghast was already wrapping his head and face in his rags like a bedouin and then he helped Marlowe with his coverings, too. That was when an awful muffled popping sound reached them. Marlowe peered cautiously out. Something was shuffling between the buildings across the yard, a tall figure leaning on a staff, wearing a dark gray robe. A wreath of smoke obscured its eyes. A heavy iron chain was slithering all up and down its arms. It paused to sniff the air and kneeled in the muck to sniff the ground and then it rose again and that was when Marlowe saw the yellow ribbon tied on its finger.

He began to tremble.

The carykk turned its skull-like visage from side to side and then moved, slowly, horribly, toward the nearest building. Its glistering skin, baggy and robe-like, gave off a faint haze of soot as it moved; with each step its heavy feet sucked powerfully up out of the mud. Marlowe felt a tap on his shoulder. Berghast pointed off to the right. A second carykk was drawing a strange line in the muck with its chain, as if tracing the way they'd come.

Berghast waited until the first carykk had gone into the far building, and then he pulled lightly on Marlowe's sleeve. They rose like smoke and slipped noiselessly out the door, across the crumbling porch, around the side of the building. It was the same way Brynt had gone; and she was flickering there at the corner, as if awaiting them.

As soon as they appeared, she turned and slid behind the next building and disappeared down an alley.

Marlowe was surprised at where they were. He'd been too exhausted when they stumbled in to explore. It was a kind of labyrinth of rotting and ruined buildings, erected to no purpose, all of it built in the shadow of the gloomy river, the sheer gray cliff rising up beyond. Some fifty yards in the other direction, lost now in fog, lay the trestle, the drop to the plain below. There were twisted and blackened rail lines leading in both directions along the river. And looming in the cliff, as tall as Mrs. Harrogate's terrace house, were the three cave entrances Dr. Berghast had warned him about, utterly black, eerily cold. The gray rooms. There was an unspeakable horror about them. He tried not to think about it.

Dr. Berghast stopped. Something was wrong.

Marlowe thought he could hear the faint popping sound of the carykk behind them, somewhere among the buildings, as if they'd got wind of the pursuit. But Brynt appeared out of the fog, radiating fear, and slid past them, back the way they'd come. After a moment Dr. Berghast, wordless, followed.

Only Marlowe hesitated. He couldn't have said why. He pressed a hand into the soft wooden wall and stood looking ahead and he saw *something*—a huge dark figure, emerging out of the mist, making no sound at all—and he started to shake with fear. It came up out of the fog toward him. A clawlike hand covered in thorns reached out, grasped the wall of the building, as if to drag itself forward. It had too many fingers, ten, twelve. Then a second hand, and a third, appeared.

Marlowe couldn't move.

And then the thing was in front of him. It was not a carykk. Still ten feet away, it towered over him, horned, with four long, muscled arms, and enormous hands, a thing not wrapped in shadow so much as in the absence of light, with eyes that burned with darkness.

A drughr.

Time seemed to slow down. For an impossible moment Marlowe stared at the creature and it stared back and something passed between them, a kind of . . . recognition. His blood slowed. His fear drained away. He felt calm, deep in his heart, and his mouth opened softly in amazement. Such gentleness, he thought, such power. What harm could lie in his own relinquishing, if he could just give it what it wanted—

Something exploded to his left. A whirl of gray fury. It was Berghast, hurtling forward, the armored glove he wore raised high to shield Marlowe. Gripped in its fist was the ancient knife. He'd ripped away his coverings. As he threw himself forward, he cried out.

And the drughr's spell was broken. Marlowe stumbled backward, horror rising in him.

He was shining.

"Go, boy! Run!" Berghast was shouting. He swung the blade at the drughr and when it struck, the dark figure gave out a terrifying roar, and recoiled. Its many arms were smashing the air. Darkness like dust burst in clouds from the drughr's fists.

Berghast fell back, his skin bloodless and gray in the mist.

Marlowe felt a coldness at his neck and turned and saw Brynt behind him, urging him to follow.

"Dr. Berghast!" he cried. "We have to go!"

Now a carykk was emerging from between the buildings to their right, its chain sliding in a liquid clatter from under the skin of its forearm, lashing out in a sharp whistling arc. But Marlowe fell back into the muck, the ooze sliding up between his fingers, and the heavy iron links missed his head.

"Dr. Berghast!" he cried again, scrambling backward.

And then the older man was with him, seizing him under the arms, dragging him up onto his feet, and they were running, running after the flickering visage of Brynt, wending their way through the fog between the buildings. There were more carykk emerging, stepping now out of the gloom, their chains spinning, and Marlowe could feel something dark and huge and terrible pursuing them. He was so afraid. They turned, turned again, stumbled out over the Tracks into the open and across from the roundhouse. Somewhere deep in Marlowe's brain he understood they were being herded, pushed onward. The fog swirled all around. In his fear he could hear Dr. Berghast gasping, the squelch of the muck. Then they were stumbling in the middle of the turntable, the deep greasy pit opening out all around them, and there were carykk creeping forward through the mist. One of them came closer, its skull wreathed in smoke. It was the carykk with the yellow ribbon. But it held back, waiting. Marlowe felt a coldness go through him. There was nowhere to go but backward, across the river, to the face of the cliff.

Brynt was guttering like a candle.

"Marlowe—!" Berghast cried. "The bridge! Go into the gray rooms! They will not follow!"

Faint through the mist the huge dark figure of the drughr was appearing. He could hear its roar. But Berghast was already hurrying past the spirit of Brynt, onto the bridge, the rags hanging from him like ribbons. Marlowe's blue shine cut the fog like a blade.

He was running, too. He scrambled across the span, half sliding on its slippery stones, scarcely daring to glance at the slow river beneath. At the cavern entrance, Berghast paused, just long enough to meet the boy's eye. Then he ducked his head and disappeared. The darkness swallowed him whole.

All around in the fog the carykk let out a fierce and awful scream, as they realized what was happening. Above all, sounded the deep roar of the drughr. The mists draping the bridge were shivering; things were coming across, coming closer.

Marlowe put his hands to ears, and followed. Brynt was flickering at the edge of the darkness, her face filled with dread. And then Marlowe too entered, and it was like a curtain of coldness fell across him, and all the light behind him winked out, all the screams and cries ceased, and there was only his own frightened breathing and nothing to be seen, not Berghast, not Brynt, no one, just a darkness that had no beginning and no end.

RISE
of the
DRUGHR

·

26

THE VILLA AT AGRIGENTO

No one knows why the drughr chose the form of a woman, children," said Abigail Davenshaw. She listened to the rustling of bedclothes cease. She could feel their young eyes on her. "Some believed it could make itself look like anyone it had devoured. Others believed the reason was stranger than that, that the drughr took on the resemblance of one that it grieved over. That there was a kind of . . . love in the creature."

"Could it pretend to be one of *us?*" asked Zorya. "If it wanted to?"

"No, my little one," she said with a smile. "Not anymore."

"Because it's dead," Antony piped up. "Marlowe killed it at the orsine."

It had been Dr. Berghast, in truth. According to Charlie, who'd seen it. But she did not correct the little one. Let them believe it was Marlowe.

"But what if it didn't die?" asked Zorya. "What if it was just *pretending* to be dead?"

"What if it's Michael!" Antony called out.

Michael made a spooky sound from across the room. Someone giggled.

"Hush, now. It wasn't like that. It would come in dreams, or in waking visions," Abigail Davenshaw replied. "It didn't climb into a bed wearing a nightshirt."

"Did *you* ever see it?" asked little Shona.

Abigail Davenshaw paused. The warm Sicilian night was coming in through the shutters. She could smell the gardens beyond. She shifted where she sat at the edge of Zorya's bed.

"*See* it?" she said, with a faint smile.

There was a quick intake of breath. "Sorry, Miss Davenshaw. I didn't mean—"

She held up her hand. "It's all right. I know what you meant. And no, I was never in the presence of the drughr, thank goodness. But we must always be careful."

"In case it comes back," the child added sturdily.

She made a face. "Well, let us hope not. Now, to bed."

"But, what if there's another, Miss Davenshaw? What if the drughr had a . . . a friend?"

Zorya spoke quickly: "Or two friends?"

Now Antony's bed, across the room, creaked. "What if there's *fifty* of them?" he whispered.

"Or a million!"

Abigail Davenshaw got to her feet, clapped her hands for attention. They all fell silent.

"The important thing to know, children," she said sternly, "is that you are safe here. Now. Enough talk of such things. Sleep. Dream good dreams. Dream of the saint's festival. And remember, you have your studies in the morning."

She wasn't sure it was the best thing to speak so openly with the little ones about the drughr. She knew Oskar didn't approve, though he'd never said it directly. But she'd come to believe a part of what made the burning of Cairndale possible was all the secrets. She was determined not to ever let such destruction into their lives again. And these children were too vulnerable, too exposed—even here, at this new refuge she was trying to establish—for her to allow them a normal childhood. They were *not* safe; and it wouldn't make them any safer to pretend otherwise.

She left their door standing half-open and glided along the hallway, trailing her fingertips over the walls. The white blindness of her vision was dim; she was moving through the dark villa, her feet careful, her steps silent. She paused to listen to the creaking of the ancient house. A sprawling Italian villa with a view—she'd been told—of a ruined Greek temple on a hill to the south, and beyond that the sea. A narrow dirt road wound its way down from the villa all the way to the village, and beyond that, to Agrigento. What the Sicilians must think of them, strange English visitors with their peculiar children and their solitary ways, she could only imagine.

The villa was not large, not like Cairndale. The eastern half had fallen into ruin, the roof collapsing, so that the rooms stood open to the sky. But the rest of the villa remained habitable. It had been built in the balanced, classical style of the Enlightenment, a two-storied, many-windowed stone edifice, with a wide balcony running the length of the facade, and a curving grand staircase down to the carriage walk. In the rear of the house the gallery opened onto a vast rectangular terrace, latticed and intertwined with foliage, and it was here, above the private gardens, that Abigail Davenshaw slipped out into the warm night air, and found her way to where she knew Komako Onoe stood guard.

The girl had changed much, since the burning of Cairndale. She'd grown thin, muscled. Abigail Davenshaw could feel it when she wrapped her arms around the girl. She'd always been clever, and reliable, but now she'd turned inward, and there was in her voice a severity that broke Abigail Davenshaw's heart to hear. Worse, since returning from Spain, since the horrors of the glyphic there—and Abigail had not been told the half of it, she was certain—Komako seemed filled with a fury, a fury that had to do with the death of that awful man, Bailey, and all the others they'd lost in the past year. She'd brought back such troubling news—word of the second orsine, sealed, its glyphic murdered; dark warnings about the Abbess, whom Abigail Davenshaw had only heard of in stories; the cryptic hints about a Dark Talent, which Komako had been unwilling or unable to explain; and the glyphic's own warnings about how meaningless it all might be. She could sense how heavily it weighed on Komako. It wasn't fair, these children, what they had to carry. Oh, Abigail worried about the girl, yes. She worried about all of them.

Komako had been back from Málaga for ten days, now. And she'd sat up every night watching for the thing that prowled outside the villa's walls. It was like she needed to hunt *something, anything*. They'd found no more mutilated carcasses, so far. But they would, Abigail knew; the thing was still out there, waiting.

She walked the long still length of the terrace, then stood waiting. The night was shirring softly all around her, the warm air on her hands and face. She could hear Komako's breathing shift.

"The little ones are asleep?" the girl asked.

"Asleep?" Abigail allowed herself a smile. "I expect they're wide awake, Miss Onoe, telling stories about your exploits in Spain. Miss Crowley will be up in a moment, shushing them. You and the drughr are their favorite subjects." She hesitated. "They're glad to have you back. They feel . . . safe with you."

"They shouldn't. They're not."

She inclined her face, to acknowledge this. "And how is your face? Is it healing?"

A pause, as the girl perhaps turned her eyes again back to the walls, to the darkness beyond. "The ointments help," she said at last. "It's like a bad sunburn now, I guess. I heard a carriage in the front drive earlier. Did you hear—?"

"I heard no one." Abigail Davenshaw smoothed the blindfold at her face with her fingertips, then glided forward. If they had visitors, she would know soon enough. And she had pressing concerns to discuss first. "What of your vigil?"

"It's been quiet. Calm." The girl's voice was low. "Still no sign of whatever it is. The stars are out; I can see all the way to the temple. There are shadows of course. You're sure it's not just a wild animal?"

"I'm sure of nothing."

The girl was silent.

Abigail Davenshaw added, "But what sort of animal takes the head from a wild dog? And spreads its insides in a circle?"

"Oskar thinks it's the drughr. He thinks it's come back."

"I know what Mr. Czekowisz thinks."

The girl cleared her throat. "When I was in Barcelona, I saw . . . bodies," she said quietly. "Taken apart. Mr. Bailey was certain it was the drughr that did it. He said it had taken a boy, a young caster. He was convinced the drughr was hunting him. He was so frightened. I told him what happened at Cairndale but he wasn't convinced. I think maybe it's why he sacrificed himself to the Spanish glyphic. I think he thought it was better than waiting for the drughr to find him."

"Dr. Berghast destroyed the drughr at the orsine. Young Mr. Ovid saw it. Mr. Bailey did not."

"Yeah. Well. Charlie saw *something*."

Abigail Davenshaw felt for the flat expanse of the stone railing, allowed herself to lean into it. She drew her shawl around her shoulders. Everything Komako was saying made a terrible sense. A warm breeze moved through the gardens, stirring the lemon and orange trees. She could smell the creeping rosemary, the faint bite of salt from the sea.

"Are we all just afraid of a thing that's already gone, Miss Onoe?"

she wondered aloud. "Your Mr. Bailey in Spain. Mr. Czekowisz, here. In Miss Quicke's last letter, she said something was stirring in Paris, she could feel it. The drughr casts a long shadow. I fear we are still in the dark of it."

She felt the girl's gloved hand cover her own. The cool of it.

"Or maybe there's more than one," the girl murmured.

Abigail Davenshaw didn't answer. It so perfectly echoed the children's fears from earlier. She'd had the thought too, of course, knew the old stories of the five talents who'd gone into the orsine, only to be corrupted and lost. They'd always just been stories. But even in the stories they'd all vanished long ago, all but one; and she wasn't prepared to consider the alternative, not just yet. Let us have our peace awhile longer, she told herself.

She laid her other hand on top of Komako's gloved knuckles, gently. "Do your hands still hurt you?"

"Only when I work the dust," the girl replied.

Just then the gallery doors opened behind them. Abigail Davenshaw heard several figures step through, the click of their shoes, the rustle of their clothing. She tilted her face, inquiring. And then Komako was catching her breath sharply, and pulling away, and someone laughed, and a voice called out to her that she hadn't heard in more than a month. All at once strong arms were encircling her, stronger than she'd remembered, and her face was crushed gently into a rumpled shirt, a shirt smelling of sweat and dust, and her eyes were suddenly sore, her cheeks were wet.

For it was Charlie.

He'd returned.

Caroline Ficke, old, weary, stood in the pool of candlelight at the edge of the terrace, breathing in the warm Sicilian night, watching as Charlie was swarmed by his friends. The pale soft boy, Oskar, his white-blond hair a mess; the dustworker, Komako, her dark eyes shining; the thin hard lady with her eyes blindfolded, who must be the Davenshaw woman, whom Charlie was holding like she was his mother. They'd forgotten her for the moment. Caroline's heart had not ceased hurting since London, since the Falls, since stumbling back up into the fog-enshrouded alleys to their wagon and finding her own little ones gone, lost and gone for good. For somehow she'd known, even as they'd gone on with Deirdre, and carefully brought her down to the docks, that the others were dead. It was a feeling in her, a certainty, like a kind of message sent to her from the beyond. The grief had stained her days since.

Only now, all these weeks later, seeing Charlie reach down to hold that blind woman, watching Komako wipe angrily at her cheeks, hearing Oskar's laughter, did she start to feel human again.

For she still had Deirdre, who sat now just inside, veiled and cloaked, a weird lumpen shape in the gallery candlelight, Deirdre who was slowly twisting into a glyphic and away from the human, Deirdre who rustled like leaves when she stirred, who needed her now more than ever. And there was Charlie, too, Charlie with that sickness in him, the corrupted dust, that had bonded to him and him alone and that she understood so poorly. She watched him there in the moonlight, how gingerly he held his arm, and she knew that Marber's dust was alive in it, creeping.

That dust had destroyed Jack Renby—Claker Jack—had torn him open and then collapsed under its own weight, crushing him until he burst. She saw it often in her dreams, and woke in the night sickened. Yet she'd learned a few truths since, suspected more. She knew the dust in Charlie—the dust that had been in Marber, and outlived him—was the very substance of the drughr itself, the same substance that the other world, the world of the dead, was made of. It seemed it could bond to only one living talent at a time. Why it had bonded to Charlie and no other, why he was safe from Mr. Renby's gruesome fate, she couldn't guess. But she knew what she'd seen in Renby's final moments: an orsine, a window onto that other world.

And other drughr within.

She'd said nothing to Charlie about it, since those confused first moments. She wanted to know more, first. But it was clear to her that Marber's dust, the corrupted dust from the drughr, was a rare and powerful substance. Mr. Renby had wanted it. His bone witch had wanted it. Those sinister urchins, with their little blades, had stalked it on behalf of the Abbess. But if the dust was capable of restoring a talent and, more, of opening a path through to the other world, then it was no wonder why.

She and Deirdre slept that night in a long desolate room, nearly empty, with faded cherubs painted on the ceiling, and water-damaged walls. But when she awoke in the morning, she found Deirdre asleep with her warm head resting on Caroline's arm, and the twiglike tendrils of her shoulders leaning into the sunlight where it poured in through the tall windows, and the light was green in the little heart-shaped leaves in her fingers, and Caroline felt a great upwelling of relief. The child was safe; they'd reached the villa at Agrigento.

She rose quietly, and put on her artificial arm. Someone had brought in her steamer trunks during the night, with her powders and tinctures and oils packed carefully within, and her rare manuscripts, her journals. She thought of her brother back in Edinburgh, alone, and hopefully, please God, still safe. The flagstones on the floor were dazzling and white. Children's voices drifted up from the gardens below her window.

She left Deirdre in the peace of that place and made her way through the tall corridors, past the crumbling plaster, toward the kitchen. The villa seemed deserted. The walls were pale and the doors a very dark hardwood, and the emptiness and light from the windows made it all feel as unlike Cairndale as it could be. Cairndale with its dark passageways, its secrets, its ancient sorrows. She understood, slowly, that this was a new beginning for the children here, for the survivors. That Miss Davenshaw's vision of a refuge for talents might, in fact, be possible.

And her heart broke anew, thinking of the children she'd lost, Brendan and Seamus, Wislawa and Maddie, all of them, who'd have been so happy here.

The kitchens were vast and stark and there were terracotta pots soaking in the big washbasins on the counters. The ashes in the oven were cold. She wasn't hungry. She unbuckled the straps of her artificial arm and left it on the rough plank table. A blue bowl of oranges gleamed. Beside it, her apparatus looked old, battered, worn by long use. It would need oiling. Gingerly, she rubbed at the stump.

She was at the open window, watching the children at play in the gardens below, their governess standing under a lemon tree calling out instructions, when a stink of rotting flesh wafted into the room. A moment later Oskar came in from the hall. He was not alone. A massive creature, slick and marbled with blood, squeezed through the doorway behind him. With each step, it squelched softly, leaving a viscous trail on the floor tiles.

Shyly, Oskar pushed his wire-rimmed spectacles into place. Those, she realized, were new. "Mrs. Ficke," he mumbled. "I, I, I hope you had a good sleep. Did you find something to eat? There's hard-breads and, and lemon preserves in the pantry—"

But Caroline just stood, staring at the flesh giant, fascinated. The sunlight was all around her.

Oskar glanced uncertainly at his companion, then back. "Oh. Um, you haven't met Lymenion," he said. "Lymenion, this is, uh, Mrs. Ficke. She's the one we snuck out to see at the chandler's shop, that night before the fire. I told you about her."

"Rruh," said the flesh giant, a fold of darkness appearing where a mouth might have been.

"Lymenion," said Caroline, with careful politeness. "It is a great pleasure to meet you."

"Rrhh-uh," he rumbled.

"I told you she was nice," Oskar whispered. He looked back at Mrs. Ficke, grateful.

She collected herself. "And you, Oskar Czekowisz. You have grown. When did you get spectacles?" An unfamiliar warmth was expanding in her chest. It was happiness. She was remembering when he'd come to Albany Chandlers with his friends, a lifetime ago. The fear in him, then. How small he was.

The boy blushed.

"Miss Davenshaw said you'd be willing to look at the inscriptions we found, under the wash-house. In the secret room."

Caroline blinked. "I thought Charlie would take me."

"Charlie?" Oskar rolled his eyes, grinning now. "He's been in with Miss Davenshaw since the sun came up. Anyhow, he'd be no use to you in there. Except maybe to hold a candle to see by. But I've been in that room since we found it, trying to make sense of it. They carved it right out of the limestone, I'll show you. Come on."

She glanced at the flesh giant, oozing softly in the doorway.

"Rrh," it rumbled.

She picked up her artificial arm. "Show me," she said to the boy.

Oskar led her through the crumbling villa, along the wide pale hallways, through the empty rooms. The eastern end was in ruins, with walls open to the sky, and water damage in the ceilings. The roof had given way in places. She saw what might have been a ballroom once, filled with furniture, all of it covered in white sheets. The flesh giant, Lymenion, loomed at her side. Oskar stopped to collect a lantern. Then they turned left, through a wide doorway, and outside into the yellow wash of light. They were at the eastern end of the gardens, and proceeded along a tall hedge until they'd reached the wash-house. It was an empty brick outbuilding, nestled among the foliage. Daylight filtered in through small dirty windows. Inside smelled of animals.

But then Oskar lit the lantern, and showed her the far corner. A trapdoor had been built into the floor. Lymenion seized the iron pull and hauled, lightly, up, and there were stone steps descending into darkness below, and Caroline felt a shiver of excitement.

Oskar took her down. Lymenion did not join them. At first, Caroline could see little. The skeletal shapes of ancient candelabras, arranged on the cavern floor. But then the boy was going from candle to candle, lighting each, and soon the buried room was bright with an orange and flickering glow. His blond hair was stained with shadow, his glasses discs of light. He smiled at her, and opened his arms wide.

And she caught her breath.

She had never seen anywhere so beautiful. The cavern had been carved out of the limestone, just as Oskar had said, and its walls glittered with a white light, as if molten. The room was long, and smooth, with a high ceiling and recesses carved directly into the stone, each filled with scrolls and leatherbound tomes. The air smelled of age. At the far end, half-visible in the gloom, she saw what looked like a long stone altar. Behind it hung a tapestry, dazzling in its colors. She saw in that instant a lifetime of study, of learning.

But most extraordinary of all were the carvings. On every available surface, on the walls, the floor, the ceiling, she saw the inscriptions. The strange runic writing, which Charlie had brought to her in Edinburgh. They were carved in haphazard lines, as if by many hands, across many generations. And there were images, too—figures and shapes and swirls and geometrical patterns. Her eye could not take it all in.

"I felt like that too, when I first saw this," said Oskar. He was smiling.

She picked up a candelabra in her artificial claw and walked slowly along one wall, tracing her fingers lightly over the limestone. It was cool to the touch.

"Can you read it?" asked Oskar. In the hush, his voice echoed off the walls.

She wasn't sure. She walked the length of the cavern, all the way to the altar, the mysterious tapestry sagging behind it. It had been nailed into the stone centuries ago. An eerie thing, the bottom half was a reflection of the top, with all the colors reversed. A frayed landscape: a road with trees, a medieval city on a hill, a river in the distance. She saw small figures like children, and dark horned shapes standing among them, five of them, which she understood must be the drughr. In the very center of the tapestry had been woven a symbol, different in style, but nearly the same: a symbol she knew. Twin crossed hammers, in front of a rising sun.

"It's the crest," said Oskar quietly. "From Cairndale."

And yet, Caroline saw, in the tapestry, an enormous drughr in chains—much bigger than the rest—was entering that sun from above, and emerging out of it below, out of the fiery eye of it. As if the sun were a doorway between worlds. Her gaze lingered on the monster's face, its gruesome teeth, its red eyes.

"It's the orsines," she said, reluctantly turning away. "That's what it's showing us. The banishing of the First Talent and the making of the orsines." She raised the candelabra and looked at Oskar where he stood, rubbing his spectacles on his shirtfront. He was listening intently. "That's why there are two hammers in the crest, see. For the two orsines. I don't know if Henry understood its meaning, when he made it the Cairndale crest. But it's older than the institute, much older." She came around the altar and studied the carvings in the floor. "Here, see. Here it is again."

"Who were they?" the boy asked. "The ones who built this, I mean."

"They called themselves the Agnoscenti. The last of them died out hundreds of years ago. They weren't talents, but they lived alongside talents. Sort of like . . . guardians. I doubt chambers like this were common. I think this must have been a particularly valuable library. Extraordinary. In the old stories, the Agnoscenti would find talents and bring them into their sanctuaries."

"Like Alice and, and, and Mr. Coulton."

"Aye. Except the Agnoscenti were also the repositories of talent knowledge and history. They were more like . . . heretical monks. With very sharp knives. There were communities of them throughout Europe and North Africa during the Renaissance. Even before that. There is an account of Agnoscenti in the Holy Land on the First Crusade. The Templars were founded on similar principles. Most of the Agnoscenti sanctuaries were destroyed during the witch hunts of the seventeenth century, their communities slaughtered. I'd always thought they were too secretive for their own good. What they preserved was lost, when they were lost."

Oskar was watching her, his pale eyes huge in their lenses.

"But. Mrs. Ficke? Will . . . will any of this help Marlowe?"

Caroline became aware of the weight of rock pressing down, the deep silence in the earth. This buried chamber was maybe the key to everything, all of it. She could feel the intoxicating pull of a secret knowledge all around. She withdrew a notebook and pencil from the pocket of her petticoat.

"Ach, child," she murmured. "That I cannot say."

Charlie Ovid walked wearily down the terrace steps, into the garden, its gravel paths bathed in the red of the setting sun. The scent of rosemary and lemons reached him. He'd spent the day with Miss Davenshaw in her dark study, telling all that had happened in Edinburgh and London. It had brought it all back again, the rains and the terrifying girl who could snap bones with a flick of her fingers, and the vast flooding underground world of the exiles, collapsing all around him. The litch in the cage. The merciless cruelty of the three urchins, the eldest who'd snatched his father's ring and called him by his father's name. That last he did not tell her; it felt too close, too private, maybe. But she'd been particularly interested in the corrupted dust, how it had rubbed into his cuts, infecting him. She'd run her fingertips lightly along the back of his arm, tracing the horripilated flesh, feeling its spread down his ribs, onto his chest. She'd asked him to repeat the little he'd heard about Claker Jack's contact, the mysterious Abbess, whom Mrs. Ficke had mentioned. Her face, he thought, looked tired. Her hands were older.

"And your talent has returned?" she murmured.

"Mrs. Ficke says it's not my talent. It's the dust. That it's like a parasite, feeding on me."

"But you *can* heal, Mr. Ovid?"

"Yes. But it leaves little white scars sometimes, though. You can hardly see them. But they're there. They look like strands of spiderwebs."

He'd watched her absorb this. Then she'd sat down again at her empty desk and rested her old hands in front of her and told him, slowly, about what had happened while he'd been away. She told about the torn-up bodies of the wild dogs outside their walls, about Oskar's fear of what was stalking them. She told about Komako, how she'd changed. Her journey through Valladolid, Barcelona, Mojácar. How the Spanish glyphic had burned the skin of her hands and face. What it had said about the second orsine, confirming its existence. "It's real, Mr. Ovid. It lies underneath Paris somewhere. I have heard from Miss Quicke; she and Miss Ribbon have nearly found it. But the Paris orsine was sealed long ago, when its glyphic was murdered. Dr. Berghast told this to Miss Quicke; now it seems he was telling the truth."

Charlie had looked up sharply, a sinking feeling in his chest. "It *is* sealed? So it exists, but we can't use it? We can't get to Mar?"

Miss Davenshaw had held up her hands for calm. "Sealed is not the same as destroyed. There may yet be a way. I rather feel that there is much we don't yet understand."

"Do we have anything to go on?"

"We know one thing. The woman who murdered its glyphic, all those years ago, who sealed the second orsine, is known as . . . the Abbess."

Daylight fell through the slats of the shutters in oblongs of shadow, light.

Charlie swallowed. It made a terrible kind of sense. "The same person?"

"I cannot imagine there are two."

"It's all leading back to her," Charlie had said slowly. "She wanted Jacob's dust, Miss Davenshaw."

"And I rather expect she still does," Miss Davenshaw had continued softly, "or someone does, in her name. The Abbess has been . . . known of. A rather sinister recluse, on the continent. She was in control of a commune in Paris for many decades, old even when I was young. The commune's precise location is lost now. I expect the orsine will be nearby. According to the Spanish glyphic, the Abbess sealed her orsine long, long ago. Therefore she is either dead now, and a different Abbess has taken her place, or else—"

"—or else she's a haelan," Charlie finished. He made a fist and felt the dust slide lazily under his skin. "No one else lives that long."

Miss Davenshaw nodded.

"Or else she's a haelan," she repeated grimly.

Now, drenched in the red light of the setting sun, watching the fountain and the gardens darken around him, Charlie lay down on a stone bench and closed his eyes and tried to make sense of all he'd heard. The second orsine was *sealed*.

Mar.

Mar was still lost in that other world.

But before his thoughts could darken further, he heard a familiar voice. He slitted his eyes. Komako's silhouette loomed over him, dark against the sinking red sky. The air had a grainy quality to it, as if filled with smoke. He sat up. She was watching him with a strange expression.

"So?" she said. "You want to tell me what happened to your arm?"

Reflexively he flinched, folded his arm up under the other, as if to hide it. But there was no point; word had spread quickly about his infection, his injury.

Komako was dressed in a long dark dress. Her face looked tender, sore, as if she'd been in the sun too long. That would be the burning from the Spanish glyphic. He was surprised to see she wore no gloves, and he could make out the painful rash on the backs of her hands. There was that new wariness in her eyes, as if she feared him, as if she wanted to turn and walk away. Her braided hair still fell long and heavy down her spine and she looked, he saw, both grave and pretty.

But she was still Komako: direct, commanding. "Let me see."

Watching her, Charlie felt an ache in his chest, both painful and pleasurable. He rolled up his sleeve, turned his hand in the light of the setting sun. The corrupted dust writhed and twisted in its inky tattoos, up to his elbow, beyond.

"The Bringer," Komako whispered, before she could stop herself.

He pushed his sleeve quickly back. "The what?"

"Nothing. Just something I . . . heard." She shook her head, uneasy. "*The Bringer of Dust brings more than he knows.* It's something the Spanish glyphic said."

"What's it mean?"

"It was like talking to a person underwater. I don't know if I'll ever know what it all meant." But then it was like he could see the shutters closing behind her eyes, locking down. She was looking at him strangely. "How does it feel? You're different, but . . . the same, too."

"Uh, thanks?"

She didn't look away. There was a quiet intensity to her, as if she were talking about something he wasn't being told about. "I mean, you're still you," she said.

He tried to give her a grin. "Well, I'm not *not* me, if that helps?"

"Does it hurt you very much? The dust, I mean?"

"I don't know. It's fine, it's nothing." But then, because it obviously wasn't fine, he told her about Jacob Marber's corpse, the vial Mrs. Ficke had collected. He told her about the little cuts on his hand, the corrupted dust getting rubbed in. The infection. He added, "It . . . it hurts a little, I guess. Mostly it's just . . . I can *feel* it in me, under my skin, all the time. Moving. But it lets me use my talent again. There's that."

"I heard. Oskar told me."

"How did Oskar—?"

At last, she gave a cautious smile. "Lymenion has excellent hearing, Charlie. He's been standing under Miss Davenshaw's office for half the day."

"I thought I smelled something." But he couldn't help smiling back, as he said it.

She had come out to walk the perimeter of the property, she explained. He knew about the carcasses, the thing that was supposed to be out there. He knew what Oskar feared it was. But in the quiet Sicilian evening, Charlie trudged alongside her and was surprised to find he wasn't afraid. They walked to the far end of the garden and passed through an ancient rusting gate and crossed a field of long grasses and stones, to a low stone wall. It was unwarded for they had no glyphic at the villa and Charlie didn't understand why anything—drughr or not—would not cross the walls.

Komako shrugged. "It's a villa full of talents. Most anything would think twice."

"*Most* anything. Not the drughr."

She gave him a withering look. "You know better than anyone. The drughr's dead, Charlie."

They walked on. The air was warm. The sky in the west changed to a deeper red. Charlie could see the skeleton of an ancient temple on a facing hill. Beyond that would lie the sea. He'd missed this, he realized suddenly, had missed being close to her, and he kept glancing furtively at Komako, wondering. Her dress was heavy and stained with a pale dust as if she'd worn it too many days in a row and there was something about her, something different, that filled him with sadness. He didn't know how to talk about what he felt, not with her. He wished Ribs were with them. She was easier to talk to. Then, for no reason he could think of, he remembered Ko's kiss, back at Cairndale. The feel of her lips. A heat came to his face and he was grateful that she wasn't looking.

But then Ko stopped in her tracks and he stopped and she reached a hand toward his throat. He swallowed. But it was just the cord at his neck, the iron artifact hidden there, that she was seeking. She drew it out and held it in her palm. She was so close, he could smell her hair.

"I didn't know you still had this," she said. "I thought you lost it. This was your mother's ring, wasn't it?"

He half cocked his shoulder, uneasy. He pulled it gently from her grip. "My father gave it to her," he said. "It's all I have of her. Of him. Why?"

"Nothing. I just . . . it's nothing."

He gave her a quizzical look. He wasn't going to tell her and then somehow he was doing it, telling her about the white-haired urchins in London, their bloodthirstiness, what the boy Micah had said about his father. That he'd worked for Claker Jack, that he'd stolen the ring. "I . . . I got the sense that he wasn't a good person," said Charlie softly. "That he took us to America because he was running away. I guess I understand that. The Falls was terrible. But why steal Claker Jack's ring? It's an artifact, it lets us go inside the orsines. Did my father know that? Did he know what he'd taken?"

A shank of hair crossed Komako's eyes, darkening her expression. She was quiet.

"I don't know who he was, Ko. I have no memories of him. I don't even know what my mama knew about him. What if he was really awful?"

The dirt where they stood was soft and pale and there were low scrub bushes and long grasses. Komako met his eye. "We're not our parents," she said.

"Yeah."

She gave a slow, regretful sigh. "For what it's worth, I don't think your father could have been all bad. Your mother loved him, didn't she? And she was good."

"Was she?"

"She stayed with you, until she couldn't anymore. When it would've been easier not to. That's pretty much what good means, Charlie."

They started walking again. Charlie wondered about snakes. Here and there on the slope down away from the property he could see the dark gnarled shapes of olive trees.

"Ko?" he said softly, after a time. "What happened to you in Spain? You seem . . . different."

Even in the settling twilight he saw her eyes flash. "Different how? Is that a bad thing?"

"No. No, just . . . sad. You seem sad."

She stopped, drew a stray hair out of her face. She looked like she might say something else, but then she stared off at the coming night. The stone wall at their backs was dark. "I'm tired, Charlie," she said. "I just feel like I'm the only one, sometimes."

"The only one what?"

"Just . . ." She held up her hands. "Just, the only one."

He was quiet for a moment. Behind them the villa rooms were lit with candles. The pianola could be heard faintly, off-key. He nodded. "Yeah. Me too."

"I keep thinking about Marlowe. Where he is. What he's going through."

"I think about him every day," said Charlie softly. "I had this ... this dream of him. In London, after I got infected. I saw him in the dream, except, it just, it didn't feel like a dream. He was alive, in it. And scared. But he wasn't alone, wherever he was. There was another *him*, a second one, and it was talking to me, but it wasn't him. And I just kept thinking, if I could remember what it was like, in there ... Maybe I could find a way to get him back. To save him."

"He *is* still alive. The Spanish glyphic said so."

Charlie couldn't keep the bitterness from his voice. "It also said the second orsine's been sealed."

She let this pass unremarked, said instead: "It's not your fault. What happened to him."

"Yeah."

"We all want him back."

"Yeah."

"And we'll do it. We'll find a way." She was blinking quickly and turned her face away but he saw the water there in her eyes. She said, "I *am* different, Charlie. I am. I can't stand all the killing, all the dying. It's what I'm good at, I think. What my talent is for. But I don't want it."

Charlie swallowed. His heart was very loud in his chest.

Suddenly Komako pulled away, and glared out into the dusk. And then Charlie heard it too: a low growling, and the moist hushed ripping sounds of flesh. It was coming from somewhere to their left. Komako was already moving into the long grass.

Charlie followed her around an outcropping of rock, his eyes straining. The twilight deepened. A smell of blood was in the air. Something huge and heavy was crouched in the grass, black-furred, ripping into the carcass of a wild dog. Charlie couldn't make out what it was. The dog's head came away with a wet crackling sound, and then the enormous thing paused, and Charlie felt the skin of his arms began to prickle, to burn with a cold, unfamiliar pain. Komako was already drawing the dust to her. Charlie couldn't move. And then the huge thing rose up before them, and turned, and they saw it.

It was the keywrasse. Alice's keywrasse. Many-legged, half-feral, with its four hourglass eyes narrowing in displeasure, its tail whipping around the carcass.

"Jesus," Charlie hissed, his heart hammering away.

He'd heard stories of it from the others, though he'd never seen it. No one had, not since Cairndale, when it had fought with such fury in the blazing manor, when Alice had given back its weir-bents and the creature had swallowed them, suddenly freed. It looked wild, Charlie thought, terrifying. This was the thing that had fought a drughr in London, the thing that had killed Jacob Marber. But even as Charlie took a nervous step back, the keywrasse diminished, shrinking down to the size of a steamer trunk, then the size of an armchair, then the size of an ordinary cat. The wild dog had been torn apart and its innards spread in a circle around the carcass, like a warning, but the keywrasse just peered at Charlie with indignant yellow eyes, as if to say: *What? Like you never did anything like this?* Lazily, it began to lick the blood from its white forepaw.

"Charlie—?" Komako whispered.

Her voice sounded strange. He glanced over at her in the twilight. She had a rope of dust encircling her fist, still wary, but she wasn't staring at the keywrasse now. She was staring at him.

He followed her gaze down. The marks in his infected hand were shining blue. And hovering over them—incomprehensibly, impossibly— was a thin rope of dust. It twisted and writhed as he turned his wrist in wonder and when he opened his fingers it dissipated in a cloud of smoke.

He looked up, dumbstruck.

"It's not possible," Komako whispered in horror. The red sky in the west was seeping away into darkness. He couldn't see her eyes. "How did you do that, Charlie? *How the hell did you do that?*"

27

Monstress

It was an ordinary steamer and it left Folkestone with a full manifest on a slate-gray morning in the last weeks of the winter calm of 1883. It crossed the Channel waters slowly, its English families leaning out over the rails, pointing at the clouds of gulls, watching the white cliffs sink away. None could imagine the evil on board. At Boulogne-sur-Mer the fishermen on the wooden pier stopped mending their nets long enough to observe the passengers' arrival, pouring happily up toward the customs house, while the hotel touts and drivers hollered from the street. The wooden bathing machines were already wheeling in out of the tide, the long sandy beaches pale and cold-looking under swept skies. On the hill, the old walls gleamed.

No one noticed the girl in the blue cloak who came down last, who glided silently with her hair twinned into ragged braids over her shoulders, a multipatched and colorful dress swishing as she walked. Her eyes were bruised; a coin at her throat winked in the daylight. Or if they did notice, some peculiarity made them look at once away. She might have been a young governess, or a maid, her face dark, her gloved hands folded and impassive, except she accompanied no one and carried no luggage. At the customs house ramp, the tourists leaned unthinkingly away from her, as if from an icy draft.

But any who might have glimpsed that girl, and followed her with their eyes, would have seen her slide quietly out into the tree-lined lanes, passing the English visitors at the coin-operated telescopes, passing the hotels, stopping neither for lodging nor food. They might have seen the shadow she cast on the cobblestones, elongated and monstrous, and wondered at it, while she crossed the ancient square under the cathedral and descended to the far edge of town, before disappearing down the old road to Saint-Omer, toward the ancient road to Paris, the ancient road to Rome.

There goes a girl unprotected and alone, they might have said. *The poor thing.* As those who did, who did not know any better.

But she was a girl who needed no protection, and was never alone.

For even as she walked tiredly away from Boulogne-sur-Mer, into the bare countryside, Jeta Wajs could feel the drughr stretching out behind her, a wisp of presence, a trail of smoke.

That was the thing about your shadow. You could only get away from it in darkness.

She'd grown thin in the long weeks since the devastation at the Falls. Thin in body, thin in soul. She felt scoured out, alone in her grief, and didn't know what to do with it, with Claker's death, with his sending her into the cages, with the cruel words he'd said to her. For a long time after, she'd huddled in her rags in the alleys of Whitechapel, taking what she needed—food, coins, the raw satisfaction of violence—from unlucky passersby. Drunks. Streetwalkers. The indigent poor. She'd lurk in her patchwork dress with her hair loose and tangled and watch the city drift past in the fog, her eyes hollow as any opium addict. Claker Jack had left her to die at the hands of a litch. Claker Jack, who'd saved her once, who'd kept her safe all these years through Ruth. The only one who'd shown her kindness. She felt so stupid. And now he was dead, gutted by his own mother, or crushed to death in the collapsing Falls, and his entire kingdom was drowned.

And all the while the drughr was there, hovering just at the edge of her vision, saying nothing, demanding nothing, but not abandoning her either. The drughr, with its own sadness, with its own sweetness. And gradually, as the horror of the Falls faded, while the yellow fog of London swirled around her ankles, her thoughts turned to the young man, the young man who'd taken the corrupted dust, the young man known as Charlie Ovid.

Micah had killed him. He'd told her himself. And yet he'd been there, at the Falls. And survived it too, the drughr had said.

She remembered him from the cathedral in Edinburgh, the way he'd tried to show her kindness, how he'd begged her to hear him out. Lurking in the alleys of Whitechapel, or drifting down by the dock-yards, where the brown Thames muscled past, she came to understand, at last, that Claker Jack's version of talentkind had been a lie. She was not a monster, not grotesque. As the weeks passed, the drughr—silent, sorrowful—began to speak again, whispering that she had worth, that she should live, that now she could choose who she might become. *Who will you be next, Jeta Wajs? Your life is your own. Live it.* And slowly, as if rising from a sickness, Jeta began to believe; she'd dial her face toward the voice, seeking out the drughr in her darkness, while wagons clattered past on the cobblestones.

Daily the drughr grew stronger. No longer did she appear as the child she'd sought, the child she'd lost. Now she was only ever a woman with black hair, parted in the middle, bundled severely on either side of her face. She wore a black high-collared dress, like something from a portrait out of Georgian England, and silver rings over the fingers of her long black gloves. She looked elegant, and somber, and like one who was once alive. She had no name.

It was the drughr who'd brought her to France. The dust would find its way to Paris, to the second orsine. That is where they would wait, spiderlike; it would come to them. Always, it was about the dust, and Charlie Ovid, the drughr seeking a way back to the powers stolen from her, the powers that would let her cross the divide and reach her son. *Most of what I am was taken from me at a . . . doorway between the worlds. By Henry Berghast, Berghast who is in the other world even now. He left me like this. It is a . . . strain, simply to appear before you . . . To make myself seen. This world is poison to me. Even as I grow stronger, I grow weaker. I cannot stay here much longer.*

Some days her grief and anger would recede, like a tide, and she would have questions. "The dust, what we're hunting. Is it yours, then?"

It was. It will be again.

"So you knew him? The body in the mortuary?"

Jacob had lost his brother. I wished to help him. He was my . . . companion, in this world and the other.

"Did you kill him?"

I did not.

Some days the drughr would speak unbidden, telling fragments, scraps of events long in the past. How she had volunteered with four other talents to enter the orsine. How they'd stood guard against a terrible evil imprisoned there. *But somehow, gradually, the task we'd been set changed us,* she murmured. *Centuries passed, in this world. Slowly the one we were sent there to guard, to keep the world safe from . . . his dreams began to become our dreams. The dreams of my brethren. And we saw what it was he was afraid of. We saw what it was he'd been trying to do. He'd wanted to protect talentkind. And instead? His kind had risen against him, had sentenced him to a living death. But he was a liar, that one. He was not to be trusted. His dreams were not true.*

Jeta lifted her face. "Who was he?"

The First Talent. The one my brethren serve.

Jeta lifted her face. "But not you?"

Not me.

And she believed the drughr, though it felt like madness to do so. Some sort of bond had been forged between them, in the sewers below the Falls, and it was in her like a fever.

W as all that only weeks ago? It felt like a lifetime.

Jeta walked now into the French evening, until there was almost no light left. In the dusk she crunched her way through the dry sticks of a beech copse, gathering brush, and then she withdrew from a pocket in her skirts a flint and soon a small fire burned. The night was cold. It didn't matter if anyone saw the fire. They were some ways off the road and she didn't fear highwaymen or thieves and the drughr was with her anyway.

She sat at the low fire, feeding it as she could. Leaning into the little warmth she could get. She started to speak, feeling hollow, speaking to the drughr a little, but also maybe more to herself, hearing her own voice as if it were coming from another. "This is like when I was very little, with my family. My uncle's tabor. We used to sit around the fires in the night and there would be talking, or just listening. O lungo drom. The long road. That was what they knew."

She leaned her head back and peered up at the stars.

"Our wagon always smelled of oil. My aunt used to make these beautiful tassels out of scraps of cloth, and they'd fill the little window with colored light. I don't know why I thought of that. I haven't thought of that in years. We used to leave patrin at crossroads, little bundles of twigs tied off, or stones stacked just so, to send messages to other caravans. My uncle rode in the first wagon and it was his honor to read the signs when we came to any, and to answer them. He was good at it, respected. I was proud of him. The gadje took them for the devil's work, and left them alone. When we'd go into a gadjikane village for food or supplies, I'd make a point of touching everything in the store. The shopkeep would sell it to my aunt at a discount, after that. Just touching it was enough to make it unusable. To them, we were mahrime. Unclean."

We are the same, Jeta Wajs. We will always be wrong, in their eyes.

She rubbed the ancient coin at her throat. "My uncle left me this, the day he let Cairndale take me. It's all I have of him, now. That, and memories. Even the words I once knew are fading. I don't know if I was ever happy, but I might have been. Maybe I was once, before I knew what was in me. What I could do."

You have been betrayed by all of them. I am so sorry, Jeta. Sorry for what your family did. For what Claker Jack did. But you are allowed to move past it. To change.

She closed her eyes. She could almost hear the strains of songs from her childhood, the soft laughter of the tabor's adults in the darkness. The pull of their bones from around the fire.

In the end, no one is to be trusted, except yourself. No one can be depended upon.

"I don't know if that's true," she said quietly, and as soon as she said it she realized she meant it. "I think maybe I've just trusted the wrong people, all my life."

There was a small puddle near the fire and she saw the drughr lean over it, suddenly the child again, the face of the child she'd first glimpsed, the little boy with black hair and blue eyes. The face of the child the drughr had lost. The drughr was staring at her own reflection in the puddle, touching her own cheek, her little boy's cheek, with gentleness.

I submitted willingly to go into the orsine, long ago, she said. I thought I could protect the talents, all of them, the weak ones, those who hadn't yet been born. We all did, who went through. But I had a baby. A son.

Jeta blinked quickly, hearing grief crack the drughr's voice.

They promised me I would be able to return, to see my boy, to watch him grow up. To tell him that I loved him. But it was a lie; there was no returning from that world. I tried. For many years, I tried. But we'd been changed, myself and the others, changed into what you see now: drughr. Monsters. We cannot exist in this world now, not for any length of time. Over the centuries we located and crafted artifacts that could bridge the worlds, and there were bonebirds that could carry messages back to the living. But it was too late for me, for my boy. Oh, the others had left their lives behind too, it is true. But none of them had children. Only me. They did not understand. My son lived out his life, grew old, died, and I did not ever see him again. I . . . I was supposed to accept it. But I could not. How could I? What mother could?

"But you . . . you got him back," she said. She curled her bone fingers into a fist. "He was inside the orsine, right? You found him."

I did not get him back. The child I seek is not the child I lost. This child was made in the gray rooms. It does not make me love him less.

"How do you . . . *make a person?*"

The drughr was quiet, sorrowful. Her eyes were craters of darkness. *Beyond a river in that world, if you are lucky, if it will let you, you can reach the gray rooms. It was said something powerful was buried there, hidden away, something living and yet not alive. I found my way in by accident. And there I found a baby, a living baby, inside a stone. And the baby looked exactly like the one I had abandoned, my own baby, my sweet little one . . .*

"How is it possible?" Jeta whispered.

It was the orsine. I knew it even then, knew the orsine was using me for some reason. I didn't care. I don't care. When I got out of the gray rooms, I was weak. The baby was taken, stolen from me . . . Taken to Henry Berghast. And Berghast has him now, even now, inside the orsine. I deserve whatever punishment comes to me, Jeta. But he does not. My boy does not.

Jeta wasn't sure she understood. The drughr was waiting, as if she was supposed to ask something more. "What was his name? Your baby?"

He calls himself Marlowe.

"But what did *you* call him?" Jeta asked, gently. "I mean, before everything?"

The drughr drifted to the edge of the fire. *His name was Tomasz,* she said softly.

They reached Saint-Omer in the late morning and Jeta walked through the colorful market stalls, breathing in the earthy smells of produce and worked leather and tools arranged in tin buckets. There were dead leaves in her hair still from sleeping and her patchwork dress was a mess and she must have looked wild. The farmers all fell silent as she passed, some with pity in their eyes. At a potato stall a child offered her a roasted potato in its jacket but her mother would take no coin in return and Jeta took it with her eyes wet and wondering what was the matter with her.

She walked on. The sun burned a white hole in the white sky. She ate the potato in the ruins of an ancient abbey, its mossy arches standing yet amid the long grasses and tumbled stones. The world seemed far away. She was tired already. The drughr looked stronger, more substantial, more solid in the daylight.

"It weakens me, doesn't it?" Jeta mumbled, lying back. "Whatever you're doing, however you're getting stronger?"

Yes. But only until I have gathered enough strength. Then I will be able to . . . feed myself.

She closed her eyes in the brightness. The sun was warm on her face. Her bones seemed to be humming. She murmured, "What good will I be to you, if I get too weak?"

But she was asleep in the sunlight before the drughr answered, if ever she did.

She awoke in the late hours of the day. It was not yet dark. Rain clouds had blown in during the afternoon and loomed now, grim, black in the east. The drughr stood as always, some feet away. Silent. Watching.

Three miles from Saint-Omer it started to rain. They found a convent of aging nuns, its doors open to female pilgrims braving the walk to Rome. The nuns did not like the look of her. The mother superior spoke in a curt French to a bewildered Jeta, her green eyes fierce. A tiny, wizened nun took her by the glove, nodding gently, as if she might be simple. There seemed some doubt as to whether Jeta was a Catholic at all and when they brought her before a cross she kneeled, as she had no idea what else to do. This seemed to mollify some.

She was granted a spartan bedchamber on the second floor, overlooking a devastated winter vineyard. The light was already going when she was led down to dinner. It was a spare meal of chicken bones in broth but every table had its own bottle of wine and the nuns drank every bottle dry. Jeta wore her gloves despite their damp and she tried to ignore the looks on the nuns seated at her table. All ate in silence but for the wizened nun who had taken Jeta's hand when she'd arrived. That nun stood at a lectern above the others and read out in Latin verses of scripture in a thin, reedy monotone.

When they had eaten, the nuns rose one by one and left the hall, wordless, severe.

And yet all of it left Jeta feeling immensely calm, at peace, amazed that such a world could exist alongside the one she had known in London. She returned to her room to find the drughr standing in the far corner, her dark high-collared dress transparent in the candlelight, the wall visible through her.

I have found a way to warn him. Marlowe. I am . . . strong enough now.

She nodded. "Is it dangerous?"

Yes.

"Then you shouldn't do it," Jeta said at once. "Even if you find him, you can't go to him. Not without the dust."

The dust will be in Paris.

Jeta crossed to the little nightstand and set the candle in its dish down and then she peeled her gloves off, one finger at a time. Her yellow bone fingers were sore in the cold. She sat and took off her boots and then she stood and turned around and unbuttoned and took off her patchwork dress. She laid it on the back of the only chair. The drughr still had not moved. Jeta tried to imagine how it must be, not knowing the safety of your child. She couldn't.

"All right," she said at last. "How dangerous? What could happen?"

I will go into the Dreaming. My . . . Marlowe will be there. Perhaps. It is . . . not always clear. But all talents can be found in the Dreaming. It joins us all. Including the other drughr. I will be weak. If they are looking for me, they will . . . find me. Find me, and destroy me.

"I won't let that happen," said Jeta in the soft candlelight.

The drughr closed her eyes. The edges of her body blurred, and for a moment she seemed to flicker in front of Jeta, like the filament in an electric glass she'd seen at a street display years ago. Her face smoothed itself out; there was a sudden feeling that Jeta was alone in the bedchamber, absolutely alone, although the drughr's form remained. But otherwise nothing happened.

Jeta stood watching for a time and when she got tired of that she went to the window and threw open the shutters onto the rain. Despite the weather it was not a dark night. She could make out the shapes of the vineyard below, the wooden box gardens of the nuns at the edge of the property. Footsteps passed in the hall outside. The candle burned down.

A long time passed. Jeta felt a vague prickling sensation at the base of her neck, and turned. The drughr's eyes were open.

"Did you find him? Did you find your son?" she asked in a whisper, afraid of waking the nuns.

But then the drughr's expression filled with dread. She turned and turned in place, as if confused, and then suddenly she reached out and seized Jeta's wrist. It was only the third time she'd felt the drughr's touch and she recoiled from it. Her grip was soft, and oily, and yet somehow too like air.

We have to go, the drughr whispered in fear. *We have to go now, Jeta Wajs! Hurry—!*

Jeta recoiled. "Why? What did you see?"

There is no time! They have found us!

And suddenly, in the stillness, Jeta heard it: a creaking on the roof above. Something heavy was up there, something big. Fear was like smoke, choking the bedchamber. Jeta stood very still, breathing. The light from the candle pooled weakly at the edge of the bed. She heard the clay tiles on the roof clink, clink, clink. Her eyes tracked the sound across the ceiling, slowly.

The drughr hissed from the doorway.

And all at once Jeta came back to herself. She didn't know what was up there, and she didn't want to know. She snatched up the bundle of her patchwork dress, her cloak and wet gloves, her muddy shoes, and then she was running barefoot in her stained yellow shift, through the candlelit halls, down the narrow staircase, across the receiving chambers toward the entrance. The drughr was a shade of darkness just ahead, leading her on. At the ancient door, Jeta threw back the latch in a panic, but then hesitated. She stared at the drughr who stared back at her. Then she threw open the door.

It was raining. The cold night looked blacker now, beyond the reach of the door lantern. The courtyard was churned into mud. Jeta could see nothing, no creature, no monster, nothing.

But the drughr's fear beside her was palpable; Jeta swallowed and, glancing one last time behind her at the dim convent, at its great stone ceilings lost in shadow, she plunged out into the rain, barefoot, and ran doubled over into the staked rows of the convent vineyard.

They didn't go far. She ran from row to row and then, suddenly, the drughr had stopped and was crouching under the dripping dead vines, peering back at the convent in the darkness. Jeta fell to her knees beside it, and parted the wet hair at her eyes, and saw something terrible.

A huge darkness was creeping slowly across the roof, back and forth, as big maybe as a drayhorse. In the rain it was difficult to make out its shape. But then it crawled to the edge above the window of their room, the room where they had been only moments before, and Jeta watched as it crawled down the wall and pried back the shutters and squeezed itself out of sight. It had too many arms, and moved like a spider, and its squat skull was antlered.

A moment passed; a second. The creature did not reappear. In the rain Jeta's blood was loud in her ears. She was afraid suddenly that the monster must hear it and she stared hard at the window, lit with a feeble light from their candle. Then the candle went out.

"How did it find us?" she whispered.

But before the drughr could answer, Jeta saw two enormous clawed hands emerge out of the window, and then two more, and then the horrifying bulk of the creature poured out into the rain. It gripped the walls with its manifold fingers and turned its skull from side to side, sniffing the air. Then it folded itself higher, back up onto the roof tiles, and there it crouched with its four elbows winglike, its knees high. Its antlered skull turned and turned in the night.

He has my scent now, said the drughr. *He will not stop.*

He, she'd said. Not *it.*

Jeta absorbed this, her heart bursting with fear.

The rain fell. Carefully Jeta's companion rose, water cutting through her insubstantial form, and carefully she picked her slow way out through the stakes. The terrible creature on the convent roof remained hunched, like an enormous gargoyle, its four monstrous arms gripping the roof tiles, the water pouring like silver all around its darkness.

Come, murmured Jeta's companion. *We cannot stay.*

And so Jeta followed, half-crouching still, creeping in her soaked shift and bare feet through the muddy rows of the vineyard, away.

One hundred sixty-five miles to the south, a ragged boy without a coat, in shoes two sizes too big, walked noiselessly across the Pont Neuf, into the gleaming Sixth Arrondissement of Paris. His heart too was filled with grief, his heart too was filled with murder. His sisters. His sisters. His sisters.

He was twelve years old and never less a child than now. The midday light was strange, the sky a murky yellow. A drizzle was flecking his face. The Seine glittered like a pebbled road and the wet streets all around were quiet as in a dream. He walked unhurried in the middle of the sidewalk, his head uncovered, his swollen knuckles bare, half hoping some bastard would appear and say something. No one did.

Up Rue Dauphine the boy went, to Rue Mazarine, then across Boulevard Saint-Germain, winding through the small lanes to Saint-Sulpice and from there to the edge of Jardin du Luxembourg. He'd been in Paris three days now trying to find his way. Here at last were signs of life. Mustachioed men in dark hats and brightly colored ties walked the rows with umbrellas, one hand in their fashionable pockets, women in long dark dresses leaning into their elbows. The gardens too were hushed; the streets of Montparnasse smelled of manure and rotting vegetables. The boy walked on, murder in his heart. He heard his sisters' voices in his head, he saw his sisters' silhouettes slipping around the pillared arcades, their grubby faces grinning meanly. They were worth more to him than all the beauties of Paris entire and he would burn the city to the ground if he could. At Boulevard du Montparnasse he waited for a break in the traffic and then, ducking between the horses, his shoes slapping on the shining cobblestones, he found Rue Boissonade and the ancient gray walls that had stood since long before the Revolution, before the Sun King himself.

The walls of le Couvent de la Délivrance.

Micah stood staring at the decaying, heavy door and then he spat and went around the side to the service door he knew would be there. He went in, not caring who might see. His white-blond hair was damp, his shirt loose almost to his knees. He stood in the dimness of that convent, and listened.

Footsteps, faint, approaching slowly.

An old acolyte in red came around the corner, her hands clasped, her gray hair shorn. A second descended from a stair, and studied him also. Both had no eyebrows. The taller looked down at the bedraggled child as if she'd expected his arrival. They would be *talents*, he thought in disgust. Smug in their power.

"I'm the Micah what kept an eye on London for her," he said, glowering. "Where is she?"

The taller red sister breathed. She might not have understood him.

"The *Abbess*," he snapped, exaggerating each syllable. "Where's the *blood-y Abb*-ess? Tell her I come from the Falls, an I bloody well walked half the way. Tell her I come with news, like."

The white rainy daylight filtered in through a lattice high up in the walls. The taller acolyte's face looked pale and drawn. The stillness in the convent was exquisite.

"Tu es Micah. Mais Prudence et Timna ne sont pas ici," she murmured. "Où sont tes soeurs?"

Micah spat. He didn't speak French but he knew what she was asking. She didn't care about his sisters, of course. He imagined his face told all that needed telling, that she was asking just to twist the knife. But he met the acolyte's eye, and his voice betrayed no emotion.

"My sisters is dead," he said.

28

WEAVERS AT THE LOOM

Word spread quickly about the keywrasse. And Oskar Czekowisz—plump, soft-fingered, so pale in the villa darkness as to look almost white-haired—should have felt only relief.

For there was no drughr.

Just Alice's keywrasse, prowling the warm Mediterranean night. Alice's keywrasse, leaving its inexplicable and bloody warnings.

He'd been so certain, so afraid. But instead of relief, in the days after the keywrasse was sighted, he would ball his hands up into worried fists and watch Charlie, with an awful pity filling his heart. His friend had grown tall, gaunt during his weeks away. And though they'd hardly talked yet, Oskar knew Charlie was sick, had heard all about Jacob Marber's dust, and how his healing talent had rekindled. Except it wasn't right, what was in him, anyone could see that; it had changed him from the inside, out.

Now Charlie'd seen the half-feral keywrasse, Charlie and Ko together, had seen it mutilating a wild dog in the long grasses outside, and as the days crept by it became painfully clear to Oskar just how changed his friend was. Charlie would slide unhappily through the afternoons, his eyes sunken with exhaustion, his infected arm cradled at his chest. And Oskar would push his spectacles up the bridge of his nose, and blink furiously, and worry.

It wasn't just Charlie he worried about. Oskar worried about Komako too, solitary, angry, Ko who'd always been too intense at everything she did. And he worried about Ribs and Alice, who should've been back by now. He worried about the villa, and how it was taking its toll on Miss Davenshaw, and he worried about the little ones. Oskar didn't like what was happening to all of them, to everyone he loved, but he didn't know what he could do about it. He'd sit with Lymenion in the morning sunlight on the terrace bench and watch the blue shadows creep down off the temple ruins, far across the valley, and watch too the shining pebbles of sunlight in the deep black sea beyond, and he'd think about Marlowe, so terribly alone. Oskar had always had Lymenion, as long as he could remember, even back at the edge of the Baltic, in Poland, when he lived alone in the crumbling old ruins and feared any outsiders who approached. But Marlowe—little Marlowe, who'd never been anything but kind, who was trusting and open with all of them, who didn't ask to be different and who'd never wanted the power that had sent him, in the end, through the orsine forever—*he* was in a land of the dead, suffering terribly, without anyone at all. While Oskar got to sit in the sunlight with Lymenion, well-fed, safe. It wasn't fair. And when he thought about how Marlowe probably had no idea they were even trying to get him back—? Well, it just about broke his heart.

At least there was Mrs. Ficke to distract him.

He'd scarcely known her, when first she arrived with Charlie. She looked so much older, grayer, as if she'd suffered terribly. As she had, he learned from Miss Davenshaw: losing the glyph-twisted children she'd cared for all these years. All but one, all but that sweet, gnarled girl, Deirdre.

He and Mrs. Ficke worked long days and late nights in the secret room under the wash-house. The limestone stairs down were soft and rounded from ancient use. The old alchemist demanded extra candelabras so that the cavern was ablaze with light, the carved inscriptions starkly clear. The smooth blue walls turned orange in the flickering light.

The work itself was fascinating. Mrs. Ficke had brought some few books with her, which Lymenion carried down from her room, and these she spread out on the floor. She explained as she worked the different letters and alphabets which she could identify, and she let Oskar read his way through the strange texts. Often she would point to a symbol or letter and ask him to find its every use in the chamber, and for hours he would rise and dip with a candle in his hands, poring over the strange markings.

One morning he came down to find her still at work. She looked like she hadn't slept all night, her eyes crosshatched with tiredness. Something shifted in the depths beyond the altar and then the lights were reflected in four fiery eyes and Oskar saw it was a cat, black like charred wood. It stood and stretched and yawned with more teeth than it should have had and then he knew it, knew it well.

"That's the keywrasse, Mrs. Ficke," he whispered suddenly. "Don't move."

She glanced at it, nodded. "'Tis been here half the night. I do believe it's been sleeping here when we retire. There must be a second way in."

He took an uneasy step back, until he felt the wall. "But is it . . . is it safe? Charlie and Ko said—"

"Aye, I heard what they saw." Mrs. Ficke shrugged. "But if it wanted to hurt me, I don't see as there's much I could do. Now, Oskar, come closer. I found something."

She stood and ran her fingertips lightly over the wall to her left, back and forth, stretching on her toes to her highest point. She'd attached a candle, melted now down almost to a stub, to her artificial arm, and this she held high.

384 • J. M. Miro

"It reads backward *and* forward, Oskar. That's why it wasn't clear before. It's a palimpsest of itself. Extraordinary."

Oskar wasn't sure what she was talking about. He wondered if her exhaustion had drained her senses. The keywrasse rose suddenly and flickered past and up the stairs to the daylight, gone.

"Ach, leave it," she scolded. "Now, see here. Tis an account, an eye-witness account, of the war between the talents, and what happened all those centuries ago."

"A war between—?"

"Aye." She bent down and rummaged among the mess on the floor and found a scroll and pinned it open and waved him closer. "This is a partial copy of the wall there. But it leaves so much out." She stood again, excited. "Whoever wrote this *knew* Alastair Cairndale, knew him by *sight*. An they was there, at the Grathyyl, at the making of the drughr."

"At the what? The making of the—"

The old alchemist made an exasperated noise. "Aye, Oskar. The drughr was *made*. What *did* Henry allow you children to learn at that institute of his? Listen—" And she began to translate the inscription, back and forth, haltingly. "*Here follows an account of the fall of the First Talent. He appeared one day among us, the wielder of all five talents, as had been foreseen in the chronicle. More powerful than any before him, he was. We believed he would deliver us. We knew not where he came from. His pride was his weakness.*"

Mrs. Ficke paused, studied Oskar in the candlelight. "Tis Alastair Cairndale it means. It goes on. It tells how he founded Cairndale Manor and drew other talents to him with promises of safety, of refuge. This would be three, four hundred years ago. It says here the First Talent wanted, above all others, glyphics at his manor. He gathered many. And when he had enough, he used them."

Oskar shivered. "Used th-th-them?"

"Aye. Used them to create a 'weaving,' Oskar. You'll not have heard of it. Tis a kind of net. Glyphics have access to the dreamscape where all talents are connected, like threads. But the First Talent wove those threads into a pattern, a complicated pattern with himself at the very center. It became more like a web. So that, to cut his thread, would be to cut all threads."

"I don't understand, Mrs. Ficke."

She lowered the candle, looked at him. "Alastair Cairndale made it so that, if he died, all of talentkind would be extinguished along with him."

"But why? Why w-w-would he do that?"

"Ach. Men and power. Isn't it always about that? He'd discovered a way to feed on his fellow talents, you see. A way to increase his own powers by devouring theirs. Well. A great struggle followed, a war between talents. Lasted a long time, it did. There were those who fought alongside Alastair Cairndale, and those who resisted him.

"Now, listen. Here's the parts I never knew. Alastair Cairndale had taken a wife. Her name's not recorded here. Women's names never are." She grimaced. "But she fled with their baby to Paris and there told all about what he'd been doing. Tis that what led to the war. The talents rose up against him as one, for the first and last time, and in the struggle that followed the First Talent was defeated. But the talents could not kill him, not without destroying themselves. And so instead he was sent into a sleep, a sleep from which he was never to awaken. And to be certain of it, a prison was built, a prison that could not be reached by any who might still support him, a prison to hold the most powerful talent of all time. A prison in the land of the dead."

"Oh," whispered Oskar, horrified almost despite himself. He took off his spectacles and rubbed the heel of his thumbs against his eyes and put his spectacles back on. "So the orsines—"

"—are the doors to that prison. Aye."

"So they buried him away, just as if he was really dead. But he wasn't dead."

"Aye. An they did it all in the Grathyyl. Tis there the orsines were made, an the First Talent was committed, an the drughr volunteered to be bent, so as to guard him. The effort must have been . . . extraordinary. There are skills they must have possessed which we will never have again."

There it was again, that word. He didn't know what she meant. She'd turned back to read the lower inscriptions on the wall and he could no longer see her face.

"Mrs. Ficke?" said Oskar. "What's the Grathyyl?"

She answered him without turning, her voice rising disembodied around the rock walls of the chamber. "The Grathyyl lies west of the fallen sun. Tis a space between worlds, between the living and the dead. It existed before talents, and will exist long after. Some believe the talents came from the Grathyyl itself, from what it is made of. The orsines are made of that substance. As are the drughr themselves, who were once talents, and who offered to be changed horribly, to guard the First Talent in that other world for all time."

"The drughr were . . . good?"

"Once. Long ago. They are no longer." She pressed her small pale hand flat to the stone. "Here is where the account ends. *We must change our ways,* the writer says. *There is a better life.*"

For a long moment Oskar was quiet. Then he crossed to the altar, to the tapestry hanging behind it, and he studied the dark, horned figures there. "How does it help us, Mrs. Ficke? How does it help us find a way to rescue Marlowe?"

"Ah," she replied. "But we've been in the right place all along." She collected a massive, leatherbound tome from the floor and opened it flat on the altar. A bloom of dust rose and settled. "This is a compendium of knowledge about glyphics. It's . . . fascinating. Alastair Cairndale threaded all the talents together centuries ago, did he not? Now, the glyphics are the ones what can go into that . . . 'threaded' space. This text calls it 'the Dreaming.' Glyphics can sense other talents in it, can move through it. And, if powerful enough, they can even brush up against other glyphics. Touch them."

"But—"

She held up a sharp hand. "The glyphic in Paris was murdered, and its heart was put into the orsine to seal it fast. That glyphic died. But its heart is still . . . alive. Its heart is what powers the seal. An I believe the glyphic's heart is still connected to the Dreaming. It can still be felt and touched by other glyphics."

Oskar was nodding, trying to follow the old woman's meaning. She turned the brittle pages carefully, looking for something. Oskar peered at the strange Greek lettering, the brown faded ink.

Mrs. Ficke continued. "It is not easy for a glyphic to navigate the Dreaming. The further a glyphic wants to travel in the web, the stronger its power needs to be. They can become lost for years. But a glyphic with enough power can . . . well, it can *walk* along the threads. All the way to Paris, say."

"Like a spider."

"Exactly. Not in the flesh, of course."

"But we don't have a glyphic, Mrs. Ficke."

"Aye we do."

Oskar blinked. Then he understood. "That girl you and Charlie brought? Is that who you mean?"

"Her name is Deirdre." Mrs. Ficke's eyes flashed in the candlelight. "An if she was to know what she was looking for, an if she could work her way around to the glyphic's heart, she could *touch* it. *Quiet* it. It would unseal the orsine. It says it right here; tis possible."

Oskar put a slow hand onto the old woman's sleeve, suddenly disappointed. "But she's glyph-*twisted*, isn't she, Mrs. Ficke? She's not a real glyphic. She doesn't have any power."

The old woman closed the book. Her eyes were bloodshot, her gray hair wild. She pushed the book to the side of the altar and walked around to the far side, tracing her fingers over the rough stone. It wasn't level, Oskar saw, but scooped and hollowed in strange impressions. He thought at first she was upset but that wasn't it, not at all.

Her voice was quiet, measured. "There were certain places, Oskar, that were holy to the Agnoscenti. Hidden places, where the worlds of the dead and the living drew near. Cairndale was one. As is the commune in Paris, I assume. That will be one of the reasons the orsines were located there. But there were others. In such places, glyphics tend to live, for their power is increased dramatically. Tell me, what does this look like, to you?" She gestured at the altar.

"I don't know. A place where they . . . worshipped?"

"Look closer, Oskar."

He did; and suddenly he saw. The impressions and divots in the stone were like the outlines in a mattress after a person has lain a long time. It wasn't an altar at all; it was a bed.

"I believe this is one such place," murmured Mrs. Ficke. "I believe a glyphic lay here, for long centuries, once upon a time. We are standing very near the Dreaming. And if Deirdre were brought in—"

"—then she could enter it, too," Oskar finished, his voice hushed.

Mrs. Ficke nodded. The candle fire carved hollows of shadow from her face.

"Shall we find out?" she whispered.

It seemed to Charlie Ovid, in the long days that followed the finding of the keywrasse, that his body—his horrible, bruised, infected body—wasn't entirely his own.

As if the corrupted dust that was crawling inside his skin had its own will, its own desires, and at any moment it could make his body do things it didn't want to do.

Such as heal.

Or twist a rope of dust around his knuckles.

Worse, he'd started having the dreams again, dreams like the one he'd had that terrible night in London, in Mrs. Harrogate's old rooms at Nickel Street West, that night when Mrs. Ficke had tried and failed to cut Jacob Marber's corruption out of him. He would wake with his thin sheet drenched and his heart hammering and in the darkness he'd rise, trembling, and stand naked at the shutters, breathing in the quiet garden air, the dust under his skin silvering faintly in the moonlight. The dreams were of Marlowe, of course. Marlowe, alone, crying out in fear. His friend would emerge slowly out of a darkness, first a hand, then an arm, then his whole body, creeping as if blind, but when his head emerged it had no features at all, and where his face should have been was only that same darkness, as if he'd become the very thing that terrified him.

Not all dreams are warnings, he'd tell himself, still shaking, and try to believe it.

Meanwhile Komako, disgusted maybe, or maybe just frightened, avoided him. He could see it. She'd leave a room as he entered, rise from a table as he sat down. He knew it was wrong, what he'd done, twisting the dust, freakish. Still, left alone, he'd try sometimes to drag it into his hands again, snapping his fingers, clenching his fists. Nothing worked. It was like it had happened *to* him, not *by* him. But she wouldn't let him explain. So he walked the grounds instead. Went looking for the keywrasse with a bowl of fresh milk, leaving the bowl in the long grass just in case. Sometimes after lunch he'd stand at the enclosure fence, watching the villa's black goats, thinking of nothing at all. In the stables he'd find Lymenion, drawing hay, shoveling out the stalls, the horses calm and acquiescent in his presence, and later in the afternoons some days he'd play with the littlest talents in the halls, tag or hoops or catch-as-catch-can, their sturdy legs pumping as they ran from him, laughing.

Only once did he call out to Komako, lurking on a balcony, her eyes following him.

She didn't answer.

Caroline found the girl lying in an oblong of sunlight, near the window of their bedchamber. She was not alone; one of the talent children was with her. His hands were dark against her pale skin. He had a small dish of water and was wetting his fingertips and running them over her gnarled roots. Her face was turned to the light; her eyes closed. Her neck was twisted strangely, but she seemed at peace. She was keening, a low musical sound, very quiet.

The boy scrambled to his feet. "I'm so sorry, Mrs. Ficke, I uh, I just thought she might be lonely," he said.

Jubal. That was his name. She remembered him, carried into the chandler's shop by Alice on that first morning after the burning of Cairndale. He could not have been older than ten. He looked so small and brave and good now, to her eye. Dressed in breeches and a shirt too long in the sleeves and with his curled hair cut short. His face was soft and trusting. He'd come out of Cairndale burned all on his left side, his nightshirt drenched in his best friend's blood. Unable to sleep from the nightmares, he'd curl in among the glyph-twisted children. And now here he was, extending a kindness back to Deirdre. Caroline thought of Berghast and of what he'd done to his wards, how little he'd valued them, and it made her angry all over again. She thought of her own little ones, lost in London—No, she told herself viciously, say it, say the word: dead—and for a moment she couldn't speak.

Jubal watched her, eyes big.

"'Tis fine, Jubal, thank you," she managed at last. She was aware of her own wild appearance, her bloodshot eyes, tangled hair. Oskar had thought her half-mad.

When the boy had slipped away, she lay on the hard floor next to Deirdre. She smoothed the buds at the ends of the littlest branches, cupping them softly in her palms.

"You've made another friend," she murmured. "Charlie says he wants to see you. He was wondering when he could stop in. I told him any time."

The girl gave no response. But Caroline sensed she was listening.

"Deirdre—" she began, gently.

The bark had grown up over the nape of her neck, again, curling like a shell around one ear. Her hair was embrangled with green shoots and tiny heart-shaped leaves. There was a faint smell of the earth in her, of sunlight and deep waters.

"Deirdre," Caroline said again, closing her eyes. "I need your help. We all do."

29

Sotto Voce

And then, one morning, Charlie saw rain across the valley, great gray sheets of it moving quickly out to sea, and on the long road leading down to Agrigento an open carriage, shining with the wet.

It was Alice and Ribs, back from Paris.

They were tired and still dripping from the rains as they climbed down. Charlie was the first to meet them. They were alone and their eyes were tight and shadowed and he saw this and knew at once their mission had been a dark one. Alice, in her old, stained oilskin coat, with her collar turned up against the weather, took off her hat and clawed her fingers through her tangled yellow hair, just like she'd always done, and Charlie felt a surge of joy. He saw a livid red scar running across one eye, down her cheek, where she'd been hurt somehow. But this she shrugged away. She stood staring up at him a long moment.

"You got tall," she said.

He smiled and ducked his head, suddenly shy. He was finding it hard to speak.

"I heard you'd gone to Scotland. You're back already?"

"Yeah," he said.

And then she stepped forward and drew him in close into a powerful, bone-crushing hug. She smelled of leather and sweat and the sea. The carriage creaked on its springs and he looked over the top of Alice's hair and saw, climbing down, with her arms bare, Ribs. Except she didn't look like the kid he'd remembered, the ropy kid who'd survived Cairndale and gone off with Alice Quicke to find other missing talents. She pulled back her hood; her red hair was tied high off her neck. Her green eyes were quiet and her face was older and under her cloak she wore a green dress bought in Paris. In the pale wash of light she looked regal and beautiful. She met his gaze boldly and lifted her chin and scowled.

"What?" she demanded.

Charlie blushed. "Nothing. I—it's just . . . it's been a long time since I saw you."

"Well, I can fix *that*," she whispered.

And suddenly she grinned, and there she was again, the old Ribs, the irrepressible mischievous Ribs he'd missed, and he felt a lump in his throat and had to look away.

"Mi scusi," said the driver, leaning down in his sopping cloak, "ma chi pagherà?"

Charlie had forgotten all about the man. He cleared his throat. Just as Alice turned, pulling open her coin purse, there came a cry from the villa and the front doors burst open and there was Komako, descending the stairs two at a time with her white skirts in both fists, and Charlie watched the girls embrace, Ribs the taller now of the two, and he was surprised at the sadness he was feeling. Alice gave the girl a quick fierce hug. Komako didn't even look his way. Then Ko hooked an arm around Ribs, and drew her away, inside, Ribs smiling over her shoulder at Charlie and mouthing wordlessly some exaggerated apology as she was whisked away.

"You were supposed to be back by now," Charlie said, turning back. "What happened in Paris? What did you find?"

But Alice's face only darkened. She'd lifted her eyes and was gazing past him, up to the terrace railing, where Miss Davenshaw had appeared in her black clothes, like an omen.

"We found the orsine," she said grimly, the long scar at her eye creasing. "Or got near enough. It's there, it's in Paris. Just like Berghast said. It's in the catacombs."

Charlie watched her. "You don't sound happy about it."

"Yeah, well," she said with a grimace, moving past him. "That's not all we found."

In the entrance hall of the villa, Alice Quicke stood listening, the hushed air washing over her. She banged her hat against her coat to get the rain out of it, put it back on.

It felt strange to be back, after so long away. The polished floors, the cool light. The white busts in their alcoves, peering blindly out. Behind her, Charlie was helping the Sicilian driver unlash and unload the trunks. He was changed; she'd seen it at once, worried. A breeze was coming through an open door somewhere. She could hear the muffled shouts and laughter of Miss Crowley's wards running in the corridor upstairs. It made her feel old. But when had it ever been different? She'd never cared enough to look for peace, not since she was eleven years old. Not since her mother had stolen her away to Adra Norn's religious community at Bent Knee Hollow, desperate for it, for peace that is, finding instead only madness, burning those poor women in their beds in the hope of—what? A miracle?

No wonder she was such a mess, she thought.

She knew Davenshaw would be expecting her. There was such a brittle intelligence in the woman, it made Alice uneasy. She'd want to—*need* to—hear about Paris, and their return through Naples, and what they'd seen there. The shadowy horror of it. But Alice trudged upstairs to her bedchamber instead, her boots leaving marks on the washed stone floor, telling herself there'd be time enough to debrief later. It all seemed far away, now that she was back. When she'd departed for Paris, she'd been clear with Susan Crowley that no one was to disturb her room; and so even the shutters hadn't been opened, and the air was stale. She took off her battered coat, unbuttoned her collar. Sat at the edge of the mattress and studied her reflection in the looking glass. The long red scar over her eye. The sad mouth.

It wasn't the journey that wore her down. Half the time, in this part of the world, she was spoken to like she was a man. Both men and women did it. It wasn't just the clothes she wore, the men's trousers and greatcoat and the frayed American hat that hid her hair. And it wasn't just the ways she'd meet a man's eyes in the street, hard, cold, uninterested. It wasn't the bruised knuckles, or—now—that scar at her face.

No, it was something else, she decided, some acknowledgment that she wasn't a part of their world, a part of the order to things that they understood and took their solace in.

She didn't mind it. Not really. But it was exhausting, all the same. And sometimes she just wanted to be talked to like the differences didn't matter, even if they did.

There came a timid knocking at the door. "Miss Quicke?" A child's voice, one she didn't know. "Miss Davenshaw would like to see you, please, miss?"

Alice just fanned her fingers up over her eyes, didn't answer.

The footsteps receded.

She lay back and untucked her shirttails and tenderly probed the old wound at her ribs. The crescent scar, dark as a bruise. The angry skin around it, red. It was aching again, just softly, and she looked all around at the dim room, its bare white walls, trying to understand why. On the roof of a speeding train carriage, Jacob Marber had impaled her with some evil substance, an evil that was inside her still. It was, she'd been assured, harmless. Inert. Because she was no talent, it could have no lasting effect upon her. But she felt it there, the corruption, its slow clouds of poison, the kiss of the drughr in her blood, and wasn't so sure.

Some nights when the dust was bad in her she would lie awake and think of Jacob Marber, his body wracked by the stuff, like the spectral poor in their rags in the tar sheds of Shadwell, the opium in them like a dark mouth. And she'd tell herself she was lucky, lucky it was so little in her own flesh.

But opium wasn't alive.

And whatever black rot Marber had left inside her was. It connected her not just to Marber, but to the orsine itself. She'd felt the orsine's presence in the dark arched tunnels under Paris, her hand pressed to the limestone walls; she'd felt it *because* of the wound in her side, had felt it hooking her, like a small talon, leading her on in agony.

Maybe the orsine had felt it, too. The thought made her shiver.

She must have slept. She awoke knowing she ought to go to Davenshaw but she rolled off the bed and stuffed her shirt back in and stood at the shutters staring out. Something was out there, she could feel it. Her wound still prickled, as if tiny jaws were gnawing at it. She thought of Charlie, their brief reunion outside. He'd be wondering about her. But she stood on her toes and fumbled at the top of the wardrobe until she pulled down a cloth-wrapped bundle and she withdrew the small pistol that had once belonged to Frank Coulton. It was still loaded, by his hand. She didn't think he'd used it even once, in all his days.

She supposed he really hadn't needed to.

To hell with it. Davenshaw could wait. She wrestled into her greatcoat and stuffed the small pistol into one pocket and went out. Susan Crowley was in the bright corridor and Alice went the other way, down the servants' stairs at the back of the villa, through the crumbling, roofless rooms, into the garden. She hurried past the fountain, the feeling in her intensifying, and out through the creaking iron gate to the rocky slope beyond. The stone wall had been repaired, she saw. The ground gave way gradually to long yellow grass, shrubs, and a stand of twisted Sicilian trees near the bottom.

She started east. The grass scissored at her knees. She walked with her shadow long in front of her and the Greek ruins across the valley gleaming.

Thirty yards on, she stopped.

A black creature, very much like a cat, had emerged from under an almond tree, downslope. It pooled like a molten darkness under the leaves, its tail curled at its feet, its eyes glinting. It had one white paw, glowing like a sock.

"Hi you," said Alice, in a happy whisper.

The keywrasse leaped lightly down and padded toward her, its four eyes narrowing. Alice didn't move. It came around the long grass and across the rocks and rubbed its cheek powerfully against her ankle, as if to knock her off-balance. It began to purr. Then it continued past, behind her, as if that was where it had been going all along. But after a moment, when Alice still didn't move, she felt it come back, and thread itself between her legs, its purr thrumming like a turbine.

She kneeled, extended her hand. "I missed you too," she murmured. "How did you find us?"

The keywrasse sniffed at her fingers, as if she might have brought a treat. Then it stood on its hind legs and put its forepaws against her chest and sniffed at her face, at the livid red scar there, and after a moment she felt the sandpaper tongue. It dropped back down, disapproving. Its four eyes turned to slits.

"Yes," she whispered. "I know. I was stupid. I get stupid sometimes."

The keywrasse pressed the back of its head up against her hand, as if to say: *All right. Go on, then. Make yourself useful.*

Alice ran her hand along its back. Its tail rose up like a whip, rolled under her hand, away. She gave a brief, sad laugh. "You know I thought maybe it was you that I felt. In my side, I mean. But I wasn't sure. I guess you came to watch over the little ones, hm?"

She could see the villa terrace from where she knelt, the figure that had emerged there. It was Davenshaw again, of course, facing her just as if she could see her clearly. Guiltily, Alice lowered her face into the keywrasse's fur. This was her friend, her companion. The keywrasse had saved her life more than once. She thought of the terrible weirbents, which she'd offered the creature on that night at Cairndale, after it had stood against Jacob Marber. The ornate wooden key, the heavy iron key. The fury with which the keywrasse had swallowed them, and been freed, while the manor blazed around them. She raised her face in the evening sunlight. Davenshaw's silhouette was still there. She thought of what she'd seen in Naples, the horror of it, as she and Ribs made their way back from Paris. How she'd have to go to Davenshaw, warn her about it. And that doing so would make it, somehow, more real.

She sighed.

But not just yet. The keywrasse, as if sensing her unhappiness, poured suddenly through her hands to curl up against her, warm and heavy, a lit brazier covered in fur. As if to say: *This is mine and this is mine and all this that you are is mine.*

And Alice, feeling it too, let herself be claimed.

Meanwhile Komako wandered with Ribs through the villa's rooms, feeling how good it was to have her friend back safe, her oldest friend, who somehow always managed to ease Ko's moods. As they went, Ko told all about Spain, and Mr. Bailey, and the savage hunger of the glyphic there. How Mr. Bailey wanted to leave Marlowe in the land of the dead, on account of the Dark Talent. The horror of Mr. Bailey's death. But she didn't tell about her own vision, what the glyphic had shown her; she didn't tell what she'd seen. The no-longer-innocent face of the Dark Talent, staring out at her, all those broken bodies sprawled around it. She'd kept it to herself all these weeks and now, with Ribs, she thought she might let it out, but something stopped her.

"What is it?" asked Ribs.

She put a cool hand to Ko's cheek, where she'd been burned, as if to feel for herself the heat in the skin there. But she didn't try to say anything reassuring, and Ko was grateful for it. Instead, Ribs told of her and Alice's time in Paris, of their hunt for the orsine, wandering lost in the limestone galleries of the catacombs. Of the darkness that was in Alice now, or that maybe had always been there but now was nearer the surface, harder to ignore. She said she feared for Marlowe. That she was tired of always being afraid.

Komako knew what she meant. "It's just how the world really is," she said quietly. "We just forgot it, after so long behind the walls of Cairndale. There's nowhere safe. Not really."

They'd drifted by then all the way upstairs, to the ravaged loft that held the bonebird. It was quiet in the high places of the villa, lonely. Water-damaged cherubs on the ceiling watched from behind pink clouds. Herringbone floorboards, once elegant, had rotted after long years exposed to rain. The plaster had come away in places, leaving yellow scars. Against one wall stood the high wire cage that held the bonebird. Komako went to the broken wall and looked down at the gardens, at the lemon trees and the fountain and the children with Susan Crowley.

The bonebird clicked softly from its perch. It had been taken out of Nickel Street West at Miss Davenshaw's instruction all those months ago, hidden in the girls' cabin during their first crossing to Sicily. In the greasy light from the porthole Ribs used to try to teach it tricks. She'd even named it. Now Ribs hooked her fingers in the wire mesh, lowered her face close. "We ought to of brung his friends," she said. "It's cruel, it is, leavin Bertie caged up."

Komako shrugged. "He gets out. Miss D sent him to Barcelona, while I was there. And anyway, he's not *alive*, Ribs. He doesn't feel . . . anything."

"Neither's Lymenion alive. An he's got feelings."

"Does he though?" From where she stood, Ko could see Lymenion. He loomed submerged to his hips in the water barrel near the wash-house, a huge lumpen figure, half again as thick as the lemon trees. Anywhere he went, great clouds of birds would screech out a racket.

"Aw, Lymie?" said Ribs, with a wink. "He's more sensitive than *Oskar*."

Komako smiled. "*No one's* more sensitive than Oskar."

Ribs laughed.

Komako watched her friend. With everything, all that was going on, it felt so good to see her again, to have her back. Already the villa was feeling full, lived-in. Then her expression altered. "Charlie's changed," she said softly.

Ribs paused. There was something in her eyes, some buried intensity. "We all have."

"No. I mean something happened to him. In Edinburgh." There was so much she wanted to tell. And she began then, uneasily, feeling as if she were betraying his confidence, even though she knew she wasn't, that this part of it wasn't a secret, that Ribs would need to know about it, like they all would—even with all of that in her heart, still she told what she knew with her eyes averted, as if ashamed. She told how Mrs. Ficke had found the corpse of Jacob Marber, dead, truly dead, so that he could no longer hurt them, and she told how Mrs. Ficke had stolen the dust that remained at his body. She told how Charlie had been infected by it, and how even now it was spreading through his flesh, like a sickness. "The dust . . . it's restored his talent, Ribs. He can heal again. But something's not right inside him. He says he can feel it there, like it's alive. It's the drughr's dust, is what it is. It's the part of the drughr that was inside Jacob Marber, that bonded him to it."

She saw Ribs flinch at that. The bonebird behind them shifted on its perch, its wings rustling like a handful of knives.

"You think maybe . . . it's bonding Charlie to the drughr, too?"

"No," said Komako quickly. "No, nothing like that. That drughr's dead. And Charlie doesn't seem . . . influenced, or anything. He's just, I don't know. Different."

What she didn't say, of course, was that she'd seen him twist a rope of dust around his knuckles. That he'd acquired a second talent, impossible as it was to believe. That maybe whatever evil was inside him was doing the changing for him, and that Charlie, good as he was, good as he tried to be, maybe wasn't always going to be the Charlie they knew. That darker things were coming.

Ribs was watching her face closely. She said, "Well, he worries about Mar. Maybe that's it?"

Komako forced herself to shrug. "Yeah."

"So he talks to you, then? Still, I mean?"

"Yeah. Why?"

"Nothing," said Ribs casually. "I just remember how, at Cairndale, he was always, I don't know. Looking for you, like. To talk an all."

"I mean, he's not exactly brilliant at keeping his thoughts hidden. You just kind of stand next to him and he'll start telling you his feelings."

"An what kind of feelings is that, then?" asked Ribs. "Feelings about you, like?"

Komako blinked. "What? No. Jesus." She screwed up her face. "Seriously? I don't think of Charlie like that, Ribs. I'm not . . . you know. Interested."

"Sure," said Ribs, a bit too quickly.

"I'm not."

"Okay. Good."

She gave Ribs a sidelong look. Her friend's face was half-hidden by her hair. Ribs was blushing, her cheeks the same red as her hair. And then she understood.

"Riiiiibs . . . ," she began, smiling.

"What? What. Stop. *What?*"

Komako poked her friend in the side, hard. "You an *Charlie?*"

"Oi, *me* an *Charlie?*" her friend exploded. "Jesus, no! Blech." Ribs paused. "Why, you think maybe *he* might—?"

Ko shrugged, smiled. "He'd be a fool not to."

Ribs grimaced. "Yeah well he is a fool. A bloody big fool."

"The biggest," Ko agreed. But her heart was filling with an unexpected unhappiness, thinking suddenly about the glyphic in Spain, and the tattoos writhing under Charlie's skin, and that thin rope of dust that had manifested in his fist. Poor Charlie. She could scarcely look at him, sometimes. And Ribs knew none of it, not really. Komako was thinking all that, all the while watching her best friend's blushing face and the hopefulness lighting in it, and wishing things could be the way they used to be, but knowing they couldn't, not yet, maybe not ever again.

Later that day, Charlie tapped gently at one of the empty rooms, then opened the door, and saw Ribs asleep in her traveling clothes, her mouth half-open, drooling. He left her like that. He'd gone looking for Ribs and Ko all afternoon but not found them. He went back down to the kitchens looking for food. The little ones were with Susan Crowley in the classroom on the other side of the wall, reciting their letters before dinner. He felt relief, knowing everyone was safe, that Alice and Ribs were back. He hadn't realized how he'd worried until he saw their carriage approach. His fingers were sore from helping the driver unload the trunks from their lashings and this too surprised him, how tender his hands had grown, his hands that all his life had been used badly in hard work. But that was another life, he thought. And maybe it was just the infection in him, eating away. Alice would be with Miss Davenshaw, he supposed, reporting her journey's events, no doubt hearing all about the corrupted dust that was in him. It made him unhappy, thinking about it. He'd wanted company all day but even Oskar and Mrs. Ficke were occupied, holed up with their researches under the wash-house, and Lymenion would not let him pass.

It was evening when he thought of the keywrasse and how much Alice would want to see it. He filled a bowl with milk and covered it with a cheesecloth and went out past the gardens. In the creeping shadows of the day he called softly but the keywrasse did not appear and then, as he came around the corner of the stone wall, he came face-to-face with Komako. She was also holding a bowl of milk.

"Jesus," she said, sounding angry. "You startled me."

He mumbled an apology, searching her face. But she didn't appear, in that moment, uncomfortable with him. It was like he'd been imagining things, like she hadn't been avoiding him at all.

"You're looking for him, too?" she said. "I guess he'll make himself known when he wants."

He nodded, awkward. "I just thought, maybe Alice would want to see him. That's all."

"Yeah."

"And maybe he's out here because he doesn't know if he's welcome at the villa. Like if, if anyone wants him around."

She gave him a curious look. "Yeah?"

He shrugged, looked away. They'd not talked about what had happened, the dustworking he'd somehow done, and now that he had the chance he didn't know what to say. Instead a feeling rose in him, a crawling feeling, as if the hairs on his arms and chest and neck were lifting, pulled like iron filings toward a magnet. It got worse. He shook his head to clear it.

The dust was waking in him. Just exactly as it had done in the Falls, all those weeks ago.

Komako had started walking again, her shoes crunching through the rocky soil. His heart started to beat faster. There were trees on the slope below, twisted and bent as if against a great wind. To the south the ancient temple glowed in the fading day.

Moments passed before Charlie realized Komako was staring down the slope, across the long grasses, to the treeline. Slowly she crouched and set her bowl of milk aside and Charlie followed her gaze down and the dust in his skin felt like it might burst.

Through the trees, maybe fifty yards away, he could see the key-wrasse, crouched in the rocky grasses. It had grown huge, heavy, the size of a carriage. Its tail was whipping back and forth, its legs were coiled as if ready to spring. There was in the blades of its shoulders an awful tension.

Something else was moving down there. It came forward, and stood very still. And Charlie knew it for what it was.

A drughr.

But not the drughr he'd known at Cairndale, not the drughr he'd seen Dr. Berghast cut open at the orsine, smoldering with black soot. Not the creature whose dust infected him now. A *different* drughr. Wider and squatter than the other, with long whiplike tentacles rising up off its back, six, eight of them, writhing and twisting and entangling in the twilight. They were darting all around into the grasses and the low trees and then Charlie saw something horrifying, even at that distance—one of them caught something, some kind of small rodent, and the tentacle stripped the skin from the living creature like it was peeling a grape, and suddenly the bloody marbled meat of the thing poured off its own bones, spitting them out, and reshaped itself into a lumpen knotted mass. And then a second tentacle caught something else, a bird, and did the same, and a third, until—to Charlie's horror—he saw the small fleshly creatures massing around the feet of the drughr, like a tiny fleshly swarm.

"It's a caster," whispered Komako in horror. "It's like Oskar, Charlie. It's a *flesh caster*—"

And he saw, in disbelief, that it was so.

The bowl of milk fell from his hands. He feared he might be sick. The keywrasse in the clearing below screamed once—a fierce, catlike scream that made the birds burst up into the sky in the hills all around—and then it was launching itself at the drughr, hurtling through the long grasses like a scythe, its powerful muscles gleaming under its coat. The two creatures collided with a sickening crunch, the keywrasse rising up onto its hind legs to grapple with the drughr, swatting at the tentacles with its many legs, sinking its fangs terribly into the drughr's neck.

But then the little fleshly swarm was crawling up the keywrasse's legs, and biting, and leaving bloody punctures, and the keywrasse flipped and twisted and snapped its jaws, trying to dislodge the things.

"Charlie!" Komako snapped, breaking the spell.

He looked at her.

"We've got to do something. We've got to help."

The dust was already gathering around her, thick, powerful, stronger than Charlie had ever seen it. She had her arms held out wide and her face was wincing with pain but her eyes were filled with fury, almost black with the power that was in her.

"Now you, Charlie," she hissed at him. "Use the dust. Do what you did before."

"I can't, Ko—"

"Yes you can. *Try!*"

But he couldn't. He could feel the panic rising in him. He was clenching his fists and grinding his teeth and trying, for God's sake, trying so damned hard, but it was no use, there was no dust, nothing. The tattoos in his flesh were burning and blazing a bright blue but there was no dust. He looked at Komako in desperation. His cheeks were hot with his humiliation.

And that was when she seemed to understand. She turned suddenly, a whirl of darkness, the dust vortexing up around her like a cloak of wrath, whipping up the broken twigs and clumps of dirt and small rocks, and she sprinted away down through the trees, leaving him.

Charlie swore, feeling like a failure. He was still a haelan, wasn't he? He was still of some damned use, wasn't he? He shook the blinding pain from his eyes and ran after her.

He caught up to her at the edge of the clearing, half stumbling down the rocky slope, the grasses slicing bladelike at his shins. The keywrasse, massive, quick, was lashing out with its many paws, crushing the little fleshly creatures into wet puddles, pulling them apart and leaving them twitching. The drughr itself was clutching the wound in its throat and had one shoulder turned sidelong to the keywrasse, its tentacles sawing through the air, its horned skull dropped low.

Charlie was halfway across the slope when the drughr looked up toward him and Komako.

Something passed through it, then, a kind of shudder, as it saw them running. Charlie was filled with fear, absolutely terrified, and yet he couldn't slow down, he wouldn't, he'd be damned if he'd let Komako throw herself at the thing without trying to help her. Komako's dust was whirling around her, a storm of fury. She cried out in her anger.

They didn't even get close.

The drughr took two shaky steps backward, and then—smoothly, inexplicably—it melted into the darkness of the treeline and was gone. The reeking fleshly things it had created all at once ceased their wriggling, and collapsed, dripping and congealing in the yellow grasses. The keywrasse turned and turned, as if all at once confused. It poked at one of the gooey bits with a tentative paw, sniffed the mess.

The stillness was sudden, awful. Komako ran to the edge of the trees but stopped there, the dust diminishing. It was no use; the drughr was nowhere.

Charlie was gasping, his blood hammering in his chest. The corrupted dust under his skin was swarming all over, on fire. As if a carpet of insects were eating its way through him. Komako glanced over her shoulder, her eyes dark and magnificent.

And then, to his mortification, Charlie doubled over, and threw up.

It was Lymenion who took the child.

From their bedchamber, upstairs in the villa, in the calm evening light.

Caroline Ficke watched impassive as the flesh giant stooped under the doorway, its powerful neck and shoulders glistening in the failing dusk. Its smell was powerful. She kneeled on one side of Deirdre, ignoring the ache in her joints, and pressed her palm to the bark-like skin of the girl's arm to calm her. "It's all right," she whispered, "it's all right now, there child, it's all right."

But if Deirdre felt fear or pain, she gave no sign. Lymenion stamped heavily near until he loomed over them, his visage sliding and almost featureless so that Caroline wasn't sure where to look; and then, with the gentlest of gestures, the creature scooped the glyph-twisted girl lightly up into his arms, and straightened, and stood waiting in a rustle of leaves and roots. The child's dark eyes studied Caroline, trusting.

"Rruh?" he said.

The boy, Oskar, cleared his throat. "Mrs. Ficke? Lymenion wants to know if we should go?"

Caroline looked away. "Yes, thank you," she said. She reached for the side of the bed, leveraged herself upright. "Let's go."

The low sun was red in the sky and the shadows long in the gardens as they wended their way back to the wash-house. The lemon trees were on fire. Across the valley Caroline could see the dazzling red pillars of the ancient temple, all ablaze. There was such beauty in the world, she thought suddenly. And her at her age, to still be surprised by it.

There was fear in her though as she walked. Fear that she was mistaken, fear that it might not work. Fear that she might cause the girl pain, or worse. They went single file and in silence with Caroline in the front, and Lymenion just behind her, and they saw no other as they went. The villa might have been deserted. For one terrible moment they heard a shriek—something harsh and inhuman and vicious—rise up from the broken ground beyond the walls. They stopped, listening. But the sound echoed off into the hills and did not come again. The boy, Caroline saw, had gone very pale. Deirdre had dialed her face toward the shriek.

They hurried.

Into the ramshackle wash-house, down through the trapdoor, down the sloping limestone steps they went. Into the dim chamber of the Agnoscenti, silent still with its thousandfold secrets. Caroline was having trouble catching her breath. The air down here was thick with candle smoke though few candles now burned, and those that did were low in their lakes of wax and guttering.

Lymenion, at Caroline's instruction, laid Deirdre gently upon the altar. It might have been carved for her and her alone. Her head fit the impression perfectly, resting gentle, her elbows in their own shallow cups. The long tendrils of wood and leaf fell into smooth channels of stone, or rose up calmly overhead. Deirdre's eyes, Caroline saw, were closed. Her rough chest rose and fell. Lymenion stepped away. Oskar's hands were clasped in front of him, as if he were praying. No one spoke.

"Is, is, is something supposed to h-happen?" Oskar whispered at last.

And then something did. Suddenly the girl's eyes opened wide in startlement and she turned her face and met Caroline's gaze. Her eyes had changed color, they were a dazzling golden hue, and the blacks in them shrank away until there was only gold. Her body seemed to be thrumming, as if with a silent electricity, and all at once the tendrils and twigs burst into bloom, golden blossom upon blossom, and the beauty of it made Caroline hold her breath in astonishment. The girl looked very grave, very serious. And that was when Caroline heard it: the voice.

A sweet voice, the voice of a fifteen-year-old girl.

Mrs. Ficke? it said in wonder, from somewhere inside her own skull. *Oh this feels so . . . strange . . .*

30

Every Monster Ever

Jeta and the drughr were just north of Roye when the monster found them again.

It was the third night since the convent at Saint-Omer. By the reckoning of locals they were maybe halfway to Paris by then. Jeta had slept in a ditch for two nights running, covering herself as best she could by underbrush for the warmth, trying not to think of the creature with all its arms and fingers and its terrifying sniffing noises, almost exactly like the litch back at the Falls. But she couldn't keep it out of her head. During the days she stumbled along, drained, weakened by the drughr that seemed always to be growing more solid, more real, feeding somehow off her own talent. Her heels were bloody. Her calves throbbed. She was hungry all the time.

The drughr had gone quiet again, after so many days of talk. She seemed saddened by her failure to locate her son. Jeta didn't understand the Dreaming, whatever it was, the thing that allowed her to seek out the boy, but she knew the disappointment of looking for someone and not finding them. She knew that.

But then, at sunset on that third day outside Roye, she wandered off the road across a barren field and saw a barn, blazing red in the red light of the failing day. There was no one within sight for miles. And the big wooden doors were sturdy, and the roof was intact, and the loft was packed with old hay. She could scarce believe her luck. She climbed up an old ladder and laid her cloak out and felt the fragrant lightness of the hay fold itself under her body, and she slept.

She awoke after midnight, curled fetal on her left side, a stink of ash in her nostrils.

Opened her eyes, and saw.

The monster was inches from her face. The hollows of its features leaned in, its nostrils like slits, snuffling its wet, warm breath, the burning darkness where its eyes should have been boring into her. Her blood was loud in her ears. She couldn't breathe. Its crowned skull was antlered with shadows and as large around as a barrel and at the corners of her vision she could see its four arms splayed out, elbows crooked, its massive many-fingered hands chewing up the wood floor of the loft where it crouched.

But under it all she could feel something else, the low aching pull of something very much like bone, inside it, everywhere inside it, impossibly heavy and thick. Bones she did not know, bones she could not have named. Bones where they should not have been. Bones like cudgels, bones like splinters, bones like the knives used to slit out the bellies of fish.

Then Jeta heard its voice, not speaking, but ringing somehow in the air itself, like a bell.

Where . . . is . . . she?

And she started to shake. She didn't want to believe her drughr would flee, would abandon her, but every sinew in her flesh was screaming out in fear. She tried to shut her eyes, to stopper her ears, but could not.

The thing made a low rattling sound in its throat, almost like a growl, like kernels being shaken in a hollow tube.

Jeta's eyes were wet. And then, almost without thinking, she curled her bone fingers into a fist. There, alongside her ribs, where her hands were still crushed up as if in sleep.

And she felt the pull of the monster's bones, and she *pushed*.

She pushed with all the talent she had in her, she drew her talent to herself and willed the bones in all its four arms to snap, she willed the bones in all its fingers to shatter, she willed its wrists and its shoulder plates and its ribs and all the manifold inhuman and unnatural bones in their impossible thickness to split and shiver and fracture apart.

The monster reared back and roared and fell, massively, heavily, through the floor of the loft in a great explosion of hay and a splintering of wood, it plunged down into the darkness of the barn below. Hay and dust were afloat in the gloom like pale seeds. The barn groaned.

Jeta had been thrown backward and for a long moment in the ringing stillness she lay still herself, uncertain. Her nose was bleeding. There was blood in her mouth. Grimacing, afraid, she crawled to the edge and looked down.

She could *feel* what she'd done, even before she looked. The monster lay with its massive arms bent at strange angles, its legs folded up under the bulk of its torso. Its skull had been twisted half-around again to peer backward. But even as she stared in horror she saw it twitch, she saw the thing—impossibly, horribly—fold itself over on its own broken limbs, the bones still shattered and yet the strength of the thing propelling it upright again, twisted now, but the muscles and thews wrapping and double-wrapping themselves around their own broken bones, as if lashing them into place, and the monster lurched to the beam that held up the loft, and with a single massive hand it reached out and ripped the beam down.

And then Jeta was sliding forward, sliding with all the hay and detritus, plummeting down into the floor of the barn where the monster stood, implacable.

Where . . . is she? its voice rang out again, not angry, not in pain.

And Jeta, her heart in her throat, scrambled to her feet and backed away.

"I don't know!" she screamed. "I don't know!"

And then, suddenly, she did. The drughr was there, on the far side of the barn, and the monster turned with all its four arms rising ropy and muscular. Except the drughr wasn't the woman in black, wasn't the child she'd lost, wasn't anything human at all. She was her true self, the self she'd shown Jeta in the sewers under London, towering and smoldering with a sootlike dust and with her great twisting antlers rising from her and her own second pair of arms, folded like wings, ending in claws. A cloak of dust whirled around her.

For just a moment the monster hesitated.

And yet she was not strong, the drughr, not yet, not enough. The monster launched itself forward on its weird broken legs, punching into the dust. One massive hand seized the drughr's throat, lifted her to her toes.

"No!" cried Jeta.

She crushed her fists tight and fell to her knees and pried back the bones in the monster's hand, finger by finger by finger. And then she snapped the awful hand back over its wristbones, horribly, and felt the breaking, and the monster's hand fell away.

The drughr staggered. Her dust was ropy and thick and it dragged the monster down to the floor by the neck. And yet the monster did not stop; it punched a second fist upward, and through, and a third, and it seized the drughr by her shoulders and pulled her down close in an awful embrace.

And began to squeeze.

Again, with her vision beginning to blur from the pain of it, Jeta sought out the weak points in those arms and again she split the bones, one by one, grinding them down to powder, grinding them into dust. And again the monster's grip fell away.

The drughr was on her knees. She looked sideways and reached out a clawed hand and the dust smashed one wall of the barn. She threw herself backward. And as she did so, her dust drove the sharp fragments and scantling from the wall deep into the monster's flesh. It staggered back, its arms loose and trying to lash themselves together. All along one side the daggers and arrows of wood shivered like so many quills.

And then, almost lazily, it reached its one good arm up, brushed them snapping away.

It turned to Jeta then. And started toward her, shambling strangely on its broken bones.

It was at that moment she understood, truly, for the first time, that a drughr could not be stopped. Not by her. Not by any talent. She crabwalked in horror backward, trying to get away.

It came on.

And then her own drughr was there, somehow. At her side, a great storm of dust and fury, her skin like coils of cable writhing over itself, if cables were made of darkness. And she drew back her arms and the curtain of dust rolled forward, like sheets of rain, and overwhelmed the monster where it stood in all that wreckage and darkness.

And Jeta saw the dust swirl around the monster as if seeking some way inside and she saw it pouring in through its nostrils and then she felt the bones themselves, the bones she'd ground to dust, rising up, tearing their own way through the monster's flesh, cutting it to ribbons from the inside, but her eyes could see nothing, so absolute was the storm of dust surrounding the thing.

She felt a familiar, oily grip on her wrist, and looked up.

The woman in black was there, shuddering, heaving for breath, her face looking gaunt and weak.

We must go! she said. *Come! While there is time!*

And then they were running, fleeing out into the blue mist in that still and barren field, the night cold all around them, their skirts heavy and awkward, hair in tangles, running together hand in hand, like sisters, like lovers, two women unlike any others in the world entire and so alike in their unlikeness, both human and yet not human, one young and one immensely old, but fleeing together broken and bloodied and afraid over the muddy earth as if there were no difference between them, as if they wanted the same thing, fleeing south, toward Paris, toward the dust, away.

Micah sat on the high stone bench, under the weeping statue, and swung his legs slowly.

For weeks he'd been able to stopper his heart against the deaths of Prudence, of Timna. But now, here in the pale hallways of the convent, all he could hear was the quick snickering of his sister, the slap of their bare feet running on wet flagstones. They'd wanted to get to this convent for years. He'd not thought he loved them, not known the meaning of the word, not in all his brutal bloody twelve years. Now he knew otherwise.

An acolyte in her red cloak came to him, gestured for him to follow. She too was old, her face lined and grooved. Her eyes were the blue of veins under glassy skin. Her eyebrows were shaved, her hair was shorn, in the manner of all the Abbess's talents.

They passed a mural, a display of terracotta bowls, they passed a small chapel with its empty pews. But it was no religious order the Abbess commanded. *Faith in an invisible power that might or might not affect your life,* she had told Micah once. *What good is that? I want a power that can be seen.*

All of the talents in le Couvent de la Délivrance were very old. They came from all over the world, women of a religious bent, a gleam of madness in their eyes. How the Abbess found them, Micah never knew. They had renounced their gifts, and lived now chaste lives, refusing their talents. Micah did know some things, had guessed at others: that their talents helped feed the Abbess, helped keep her strong; that they guarded an object of great power and value, in the catacombs below the gardens. Claker Jack had had no idea the nature of what he'd tried to betray. The Sisters of Deliverance would have destroyed him.

Micah followed the acolyte along a wide hallway, through an antechamber, down an ancient curving stairwell. He scarcely reached her elbows. There were brackets for torches on the walls and candles burning when they reached the basement.

Somewhere: old women's voices, in a slow chant.

A scraping, as if someone were scrubbing out a stain.

Down they went, deeper into the earth, the hallway twisting and sloping away, the air warming as they went. The hallway ended at two great wooden doors, with iron pull-rings low in their centers. The acolyte opened the doors with both hands, clouds of vapor pouring out around them. Micah went through, into the mists. A green light seeped poisonously through the steam. The doors shut behind him; he was alone.

He stood breathing. It was an ancient Roman bathhouse. The steam was thick with strange herbs, making him light-headed. He could see little. The faint greenish outline of a pillar to his left, the glistening tiles underfoot. Heat plastered his hair to his face.

From within the steam, within the hot pool somewhere ahead, the waters splashed softly.

Micah blinked, uneasy.

Something approached, a dark shape moving through the vapors like a languorous slow serpent. It was the Abbess. She did not ask about his sisters; she did not ask about him. She lurked half visible in the cloudy green light. "Ah, mon enfant" came her voice, deep, dangerous. "Tu es revenu."

Micah shoved his little fists deep in his pockets. "Claker Jack's dead," he said abruptly. "It were the dust what killed him. He were trying to use it, to get his talent back."

"He was a fool," she said, switching to his language. "Where is the corrupted dust now?"

Micah spat. "Some kid took it. A talent, out of Cairndale. But he weren't alone. That Ficke woman from Edinburgh, she were with him."

"Ah."

Micah swallowed uneasily. He had the uncomfortable feeling she knew everything he was going to tell her already. "Listen, I . . . I saw something at the Falls. It were . . . I don't know. I don't know what I saw. Claker's bloody body just opened up, like a . . . like a window. An I saw, inside him—"

His voice faltered, remembering the horror.

A stillness filled the chamber. And then at last the Abbess emerged slowly out of the vapors, the green mists coalescing around her, then parting, and she came forward, her white robe wet and dragging shapeless at her shoulders, her silver hair gleaming like molten ingots. There was a catlike grace to her walk, her bare heels making a sucking sound on the tiles. Micah craned his neck. She loomed above him, taller even than any man. Her silver eyes had gone absolutely black. Her cheekbones were flat, her face uncannily smooth. An overwhelming awe filled him.

"You saw *them*," she murmured. She reached a huge hand out, cupped his chin. "You saw the risen drughr. They are awake."

"They'll be coming," whispered Micah, afraid.

"Non, mon enfant," replied the Abbess softly. "They are already here."

31

THE AGRIGENTO COUNCIL

Word of the drughr's attack, in the rocks below the villa grounds, spread fast. The littlest children were afire with it, whispering in the halls, huddling together at the edges of the terrace, peering through the windows at the hills beyond the garden. The bravest among them flared their own talents, wishing they'd seen it themselves. Zorya said Charlie and Komako had scared it off. Michael said the keywrasse, like an avenging angel, was back, and had delivered them like it had done in the last days of Cairndale. Little Shona swore she'd seen Charlie twisting dust in that gallery after, and that the drughr had done something to him, something awful. When Charlie came into the dining room in the morning they all fell silent, peering sidelong up at him, until Miss Crowley clapped her hands and glowered.

While Charlie, bewildered, heard what he heard and tried not to care.

But there was something else, a wisp of another rumor, more eerie, more intriguing, just at the edges of all of that. It was said Oskar and Mrs. Ficke had found something, something important, something that might change everything. Both kept themselves locked now in the buried chamber, late into the night, with Lymenion like a soft reeking guardian standing patiently in the dark wash-house. Twice Charlie tried to talk to them but Lymenion—gently, firmly—refused to let Charlie pass. When he went to Mrs. Ficke's room, he found little Deirdre missing, too. Komako was a ghost, avoiding him now more than ever, and Alice spent her days in Miss Davenshaw's room, recounting no doubt whatever she'd seen in her travels. And so Charlie lurked with Ribs in the villa's rooms, distracted, tired, trying to keep an eye on the villa's grounds, as if the horror he'd sighted might rise up at any hour, trying not to notice the sidelong way she'd look at him, like he was an invalid, a pitiful child, a child with an illness that couldn't be cured.

But in the night, alone in his room, he'd unbutton his nightshirt and peel it back and stare at his torso in the clouded mirror, the inky swirls of dust in his skin, always moving, moving as if to some purpose he was not privy to, though it be writ on his very skin. And he would shudder.

The marks continued to spread.

Then one night Charlie received a summons.

He was to report to Miss Davenshaw in the villa's lower library, at nine o'clock. He was not the only one. As he came around the corner he could see candlelight shining under the door. Voices, muffled, drifted through the wall.

He was the last to arrive; the small library was already full. The lamps had been lit and in the leather armchair in front of the fire sat Miss Davenshaw, all in black, her grave face turned toward the room. Alice and Komako sat on the far side of a low table, Oskar facing them. Komako would not look at him. Her hair was not in its usual braid and it fell all about her face and she looked, he thought, wild and angry. Ribs, who'd been lounging against a bookshelf, drifted over toward him. She winked out of sight, so that only her disembodied smock and shoes remained.

"Just take your time, then," the clothes whispered.

"You are late, Mr. Ovid," said Miss Davenshaw curtly. But her voice sounded tired, her skin looked gray. "Miss Quicke, do continue."

Alice set a tumbler with some amber liquid in it on the low table, ran the back of her hand across her lips. "We got close to the orsine in Paris. I could *feel* it, through the wall of the catacombs. But we couldn't find our way to it. It's a maze under there, and there are dozens of ways in. But it's there. It's real.

"It's what we found on our way back here that's more disturbing. We sailed to Naples. There was a lead on a talent there, a kid, from the old glyphic at Cairndale. We found him quickly. But he'd been taken, just before we got to him. The bedsheets were still warm." She withdrew from a pocket of her coat a burned journal, which had been saved from Cairndale. She laid it softly on the table. "The ache in my side was bad. I tracked what took him. Ribs and I caught it in a warehouse near the docks. It was the drughr."

Charlie ran his tongue over his teeth, leaned forward. This was new.

"But it was different, changed from what it was in London in the fall. Still huge, shadowy, antlered. But now it has a kind of—what would you call it, Ribs? This red, burning hollow in its chest. It was ferocious. When it attacked us, the hole just sort of burned up all through it, until we couldn't see the drughr anymore. It was still there, just . . . invisible. Like Ribs can do. My bullets did nothing to it. It grabbed Ribs like it could see her and threw her over the pier, into the harbor. It's where I got this." She touched the long, angry red cut on her face. "I don't scare easily. But I've never been so scared."

"Jesus," whispered Oskar.

Charlie frowned. "How long ago was this?"

"Six days, maybe." Alice pressed a hand to her ribs, gingerly. Her voice turned thoughtful. "But why didn't it kill us, in that warehouse? Or kill me, and take Ribs? I think maybe it wasn't done with us, yet. I think we were still . . . useful. It's been following us."

"An now it's followed us here," said Ribs angrily. "It came after Charlie an Ko."

"But ours had tentacles," Charlie interrupted. "Not a hole in its chest. It made these little flesh things out of whatever it could catch, birds and mice and such. They were like these little . . . Lymenions."

"Charlie!" Oskar protested. "You know Ly's just outside, right? He, he, he can *hear* you—"

"Could there be two of them?" asked Alice.

Oskar fell quiet. All eyes turned to Miss Davenshaw, her pale fingers interlaced in her lap.

"It would seem the drughr are rising," the blind woman said softly. Her voice cut through the firelight like a blade. "You were right to return, Miss Quicke, Miss Ribbon. This is no time to be reckless. They are growing bolder."

The room had gone very still.

Alice leaned forward, her chair creaking. "So there *are* more than one?"

"There were five, once," Miss Davenshaw replied. "Each commanded a different talent. One, we know, was destroyed by Dr. Berghast at the orsine, at Cairndale. She was, we believe, the dustworker. Which leaves the caster, the clink, the turner, and their own corrupted glyphic. The caster will be what Miss Onoe and Mr. Ovid faced two days ago. The turner will be what you and Miss Ribbon encountered in Naples. As for the others . . ." She opened her empty hands. "The drughr have been silent for centuries; it seems they are back. Why now? The shining boy returns to Cairndale, and the lost drughr rise only a few months after? The timing is . . . interesting."

"You think this has to do with Marlowe?" said Alice.

Miss Davenshaw drew a long, careful breath, almost a sigh. "In more ways than one, I fear."

The candlelight was craggy in Alice's features. Charlie watched her until she felt his eyes on her and looked his way.

"Marlowe is my ward," Miss Davenshaw went on, "your friend, one of us. But more than that, he is unlike anyone who has lived before. There are many who believe he was foreseen, that he has a role to play in the struggle that is coming. That he—and he alone—will prove decisive against the drughr."

Charlie shook his head. "I don't care about any of that. I just want him back."

"We do too, Charlie," said Alice.

"The Spanish glyphic said the Abbess is the key," said Komako. "If we find her, we find the entrance to the second orsine."

"It also said the orsine was closed," added Alice. "You'd still need a way to open it."

"Oh, but there *is* a way," said Mrs. Ficke, in her creaking voice. "Oskar and I have found it."

The room went still. Charlie looked at the old Scottish alchemist in surprise. They all did. She stood grizzled at the fireplace, a blade where her one hand should be. He felt a heat flooding his chest. The frail woman he'd traveled with was gone; in her place was a figure carved with purpose, glittering with intelligence.

"Oskar?" she said. "Would you like to tell them?"

Now Charlie noticed Oskar's shy eagerness, the way he kept chewing at his soft red lips. "It's true, the, the orsine in Paris can be reopened," he said, looking all around.

"Reopened how?" asked Alice.

Oskar started to smile, faltered. "By, by—"

"By using the chamber below the wash-house," said Mrs. Ficke. "It contains a kind of . . . nexus point for glyphics. A way to channel their power. Whether this nexus was made, or already a part of this place, I cannot say. Before this villa existed," and she swept the blade of her arm around the room, "all this belonged to the Agnoscenti. There must have been a monastery once, on this spot. The underground chamber dates from then. The Agnoscenti were the builders of the orsines. They kept careful records until their kind were scattered, nearly four hundred years ago. They are all dead now, alas. Much to our misfortune. They would have been a great help in fighting the drughr." Her voice darkened. She unrolled a parchment rubbing from where it had been on the mantel-piece and she set it down on the table. "We found this symbol carved into the floor and the walls of the chamber here. 'Tis very old."

"It's the Cairndale symbol," Oskar said helpfully to Miss Davenshaw.

"Thank you, Mr. Czekowisz," she said dryly. "I am aware."

Charlie reached a hand to the cord at his throat, the ring he'd threaded there. The ring his father had given his mother, the ring Dr. Berghast had told him was an artifact. The crossed hammers before a rising sun.

Mrs. Ficke said, "One of the Agnoscenti must have been present at the founding of Cairndale. This mark appears in writings that reference the orsines. There are two hammers, we believe, because there were two orsines. The chamber below the wash-house is one end of a path that leads directly to the orsines. A path for glyphics. All that we are in need of, it would seem, is a glyphic to walk it."

Charlie watched Komako shake the hair from her eyes. She looked from Oskar to Mrs. Ficke and back. "I've seen two glyphics now," she said. "Both were . . . terrible. I wouldn't trust either to do what was asked of them."

"Glyphics are just people, like anyone," said Miss Davenshaw softly. "They can do good, or fail to. But we cannot judge the all, based on the one. Not every glyphic is like the Spanish glyphic. Any more than every dustworker is like Jacob Marber."

"And how many glyphics have you met?" said Komako sharply. "Or you, Mrs. Ficke?"

"Ko—" said Charlie, shocked.

She glared at him. "What?"

Mrs. Ficke watched them both with hooded eyes. "The orsine in Paris lies dormant," she said. "But it was not destroyed, not like the orsine at Cairndale. Its glyphic's heart burns within it still, like a key stuck in a locked door, keeping it sealed. And that heart is still a part of the web that connects all talents. Deirdre, in the nexus, might just be powerful enough to . . . unstick it. And then we might unlock the door."

"What do you mean, unstick it?" said Alice.

"She means kill it," said Komako. "Say what you mean, Mrs. Ficke. You want to kill it."

"Its glyphic is already dead," the old alchemist replied. "Only its heart beats on."

"All this dying," whispered Ko angrily. "All this damn dying."

"I need hardly remind you what happened at Cairndale. An orsine without a glyphic is in danger of tearing open. The spirit dead will pour through. The glyphic's heart must be kept whole, to be returned to the orsine after the child is rescued. The orsine *must* be sealed again."

Nobody spoke.

Alice got to her feet. She looked tired. "Okay. So we move fast. Your Deirdre unsticks the glyphic's heart. And one of us finds the Abbess, and enters her orsine, and pulls Mar out of it?"

"Why does that sound so filthy?" Ribs sniggered in Charlie's ear.

"Even if Deirdre *can* unlock the orsine," said Mrs. Ficke, "she still cannot actually *pull open* the door. Nor close it after. Not without actually *being there*, touching it. That's why the orsine at Cairndale needed Mr. Thorpe, and why Dr. Berghast was so desperate to make another glyphic to replace him. And without a glyphic, no living thing can pass through an orsine safely. Only the spirit dead. And the drughr."

"Jesus," breathed Alice.

Ribs again, whispering dryly: "Him too, probably."

But Charlie was only half listening. He felt strange, nervous. He cleared his throat.

"I can go through," he said quietly.

He came around the back of a chair and unbuttoned his cuff and rolled back his sleeve, shoving it the last of the way up to his armpit. Then he held the bared arm out. In the firelight the corrupted dust writhed in smoky crescents, his dark skin glowing faintly with its eerie blue shine, as if the light were deep inside him. He turned the flat of his hand. The library was utterly, terribly silent.

He forced himself to meet their upturned faces. To see the fascinated horror in their eyes.

"It's the drughr's dust," he said. "It's what the drughr left in Jacob Marber, what bonded them. It made him more than a dustworker, more than a talent. And it allowed him to pass through into the other world. If he could go through, I can go through too."

"Charlie—" murmured Ribs.

"The Abbess in Paris wants this dust, just like Claker Jack did. You remember, Mrs. Ficke. She'll be only too pleased to receive me, if I seek her out. Once I'm inside, I can find my way to the orsine. No matter what gets in my way."

"How?" said Alice.

He shrugged. "I'm a haelan, aren't I?"

"Are you?" said Komako softly, with an edge in her voice. Her dark hair was in her face, hiding her eyes. "Is that what you are, Charlie?"

Charlie looked at her.

"Mr. Ovid is correct," said Miss Davenshaw, after a moment. "The Abbess will receive him. I do not know her reasons for desiring the corrupted dust, but desire it she does. And once the orsine is unsealed, the dust should indeed grant him safe passage."

426 ◆ J. M. Miro

"Should?" said Komako.

And now Ko did look at him. He thought it was anger in her expression but she held his gaze just a moment too long and he saw that wasn't it, that wasn't it at all. It was fear.

"Ummm," said Ribs. She cleared her throat.

"Miss Ribbon?"

"I'm just thinking, like. If this Abbess is as awful as she's supposed to be, an she wants this dust so bad, do we all reckon it's such a good idea for Charlie to just walk up an knock on her door?"

Charlie started to shake his head but then said, quietly: "Do you have a better way to get to Mar?"

Ribs was silent.

"And he will not go to Paris alone," Miss Davenshaw went on. "We will see to that. He will be protected."

"Charlie couldn't find his own feet in a dark room," said Komako. "I'll go with him."

Miss Davenshaw held up a long hand. "Not you, Miss Onoe. We will need you here, to keep the villa safe. You are the only one who can stand against the drughr."

"The keywrasse—"

"—will be here, too. Yes. But the drughr are . . . unpredictable. If one lurks still outside our walls, it will have stayed for a reason. Perhaps it wishes simply to feed on the little talents. But perhaps it is here for another reason. Perhaps it suspects what we are attempting to do. The young glyphic, Deirdre, must be protected."

She was right, of course; Komako's face betrayed it. She looked at Charlie and then away.

"Me an Alice'll go back," Ribs called out. "Right, Alice? We hardly even unpacked. It'll be right simple. We'll keep Charlie safe."

"We can be in Montparnasse in five days," said Alice. "We didn't know about the Abbess before. It would've made things easier. Ribs can make the inquiries. She speaks excellent French."

"I have a contact there, also," said Miss Davenshaw. "An old exile. She may know how to find the Abbess."

"She can be trusted?"

"She will have to be."

But Charlie was looking in surprise at Ribs's disembodied smock. "Wait. You speak French?"

"What?" she muttered. "It weren't my idea to learn. It just comes easy, is all."

Charlie grinned. "I'm just surprised. You barely speak English."

"Ass," she hissed.

The library had gone quiet. Everyone was watching them. Charlie felt the heat rise to his face.

"If you two are quite finished—?" said Miss Davenshaw crisply.

As he left the library, Charlie could feel something rising in him, something strong and joyful and dangerous, something he hadn't felt in a long time.

Hope.

Back in his spartan room he began at once to pack for the journey. The battered sea-green trunk beside the wardrobe was small in the candlelight and not his own and he packed only what he needed, nothing more. It had been agreed they would depart at once, in the morning, making their long overland way to Palermo and sailing north from there, for Provence. He remembered Mar crawling into bed with him on a cold night at Cairndale, his little toes icy and making Charlie jump, his hot breath on Charlie's arm. And he remembered how Mar would walk along the low stone wall in the courtyard, arms out for balance, grinning at Charlie in pride. Just like any little kid anywhere. Something low in his chest hurt. He dressed for bed and then rolled his sleeves high and looked at his tattooed arm. It was just chance that he'd been infected, that the bone witch in that cathedral in Edinburgh had attacked him. And yet, without all that, he'd have had no way to go after Mar.

Mar, he thought. *Hang on. I'm coming.*

The shutters of his window were closed to the night darkness. When he was packed, he sat at the edge of his bed and allowed himself to imagine how it would be to see Marlowe again. Shadows gathered in the cornices. The villa was quiet. His bare feet on the flagstones felt cool and in the stillness he lay down and studied the water-stained ceiling, wondering at the strangeness in his life. He thought of his mother, their final days together in her sickness. He tried to remember his father's face, but it was like a sun was too bright behind him, and Charlie couldn't see the features anymore. He remembered Cairndale, how it had been on that first morning, when Komako and Ribs had woken him and Mar up. He remembered Mar.

He sat up, his blood pounding. Slowly, softly, he curled his fingers and tried to call the dust to him. He could feel the skin all over his forearms burning and prickling as if rubbed with sandpaper, and he cupped his palms and lifted them to his face. A thin tendril of dust, like a dark candle flame, wavered weakly in his hands.

It was real. Jesus.

And then there came a knock at the door, and the dust dissipated, and he got guiltily to his feet as if he'd been doing something wrong, and lifted the candle in its dish for the light.

It was, to his amazement, Komako. Grim, still in her dark clothes from the day before.

"Walk with me," she said.

He blinked, confused. Then cast around for his shoes and, still in his nightshirt, stumbled after her down the stairs, into the garden. She'd exited through the ruined east hall and as he emerged Charlie glanced back at the villa. The far gallery was bright and cast its lantern light in oblong squares across the terrace, then steeply down onto the foliage and the gravel paths. Charlie saw Miss Davenshaw and Alice and Mrs. Ficke all moving within. He saw Oskar's window, lit up. But Komako had scarcely paused, and just led him deeper, away from the villa and his friends, along the moonlit pathways, toward the fountain at the heart of the garden.

She was seated at the edge of the fountain when he emerged into the moonlight. He looked at her awkwardly, feeling suddenly foolish in his long shapeless nightshirt.

"I never told them," she said. "I never told them about what happened. The dust."

He nodded. "Yeah."

"I guess I feel it's your truth to tell. Not mine. Has it happened again?"

"No," he lied.

She seemed relieved by it, though he was puzzled. He sat beside her and clasped his hands between his knees and leaned forward. Her hair smelled of milk and almonds. The lemon tree over the bench was black with its own stillness. Her eyes were very clear in the moonlight.

"How will you find him, once you're in?" she asked. "Isn't it a big place, on the other side?"

"I don't know. I think so? It's a whole world, isn't it? But I just have this, this feeling. Like he'll be there, where he's supposed to be, when I get through."

"A *feeling*."

"Yeah."

"A lot's at stake, to depend on a *feeling*."

She half turned then and trailed her fingers lightly through the fountain, shattering its reflection into jewels of light. Charlie tried to hold this moment in his mind, to remember it. He felt like he would be losing all this, the peace, the stillness, the friendship. He felt like everything would be changed, if ever he returned.

Komako asked, "You don't think Marlowe's going to be mad? He went into one orsine in order to close it forever, to stop the spirit dead from getting through. And now you're going to open another, to get him back."

Charlie hadn't thought of it that way. It made him uncomfortable. He'd never seen Marlowe angry, not really. Not at him. "You heard Mrs. Ficke. We can use the glyphic's heart to seal it back up again, once I've got Mar out."

"And if she's wrong?"

"I don't think she's wrong about much. But what can I do, Ko? It's *Mar*. He's still *in* there."

"The drughr are in there too, Charlie."

"Yeah."

They sat then for a time in silence. Their legs were touching. Charlie could feel the heat of Komako's thigh pressing against his own. He screwed up his courage. "Ko? Why did you bring me out here?"

He could hear her swallow, uncertain. "I needed . . . to talk," she replied. "Alone. I didn't want anyone to see us."

Charlie too swallowed suddenly. It was like there was too much saliva in his mouth. He felt a heat come into his cheeks and he didn't dare look at her. "Uh, Ribs is probably right beside us," he mumbled.

But when she didn't laugh he risked a glance, and saw the seriousness in her face, and faltered. "Um, I'm sorry you can't come with us," he said. "I—I wanted you to."

But she shrugged that off. "I keep thinking about that drughr. Outside the walls. Why did it run from us? We're not much danger to a drughr."

Charlie tried to grin. "Well. You're scarier than you know."

"*We*, Charlie. *Both* of us. And that's just it. Neither of us *should* be scary to a drughr." She was scratching miserably at her sore hands with her nails and she stopped. Her voice was grave. "There's something else, something I haven't told anyone yet. Something the Spanish glyphic showed me."

Charlie looked up at that. He had the uncomfortable feeling something bad was coming. "About Mar?"

"Well, him and this stupid . . . vision. The Spanish glyphic is the one who saw it, originally. Did you know that? And I was forced to see it, too. It made me watch. While it killed Mr. Bailey. I didn't understand it, or maybe I just didn't want to understand it. It was like the whole world was ending, and the sky was on fire, and there were dead little ones all around . . ." She shuddered. "The glyphic showed me everything. It was the Dark Talent."

Charlie couldn't keep the skepticism from his voice. "The Dark Talent. Who brings about the end of talentkind."

She nodded. "Mr. Bailey believed it."

"You don't though, right? It's just a story."

"Sometimes stories have their own ways of coming true," she said softly. "After I saw it, I couldn't . . . I couldn't remember how to put it all together. It was like I knew it, but I didn't know what I knew. I can't explain it. Then, when you started dustworking, when the keywrasse appeared? Suddenly it all came back to me. That's why I got so angry." She gripped his wrist suddenly, hard, and her eyes were fierce. "Listen, Charlie. The thing about this vision is, it's not real. Or it doesn't have to be. It's just a *possible* future. That's what the glyphic wanted me to understand."

"Okay. So this vision you saw, it's more like a warning?"

"I guess."

"Mar would never hurt us, Ko."

She looked away, out at the garden. Her voice was troubled. "But that's just it. Everyone thinks it's about Marlowe, how he's going to destroy everything because he's different, not like the rest of us. The shining boy, right? Except they're *wrong*. This vision or whatever, what Mr. Bailey was talking about, a living boy born in the land of the dead, the Dark Talent? It's not what the Spanish glyphic saw. It's not what I saw. It's got all mixed up somehow, in all the centuries since it was seen."

He could feel his blood stilling inside him. It was like everything slowed down. His wrist hurt where Komako's nails dug in. He looked down and saw the dust writhing in his arm, glowing a faint blue.

"Mixed up how?" he asked, suddenly afraid.

"Marlowe *is* the living boy, he's got to be. But he was never the Dark Talent, Charlie. It's two different people. And I saw the Dark Talent's face in Mojácar, the Spanish glyphic showed him to me. He was ... awful. Frightening."

Her eyes were all shadows as she raised her face. He'd never seen her like that.

"It was *you*, Charlie," she whispered. "That's why the drughr ran from us. You're what I saw."

32

Risen

They were three, hulking and dark, pouring like liquid across a dank and rotting road. In the feeble light their edges looked blurred, but their antlered heads dipped and shifted as they went, unmistakable. The squat wide one out front swung its four powerful arms as it walked, each shovel-like hand with too many fingers. Beside it came a smaller drughr, faceless: all over its torso and arms blinked slow dim eyes, like the buds of a tree. The tallest came last, a smoldering red hole in its chest pulsing darkly, its edges eating away at the flesh, then retreating, the roadbed behind them visible through the hollow. That last one carried a bundle of rags under one arm.

The wraiths of the dead flickered and vanished as they came up the road. Bonebirds circled overhead. In front of them loomed the crumbling gate, its stone pillars slick now with black moss. The wall the gate was attached to was moving softly, stirring like long grass in a wind. It was a wall of bodies, bodies lashed together by chains, chains that twisted in and out of their flesh, wormlike, alive. They were carykk, smoke wreathing their eyes, their heads slumped into the robes of their flesh. The wall went on into the mists.

And beyond the gates lay the driveway, curved, and the dead grounds, and the manor itself silhouetted against the sky, the manor where their master was imprisoned long centuries ago, the First Talent, the greatest and wisest of them all, the betrayed man, Alastair Cairndale. The man who would preserve their kind. The man for whom this entire world had been constructed.

The light all around them flickered, grainy as blown ash. They came on, silence moving through them like blood in a vein. Where they walked the cobblestones sank under their weight, such weight there was. An overturned barrow with its wheel missing dripped in a watery ditch. The dead air was still.

A fourth drughr awaited them outside the gate. Unmoving but for the tentacles writhing from its back, six in all, tangling and lifting and sliding with a rasp off themselves, slippery and wet-looking. It had no face but a greater darkness where its face should have been.

This one spoke from out of its darkness, in front of the gate. *You have the child?*

The others gathered in a rough circle. The tallest, the drughr with the smoldering hole in its chest, lifted the bundle in its two hands. Small legs, ending in small shoes, dangled limply. It set the bundle down with gentleness on the wet ground between them.

It is still alive?

The tall drughr nodded.

The drughr with the thousand eyes said, *There are trespassers. Here, inside the orsine. I have dreamed them.*

Its heavyset companion folded its many arms. *What you have dreamed is that fool, Berghast. He has come through himself, again. This world will devour him. But he carries the scent of our sister. He has taken her essence, somehow.*

And what has become of her? said the tall drughr. *I can smell her on you.*

She . . . surprised me. But she is weak, brother. I had to leave Berghast, in order to deal with her. She has bonded to a new talent, a bone witch. She is not reformed. She cannot be saved. I will hunt her down.

She has made her choice; she is no longer important, said the first drughr. Its tentacles writhed over the bundled child. *Nor is Henry Berghast. It is the boy we must concern ourselves with. He will know himself soon.*

The Ovid boy.

Yes. That is who Lord Cairndale seeks.

The heavyset drughr took a grim step forward. *Lord Cairndale is not free, sister,* it said. *He can seek no one. We cannot be sure he is even awake.*

He is awake. And hungry.

The drughr were quiet a moment, looking down at the unmoving bundle. Then the drughr with the four arms, powerfully built, stooped and lifted the child.

Forgive us for all that must be done, the first drughr murmured.

For all that must be done, the others echoed.

They turned then and passed through the broken gates, and as each stepped through they felt the sharp prickling heat of the wards in the carykk wall, and the air seemed to ripple and shift, and then each drughr was again the human visage of who they had once been, one woman and three men, each as different from the others as could be, the woman with her dark skin and long white hair, the tall man with his shaggy blond beard, the stout red-faced man who had come once, long ago, from an island in the North Sea. The smallest among them, a man with the body of a boy, walked with one hand on the shoulder of the woman, for he had no eyes. All four wore glinting black clothes, their sleeves cut into ribbons, and long oilcloth cloaks that gleamed like black leather. The blond man carried the bundled child in his arms.

The sense of wrongness only increased as they neared the manor.

It was always thus. A vast stone house loomed above them, the ancient manor of Alastair Cairndale, a replica of the very seat of the First Talent. They passed the carriage house, crossed the slick flagstones in the courtyard, the rot in the air heavy here.

At the great wooden doors they stopped. Burned into the very center was the old symbol, the crossed hammers against a rising sun. A keyhole edged in gold sat in the middle of the design, a single key sticking out of it like a broken finger. Over each hammer was an empty silver-edged keyhole, twin keys, lost long ago. Keys that could free their lord and master.

Without them, they dared go no further. For nothing that passed that threshold could ever get out. And somewhere inside, they knew, in those dark halls, the First Talent was stirring, strengthening, biding his time. Those who'd imprisoned him had believed he'd sleep forever; they'd been wrong.

The woman, very carefully, reached out and opened the massive door.

A roaring of wind filled their ears. They could see nothing within, only a reflected darkness, as if they were staring down into a lake at night. Then the blond man hurriedly dumped the bundled child into the blackness, and the woman drew the door shut with a bang.

The dead world all around them was still.

They stepped back, facing the manor, and stood all in a line to be sure. The windows all were dark. And nothing happened: the child did not, of course, somehow open the door; the First Talent did not show himself.

And you, sister, said the stout man. *Did you find what you were sent for?*

She stepped forward, pressed her hand to the symbol burned into the door. She could feel the hollows of the two keyholes over the crossed hammers. The old ache of its wards ran through her, awful, sickening, but she held her palm there anyway letting the ill of it wash over her.

I did, she said quietly, and turned to her companions. *It is at Agrigento. At the villa of the Agnoscenti.*

We know the place, said the man with no eyes.

Faintly then, as if from very far off, they all heard the sounds of the child within. He was screaming.

In the
GRAY
ROOMS

•

33

THE THING IN THE MIRROR

Marlowe was screaming.

Falling forward, into darkness. His scream made no sound in the tunnel as he fell and he could feel neither wall nor floor nor air nor anything at all. Only the plummeting sensation in his skin, a falling that went on forever. The drughr and its horrifying carykk were gone, severed by the curtain of darkness. Brynt had vanished; Dr. Berghast, too. There was a darkness inside Marlowe and a darkness outside and as he fell the two were one and the same.

He felt a touch at his arm. Firm, solid.

Heard breathing.

The darkness righted itself and he opened his eyes and saw then in the blackness, faintly, ever so faintly, five spectral blue filaments, lifting eerily up toward him as if through deep water. It was his own hand, cupped, his fingers beginning to glow. Then his palm too filled with a blue light and Marlowe could see now the old man's face, very near his own, the swaddling drawn back and away. He saw the shorn scalp and the blistered skin where one ear should have been and the eyes, reflecting the blue shine.

"You're all right, child," said Berghast, and his whisper echoed all around. Roughly he unwrapped the rags at Marlowe's hand. "It's only the dark. Go on, focus. Find the light."

He'd never been able to control what he could do. At Cairndale, Miss Davenshaw had told him to be patient, to trust himself, to let its power come to him. It never had. But here, now, to his amazement, he made a fist and it was like he could feel a warmth draining into it, like a heavy syrup in his skin, and when he raised his fist it was a bright lantern of blue light, the bones visible within, small dark shapes.

Berghast grunted, and stood. His feet crunched in the loose stones.

Marlowe turned his fist back the way he'd come. He saw no sign of Brynt. There was only a carved rock wall, carved with elaborate stone vines.

"She won't be in here," he said. "Nothing will have followed us."

There was certainty in the old man's voice, but something else, too. Fear.

Marlowe asked, "Why not, Dr. Berghast? What is this place?"

Berghast raised Marlowe's hand high, illuminating the curved archway of a stone passage. It looked ancient, and damp, and there was a black moss growing on its walls. In places the stones had loosened and tumbled to the floor. Marlowe saw now that the black glove, the artifact Berghast wore on his other hand, had been cracked in his fight with the drughr. Several plates were missing. Berghast's pale fingers poked through in two places.

"We are in one of the oldest parts of this world," said Berghast, paying it no mind. "We are in one of its own memories. We are in the gray rooms."

"I don't think we should go any further," said Marlowe, in a small voice. He felt strange, as if the very air itself were brushing up against him, taking the measure of him, licking at him. "I don't like this place."

"We must go where it leads, child," Berghast replied. "There is no other way now."

The tunnel led steadily downward, curving always to the left, descending. At times the floor they walked upon crunched softly, as if a carpet of shattered bone; at times the tunnel widened, or ended abruptly in broken stairs, which they would descend with caution. Once Marlowe put his hand to a black fungus on the walls and it came away covered in grime: it was not moss at all but dust, a thick dust like soot, and he saw then that it was everywhere, all around them.

Otherwise there was nothing, only their own lonely progress. It felt strange to Marlowe, after so long in that other world, to see no shimmering columns of spirits, to breathe air that was not thick with rot. The gray rooms felt desolate in their stillness. But they did not feel empty: something walked with them, invisible, all the way down.

Berghast paid it no mind. Or perhaps did not sense it at all.

Gradually the turnings eased, and the arched tunnel flattened, until they came to the edge of a greater darkness. Carved out of the stone walls were two statues, worn smooth from age, their figures covered in that smearing black dust. Berghast stopped in front of one, drew his sleeve across the face, wiping it clear. Then he beckoned Marlowe close, for the light.

It was the face of a little boy, carved to look like life.

Marlowe looked at Berghast, eyes wide with questions. But the old man did not pause. He crossed to the other statue and did the same and it, too, was the face of a child, a small girl. She bore no resemblance to the boy.

"Who were they?" Marlowe asked, unable to contain himself. "Why are they here, Dr. Berghast?"

But the old man gripped the ancient knife at his belt, and did not answer. Instead, he stepped forward into the vast dome of darkness that lay before them.

And as Marlowe followed him in, afraid to be left behind, a gradual pale glow began to rise up out of the floor and walls all around them. It was the dust, the dust that covered everything, shining as if in response to their presence. Where they walked the dust shone brighter, illuminating the cavern, then easing back into a dull glow after they'd passed. Marlowe felt a peculiar foreboding, just at the back of his mind, like a warning: Go back. *You should not be here—*

But when he looked across, Berghast did not seem to share his unease. He screwed up his face, and went on.

It was a vast underground chamber, its ceiling lost in darkness, pricked here and there with tiny blue lights, like fireflies. That was the dust, adrift. All along the walls where they curved away Marlowe could see the carved stone reliefs, the figures of children, a few big enough to be grown, each one distinct. But it was the floor of the cavern that drew his eye. For stretching out before him he saw a strange sculpted city, its buildings no higher than his ankles, but sculpted in such detail as to astonish. It too pulsed with that same blue shine. There was a river running through the city, a river of dust, a low smoke of dust hanging over its currents. And Marlowe saw the river moved and shifted in its own strange course in just the way the map in Berghast's office had once done. Berghast had sheathed his knife. He was stooped in front of a statue, silent.

Marlowe turned back. The miniature city of stone, laid out before him, was London. He was sure of it. But it wasn't the London he'd passed through months ago. There was St Paul's, its dome rising up. And he could almost see the very building where Mrs. Harrogate had lived. But the Houses of Parliament were not there, Westminster Bridge was not where it should be, the Embankment wasn't there.

"It is the city as it was, but more than a hundred years ago," said Berghast softly, approaching. "I should think it, ah, 1775 or so. What could its purpose be here, I wonder?"

Marlowe didn't know if he was supposed to answer. He looked at Dr. Berghast, swallowed.

There was steel in the old man's voice. "We have been led here for a reason," he said. "Come. Do not step where the dust moves. Let us go the long way round."

They kept to the walls after that, their footsteps loud in the glimmering cavern. Marlowe's legs began to tire. His feet were sore. Where they walked the statues of the children peered out, their expressions troubled, anxious. They passed the far edges of London and the floor of the cavern shifted in its landscape of stone and soon a second city appeared, a different city, also miniature, and precise, and made of thousands of buildings, and after that a third again.

"What is this place?" asked Marlowe. "I mean, what is it for?"

"These are the makings. The central mystery of this world."

"What does that mean?"

Berghast hesitated. "That," he said, "was not recorded. Who can say? Perhaps it is here the Agnoscenti wrought their bindings. Or here the drughr were born. Perhaps it held some other secret, some other purpose."

Marlowe's feet were aching. "Does it ever end?"

"Everything ends, child."

Marlowe slowed in his walking. That eerie foreboding washed over him again. "Dr. Berghast? You said it . . . this world . . . led us here. Like it *wants* us to see this."

"It would seem so, yes."

"But how can the land of the dead *want* anything? It's not a person, Dr. Berghast."

"The land of the dead," Berghast murmured. "Is that where we are? Perhaps . . ." His voice trailed off. He'd stopped in front of one of the statues and was staring intently at its face. Marlowe waited, quiet.

"I . . . know this boy," the old man said. He straightened and looked sharply back the way they'd come and then he kneeled and looked more closely at the statue. "Yes. His name was . . . Elias. He was a clink. He was thirteen years old when he went missing. Mr. Bailey and I came to believe . . ."

The old man fell silent. He rose and stalked out to the edge of the tiny city, his expression fierce. He gestured with his hand at the cavern. As far as the eye could see, there were statues carved into the walls.

"We came to believe Elias was taken by the drughr," he said. "He ran away to his home in Cornwall from the institute ninety years ago. He never arrived. It was before Mr. Bailey's time, of course. And that girl there, that is Therese. She came to us from Calais. We found what was left of her, after the drughr had fed." Berghast's eyes flashed. "These are not statues, Marlowe. They are . . . memorials. These are the faces of those the drughr took, over the years."

Marlowe stopped. "But there are so many," he said.

His voice faded in the darkness.

"Yes," said Berghast. "The drughr have been hunting longer than we knew."

Marlowe looked all around in dread at the cavern. He was afraid of this place, though he couldn't explain why.

There must have been something in his face that gave the old man pause. He sat heavily, leaning his back against one of the statues. He unbuckled the shattered artifact and pulled it from his wrist. The fingers on his hand were blackening.

"I told you the First Talent was imprisoned here, in this world," said Berghast. "He could not be held by chains and was subdued only in a sleep, a sleep brought on by the Agnoscenti and their glyphics. An unnatural sleep. And banished into this world for all eternity. I told you the drughr were once talents, talents who'd volunteered to remain here, to guard him. They were changed in order to go through the orsine and survive. It was a cruel fate. It meant they could never return. Such was their choice; and we were grateful, too, grateful that they would keep the First Talent imprisoned. But the orsine was built *out of* the Dreaming, built *out of* the First Talent's endless sleep. It was meant to be a living prison, feeding his dreams back at him. His longing was to be used against himself. And it worked, for a long time. But gradually, strange reports began to come back. It was said the prison was growing, growing past itself. And it kept growing. Until the prison became a world."

"*This* world? The whole thing? I thought it was the land of the dead—"

Berghast shook his head. "Ah, there are greater mysteries yet. No, the orsine was created by the Agnoscenti, using what they had to work with. Meaning us. Talentkind. And our talents draw from our own dying cells. It must have seemed natural to locate their prison at the edge of the abyss, perched in the gulf beyond life." Berghast smiled coldly at his expression. "The abyss, that is the real death. Imagine a soap bubble, stuck to the edge of a larger soap bubble. That is where we are, what this world is, in relation to the abyss. The orsine was never supposed to ensnare passing spirits, the passing dead. But then, it was not supposed to harbor carykk either. Or to grow, as it has grown."

Marlowe swallowed. "What *are* the carykk? If they're not dead, or spirits, are they . . . alive?"

"Not what," said Berghast. He waved angrily at the statues. "Who."

Marlowe stared at the thousands of statues in the cavern. Slowly he understood. "They're . . . the *children?*"

The old man said nothing.

Marlowe felt his eyes grow wet. He thought of the drughr—his mother—stalking him through Jacob Marber. He thought of Charlie, nearly taken all those months ago. All those young talents Alice talked about sometimes, the ones she and Coulton had never found. He felt a revulsion growing in him.

"Drughr have been feeding on talents for a long time, child," said Berghast. "Not only your mother. We just did not realize what they were doing. Some they would have used to nourish themselves. But most, I think now, were brought through. To the First Talent, in his prison. They've been *strengthening* him. These little ones would have been fed to him until nothing was left, nothing but carykk."

Marlowe felt a sudden lurch in his stomach. He thought of the carykk with the yellow ribbon, its grinning visage, its soft, human eyes. The eyes of a child, trapped in its pain. "No," he whispered. "Oh—"

Berghast was quiet.

"Why are they *here*? Why are their faces *here*?"

"That I don't know," the old man replied. His voice faltered. "The orsine has preserved their likenesses. Is it because the First Talent dreams of them? Or does the orsine itself grieve?" He laid his palm flat on the flickering blue stone underneath him. "All this is a part of the prison, the orsine itself. The dust that's in you, that's all around us, that's in the drughr . . . *that* is what this world is made of. It sculpted these rooms. It forms the buildings and the rivers and the trestles and all that's back out there. But it is not the world itself, any more than your talent is you."

Marlowe sniffed. "Is . . . is Brynt even real?" he asked.

The old man held his eye a long moment. Then he looked away.

Marlowe remembered how hollow Brynt had seemed, how empty and confused her eyes. She was herself, and yet not. He thought he might cry but he pinched his arm hard instead, so he would feel something else.

"Why does the orsine want to show us all this, Dr. Berghast? Why us?"

Berghast shook his head, grim. "It has its reasons, I'm sure. Maybe it's just that we're the only ones ever to come so far."

Marlowe blinked, thinking about that.

"That's not what troubles me," the old man continued. His eyes were dark. "Look around you. Everything here—everything you see, every stone we walk upon—comes out of the First Talent's dreaming. It's a dream outside of himself, an entire *world*. But if he were to awaken, and be freed...what would become of this place? Of this dream he has built?"

The shadows seemed to press in around them.

"It would disappear?" whispered Marlowe.

Berghast glanced at him sharply. "Or become real," he said.

They went on.

Berghast would stumble now and again, rubbing at the blackening fingers where they stuck out of the artifact. He seemed weaker. Marlowe peered up at him with a worried eye as they trudged along. The cavern had lost any bit of wonder it had held, and seemed now only sinister, grim. He knew now what it was that filled him with foreboding. It was the darkness itself. The orsine.

The sculpted dead stared out, face after face. Each had been loved in their time, had had a mother, a father, a friend. Marlowe tried not to think about it but couldn't help it. He turned his face the other way. Sprawled across the cavern floor, the tiny sculpted cities passed, each one stranger than the last. For a while Berghast would nod and name them: *Prague. Persepolis. Benin. Alexandria. Beijing.* "The great cities of the talents, once upon a time," he'd mutter. "Each had their time in the sun."

Gradually Marlowe became aware of the blue shine dimming, ahead. The dread in him rose up. It seemed that the vast cavern ahead was plunged in darkness, abruptly, that the eerie light they walked by simply ceased. But as they neared he saw, in the blackness, the faint rippling blue shine of twinned figures, moving closer toward them, and then he saw that it was their own reflections. They'd reached a vast polished basalt wall, like a huge black mirror. And they could not go any further.

In front of the basalt wall was a huge stone, cracked in half. Its center had been hollowed out, and held the negative molded shape of a human baby.

Marlowe's heart was beating very fast. His skin was shining very brightly. He stared at the empty shape and his eyes, he was surprised to feel, were wet.

"What is it, Dr. Berghast?" he asked.

But the old man did not know. He crouched beside it and ran his fingertips lightly over the stone and he shook his head. "It is only a rock," he said. "I've never seen such a thing."

Marlowe shivered.

"Child? Are you all right?" The old man rose and went to him.

But Marlowe didn't know what to say. He went to the glass wall, trying to clear his thoughts, to calm his blood. His reflection was pale and otherworldly.

But there was something wrong with his reflection, too. He sensed it at once. It was him, and yet it was not him—it had his eyes, his hair, the hatchet-sharp line of his mouth, its fist too glowed dully, and when he raised his fingers to touch the glass, the reflection too raised its fingers. And yet it wasn't him, it wasn't the reflection of him at all. It was something else.

Marlowe stepped back, afraid.

"Dr. Berghast?" he said softly. "I don't think we should be here."

The old man had pressed his palm flat against the mirror and now, to Marlowe's horror, the hand went in, smoothly, and the mirror rippled around it like a viscous darkness. He put his hand in all the way to the wrist, and then pulled it out, and looked at Marlowe in amazement. The hand was smoking with a thick sooty dust, a dust that had no shine at all.

"We're supposed to go through," he said, rubbing his fingers together. "This is the way out. I'll go first."

Marlowe was shaking his head. "I don't think so, Dr. Berghast. I think it takes us deeper."

The thing in the mirror that was not him was shaking its head also.

"Dr. Berghast?"

But the old man had drawn himself up and he wrapped and double-wrapped the rags at his face and scalp again, and then his hand, and then he adjusted the shattered artifact and flexed his sore fingers, and gave Marlowe a calm look, as if to say: *I will go first; you must follow.* And he stepped through. The black mirror smoked and rippled and Berghast's reflection bent weirdly away from itself and then suddenly he was gone, and the mirror was still.

Marlowe swallowed, afraid. He looked at the thing in the mirror and the thing looked at him. He waited but Berghast did not step back through. He became aware of the vast glinting cavern at his back, the statues of the living dead with their sorrowful faces, the feeling that something was back there. The broken stone with the baby's outline inside it. His heart was beating very fast. He wished, not for the first time, that Charlie was with him.

"Okay," he whispered to himself, to make himself brave.

But his words shirred away, off the walls, making him feel even smaller. He gave his reflection a stern look. "Don't hurt me," he said firmly. "Okay?"

And then he shut his eyes, because that always seemed to make him feel a bit braver, and he stepped up toward whatever it was in the mirror, and he felt the cool liquid give of it against his little body, and he pushed through.

34

THE THRESHOLD

And stepped, lightly, down into a pale gray room.

He blinked. There was a strange taste in his mouth, a taste of ash and soot. He was squinting against the brightness and raised a hand to his eyes and saw Dr. Berghast, at a crumbling window, watching him. He had removed the broken glove.

"You certainly took your time," the old man said grimly. "I thought you'd decided not to follow."

Marlowe swallowed. His throat didn't work right. He turned in place but there was no mirror behind him, no sign of a passage through at all, only a wet brick wall, running with a faint ooze. When he wiped at the rags on his arms a greasy black soot was smeared there.

"Dr. . . . Berghast?" he mumbled.

And then he saw where he was, and started to cry. He couldn't help it. There was the broken and leaning chair he'd wrestled free of. There was the balcony where Charlie had hid, and the ceiling ripped open to the sky. And there was the broken door where Jacob Marber had appeared, wreathed in smoke. He and Dr. Berghast had gone so far, and seen so many awful things, and now he was back here, right where he started, back in the room where he and Charlie had found the artifact glove all those months ago. The mummified talent still lay propped against one wall, though Dr. Berghast had wrestled the corpse out of its vest, and covered its face.

"We haven't got anywhere!" Marlowe cried in despair. "This is the room where we found your glove, Dr. Berghast! I came back here. We're . . . we're right back where I started from!"

The orsine had played its trick on him. He saw that now, saw now that it had all been for nothing.

Numbly he went to the balcony and stared out. Saw the strange white tree in the square below. The dark shingled rooftops of London, stretching out all around, their chimneys twisting in the fog. He could see the paler mists of the spirit dead, adrift over the sinking cobblestones. Water, seeping in doorways. And all the cast-off detritus, shoes, bits of softened broadsheets, clothes twisted and limp in the gutters like dead things. The rot of it all. He just wanted to see his friends again, just wanted to go home. Why wouldn't the orsine let him go?

But then he felt Dr. Berghast's hand on his shoulder. He looked down. The knuckles were black, the fingernails rotting away in strange horns.

"Marlowe, child," he said.

It was one of the few times he'd said Marlowe's name aloud and the boy sniffled and let himself be turned by the shoulders, and he looked up at the old man.

"We're not back where you started from," said Dr. Berghast. "No path goes backward, child, not really. For the shoes that walk it grow more worn, at every step. Come. Look."

He led Marlowe across to the other side, to a small circular window high up in the wall, and he dragged the wooden chair across for the child to stand on and look out.

The city ended abruptly, one street further on. It hadn't been this way before; the city of the dead had just gone on, and on, into the fog. He and Brynt had walked in it for days, weeks, getting nowhere. And yet here, somehow, now, he'd reached the edge of it. And beyond it was a slimy cobbled road, its setts uneven and missing in places, leading up to a vast, curving wall. Marlowe held his breath. In the fog the wall seemed to be moving, swaying like long grass in a wind. He could make out a high iron gate fixed in it, stopping the road. And then the fog sifted apart for a moment and beyond it he glimpsed the unmistakable silhouette of Cairndale Manor.

"It's what we've been seeking, child," said Berghast, and there was a dark hunger in his voice. "The very center of the orsine. The First Talent's prison."

Marlowe stared in disbelief. "But it's, it's Cairndale—"

"Yes it is," the old man whispered. "It always was."

It didn't look much like a prison to Marlowe. There were no bars, no iron grates at the windows, no guards. The faint wall that encircled it didn't look spiked. And the iron gates stood open, like an invitation. He wondered aloud if maybe it was an illusion.

"Ah, but it is real," said Berghast. "I went down and looked. When you didn't come through the glass. I was careful not to stray too near the wall. I was not seen."

Marlowe squinched his face up in confusion. "How long was I inside the mirror, Dr. Berghast?"

The old man shook his head. "Hours. Maybe half a day. It is . . . difficult to be sure, here."

Marlowe didn't know what to say. It had felt like only just a moment, to him. He grew suddenly afraid again, confused. The sooner he got out of this world, the better. "And somewhere in there is the way out?" he asked. "I mean, for me?"

"The Passage of the Drughr, it's called," Berghast replied. "You cannot see it from here. But beyond the manor lies the loch, and the island, just as in our world. On the island is the monastery, and under it . . . the mouth of the second orsine."

"Is it safe?"

Berghast smiled thinly. "Is anything safe?" He drew his finger smudgingly across the warped glass. "It has been sealed for a very long time. But there is always a way to open a door. Even if one must break it down. Look, there," he said. "Those figures. Do you see them?"

And Marlowe did, four figures, one quite tall, dressed in black overcoats and two with hats. One walked a step behind, his hand on the shoulder of the figure in front, as if blind. They were emerging out of the mists, leaving the manor grounds, approaching the iron gates.

"Who are they?"

"Watch," purred Berghast.

As they passed under the gates they were suddenly transformed, elongating and darkening and twisting into the unmistakable silhouettes of drughr. Marlowe shuddered and ducked his head.

"They cannot see us here, child. This room is . . . warded. It is the safest space we have, here. Watch them. Watch."

Marlowe raised up again. Through the sulfurous fog it was difficult to see what they were doing. They stood for several moments in the cobbled road. And then there were three, and then only two, and the one who strode down the oozing road and disappeared into the city of the dead was a drughr with tentacles writhing from its back.

"The one at the gates, still. Do you see him?" murmured Berghast. "That is their glyphic. He will be . . . occupied. He is the one who can fold the edges of this world and let the others slip through. That is how they travel, I believe. Using him. He cuts little holes between the worlds."

The drughr was long and thin and it looked like his back and arms were covered in sores. Then he saw they were not sores, but eyes. He was drifting along the wall, disappearing into the fog.

"Could he send *us* back? If we forced him?" asked Marlowe.

Berghast shook his head. "He would eat you, child."

"But is it possible?"

Berghast hesitated. "I do not know. You are not like the rest of us. Perhaps. But I would advise using the second orsine is a . . . preferable option. Now, that wall . . . Do you see how it moves? It is made of carykk. It is the first line of defense."

Marlowe swallowed, afraid.

"They have been chained fast, unable to break free," the old man said. "I expect they are rather useful for frightening off any wayward spirit dead. And if any intruder approaches, they will begin to scream. You remember that sound? It draws the drughr and their bonebirds like a wolf whistle."

"Will the drughr be near?"

"They are always near."

Marlowe swallowed.

Berghast went on: "The First Talent is asleep inside the manor. I do not know where. No one has ever entered and returned. The only way in is through the front door. That door opens only one way. Any who cross its threshold cannot return. Not while the door remains locked."

"Wait. There's a lock? Could it be unlocked, then?"

"The keys were lost long ago. There is no unlocking that door. And thank God for it. Without it, there's no way for Alastair Cairndale to get free. No matter how his strength grows, no matter if he were to awaken entirely."

"You could just leave him there, and come back with me," said Marlowe quickly. "If there's no way he can get out."

Berghast paused. "You still wish to leave, then? I cannot persuade you to help me?"

"What . . . what would I have to do?"

"Ah," murmured the old man. "I've been thinking about that. You are the progeny of a drughr, the inheritor of her abilities. Originally, the drughr were made to resist the First Talent, to keep him weak. I believe," said Berghast, his eyes bright, "that your presence will act as a . . . muffling effect on his own powers. You will weaken him, child, simply by being in his presence. So that I can kill him easily."

"Could we even get out? After, I mean?"

"Ah, the prison was built to hold Alastair Cairndale. It is not a physical space. If he is dead, perhaps the prison too will . . . cease? But I do not know that for certain." Berghast sighed. "I cannot promise you safety, child."

"But isn't all of this, everything here, part of it? This whole world?"

Berghast nodded.

"So *everything* could . . . cease?"

Again Berghast nodded.

Marlowe wanted to cry. He climbed down from the rickety chair, feeling the heat rise to his face. He felt ashamed as he said, "I'm sorry, Dr. Berghast. I just want it all to be over. I . . . I just want to go home."

It came out like a plea.

The old man studied him from his great height, his ravaged face twisting with some unnamable emotion. At last he relented. "Of course you do," he murmured. "And maybe it is for the best. You have been through enough."

Somehow the gentleness of it made Marlowe feel worse.

Though the weird light in that world did not change, the hour had the feel of evening and Marlowe was tired. He curled up against a wall, as far from the desiccated talent as he could get. Even with his face covered, the dead man made him uneasy.

"His name was Azhar Leghari," said Berghast. He had laid out on the floor his knife, and the broken artifact with its missing plates, and a roll of ragged cloth he had taken from around his arms. His hand looked bruised and soft to the touch and he cradled it carefully, Marlowe saw. He'd taken a whetstone from the dead man's waistcoat pocket and was sharpening the knife for something to do.

"He was a turner," Berghast went on, in a calm voice. "He came to Cairndale from the Raj, somewhere in the north. Stowed away on an East India Company ship. He loved the taste of iced creams. I remember he used to say they ate something like it in the mountains in the summer, when he was a boy. With honey." Berghast's voice trailed off. "I did not think it would be he, that he would be the one to have found this room. I wonder what happened here?"

Maybe it was being here, in this room again, or maybe it was just he was so tired, but suddenly he could remember the sound of Charlie's voice as he said he'd come back for him, he could remember the smell in Charlie's shirt, all of it. This was almost the last place he'd seen his friend.

"Dr. Berghast?" he said, trying to think about anything else. "Your hand looks bad. Is it because the glove got damaged? Will you be okay?"

The old man was quiet. At last he said, "It's not just the artifact getting damaged. What I did at the orsine, taking your mother's power into me . . . It was never meant to be contained in a human body. Not even one with your friend's healing talent."

"Does it hurt?"

Slowly the old man nodded. "It doesn't feel like a talent. It feels . . . inverted. Unnatural." He pulled down the rags at his mouth to regard the boy square. "I've hated the drughr for so long it's like that hate is a thing outside me, now. I hated them for their betrayal. I hated them for killing all those children. I thought using their power against them would make me feel . . . satisfied. It does not. I can feel a part of your mother inside me, eating away at me, having her revenge."

"Oh," said Marlowe.

"Yes. Well. You're not responsible for where you come from. Only for where you choose to go. Your mother made her own choices." And then, in a low voice, Berghast told how he'd slipped from her claws as they plunged through the orsine. She'd been too weak to keep him close. She was most likely trapped between the worlds, even now. Perhaps she would always be.

"Do you think she's in pain?" asked Marlowe.

"She was very wicked," said Berghast. "She wanted to consume you, child. To absorb whatever it is you have inside you. She would lie and dissemble and commit any cruelty to get close to you. I hope she is in great pain. Yes."

"I feel bad," said Marlowe, in a small voice. "When you talk about her, I feel bad."

"We all have family, child. Or had. We are not what they are."

"Who did you have?"

Berghast drew the dark blade in a slow rasping gesture across the whetstone. "A baby brother, dead in the cradle. A wife and little girl, long ago. And . . . a sister," he said at last. "She was a haelan, like me."

Marlowe looked quickly up. "But I thought talents didn't run in families."

It was strange, trying to imagine Dr. Berghast with a sister. Like he'd been a boy once, too.

"Not as a rule, no. But there is every kind of variation in the world, in talentkind as in any other. Why wouldn't there be?" Berghast studied him. "You'll understand when you're older, perhaps. I was born in Würzburg, in the year of the first great witch trials, just before the outbreak of war. It was 1617, by the current calendar. Later, even my year of birth was counted against me. The city was small, dirty. I remember the smell of bread, and my sister showing me animals in the stars. She was older than me. I was happy, I think. But the Catholics were taking back the country, and there was great fear. Highwaymen were on the roads. Soldiers who had fled the horrors. Famine was already in the north when I was eight years old, my sister eleven. That year the vines died from a strange frost and sorcery was blamed. Our talents had shown themselves, by then. We, alone of all the children in our street, never fell sick. I had fallen into the fire twice, without injury. When our mother struck my sister for speaking to a soldier, her strap left no mark. It was our mother who turned us in, to the bishop. Witchcraft? Ah. Our torture only enraged them. In the trial my sister demanded a test by water. That is where, if you do not drown, you are considered judged innocent by God. Of course, you cannot drown a haelan," he said sharply. "But they looked at us differently, after that. No one believed it was the hand of God that had saved us. We were the devil's spawn.

"My sister was a tall girl, and strong for her age, and the very day we were released she carried me on her back and started walking. We left Würzburg, we left our mother, we left all of it behind. The roads were full of soldiers, starving. It was safer than our home.

"She never left me," he said softly. He turned the knife he was sharpening and tested the blade. Then he went back to the slow, steady work. "We didn't know then, of course, what it would mean. Our talent. How we would live on, and on, seeing the years pass. The first talent we met was a caster, a bone witch named Miguel, who was working on a commercial ship in the Netherlands. He is the one who taught us about the others. Who told us there were safe places, for those like us."

"Is that why you took over Cairndale, Dr. Berghast? To make a place like that for others?"

Quietly Berghast set aside the blade, quietly he wrapped his hands in their rags.

"No," he said.

Marlowe watched him, afraid.

"We saw such things as now seem dreams," he murmured. "We were too young to be a part of the war when it broke out, the war to stop the First Talent from imposing his will. But we saw what it did to talentkind. How it broke them. How it turned them against each other. We are few enough in number without such violence, child. I saw Alastair Cairndale once, from a distance. At the end, after he had been defeated. Even then I remember the pull he had on me, the way I felt myself wanting to . . . go to him. To raise his head, to offer him a drink. He was terrible because he was loved. That was his darkest power."

"But you came here to kill him," whispered Marlowe. "If you felt that way—"

"It is *because* I felt that way. And because I understand that others will too, one day. He must not be allowed to be free. Even the drughr are drawn to him, the *drughr*—who were sent here to keep him secure. Now they reap among us, slaughter our children at *his* urging. No. I have watched too many little ones die. I would do worse than cut his throat, if it meant a simpler world."

"Oh," said Marlowe.

Berghast paused. "Do I frighten you?"

Because he didn't know what else to do, Marlowe answered truthfully. "Sometimes," he said. "But I think you don't mean to. I think you want to be kind. It's just . . . hard for you."

Berghast smiled a grim smile. "I imagine I have frightened many, across the centuries. Did they tell stories about us to their babies, I wonder, stories about the wicked brother and sister, who spoke with strange accents, who did not age, who walked the world like witches? We were in Spain as their stolen gold poured in from the New World. We saw the sugar fields in the West Indies, where the desperate slaves were ground down. We were in New York when it was still an island of trees. I remember the frenzy in the crowds in Paris, as the revolution turned dark. My sister and I watched the guillotine do its bloody work the day they cut the head off their king. There were sweetbreads for sale in the square."

"Where is she now? Your sister?"

"We grew up," said the old man quietly. "We grew apart. We ceased to share a common . . . sensibility." He tapped his heart with his blackening hand, three times, wincing as if it hurt him to do so. "But she lives on, in here. She is with me, always."

Marlowe studied the grief in the old man's face, his heart breaking. "You've not said her name, Dr. Berghast. Not even the once."

The old man ran his thumb over his dried lips, lost in his memories. But then he came to. He drew the rags up over his face and turned away.

"No more questions," he muttered, through the cloth. "You should sleep. We'll not be here much longer."

35

CHARLIE IN THE DREAMING

That night Marlowe dreamed of Charlie.

Except it wasn't a dream, not really. He knew it even as he stood in the fog of his dreaming, even as he stepped forward. He was standing again in the gray rooms, in front of the polished black glass.

But instead of his reflection, inside the mirror was Charlie.

Charlie, who turned his face at Marlowe's approach, who rose and came forward to meet him.

His friend looked surprised, disbelieving. Marlowe pressed his small hand to the mirror and Charlie, too, like a perfect reflection, kneeled and did the same. Charlie looked taller, older, and there was a sadness in his face that Marlowe didn't remember being there before. The hand he pressed to the mirror was dark with shadows crawling across it, shadows that curled and writhed and split apart, and Marlowe knew what it was. The dust. The dust that had been in Jacob Marber.

And yet he wasn't afraid, seeing it. That surprised him. He felt instead an overwhelming loneliness, and he blinked sharply and ran his cuff across his eyes so his friend wouldn't see him cry. He didn't know if he was seeing what he wanted to see, or if Charlie was looking for him still. He just didn't know.

And then his friend spoke.

Mar? he said, uncertain. *How is it—Can you hear me? Mar, is it you?*

In the dream Marlowe felt himself nodding gravely. He wanted to speak but something stopped him. He looked up at his friend's face, as if from years away.

We're coming to get you. Me and Alice and Ribs, we're coming. There's a second orsine. We're going to find it and then I'm going through it, to find you. I'll bring you out. Can you hear me? Mar? Can you hear me?

Marlowe felt a sudden surge of love and fear and hope pour through him, so powerful his legs weakened. He was rubbing at his eyes, wanting to speak. He wanted to say that he'd known they'd come, he wanted to say he was here, he was waiting. Then in the dream he thought about Dr. Berghast and what he'd said about the First Talent growing stronger and the light seemed to darken in the mirror, to darken all around his friend where he kneeled, his palm still pressed to the glass. Marlowe knew it wasn't safe; it wouldn't be safe for Charlie to come through, for any of his friends. Not with all the carykk, not with the drughr. Not with the First Talent. They'd be overwhelmed, and devoured.

He shook his small head. He tried to warn Charlie but no sound came out. *Don't come here!* he wanted to say. *Don't! Don't!*

The dream faded. He opened his eyes in the gray light of a dead world.

His back was stiff. He rolled onto his side and saw Dr. Berghast, some feet away, staring out at the ghostly silhouette of Cairndale Manor. Even at that distance Marlowe could make out the wall of carykk, stirring weakly. His heart was filled with pity and anger.

He rose and went out to Dr. Berghast and sat beside him. A bonebird was wheeling far out over the lake. Marlowe balled his little hands up into fists.

"I'll do it," he said, in a creaking voice. "I'll help you stop the First Talent."

The old man did not turn, not at first. The wound at his back was seeping again, through yellow rags. "You understand there might be no getting out, child?" he murmured. "That you might be trapped in there, forever?"

"I understand," said Marlowe.

Now Berghast turned. There was no kindness in his face. His fierce blue eyes were bright with hate, and for just a moment Marlowe saw the old Berghast, the one from the institute, the one who had cut him badly at the edge of the dark orsine so that his blood could draw the drughr out. The one whose hunger was all.

"Good," the old man said softly.

The DOOR
at the
CENTER
of the WORLD

36

LA BELLE ÉPOQUE

On the passenger liner, Charlie awoke from troubled dreams. He'd been dreaming of Marlowe, again. Thin and glowing and distorted, as if behind dark glass. He rose from the folding cot and peered through the porthole at the passing night. There were jeweled lights, far out on the water. He rubbed at the glass with the cuff of one sleeve. The cabin was cold.

"That's Marseille," said a voice. It was Alice, awake. Sometimes it seemed like she never slept. "We'll anchor offshore and approach in the morning. You should go back to sleep. It's still a long train ride to Paris."

He pressed his forehead against the cool glass, closed his eyes. The thrum of the steamship's engines could be felt, faint, steady, like a monstrous heartbeat. Ribs was snoring in the bed. He could just see her hand, flopped out over the edge. Alice was a pale face in the darkness, in a chair near the door. He heard a click as she put her revolver down. He tried not to think about Komako and what she'd told him about the Dark Talent. All his life he'd been told what he was, what he could or couldn't be, and he'd come to see it wasn't for anyone to say. His life was his own. He didn't believe in fate or the visions of a glyphic gone mad with bloodlust, he didn't believe that there was a possible future where he would hurt anyone he loved. He knew enough about himself to know that. And yet ever since that night when Ko had told him what she'd seen—himself, Charlie, as the Dark Talent, wreaking slaughter—he'd slept badly. Because he knew the corrupted dust had its own wants and needs.

And something in him *was* wrong, something more than the infection, and it was this that scared him most. It was the slow realization that he'd been a part of it all his whole life, without knowing. That his father had served Claker Jack, had betrayed him. Charlie, a haelan, had been born to another talent, and all this horror around him was a kind of birthright. And now he could heal, again; and he could twist dust; and his dreams were becoming as vivid as any glyphic's.

New talents were rising in him, whether he wanted them or not.

He confided none of this to Alice, to Ribs. It was like he was back in Mississippi, hoping if he didn't think too much about what was happening inside him, it would just leave him be, just let him go on pretending. Instead he let his thoughts drift to the orsine, to the monastery convent they were seeking.

He reached for the cord at his neck, his father's ring. Rubbed it distractedly. "Alice? What do you think the Abbess will be like?"

He heard Alice snort. "She calls herself the Abbess. What do you *think* she'll be like?"

"I think she'll be dangerous."

"She'll be a pain in the ass," Alice muttered, tipping her hat over her eyes. "They always are."

But Alice wasn't sleepy. She kept a watchful eye on Charlie, on him and Ribs both. Worrying about how much they'd changed since Cairndale.

She sat up late with her arms folded and Coulton's ridiculous little pistol tucked up under her armpit, brooding, her eyes tracing the movement of any footsteps outside their cabin door.

They went on. Disembarked at the port in Marseille, trudging through the customs house, then buying tickets in the new station, passing Lyon, then Auxerre, then finally the grimy outskirts of the center of the world: Paris, France.

She saw the new unhappiness in Charlie, no longer at ease in his own skin. She knew about the corrupted dust, of course, knew that it pained him and made him shy around her, around all of them. Like he was afraid they'd want nothing to do with him, if they knew what was really going on.

But she *did* know, knew how it was to have the corruption eating away at you from the inside, at least a little bit, and when she looked at Charlie she was half-afraid of seeing her own reflection.

She'd stand over him sometimes in the night and watch his breathing and remember the boy he'd been, only just half a year ago, a boy who knew nothing of the world and yet too much of it, more than most ever knew in their lifetimes, the cruelty in it and the unkindness of fate and all the many ways a body could be made to sing with pain. She remembered the locked room in Natchez where she'd first met him, how he'd dug a blade out of his arm, the hard intelligent look in his eye as he'd considered Coulton's offer. Jesus, she'd think to herself. Surprised still at how much it made her heart hurt.

That was the same trip back to America that she'd gone out to her mother's asylum, and learned of her death. Her mother, who had failed her, failed herself, failed her own god. It all seemed so long ago, what had happened, how that community had burned, half the bodies found charred in their beds in the morning. The woman Adra Norn, who had seduced her mother into madness, who had walked through fire and claimed it was her holy purpose to cleanse the souls of her community, that they too might be untouched by the fires of sin, or whatever—her body had never been found.

But then, that's what you get for burning the house of a woman who walks through fire, she thought bitterly.

The sky in Paris was the mottled brown of an old bruise. They drifted up out of the railroad station, a strange threesome, Alice and Ribs in front, back in the city they'd only left a short while before, and Charlie tall and grim just behind. They might have been a governess and her ward out for a stroll, their manservant accompanying. Except no one could mistake Alice, with her scarred face and dark expression and man's trousers, for a child's governess. And Ribs, with her bold grin, and her sly hands, hadn't ever quite been a child. And Charlie's proud bearing resembled a master's more than a servant's.

No, what they most resembled, Alice supposed, as she met the startled looks of gentlemen and ladies hurrying past, were three criminals newly arrived in a city ripe for the taking.

Her French was execrable. It was a part of why she disliked Paris. She'd been here several times with Coulton, finding it oily and full of judgments and quietly sneering. The boulevards were still a reminder of those days. She remembered her friend's gruff face, his whiskers riding his cheeks as he chewed in that fish restaurant overlooking the Seine; and the tailor he'd insisted on visiting, carrying a *walking stick* to the appointment, of all things, that tailor with the long mustaches who made Coulton's brightly colored waistcoats to order; and she remembered, too, how her friend's very manners grew more delicate in this city, as if he were becoming another person, a gentler one, more urbane. Of course, he'd been that person all along.

Coulton, damn you, she thought sharply, as the old ache rose up in her chest.

At least she knew, this time, where they had to go. Mrs. Ficke had written to an acquaintance of hers in the grubby streets of Montmartre, an acquaintance who could help them locate the Abbess. They crossed the grand boulevards on foot, making for the tight steep streets of the butte, beyond the Seine. They passed serving girls with ribbons at their throats, butchers in aprons with shanks of meat on their shoulders, blood running over their arms. They passed women dressed as men and men dressed as women. They passed artists in red and yellow waistcoats, paint on their knuckles, carrying canvases through the streets. There was a light emanating out of the cobblestones and the pale buildings and all the many windows of brasseries and patisseries that made the city feel dazzling and otherworldly. All this despite the grime and peeling paint and the apples of horseshit underfoot. They passed ancient wind-mills. The streets narrowed. They ducked under lines of drying laundry, listening to the roar and laughter in the milling crowds.

First, they found lodging. It was a house shared by three families; Ribs did the talking. And the talking. And the *talking*. Alice and Charlie sat through a smoky meal of stew and pie while Ribs had the families in stitches, gabbling on in her perfect French, with her red hair twisted off her neck and wearing a green ribbon at her throat and an enormous hat with flowers in it, and she was dressed in a green and purple frock lent her by a daughter of the household. She looked pretty, and mischievous, and much older than Alice had ever seen her. Alice could only glance across at Charlie over the scraping of plates, and meet his bemused expression with her own.

The streets came alive at night. Alice led Ribs and Charlie to a base-ment brasserie, at the foot of the hill, in search of Mrs. Ficke's acquain-tance. But the woman did not show that first night; nor did she appear on the second. On the third night Alice saw through the gloom and crowds, an old lady, wrapped in a shawl, seated in front of a smoky glass of absinthe. She had her feet up on a chair, and her white hair was loose over her eyes. The lady knew them at once. In the long mirror behind her, drinkers moved through the smoke like apparitions.

"Vous êtes les amis de Madame Ficke," she said, her voice like stones in a sieve.

Alice glanced at Ribs, who shrugged. "She's just sayin we come to the right biddy," Ribs translated. "She knows us, like."

The old woman's eyes shifted between them, weighing them, assessing them. "Vous la trouverez au Couvent de la Délivrance. Dans Montparnasse. Votre travail est dangereux. C'est la morte qui t'amène ici."

Alice waited for the translation. In the noise of the brasserie, Ribs held a hand to her face to conceal her expression from the old woman. She rolled her eyes exaggeratedly at Alice. "Seems what we're doin is *dangerous*," she whispered, "an I don't reckon she approves. Dangerous don't sound like us, now, do it?"

The woman worked her toothless mouth, gestured at Charlie with her thumb. "Ce garçon est malade. Quelle est ca corruption?"

"Uh, Ribs?" said Charlie uneasily. "Why does she keep looking at me like that?"

Ribs shrugged prettily. "She says you got a stink to you."

Charlie sniffed. "I don't. I don't stink."

Ribs grinned. "O-kaaay," she said, making her eyes very big.

A dread flickered across the woman's ancient face. She said something very fast in French. As she spoke, she mixed the absinthe, waving the fumes toward her. Then she stared into the glass, hunched as if to read its secrets. Alice didn't know if the old woman was mad or gifted with some talent she'd not yet heard about. All around in the brasserie women were laughing, men were moving in the smoke. An accordion struck up in a corner, wheezing mournfully. Alice felt herself jostled and she shoved a man angrily off. He stumbled backward, losing his hat, regarding her with surprise, but she was already turning away.

The old woman's face looked green as it leaned in very close to the table. Her lizard-like eyelids were creeping shut. She spoke in a low menacing tone, words Alice didn't catch. She belched softly.

"Aw, I think she's like to be sick," Ribs whispered.

Alice scowled. "Does she know where we have to go, or not?"

"Deliverance Convent," said Ribs. "We'll be all right. She says it's in Montparnasse, across the Seine. She don't know about any orsine, though."

Alice grimaced. "We're not asking her advice. We just need to know the way."

Ribs's glance strayed past Alice. "Oi, Charlie," she called. "Don't look so glum. It ain't nothin a hot bath can't fix."

"It's not me," he muttered from the gloom behind.

That night Alice sat up in the lodging house high in Montmartre, listening to the streets of Paris come alive. They slept in a half room with a sheet strung up for privacy and she could hear the two grown brothers, bricklayers both, snoring through their mustaches beyond. Ribs was asleep under the little window and the light fell across her features and Alice, not for the first time, wondered what sort of a life the girl might have had, if she'd been better born. She was smart and there was a sweetness to her that she tried to hide but couldn't. The moonlight fell aslant her features and carved out her cheekbones and her snub nose so that she looked very much like the woman she would one day be.

Charlie was watching her, too. Alice was surprised to see his eyes open and his face alert and she studied him where he lay, curled up in the far chair. He looked at Alice. His Adam's apple moved awkwardly.

"You should sleep," she told him. "You'll want your rest when tomorrow comes."

"Yeah."

But she knew he wouldn't. She was the same; she'd never been able to sleep much, not even when she was just starting out as a detective, not the night before a case broke. After a moment she rose and went to him and crouched in front of him.

"She looks so peaceful," he said. "I wonder what she's dreaming about."

"Probably lifting some jack's pocketbook and kicking his jill down a stair," Alice said with a smile.

"I don't know how she can sleep."

"If I've learned anything, it's that Ribs can sleep anywhere. Anytime."

Charlie smiled too. "She's kind of amazing like that, I guess?"

"Kind of."

He was rubbing at his forearms with both hands, slowly, methodically, as if trying to massage a bruise. Alice blinked and frowned. "Does it hurt? The dust, I mean?"

Charlie dropped his hands, shrugged. "It's not the hurting. It's the feeling of it, something inside me that shouldn't be there. That's not me." He rolled up his sleeves to show her the tattoos, swirling and coming apart and together, like a strange kind of writing, like a pattern that almost transcended meaning. Alice stared at the dust in fascination.

"I'm sorry," she said at last.

He looked at her in surprise. "For what?"

"For all of it. For taking you to Cairndale. For everything that happened there. I . . . I didn't know. I didn't know what Henry Berghast was. What Cairndale was."

A faint smile played at Charlie's lips. "That's stupid, Alice. None of it's your doing."

"Maybe."

"And what? You think I'd have been better off in Natchez?"

"No," she said quietly.

In the stillness that followed, Alice pulled out the tail of her shirt, and lifted it high at her ribs. "I've got it in me, too," she said. "The dust. From Jacob Marber. Some of it was left in me after he attacked us all on the train, on the way to Cairndale."

Charlie stared close at the dark scar on her ribs, its unnatural coloring. "I remember," he said.

"It's not like what's in you," she went on. "And I'm not . . . special. I don't have a talent. So it doesn't have any effect on me, really. But when I went to London with Margaret, to try to find Marber, I could . . . feel it. Tugging at me. Like stitches getting pulled. I had the same feeling when I was here before, hunting the second orsine. Like the dust was . . . guiding me. Like it's alive."

"Yeah," said Charlie. "It's a bit like that."

She swallowed. "I didn't like it. I don't."

"Yeah," said Charlie again.

Ribs was snoring softly. Alice traced her fingers lightly over her scar, its weird toothlike edges.

"It . . . wants things," Charlie whispered suddenly.

She looked at him in surprise. He seemed so vulnerable. "What do you mean?"

"I don't know. Nothing." He got to his feet, as if embarrassed. "It's stupid."

"You feel like the dust is changing you," she said quietly. "Like you're not you, anymore."

He nodded slowly. His eyes were in shadow.

She was quiet.

"I'm . . . afraid," he whispered.

"Don't be," she said. "Don't be afraid of it. You're stronger than it is."

"No, Alice," he whispered. "I'm afraid of *me*."

But he didn't explain; and she didn't ask him to. Later, after he'd fallen asleep, she laid her head back. She tried again but couldn't sleep herself. She was thinking about him and what he'd said but when she closed her eyes, it was Coulton she saw. Coulton again, always Coulton, his wide face twisted into a litch's leer, his sharp teeth clicking. She'd lost friends before but never killed them herself. It didn't matter that he wasn't himself in the end. Coulton, the three bloodlike lines at his throat. Coulton, begging her to pull the trigger. The slight pressure in her tendons; the bang of the hammer, igniting; the buck and recoil. And then suddenly there was no more Coulton in the world, he was just gone, gone forever, his voice and his thinking and that look he'd get in his eye like he knew what she was going to do even before she said it, which she'd hated about him, and which now she'd give almost anything to have back.

He was just gone.

Sometimes it was like living wasn't anything more than just surviving. And surviving? That was just a matter of how much you could stand to lose, before you weren't you anymore.

In the morning Alice was careful to pay their landlady in full. Making her excuses for Ribs's absence in a halting, awful French. They walked out into the pale Paris daylight, Alice and Charlie, wending their slow way across the city toward Montparnasse, the Jardin du Luxembourg, the mysterious Deliverance Convent somewhere beyond that. They caught an old fiacre, stumbling through the directions. A third rode with them, of course, Ribs, muttering in Alice's ear as they went. Complaining of the cold air on her legs, the chill on her arms, making Charlie's cheeks hot with the things she said.

Alice had insisted on Ribs's invisibility. She didn't know what the Abbess would be like, but if the world of talentkind was any measure, she expected a less than pleasant welcome. Any advantage would be needed.

They got down at a quiet boulevard in Montparnasse. The convent was not difficult to find. It was a grim, weathered building, constructed for a darker century than their own, fortress-like in its implacable stone facade. And yet Alice suspected there were gardens beyond, and quiet, and a steady peaceable stillness.

They climbed the few steps and knocked sharply at the door and waited. It opened to reveal a sour-looking nun, in a faded red woolen frock, peering suspiciously out.

They'd never agreed on the best way to get inside, to get near to the Abbess, and locate the second orsine. Ribs had wanted to sneak in on her own; Charlie thought they should wait for nightfall, and try to pick the locks. Alice had her own method.

"We've come to see the Abbess," said Alice abruptly. She glared at the nun, weighing the woman's size. "We've come a long way. We have business to discuss."

But the nun in red only nodded and glanced past at the carriages in the street and then ushered them inside. There were whiskers on her chin and upper lip. She clapped her hands sharply.

"Marie!" she called. Out of the dim interior emerged a second figure, also in a red robe, a hood covering her eyes. "Marie, voici les Anglais. Ils sont attendus."

"L'Abbesse?"

"Elle est à ses dévotions dans le pavillon."

Alice wished, suddenly, that Ribs wasn't the one who could speak fluent French. She looked from nun to acolyte, trying to follow their exchange.

The ancient acolyte, Marie, gave a slow nod. She gestured for them to follow. Alice saw her left arm was wizened into a claw. "Come, English, I will take you to the Abbess," she said haltingly. "You are expected. The Abbess is most holy. You are blessed to be granted an audience."

Alice gave Charlie a wry look, raising her eyebrows in disapproval. Charlie's expression remained worried. She had little patience for such fanaticism. Her childhood at Bent Knee Hollow, her mother's madness, had cured her of such things. Allan Pinkerton had taught her to doubt everything, her own certainties most of all, and that had served her well.

They moved quietly through the quiet convent. She saw few signs of life. The floors shone where daylight fell from high windows, hidden from view. Motes of dust hovered in the air. The acolyte, Alice saw, walked barefoot in the cold, her shriveled toes vanishing under her red robes at each stride. They passed no crucifixes, no holy paraphernalia. Whatever sort of nuns these were, Alice knew they were not daughters of God.

"I'm surprised she knew to expect us," whispered Charlie.

But his voice carried, and the acolyte heard. "For those touched by God," she replied, without turning, "anything is possible."

Alice slowed, the words ringing in her mind. They were strangely familiar. "Wait. What did you say?" she asked.

But the acolyte did not repeat it. She had reached a heavy white door and now she opened it onto a cold sunlight, the monastic gardens spreading out before them. There was a skeletal chill to the trees, still barren from winter, and despite the wide gravel paths and the elaborate plantings, everything looked weatherworn and shabby. A glasshouse stood to their left, its panes dirty and broken. Tall terracotta pots, filled with dirt, lined the outer wall. The gardens were vast, so that Alice could not see their end, though she glimpsed through the shrubbery and bracken flashes of red robes, where other acolytes were at their silent labors.

The air felt cool and otherworldly on Alice's face and hands. Her oilskin coat was heavy at her shoulders. She drew the brim of her hat low and steeled herself to whatever they might find.

The path they walked led to a low white pavilion, built of stone, at the middle of an empty square, with benches lining the edges. As they approached, the daylight fell whitely through the delicate filigreed roof. Everything felt pale and bright. On the steps of the pavilion were small clay dishes, with fires in them, fires burning down some scented oil, giving off little smoke. In the center was an entrance into darkness, with steps leading downward into the earth. To one side stood a brazier, the flames in it nearly invisible in the afternoon light, and standing behind this, with her back to them, was the ancient holy figure of the Abbess.

The acolyte stopped at the base of the pavilion, and waited. Alice and Charlie waited too.

And at last the Abbess turned, and came toward them, her face lined with age, her gray hair cropped short. She was immensely tall, six and a half feet at least. She wore a rough-spun white robe, plain, tied with a rope, like an ascetic. When she held her hands out to greet them those hands were massive, and callused, like the hands of a sailor.

"The fire is holy," said the Abbess in her deep voice. "Only the pure will pass through it, untouched."

Hearing that voice, Alice felt like she'd been punched. She stared, shocked. Everything, all of her childhood, all of her fury and sorrow and grief all came rushing up at her at once. For she knew that woman, she knew that face and those words, had suffered them in her dreams since she was a little girl.

Standing before her was the woman who'd seduced her mother into madness, the woman who'd founded the religious community at Bent Knee Hollow, all those years ago.

Adra Norn.

"Jesus fucking Christ," she swore. "No—Stop. Charlie? No, no no no no . . ."

She seized Charlie by the sleeve, pulled him back. Adra Norn had always been tall but she looked now almost monstrous, peering down with silver eyes, her lids rimmed with red, her face impassive as stone. But it was her; there was no mistaking it.

Adra Norn too had stopped. Her dead eyes at first had seized on Charlie with a grim satisfied hunger, but now they shifted, reptilelike, to Alice. A flicker of recognition flared in them.

"Ah," she said simply. "I know you."

Alice was breathing hard, staring. Before she could think, she'd pulled

Coulton's pistol out of her pocket and cocked the hammer and held the gun level at the old woman.

"Uh, Alice?" said Charlie, his voice reaching her as if from a long way off. "Alice, what're you—?"

Adra Norn merely stood in her rough robe, peering down. If she was unnerved by the loaded gun, she gave no sign. At last, she nodded. "You are Rachel's daughter. Yes."

Alice's head was spinning. She wanted to throw up. She felt so stupid. She remembered her conversation with Margaret Harrogate, nearly two years ago now, when she'd first interviewed for the employment. How the woman had asked about Bent Knee Hollow even then, how she'd conceded that it was her experience with Adra Norn that had drawn them to seek her out in the first place. This was no coincidence, she saw; it was all interconnected, always had been, from long before her time. Adra Norn, Dr. Berghast, Margaret Harrogate. Talents, and children, and the deceived believers at Bent Knee Hollow. This. This woman. She'd hated this woman, hated her even more than her own mother, had imagined all her life finding her again, and now she was standing in front of her and she realized it didn't matter, there was nothing about it that could make anything right, no amount of vengeance or fury could fill in the hole that was inside her, the hole that was her grief. She could pull the trigger or not, it wouldn't change a thing, and did that make her weak or strong?

But she thought of Charlie and of Marlowe and the reason they'd come to this place and she knew she'd sooner die than be the reason they failed. And she raised the gun sharply away and carved her tongue along her eyeteeth and then she slipped the weapon back into her pocket.

"It's her," she said angrily to Charlie. "She's the woman who ran the commune, when I was little. Who made my mother think it would be a good idea to burn a house full of people in their beds."

"Bent Knee Hollow has always filled me with regret," murmured Adra

Norn. "I am so sorry for what happened there, child. I'd sought women for my community here, women who were not talents, but capable all the same. It was a mistake. Only talentkind can do the good work we do here. And your mother suffered for my mistake, as did those she hurt."

Charlie, bless his heart, stepped forward, his hands balled into fists. He glared up at the towering figure. "You can't apologize for a thing like that," he said angrily. "There's no apologizing for it."

Adra Norn, implacable, unmoved, merely watched Alice's face, her great slabs of hands still flat and upturned. "Interesting. I thought I'd found none suitable, at Bent Knee," she murmured. "And yet here *you* are. Perhaps I was not so mistaken after all."

Alice felt sick, furious that she couldn't just turn and walk away.

Adra Norn shifted her gaze back to Charlie. "You. You are the one who carries Jacob Marber's dust," she continued in her deep voice. "The famous Charles Owydd. You have come here to me."

Famous.

Suddenly Alice felt afraid. Sharp memories of Adra Norn from all those years ago were coming back, memories of how the women at the commune had worshipped her, emulated her, adored her. She remembered watching Adra Norn move through her disciples like a farmer through her sheep, trailing her fingers over their heads in benediction. The cold assessing light in her eyes. Then she remembered what Abigail Davenshaw had told her about the Abbess, how dangerous the woman was, how she had been hunting the dust that was in Charlie for her own ends, and she knew he was in real danger.

"I didn't come here to *you*," Charlie told her, fierce. "I came for the orsine."

"Oh? And what would you want with an orsine?"

"Nothing he can't manage on his own," interrupted Alice.

A flicker of a smile crossed Adra Norn's lips. "Nothing to do with a child lost in the gray rooms, then?"

Charlie turned to Alice. "She *knows* about Mar," he hissed.

"Paris is the center of the world, child," said Adra Norn, raising her hands. "All news reaches here, eventually. But you may relax, young Charles Owydd. I will not impede your efforts. Though I fear there is little I can do to actually help. Our orsine has been sealed for centuries; there can be no passage through."

The Abbess glided closer, towering. Alice took an involuntary step back, but she needn't have feared; the woman dismissed her acolyte with a flick of her fingers, then stopped at the base of the steps. Her clothes smelled faintly of sulfur and sweat. Her teeth, when she smiled, were blackened at the edges, as if from sugar.

"You have brought the dust, I assume?" she asked. "Show it to me."

"Don't, Charlie," said Alice. "Don't do anything she asks."

But Charlie, ignoring Alice, folded back his sleeve, exposing the writhing tattoos. "It's inside me," he said calmly. "I can feel it. It . . . it got into me, somehow. And now it's spreading."

"Yes," Adra Norn murmured. "Because it has bonded to you, child. Good. So it is safe." She nodded twice, and her eyes darkened. "I am relieved. I have been so afraid for its safety. The outcast drughr will be hunting it, even now. It will make her powerful again. But in you it is contained, child; in you, it is stable." She frowned down from her immense height. "You are a haelan, are you not?"

Alice scowled. "And what if he is? He'll be of no use to you. He's not about to join your cult."

"We are only women here, Alice, daughter-of-Rachel," said Adra Norn. "There would be no place for Charles, among my acolytes. But these women—these talents—have devoted their lives to guarding the orsine, keeping it sealed. Keeping what lies on the far side of it at bay. They are deserving of your respect, not censure."

Alice could have spat in her eye.

"Why would you help us?" asked Charlie.

"Because I loathe the drughr even more than you do," she said calmly. "All my long life I have labored to keep talents safe from their hungers. My task has been to watch over this orsine, to keep the terrible things on the far side contained. The world beyond is not a fixed place; it is always growing, mutating. It cannot be withstood. It can only be refused. Henry, alas, thought differently. He wanted to enter Cairndale's orsine, and destroy the evil that is inside it. He believed he'd found a way to absorb a drughr's power, its . . . talent. That an exile's emptiness was a kind of strength. He thought he could *become* a drughr, and carry that power into the land of the dead. I warned him it would destroy him instead. But he always was stubborn; he would not listen."

Charlie was staring at her, his mouth half-open, astonished. "You knew Dr. Berghast?"

"Of course I *knew* him, child," replied Adra Norn. "He was my *brother*."

Alice laughed angrily. "The hell he was."

"You don't . . . look like him," said Charlie doubtfully.

"Because it's bullshit," Alice said. "Don't believe anything she says, Charlie. This is what she does. She gets in your head."

"You are skeptical. Of course you are." Adra Norn's gaze flickered over Alice, untroubled. "I expect Henry shared a great many truths with you. But there are truths of spirit, and truths of fact, and he did not always distinguish between the two. Did he tell you I too am a haelan? How else could I walk through fire and live?"

"Damn you," whispered Alice.

"If there is a God, I am certain that damnation awaits," replied Adra Norn calmly. "Thank goodness there is no such thing. My brother and I were . . . chosen to guard the orsines. When we ourselves were still young. Chosen, on account of our talents. It was known we would live long enough to see the gateways safe. Such was our charge, many centuries ago. But in a long lifetime, there is space for many mistakes, hm? That is what you are thinking, is it not, young Alice?"

Alice glared, trying to get a sense of the woman. Her thin lips, her silver eyes betrayed nothing.

But then, unexpectedly, Adra Norn reached out one massive hand and gripped Alice's shoulder, too quickly for her to pull away. The hand was hot, crushing. It felt like a burning weight was pressing down upon her and she could only stare up, startled, rooted to the spot.

"What happened to your mother was awful, child," said Adra Norn, her voice lowering to a purr. "There is no excuse for such suffering. I am so deeply sorry."

"What if your brother was still alive?" said Charlie. He turned his face to Adra Norn like a flower to the sun. "I mean, Mar is. We *know* he is. So maybe Dr. Berghast is inside the orsine, too? What if we could get him out, too?"

Adra Norn withdrew her heavy hand. Alice felt her knees go weak, as if something had been drained from her.

"My brother is dead," said Adra Norn flatly.

She turned away, and rose impassively back up to the pavilion, to the dark entrance there. She raised a hand and several acolytes emerged at the edge of the gravel path. "Nor, I regret to say, is there salvation for your friend. I will show you the orsine, Charles Owydd. You will see, and understand. Yes?"

"Show us," said Charlie firmly.

Adra Norn nodded. "Come. The both of you. Come."

Charlie followed the Abbess down, into the dark.

Alice was right behind him. Behind her came three acolytes, heads bowed, hands clasped. The stairs led into the catacombs of Paris, a rough-cut maze of ancient quarries, the walls smoothed in places and slimy to the touch. At the first branching the Abbess took a torch from its bracket on the wall, held it high. A blue flame folded itself in transparent sheets, the heat strong. Alice, Charlie saw, kept a hand deep in her pocket, where Coulton's old pistol lay. The ancient acolytes followed at a distance, in near darkness, as if they'd walked this way often and knew it blind.

The Abbess went slowly down, into the earth. The floor was smooth from long centuries of use and gradually they passed alcoves filled with human bones. There were ribs arranged on shelves, and stacks of skulls with solemn dark sockets, and the chambers they passed were shrouded with sadness. They approached a reservoir of black water, the Abbess's torch glittering fiercely in its reflection, entered a gallery with red walls. A long corridor branched away, lined with the bones of children, at the end of which stood an altar with a silver chalice. The Abbess explained nothing. She led them down a winding stair that seemed to end in a wall, then turned left, and they slipped into a narrow passage Charlie hadn't noticed. All the while he could feel Alice's anger, like a hot wind on his skin, and the eyes of the acolytes far behind.

At last they came to a great limestone cavern, not unlike the cavern below the island ruins at Cairndale. Its ceiling glittered with strange calcified shapes, twisted by age. They might have been bodies, suspended frozen in a rictus of pain. All along the walls were bones, skulls and humeri and fibulae stacked like firewood. The skulls grinned in the flickering light.

And there, in the center of that cavern, was the second orsine.

Charlie knew it at once. He felt a sudden heat under his skin, as if all the capillaries there were burning. He knew the Abbess was watching him but he didn't care. He took a step forward. The orsine was a limestone reservoir, with a railing made of wood that ran its perimeter. Stone steps, worn by age, led down into it at each end. It might have been carved with care once, lovingly even.

But there was no water within, no strange blue glow like at Cairndale. The orsine was crusted over with black vines, strange bud-like contusions grown up out of it, like little horns. It was not vegetal; whatever it was, it had grown up out of the orsine itself, entwining and roping over itself and looping all around the railing and the stonework and spreading even across the floor, like an infection.

Charlie shuddered.

"That happened around the time Cairndale burned," said the Abbess softly. "It is . . . leaking."

Charlie went over to it. And then he saw the corruption more clearly. They were not vines, but arms, hundreds of arms of all different strengths, twisted at the elbows and wrists; they were not buds but fingers, curled painfully. The firelight did not reflect off the black limbs, but seemed drawn into them and eaten by their own dark nature. He stepped cautiously between the arms on the floor, crouched low. He reached out, touched one of the charred hands.

"Charlie—" called Alice, uneasy.

The dust in his skin began to shine a soft blue. At his touch, the hand gave off a loud sigh, and crumbled away. He rubbed his fingers together. The hand was made of a thick, greasy soot, or something near to it, and where the corruption had been a black smoke now rose up off Charlie's skin, and off the broken black wrist.

The shine in his hand grew brighter. He waved his fingers sharply and the black smoke dissipated. But the broken arm was still smoking; gradually, as Charlie watched, the tendril of smoke thickened, hardening into a new arm, congealing like wax and folding over itself under its own weight before freezing into place.

"What the . . . ," he whispered to himself, leaning nearer.

"If you touch it, it will spread," called the Abbess. "I would advise you to step back. It has a . . . tendency to grow toward living things."

Charlie turned his face. The tattoos in his hands were pulsing, casting their eerie blue shine. He rose and returned to the tall woman with the torch, to his friend with her loaded pistol.

"There'll be a glyphic's heart inside that, then," said Charlie.

The Abbess nodded.

He was wondering how they'd ever get it out, if Mrs. Ficke and the girl Deirdre should manage to unseal it. If he could just wade through the arms and plunge into the heart of it. "What happens when the corruption gets onto a living person?" he asked.

"It has been many months since anyone has approached the orsine," said the Abbess. "The last who did so are still there." And she gestured toward the black rot in the middle of the floor, her eyes grave.

Alice's eyes were dark. She stood some feet away, grim.

"But what is it? What *is* that stuff?" asked Charlie.

"It is what the orsine is made of," replied the Abbess, "and the world beyond it. The same substance has infected you, young Charles Owydd. Though the dust in you has been altered by the drughr. Some believe a variation of this substance can be found in all talents, that it is the very substance of death-in-life. The source of talentkind. Who can say? The ancients called it *stille*, but we have lost that word. It is, how do I say . . . ," and she opened the cage of her fingers, as if releasing a small creature, ". . . a *wrongness*, on this side of the divide."

Charlie wet his lips.

"You see now why it is not possible to use the orsine," said the Abbess. "I am sorry. Perhaps we can find another way to your friend."

But Charlie wasn't so sure. The Abbess knew nothing of Mrs. Ficke and Oskar and Deirdre, what they were attempting. And if the glyphic's heart could be stopped, what would happen to the corruption then? He was careful to keep his face neutral as he turned and studied the orsine. It had not hurt him, as it had hurt those others who had gone near it. He, Charlie Ovid, for whatever reason, seemed immune to it. Perhaps it was the drughr's dust, already in him; perhaps it was his nature as a haelan. But it meant he could still maybe find his way to the glyphic's heart when the time came. All this was in him while the Abbess peered down, her silver eyes assessing him, her mouth cold and downturned and seemingly filled with regret.

"Young Mr. Owydd," she murmured then. "If you would follow me, there are matters I would discuss with you. I would be honored to show you to your sleeping chamber." Her eyes flickered over Alice. Alice looked, Charlie thought, very small next to the Abbess and yet hard and tough as a bent nail. The Abbess continued: "For obvious reasons, it would be inappropriate for a young man to share arrangements with a woman. But you will see your companion again, soon."

Alice spat, squaring her shoulders. "The hell with that. We'll go together."

The acolytes near the entrance rustled, like long grass where a predator lurked.

But Charlie shook his head. "It'll be fine," he said quietly, taking her aside. He gave her a quick unhappy grin. "Really, I'll be fine. I mean, what can she do to *me*?"

The red scar at Alice's eye was creased with worry.

"You'd be surprised," she muttered.

37

PAYING THE GATEKEEPER

The land of the dead was still.

Marlowe followed the ragged figure of Dr. Berghast down the creaking stairs, through the house, out into the square. The cobblestones seeped at their edges. The white tree in the mist looked spectral and bare. There were some few spirit dead adrift near the far tenements but they took no notice of him.

Berghast hurried. Tall and thin and double-wrapped again in his rags like the Egyptian dead, his hand armored in its fractured glove of black metal plates, gleaming black wood. The teeth within it had raked his wrist raw. His rags were the yellow of the mists and when he moved he almost disappeared. Only his eyes were visible and those eyes were blue and fierce.

Around the corner they went, wending between bollards, splashing softly through the muck. Past a small charnel house and down a steep stair, the high narrow walls dripping with water. There were ancient shop fronts, their windows smeared and dark. Signs on rusting chains hanging still above. And then they were there, at the edge of the city, staring out at a road shining in the brown fog. Their breathing was loud in the stillness. The whole world was lit as if from within. Ahead, Marlowe knew, stood the wall of carykk, and the terrible prison of Cairndale. A man asleep, with his throat exposed.

Berghast hesitated. Something strange was happening. A light ash began to fall, softly. Marlowe held out his hand, watched the flakes settle. In all his months trapped in this world, he'd never seen its light change, never seen its weather. Behind him, he could see his and Dr. Berghast's footsteps, already filling in. It was like the orsine sensed what was coming. But whether to help them or hinder them, he didn't know. He looked at Dr. Berghast with dread.

"Never mind it," the old man whispered. "Focus, now. You must go as if you belong here. Do not slow when you reach the gates."

"But the carykk—"

"Will not trouble you. You are the child of a drughr. They will let you pass, and me with you."

Marlowe wasn't so certain. "The other carykk were after me. They didn't let me . . . pass."

"You must go first. It is the only way. Watch the skies."

Marlowe stared at the old man in sudden panic. He didn't think any bonebirds would be able to fly in this ash, or see much if they could. But the idea of going first past the awful carykk left him frightened. They had been talents, like Charlie, or Oskar, or Komako, talents who'd been seized by the drughr before Coulton or Alice or anyone like them could get them safe. But they weren't that anymore. He thought of the creature with the yellow ribbon, the one that had hunted him.

"I don't like this plan," he said. He tugged at Dr. Berghast's sleeve. "I don't think it will work."

Berghast kneeled before him in the thickening ash. "Trust me, child," he said. "I will keep you as safe as I can. This is the way we will end it."

He straggled along behind Berghast, running every few paces to keep up. The old man strode down the middle of the road, straight and sure, and he did not slow until they could hear the faint moaning of the carykk wall, a low unhappy sound, like when Marlowe would press his ear to the wall of the circus wagon as they moved from town to town, and hear the rumble of its wheels. Like that.

And then Marlowe was out in front, somehow, walking slower and trying to remember Dr. Berghast's words, that he must go as if he belonged there, and not be distracted, and not stare at the creatures he saw now emerging through the fog and ashfall, the terrible creatures, taller even than Dr. Berghast, weirdly upright, their skulls stirring and swaying on their long necks.

He set his jaw. He walked on.

The carykk were lashed each to each, with slick chains piercing their flesh, their bodies crushed up against each other, their long arms pinioned fast. Only their heads were free, most with their long hoodlike skins fallen back, baring their bonelike scalps. Thick wreaths of smoke hazed the air where their eyes should have been. But their teeth were sharp, their lips peeled back in a rictus of pain.

The wall vanished into the fog in both directions, as far as Marlowe could imagine, maybe as far as the world itself. He shuddered. The ash fell silently.

And then he was there, nearing the black gates. They stood wide as if no trespasser would dare cross them. A dusting of ash across their spikes. Marlowe saw the intricately worked metal, the pattern of the Cairndale crest, all of it rusting and giving way to the orsine's rot. He could hear Dr. Berghast breathing behind him.

The nearest carykk in the wall had gone weirdly quiet. They twisted their unseeing faces, as if trying to make sense of what he—Marlowe—was. They were maybe seven feet tall, towering over him.

You belong here, you belong here, you belong here, he told himself, over and over.

He heard the awful popping noises, as the carykk turned their faces, following him.

He swallowed. His shoes were silent in the deepening ash. But as he began to pass through the gate the fog far ahead parted, just for a moment, and he glimpsed the dark glittering loch beyond Cairndale. There was no island. The island of the monastery, the island that had contained the glyphic and the orsine and his way out—simply *was not there*. Dr. Berghast had lied.

All at once Berghast was hissing into his ear: "We are discovered. Run!"

Marlowe looked up; and the nearest carykk screamed.

It screamed with the awful airless endless scream of the undying, a scream of fury and hunger and pain, and Marlowe clapped his hands to his ears, afraid. The carykk was thrashing at its chains.

And then the next carykk began to scream, and the next after that, and the scream was a wall of sound muscling the air, rooting Marlowe to the spot in terror.

"Run, boy! Go!" Berghast was shouting over the din.

He seized Marlowe by the shoulder, roughly, and shoved him stumbling forward. And then Marlowe saw it, the swift dark monstrous shape of the drughr, striding up the cobbled road toward the gates. It was the drughr with all its dozens of eyes, each one blinking sorrowfully, but the creature's speed and long sharp claws betrayed its purpose.

He started to run. Berghast was with him, not leaving him, running with his head turning back all the time to see what followed.

Marlowe ran as fast as his small legs could carry him. Past the rotting carriage house, across the courtyard in the fog, his and Berghast's tracks clear in the carpet of ash. He was sliding, getting to his feet, running onward.

When he glanced back, he didn't see the drughr, but instead a man in a long black oilskin cloak, a man with black hair, running wildly after them. He had no eyes.

"The door!" Berghast was shouting. "We must go inside! Go!"

And then he was stumbling at the steps, clambering up, hesitating only a moment at the massive carved doors to Cairndale, so different from the ones in his world, these doors with the Cairndale crest burned into them, as if with a branding iron, and the ornate keyholes where the heads of the crossed hammers would have been, both empty, and a single keyhole edged in gold with a gnarled key sticking out of it.

But then Berghast was pushing at the doors, and Marlowe leaned his shoulder in too, and pushed with everything he had, but the doors wouldn't open. The drughr with no eyes had entered the courtyard and was already almost upon them. Marlowe saw from the corner of his eye three small cages, suspended on chains, two with the mummified remains of some small furred creatures. He pushed and pushed.

The doors opened a crack, no more. The air that seeped out was like a poison. Marlowe glimpsed a darkness beyond, a darkness like the obsidian mirror in the gray rooms, a darkness that smoldered with its own soot. He could hear Berghast groaning with the effort. Marlowe pushed, he pushed with everything his little body had—

—when all of a sudden the doors gave way.

And he and Dr. Berghast plunged, like wraiths, into the First Talent's prison.

In Paris, it was almost raining.

The white sky was darkening. The bone witch Jeta Wajs lurked in the shadowy bell tower of a church in Montparnasse, her naked hand on the cold mouth of the great bell, the two bone fingers clicking softly. Her eyes were sunken from lack of sleep, her cheeks hollow. Her braids were dirty and tangled with bits of straw, dead leaves. The sharp fishy stink of the gutters was in her shift.

She was too tired to care. She peered down at the tiled rooftops, the public gardens with their fountain, the distant Seine vanishing in the haze, and she grimaced. Several hours had passed since she'd sighted the boy, Ovid, his unmistakable lanky stride, crossing Boulevard du Montparnasse. Just as the drughr had predicted. But he wasn't alone: a woman in a broad-brimmed hat, wearing men's trousers and a filthy oilskin coat, had led him carefully through the carriage traffic. There was something about her, the way her hands hung at her sides, red-looking even at that distance, that gave Jeta pause. They'd turned down Rue Boissonade and knocked at the ancient convent doors where the drughr, three days ago, had felt the sealed orsine's pull.

Now, somewhere in the gloom above her, stirred the drughr, the bell tower's shadows coiled like a serpent around it, waiting. She could *feel* its presence, up in the heavy ropes, a wrongness in the air.

Her exhaustion was not just in her body. She knew this, knew there was something the matter with her, ever since that barn outside Roye, when that terrible other creature had smashed its way out of the mist. Montparnasse was a thick miasma of human bones, tugging at her, dizzying her, making her ill from a lack of sleep. And yet, somehow, she didn't collapse. The drughr itself was stronger now, so much stronger. It could take on physical form, could reach out and grasp her arm with its cold touch. All that it lacked was the corrupted dust, its own dust.

Jeta, rubbing the coin at her throat, her dark eyes bloodshot, turned to the corner of the bell tower. The drughr had descended silently.

"They aren't coming back out," she said quietly.

Ah, said the drughr. *My dear Jeta. I am grateful.*

Suddenly she was in front of Jeta, so close. She raised a gloved hand, the many rings glittering upon it, and touched Jeta's cheek. The feel of silk was unmistakable.

Let us follow them, then, murmured the drughr. *Let us finish this.*

Jeta swallowed. "What's inside? What am I walking into?"

The convent is nothing, replied the drughr. *It is what lies below it that we should fear.*

"And what's that?"

Our ends and our beginnings, Jeta Wajs. As it has always been.

Getting into the convent was easy.

Jeta stood on the chipped stairs and banged on the door and when an old acolyte in a red rough-spun robe, her hood pulled low at her eyes, opened the door in displeasure, Jeta felt through the ache in her fingers for the woman's vertebrae, and tore them brutally apart.

The woman's eyes rolled up and she collapsed in the doorway, dead.

The drughr was at Jeta's ear, warning her. *They are all talents here. You must go swiftly.*

Jeta glanced around but the carriages in the boulevard were still some distance off, and no pedestrians were near. She squeezed past. Inside there was no place to conceal the body. The entrance hall was bare, the corridors quiet. She stripped the woman out of her robes and pulled them roughly over her own clothes. Then she turned the dead woman in her yellowing shift, so that she didn't have to see the face. Surprised at the lack of remorse she felt. She crouched over the body and, satisfied that she was still alone, she opened the door and dragged it by the wrists out, onto the stoop, and dumped it unceremoniously into the bushes under the small barred window. She stuffed the feet back under. And hurried inside.

The drughr was standing in the shadows, her hands clasped before her. Her dark hair was parted tightly in the center. Jeta studied her. She looked, she thought, severe and beautiful.

It is this way, said the drughr.

And she led Jeta through a small wooden door, up a narrow staircase, out into a private chapel. On one side she could see, through a row of arches, a kind of courtyard, where several red-robed acolytes scrubbed at the flagstones. No one glanced up at her.

She hurried on. Past the altar and left, down a second stair, along a bright windowed corridor, spare and white, and through a second door into a vast garden.

The garden was bare and skeletal from the winter and its paths were white as chalk. The drughr glided unerringly forward, along the maze of hedges and dead trees, past the cold-looking terracotta pots, toward a pavilion somewhere near the garden's center. The air was brisk on Jeta's face. She was alert, afraid, listening for sounds of pursuit. But all was still.

At the pavilion a brazier burned with a low orange flame, its coals soaked in oil. There was a fine filigreed detail worked into the posts and under the roof that belied its presence in a holy refuge. Jeta slowed and drew back the red hood and stood looking around. The drughr was in the pavilion, staring at the flames. There were wizened figures far back in the garden, kneeling in the dirt.

Something was making Jeta uneasy. It wasn't just the convent itself. Her bones were aching as if dipped in a fiery cold and she went down to one knee and, fearfully, pressed a hand flat on the earth.

And there it was, pulsing up through her, a terrible painful pull. Something under them was washing over her, dragging her talent toward it, agonizing. Bones. There were bones beneath the garden, thousands upon thousands of bones. She swayed, unsteady, and looked anxiously around.

In the center of the pavilion stood an open door, stairs leading down into the earth. Jeta's blood was loud in her ears. She knew what she was supposed to do.

"It's bones," she whispered. "It's more bones than I've ever felt. I can't . . . I can't go in there . . ."

This is where they have gone, said the drughr dispassionately. *The dust is near. I feel it.*

"No," murmured Jeta. But she got to her feet anyway, she moved woodenly toward the stairs.

Come, Jeta. The orsine lies below us. The dust has been brought to it.

She nodded weakly. "Okay," she whispered.

Swaying unsteadily at the top of the stairs, peering down at the blackness. She steeled herself; she forced herself, once more, to contain what she could of the pull from the bones. It was not different in kind from being in a city like London, surrounded, overwhelmed. Not different in kind, only in degree.

There were just so *many* bones down there.

But just then there came a cry from the monastery behind them. Jeta turned weakly. Figures in red robes were running into the garden, some carrying weapons. One of them twisted a rope of dust around her fists. A second was accompanied by a molten, fleshlike *thing*. Jeta could feel their bones too, but just faintly, as if they were too thin, delicate as china. The pull from the catacombs below nearly drowned out all else.

The drughr in her black dress glided halfway down the stairs, turned her white face back upward.

You must come now, Jeta, she whispered.

Wincing, Jeta flicked her sore wrist back at the nearest acolyte. The woman's left tibia snapped cleanly. The acolyte, maybe seventy years of age, heavyset, screamed and fell in the path, clutching at her leg. The others slowed, confused.

Jeta stumbled down into the catacombs. She slammed an iron grille, snapped its bolt into place. It would not hold them long. The pain of the bones was like a sound, was like a rustle of voices just out of earshot, making her shake her head, making it hard for her to think clearly. There was a torch in a bracket at the first branching of the tunnels and she stumbled toward its light, took it from the creaking iron ring, held it high to see.

Slick limestone walls, ancient and stained with centuries of grime. A rough-cut floor. The drughr turned right, and led her along the dark gallery. Soon she was passing skulls in their stacked hollows, arches filled with femurs and humeri all arranged with a terrible precision. As she swept past she could feel the skulls turning, as if drawn to her, she could feel the tremble of the humeri as if some heavy carriage were rumbling overhead. But it was her, just her, just the thing that was in her, doing it.

Her head was throbbing. She knew the talents in red robes would be following, raising an alarm. But she could hear no sounds of pursuit. The drughr led her deeper, down steep stairs, along narrow galleries. Past a reservoir of black water, a gallery of skulls with its curving walls painted a strange ochre.

She could sense the dust, she told Jeta, it was near, it was *near*!

Sweeping always just ahead, the black lace of her collar creeping at her neck, as if the darkness were eating away at her, twisting her, accentuating her size and power, and Jeta kept glimpsing, at the edges of her vision, antlers and a monstrous stooped form, but it was just the drughr, the woman in black, sorrowful, suffering, her poor friend—

And then, suddenly, the drughr went still.

Jeta, gasping, slowed beside her. There were bones, scraping along the rock floor, slowly drawn to her like iron filings to a magnet. She tried to still the power that was in her, that was making her sick. The drughr's white face was turned to the darkness.

Do you feel that? it murmured. *What . . . what is it?*

Jeta's ears were roaring with all the thousands of bones. She splayed a pale hand against the wall, feeling the cold limestone. She closed her eyes.

"I don't think you're feeling the same thing I am," she muttered. "Is it him, is it Charlie? Where is he?"

No, it is . . . something else. At the orsine. There is another . . . I feel another, Jeta Wajs . . .

Jeta crushed her eyes shut. "I can't . . . stay here," she whispered. "Let's just get the dust, okay? I . . . I need to get out of here. Which way do we go?"

The drughr did not answer. Jeta stood with her eyes closed, head aching, trying to breathe. Her heart was pounding. At last, wincing, she raised her face, looked around. The torch smoldered with a weak orange flame. The drughr was no longer beside her.

"Hello?" she called out, as loud as she dared. She turned in place. "Hello?"

But the tunnels were empty; the drughr was gone.

38

HAUNTINGS

The Abbess held the torch high as she led Charlie through the catacombs. Its soaked cloth burned a frail blue flame, translucent as glass. In alcoves as they passed Charlie glimpsed stacks of bones arranged in patterns, skulls lined up by the thousands. The bones, bronzed with age, glinted with a patina of firelight. The gallery they walked was low and the Abbess had to stoop and their footfalls were loud in the stillness.

"Is Dr. Berghast really your brother?" Charlie asked quietly.

"Yes." She paused, studied him with dark eyes. "Do you have a sibling, Charles?"

"I've got Marlowe," he said, peering up at her. "He's what I've got."

They descended a rough-cut stair and turned left, passing through a chamber half-filled with water. Charlie soon lost all sense of direction. The Abbess led him into a narrow passage, one Charlie hadn't noticed, and then they went deeper still. There were limestone sarcophagi along the walls, bones arranged on shelves above them.

"The quarries go on for miles," the Abbess told him. "But these tunnels we are in now are cut off from the others. There can be no reaching the orsine, except from the gardens above. We are quite safe here." She lifted the torch as she walked, to see his face more clearly. Her own eyes glittered with reflected fire. "Is it strange, how the corrupted dust has changed you?"

Charlie slowed. "You . . . you know about that?"

"I have been alive longer than half the countries of Europe, child. You are not the first talent to be infected with a drughr's dust. Your gift will be different now, though. Does it feel like some other is within you? Like there is a hand upon your hand, guiding you?"

"Yes," said Charlie.

"Mm. How awful it must be." But the Abbess's voice did not sound unhappy; it sounded pleased.

Charlie didn't know if she knew about the dustworking, ineffectual and impractical as it was, or about the dreams that felt so real. He didn't know if she had any suspicions like Komako had, if she knew anything about the foretellings of the Spanish glyphic. He made a careful fist; a hot prickling pain rose in the wrist. The corrupted dust under his skin was glowing a faint blue, and he tugged at the cuff of his sleeve to hide it.

At last the Abbess slowed. "We are here," she said, in her deep voice.

The passage ended at a wall. A small iron door, as if built for a coal scuttle, or an ancient children's prison, was fastened into the limestone. Standing beside it, with her red hood drawn low to obscure her features, was a small acolyte. Much smaller than any other he had seen thus far. She held a candle in a dish, its orange light pitifully weak.

Laboriously, from deep within her red robes, she withdrew a heavy iron key, and unlocked the door. It all felt sinister, and Charlie stopped some feet away. He gave the Abbess a quick perplexed glare.

"You're *not* putting me in there," he said firmly. "No."

She turned. Her head was angled weirdly because of the ceiling and she smiled grimly down at him. "You are afraid, child?"

"Yes," he said truthfully.

"And what," she said, her voice dropping to a whisper, "are you afraid of?"

He shivered, despite himself. A cold air was seeping from the open door. The blackness beyond was absolute. He became aware of the weight of rock above them. But he was a haelan, and somehow a wielder of dust, and he knew that there was little this woman could do to him, powerful as she might be. A locked room could not hold him. No injury could stay him.

But the Abbess just held the torch wide, her broad shoulders in their burlap blocking the darkness, and said, "Relax, Charles Owydd. I only wish to show you something, something for your eyes only. So that we understand each other."

"Is it to do with the orsine? With how to unseal it?"

"It is to do with your father."

Charlie froze. The shadows in her eye sockets and under her nostrils made her look monstrous, like a drughr pressing through a human face.

But she was just Adra Norn, a haelan who had lived too long, who had seen too much, and who was as hard and cruel and inhuman in her way as her brother Henry Berghast had been in his. He saw this suddenly, without quite knowing how, and he knew he must be careful with her. She turned, pushed the burning torch through the doorway, and disappeared inside.

Charlie, wary, followed.

The gallery was surprisingly wide. He could just make out the far wall of bones, in the firelight. The ceiling was higher here and domed and the Abbess could stand comfortably. She set the torch in a bracket away from the door. In the middle of the floor stood a stone well, a few feet high, not unlike the orsine. All around it stood a complicated pattern of bones. A heavy mound of ancient chains was stacked beside the well and a complicated iron brace with a winch and hook had been constructed over the water. Its surface, Charlie saw, was very black and still.

"I *knew* your father, Charles," said the Abbess, her back turned. "We shared many beliefs."

She crossed the chamber and plucked a skull from the wall. Lifted it reverently in two hands.

"No—" Charlie whispered, horrified.

The Abbess laughed. It sounded unhappy, strange. "Ah, no," she said. "Your father is not here." Her powerful hand tightened and the skull burst into a cloud of white dust. Bone fragments and teeth scattered on the floor like pebbles. "Tell me, do you have the artifact?"

Charlie reached a hand to the cord at his neck without thinking. Caught himself too late.

Her eyes glittered. "Good. What do you know about your father? Did Mr. Renby tell you he was a thief, a coward? An exile?"

Slowly, Charlie nodded.

"You must not believe it. Your father was no coward. He went down to the Falls deliberately, to gain Jack Renby's trust, in order to locate and steal the very artifact you wear. Steal it *back*, I should say. It had been his by rights, all along. When he understood who he was, what he was, what other choice did he have? Meeting your mother, having you—that was his mistake. He would still be alive today, had he not tried to protect you both. To take you with him, when he went in search of the Grathyyl." She paused, her eyes filled all at once with a dark concern. "Oh, child. Have you not yet figured out who your father was?"

Charlie ran his tongue along his sharp teeth, wary. He knew there was no answer he could give that would be correct. He thought of his mother, how she used to speak about him. How much she had loved him. Whatever this Abbess would say, he tried to hold on to that as the truth. He remembered Alice's warning, to trust nothing the Abbess said. That she would twist the truth until it became a lie.

"Your father," said the Abbess, taking a step toward him, "was descended from the same bloodline as Alastair Cairndale. As are you, of course. You and the First Talent are kin."

"The First Talent—?" whispered Charlie. "But I'm not . . ."

"And do you know what made the First Talent *preeminent?* First, among all others?"

Charlie shook his head.

"All five talents manifested in him. He was the only talent ever to do so. But the gift was in his blood; it was believed that another like him would appear. *Emergent of the drughr*, the old writings claimed. *A child of the First*. And that this descendant would bring the fire that would burn all to dust."

Charlie wet his lips. "But talents don't run in the blood," he said. "They're not . . . passed down. Right?"

"Who told you that?"

"We learned it. At Cairndale."

The Abbess sighed. "Oh, child. Talents are as varied as anything on this earth. There is no rule, one way or another. Merely probabilities. It is unlikely for talents to be blood. But it happens. My brother and I, for instance. Your father and yourself. Tell me, now. How many talents have manifested in you, Charles Owydd?"

"One," he whispered.

"Mm. I think more than that."

Charlie followed her gaze down to his fists and saw, to his horror, that a thin spiral of dust was orbiting his knuckles. The skin was on fire. He heard a scraping behind him: the acolyte in her red robe had entered the chamber, her little hands loose at her sides. It would have been a laughable attempt to restrain him, had he intended to fight. But Charlie wasn't laughing.

"Your father was supposed to be the one," the Abbess continued. She took another step, looming closer. "The one that had been foreseen. The one who was to bring about the destruction of all talentkind. I saw the five talents manifest in him with my very eyes. The glyphic at Cairndale had granted him a vision of what was to come. A vision of the artifact and its use, and of the First Talent in his cell, and of the Grathyyl where it all began, and will end. Your father did not want to be what he was, but he took the artifact from Mr. Renby, and went in search of the Grathyyl, because there was no other way. He believed he had found a back door, a hidden way in. He intended to destroy the world beyond the orsine, the prison that holds the First Talent captive. Hywel Owydd wanted to find the source of talentkind, and *smother* it."

"But he didn't make it," whispered Charlie.

"No. He did not."

"Because of us? My mama and me?"

The Abbess inclined her head. "He was weak, yes," she said, "and he didn't dare leave you in London, to be found by Mr. Renby's exiles. But that is not the reason he failed. The truth is, we were . . . mistaken. Your father failed to reach the Grathyyl because he was *not* the one, after all."

Charlie was shaking his head. *Don't listen to her, don't!* he told himself sharply. But he knew what was coming, even before she said it, knew it and felt a rightness in it that made him sick.

"You are the one, Charles Owydd. The one who will destroy our kind."

"I won't," he protested. "I just came to save Mar. That's all."

"You will not mean to, no," agreed the Abbess. Her eyes were terrible in the firelight. "But it will be so. You have brought the dust to the catacombs, as was foreseen. And you can do more than heal, also." Her eyes flared at the emotion in his face. "Hush. I mean you no harm. I want to keep you safe. If you were to die, Charles, then some other would acquire the dust; the foretelling would change, and yet not change. Killing you would not stop anything."

"Killing me—?" Charlie took a nervous step backward, toward the door.

"Of course, killing a haelan is nearly impossible," continued the Abbess. "It rather makes you the perfect vessel for what is in you. The perfect . . . containment. You will live to a great age, with the drughr's dust inside you."

The acolyte behind him withdrew something from her robes. A long thin blade.

"Jesus—" Charlie hissed. "Tell her to put that away. Or I'll hurt her. I mean it."

"I ain't a bleedin *her*," whispered the acolyte. Pulling back the red hood to show a boy's face, pinched and mean, with hair so fine and blond as to look white.

It was the murderous urchin from the Falls, the one who'd attacked him in the London fog, who'd cut him badly and stolen his father's ring and left him for dead at the docks.

Whose sisters had died in the devastation.

"Alice will come looking for me," Charlie said wildly, an unbridled fury rising in him all at once. But even as he said it he knew it wasn't true; she'd never find him. "And not just her," he spat. He turned his face from side to side, trying to keep both in his view. "We fought drughr, we stopped Jacob Marber and his litches. We stopped your *brother*. What are you? You're *nothing*."

But already the urchin was moving, swift as firelight, sliding alongside Charlie with his thin blade flashing and Charlie felt the tight hot seep of blood in his side where the knife passed. He stumbled, spinning around. And then the dust was at his fist, thickening, rising up out of his skin and being sucked up from the stone floor, a great dark webbing of it, and he unleashed it on the boy and the boy collapsed, choking, under its pall.

Suddenly the Abbess loomed up, one enormous hand enclosing his throat. Her grip was strong, impossibly strong. She lifted him onto his toes, crushing his windpipe slowly. Her eyes were flat, uninflected.

Charlie was scrabbling with his hands, trying to pry her grip loose. Her arms were too long and he couldn't reach her throat, her face, her eyes. He fumbled for the dust and felt it spin ropelike from his knuckles, he felt it enclose her throat and begin to squeeze.

But some eerie change came over her then. Her throat shifted, thinned under the pressure, as if adjusting to the new envelope of its flesh; he realized, in horror, that it was the mortaling: she was a haelan of tremendous power.

His vision was blackening around the edges. He glimpsed, for only just a moment, her free arm snaking weirdly across the floor, dragging back the heavy chain. He kicked weakly out. The dust was thinning, he wasn't strong enough.

That was when he felt the urchin's fierce angry grip on his wrists, twisting his arms behind him, looping with incredible speed a rope into place and tying him fast.

The Abbess released him. He fell, coughing, to the floor, the bloodied wound in his side already healing. He was shaking his head, glaring up at them. They couldn't hold him; surely she knew that? No chain could hold him.

Already the urchin was kneeling, looping the chain with cold precision around his body. Over his shoulders and around his legs and ankles, back up across his ribs, pinning his elbows fast, his wrists still tied behind him. Over and under and around. Again, again, until the chain was fastened.

And then the Abbess reached down and picked him up, chains and all, as if he were no more weight than a sack of dried apples, and she carried him to the edge of the well. The heavy hook that dangled there was attached to an open link of chain. And there Charlie balanced in horror, at the edge of the well, slowly beginning to realize what she intended. He looked all around. The chamber was dim, deep in the halls of the dead, and hidden from all living memory.

"You will not drown here, Charles Owydd," she said softly. "Or rather, the drowning will not kill you. It cannot kill you. But the water will stop you from working the dust. And the drowning will stop you from trying to get free."

Charlie was shaking his head. "Why are you doing this? You said you'd help us!"

"And I shall. I shall help all of our kind."

The urchin lurked in the shadows, his filthy little face grinning. There was blood in his teeth.

And then the Abbess raised one enormous heavy foot, pressing it to his chest, and she tipped him over into the black water. He felt the shock of the cold close over him. The winch was loosed and it spun wildly as he plunged under. He sank swiftly, his panicked eyes watching the circle of firelight above grow fainter, like an eyelid closing. In the blackness he collided with the well's bottom. His blood was pounding in the roar. After that there was only the furious pain of his lungs, bursting, filling with water, the muffled sound of his screams, their bubbles soon extinguished, and then the endless thrashing of his legs and arms as he died and healed, died and healed, died and healed again, returning to consciousness only long enough to drown all over again, for all time and for never in the awful endless circular agony of his flesh.

Marlowe opened his eyes in the gloom.

His heart was battering away at his ribs like a caged thing. He rolled onto his back to catch his breath and he saw Berghast, on his knees, gasping also. They were alive.

The drughr had not followed.

They'd not closed the door behind them and yet it stood closed now, the drughr somewhere on the far side. A massive door, black and imposing. The smooth wood was unmarred by any kind of pull or handle, Marlowe saw. Dr. Berghast had spoken the truth: it could not be opened.

He was sprawled on the floor of the great hall at Cairndale. Nearby, a reeking blanket lay in a tangle; beside it, a solitary child's shoe. All around in the shadows the manor rose up around them, thick with silence, its walls bare, its sconces dark. His ears were still ringing from the screams of the carykk outside, but here no sound penetrated. Yet they were not alone; he could feel it, the presence of others, like a draft from an open window. He glanced anxiously at the cold hearth. Slowly, he understood.

"I couldn't have got through, anyway," he mumbled. He dialed his face upward, looking to Dr. Berghast. "If I'd tried to just go home, I mean. I *looked*. There was no island. Just the loch, with nothing in it. I couldn't have got home, could I? And that drughr would have caught me. I *had* to come here."

"Yes," murmured Berghast. He did not seem surprised.

Marlowe scowled, all at once suspicious. "Did you know? Did you know the island wasn't there? That the carykk wouldn't let me pass?"

"Lower your voice," Berghast replied sharply. He began to unwrap the rags and scarf at his head and face, until he stood bare. He withdrew the ancient knife from his belt. "The drughr will not follow us in here. But it does not mean we are alone."

The artifact glove clicked as Berghast worked the fingers of it. His shoulders were long and narrow, his eyes lost in their hollows. In the half-light of that place he looked almost, thought Marlowe, like one of the carykk. He shivered.

"I suspected," said Berghast softly, when he was ready. "But I did not know. Now, let us finish what we started."

It was Cairndale and yet it was not Cairndale, Marlowe saw almost at once. That was maybe the worst thing. The gloom was thicker, darker. The ceilings seemed to bend away into the shadows. The carpet under his feet thrummed softly. How much it was like a part of his own memory, how close it was to the place he'd found his friends, his true family, and yet how much it was not that at all.

The house creaked and shifted. They made their slow way up the great curved staircase. The wallpaper was peeling, spotted with mold in places. The floor was soft with rot. At the edge of his vision, Marlowe kept glimpsing flickers of movement, but when he turned always there was nothing. Berghast continued to climb.

Now the light changed, the light that had been gray and exhausting for so long. It filtered in through the grand stained glass windows of Cairndale, the huge elaborate windows. Marlowe's hands and face were stained green, then red. Berghast walked on, glowing with all the colors of that place.

And then they were at the upper landing, and the corridor stretched out ahead of them, narrow and peeling and dim. A patch of carpet had been rubbed raw, was curling back on itself. A small table, under a rusting sconce. There were doors on both sides, waterstained doors Marlowe did not recognize. He shuddered. Once again he had the unmistakable feeling that they were not alone.

And then something flickered up ahead, a figure. It was a woman in white, clearly visible, but sliding around the corner of the hallway, just out of sight. Marlowe froze. Berghast put out a cautious hand, shook his head silently. He withdrew his knife. Then he led them carefully along the passage, following the specter. Around the corner, with his knife held low.

The hallway went on, the same as before. Marlowe saw the waterstained doors on both sides again, the same doors they had just passed. The same little table, under the same rusting sconce. The specter of the woman was just turning the corner ahead again, vanishing.

This time they stood still for a long moment. The house creaked and groaned.

"I don't like this place, Dr. Berghast," he whispered.

"It is the prison that makes you feel afraid, child. We are in its turnings now."

Grimly the old man approached the corner, Marlowe at his heels, and grimly again they found themselves back in the same hallway. Ahead, the specter was gliding around the corner, vanishing.

"We must find a different way," the old man murmured.

Cautiously, he opened the first door on the left. The chamber was small, and heavily furnished, the gloom cut by a window in one corner. Berghast was still. Gradually Marlowe became aware of a figure within, moving slightly. It was the apparition of the woman. She wavered, blurred at the edges, but not like the spirit dead in the city. She looked youthful, pretty, with brown hair falling in curls past her shoulders. She wore a white dress without any kind of stitching on it, a simple gold cord tied at her waist. She wore a ring on a chain at her breast. She was seated at a dressing table, with a small mirror on a hinge in front of her, her face tilted to one side as if listening to a voice in the shadows. As Marlowe watched, she lowered her chin, her eyelashes long and dark, and then she rose and crossed to the window and the window glowed through her features, as if she were parchment held to the light. After a moment she turned back, her expression frightened. She returned to the dressing table.

And then, to Marlowe's confusion, she repeated her movements, identically. Her face tilted; she rose, crossed to the window. Looked frightened. And then again. Again.

Marlowe felt a chill go through him. But Berghast was already pulling at his sleeve, breaking the spell. "Come, child," he said, gesturing at a door in the far wall, a door that should not have been there. "Do not be afraid. She is not real; she cannot harm you."

Yet Marlowe lingered, watching her gravely. "Who is she?"

"I do not know her," the old man said quietly. He crossed to the door. "Someone who mattered a great deal to the First Talent, it would seem. We are in his dreaming, now; these are his innermost memories. We are close. Come."

And yet it was eerie, all the same. It seemed to Marlowe, as he followed Dr. Berghast across the chamber, that the apparition's eyes tracked his movements. He shivered, hurried on.

The door opened onto a hallway, identical to the one they had just left. The small table, the rusted sconce. The waterstained doors. And the specter, of course, just vanishing at the corner. But Berghast did not hesitate, this time. He opened the same door, the door on the left, and together they went through.

The chamber was different, longer, darker. The woman in white was the same, though there was a new sadness about her. Now she sat at a fire, rocking in a chair, staring into the flames. She raised her face as they entered, but it was not them she saw. Her eyes followed some invisible presence to the hearth. She nodded in some agreement. And then she smiled, sadly.

Berghast led them through, to another door; this door too led to the same hall. The woman was in the next room, also; she was trapped in some repetition in the room after that, as well. Berghast began to mutter to himself.

"It is close now," he muttered. "Just ahead. He will be just ahead, through the next door."

Hurrying past.

Gradually Marlowe became aware of the apparition's face, turning to watch them as they crossed each room. It was a feeling at first, more than anything else. But then he became certain of it: the ghost would cease in her repetitions, and even stand up, hands falling to her sides, and she would watch them with a look of increasing fury as they strode by.

Berghast too had noticed. He hurried them now from room to hall, from hall to room, in the endless twisting labyrinth. He scarcely hesitated now as he went. Marlowe had to run to keep up with him. He was growing tired, confused, and he tried to get the old man's attention, but could not.

Now in each room the woman would speak, in a voice that was no woman's. "You should not be here," she said, uncertain. "This is not yours to enter. Why are you here?"

Berghast ignored her. Now Marlowe could hardly keep up with him, so long were his strides, so quickly was he moving. The woman began to raise her voice. She was shouting at them, her eyes ablaze each time they entered. "You!" she cried. "You do not belong! You do not!"

Berghast was halfway across the next room when Marlowe entered. He was already at the far door of the room after that. Marlowe couldn't keep up, he couldn't, and he was shouting at the old man to wait, please, wait up, but the rooms kept racing past, faster and faster.

And then Marlowe stopped. He just stopped.

He stood breathing in the middle of the chamber and he looked at the apparition who was screaming at him in her hatred and he turned his face and he saw a second door. It was small, big enough for a child, and it was half-hidden behind a dark velvet chair. But it was there.

"Dr. Berghast!" he cried. "Come back! Dr. Berghast!"

But the old man was gone; and Marlowe, ignoring the furious ghost, hearing his own blood loud in his ears, squeezed between the furniture in the gloom and opened the little door and crawled through.

Suddenly everything was still. He was in a corridor, a corridor with no doors but one, at the far end. It was painted red. He looked behind him, and saw Dr. Berghast. The old man was gasping, his ravaged face red with exertion. His eyes were wild. He looked all around him and then down at Marlowe and then he pressed a big hand to the peeling wall, and nodded, as if coming to himself.

"Enough of this," he said angrily.

He withdrew the knife again from his belt. It made a long, slow rasping noise, a sound Marlowe had not heard before. It looked almost to be glowing faintly. And then the old man swept forward, toward the red door at the end of the hall.

Marlowe followed. The corridor was narrow and badly lit and he couldn't seem to peer around the old man's frame. He heard the red door open, softly, with a tired groan of hinges; he heard Berghast's grim steps as he entered a room filled with light. He felt the air go cold.

And then Berghast made a strangled sound, deep in his throat, and Marlowe tried to see what was happening.

"No," the old man was whispering, stricken. "But I came . . . I was here—"

Marlowe, all at once afraid, pressed his small body around one side of Berghast, and saw. In the middle of the barren chamber stood a bed, very simple, very old. Its gray blankets were peeled back. The mattress was yellowing and stained and held still the visible imprint of a body, a body that had lain there for centuries.

But the bed itself was empty.

The First Talent had awakened.

39

THE DRUGHR AND
THE DUSTWORKER

The sun descended into the hills outside Agrigento, a vast orange disc of fire. Komako trailed her fingers through the long grass, listening.

They were ready. Or nearly so. Day after day, Miss Crowley had insisted on the little ones learning to harness their talents for self-defense. Forgotten now were their long classroom hours of sums and letters. Instead, they'd muster in the courtyard in the early sunlight and square off against each other, their shadows long and ribbonlike over the gravel, their soft faces turned gravely toward the sun. Their cries were fierce, high-pitched, like children arguing over a game of kickball. Some mornings they would spar against Komako, spar against Oskar and Lymenion, trying to break through their defenses, trying to score a hit. Little Jubal and Meredith, both nine years old, both clinks, could make themselves strong and dense enough to throw Lymenion into the dirt, but not for long. Tiny Shona, with her quick dark hands, could manifest a single tight rope of dust to pinion one of Komako's wrists, but Ko's other wrist stayed free to counter it. The two young turners, Michael and Alua, could turn invisible and creep up on Oskar, but Oskar would always end up seizing them by the arms and hauling them up short, breathless, grinning.

What intrigued Komako was the way Miss Davenshaw guided Miss Crowley's methods. On their own, the children were so young, so ill-prepared. But Miss Davenshaw would whisper to the governess and Miss Crowley would clap her hands sharply, her white dress blinding in the sunlight, and she would move the children into different arrangements, into different rows. Gradually they learned to work together, for some to create a barrier of defense, others a distraction, and yet others to attack quickly while their talents held.

And Komako would stand at the edge of the courtyard, unnoticed, and watch in approval. Miss Davenshaw had told her once that she'd not allow what happened at Cairndale to happen again, if she could prevent it. That the children should know the nature of their peril, and be taught how to fight it. It was no protection to pretend the wolf was not at their door.

Komako agreed. She knew, if evil descended upon them, these little ones would not withstand a drughr. But they just might hold it off long enough to stay alive.

The drughr itself had vanished. There had been no sighting since she and Charlie had stumbled upon its fight with the keywrasse. The keywrasse, for good or ill, no longer left mutilated carcasses outside the villa's walls. It had taken to crouching, watchful, in a corner of the chamber under the wash-house, while that poor glyph-twisted girl Deirdre lay on the altar, keening softly, going deep into the Dreaming. But poor was no longer the word for her, Komako thought, seeing the golden blossoms that had burst in a riot of beauty from the girl. She seemed gorgeous and remote and, at last, *right*. Komako had walked around the strange walls, worrying about their safety, while Mrs. Ficke studied her ancient scrolls by lantern light and scarcely looked up. There was only the one way in or out. If the drughr came after Deirdre, it would be a massacre.

The perimeter walls had been rebuilt; a weak warding had been cast by the glyph-twisted girl, a warding amplified by the mysterious nexus in the Agnoscenti chamber. It would *discourage* the drughr, Mrs. Ficke explained, though it would not keep the creature out entirely. But it was not yet strong enough, Mrs. Ficke continued, to remain in this world for long; if they could detain it long enough, it would weaken, and return to the far side of the orsine, to the land of the dead. "Tis why it will not linger," the old alchemist had said, pulling an ancient tome toward her, finding the page she sought. "Tis kept in check, child. See, here. The drughr will not find its full power while the First Talent remains in his prison. Aye. We must be thankful for the small mercies."

And so Komako had insisted the front drive be left unwarded: she wanted to funnel the drughr to a chokepoint, control its progress. There she and Oskar could try to contain it. The children would wait in the villa; and if they needed to fall back, the children would have time to retreat to the ruined ballroom. The villa would stand between the drughr and the wash-house; Komako hoped it would help them trap the monster in its rooms, delay it long enough to drain it. The keywrasse—God willing it cooperated—would be locked in the chamber with Deirdre. It alone was strong enough to withstand the drughr. Maybe even destroy it.

Or so Komako hoped. But each night, as the sun sank away, and the blackness took over, she felt her dread grow. It was then her thoughts would turn to Charlie and Ribs and Alice, and whatever they might be finding in Paris. She would turn her face in the fragrant darkness, and worry. All around her, the Sicilian hills stayed quiet.

But she felt it, with a terrible certainty, deep inside her flesh: the drughr lurked there still, watching. It wasn't finished with them yet.

And yet it did not show itself. Komako brooded in the empty hours, knowing how different she was now from the girl who'd faced down Jacob Marber back at Cairndale. How she would not hesitate now. She had seen too much death, too much suffering for her to flinch in the face of it.

She would protect the children here at this villa, protect Deirdre, Miss Davenshaw, all of them, even Oskar and Lymenion who were prepared to stand alongside her, she would protect them by being more vicious, more brutal, more ferocious than any of them. And in this way spare them from their own horror.

Some evenings, alone in the garden, or drifting through the villa's ruined rooms, she would think of her sister, Teshi, Teshi whom she'd made a litch, without meaning to, using some secret part of her talent that she'd never used since and wanted never to use again. Jacob Marber had made two litches, both awful, both in pain. But Teshi had just seemed confused, hollowed-out, sad. Teshi, whom Komako had loved most of all.

It made her heart hurt to remember.

On the eighth night, the night of the new moon, Komako went to Miss Davenshaw's rooms. She wanted to ask the older woman's advice but found Oskar already there, standing in the dimness. Lymenion was beside the doorway, hulking, soft, a strong smell about him.

"Rruh," he said.

"Yeah," she murmured. "Me too."

The blind woman was deep in conversation with Oskar but broke it off when Komako called in. Both got to their feet, Oskar with a curious expression on his face. He looked, she thought, unhappy.

"You are worried about what is coming," said Miss Davenshaw, before Komako could speak.

"Yes," she replied.

She watched her old teacher glide smoothly through the unlit room, her fingers tracing a line across the surface of her desk. She stopped and picked up a book and returned and pressed it into Oskar's hands. She was not wearing her blindfold and her irises were opalescent. They were, thought Komako, stark and beautiful.

"You are both stronger than you know," said Miss Davenshaw. "You, Mr. Czekowisz, are a powerful caster. I have observed your growth these past months. Lymenion is a remarkable creature. The drughr would be right to treat you both with respect." She raised a hand to silence whatever mumbled reply Oskar might make. "They will *not* respect you, of course. You are a child, in their eyes. That will be useful to us. You will see how well-bound Lymenion has become, when he meets the drughr."

Komako put a hand on her friend's soft shoulder. He looked at her, afraid, but with a different kind of light in his eyes.

"And you, Miss Onoe? Are you afraid, also?"

Komako's brow furrowed. "I am."

"It is wisdom, to fear that which can destroy us. But to know yourself is a greater wisdom. You are the most dangerous of dustworkers," the older woman murmured, "more dangerous than you know. For you have been spared by the Spanish glyphic." She beckoned with her fingers and Komako came closer, took the older woman's hands. The skin was soft, very warm.

"I don't know how to fight them, Miss Davenshaw," she said. "I keep pretending like I do. But I don't."

"Oh, child. You will fight them with your heart. That is the one thing they lack."

Komako shrugged helplessly. "I don't know what that means. What does that mean?"

"You will know, when the time comes." The old woman's voice went deadly quiet. "Just remember, they are creatures of dust. Creatures of the orsine itself, twisted by the very substance of that world. Dust is your domain, child; you command the very thing they are made of."

Komako studied the lines at the older woman's eyes, the set of her thin lips, the delicate flared nostrils. "But it isn't the same, Miss Davenshaw. I've been in a drughr's presence. I can't . . . *command* a drughr."

"Perhaps. But you will feel its *pull* on you, child." The old woman's cadaverous cheeks were tight with some controlled emotion. Her eyebrows softened. "Remember: *you* may pull *on it*, in return."

There was a commotion, far down the corridor. Komako heard children's voices but for a long moment she ignored them. She held both of the older woman's hands in hers and then she stepped forward and hugged her, hugged her old teacher, this woman who had seemed so remote, so intimidating back at Cairndale, and who now had proved a kind of mother to them all. She felt the frail bones in the woman's spine, the ladders of her rib cage as she breathed. And then the sudden fierce embrace as the older woman hugged her back. Komako's hands closed, like flowers. She could hear Oskar, breathing.

"We can only do our best, child," Miss Davenshaw murmured into her ear. "Our best, and no more."

She thought of little Marlowe, abandoned in the land of the dead. She thought of Charlie, afraid of what his body was doing to him. Her eyes were wet.

Just then the footsteps in the hall grew louder and the door burst open. Little Michael was gasping breathless in the doorway, his hair wild.

"It's the drughr!" he managed. "At the front gate! It's here, Miss Davenshaw! Come *on!*"

Komako pulled back. Oskar was already at the door, adjusting his spectacles, gesturing for Lymenion to hurry. He called to Shona to run as fast as she could to Mrs. Ficke, to let her know to lock the chamber and open it for no one. "And then get back here, quick as a rabbit, okay? Go!"

Komako felt an ache bloom in her wrists as she drew the dust toward her, and ran past the gathering children, their pale faces emerging in doorways, their frightened eyes peering up at her, a sheet of black dust billowing out behind her like a cloak.

"Snuff the candles! Keep yourselves hidden!" she cried as she ran past. "Remember to assemble in the ballroom, if we cannot hold it!"

But when she threw herself forward, leaping the stairs three at a time, hurtling out the front door, she skidded to a sudden halt in the gravel drive. For it was not one drughr that stood at the gates, as if awaiting her challenge, but two.

They stood hunched and quiet at the very edge of the property, where the road became drive, but massive and thick with darkness in the settling dusk. There was the one she'd already seen, the flesh-caster, its tentacles stirring like weeds in a current, swaying on their slender stalks. Its shoulders were rolled forward and it leaned almost into its knees where it waited. But beside it stood another, a drughr she'd not seen before, thick around as a stone pillar, with four arms, and too many fingers on each shovel-like hand. She could see, at once, that it must be their clink, its antlered skull like a heavy boulder upon deeply mus-cled shoulders. It had almost no neck, so thick and broad was its chest. Its eyes, as they sought out hers, burned with a lightless fire that was blacker than even the darkest night.

Oskar and Lymenion had fanned out across the white gravel, Oskar looking impossibly small and soft against the monsters. Komako gritted her teeth, and held out her fists, and the dust came to her sweetly, gently, as if it longed to be close to her, to caress her. She let it tighten and ripple around her, lifting her hair.

The two drughr did not stir.

The dusk deepened; night crept in all around them.

Slowly Oskar crunched his way over to her, his eyes never leaving the creatures at the gate. "Uh, K-Ko?" he said under his breath. "Wh-what are they w-w-waiting for?"

But she didn't know. Her eyes scanned the carriage house and the remains of the ancient fountain below the wall. She glanced quickly back at the villa, at the rows of faces in the windows, peering out, frightened. She scanned the skies.

That was when they moved. It was so sleek and strange a movement that it seemed they simply went from being on one side of the gate, to the other; the darkness that was their form rippled and something in her eyes had trouble following what was happening.

She blinked sharply, tightening the dust that was swirling around her. And then she remembered what Miss Davenshaw had said, and she willed her eyes closed, and she fumbled uneasily outward, feeling for something, something dustlike, something that was coalescing and drawing apart with its own alien intelligence.

The dust.

The dust that was a part of the drughr themselves.

She felt it, as if an invisible rope extended between them, and she caught it in her hands. She drew her fists together as if to shackle them fast and felt the impossible mass at the far end of it, as if she were hauling a ship into shore, and she fell to one knee, gasping, and planted her fists hard down into the white gravel, screaming with the effort. Across the courtyard the massive drughr—the clink—fell heavily to one knee, also. Twisting and shuddering as if to break free. Then it raised its terrifying face, and roared in fury.

She could hold only the one. She opened her eyes and saw through a screen of her own swirling dust the second drughr, the flesh-caster, hurtle itself forward at Oskar.

He stood fast. His plump hands were in fists at his sides and he was leaning toward the creature as if into a strong wind and that was when Komako saw Lymenion crash into the drughr, sending it flying, scrabbling with its many claws, sliding through the gravel and colliding into the carriage house. But it rose up on its tentacles almost at once, shaking the rubble free, even as Lymenion seized two long mouthlike tentacles and snapped them backward, drawing the drughr inward, and then he enclosed one massive fleshly palm over the drughr's face, and began to crush.

The drughr's tentacles and claws were ripping at Lymenion's body, but they had no effect. At last the flesh giant twisted the drughr backward and threw it toward the gate. The gravel shook with the weight of the creature's landing.

She could hear Lymenion breathing, snorting like a horse, but the weight of the drughr she held was all she could manage. Already she was weakening; she could do nothing against the second.

And then, as it had before, the flesh-caster began to drag from the ditches and the grasses and the very earth itself, as if some song drew them near, the small animals of that place; it ripped their flesh from their skins and bones and the flesh reformed itself into tiny many-legged things and they threw themselves at Lymenion. The first leaped on his back and burrowed itself into his flesh and Komako could see, even in the dying light, how the flesh giant tensed and how something burst under his skin, spraying up into the twilight. But it had slowed him; a second, a third, soon a dozen small skittering fleshlets were crawling over him, into him, and he was staggering, bursting them inside himself, swaying with the effort.

And then the second drughr was running again, but running this time not toward Oskar or Lymenion, but toward Komako herself. It had figured out what she was doing.

Somehow she threw a wall of dust between herself and the drughr, and stumbled backward. And then Oskar was kneeling, and drawing the clumps of flesh out of Lymenion's body, drawing them with his hands outstretched, and forming them into a second body, humanoid, slender, and he sent this tottering against the drughr, its own handiwork repurposed. And the drughr screamed.

Something made Komako's blood go cold. She couldn't explain it; but she turned, her eyes scanning the villa grounds. It was like she could feel something there, a wrongness. She could still see, lined up at the windows, the pale faces of the little ones. Her eyes continued upward. Something massive and antlered was crawling across the villa roof. Her blood slowed.

It was a *third* drughr.

And then, as she watched, it rose up to its full height, a fiery red circle ablaze in its chest, and quickly the edges of that circle ate their way outward, devouring the silhouette, until it was gone, invisible.

A second passed, another. Then the tree out front swayed wildly, as if a massive weight had fallen into it; it swayed wildly and bent almost to the earth, then whipped back upward, released. Moments later the villa's front door exploded inward.

"Oskar!" she cried, in a sudden terror. "There's a third drughr! It's gone inside, after the children!"

Across the gravel drive, Oskar raised his face. A sheen of sweat was on his cheeks. Lymenion, tearing at the small fleshly creatures, roared.

But Komako didn't wait. She was already running, loosing the twists of dust behind her, letting the drughr she'd held struggle its way free.

The children, she was thinking. *No dear God not the children, not them—*

When she heard the screams begin inside the villa.

In the chill of the catacombs, Alice drew her collar close about her throat.

All around her a silence, heavy as stone, grew. The old wound in her side was burning with a cold fire. She pressed a hand to it, grimaced, hearing her boots scrape as she circled the orsine. It loomed gray and still, twisted in the torchlight like a lightning-blasted tree. Somewhere inside there lay a glyphic's heart, not safe to touch. Not unless little

Deirdre could—what was the phrase?—*unstick* it. Whatever the hell that meant. There were three acolytes standing back near the entrance, as if to guard her, but Alice paid them no mind. She'd not be hurried. Instead she walked the perimeter, a torch in her hand, passing the stacks of skulls and bones, lighting the little candles in their alcoves until the gallery glowed with light.

Charlie and Adra Norn still had not returned.

She didn't like it. But the kid was right, she thought: he could take care of himself. What could Adra Norn do to him that he couldn't just heal from and keep going?

Alice approached the orsine, allowing the faintest bit of wonder to creep in. It was all a bloom of madness, truth be told. Everything: talentkind, what those children could do, the monsters she'd seen with her own horrified eyes in the last months. What happened to Coulton. All of it. So if this really was a doorway to another world, a passage through to the land of the dead, who was she, Alice Quicke, to say otherwise?

"Ah, here you are" came a slow deep voice. "I feared you might have already departed."

Alice turned.

Adra Norn had entered the gallery. Charlie was not with her. She stood head and shoulders above the acolytes in their red hoods, her own head bare, her grooved features distorting as she passed through the torchlight, her white robes now red, now orange, now a deep yellow like the edges of a bruise.

The pain in Alice's side flared up again. She reached for Coulton's pistol in her pocket. The weapon might do little good against a woman who could heal from anything but it would feel damned great putting a bullet through her eye anyway.

"Where's Charlie?"

"Resting."

Alice knew when she was being lied to, or at least not told enough of the truth. But she said nothing. She watched warily as the woman she'd hated all her life came toward her, massive hands clasped in front of her. The woman's eyes were on the orsine.

"When my brother and I were elected to monitor the orsines, the drughr were still . . . human. Or mostly so. They had not yet been seduced by that which they'd been tasked to guard. This was shortly after the First Talent's defeat." Her voice was soft, calming. "Ah, I was still so young. I was simply grateful not to be sent to Scotland, to Alastair Cairndale's old manse. I never did envy my brother, having to live in such a haunted place. Cairndale's halls were always stained by its founder. You must have felt it, surely? A sinister presence, still there? A terrible place to bring young talents to. But what could be done? Henry did not choose the location of his orsine; and one must go where the orsine is. Or was."

Alice furrowed her brow. "He said you were a fanatic. He said your belief was greater than your compassion."

"Henry said that?"

"He said other things, too."

"Well. Brothers."

Alice glared, her face hardening. She squared her shoulders. "Why did you do it? Why did you walk through that fire, at Bent Knee Hollow? Why let us believe it was a miracle?"

"*You* never believed, I think."

"My mother did. All of those women did. You must have known they weren't talents. Why encourage them?"

"You would not understand."

Alice felt the blood loud in her ears. "Try me."

Adra Norn swept closer. She stared down at Alice with ancient eyes, her face suddenly grim. "I wasn't seeking talents, child. I was seeking the faithful. These women you see around me here are talents, yes. But they possess something more powerful than that. They are believers. They possess faith."

Alice scowled. "Bullshit. They're tools. You use them as you see fit."

"More than you know, perhaps. What of it?"

Alice didn't know what to say. She watched as the Abbess went to the nearest alcove, and snuffed out the candle there with her fingers. She drifted to the second, and did the same. Though she did not raise her voice it carried still to Alice with the same clarity.

"You have traveled a great distance, young Alice. You will be tired, I expect. Not only the journey by rail, and by steamer. There was the carriage overland in Sicily, before even you reached the port of Palermo, yes?"

Alice stared steadily at her, but her thoughts were racing. How much did this woman know?

"I am surprised, however, that you would leave the children. The littlest ones, I mean." Adra Norn turned, her eyes glittering in the half darkness. "Ah. What is that look on your face? Do not fear, Charles did not tell me about the villa. He did not need to. It is not easy to make a blind woman and her retinue of uncanny children pass through the world unnoticed. But," and she glided now to a third alcove, snuffing that candle too, "if I know of them, then others must also. Are you not afraid of the drughr coming for them?"

Alice glared. She wasn't going to answer and then she did. "We didn't leave them unprotected. We wouldn't do that. They're safe."

"Ah, yes. Your dustworker is with them. What is her name . . . Komako."

"Not just her. We have a weapon, a weapon even the drughr fear."

Adra Norn raised her eyebrows. "Oh?"

Alice saw the woman's surprise at that, and liked it. "Mrs. Harrogate is the one who found it. I saw it fight a drughr in London, it's fierce enough. It's what killed Jacob Marber. The drughr'll think twice before troubling the children with the keywrasse there."

Adra Norn froze. "Keywrasse?" she whispered.

"Yeah."

"You have the keywrasse?"

Alice allowed herself a cold smile.

"Oh, you fools," Adra Norn murmured. "You stupid, stupid fools. Do you know what you've done? That creature is not a *deterrent*. It is what the drughr *seek*."

"Yeah, well. It can handle itself."

"Against one drughr? Perhaps. But against two? Three?"

Alice shrugged. "You don't know the keywrasse."

"But I do know the First Talent." Adra Norn folded one hand inside the other, began twisting her fingers in suppressed anger. Her words were clipped, precise. "Did you never wonder what purpose its keys could serve? The drughr are servants of the First Talent, imprisoned inside the orsine. Tell me, young Alice: what do you imagine is needed to open that prison?"

Keys. That was what.

Alice swallowed. She knew not to trust this woman and yet knew too there was a truth in the Abbess's anger. Just then she felt a sudden sharp twinge in the wound at her side, as if the remnant of Jacob Marber's dust had sensed her stupidity, and was flaring with its own disapproval. She winced, reached inside her oilskin coat.

That was when she heard it: a soft hiss, almost a sigh, exhaling from far across the gallery. The three acolytes in their red robes seemed to suck themselves together in the doorway, as if squeezing together, their arms at weird angles. Their eyes were wide, their mouths open, making no sound. Then, all at once, they collapsed away, falling to the stone floor.

Adra Norn made a low sound in her throat, animallike.

Standing in the doorway, scarcely visible in the torchlight, was a woman, dressed all in black. A veil obscured her face. But the dress looked very old, high-collared and edged in black lace. She wore black gloves on her hands. Her shoulders were slight, her pale throat thin.

She lifted away the veil, glided forward.

Adra Norn strode to the middle of the gallery and held out her massive palms, as if to ward off some evil wind. "You," she said coldly. "I thought you were destroyed. They will be looking for you."

The woman in black paused. Dear God, she was as real as anything Alice had ever seen and yet she cast no shadow. Alice's throat filled with fear. It was like she couldn't swallow. And now she could see the woman's face, the unreal pallor of it, the deep-set eyes without any color at all. Adra Norn might not have spoken at all. For the woman was looking at Alice.

I can smell it in you, she whispered, her voice carrying. *But you are no talent. How is this possible?*

Alice flinched.

The wound in her side was throbbing. She pulled out Coulton's pistol and leveled it and fired. The bang echoed up off the limestone making a terrible racket. But the bullets passed through the stranger, harmless.

In a flash, Adra Norn threw herself forward. She moved swiftly and with a great power and seemed to double in size. But the stranger simply swatted her to one side, as if she were nothing, and the Abbess smashed into a wall of bones and lay still.

And then the woman in black began to change.

It was like the darkness of her old-fashioned dress elongated, crawled like smoke up over her face and arms, and she was growing, growing with it, massive and muscled and her skull was distending. Twin antlers twisted up into the gloom. Her arms turned long and simian, her hands clawed. She shifted her terrible glower upon Alice and her eyes were like twin coals of darkness, burning. That was when Alice, feeling a horror take hold in her, crumpling suddenly under the icy pain in her side, understood.

It was a drughr, the same drughr she had seen in London, all those months ago. The drughr that had fought the keywrasse, fled with Jacob Marber through a rip in the air.

But this time it had come for her.

Komako kicked her way inside, over the pieces of the villa doors, stumbling and skidding and getting back up.

Oskar was there in the gloom just behind her, his forehead glistening with sweat. He'd lost his spectacles and his wide face looked soft and vulnerable without them. "Go!" he called to her. "We've got this. We'll hold them as long as we can. Go!" Lymenion loomed up behind him in the doorway, an oozing silhouette. And then he balled up his fists and turned fiercely to block the carriage walk outside, the drughr there.

Komako didn't protest. She ran for the stairs. The villa was silent; the screaming of the children had ceased. Dread was filling her heart. She was afraid of what she'd find in the upper rooms. The little ones were so small, so ill-prepared to confront a drughr on their own. That had never been the plan. The monster would cut its way through them savagely, she knew.

She leaped the last stairs and crossed the landing and pushed open the door onto the interior hallway. The walls felt strange with all the candles doused. The hush was total. She forced herself to go still, to listen carefully.

The long corridor was very dark, its high ceiling lost in gloom. The doors to the children's rooms stood open.

Komako hesitated, lurking in a pool of shadow, straining to hear any sound, then took a cautious step forward. The floorboards creaked. She drew a rope of dust to her fist, scarcely daring to breathe. Something was twisted on the floor of the third doorway, in a pool of blood, too big to be a child.

It was the body of Miss Davenshaw.

"No, no no no," Komako whispered, kneeling in the gore, cradling the older woman's head. The sticky warmth seeped through her skirt.

Her eyes couldn't take it all in. She knew what she was seeing and yet her brain couldn't put it all together. She saw how Miss Davenshaw's leg had been taken off at the knee and how her left arm was crushed and how her head was turned the wrong way on her neck. She must have died quickly, instantly. Komako blinked back her tears, suddenly afraid for the littlest ones. Whatever had happened here had been awful. Then in the dim corner of the room she saw a second body, the body of Susan Crowley, her hair loosed from her bun and spread all around her like a pool of blood.

Komako got to her feet. Anger was in her now, a new anger that she didn't know what to do with. She crept slowly along the dark hallway, pushing open the half-closed doors with one hand, her other at the ready. The rooms had been torn apart, the beds upended, the walls scraped and scoured. But she saw no more bodies. She saw no drughr.

Grimly she rounded the corner. The hallway here went straight down to the gallery ballroom. There was a splintered pier table in the way and she stepped quietly over it, listening. Something was wrong. She paused, drawing the dust more fully to her, and turned her face from side to side in the gloom.

And that was when she felt it: a faint shirring on the crown of her head, the strands of her hair moving slightly. Like a breeze, but coming from *above* her.

Slowly in the darkness she dialed her face upward.

The drughr was splayed high up in the ceiling of the corridor, a great mass of darkness, impossibly long and vast, its antlered skull leering down at her, silent. It had no eyes that she could see. Its long sinewy arms, carved from the darkness, were pressed hard against the walls, its knees bent at strange angles to keep it suspended overhead. The small burning hole at its chest was pulsing, as if sucking at the very air itself. When it opened its jaws Komako saw the rows of tiny, very sharp teeth.

Everything happened very fast then.

Komako cried out, and threw herself backward. The drughr dropped heavily to the floor, twisting as it did so, its antlers gouging long divots in the walls as it fell. Already the burning hole was eating away at its edges, and even as Komako summoned the dust to her, the drughr was shimmering, vanishing away.

But it couldn't make itself disappear entirely. It was like Mrs. Ficke had said: they were not strong in this world, not yet. The drughr drew itself up to its full height, its skull crushing up against the ceiling. Komako clenched her fists.

The drughr fled.

Shimmering, it spun and careened off the walls and burst furiously through the gallery doors in an explosion of glass and wood.

Komako ran after it, her boots skidding on the villa floors. She tried to cry out, to warn the children what was coming, if they'd made it as far as the gallery, the gallery where they'd been instructed to make their stand. But she was gasping too much from the running and could not. She could feel the massive weight cleaving the air ahead of her, see the way the walls rippled through its form.

She stumbled into the gallery in pursuit. Her blood was loud in her ears. She scanned the half darkness, her eyes taking in the barricade of furniture the children had put up, taking in the little ones standing together, bravely, some holding hands, the little clinks making themselves strong, the little dustworkers forming their ropes of dust, all of their small faces big with fear. They were here; they were alive.

But the drughr paid them no mind. It tore past, a whirlwind of half-visible horror, and burst through the glass doors onto the terrace, sliding on the broken glass and crashing into the stone railing and bursting through it, into the gardens below.

In the dark ballroom, the littlest ones were whimpering, leaning into each other; a few of the bravest rose up over the barricade of toppled furniture. Komako had run to the shattered glass, staring out at the dark terrace, the gardens below. She could *feel* the drughr there, uncoiling, half-stunned. But her eyes could detect nothing.

She glanced back at the children. "I have to find it," she said. "Stay here. Oskar's holding the other two back. You've done well, but it's not safe yet—"

"Miss Komako?" little Shona asked, raising her hand in the gloom, improbably, as if in a schoolroom. "Where's Miss Crowley and Miss Davenshaw? Are they . . . dead?"

She could feel their eyes on her. She wanted to scoop them all up in her arms, tell them to hide. But she couldn't. That would be the more deadly. The broken glass clicked under her heels as she faced them.

She opened her mouth to tell them.

When all at once the floor under the children erupted, exploding outward, throwing each child backward in a great splintering of wood and nails and flesh and blood. The drughr Komako had pinioned in the carriage walk outside, the clink, had smashed its way upward from the rooms below, crashing into the ceiling and spinning furiously to one side to land, massive and antlered and heaving, in the ruin of small bodies.

Komako screamed. She screamed for the horror of it and the sudden fear that was in her, and she saw the little legs and feet standing out at bad angles, and the stillness of the children, and as if in slow motion she saw the drughr lift in its many arms the two nearest children and shake them horribly, shake them as if they were made of rags, and then smash them into the floor, and then crush and twist and smash whatever bodies it could find. All of it happened impossibly fast. Komako sucked all the dust she could find in that gallery to her and threw it, like a great wall of air, colliding into the drughr full force.

The drughr was lifted, its four muscled arms wheeling, its manifold claws ripping at the air, lifted upward and thrown terribly against the back wall. Plaster sifted from the molded ceiling. The villa shuddered. When the creature rose, snorting, onto its knuckles, Komako screamed again and sucked all the dust she could back toward her, the otherworldly dust inside the drughr, the normal greasy dust of her own world, all of it, yanked it back toward the shattered gallery windows behind her, to the terrace beyond, thinking only to remove the monster from the children, the little ones, whoever was still alive, and with a force she hadn't known was in her she dragged the struggling drughr across the floor, through the broken wall, and hurtled it spinning into the dark garden below.

For a long moment the villa was eerily still. Nothing moved.

Komako ran to the bodies, kneeled in the dust around the gaping hole in the floor. She was crying, going from child to child, wiping their faces, calling to them. But they were dead; all of them were dead.

Something broke in her then. It was like she'd held on so hard, for so long, to a part of her that frightened her, and all at once it burst free, this wild bottomless rage. It was like it was inside her, and outside of her at the same time, and she was shaking, feeling a deep wellspring of power rising through her that she'd not suspected before, some horrifying dark grief beyond all words, beyond all thought, as if her very talent were screaming out in pain, and she fell to her knees. She didn't want it. Her eyes were shut. But she was thinking of her sister, Teshi, all those years ago, whom she could not save, the little hiccuping laugh she had, ever since she was a baby, the warm smell of her skin when she'd hug Ko tight. And of poor Mr. Coulton, who'd take off his hat and run his hands through his thinning hair and blush before telling Ko that he was proud of her. And Mr. Bailey in Spain, awful Mr. Bailey who didn't deserve to die, and little Marlowe too, who'd never acted out of malice ever in his whole life, and all the little ones back at Cairndale slaughtered by Jacob in the fire, even Miss Davenshaw strewn in pieces back in the hall. And it was as if the dust was spiraling out from her at each beat of her heart, spiraling into all the little broken bodies in that gallery, their bent limbs and twisted necks, reaching out and enveloping them in outrage and cradling them close, Michael, Shona, Jubal, all of them, and she felt a blinding anger at what had been done, what was always done to the weakest and the smallest in this world. She staggered to her feet, the weight of it in her wrists, in her bones. And as she stood she *felt*—how?—the children all around her stir, too, stumble to their feet, paler in their torn clothing and drenched in dust and blood and yet not dead, though not alive either, and their teeth were long in their little sheaths, and there were three red lines rising at their throats, and somewhere in the back of her mind Komako knew, knew with an awful certainty what she had done, and yet she did not care. She stood in a vortex of dust and debris with her black hair wild about her and her sleeves crackling and she opened her eyes, and her small army of litches opened their terrible eyes also. And there was nothing in her heart but fury at the world as it was.

"Ko . . . mako . . . ," they whispered, as one.

Her eyes were streaming water and she had to keep running her sleeves over her face. But she would not look away; she would not.

"Ko . . . mako . . ."

Outside in the night garden the two drughr were approaching the nexus at the wash-house, slaughter in their hearts. Inside, on the villa's stairs, Oskar and Lymenion were fighting for their lives, desperate against the third drughr. In the darkness Komako could feel them all.

The dust was all around her, touching everything, leaving her gutted and raw and awash in pain. *No more*, she cried silently. *No more.*

And she swept through the ruined wall and down into the villa garden in pursuit, a terrifying queen, flanked by her litch-children. Their coming was like the winds of death.

40

THE MANY
OUT OF THE ONE

The shadow prison of Cairndale Manor was quiet. Its walls creaked softly. Marlowe saw the new fear in Dr. Berghast's face as he stood over the empty bed, and he shrank from it.

"He should be here," Berghast was murmuring. "The First Talent. He should be here."

He put his gloved hand on the rumpled bedclothes as if to reassure himself of their reality, the broken plates at his wrist clicking softly. His mouth was twisted in horror. Then he crossed the small bedchamber and peered out of the window at the mists in the land of the dead.

"Dr. Berghast?" Marlowe whispered. He looked around at the walls, afraid. "Is he in here, with us?"

Berghast turned, nodded. "Most certainly. Somewhere. But he is still weak." The old man ran a hand over his shorn scalp, his eyes bright. "I can feel him. He's in here with us, hungry. I had not realized . . . All these years, the drughr have been feeding young talents to him, strengthening him, bringing him out of his sleep. All those carykk we have seen, his victims . . . There were so many. So many. I did not know." Berghast turned the blade in his hand, studying the glint of its edge. "But we are in here with him, now. And his drughr are not. We have the advantage, child."

Marlowe swallowed. "But what if he . . . what if he gets out, Dr. Berghast?"

"It is not possible. Not without the last key to the door. And that has been lost for centuries."

"But the carykk get out. You said he eats them, and we saw them out there . . ."

"The carykk are not living creatures, child. They are liminal. They must be able to . . . pass the wards, somehow. But the drughr cannot. We cannot. And Alastair Cairndale most certainly cannot."

"How do we find him?"

Berghast smiled coldly. "We? We do not. He will find *you*, child. This house will bring you to him."

"Because I'm different."

"Because you are different, yes."

Marlowe thought about the maze of rooms, the woman in white, her rising fury. He shuddered. He didn't want to go back through it all again. But then he thought of Charlie, and Komako, and Ribs, and all of them, and what would happen to them if the First Talent were freed. He had to, if he wanted to keep them safe.

"Is he very awful to look at?" Marlowe asked. "Is he as scary as the drughr?"

"What he is, and how he appears, will not be the same thing, child. Whatever you see, do not trust the sight of it. Trust what you know. Trust what is good."

"Okay," said Marlowe. But he didn't really understand any of that.

He just wanted to know if he was going to be afraid. "Dr. Berghast? What can a knife do to hurt him? If he's already awake, I mean?"

Berghast slid the knife back into the rags at his waist. "He can still bleed, child. He will be weak. And even a haelan will die, if his head is taken from his shoulders."

Marlowe's eyes grew wide. "You want to cut off his head?" he whispered.

"I want to end this," said Berghast grimly. He took Marlowe's face in his hands, leaned in close. "Let the house guide you. Can you feel it? It *wants* to help you."

Marlowe blinked. He could feel it there, like a third person, at the edge of his vision, waiting.

He went back out through the red door, hesitated. The corridor was gone; he was in a small tack room, with leather bridles and straps hung up on the walls. He passed through a low door into a cold room, with barrels of rotting vegetables, the floor slick underfoot, and went up a flight of stairs. Berghast was just behind him, quiet as an adder. He entered a long dining room, a polished table with a dozen or more chairs. A clouded mirror on the far wall. It seemed almost as if the house itself was leading him onward, further. Through a dimly lit pantry, down a carpeted hall, to another red door.

"Here," Berghast whispered. "He is through here. I am sure of it. When I raise my knife against him, you must not watch. Do you understand? It will not be for a child to see."

"Okay."

"Good. Now: open the door."

But Marlowe hesitated. "Dr. Berghast? I'm afraid."

Berghast's eyes flashed. "There is no time for that. Open the door. Let us finish this."

Marlowe found himself on a narrow balcony, overlooking a long, dim solarium. Dark polished mahogany panels, interrupted by towering leaded windows. Terracotta pots, with dead and desiccated plants lining the floor below. Shelves with more dead plants. The ceiling was beamed with panels of glass fit between. He moved slowly to the railing, peered down. Gray flagstones, a thick carpet running in the middle. The thin mists of the land of the dead drifting past the glass. He felt Berghast creep past, onto the carpeted stairs.

It wasn't until they'd reached the base of the stairs that Marlowe realized they weren't alone. There, at the far end of the room, half-obscured by the dead plants, was a figure. Kneeling at the glass. And Marlowe knew somehow, without having to ask, that they'd found who they'd been seeking.

Alastair Cairndale. The dreaded First Talent.

He was not tall. He was bearded and kneeling at the garden window, head bowed as if in prayer. He wore a yellowed nightdress, with buttons down the left side, and there was some sort of runic writing all down the back of it. His hair was white and fell in greasy snarls past his shoulders. In the mist outside, Marlowe could see a second figure, with one hand outstretched, palm pressed to the glass too. There was something pitiful and lonely in the gesture, and Marlowe's heart ached to see it.

But then he recognized that figure—the man in black with no eyes, the drughr glyphic who had chased them in the courtyard—and at the same moment Alastair Cairndale turned, and raised his face, and Marlowe sucked in his breath.

He had been mutilated. There was old blood from the old man's mouth all in his white beard, staining it, as if he'd poured a brown soup all down his front. His lips had been sewn shut with a black thread. His eyes had been torn out, and a black blood had streaked from the raw sockets, over his cadaverous cheeks. He turned his face this way and that, as if sensing some presence, feeble, unsure.

He was not terrifying. He was a broken thing, punished to the point of cruelty.

Berghast did not hesitate. The knife was already in his hand. He moved with a predatory silence, swift and vicious, a ripple of rags. As he crept down the room the drughr outside began to bang at the glass, a steady quick banging that was full of warning. Berghast did not slow. Marlowe knew he was supposed to look away but he didn't. Berghast rose up in front of the First Talent, gripping the hilt of the knife in both hands, the black plated glove clinking, and he stabbed fiercely, quickly, into the ancient man's heart. The old man gasped. Then Berghast seized Alastair Cairndale's hair with the gloved hand and yanked his head back, exposing the throat, and grimly he began to saw away at the neck.

Marlowe started to cry. It was so terrible. So terrible.

Blood was everywhere. The poor old man, whose lips had been sewn shut, made a pitiful muffled groaning sound, as his hands fluttered in the air.

But then the First Talent's hands reached up, slowly, unhurried. One folded over the wrist that held the knife and, with a delicate gentleness, drew the blade away. The other took Berghast by the throat and lifted him up off the ground, so that he gasped and struggled.

The blade fell to the floor. Marlowe, frozen with fear, didn't move.

And then the First Talent reached up, still unhurried, and with his long old man's fingers he plucked one of Dr. Berghast's eyeballs from its socket, and inserted it into his own. And then he took the other eye.

Berghast was screaming. The First Talent dropped him and he fell in the mess of blood, his hands at his face. But Alastair Cairndale was not finished with him yet. He blinked slowly and rolled his eyes as if to find his focus and then he peered down at Dr. Berghast, and kneeled in front of him, and he took the man's jaw in one hand. With his other he reached into Berghast's mouth, and pulled out his tongue by the root. And then he picked apart the stitches at his own lips, and worked the man's tongue into the gaping hole where his had been, and then he rose and turned and left Berghast writhing on the ground.

He looked at Marlowe with Dr. Berghast's eyes. Marlowe, still on the stairs, one hand on the banister, shining his brilliant blue shine. Marlowe's face was wet with tears.

The First Talent smiled, his teeth bloodied.

"Ah," he said, in a soft voice. "Much better."

In the silent catacombs, Jeta pressed a palm flat to the wall, feeling its cold stone, trying to quell the sickness that was rising in her. There were so many bones. Her head was throbbing. Around her, the skulls of the ancient dead rattled and shivered.

She was alone.

That was almost the worst part of it. That the drughr would leave her, abandon her without word or warning. She gritted her teeth and forced herself to stumble painfully forward. Somewhere in these tunnels red-robed acolytes with talents of their own were hunting her. And Charlie, infected with the dust. And the orsine itself. Maybe the drughr had found a way through, maybe she would come back for Jeta. Jeta took another few steps forward. Maybe. There came a faint clatter as several small bones dislodged from their alcoves and were dragged behind her, like leaves in a wind.

The torch she held guttered. She forced herself to lift it higher, to keep it lit. The darkness down here was absolute; she'd be lost forever, her own bones joining the stacks. A fitting place to die, for one such as her.

You're not going to die, she told herself angrily. *Not here. Not like this.*

She forced herself to continue. She didn't know how long she walked through the tunnels. Galleries with low ceilings and strange amalgamations of bones in the dim light would give way to long roughly hewn quarries, to sudden steep staircases carved from the stone. A sense of increasing dread came over her.

And, gradually, a different kind of pull was leading her forward. The pull of living bones. She followed it deeper and saw, at last, a faint firelight glowing ahead. It was an ancient door, bolted into the limestone itself; torches burned on either side; in front of the door stood three acolytes in red, their hoods drawn low.

They were watching her approach.

And no wonder; a carpet of bones was clattering softly along in Jeta's wake. She staggered into the pool of light and saw the acolytes' alarm, saw the woman on the left draw back her sleeves, baring her wrists for some sort of attack. She felt the bones in the other two thicken, grow heavy as they condensed their flesh down.

Jeta didn't hesitate, despite the fog in her brain. She threw her hands in front of her, pulling at the bones all around her. Feeling the bits of bone and skull hurtle forward, a rain of sharp missiles, impaling the acolytes where they drew themselves up. At the same time she felt for the ankles of the nearest clink, crushing the talus and the calcaneus into powder, so that the woman screamed and fell to the stone floor. The second clink was thundering toward her and Jeta swayed and climbed her talent along all the cervical vertebrae and just lashed out, splitting them, and she felt the clink go down heavily in the torchlight. The third acolyte lay already dead, a splinter of bone sticking out of her eye.

Jeta, gasping, reached out with her talent for the clink with the broken ankles. And snapped her neck cleanly. Then she stumbled forward, toward the door. The bones all around her sifted like sand in a wind. There would be no concealing these bodies, she saw. *To hell with it*, she thought.

And pushed past, opening the thick door.

The chamber beyond was still. A domed ceiling, shrouded in darkness. A weak torch was burning in a bracket near her and its light etched the skulls in their stacks along the wall. There were two bodies slumped against the wall in red robes. Already dead. Her eyes took in the signs of struggle, the dark stone well with its chain-wheel in the shadows. When she stepped softly inside all the skulls on one wall turned slightly, as if drawn to her, as if tracking her entrance with their empty sockets.

She heard a strangled noise in the darkness. There in the shadow: a movement. It was the urchin from the Falls, Micah, in a red robe with the hood cast back, the sleeves rolled high off his wrists. She didn't understand what she was seeing at first. He looked strangely contorted, alone and wrestling with the empty air. His blade was bloodied. Then Jeta became aware of a red stain in the air, hovering in front of him, like a blur of mist; then she felt the unmistakable pull of a second set of bones, and knew it for what it was.

A talent. A turner, gone invisible.

Micah called across. "Shit," he spat. "If it ain't Ruth's bloody pet, out of London." He waved his long blade at her. "Easy, you. Walk the blazes back or I'll cut this un's throat, I will. How'd you even get out of the Falls? Got more lives than a cat, I reckon."

Jeta felt her knees go weak. There were too many bones. She forced herself to stay upright. "Where's the other one?" she said grimly. "Where's Charlie Ovid?"

"Up your bleedin arse," grinned Micah. "You got no idea what you walked into, do you. You reckoned old Claker was dangerous? The Abbess cooks up twelve of his sort for breakfast of a Sunday." He gave a low whistle. "Them acolytes of hers ain't nothin. Wait till she comes back."

"Where . . . is Charlie Ovid?" she said again.

"Down the bloody well!" came a girl's voice. It was the turner, still invisible, struggling again in Micah's grip. "They's drownding him, is what!" she cried out. "You got to pull him up! Please!"

Jeta looked again at the chain disappearing into the still black waters and at the limestone well in the darkness and she understood. Charlie Ovid was a haelan. He could not drown. He'd been sunk by Micah and his mistress to keep the dust hidden.

Micah shook the invisible girl in his fists. "You goddamn talents," he snarled. "Always reckon you're the ones in control." He glared at Jeta. "How's all these bones doin for you, down here? You feelin a wee bit peaky?"

She wavered. She felt the pull of bones, all of them shifting, rattling around her as if the earth trembled. Her head spun.

That was when Micah moved. He stabbed at the invisible girl twice, then dropped her and threw himself impossibly fast across the chamber, colliding hard with Jeta's knees. She fell backward, and the urchin was on top of her, his blade lacerating her hands and arms where she tried to keep him off. Her slippery hands found his wrist, tried to hold the blade off. Micah leaned his weight in.

"I never bloody liked your Ruth," he hissed. "An I never bloody liked you neither."

Suddenly all the rage and pent-up frustration she'd felt was loosed; time seemed to slow down; she felt the outer edge of each and every bone in Micah's slender body. She screamed.

And *pushed.*

She pushed on his bones with a terrible power and for a split second Micah's eyes grew wide in shock. And then it was like the back of his body was unzipped, and all the bones that were in him burst backward, out, up at an accelerated speed, trailing lines of gore as they flew. Jeta's eyes were closed. She heard the clatter and rattle of the bones striking the ceiling of the chamber, striking the walls, shattering. *Every bone in his body.* She felt the deflated flesh of the urchin collapse over her, a sleeve of gore, pouring with blood. The soft organs inside were still warm and heavy and contracting. She peeled it, horrified, away, like a wet blanket, and clambered to her feet. Shuddering. Appalled at what she'd done. The gore on her face and in her braids and slathered all over the coin at her throat was already cooling, congealing.

On the far side of the chamber, the chain-wheel was being turned in invisible hands. And then the head and shoulders and struggling chest of the young man appeared, and was lifted up, dripping, out of the dark well, and the invisible girl was steering the gasping figure of Charlie Ovid down to the floor.

His eyes were roving. As the chains loosened he fumbled for the girl, found her arm. "Ribs? Ribs, it was . . . the Abbess. She . . . she never meant to help us . . ."

The girl's voice sounded exasperated. "I *know*, Charlie. I been here the whole time. I followed you here. I *saw* it, Charlie."

The torchlight in the chamber was low. Jeta stood very still, her heart hammering. It was him. It was the young man her drughr had hunted, all these weeks.

He gripped her invisible wrists and held them out and the blood seeping from them was evident. The girl sucked in her breath.

"What's happened to you?" he demanded. "Are you hurt?"

"Well that's usually what blood means," her voice replied tightly. "Aw, now, it's all right. I ain't like to keel over just yet. It were that bloody wee kid with the knife what done it."

"Micah . . . was at the Falls . . . Where is he?" Charlie Ovid got up off his knees, scanning the shadows. His teeth were gritted in pain. Jeta could see the marks on his skin, the tattoos of dust swirling there, as if alive, shining with a faint light. That was when he caught sight of the bloody mess that had once been the urchin, Micah, his shattered bones fanned out across the floor, Jeta standing drenched in his gore.

"You!" he whispered, stumbling to his feet.

Jeta saw him then, really *saw* him, not as the drughr did, not as just a vessel for the corrupted dust, as something to be used. Instead she saw the young man he was, the way he moved to protect his friend, the fear that was in him and the pain but how it wouldn't stop him, wouldn't get in the way of what he needed to do. And she felt suddenly, again, that old loneliness she'd felt all her life, but now without the anger, without the hatred of other talents who'd been taken to the safety of Cairndale, to find each other, that hatred cultivated by Ruth and by Claker Jack and even, she understood, by the drughr in its own subtle way. Now there was only her own awareness. She'd wanted friendship all her life, and never found it. She wouldn't get in the way of these two.

She held out her hands, black and sticky with blood. The knife cuts were painful. "I'm not here to hurt you," she said, taking a careful step back. She could hear the pleading in her own voice. "Please. Just come with me. Talk to her. You'll see, you'll understand. Will you?"

The young man was shaking his wet head. He was shivering. He looked desperately at the air all around him. "Ribs? What's she talking about?"

"Damned if I know," said the invisible girl. "But she's what helped get you out. She's all right."

"The hell she is. She's the bone witch from London." He stared hard at her. "How are you here?"

Jeta took an uncertain breath. "The drughr," she said softly. "I came with the drughr. It's her dust you have in you. She needs it."

The limestone chamber was quiet. Her blood moved in her ears. The walls flickered in the torchlight.

"Jesus," whispered the young man. "It's like Jacob Marber, all over. She's under its spell, Ribs."

"She ain't like Jacob. I wouldn't be standing here, if she was."

Jeta had backed up, against the cold wall. Her shoulders left red smears where she leaned. She rubbed at her temples, dizzy, keeping her eyes on Charlie Ovid. She didn't know what to say.

"The dust is inside me," he said grimly. "It can't get out. I'm going into the orsine to save Mar. My friend. I think . . . I think that's why it's in me. Why it bonded to me. I won't give it to you. Or to her."

"That's what she wants it for, too."

"You can't trust a bloody drughr," said the invisible girl. "You don't know what she wants."

Jeta hesitated. "She's . . . not like that. She's so sad."

They looked at each other for a long moment. In the firelight lay the bodies of dead acolytes, bones shattered to powder, gore slick and shining blackly.

"Uh, Charlie?" called the girl, Ribs. "We got to go. There's like to be more jills comin down here soon. We got to get to the orsine. We got to find Alice."

The young man nodded. Ran a hand over his face, wiping away the water. Then he crossed the chamber in his dripping clothes. His boots left wet prints. Jeta felt her heart sink. She knew she should try to stop him, try to contain him. Summon the drughr to her, somehow. But she didn't.

At the exit, his silhouette stopped.

"We all know what it's like to be alone," he said quietly. "You don't have to be. My friend, Mar . . . he'd tell you it's a choice. That you can choose what kind of person you want to be." He breathed for a moment. "He'd say, everybody deserves a chance to be better."

Jeta studied the torn body of the urchin. Her skirts were sticky with blood. She thought of her life, all of the terrible things she'd done. "I don't think that's true," she said. "Not everybody."

"Charlie!" called the voice of Ribs.

"I didn't either," he said. "But Mar's got a way of making you see things differently." He reached out and took the torch from its bracket and in the bloom of light his face looked heavy with regret and sadness. "Come with us," he said suddenly. "We could use your talent. Mar's not saved yet."

Jeta blinked, swallowed. Something lifted in her chest, like a sudden bright hurt. She was surprised by what she felt, the strange warmth inside her.

"Okay," she whispered.

Back at the villa, Komako ran for the wash-house, the night air prickling in her skin. She knew the keywrasse would fight with a terrible ferocity. But she didn't think it could stop two drughr from reaching Deirdre, from opening the poor girl's throat. All around her in the darkness scrabbled her small pale litches, her little ones, the children she'd sworn to keep alive. She could *feel* them, a faint pressure at the back of her skull, their muffled voices in her head, whispering unnaturally. She thought of her sister, all those years ago. Her eyes were stinging. She ground her teeth and ran harder.

Ducked under trees, leaves scraping her cheeks and hair. Kicked through snarls of bushes. Circled the fountain, leaped over the stone benches. Praying she was not too late, praying the child Deirdre would be all right.

Now she could hear the sounds of fighting. The keywrasse screamed, a high wild sound, and ahead of her somewhere a drughr roared back. The wash-house materialized out of the darkness, gray and narrow. The barrels were overturned. A window had been broken. She kicked through the door that hung askew on one hinge as something enormous crashed below. They were fighting in the underground chamber. There came a whoosh, almost like a flame catching; the keywrasse screamed in fury again. Komako could hear Mrs. Ficke, shouting.

She didn't slow. She threw herself down the stone stairs, nearly falling, seeing the flickering lamplight below and the dance of shadows within it. The children were at her heels, silent, running steadily, their claws clicking on the stone.

And then, moments before she burst into the chamber, all sound ceased. The fighting went still. And Komako stumbled, her heart pounding, into the aftermath, trying to make sense of what she saw.

She was too late. There were no drughr. The keywrasse, too, was gone. The chamber stood in disarray, its books torn and strewn about the floor, wood splintered all around, the iron lamp-standards bent and twisted. A fire was burning in an alcove where a lantern had overturned. Blood had sprayed up along the walls, over the carved incantations.

Stooped against the altar was Mrs. Ficke, her long blade dripping with some viscous tar. She held her left side gingerly, and Komako could see blood between her fingers. Her skin was gray but her eyes were bright with anger. Behind her lay the glyph-twisted girl, Deirdre, in a great riot of golden blossoms and gnarled roots and branches, her eyes still closed peacefully, her chest rising and falling.

She was uninjured; she was safe.

Komako shook her head, trying to understand. "Mrs. Ficke?" she called. "Mrs. Ficke? What's happened? Where's the drughr?"

"Ach, they were two," the old alchemist said. Her face creased in confusion. "Two drughr."

Komako still had a thick rope of dust encircling her fists. She glared swiftly from side to side. "Where are they? Where did they go?"

"They didn't touch Deirdre, not at all," Mrs. Ficke murmured. She slumped suddenly against the altar, then steadied herself. Komako took a step closer. "Paid her no mind, child. Twas the keywrasse they come for. They opened some kind of a . . . a door. A door to the other world, it was. They took the keywrasse through it."

Komako blinked, her heart still racing. She wasn't sure she'd heard right. "They *took* the *keywrasse?*"

"Aye." Mrs. Ficke winced and looked at her hand with its blood and then pressed it back against her side. "But tis done, at least. The glyphic's heart in Paris, the orsine . . . Deirdre's stopped its heart. Tis done.

Our Charlie can go through it, he can go find that boy. Marlowe." The old alchemist squinted tiredly past Komako, to the small figures still in darkness behind her on the stair. "Is that the wee ones with you? But what's happened to them? What—"

Komako flinched, all of her outrage and dread rising again inside her. She held on to the anger like it was the only thing she had left and she started to explain but couldn't. She just couldn't. She turned to go. Oskar was still out there. Oskar and Lymenion and the third drughr.

But Mrs. Ficke made a strangled noise in her throat. The old woman's grizzled face was glistening in the candlelight, wet with sudden tears.

"Ach, child," she whispered. "What did you do? *What did you do?*"

41

LIKE WIND IN A HOLLOW

Alastair Cairndale turned at the window, facing Marlowe.

He was very calm. A sheet of scarlet blood had stained the upper half of his nightdress where Berghast had tried to cut away his head; his beard was matted and sticky with it; his eyes—Berghast's eyes—were hard and cold. At his feet, Berghast writhed, blinded, his mouth pouring blood.

"I so seldom get guests," Lord Cairndale was saying. "You will have to forgive my appearance. Well, *you* will, child, at least. Your companion here will not mind it, I think."

Marlowe stared in horror, eyes wide.

Lord Cairndale squatted next to Berghast. He slid the artifact glove from Berghast's fingers, exposing the limp blackened hand, twisted now in pain. The empty glove clicked softly. Lord Cairndale turned it with interest in the faint light, studying it, and then he set it aside on the ancient carpet. His fingertips slipped into Berghast's chest, as if into shallow water; Berghast grunted in pain. Cairndale closed his new eyes, taking a long deep breath. He seemed perfectly calm.

But the skin at Berghast's face and throat began to darken, began to suck up against his bones. A blue shine was emanating from his chest where the First Talent had pierced him. He was coughing, choking badly.

"Ah, a haelan," murmured the First Talent. "Of course. Alas, your talent will not help you overly much, here. Talents do not work well inside this . . . abode of mine. Which is why I must thank you for the gifts of sight and speech. I have been without, for too long. But you are not only a haelan, yes? There is something else I taste . . ." Alastair Cairndale withdrew his fingertips from Berghast's flesh. His eyes widened. "Oh, you have been busy. A drughr? You have drained one of my drughr? Fascinating. I imagine there is a story, there . . ."

He wiped his fingers, gently, in the rags of Berghast's chest. Then he made a tsking sound. On the other side of the window, the blind drughr stood very still and dark in the fog.

"You thought to kill me while I slept," he said softly. "What did you wish to do? Did you wish to protect the talent world? You wished to slay the terrible monster, and protect the little children? Is that it?"

Berghast made a gurgling noise.

"Please!" Marlowe shouted at last. "Please! Leave him alone!"

The First Talent paid him no mind. "Did you not realize that if you kill me, you destroy them too? All of your precious talents? Why do you think I was put in this prison, rather than executed, all those years ago? Do you imagine it was *mercy*? Do you imagine any of those who sat in judgment on me wished to *spare* me?"

Marlowe's hands were balled up into fists. But he didn't dare go any closer.

"And if they—your betters—did not dare to kill me, what arrogance could have brought you here, into my house, to commit such a deed?"

Berghast was groaning, trying to protest.

Alastair Cairndale reached out one bony finger, lifted Berghast's bloodied chin. "What is that? What are you saying?" He brought his ear close to Berghast's lips. "A lie? No, I assure you, it is quite true. You would have done well to have listened to the old stories. They were not lies. I *am* the Dreaming. I *am* what connects all talents. Had you destroyed me, you would have severed all talents from their source. Talentkind would be no more."

Berghast groaned.

"Isn't it *wonderful*, that you failed? Aren't you *grateful?*"

Now Alastair Cairndale looked across at Marlowe, his eyes the haunted eyes of Henry Berghast. He stood smoothly. "My life is, quite simply, of greater importance. To feed it, to help it heal . . . why, that is a *kindness* to all those you might love. You, little one. You are here because you fear for those you love, are you not?"

Marlowe was shaking.

"Do you love this man? Is it love that has brought you here? Is he your father? A mentor? A friend?"

Marlowe took a shivery step backward, up the stair. Then a second. He knew he shouldn't run, shouldn't leave Dr. Berghast, that he needed help, but he couldn't do it. He couldn't.

The older man crossed to a small pier table with a blackened aspidistra. He ran his fingers over it. "Not love, then. Something else. Fear?"

That was when Marlowe started to shine. The blue shining came up out of him, between the wrappings and the rags on his arms and his hands. The First Talent went still.

"What is this? What are you? A part of the Dreaming, and yet not a talent . . ." He curled a long finger. "Come closer. I wish to see you."

"No," whispered Marlowe.

A flicker of anger appeared on the First Talent's face. "You resist. How is that possible?"

That was when Marlowe turned, and ran. He burst through the door and found himself in a strange hall, and he ran to the nearest door and threw it open. It was an old parlor, the wood dark and splitting, and seated calmly in a wingbacked chair by the fire was Alastair Cairndale.

"Child. Why do you run?" he asked.

Marlowe ran back out. He looked over his shoulder but the First Talent made no move to pursue him. And yet when he ran through the next door he found himself in a dining room. Alastair Cairndale stood behind the farthest chair, facing him, his face composed.

"Child," he said again. "There is no running from me here. Come, do not—"

Marlowe ran back out. He ran the length of the dim hall, his footfalls muffled on the thick carpet, and rounded a corner and found himself in a long gloomy library. A fire was burning in a grate along one wall. Shelves of leather tomes loomed up into the darkness. Marlowe, breathing hard, ducked around behind a shelf, drew his knees up to his chest. Make yourself small, make yourself safe. He stuffed a fist in his mouth to quiet his breathing.

Moments later he heard slow footsteps.

"This is becoming tiresome," said Alastair Cairndale, an edge in his voice. "Do come out. You are not hidden, child."

Marlowe waited. The silence seemed to stretch out around him. He felt so little, so helpless. His heart was hammering with fear. But after a moment he got to his feet, his eyes wet, and he stepped out.

Alastair Cairndale stood in the shadows, staring directly at him.

"Better," he said softly. "Now. What is your name, child?"

"Marlowe," he whispered.

"Tell me, Marlowe. Why does the dust answer you? Why does the orsine shape itself to you? I can see how you are moving these rooms around, hoping to deceive me . . ."

He came forward in his bloodstained gown, his long white beard discolored, his fingers oddly thick and red. Marlowe could see the waxen look of his skin now, this close, could hear the faint sticky give of the wound at his throat.

The horrible man's words reminded him of what Dr. Berghast had said, how this house would listen to him, how it *wanted* to, and he crushed his fists tight and he thought of the woman in white, the woman they had seen in those strange dreamlike loops upstairs. And suddenly she was there, at the far bookshelf, removing a green leather volume and leafing through the pages, and Alastair Cairndale froze.

"Callista?" he murmured. "No. You are not here. It cannot be. It is the dream . . ."

The woman looked up, her eyes clear. But she looked *through* him, as if he wasn't there; then she tucked a strand of hair behind one ear and walked into the gloom and was gone.

The First Talent turned slowly back to Marlowe.

"You did that," he said quietly. He was not angry. "Your talent works here. How?"

But then, before Marlowe could think how to reply, with an impossible quickness, suddenly the First Talent was there in front of him, reaching down with his swollen hands, gripping Marlowe hard on the sides of his shining head, as if to crush his skull. His eyes did not look right, up close. The irises were blue with the reflected light of Marlowe. There was blood in the ancient man's teeth. He smelled like the grave.

"You are what woke me," he hissed. "You were in my dream . . . but you were not a part of it. I see that now. What a gift your companion has brought me. You are not a child, are you? You are something more . . . Ah. *Ah.*" His expression darkened with sudden understanding. Marlowe could see the veins in the whites of Berghast's ripped-out eyes. "But you do not know, do you? You do not know what you are."

"I'm just . . . ," Marlowe said, struggling. "I'm just me . . ."

The First Talent's hands crushed his skull harder. Marlowe's legs kicked. "Oh, but you are more than that, little one. You are what they built the orsine for. Has no one told you?" His voice was almost too soft to hear. "All this was built to hold you, not me. To contain you, not me. I am just the vessel. But you?" Alastair Cairndale smiled. "You are the sixth, the greater part, what they stole from me. You, child, are my talent."

Marlowe stared at him, horrified.

"We are one. We are what they fear. And we will be whole, again."

But then Marlowe reached up, just as he had at the edge of the orsine all those months ago, he reached up with his hands and clasped the ancient man's wrists and he felt the flesh bubble and sear and begin to melt under his grip. The smell was awful, horrifying.

The screams of the First Talent came out guttural and strange, shrieking like a steel cable flailing through a winch like he'd heard in the circus when he was younger. The old man tore free of Marlowe's grip and stumbled backward, holding his hands up before him. The stumps were dripping like molten wax, the clawed hands dissolving, dripping onto the floor.

The fire in the grate guttered. The First Talent's gaunt face was aghast. He stared at Marlowe and there was fear and horror and pain but also something else, some dark shadowy thing overtaking him, something very much like hunger.

And then he started forward.

42

THE KIDS AT THE END
OF THE WORLD

In the villa gardens, in Sicily, Komako, desperate, was running.

She was running from Mrs. Ficke and the glyph-twisted girl and the ruin of the Agnoscenti chamber, running from the accusations in the old alchemist's words, running from the guilt and horror she herself felt at what she'd done. Back up the stone steps, through the shed, out into the coming night, the garden dense and still in the gloom. She ran down the path, toward the darkened villa, fearing for Oskar.

And the litches, untiring, ran with her.

There were roots and creeping vines snaring her ankles as she ran and then suddenly she slowed, stopped. She didn't know what compelled her. But she turned, and started running into the dark gardens. And as she hurried toward the center she smelled the unmistakable reek of Lymenion, somewhere up ahead in the quiet.

She came out at the clearing with the stone fountain, the narrow benches under the lemon trees. Her lungs were on fire from the running.

The drughr had Lymenion pinned by the throat, and its tentacles were peeling the flesh from his legs in long strips, as if peeling away the skin of a fruit. Two of the benches had been overturned and under their broken stone she could see Oskar. He raised his head weakly at her arrival.

She should have felt fear. Any drughr powerful enough to overwhelm Lymenion would not be stopped by a dustworker. And yet she didn't; she raised her chin and felt the litch-children move as one, surging forward at her command. And then they were swarming the drughr, spinning lightly and smoothly around its tentacles and four muscular arms, dancing across its back. She watched it catch and throw her litches one by one into the darkness and yet they came hurtling back, their little teeth bared, their nails sharp. Two caught it by the throat, three swung by each arm. Slowly, heavily, they dragged the monster down to its knees, pinioning the toothed tentacles to the ground.

Komako watched all this with a terrible fury. She felt scoured out, only part human herself. There was no mercy in her. She could feel the eerie dust that was inside it, sifting through its bulk, like dark sand in a sieve. A thickness at the back of her skull was filling with a strange and beautiful music, a music coming from the dust itself. She'd never felt so powerful, so unfettered. Gradually she understood it had something to do with the children, her litches, that each was like a kind of mirror she had polished to a shine, a mirror reflecting her own talent back toward her, amplifying it, so that the power that was in her was staggering, unlike anything she'd known.

She walked slowly up to the struggling drughr. Something in the way it shifted its antlered skull, twisting its face as if to query what manner of creature she might be, gave her pause.

It was afraid.

Afraid of *her*.

Then Komako raised her two hands, fingers spread wide, and pressed them against the drughr's chest. There was a slight resistance, like the surface of a jelly; then her fingertips pushed through, and her hands dipped into the drughr's flesh, all the way to her wrists.

Her heart was beating very fast. Something was happening to her. She withdrew her hands and felt a resistance, as if she were pulling them out of a thick mud, and as her fingertips emerged she saw why.

The drughr's corrupted dust—that stuff, that shining substance from the other world that animated the drughr, gave it its form, that *shaped* it—was pulled out, unspooling, in a long smoldering line from the gashes in its chest. And Komako stumbled backward, pulling and pulling with her hands, and the corrupted dust kept pouring out from the drughr, draining it.

The creature made no sound, except a long shuddering sigh. Its enormous body sagged.

Faster Komako pulled the dust, faster and faster, her own arms aching with the weight of it, and as she pulled, the drughr began to shrink. Its tentacles sucked up into crumbling ropes. Its chest caved in on itself. Its antlers crumbled. The monster got smaller, smaller, until it was almost the size of Komako herself. And there, deep inside the massive creature that had been, Komako could see the lineaments of a person, a human being, ancient and still shriveling, its face tight over its skull, its eyes sunken and hollowed. Until at last no more dust could be pulled from the creature, the person, the talent that had once been a woman, and Komako fell to one knee, gasping, and let the dust go free.

A mummified husk lay sprawled in front of her, naked, eyes wide and staring. Her thin lips were parted in an expression of horror. Her long white hair tangled under one dark cheek. All around her, the earth was stained black.

And then Lymenion stumbled over on his peeled legs, using his powerful fists for support, and took the dried skull in his two powerful hands and twisted it from the mummified corpse, wrenching it clear.

It was done. The drughr was dead.

She closed her eyes. The gardens smelled of sweet leaves, its white flowers closed like eyelids. Somewhere the fountain made a soft trickling of water. Every part of Komako's body ached.

When she raised her face, Oskar was looking at the litches. Blinking his big slow eyes, wiping the snot and tears from his face with his bloodied hands. He didn't try to move, to crawl toward her. She could feel the fear and dread in his glance, the recrimination. The children. What she'd done. The wrongness of it. She bit her lip. She thought of Mrs. Ficke, the appalled sorrow in her eyes. She thought of Miss Davenshaw's body, somewhere in the upper villa. She didn't try to explain, didn't try to tell her friend that she hadn't done it on purpose, that they'd all be dead otherwise.

Something clinked in the rubble; silently around her in the settling dust her litches came forward, a horde of ghostly children, their inhuman eyes searching hers, their little bodies quivering.

"Oskar—" she started to say. But she didn't know how to continue.

"Rruh," rumbled Lymenion softly, sadly.

The flesh giant staggered weirdly over on his ravaged legs. Scooped Oskar up with great gentleness. Oskar's silence was like a slap, a fierce disapproval. He looked at her; he looked miserably away.

But you're *alive*! she wanted to shout. You're both alive! It didn't win, the drughr didn't win!

But the words wouldn't come; there was a lump in her throat, a painful lump, getting in the way. The eyes of her litches glittered in the darkness, awaiting her command, unmoved.

The warm night was quiet.

In Paris, Charlie was staggering through the dark catacombs, following the torch in Ribs's fist. His wet clothes clung to his skin, freezing.

He'd never have found his way back to Alice, to the second orsine; he could have been lost down here forever, stumbling along the stone arcades, up rough-cut steps, quarries carved from limestone. But Ribs, clever Ribs, had marked the path when she'd followed him and the Abbess, and she hurried confidently through the darkness. The torch in her hands guttered and swooped as she walked. She'd thrown over herself the red robes from one of the dead acolytes, and strapped a pair of sandals to her feet, and now Charlie could see her, see the tangle of red hair at her neck, the quick fierce movements of her hands.

"This way," she whispered. "Come on."

Behind them both came the bone witch, the dark girl with the braids and the coin at her throat, who had tried to kill Charlie once, who had killed the urchin Micah, who'd walked with the drughr and learned its secrets. Fragments of bone and skull clattered softly behind her as she walked, like a weird procession.

Charlie knew he was probably crazy to trust her. But he'd asked himself, what would Mar have done? And known the answer. Where would he himself be now, if Alice and Margaret Harrogate and Mar himself hadn't given him a chance, a chance to be more than he was?

But just let her make one wrong move, he told himself.

The acolytes at the entrance to the orsine gallery were sprawled in a heap of limbs just within. Ribs slipped past, the torch high, and Charlie saw at once something was wrong. Alice was leaned up against the far wall, her legs outstretched. There was blood in her hair and all down her face. She was holding something in her lap. Adra Norn lay unmoving some feet away. In the flickering light he could see the arms of the orsine had been peeled back, and were curled upward, like the hundred legs of some exotic insect, crushed. The air was thick with dust and smoke.

Alice raised her head wearily as they neared. "Took your . . . sweet time," she said.

Charlie saw then what she was holding. It looked like a calcified stone, about the size of a man's fist. But it was cracked all over with tiny fractures, fractures that were oozing with a gelid black blood.

The glyphic's heart.

"The drughr," she said with a grimace. "It was . . . Jacob Marber's drughr . . . She ripped out the heart . . . went through . . . the orsine . . ."

Charlie put a hand on his head and looked back. The bone witch stood very still six feet away, her bone fingers glinting in the firelight. Her face looked ashen, shocked. Then he glanced at the Abbess. She didn't look dead.

"But it didn't get the dust," he said. "It's still in me. How could it go through? Doesn't it need—"

Then he saw the careful way Alice held her ribs, and understood: the drughr had drained *her* wound, had taken the corrupted dust trapped inside her, the dust left by Jacob Marber after he'd hurt her on that train ride to Scotland, so long ago. Alice's face was gray. Her eyes were blurred with pain.

"Jesus," he whispered, kneeling. "Are you okay?"

She waved him away.

"It's open, is it?" called Ribs, not having heard. "The orsine's open?" She came over, gave him a little shove. "Mrs. Ficke and Deirdre, they *done* it. So *go*, Charlie. Go after Marlowe."

He nodded, slowly and then faster. He looked again at the sprawled body of Adra Norn. He thought of the dark well, the icy water. If there was any justice in the world, she'd never awake. But the world wasn't made for justice, he knew.

"You'll be okay, here?" he said. "You and Alice?"

Ribs put a small hand on his arm, held it there. The heat of it was unexpectedly human and kind.

"Go," she said again, but gently. "We can't seal it till you come back with Marlowe. An there's no telling what's like to come through in the meantime. Don't you worry none about that Abbess. We got this. Go."

He didn't wait to be told again. He rose and kicked his way through the husks of arms and clawed fingers, the appendages crumbling away now to dust with the glyphic's heart gone. The orsine was a rectangular limestone pool, like a Roman bath, not unlike what he'd seen at Cairndale, with smooth steps leading down to a black, sludge-like water. That water gave off no light. It stood low in the basin and thick like jelly and there were slow bubbles rising to its surface. As he watched, the water level shivered, then rose up an inch, staining the walls.

"Just . . . Charlie?" Ribs called.

"Yeah?"

"Try not to, you know. Die."

He looked at her. Nodded gravely. He remembered Cairndale, the waters overflowing the orsine, the spirit dead screaming and tearing at the glyphic's heart. He walked down into the dirty water, feeling the cold surface close at his ankles, at his knees, climb up past his waist to his chest. The tattoos in his flesh were writhing madly, shining with a dazzling blue shine, and Charlie cast a quick worried glance behind him. Ribs had come to the edge. Then he took a deep breath, and closed his eyes, and descended.

His clothes lifted up all around him in the waters. It was very dark. He felt cautiously for the steps with his feet, going deeper. There was a roar in his ears, the roar of the waters surrounding him, the roar of his blood within. His lungs were bursting. All at once the horror of the Abbess's well was in him, the horror of his drowning, and he did not think he could go on. But he did, he took another step, another.

Mar! he thought. *I'm coming! Just hold on!*

And when he could hold his breath no longer, he became aware of a faint greenish glow all around him, and he gasped, and it was not water but air, and darkness, if darkness could be breathed in. A sooty reek filled his lungs. He glimpsed the faint outline of stairs, turning and turning below him in the gloom.

There was a wall to one side of him, slimy and dark, and his fingers brushed it and then recoiled. Gradually he became aware of a vast chamber all around, and the stairs ended in a rough-hewn stone floor, pocked with puddles, and he fell to his knees, gasping.

He'd made it. He'd returned to the land of the dead.

Maybe not something to brag about, he thought to himself.

He got to his feet, trying to think clearly. His breathing sounded harsh in the stillness. A faint drip of water, somewhere. His tattoos were still shining very brightly. Some distance away, a faint pillar of mist glowed, twisting upon itself, silver in the darkness. Another rose up just beyond it. Charlie's skin went cold: they were spirit dead, adrift in this place.

He backed cautiously away. He knew their hunger.

There was a dull light off to one side, leading out of the chamber. Charlie hurried toward it, his boots splashing softly. Though he remembered only fragments of this world, still it seemed eerily familiar. He emerged onto the gray, mist-enshrouded shore of an island, a black lake leading off into fog. There was a long stone building, ornate, looming up behind him, deserted and dripping with moss and water. Then Charlie saw, with a shock, where he was. He was on the island in Loch Fae, below Cairndale Manor, the island of the ruined monastery where Mr. Thorpe—the Spider—had lived and had died.

Or some malformed version of it. For the water in the lake was viscous and toxic-looking, and the monastery itself shivered in and out of focus, from ruin to grandeur, while the mists curled around it. There was no golden tree, however; and the island, he saw, was joined to the far shore by a low bridge of land.

On the lake, a rowboat parted the mists, the water lapping quietly at its hull. Something stood up in its stern, something angular and robed and very tall. Then it pulled its hood back and Charlie glimpsed a skull-like visage, a wreath of black smoke obscuring its eyes. Fear poured through him. The thing, whatever it was, was looking directly at him.

He stumbled back into the fog. The island was swampy and soft, as if the seeping lake water would eat it away in time. He glanced back at the fog but the creature's boat had vanished.

If this was the island in Loch Fae, then perhaps across the loch lay Cairndale. He could sense even now how this other world shifted, how uncertain its landmarks would be. He rubbed at his eyes with the heels of his hands. Mar was in this terrible world, somewhere. In danger. He didn't know how he could find him but he had the vague idea to stalk the bone witch's drughr, Mar's mother; she might lead him to his friend. Except he had to catch up to her first.

He hurried down to the low-lying isthmus that led across the lake. He tried not to look anywhere but straight ahead, and felt relief when the sloping lakefront materialized out of the mist. The world was quiet. And there, looming high up the slope, he saw the unmistakable silhouette of Cairndale Manor, its ancient roof and spires fallen into disrepair.

"Damn it, Mar," he muttered. "Why are we always ending up back here?"

He crept off the path as he passed the manor, not wanting to get too close. The gates were nearer than in life, the gravel drive leading out was narrower and pocked with holes. The fog was thinning. Now he could hear a soft moaning and he slipped behind a sunken cart, its wheels rotting in the muck, and tried to see the way out.

The gates stood open. But there was something wrong with the perimeter wall. It was writhing, as if alive. Then Charlie saw the ghastly creatures lashed there, together, and he caught his breath.

He saw no sign of the drughr he hunted, nor of her passage. But she must have come this way, he supposed; and he was just crossing the dead grass, making for an overturned pedestal, when he heard a scream just ahead.

His blood went cold. He knew that sound, knew it with a terrible certainty.

The keywrasse.

How it could be here, and not at the villa, he didn't know. He was filled with a sudden fear for Komako and Oskar and all the children. He risked a clearer look. And there it was, just outside the gates, huge and terrible, its tail lashing the thick air. How long it might have been there, he didn't know. It took him a moment to see what was wrong. The keywrasse was swarmed by three enormous drughr. The biggest, a massive drughr with many fingers, stood crushed up behind the keywrasse, gripping its throat and two of its legs, bending the beast backward so that its belly was exposed. A second drughr, the one with the burning hole in its chest, had two other of the keywrasse's legs held fast. The keywrasse was snarling, biting at the air. A third drughr, covered in blinking eyes, like sores, crouched in front of them all. As Charlie watched, it dragged a long singular claw down the cat's chest, to its belly.

The keywrasse snarled, screamed again. Its four eyes were slits.

And then the drughr with the thousand eyes stood and went forward. It pried the keywrasse's jaws apart, and reached one long, smoldering arm deep into its throat, while the keywrasse choked and its hind legs wheeled in panic and its tail thrashed. Charlie started to gag. At last the drughr pulled some dripping thing from out of the keywrasse, dark and many-pronged, and held it up to the light. It was a key, two keys, each strange and heavy-looking and glistening in the eerie mist. The weir-bents.

The keywrasse, all at once, fell still. It seemed to diminish, to shrink back into its fur, as if cowering inside itself.

No! Charlie wanted to cry. *Leave him alone! Leave him alone!*

But he couldn't say a word. He watched in horror as the drughr with the burning hole took up a wire cage, and stuffed the keywrasse inside it, and fastened the door shut. Then all three strode in, past the gates, approaching Charlie, the mist swirling around them. As they entered the grounds of Cairndale, they were transformed; Charlie caught his breath. Each drughr became human in form, or almost human, wearing long black coats and one with a hat and leather gloves and another with a faded waistcoat and high boots. The man in the front, who carried the weir-bents, had no eyes. This Charlie saw with great certainty. But he walked with a sure step all the same, as if he had other ways of seeing. They strode unaware past where Charlie crouched.

At the front doors, they stopped. The keywrasse's cage was hooked to a chain, spinning very slowly next to two other cages. Charlie could see the keywrasse, small now, scarcely larger than a regular house cat. The poor thing was pressed against the back of the cage, terrified.

The drughr stood in a semicircle around the front doors, an air of intensity rising from them. Charlie felt a dread rising in him. He didn't understand why. The eyeless drughr spoke some guttural words, as if completing some ritual, and then climbed the steps and inserted the weir-bents into the door, above the crossed hammers, and turned each three times, with both hands, straining as if against a great weight. There was already a weir-bent standing out of a third keyhole, edged in gold, at the center of the great crest. And at last, suddenly, the great fortress-like doors of Cairndale were opening, swinging inward with a shrieking of hinges, and Charlie saw, beyond, not darkness, not nothingness, but the unmistakable blue shine of his own dearest friend.

The entire house shuddered. A deep low booming began, and grew louder, and then fell silent. When Charlie raised his face the drughr had twisted back into their true forms, antlered and monstrous. The fog all around Cairndale began to whirl up, as in a wind. A reddish glow grew in the skies overhead.

Charlie stood as the drughr, one by one, climbed the steps of Cairndale and went inside, disappearing into the blue shine within. He was shaking.

For he knew where he had to go.

✦   ✦   ✦

Jeta had watched Charlie Ovid wade down into the muck of the orsine, his shirt blooming up around him. Had watched him go under, disappear.

And her heart had hurt to think of it, how he'd do that, go into such a place, in order to find a friend and bring him back. To think that love like that was real. She saw she'd come to believe Ruth, and Claker Jack, all of them, when they created a world of cruelty and self-interest and base survival. She'd let herself believe.

The torchlight was flickering over her face and hands. She stood back, away from the woman Alice, the brash girl in the stolen acolyte robes, Ribs. All around her the bones were like a steady dizzying throb in her skull.

There were acolytes hurrying through the galleries, hurrying toward them; she could feel it, feel the soft squish of their bones in their flesh; and she drew down a great tumble of bones from the walls and packed them grindingly tight into the doorway, blocking their approach.

The effort made her gasp.

That was when she saw the Abbess had got to her feet. She was very tall, and her long face was grim. Jeta heard Alice click her revolver but she knew a bullet would do nothing against a haelan. Nor would a torch. She remembered Micah's words, how eager he'd been for the Abbess to appear.

"What . . . is this?" the Abbess murmured. Her voice was deep. She stepped angrily around the orsine, peering down at its dark waters. Then she strode forward. "You, Alice Quicke. Give me the glyphic's heart." Then she caught sight of them all. "Who are these girls?"

"They're with me," said Alice fiercely.

And Jeta felt a sudden bloom of gratitude, and doubled up her fists. She drew on the sharpest bits of bones and swung them up, into the air, hovering menacingly. At the edge of her vision, she saw Ribs vanish, kick her robe emptily to the floor.

The Abbess's eyes lit up. "Ah, marvelous," she said. "Circus tricks and distractions. While the orsine stands open and God only knows what will come through. Give me the heart, young Alice. Let me repair what I can. There is little time."

The woman, Alice, actually smiled. "To hell with that," she said, and raised her revolver. "And to hell with you."

The gallery was silent. A soft drip of water was the only sound.

"I can kill you all, you understand," the Abbess said quietly.

Ribs snorted from somewhere in the darkness. "You can try, maybe."

Alice spat. "Step back, *Adra*."

But then the Abbess looked at the orsine. The black waters had risen to the edge of the pool and begun to spill out over it, a froth of putrid liquid. The waters, very slowly, seeped out over the floor.

The Abbess took a step back.

And then something was stirring the surface, some ridged and monstrous thing. Jeta couldn't make it out, at first. It curled up over the limestone sill, all knuckles and bone. A hand.

Jeta stared. She could feel no pull from its bones, or maybe it was just drowned out in all the madness of the catacombs. She shrank back in fear.

And then the creature rose up out of the waters, a grimy smoke smoldering from its shoulders and arms, a hooded thing, enormous and shrouded in darkness, so that only a faint grin could be seen in the firelight. Something was writhing all over its chest and arms, wormlike. A chain, heavy and slick, sliding in and out of the creature's flesh. The creature loomed up over them, turning its skull from side to side, as if smelling their heat and blood.

"What the hell—" muttered Alice.

"It's a carykk," whispered the Abbess in horror. There was such fear in the woman's voice, and this made Jeta the more frightened. "The orsine is lost . . ."

But Jeta didn't run. And she saw the woman, Alice Quicke, didn't run either. She'd taken up the torch instead and held it now in her free hand, like a weapon.

"Charlie's still in there," Alice said grimly. "I'll be damned if I lose that kid again."

The carykk rose up still further, taking one unsteady step out of the pool. Its skull scraped the ceiling. Its robes were bunched and slack all over its weird body and then Jeta realized with a shock that it was not fabric but skin. The soot continued to smoke up off it, like steam. When it moved it made a clicking and popping noise. And then it drew back its hood, and its face was lean and white, and the wreath of darkness where its eyes should have been was awful to behold.

That was when Jeta realized the Abbess was gone. She'd burst through the bone barrier Jeta had made, smashed her way through it with a tremendous strength, and vanished into the catacombs beyond. Her acolytes too were gone. It was just them, now.

"Oi!" came a voice, Ribs's voice.

The carykk turned its grinning face from side to side, seeking her.

"You can just—" Ribs grunted, "—Bugger—Right—Off!"

And Jeta saw an enormous femur swing out of the darkness, catching the creature on the side of its head, knocking it staggering to one side. The bone swung again and again, crashing into the same part of its head. Such a blow should have crushed the monster's skull. But the carykk did not fall. It swept an arm angrily out, the chain sliding with a liquid clatter out of its wrist, and lashed the femur from Ribs's grasp.

And then it threw back its head, and screamed.

Jeta's blood ran cold. It was a horrifying sound, filled with despair and dread. The scream was made the more awful by the small gallery, its echoes splitting Jeta's ears.

The black water was overspilling the orsine now and creeping deeper into the chamber, and the carykk stood down into it, and splashed its way forward. It threw both its arms wide and both ends of the living chain whipped out from its wrists, snakelike and terrible. Alice swung the torch in a sweeping arc, back and forth, hollering at the thing, before leaping back. And the carykk came forward at a run.

But then it stopped, just at the edge of the liquid, and screamed again. The chains writhed forward. Alice pressed herself against the back wall; the carykk could not reach her.

It was then Jeta noticed how the smoke steaming up off the carykk itself was the same foul dark tint as the liquid in the orsine; and she saw how, with each step, the liquid seemed to sizzle and boil up under the creature.

"It needs the waters!" she cried. "It can't leave the waters! That's what gives it its strength!"

And she hurled a sharp rain of bone fragments at the creature, trying to overbalance it. Out of the corner of her eye she saw another great femur come swinging at the carykk, but even before it could connect the monster seized it in one powerful hand, and then one long loop of chain reached out and encircled Ribs's invisible body, dragging her forward. The carykk swung her up under its arm. Jeta could hear Ribs screaming, could see the way she was kicking and fighting against the creature. And then the carykk, as if satisfied, turned and waded back over to the orsine, and began to climb down into it.

"Ribs! Ribs!" Alice was screaming. She had the torch and was running through the filthy water, running and swinging the fire at the carykk. But she would not stop it in time, Jeta saw.

And she fell to her knees, and shuddered, and let in all the deep pulls of the bones in that gallery, the long-dead in their dusty sleeps, the newly dead acolytes crumpled inside the door, all of them, she let the song fill her ears with a terrible black rushing wind, and summoned more than she could hold, and built a lacework around the carykk as it tried to carry the poor girl Ribs down into the land of the dead.

Jeta's eyes were bleeding. There was blood smeared at her nose, trickling from her ears. She swayed but forced herself to look. She saw a vast web of bones interlaced and patterned across the surface of the orsine, pinning the carykk in place, and even as it thrashed and punched its chains at the bones, more were linking up, overwhelming the creature, prying it back upward, so that it staggered back, out of the pool, across the floor of the gallery. The bones were like a wall, crushed into powder by the carykk's fists, but leaping back up, forcing it backward, until at last it stepped out of the liquid entirely, onto the dry edges of the floor. And she felt it falter then; she heard Ribs's voice, crying out in fury; then the invisible girl appeared, wriggling free of the carykk's chains, scrambling to her feet in the half darkness and running clear.

And then Alice Quicke stepped forward with the torch, murder in her eyes, and thrust the fire deep into its strange skin-like robes; and the carykk, screaming, burned and burned.

Jeta collapsed back onto the cold stone floor, retching. Her head felt strangely light.

In the dying glow of the fire, Ribs leaned over. Her face was pale. Her red hair was sticking to a bad cut at her temple. But her eyes were bright.

"Well, shit," she said. "Whoo!"

And she grinned shakily.

Meanwhile, in the library inside Cairndale, the shining in Marlowe's skin had grown brighter than ever. A heat was pouring off him in waves. He was so afraid. The fear was like a blaze inside him and he could feel whatever he was, that strange power in him, burning hotter and hotter. He crawled under a table, folded his knees to his chest. The library vanished in his shining.

The First Talent was wading toward him, his slender body turned sideways against Marlowe's brightness, as if it pained him. His nightshirt was rippling all around. His wrists were folded against his chest, twisted like stumps of wax. But his eyes—Berghast's eyes—were cold and hungry.

Marlowe couldn't think clearly. He just knew he had to get away, he had to. But his feet wouldn't go, they wouldn't do what he wanted them to, he was too scared. He closed his eyes and prayed for help, any help, from anyone.

That was when the manor began to ripple, to slide sideways out of itself. He saw the First Talent pause, glance around. One wall was still the library wall, bookshelves shuddering in the shine. But directly in front of Marlowe was the long dining table from elsewhere in the house. And to his left he could see the windows of the solarium, where Dr. Berghast had been hurt so awfully.

And then the floor began to shake, as if Cairndale itself were coming apart. Marlowe folded his arms over his knees, terrified. A deep low booming sounded throughout the house, like the beating of a vast drum, then died away. The manor seemed to sink into itself, go still.

Something was different. Marlowe could *feel* it.

He crawled out from under the table. He was back in the solarium. He spun around and saw the First Talent towering over him, hands still a mess. The shine was as bright as ever.

"Mar-lowe ...," Alastair Cairndale growled, as if tasting the name. His voice was thick with anger.

That was when something leaped out from the dazzle, some ravaged thing, seizing the First Talent in a desperate grip and hauling him backward, almost off his feet.

It was the mutilated figure of Dr. Berghast, howling. Marlowe recoiled in horror. The old man's eyes were bloodied holes and his mouth was filled with blood and yet somehow he threw himself onto the First Talent's back, as if he knew exactly where to do so, and the blade in his hand was plunging again and again into the ancient talent's chest and neck and ribs.

The First Talent spun and twisted in agony.

And Marlowe, little Marlowe, jumped to his feet and ran.

His eyes were stinging with tears. The manor was folding itself around him again, eerie, as if the air were a deck of cards being shuffled, as if the house had a place it wanted him to get to. The walls were shaking. Marlowe threw open a set of French doors and found himself unexpectedly in the foyer, the vast dark stone foyer of Cairndale, its hearth black, the stained glass windows above the stairs illumined and awful. The shining that poured forth from his flesh lit all of it in an unearthly blue light.

But something had changed. The great doors of Cairndale had been opened. He could see the third key in the pattern, standing out of its lock. Through the wide open doors, the land of the dead waited, its mists curling and uncurling, whispery as hair in a breeze. It was right there, just ahead of him—a way out.

Then, ascending the slow steps into the foyer, came three drughr, antlered and horrifying and enormous in their shadowy forms. Their long claws clicked as they stepped inside, onto the flagstones. The manor seemed to creak under their weight. They stood, snorting softly, peering all around them, a black soot sifting from them as they turned in place.

Inside the prison.

Marlowe turned to flee. But the French doors he'd passed through had vanished. From somewhere deep within the manor, a muffled roar could be heard. It was the First Talent, crying out in anger. Marlowe knew Dr. Berghast could not delay him for long.

The drughr with the manifold eyes stepped nearer. It opened its wide mouth. Its teeth were small and square, like the molars of a child, but there were dozens and dozens of them. Marlowe shuddered.

It reached out three hands.

And paused. A black smoke was seeping in through the opened doors, rolling like a heavy gas across the flagstones, swirling around the ankles of the gathered drughr, clinging to them. Marlowe's heart was in his throat.

Then he saw a dark thing lean down out of the top of the doorframe, unhurried, with a predatory uncoiling, letting itself gently down with its many arms.

It was a fourth drughr.

Huge and antlered, with a cloud of darkness enveloping her like vast wings. And Marlowe *knew* her, just like that, without being told who she was. He could feel something washing over him, like a strange scent. This was the drughr who'd seduced Jacob Marber, the drughr who'd hunted him all these years, a creature out of his nightmares. His mother. Before him at last.

And the fear that was like a little nail driven into his heart just got bigger and bigger. She'd come for him. She'd come for *him*.

Her eyes found his. There was such a black love emanating from her, a love like the absence of love, a love that wanted only to devour him, and it was like an icy wind had struck his face, made his cheeks sting.

The other drughr turned to face her, slow, too slow. She expanded until she filled the doorway with a wall of darkness, only her eyes glinting, and those eyes not leaving Marlowe's own. And then she struck.

The dust snapped tight around the drughr's ankles and cracked them hard, one by one by one, against the flagstones. Then she was dragging them ferociously out, smashing their arms and skulls against the doorframe, hurtling them across the courtyard, out of the manor itself.

Marlowe watched her in terror.

Ropes of sootlike dust flowed from her body, snakelike, too many to count, wrapping themselves around the drughr's throats and arms and legs, pinioning them fast against the rough-hewn courtyard. The monsters themselves were powerful, struggling mightily, the drughr with the burning hole in its chest burning away at the tendrils as fast as they could snap into place. But she was not alone; a second figure, smaller, small as an ordinary man, had stood up from behind a sunken cart, and

Marlowe watched as a thick rope of dust was hurled against one of the drughr, strangling it.

He snuck to the edge of the doors. The shining would not die down. Where he gripped the edge of the doorframe, the wood hissed as if burned. And that was when he heard his name.

"Mar!" a voice was calling, as if from a great distance. It was the second figure, the man. "Mar! Mar!"

And there he was, Charlie, *his* Charlie, shirt ragged and clinging, arms prickling with a blue fire, dust in a storm around his fists—Charlie Ovid, in the flesh, running toward him through the mists.

He'd come, he'd come after all, just like he'd said.

The little boy looked fierce and fiery in his blue shine, his skinny arms and chest wrapped in strips of rags, blood flecking his cheeks, his mind scarred by God only knew what—and yet the moment Charlie grabbed him and pulled him into his arms, Mar burst into tears.

Mar who was alive, Mar who was here, his little body heaving with sobs, and Charlie held him out at arm's length and looked for any hurt and saw none and then he hugged him again, his eyes hot with his own crying.

Cairndale creaked above them. The drughr all around were lashing out with terrible ferocity, screaming in fury. The gray mists of the dead world drifted thickly past. Charlie knew they had to go. Now. Something large and heavy crashed into the wall of the manor, rose up, hurtled again into the fight.

Charlie crouched and turned and then turned back. He didn't understand any of what was happening. The cage with the keywrasse was spinning slowly on its chain beside the doors and he reached up, unhooked it, lifted it down. The cat within was cowering, looking very small. Marlowe was holding Charlie's sleeve, as if afraid of being left.

"We've got to run," Charlie said. "There's a way out. Come on, while the drughr are busy—"

But then the old man appeared. He burst out of the doors of Cairndale, a streak of white fire, smashing bodily into the drughr, sending her spinning across the rotting ground. He wore a long white nightshirt with blood all down the back and his beard and hair were long and matted with blood and he looked, Charlie thought, powerful and frightening. He raised his arms and his wrists were malformed into gruesome stumps but even as Charlie watched he saw the flesh rope itself together, twist into a palm, the buds of fingers, into two strong pale fists. And he knew the man before him was a haelan. But then he drew a long scythe of black dust to his hands, and suddenly vanished from sight, and the small clear part of Charlie's brain that wasn't filled with terror understood. This was the First Talent, the one they'd all been afraid of. The wielder of all five gifts.

And suddenly the old man was visible again, tearing at the drughr where she struggled, clawing away at her flesh, lashing her fast with his own ropes of dust.

"Charlie?" Marlowe was tugging at his sleeve. "Charlie? We can't stay here. Brynt will take us—"

He heard a sound, like a hiss of water in a pipe. There was an enormous spirit dead, folding and in-folding very close, its faces flickering. It was a woman, a huge woman.

Marlowe, it whispered. *This way. Come.*

"It's Brynt, Charlie," said Marlowe. "She's been in here all this time. You remember Brynt?"

And he did, vaguely, this spirit who had guided them through the city of the dead, all those months before, when Cairndale still stood, and Jacob Marber stalked them.

"We're trying to get to the orsine," he said. "On the island."

This way. Come! she said again.

She led them around the far side of the manor, through the rotting grass. As Charlie turned the corner, he glanced back, saw the ancient man in his bloodied nightshirt punch both his fists into the drughr that had saved Mar, deep into her chest, and lift her bodily from the ground. She was thrashing, helpless.

Then he ran. He ran with Mar's hand in his own the long way around Cairndale, half sliding down the rotting slopes, getting to his feet, hurrying on, the cage with the keywrasse banging against his leg as he swung it and ran, following the spirit of Brynt.

And then the fog slid away for just a moment and he saw the spit of land, low-lying, seeping with the black lake water, and the island beyond it, and Brynt was already out across it and he and Marlowe were running, their feet sloshing underfoot, the cold mists all around them.

Marlowe's face looked gray, shaken. He slowed, pulling free of Charlie's grip. He was shaking his head. "There was no island here before," he said. "This wasn't here. I looked for it. It wasn't . . ."

"Mar, we got to go," he said urgently.

But the little boy was staring up at him, his eyes wide. He stood very still. All around them the lake sloshed, quiet. "Are you real? Are you really Charlie?"

Charlie swallowed, trying to catch his breath.

"Because Brynt's not Brynt," Marlowe said. "Not really."

"I'm me. I am. I'm Charlie."

"If you're not, I need you to say it. Please tell me. Because I can't . . . I just—" And he blinked his eyes sharply and he rubbed his ragged sleeve over his little face. "Tell me the truth."

Charlie hesitated. Behind them, he could see the mists whorling above the nightmarish roof of Cairndale. When he glanced the other way, he saw the monastery on the island, very near. But he didn't grab his friend, didn't drag him free. He set down the cage with the key-wrasse in it and he kneeled carefully in the muck and he looked at Mar's face.

"Sometimes you don't get to know for sure," he said gently. "Sometimes you just got to trust what's in your heart. You taught me that yourself, long ago. At Mrs. Harrogate's house, on Nickel Street. Do you remember? You get to *choose*, Mar. If I could give you a secret word, something to prove it's me, I'd do it. But I can't. I just got this." And he held out his empty hand, palm up. "You either take it now, or you don't. But you got to choose. Because we're running out of time."

He could see now a disturbance in the mists behind them, as if something large and dark was moving down toward the lake. The key-wrasse meowed, a small kittenish sound.

At last the boy put his small hand in Charlie's own. It was warm and soft.

"Okay," Charlie whispered, holding that hand tight. "Okay, good. All right. Let's go, okay?"

Marlowe nodded.

And he picked up the cage and he hurried the boy toward the monastery, glancing worriedly back behind him all the while. It was like he could feel what was coming.

The mists far back on the spit of land parted, and a tall, slow figure emerged. A bolt of fear shot through Charlie. It was the creature he had seen in the loch, hooded, thin as bone, its grinning face leering out at him. It moved unhurriedly toward them and yet with each step it seemed to cross an impossible distance, getting close. Charlie saw they couldn't outrun it.

"Mar," he hissed. "Take the keywrasse. Run for the orsine. I'll be right behind you."

And he turned, drawing what dust he could find toward him. Willing himself to stand his ground.

But the spirit dead of Brynt was there, suddenly, flickering in and out of focus. *You must go with Marlowe*, it said. *I will delay the carykk. Go.*

"But it will . . . it will kill you, Brynt," said Marlowe. "You said so yourself."

I am already what I am, she replied. *It will be . . . a mercy. Go. Don't look back. Promise me.*

Charlie nodded. He picked up the cage again.

Marlowe was sniffling. "I promise," he whispered.

And then they were running, clambering up the slimy rocks of the island, hurrying for the dark entrance to the cavern. Charlie heard a sudden screaming, and paused, and looked back in time to see the carykk, flailing its long chains at the air, beating at a silvery fog that had enveloped it, as if it could not pass.

But Marlowe kept his promise and did not look back and instead pulled Charlie forcefully into the dark cavern. There were no spirit dead in the shadows. The stone steps led up, into darkness.

Marlowe's face was upturned, his eyes big. "Charlie?"

"You ready?" he said.

Marlowe nodded gravely. His hand was damp in Charlie's. "Don't let go, okay? Please?"

"I've got you," said Charlie.

And he did. He doubled his grip on Mar's wrist to be sure, and lifting the keywrasse's cage high, he stepped up into the water that was not water, those icy upper reaches of the orsine, and up ahead he could see the flickering torchlight of the Paris catacombs, blurred but coming clearer, and the pale faces of his friends, Ribs, Alice, the bone witch Jeta, peering anxiously down at them from the world above.

He climbed faster.

And Marlowe—little Marlowe—came with him.

• • •

Deep below, in the swirling mists at the edge of Loch Fae, in the very heart of the land of the dead, Alastair Cairndale, First Talent, terror of talentkind, stood in his bloodied nightshirt, watching the island in the middle of the lake recede into the mists and disappear. He was not angry. He was not weary. His body was stiff from his long sleep but the ache was pleasurable. He held in his two hands the broken armored glove, its black plates clicking quietly. It would be of use, yes. All around him he could feel the thousands of dead, like pricks of pain, adrift and afraid and filled with forgettings, and it was good. He could feel the carykk, hungry for what had been drained from them. He could feel the orsine itself, frightened.

Cairndale had been opened. His prison would be his fortress. *Let them come*, he thought; *let them try*. Somewhere on the flats of the dead an orsine was being built, an orsine that would carry him through to the world of the living, to his own kind, to his rightful place.

The First Talent's hands turned and turned the artifact, and his white beard was matted with blood. His hair was greasy and tangled in his eyes. But he could feel the faithful drughr gathered behind him, lurking in the fog. Waiting.

He didn't move, not just yet.

"Marlowe," he murmured. His sixth, his greater power. What had been taken from him, would yet be returned. And then, as if quoting a line of scripture to himself, he whispered: "Who will go before me, to prepare the world for my coming?"

The mist was quiet, as if the entire world held its breath.

In the cold gray light, Alastair Cairndale smiled.

43

BOOK OF UNBINDING

They came out soaked and shivering into the ruins of the orsine gallery, Charlie and Marlowe did, their eyes glassy in the torchlight with a pain they could not describe.

And even as Alice drew them safely back through the ankle-deep muck, taking the caged keywrasse in pity from Charlie, even as Ribs plunged the glyphic's heart back into the sludge-like waters of the orsine, and Marlowe stepped forward once again on shaking legs to seal it up forever, little Marlowe, spindly legged, his arms covered in fluttering rags, a dazzling blue shine erupting from his skin as the orsine collapsed in on itself in a tumble of stone and brick—even then, he and Charlie could say nothing, no words at all, only tremble with a cold that was no longer outside of them, but now within.

And all the time they were being dried, and calmed, and even all the long journey back to the villa in Sicily, after they were strong enough at last to travel, still they did not know how to speak of what had happened on the other side of the orsine. Charlie would lay his head back on the seat, feeling the railway tracks clatter up through the carriage, and close his eyes, hating the pity he saw in Alice and Ribs and the bone witch. Marlowe, small as a bird, would curl into Charlie's side, keeping close, always close, but with his own shadowed eyes open as if afraid all that he saw would vanish, if he just stopped looking at it.

And the days passed, the horror of Paris receding gradually. The key-wrasse slept in Alice's lap on the train, a soft purring engine of warmth. One evening on the deck of the steamer, bound for Palermo, Ribs said some sly thing and Marlowe laughed—he *laughed*—and Charlie raised his face at that, as if awakening from a dream. By the time they'd reached the villa outside Agrigento they were themselves again, or nearly so, more living than dead. And they greeted Oskar and Lymenion and Mrs. Ficke on the gravel drive, hearing the terrors of the drughr's attack with heavy hearts. Jeta walked all around Lymenion, fascinated, her dark eyes grave and polite, while Ribs and Oskar looked on. Mrs. Ficke gave a strange old-fashioned curtsy to the keywrasse, as if to thank it. Only Komako was absent. Charlie followed his friends into the ruined villa, trying to imagine how that frightening night had been. All wept for the dead, the lost children, Miss Crowley the governess, Miss Davenshaw whom they had loved.

In the gardens, Charlie gathered his courage at last and asked, "Where's Ko?"

She had taken herself away to a cave, in the nearby hills. Herself and the twelve children. She came out to the edge of the sunlight with sorrowful eyes as Charlie and Marlowe trudged up through the dry grass, Charlie raising a hand in greeting. She wore all black with thin gray fingerless gloves and strong men's work boots under her hem, and her eyes were painted with thick black makeup. Her hair hung loose and snarled at her shoulders.

Marlowe ran the last few steps, into her arms. She'd held him a long while, saying nothing, watching Charlie over his tousled hair. And Charlie had seen in the shadows of the cave the children, her litches, gathered there pale and quiet with the three red lines at their throats, with their unnatural stillness. He'd never felt so old, so tired, as then. His heart ached. But Marlowe went over to the nearest girl, Zorya, she had been, and kneeled in front of her, and whispered some quiet thing, and she'd folded herself into his little chest with the same sweetness Charlie had remembered from life. And then the others emerged, pale and cautious and strange, their teeth sharp, their eyes as sad as Komako's, and they all gathered around Marlowe, reaching their fingers out to brush his arm, his face, his shoulder, a family.

Miss Davenshaw and the children's governess, Susan Crowley, had been buried in the southeast corner of the garden, within view of the sea, along with several of the little ones, those Komako had not resurrected. Their small stones were white and simple and shaded by a lemon tree. The drughr Ko had killed had been burned on a pyre outside the walls, its ashes scattered, and where the fire had burned nothing now grew. Lymenion and Oskar were often down at the graves, tidying them.

In those first days, Charlie did not like to be indoors. He'd walk the dusty roads or stand at the fountain in the garden, while gradually the Abbess's strange account of his father's journey, what he had tried to do at the Grathyyl, what Charlie himself was fated to fulfill, came back to him. He told no one, not Ko, not Marlowe; he peered out at the sky, afraid of what he was, and wished he could forget. But the dark truth of it cast its red light over everything. He found a sapling, a golden wych elm, like what had grown on the island at Cairndale, pushing up out of the soil above the wash-house. And when he went down into the chamber, he saw Deirdre sleeping at peace, tendrils thickening all around her, as if she lay in a nest of roots, and he placed a hand on her cool cheek, thinking about fate and how it didn't have to be the way everyone said it was.

The keywrasse kept close to Alice. It would climb onto her lap or walk in front of her plate at lunch, its four eyes narrowing in pleasure as she stroked its fur. For her part, Alice felt weak but whole again, with the corrupted dust drained from her. Her thoughts kept straying back to Adra Norn, to her mother, to the ways her life had been altered by a callous woman with no regard for the havoc she'd wreaked. All that had happened, all that had been so important to Alice, had mattered not at all to Norn. Somewhere that awful woman walked free, even now. Alice brooded, telling no one, spending her days alongside Lymenion, her sleeves rolled high, the two of them repairing the stonework on the balcony, trying to keep busy. She liked the ache in her muscles at the end of the day, the dark dreamless sleeps as they took over.

Caroline Ficke sat in a wicker chair in the sunlight, recovering from the wound in her side. She left her apparatus unbuckled and spent her days reading. One day a letter came from Edinburgh. It was from her brother, Edward. It read, in part: *Deer Caroline, I am hapy you ar hapy. I werk hard evry dae. I miss you. It is kwiet at the shop. How ar the litl wuns?* And she set it aside, and began to cry.

The trees grew fat with fruit. Songbirds returned to the garden.

The daylight grew long.

And always everything came back to Marlowe, to Charlie and Marlowe. They were together almost from morning to night, together and quiet and often not speaking, just surprised, both of them, surprised to have found each other again, amazed and grateful. And in the evening sun, after dinner and washing up, they would go out to the broken fountain at the center of the garden, and find Ribs and Jeta, Oskar and Lymenion all sprawled about, sleepy with the goodness of it all, and sometimes even Komako would come down from her cave in the hills to join them. Insects were buzzing in the flowers. They were all alive, and together. The sun fell warm on their faces and the backs of their hands, and when they leaned back and closed their eyes they felt its light sifting through the branches above. Ribs threw bits of grass into Oskar's hair. Lymenion snorted and breathed. Jeta would hum softly, some Roma song out of her childhood. Charlie had the feeling, for almost the first time in his life, of a languid summer, made all the sweeter because he knew, like childhood, like innocence itself, it could not last.

EPILOGUE

·

Alexandria, Egypt

It was early yet, the morning warm. In the hour before the household woke, the boy crept up to the roof and reached into his shirt and took out the three little pouches he carried there always. These he unbuttoned by the light of the rising sun and tilted sidelong, sliding their contents onto a cloth.

The first pouch held a severed finger. The second held a lock of black hair, tied with string. In the third was the final joint of an old man's toe, its skin stained the color of tea.

Pieces of the dead.

The boy, taking out a broken hand mirror, concentrated on his own face then: the bleak eyes, the mouth carved into hardness, the white keloid scar on his left cheek.

Then he reached out two fingers, lightly touched the objects in their turn: toe, hair, shriveled finger. Very quickly, over and over.

Watching the clouded glass in wonder all the while.

It started with the face, as it always did. A sudden sharp pain. His features blurred and bent woozily away, each from each, and then in a blink he was another. The ancient beggar, toothless, blind in one eye, who had died in a doorway two winters ago, whose toe he had taken. The Frenchwoman with the small pretty mouth who had drowned herself in the harbor, whose strangle of wet hair he had dared to cut before the constable arrived. The big stonemason, whose nose had been broken and set badly years before, who had done unspeakable things to women, who had been knifed in the alley twenty-seven times and left for dead but who had opened his eyes in unbearable pain when the boy carved the finger from his hand.

Face after face after face, in the red of the rising sun.

For he was a turner, a skin-shuffler. And though he knew there were other talents in the world, he had met none. His name was Yasin al-Ashur and he was fourteen years old, light-boned as kindling and blue-eyed like his blood-father before him. He had lived as an apprentice in the streets of Alexandria since his fifth year. His blood-father was an English explorer who had died of fever while the child slept yet in his young mother's belly or so he had been told and his blood-mother had been that household's servant. Whether conceived in love or by force the boy would never know. She was gone now too. Her people were holy and traveled from wadi to wadi in the sands east of the Red Sea and lived by the old ways and the boy in his loneliness could not have found them even had he wished it. He did not wish it. To the denizens of the alley he was known, simply, as the English Boy. He lived with his master, the goldsmith Kamal al-Ashur, and together they were among the last of the Agnoscenti.

When he felt a hand on his shoulder, he turned. The rising sun through the wooden grille was coppering his hands and the hands of his master's wife where she knelt. "Kamal wishes to see you," she told him. "Come."

They found the goldsmith at his dressing mirror. He did not look up. He held his thick arms wide and his wife went to him and removed his robe and laid it on his bed and went out and returned with a basin of warm water. She brought in a tin tray of coffee and he drank while she stood holding it. Then he washed his face and hands and dried them on a towel and smoothed and twisted his mustache and picked a white fez from the bedpost, turning it in his fingers.

"My father retained the turban," he said. His voice was soft and delicate for a man of his size. "What would he think to see me in this? Tradition is not what we remember, but what we have not yet forgotten. Is it not so, young one?"

The goldsmith looked at Yasin, eyelids dark and hooded. In the stillness Yasin could hear the clatter of a milk-cart on its rounds in the alley below. The goldsmith's wife came back in with a caftan and helped al-Ashur dress and then he waved her away.

"Light of my eyes, may your morning be bright," she murmured, retreating.

Kamal al-Ashur did not look at her. "Walk with me, Yasin," he said instead.

They went back up to the roof. Often the goldsmith would take him there when he wished to speak undisturbed. There were pigeons flickering in cages on the high wall and a large wooden coop where yellow chickens dipped and scrabbled for seed and over the alley-side stood a green trellis of hyacinth beans and jasmine. A haze hung over the city and on all sides he saw the brown minarets of Alexandria materializing out of the dust.

"I have had a message from the shaykh," said Kamal al-Ashur. "The First has awakened. His prison has been opened. He will walk among us again, and there will be no preventing it. It has been seen."

Yasin looked up. "The First?"

His master kneeled and wiped away the straw covering the roof, baring the ancient crest, burned into the wood long ago. A rising sun, crossed by twin hammers. He placed his big hand on the insignia and

a small panel opened. Inside was a velvet bag, which he withdrew carefully. He laid out the gleaming weapons of the Agnoscenti, one by one,
their blades still sharp after centuries.

"We are few, and weak," his master said, with sadness. "But we must
do what we can. You must find the Dark Talent, young one. You must
finish this."

"It has begun, then," said Yasin softly. There was fear in his voice.

The early cries of vendors in the alley below drifted past. There came
a scrape of handcarts on the grooved stones, the clang and echo of stalls
being erected for the day.

Kamal al-Ashur nodded. "It has begun."

ACKNOWLEDGMENTS

Firstly, always, Ellen Levine, visionary agent and friend. I owe her everything. Also: Audrey Crooks and Lauren Campbell, outstanding in their support, as well as Alexa Stark, Martha Wydysh, Nora Rawn, Ana Ban and the foreign rights team, and everyone at Trident Media.

Megan Lynch at Flatiron Books: brilliant reader, even more brilliant editor. These books are absurdly lucky to have found her. Also: Kukuwa Ashun, who holds everything together. Keith Hayes, for his exquisite designs. Malati Chavali, Marlena Bittner, Katherine Turro, Nancy Trypuc, Cat Kenney, Claire McLaughlin, Elizabeth Catalano, Jeremy Pink, and all the rest of the team. Ana Deboo, my wickedly precise copy editor.

Stephanie Sinclair at McClelland & Stewart, who has taken the Talents under her wing with such grace and enthusiasm. Andrew Roberts, for his stunning designs. Sarah Howland, Tonia Addison, Martha Leonard, Ruta Liormonas, and everyone at M&S who have helped make this book happen. Melanie Little, who copyedited an early excerpt with her always excellent eye.

Vicky Leech Mateos at Bloomsbury, for her intelligence and passion, thank you. Also: Philippa Cotton, Emilie Chambeyron, Stephanie Rathbone, Amy Donegan, and the rest of the UK team. Terry Lee in Edinburgh was wonderfully informative and patient as we walked the old city and I began to dream up this novel.

Rich Green at Gotham Group remains, as always, a champion of the written word. My thanks for all he does.

My gratitude to Pamela Purves, in Nova Scotia, at whose exquisite cottage I wrote many of these pages.

Lastly, those in my life who I write for, whether they know it or not: my parents, Bob and Peggy; my children, Cleo and Maddox; my dear friend and namesake, JM.

And Esi, my love, first and last reader, a shining that will never go out.

ABOUT THE AUTHOR

J. M. Miro is the author of *Ordinary Monsters*, the first in the Talents Trilogy. He lives in the Pacific Northwest with his family. He also writes under the name Steven Price.